DARKROOM

The University of Alabama Press • Tuscaloosa, Alabama

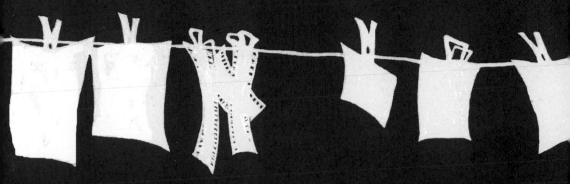

DARKROOM

a memoir in black and white

LILA QUINTERO WEAVER

The University of Alabama Press
Tuscaloosa, Alabama 35487-0380

Manufactured in the United States of America

Typeface: Franklin Gothic and Blambot

∞
The paper on which this book is printed meets the minimum requirements of American National Standard for Information Sciences—Permanence of Paper for Printed Library Materials, ANSI Z39.48-1984.

Library of Congress Cataloging-in-Publication Data
Weaver, Lila Quintero.
Darkroom : a memoir in black and white / Lila Quintero Weaver.
p. cm.
ISBN 978-0-8173-5714-6 (pbk. : alk. paper)—ISBN 978-0-8173-8619-1 (electronic)
1. Weaver, Lila Quintero. 2. Alabama—Social conditions—20th century. 3. Civil rights movements—Alabama—History—20th century. 4. Alabama—Race relations—History—20th century. 5. Argentine Americans—Alabama—Biography. 6. Alabama—Biography. I. Title.
CT275.W3497A3 2012
976.1092—dc23
[B] 2011036117

AUTHOR'S NOTE

The views expressed in this book are not necessarily shared by my siblings or other persons that witnessed or experienced the events recounted.

In memory of
Mama & Daddy,
whose gifts are without number.

To Paul,
who keeps on giving,
and to
Jude, Benjamin, & Caitlin,
who've inherited these collective
treasures.

I love you all.

CONTENTS

DARKROOM

Prologue

HOME MOVIES

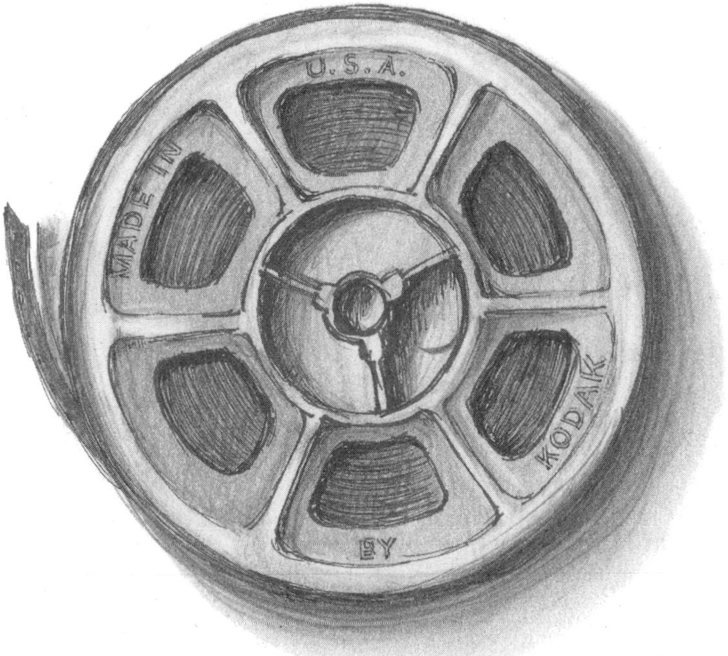
U.S.A.
MADE IN
KODAK
BY

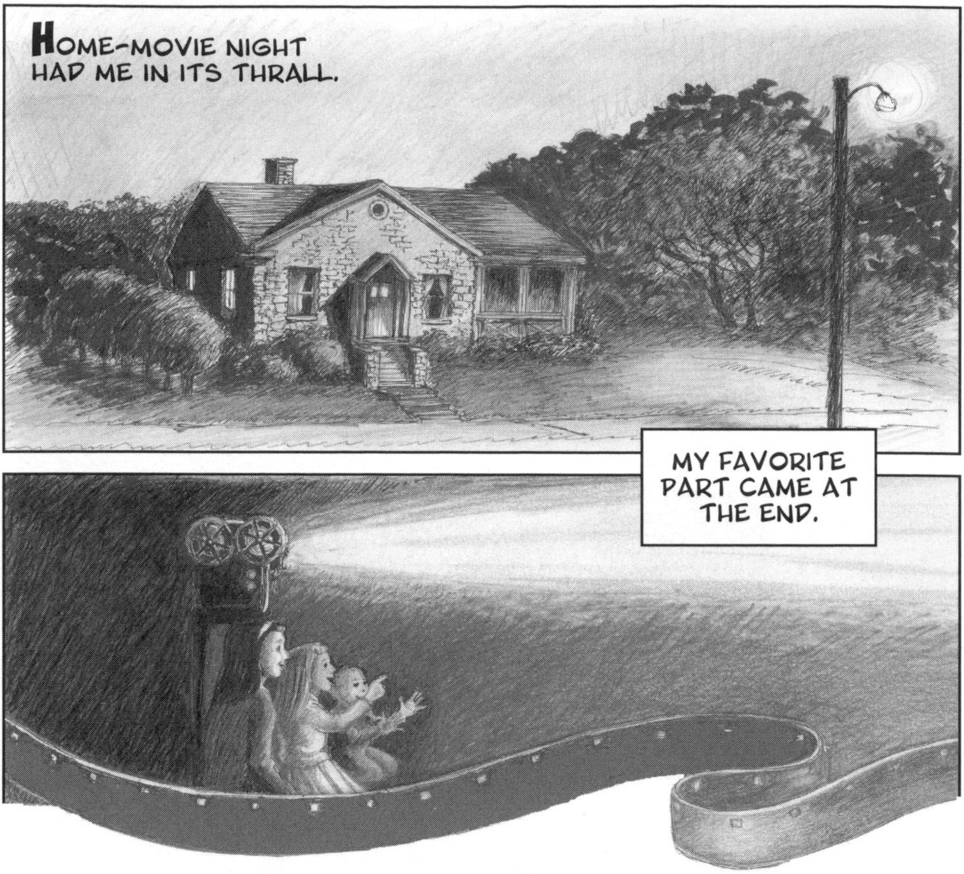
HOME-MOVIE NIGHT HAD ME IN ITS THRALL.
MY FAVORITE PART CAME AT THE END.

AT THAT POINT, DADDY REWOUND THE FILM, AND WE SAW IT ALL IN REVERSE.

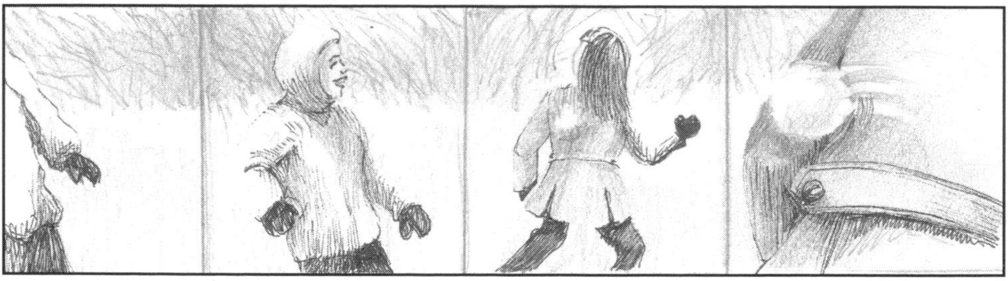

THE BACKWARDS FLIGHT OF A SNOWBALL

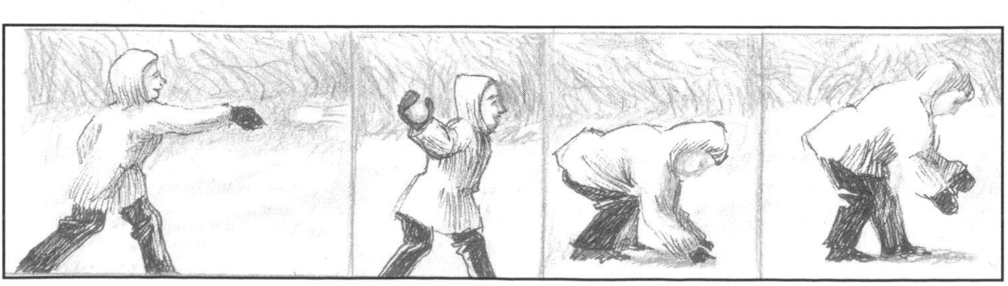

THE BACKWARDS
PEDALING OF A BIKE

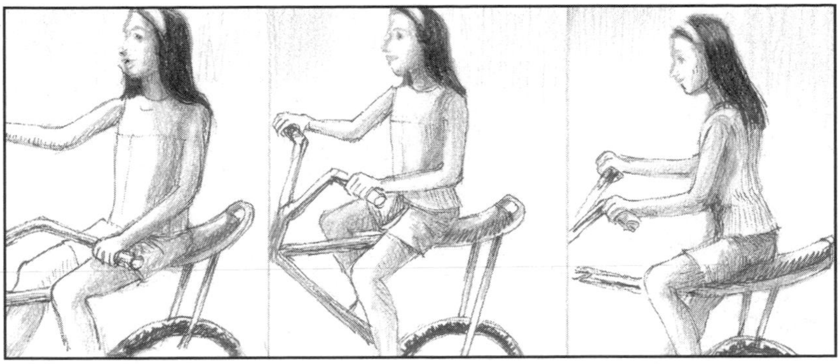

THE BACKWARDS
DIGGING OF A HOLE.

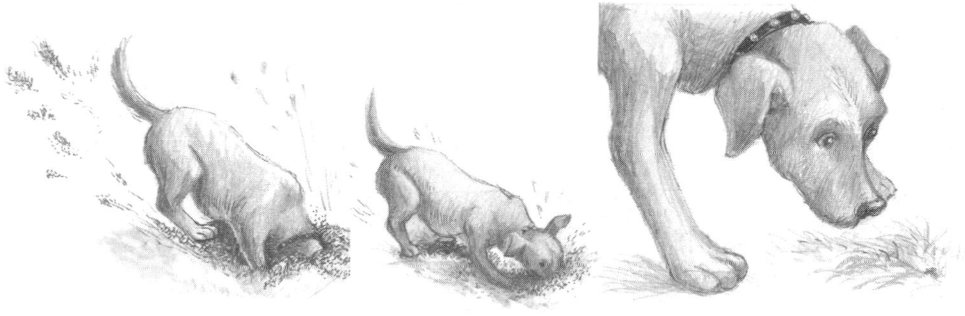

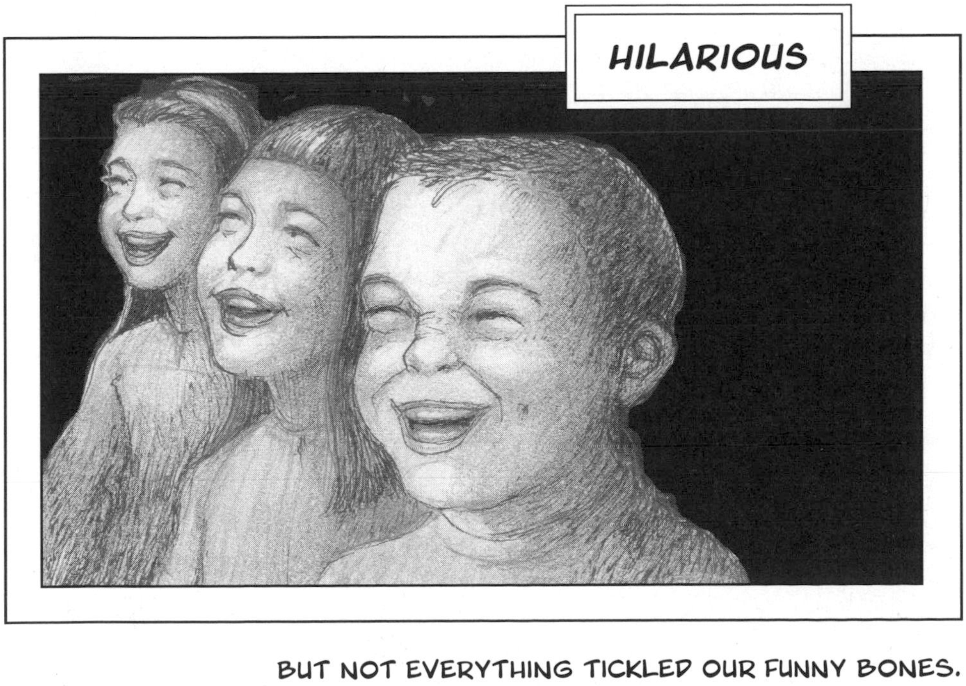
HILARIOUS

BUT NOT EVERYTHING TICKLED OUR FUNNY BONES.

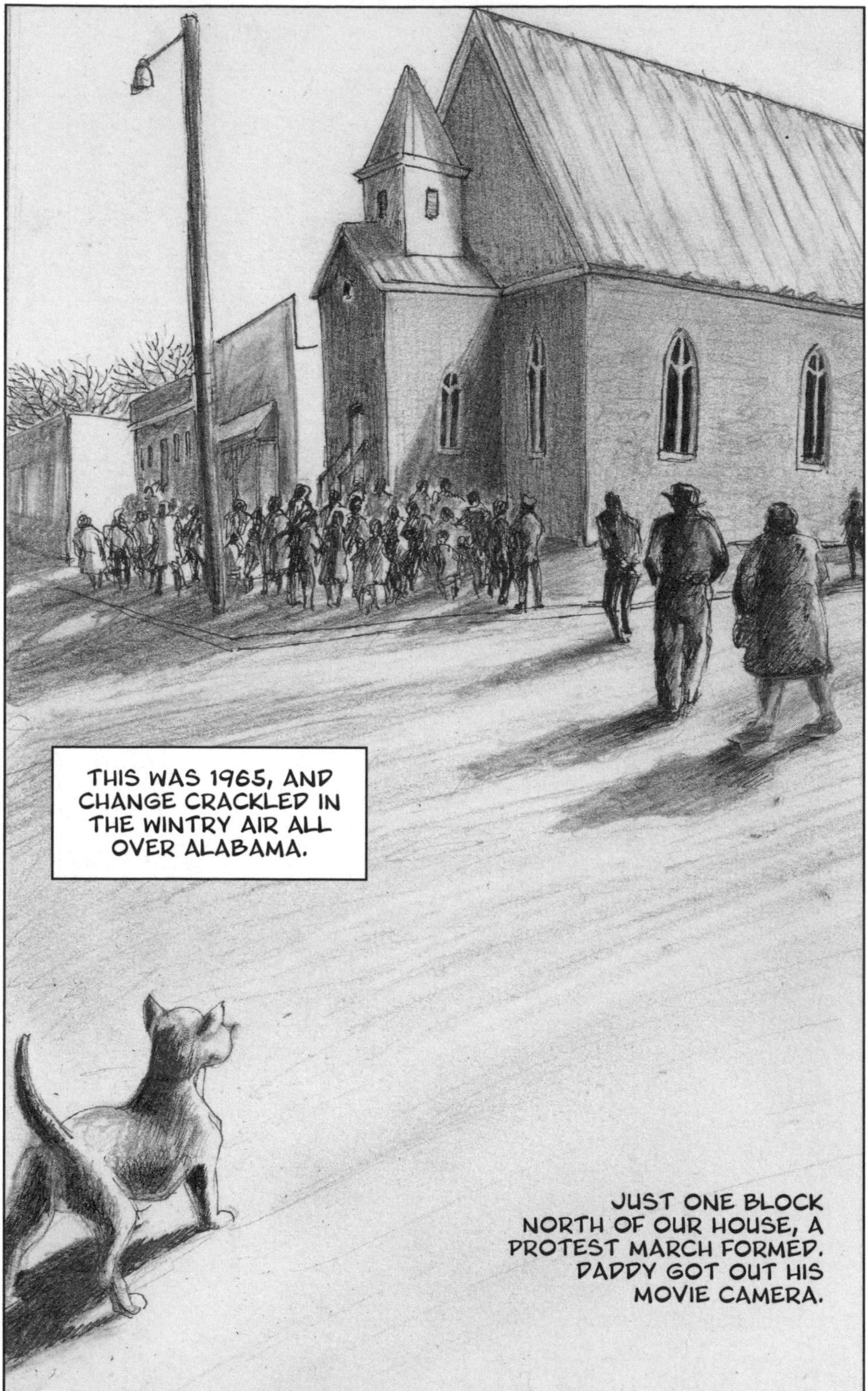
THIS WAS 1965, AND CHANGE CRACKLED IN THE WINTRY AIR ALL OVER ALABAMA.
JUST ONE BLOCK NORTH OF OUR HOUSE, A PROTEST MARCH FORMED. DADDY GOT OUT HIS MOVIE CAMERA.

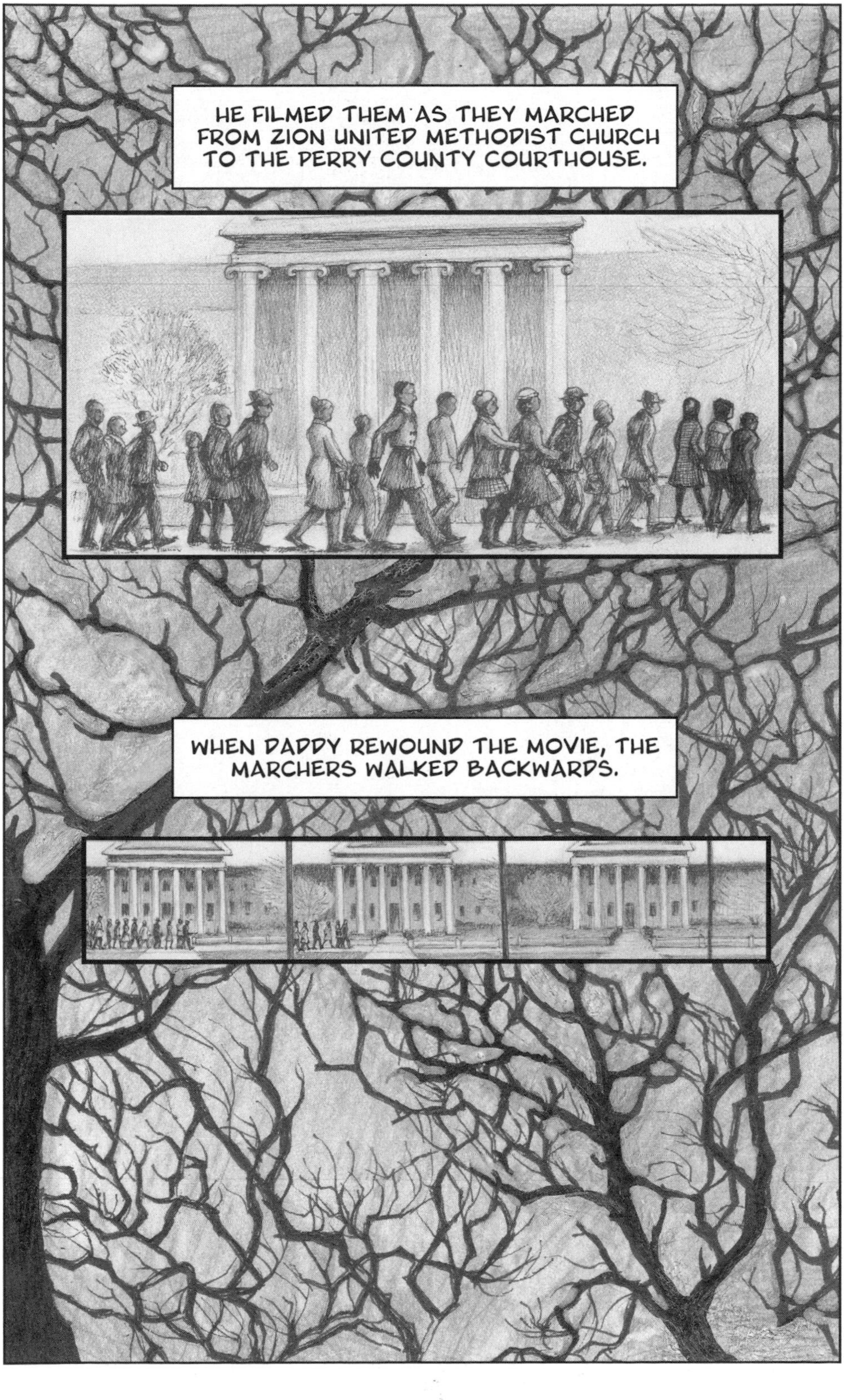
HE FILMED THEM AS THEY MARCHED FROM ZION UNITED METHODIST CHURCH TO THE PERRY COUNTY COURTHOUSE.
WHEN DADDY REWOUND THE MOVIE, THE MARCHERS WALKED BACKWARDS.

IT WAS FUNNY. HOW COULD ANYBODY KNOW WHERE THEY WERE GOING WITHOUT EVER LOOKING BACK? BUT THEY WALKED WITH SUCH APLOMB, AND THAT'S WHAT KILLED US.

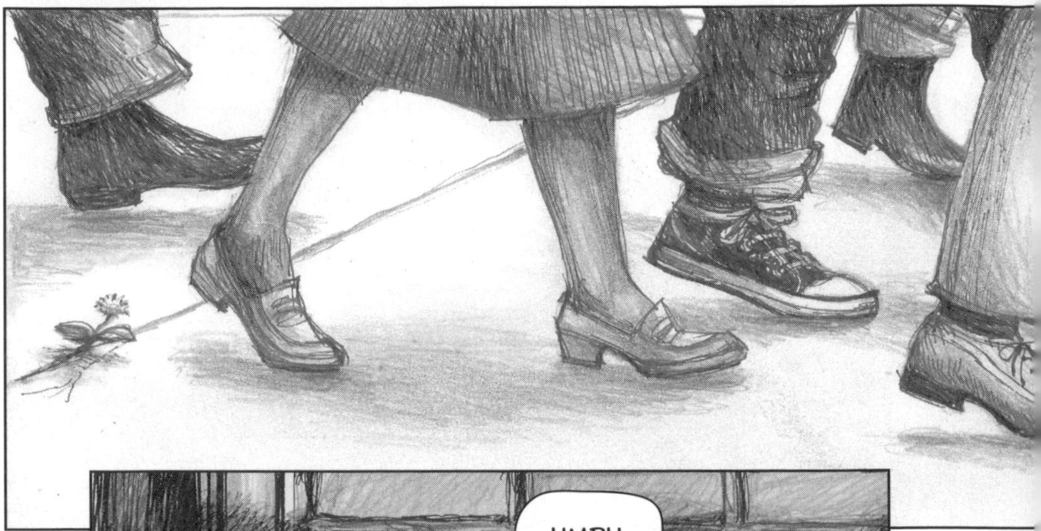

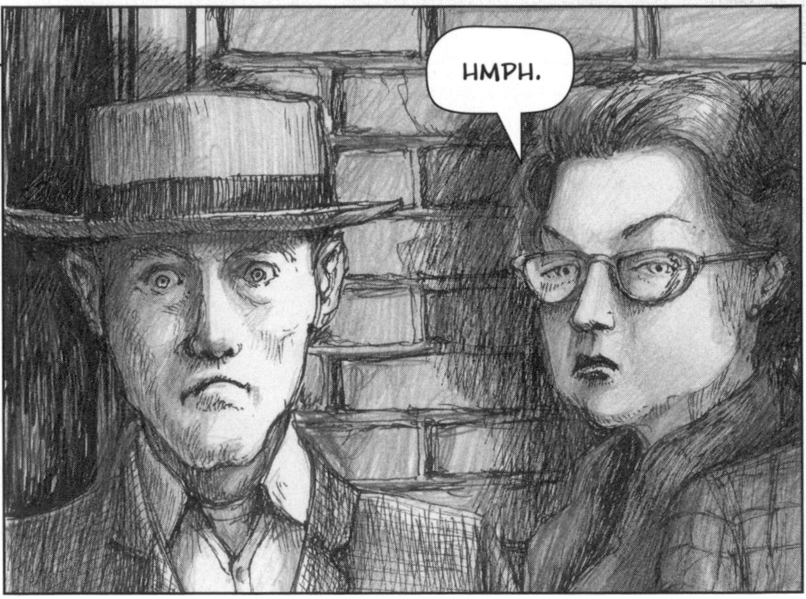
HMPH.

THE MARCH TOOK THEM AROUND THE COURTHOUSE I DON'T KNOW HOW MANY TIMES.

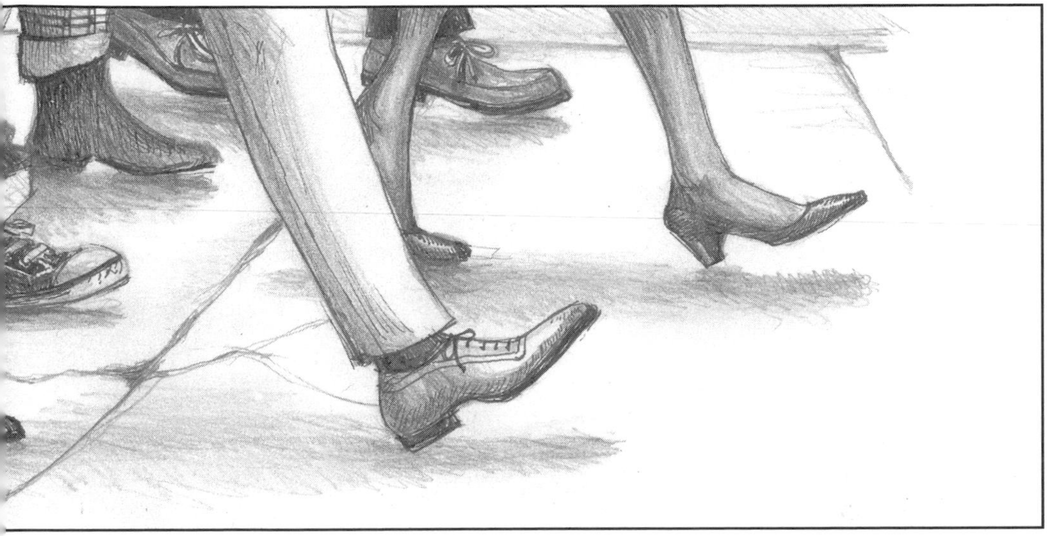

THE MOVIE DOESN'T SHOW HOW WHITE PEOPLE REACTED. BUT HAVING LIVED AMONG THEM, I CAN MAKE AN EDUCATED GUESS.

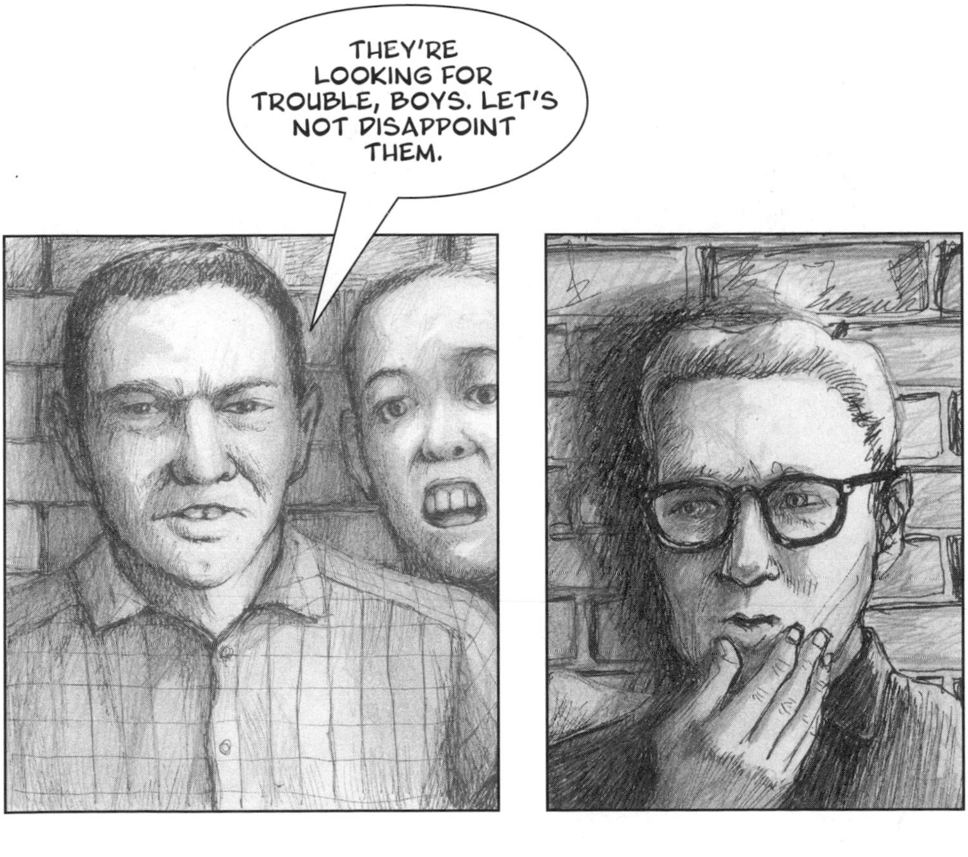
THEY'RE LOOKING FOR TROUBLE, BOYS. LET'S NOT DISAPPOINT THEM.

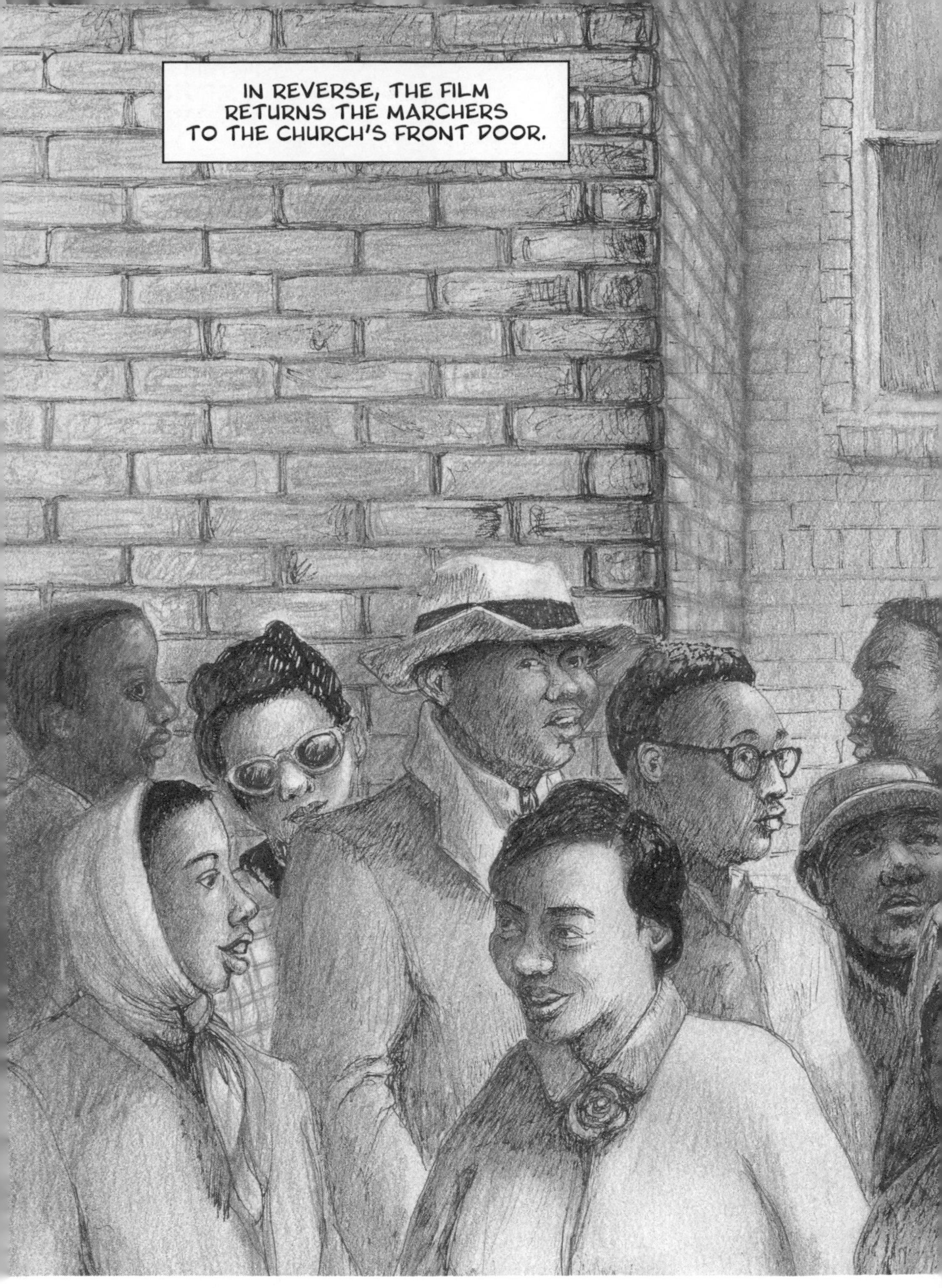
IN REVERSE, THE FILM RETURNS THE MARCHERS TO THE CHURCH'S FRONT DOOR.

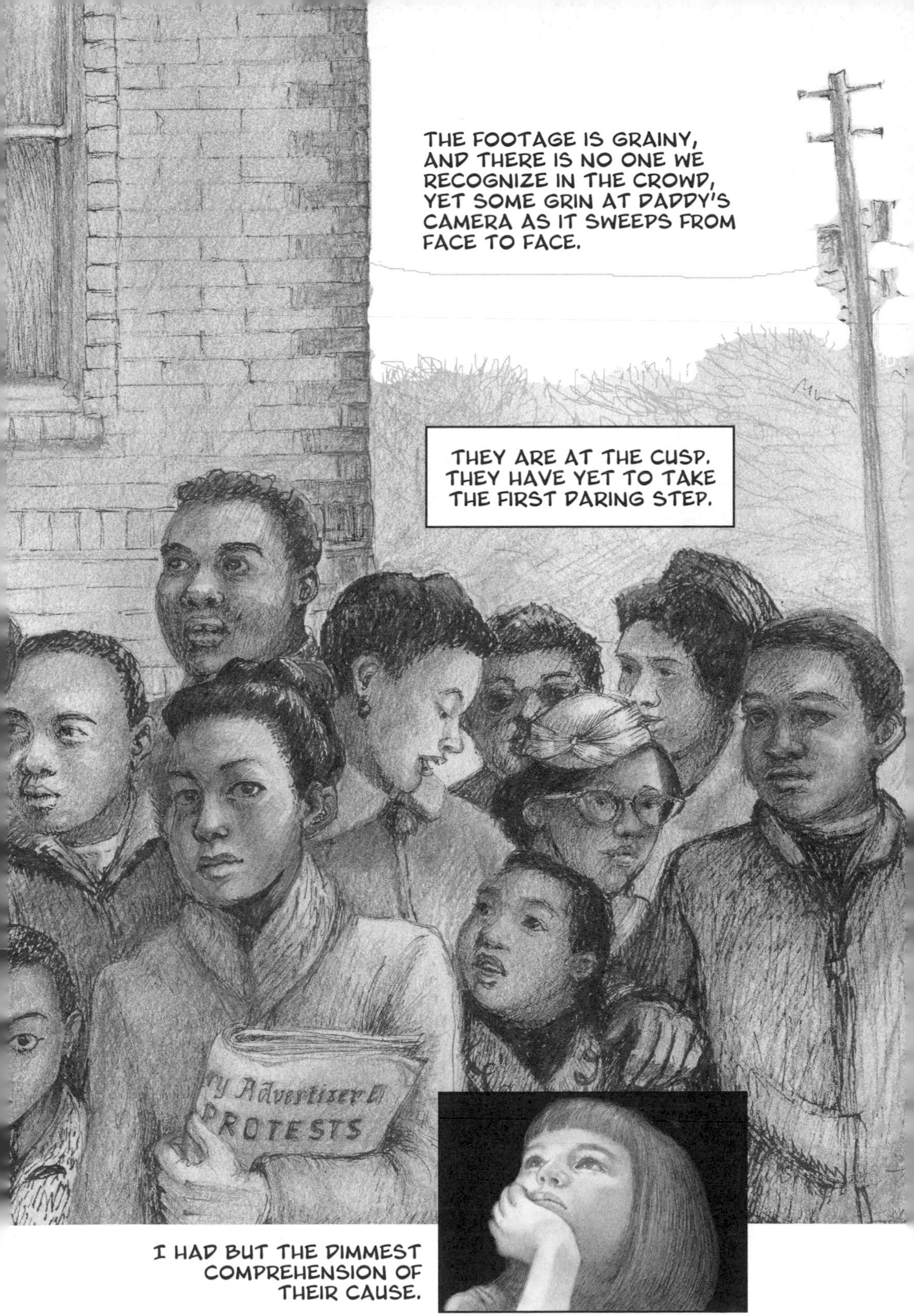
THE FOOTAGE IS GRAINY, AND THERE IS NO ONE WE RECOGNIZE IN THE CROWD, YET SOME GRIN AT DADDY'S CAMERA AS IT SWEEPS FROM FACE TO FACE.
THEY ARE AT THE CUSP. THEY HAVE YET TO TAKE THE FIRST DARING STEP.
y Advertiser
PROTESTS

I HAD BUT THE DIMMEST COMPREHENSION OF THEIR CAUSE.

A SCENE OR TWO MORE, THEN WITH A *FLAP, FLAP, FLAP*, THE TAKE-UP REEL TURNS LOOSE THE FINAL BIT OF FILM.

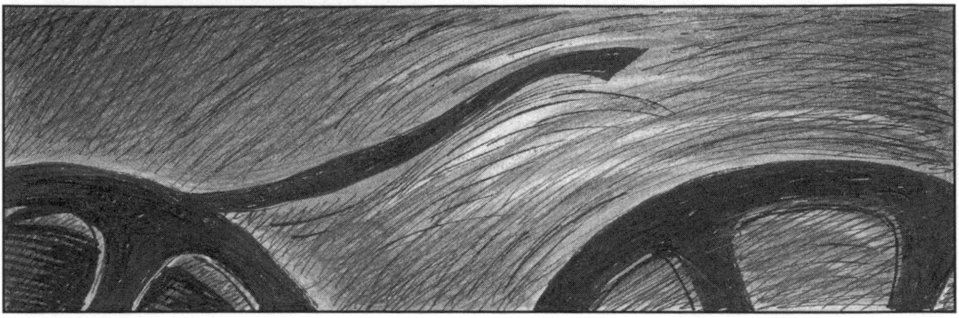

AND LIKE THE BACKWARDS UNWRAPPING OF A GIFT,

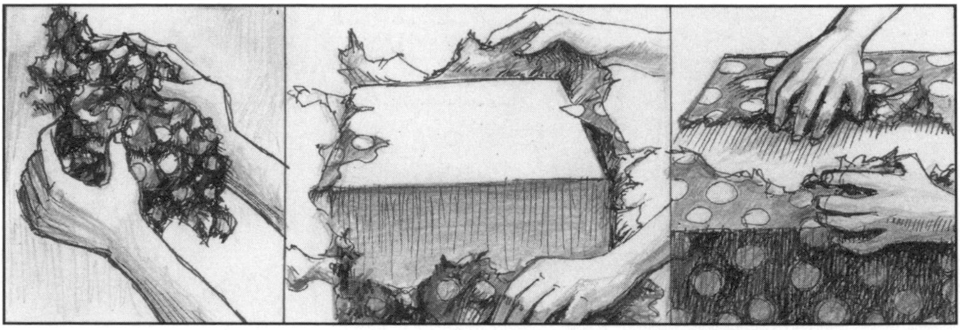

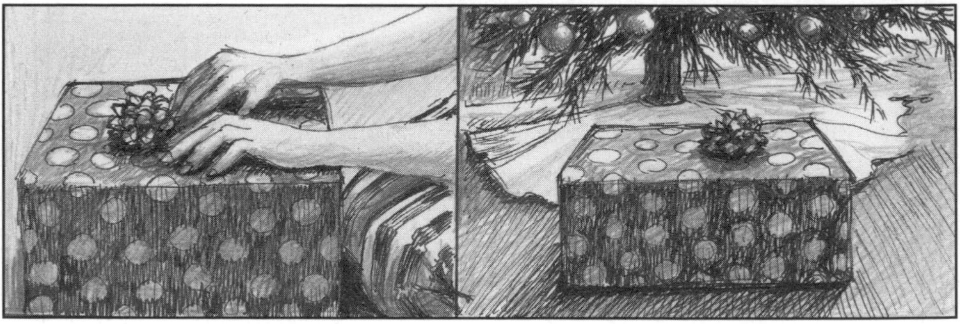

EVERYTHING RETURNS TO ITS NEAT BEGINNING.

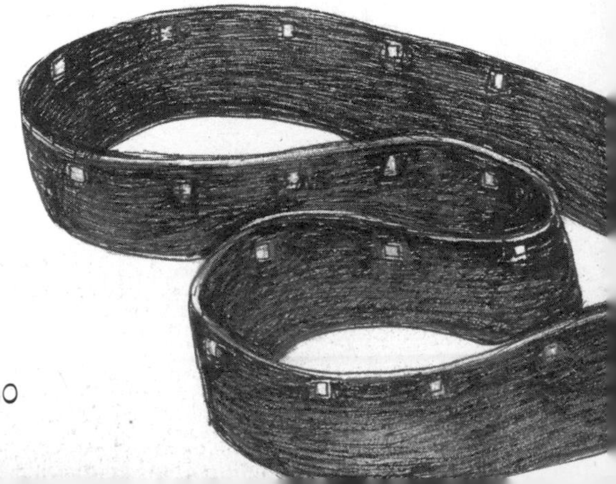

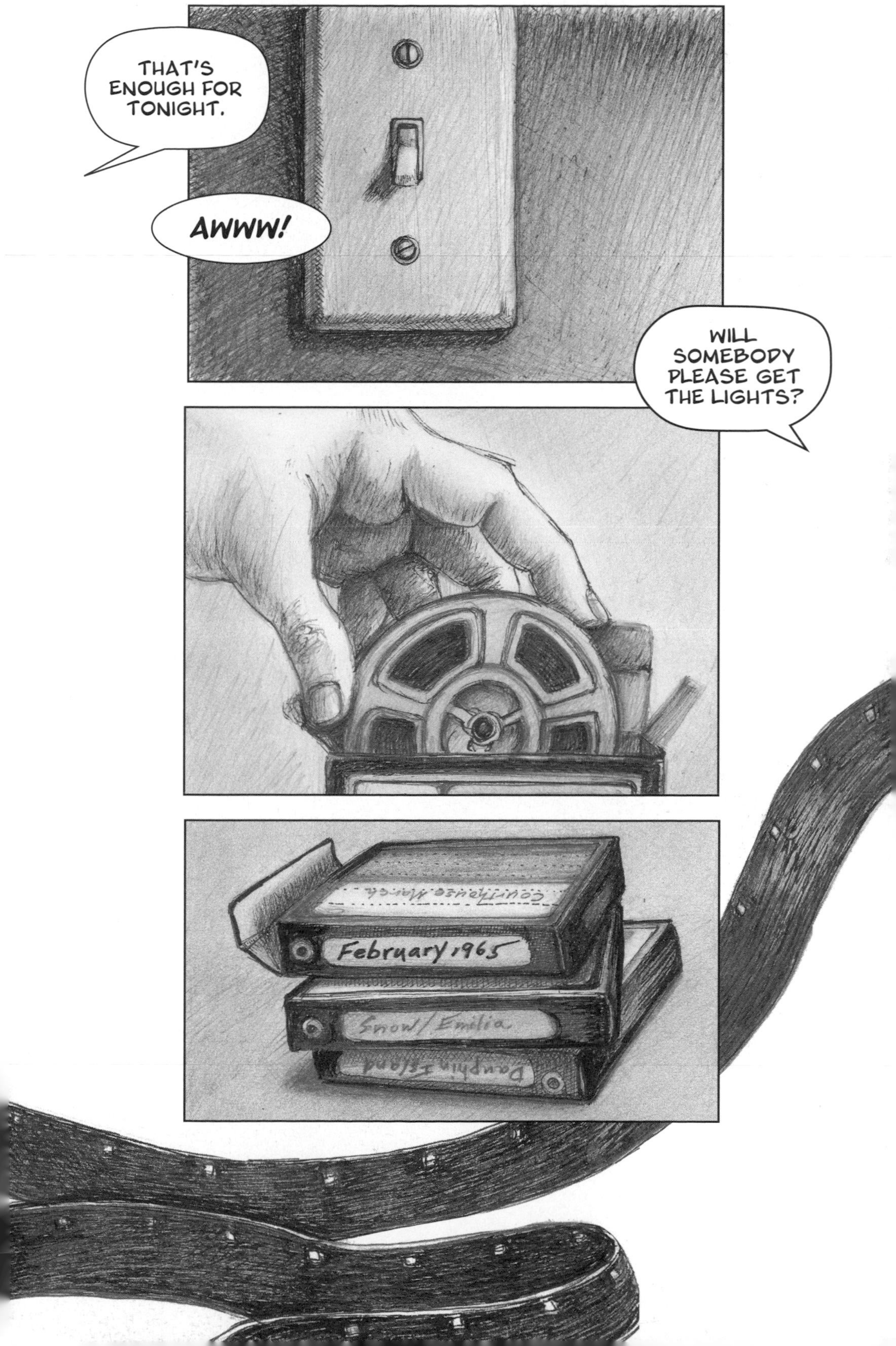
THAT'S ENOUGH FOR TONIGHT.
AWWW!
WILL SOMEBODY PLEASE GET THE LIGHTS?
Courthouse March
February 1965
Snow/Emilia
Dauphin Island

chapter 1
IN THE DARK

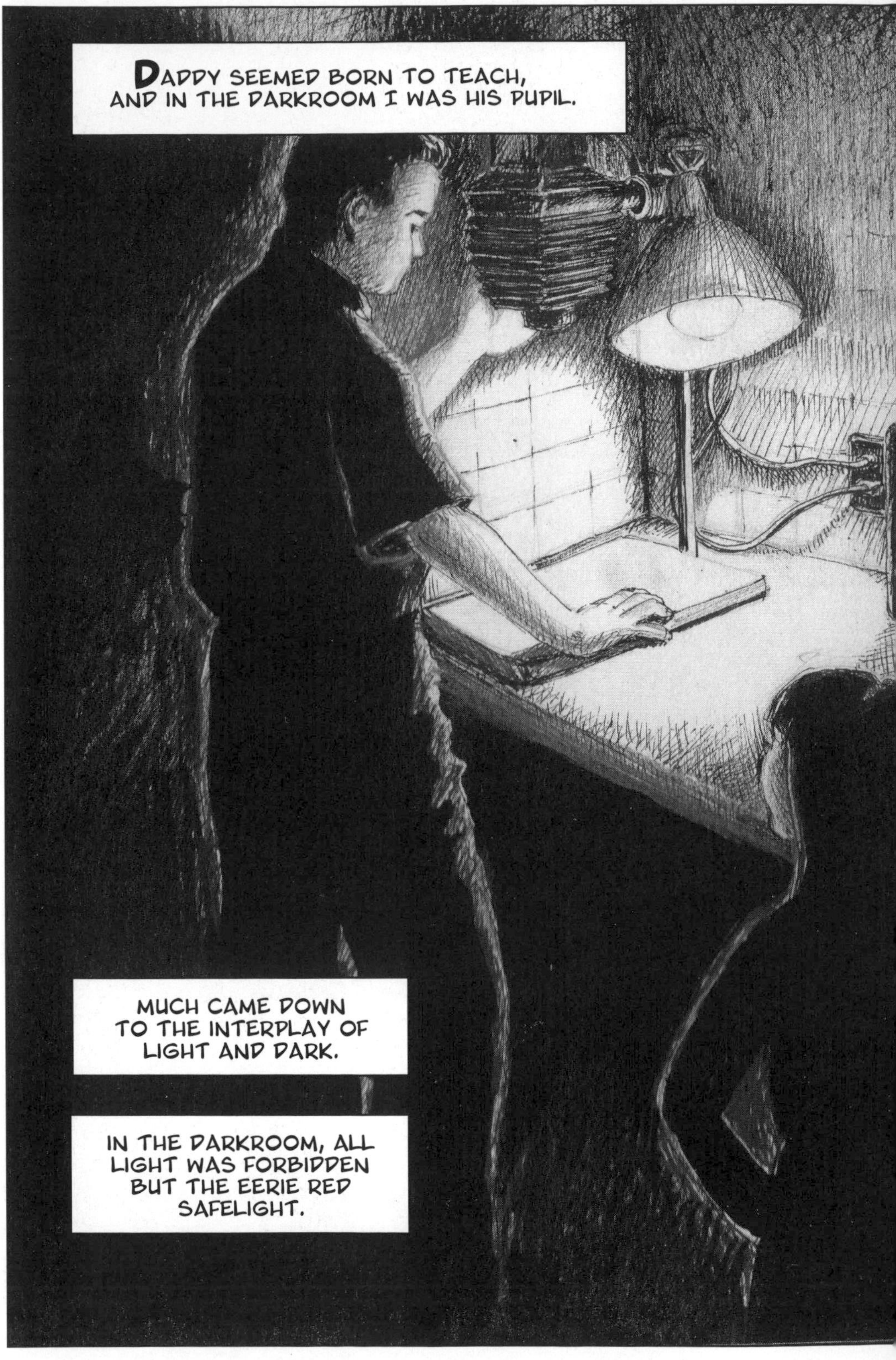
DADDY SEEMED BORN TO TEACH, AND IN THE DARKROOM I WAS HIS PUPIL.
MUCH CAME DOWN TO THE INTERPLAY OF LIGHT AND DARK.
IN THE DARKROOM, ALL LIGHT WAS FORBIDDEN BUT THE EERIE RED SAFELIGHT.

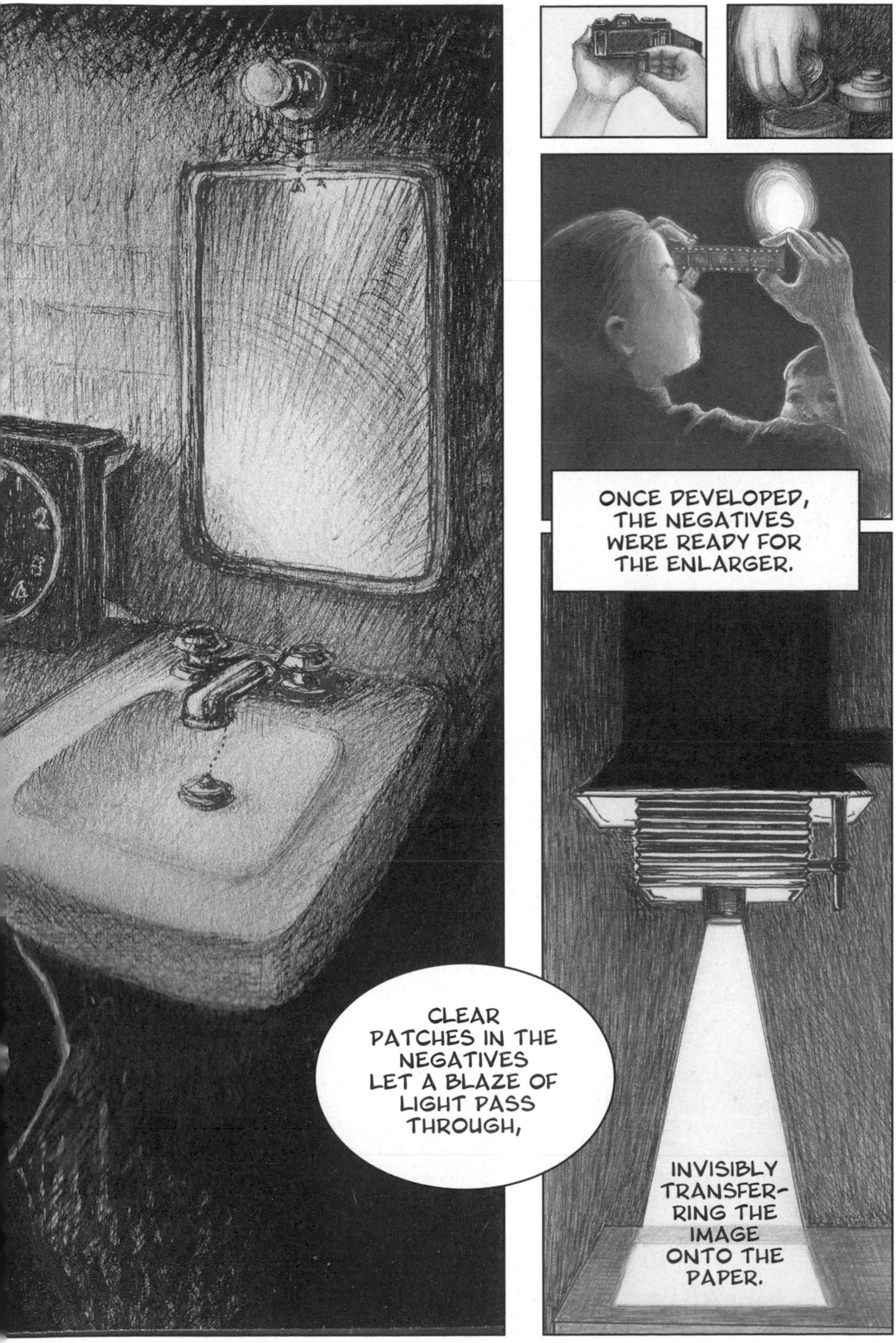
ONCE DEVELOPED, THE NEGATIVES WERE READY FOR THE ENLARGER.
CLEAR PATCHES IN THE NEGATIVES LET A BLAZE OF LIGHT PASS THROUGH,
INVISIBLY TRANSFER-RING THE IMAGE ONTO THE PAPER.

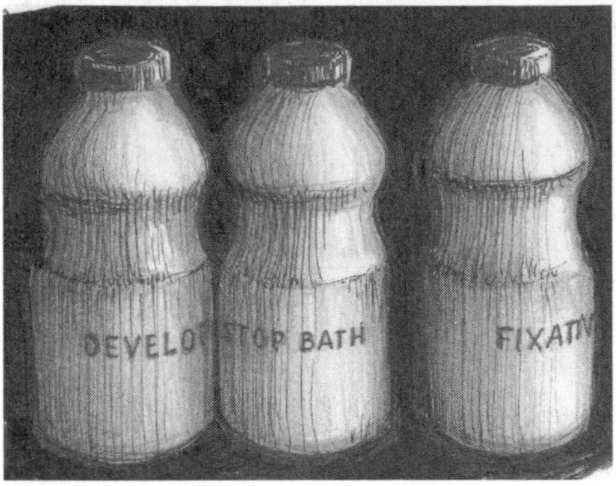
DEVELO
STOP BATH
FIXATIV

MOST OF THE DARKROOM LESSONS HAVE FADED AWAY.

BUT HOW COULD I FORGET THE ACTUAL MOMENT OF REVELATION?

WHEN THE BLANK SHEET OF PHOTOGRAPHIC PAPER...

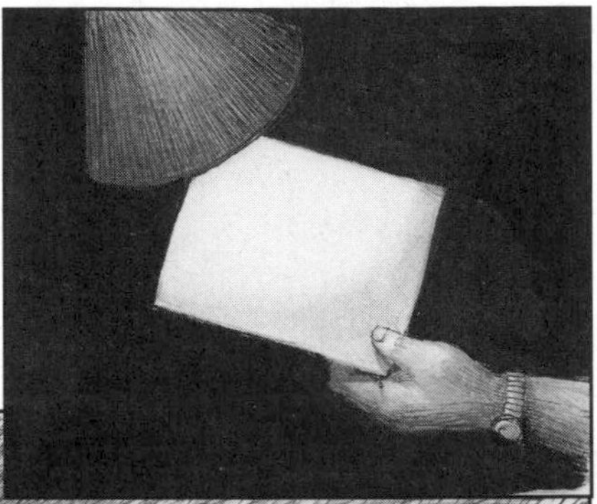

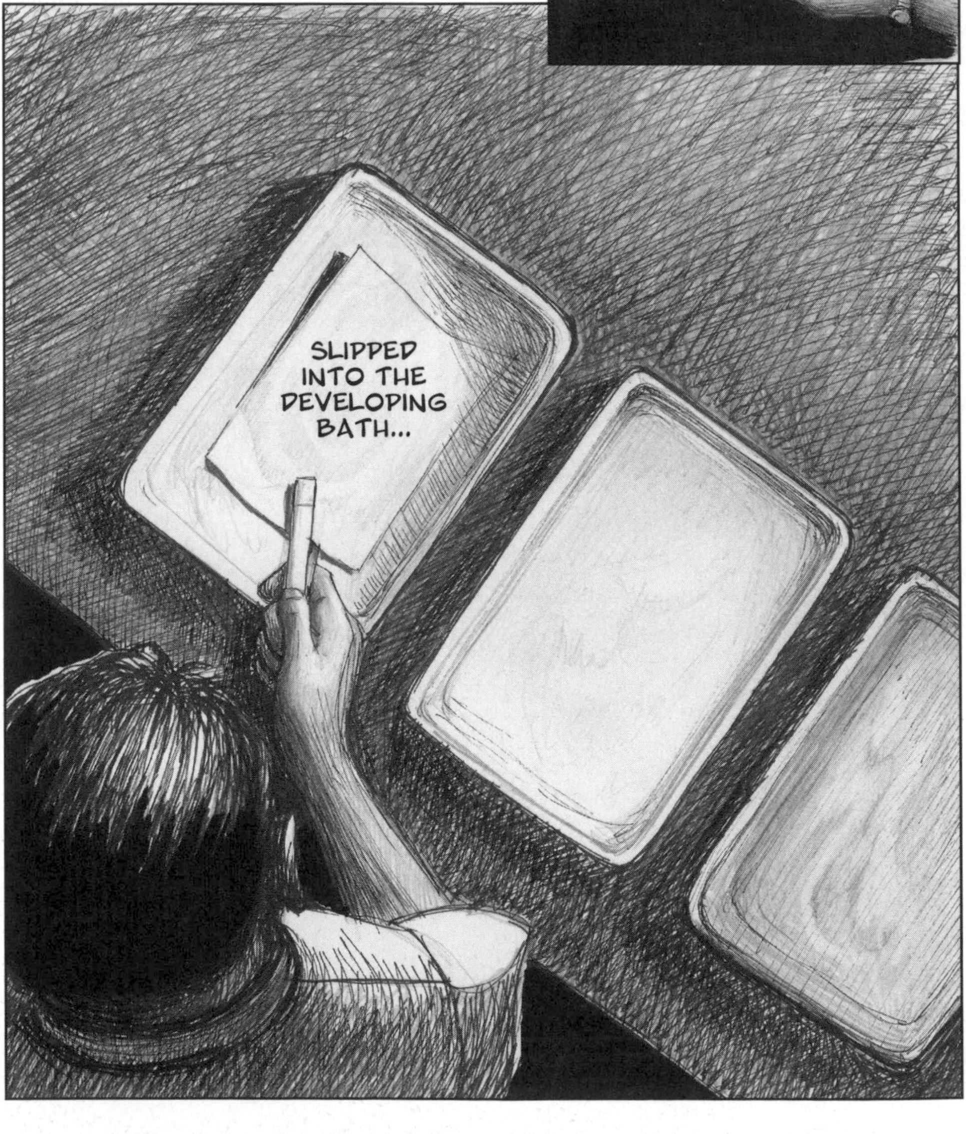
SLIPPED INTO THE DEVELOPING BATH...

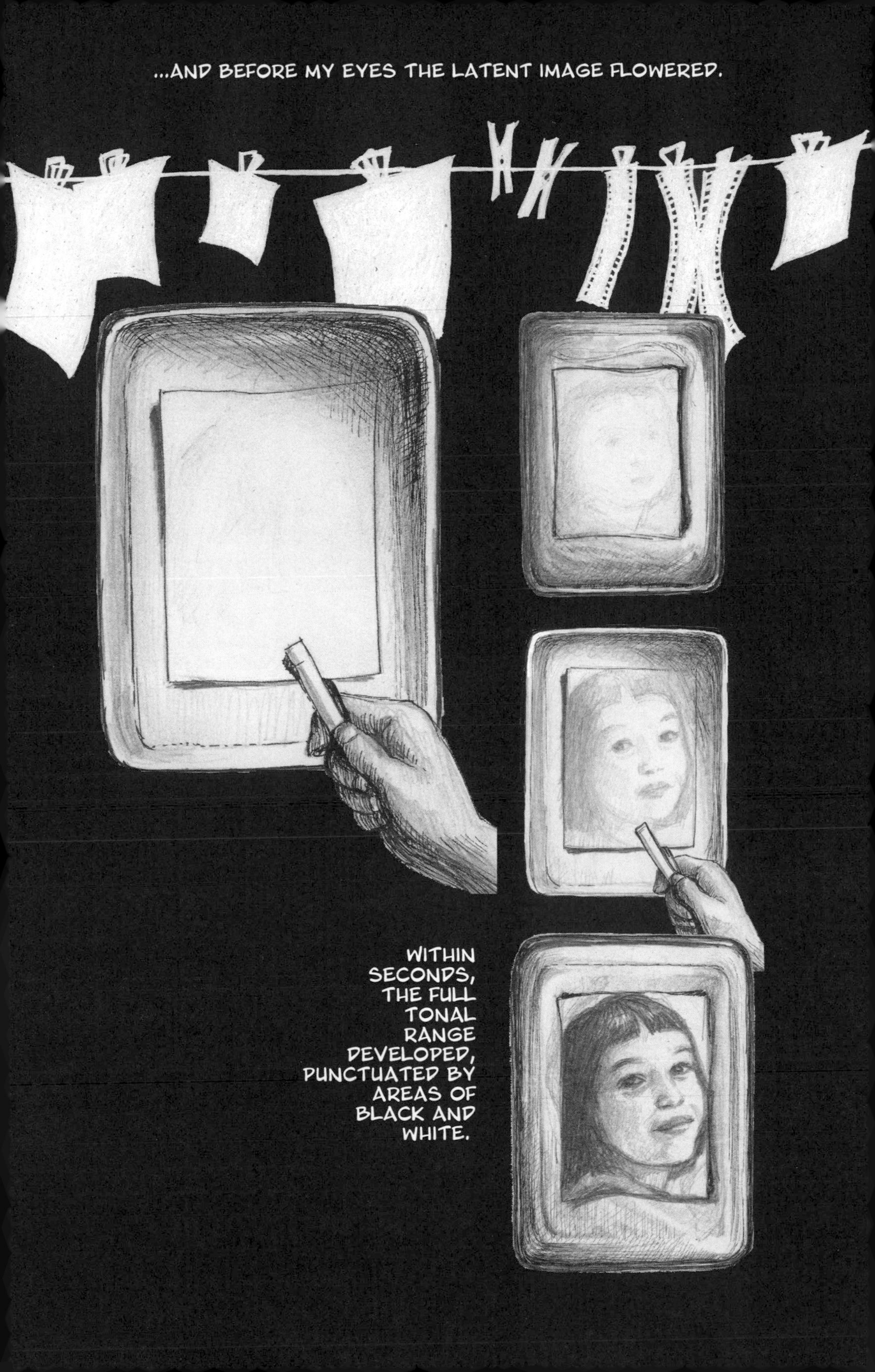
...AND BEFORE MY EYES THE LATENT IMAGE FLOWERED.
WITHIN SECONDS, THE FULL TONAL RANGE DEVELOPED, PUNCTUATED BY AREAS OF BLACK AND WHITE.

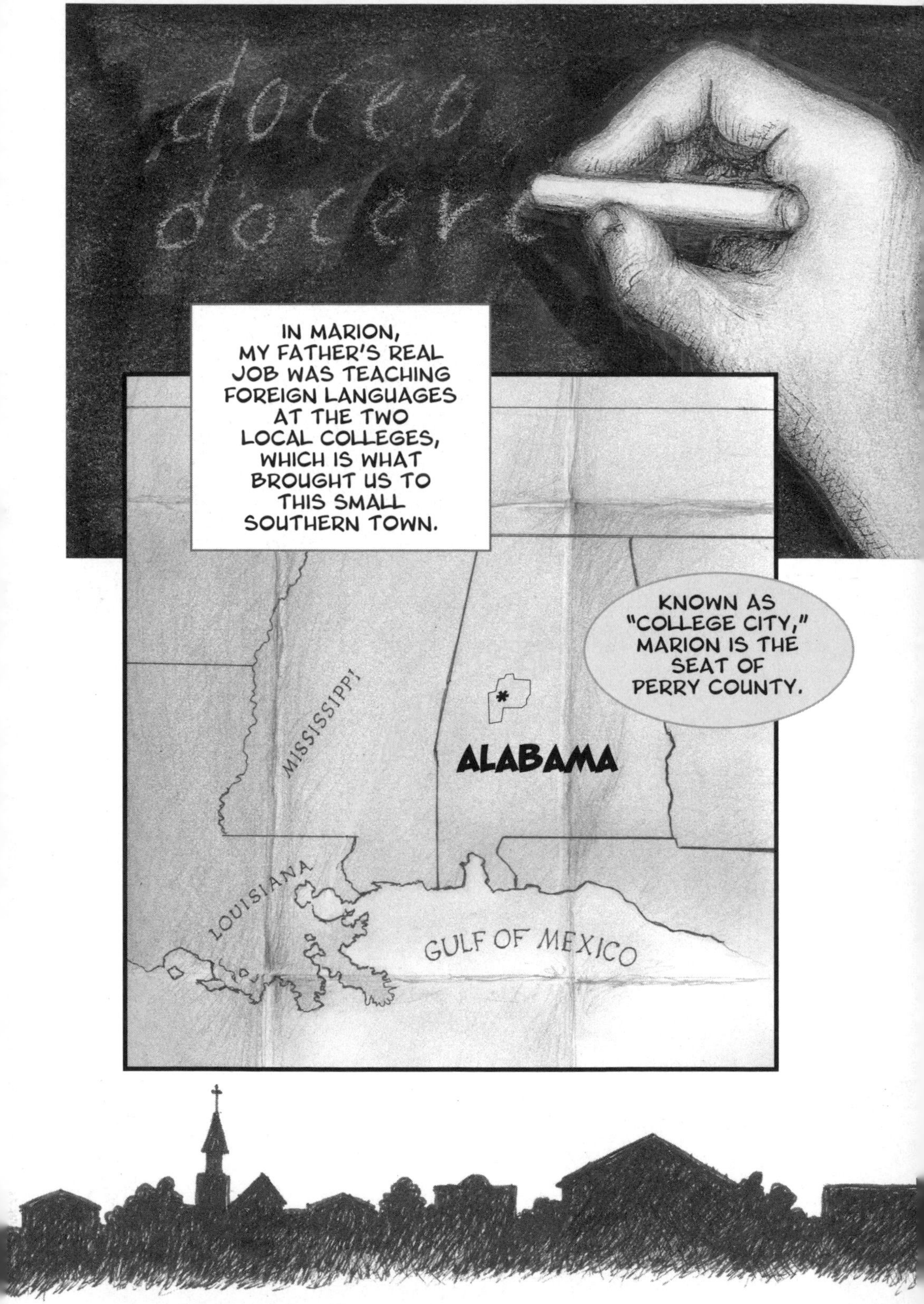
doceo
docere
IN MARION, MY FATHER'S REAL JOB WAS TEACHING FOREIGN LANGUAGES AT THE TWO LOCAL COLLEGES, WHICH IS WHAT BROUGHT US TO THIS SMALL SOUTHERN TOWN.
KNOWN AS "COLLEGE CITY," MARION IS THE SEAT OF PERRY COUNTY.
MISSISSIPPI
ALABAMA
LOUISIANA
GULF OF MEXICO

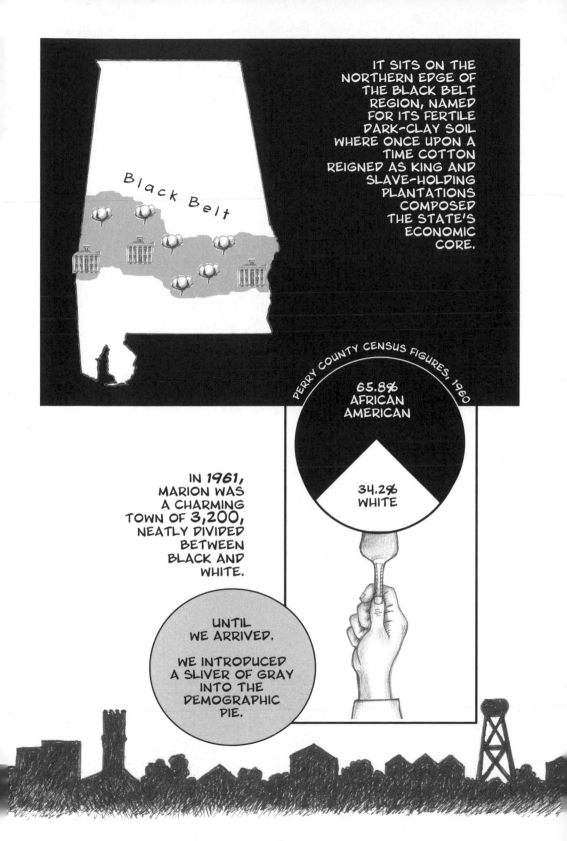

IT SITS ON THE NORTHERN EDGE OF THE BLACK BELT REGION, NAMED FOR ITS FERTILE DARK-CLAY SOIL WHERE ONCE UPON A TIME COTTON REIGNED AS KING AND SLAVE-HOLDING PLANTATIONS COMPOSED THE STATE'S ECONOMIC CORE.

Black Belt

PERRY COUNTY CENSUS FIGURES, 1960

65.8% AFRICAN AMERICAN

34.2% WHITE

IN *1961*, MARION WAS A CHARMING TOWN OF 3,200, NEATLY DIVIDED BETWEEN BLACK AND WHITE.

UNTIL WE ARRIVED.

WE INTRODUCED A SLIVER OF GRAY INTO THE DEMOGRAPHIC PIE.

IN OUR TINY ALABAMA TOWN, DADDY TRAINED HIS LENSES ON MANY AN IMPORTANT EVENT.

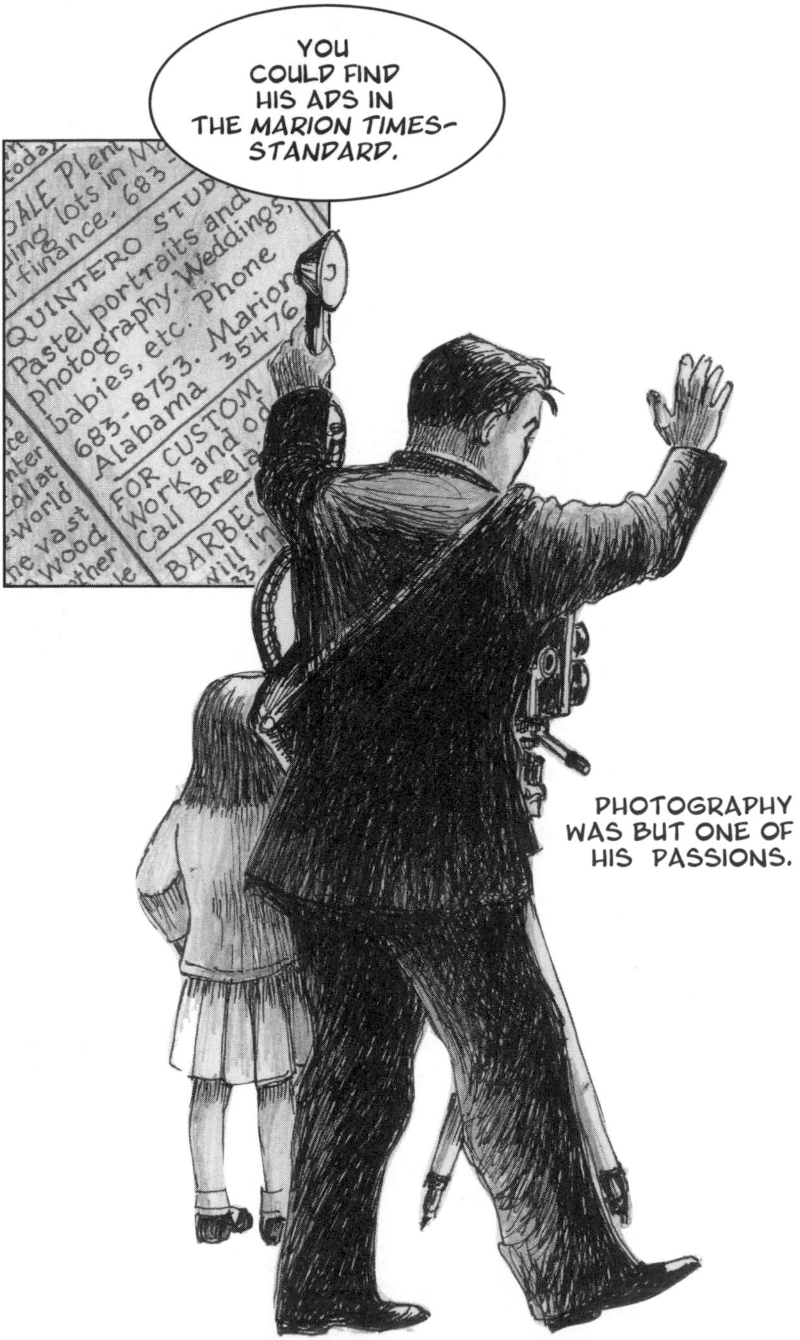
YOU COULD FIND HIS ADS IN THE MARION TIMES-STANDARD.
QUINTERO
Pastel portraits and
photography. Weddings,
babies, etc. Phone
683-8753. Marion
Alabama 35476
FOR CUSTOM
PHOTOGRAPHY WAS BUT ONE OF HIS PASSIONS.

UP TO 1961, WHEN MY WHOLE FAMILY CAME TO AMERICA, MY FATHER'S LIFE CAN BE SUMMARIZED IN A SERIES OF SNAPSHOTS:

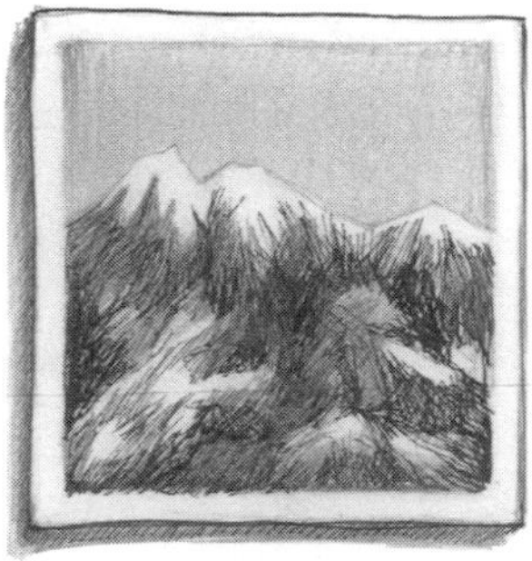

BORN IN ARGENTINA AT THE FOOT OF THE ANDES

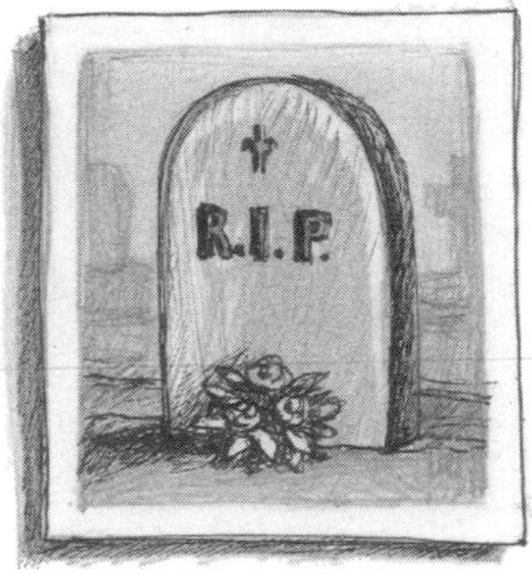
R.I.P.

ORPHANED AT AGE NINE

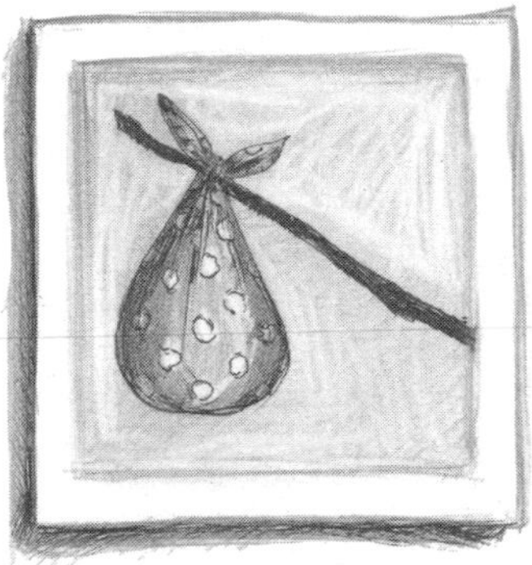

LEFT HOMELESS ALONG WITH HIS BROTHER

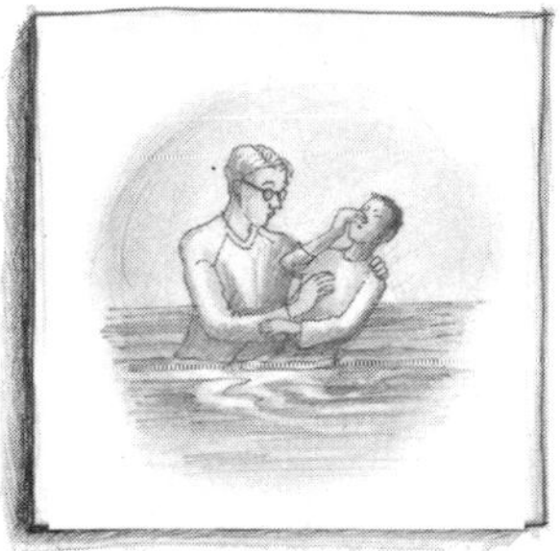

RESCUED BY AMERICAN MISSIONARIES

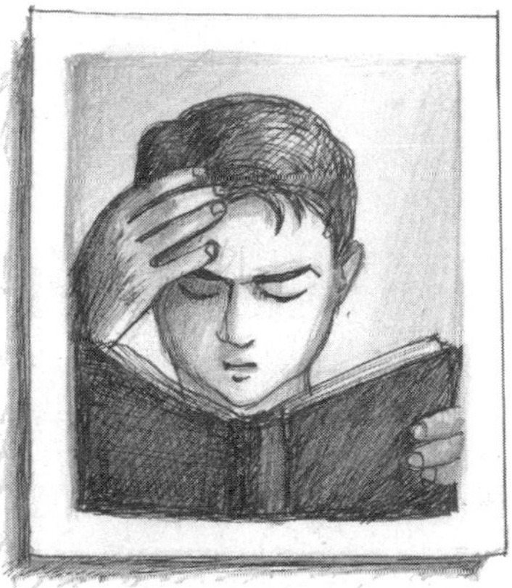

TAUGHT HIMSELF TO READ

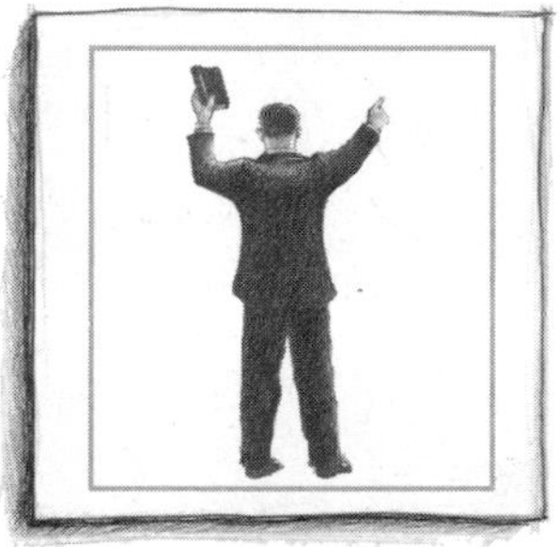

CALLED TO PREACH

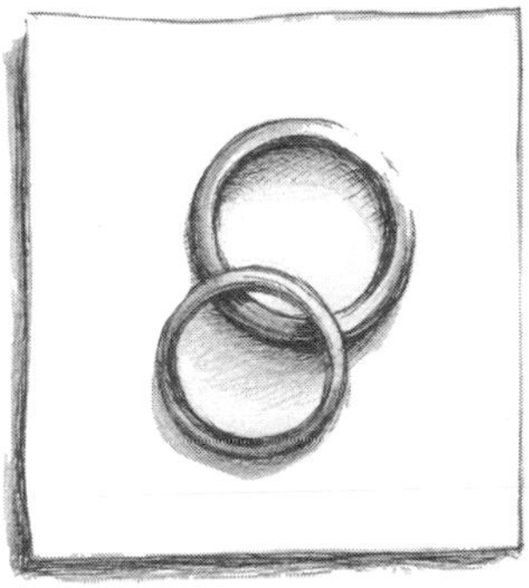

WED TO MY MOTHER

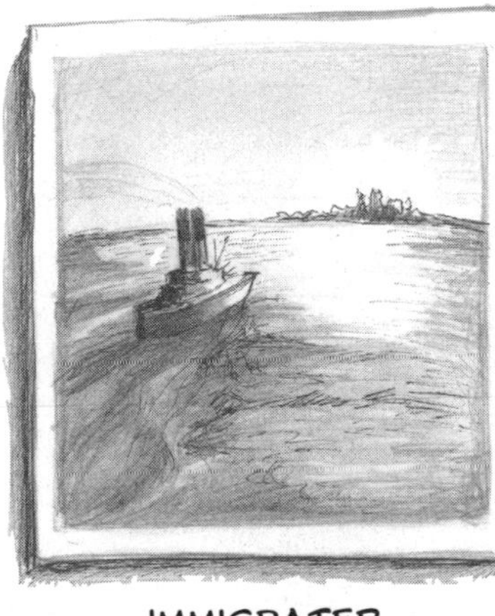

IMMIGRATED TO AMERICA

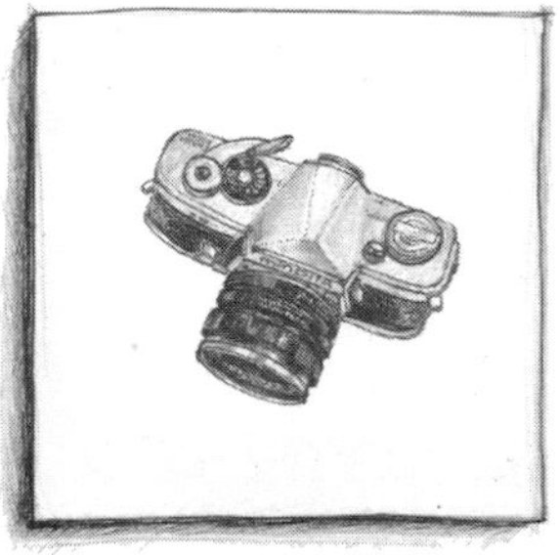

ACQUIRED THE FIRST OF MANY CAMERAS DESTINED TO RECORD MUCH OF OUR LIVES

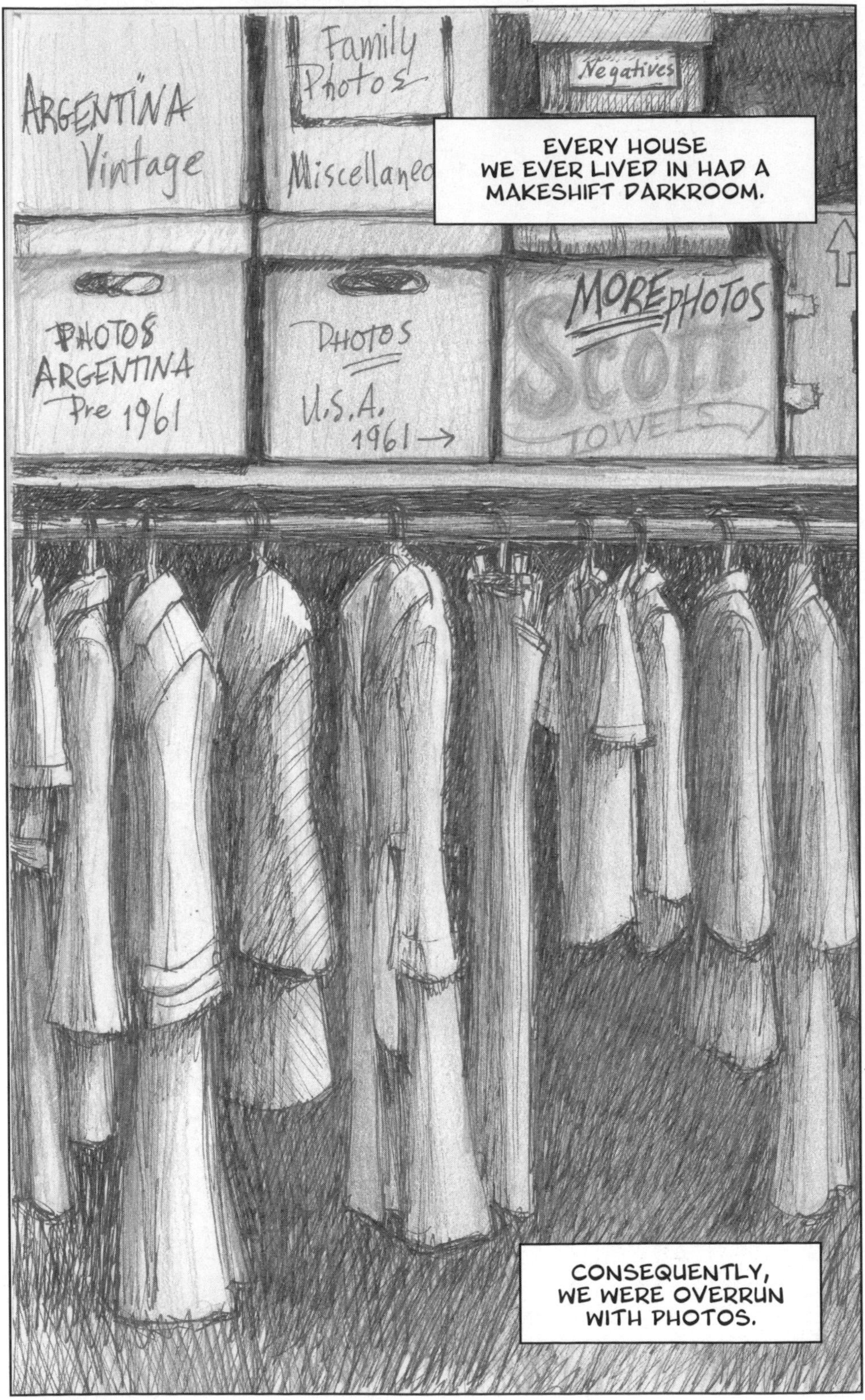
EVERY HOUSE WE EVER LIVED IN HAD A MAKESHIFT DARKROOM.
Family Photos
Negatives
ARGENTINA Vintage
Miscellaneo
PHOTOS ARGENTINA Pre 1961
PHOTOS U.S.A. 1961 →
MORE PHOTOS
SCOTT TOWELS
CONSEQUENTLY, WE WERE OVERRUN WITH PHOTOS.

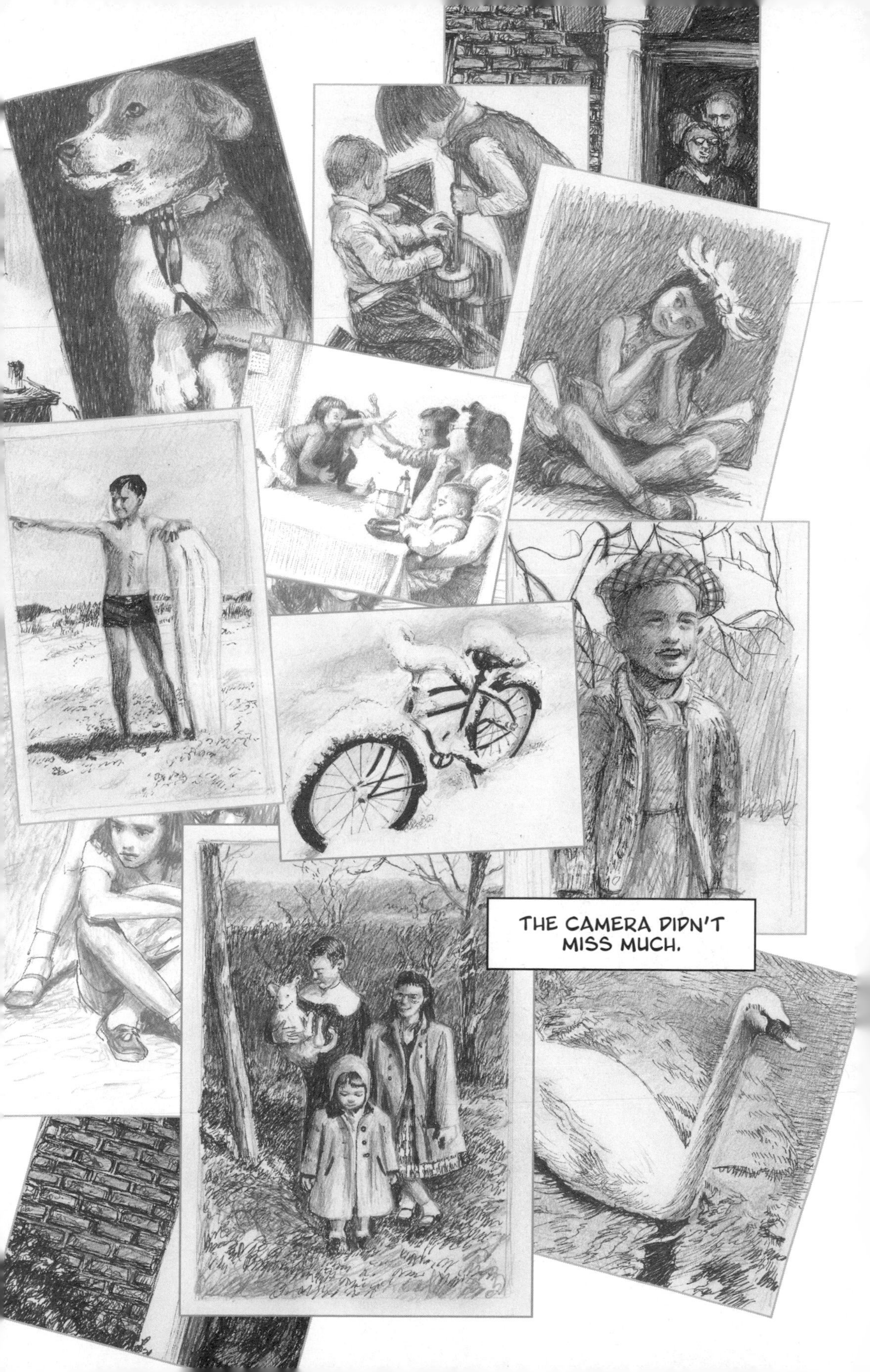
THE CAMERA DIDN'T
MISS MUCH.

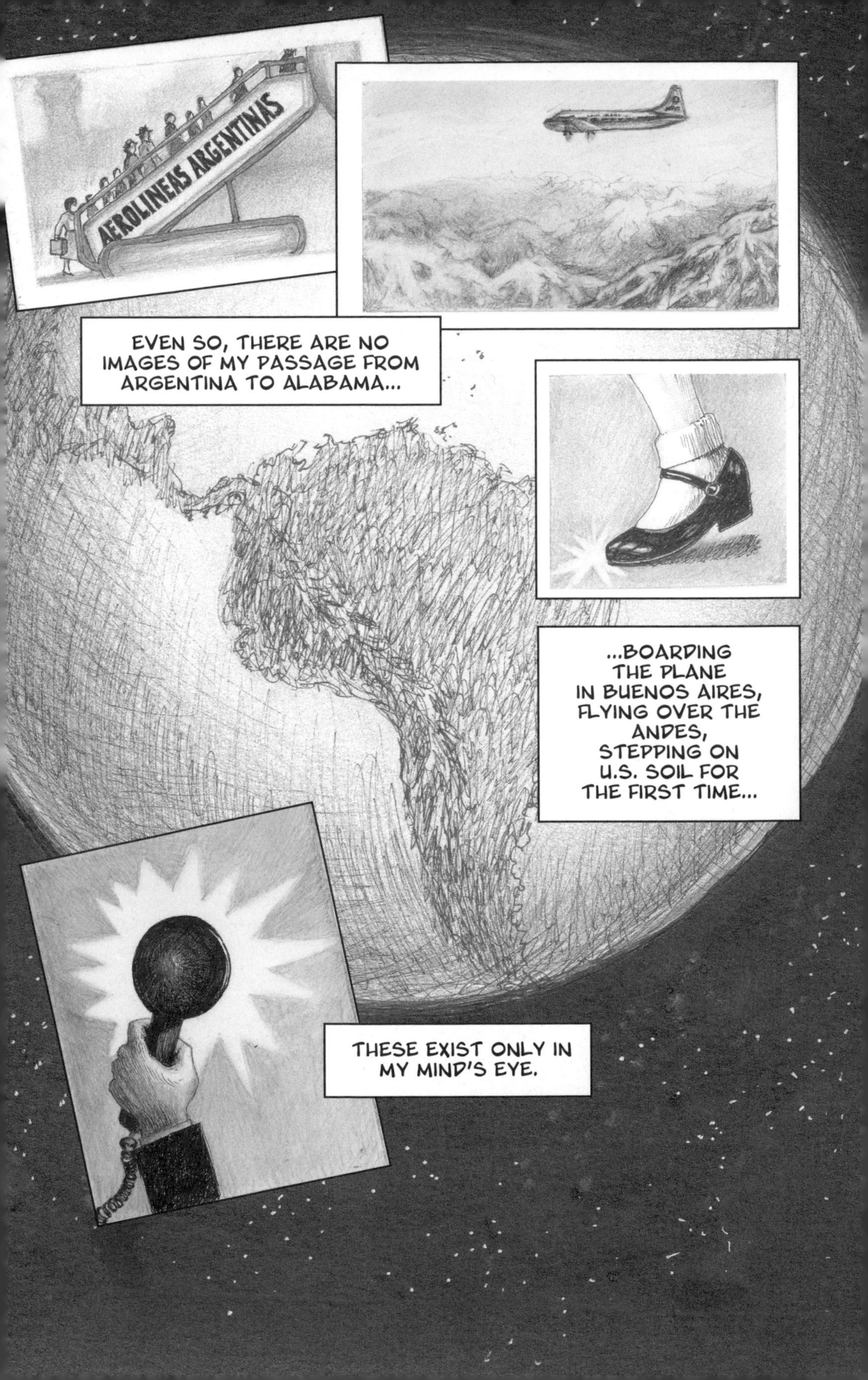
AEROLINEAS ARGENTINAS
EVEN SO, THERE ARE NO IMAGES OF MY PASSAGE FROM ARGENTINA TO ALABAMA...
...BOARDING THE PLANE IN BUENOS AIRES, FLYING OVER THE ANDES, STEPPING ON U.S. SOIL FOR THE FIRST TIME...
THESE EXIST ONLY IN MY MIND'S EYE.

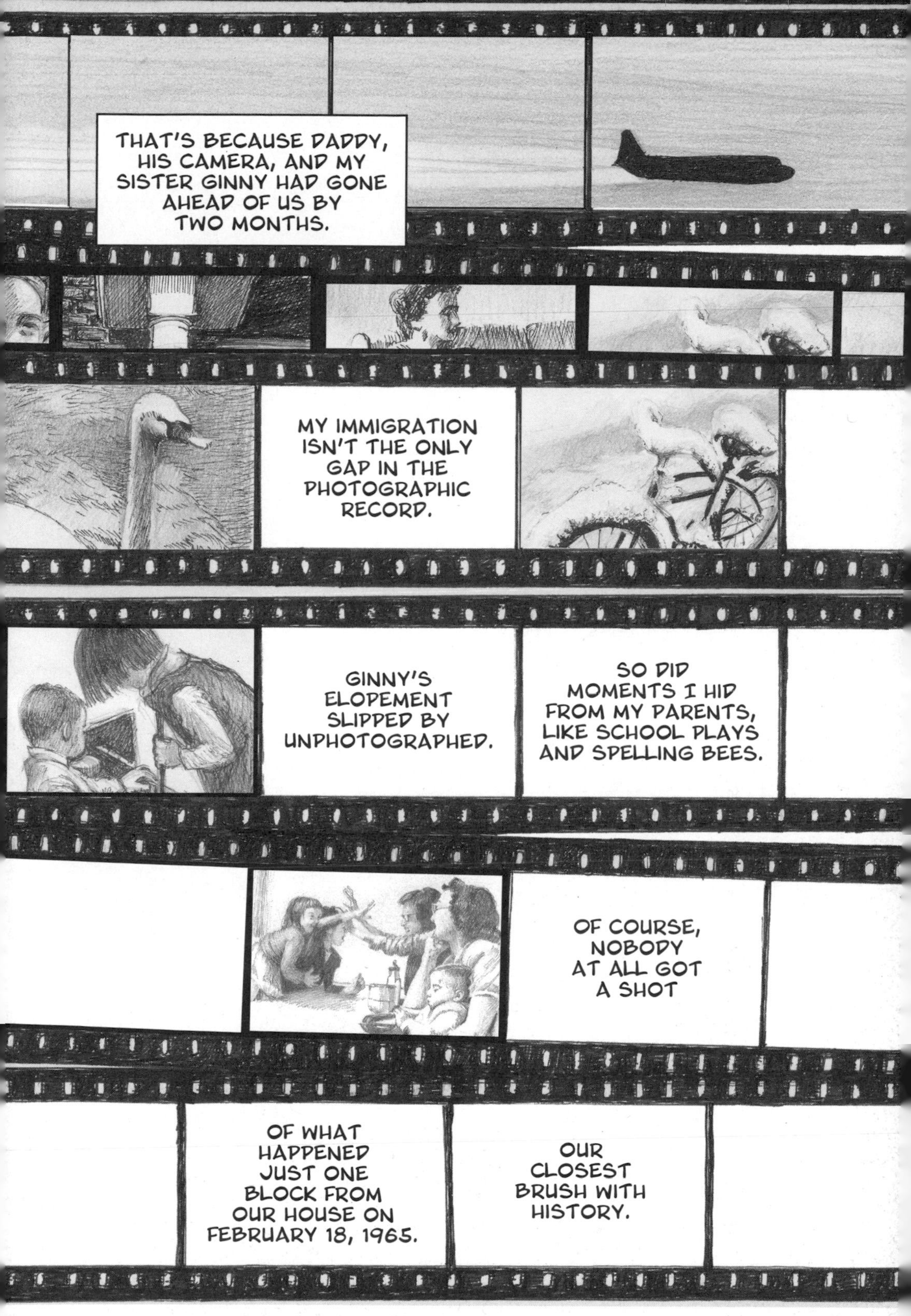
THAT'S BECAUSE DADDY, HIS CAMERA, AND MY SISTER GINNY HAD GONE AHEAD OF US BY TWO MONTHS.
MY IMMIGRATION ISN'T THE ONLY GAP IN THE PHOTOGRAPHIC RECORD.
GINNY'S ELOPEMENT SLIPPED BY UNPHOTOGRAPHED.
SO DID MOMENTS I HID FROM MY PARENTS, LIKE SCHOOL PLAYS AND SPELLING BEES.
OF COURSE, NOBODY AT ALL GOT A SHOT
OF WHAT HAPPENED JUST ONE BLOCK FROM OUR HOUSE ON FEBRUARY 18, 1965.
OUR CLOSEST BRUSH WITH HISTORY.

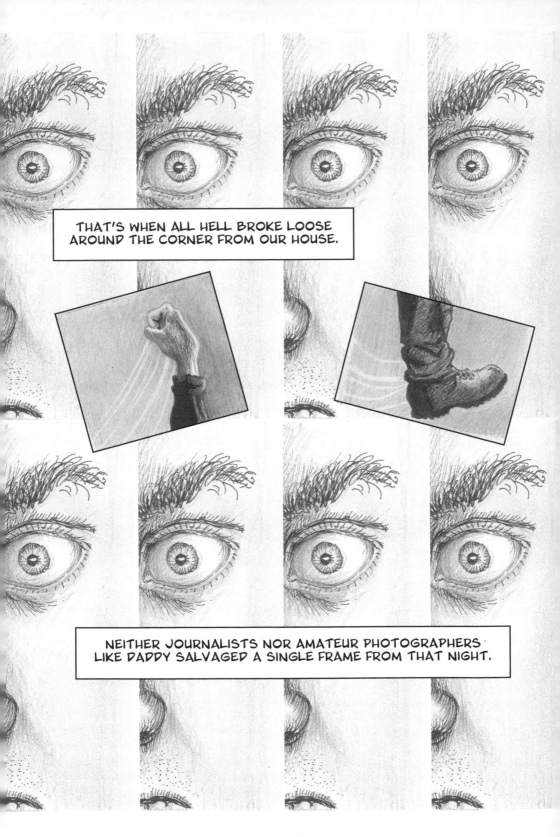

THAT'S WHEN ALL HELL BROKE LOOSE AROUND THE CORNER FROM OUR HOUSE.

NEITHER JOURNALISTS NOR AMATEUR PHOTOGRAPHERS LIKE DADDY SALVAGED A SINGLE FRAME FROM THAT NIGHT.

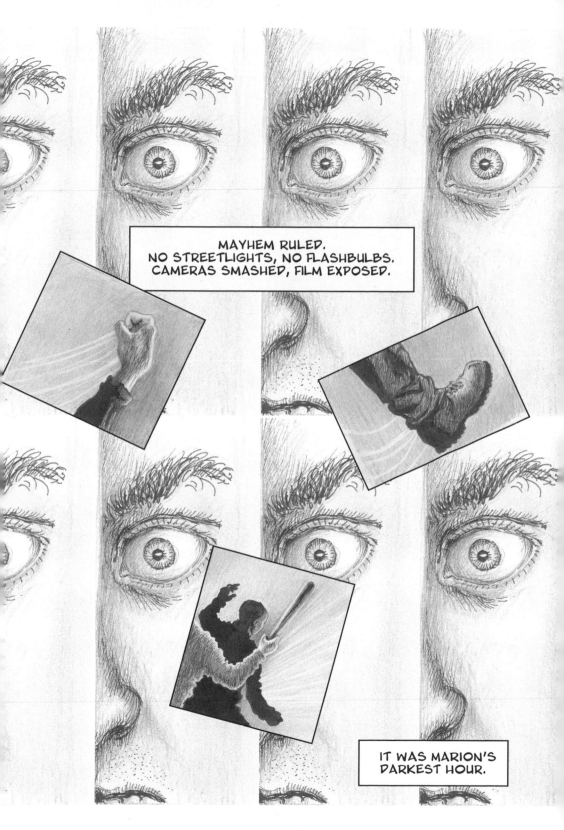

MAYHEM RULED.
NO STREETLIGHTS, NO FLASHBULBS.
CAMERAS SMASHED, FILM EXPOSED.

IT WAS MARION'S
DARKEST HOUR.

NOW AND THEN IMAGES FROM THOSE YEARS COME INTO ALIGNMENT, AND I SEE SOMETHING....

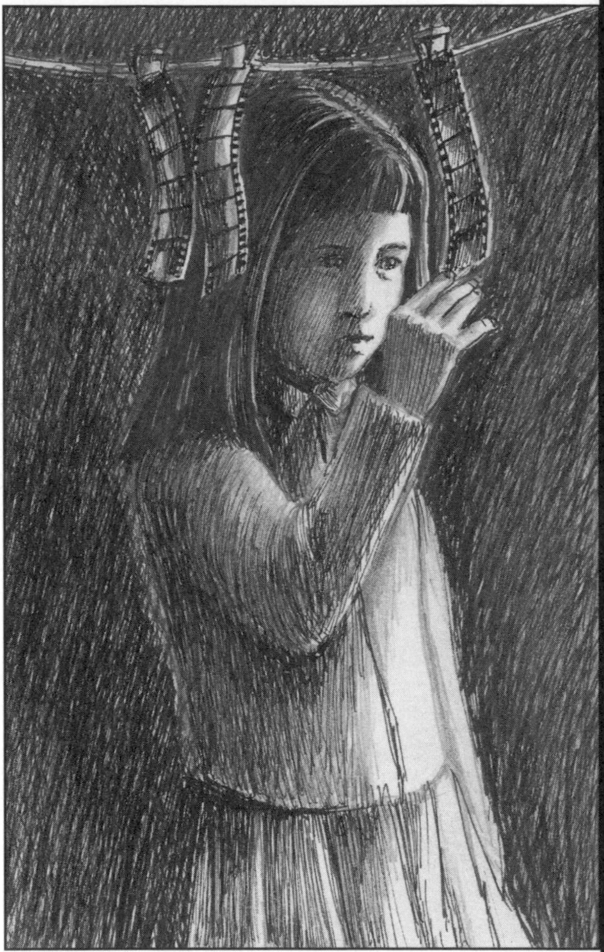

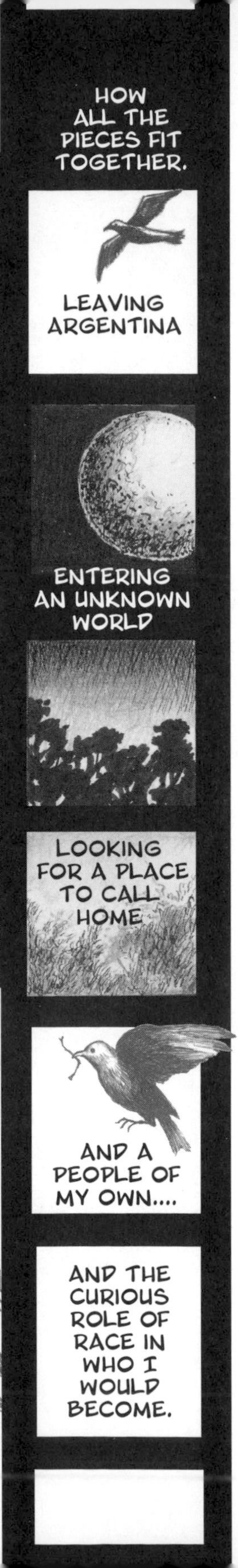

HOW ALL THE PIECES FIT TOGETHER.
LEAVING ARGENTINA
ENTERING AN UNKNOWN WORLD
LOOKING FOR A PLACE TO CALL HOME
AND A PEOPLE OF MY OWN....
AND THE CURIOUS ROLE OF RACE IN WHO I WOULD BECOME.

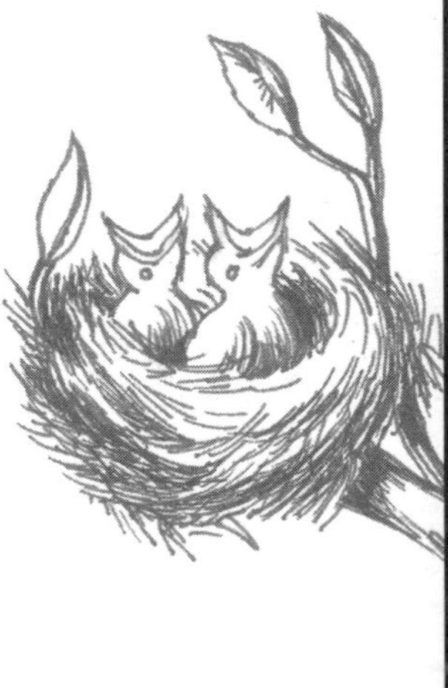

chapter 2

PASSAGE

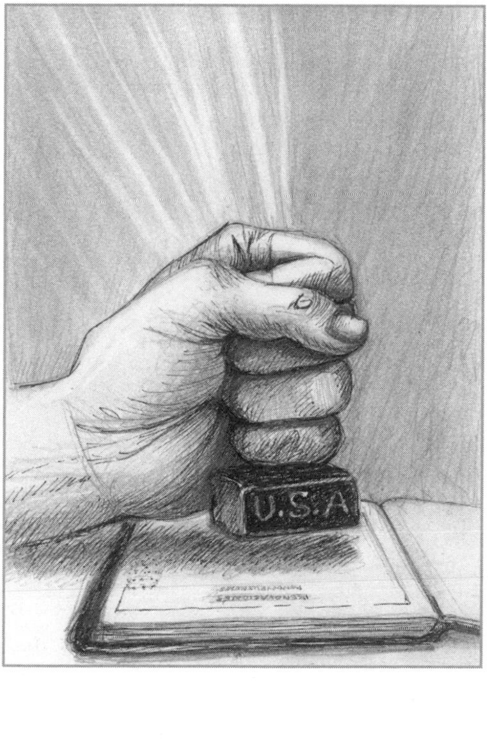
U.S.A

MUCH I HAVE FORGOTTEN,
BUT NOT THE LAST GLIMPSE.

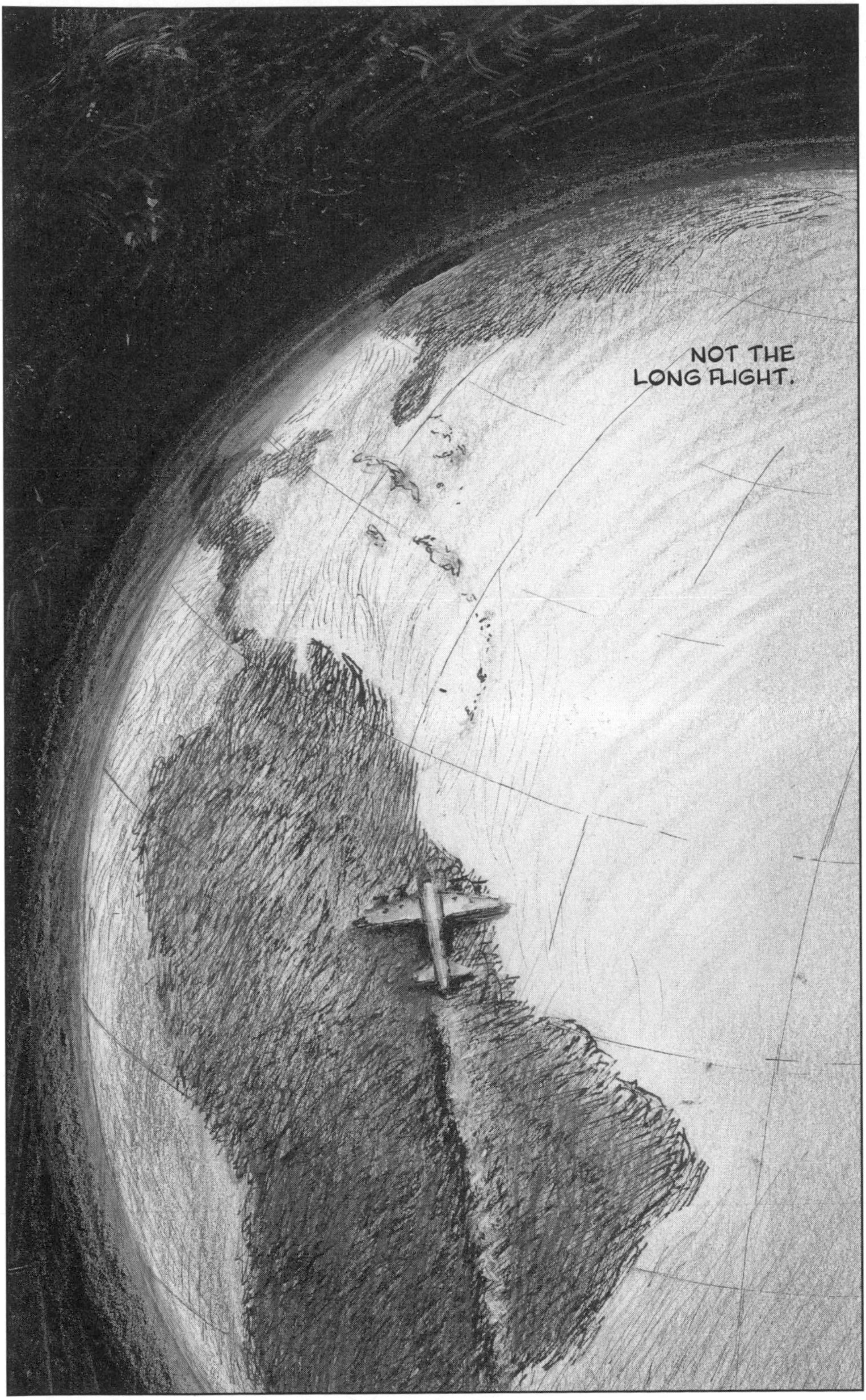
NOT THE
LONG FLIGHT.

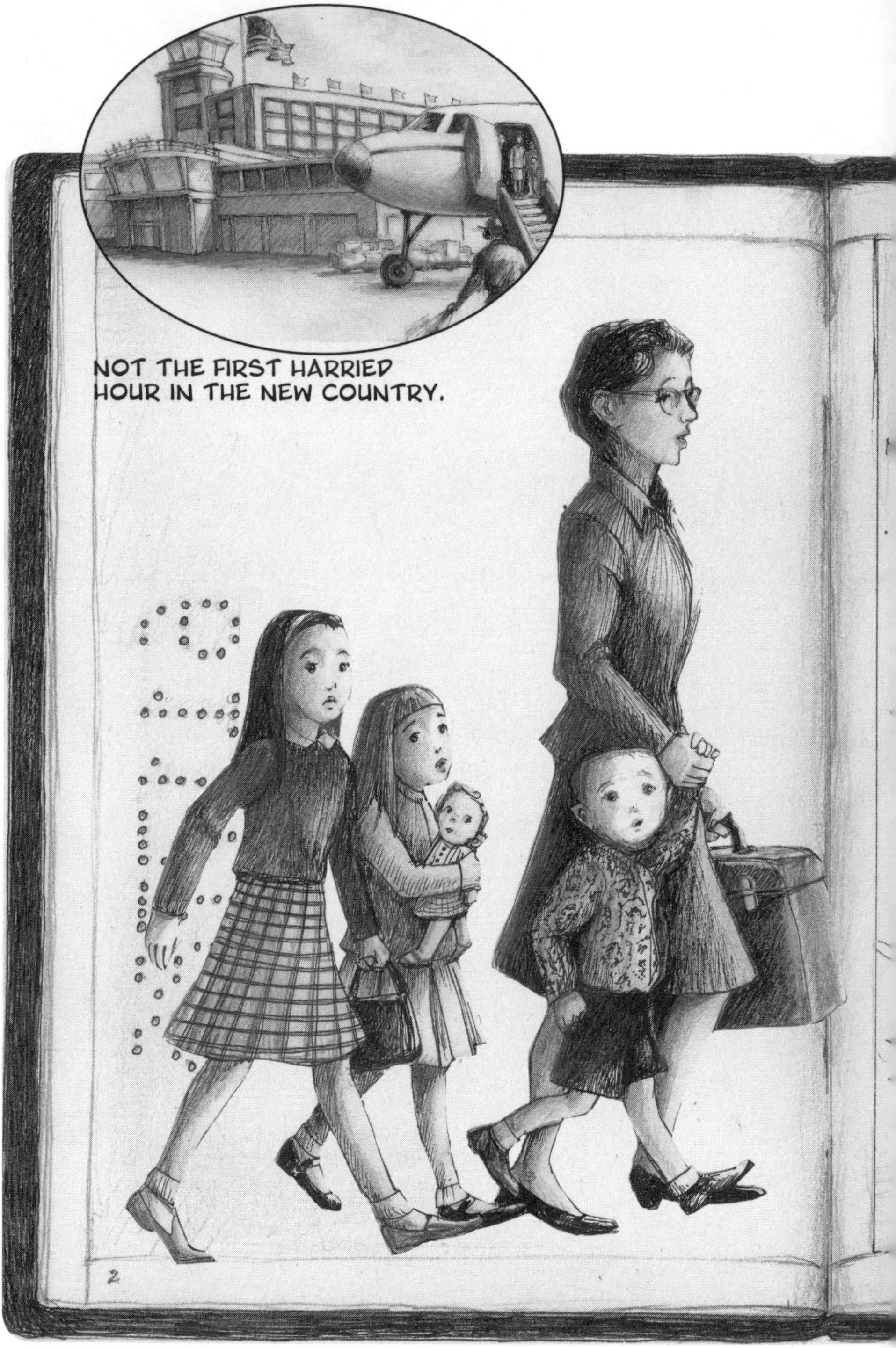
NOT THE FIRST HARRIED
HOUR IN THE NEW COUNTRY.
2

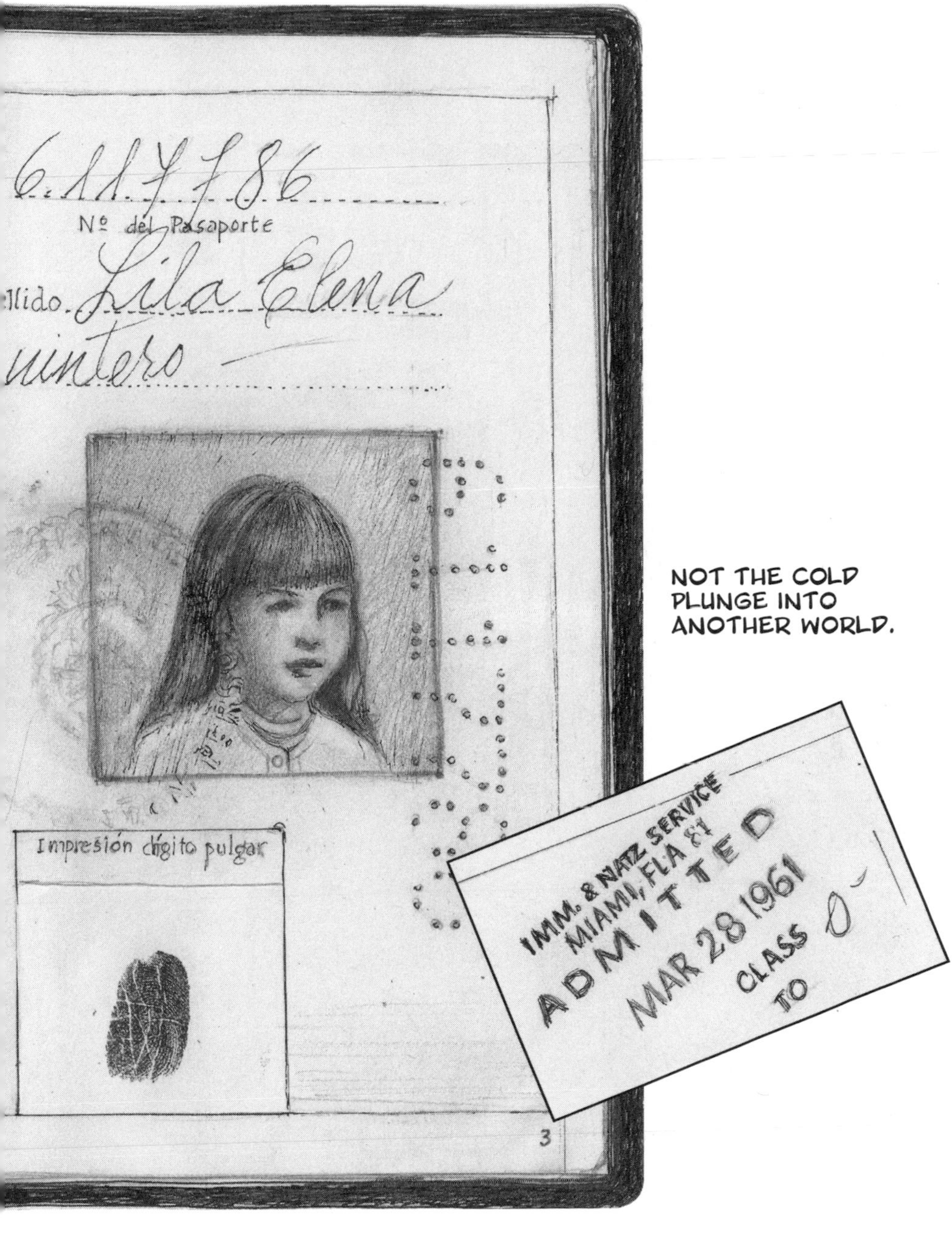
Nº del Pasaporte
Lila Elena
Impresión dígito pulgar
NOT THE COLD PLUNGE INTO ANOTHER WORLD.
IMM. & NATZ SERVICE
MIAMI, FLA 87
ADMITTED
MAR 28 1961
CLASS
TO

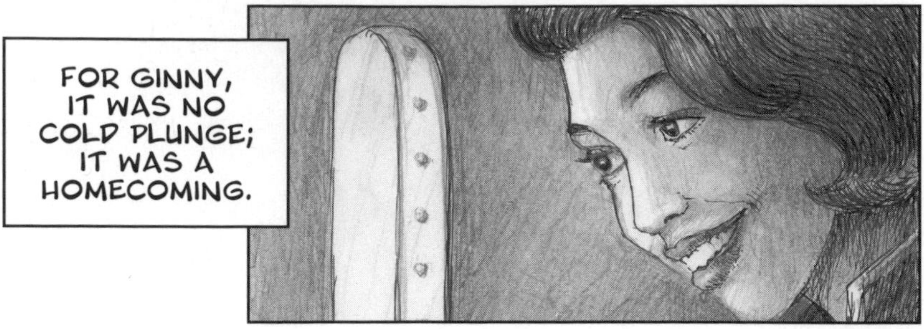
FOR GINNY, IT WAS NO COLD PLUNGE; IT WAS A HOMECOMING.

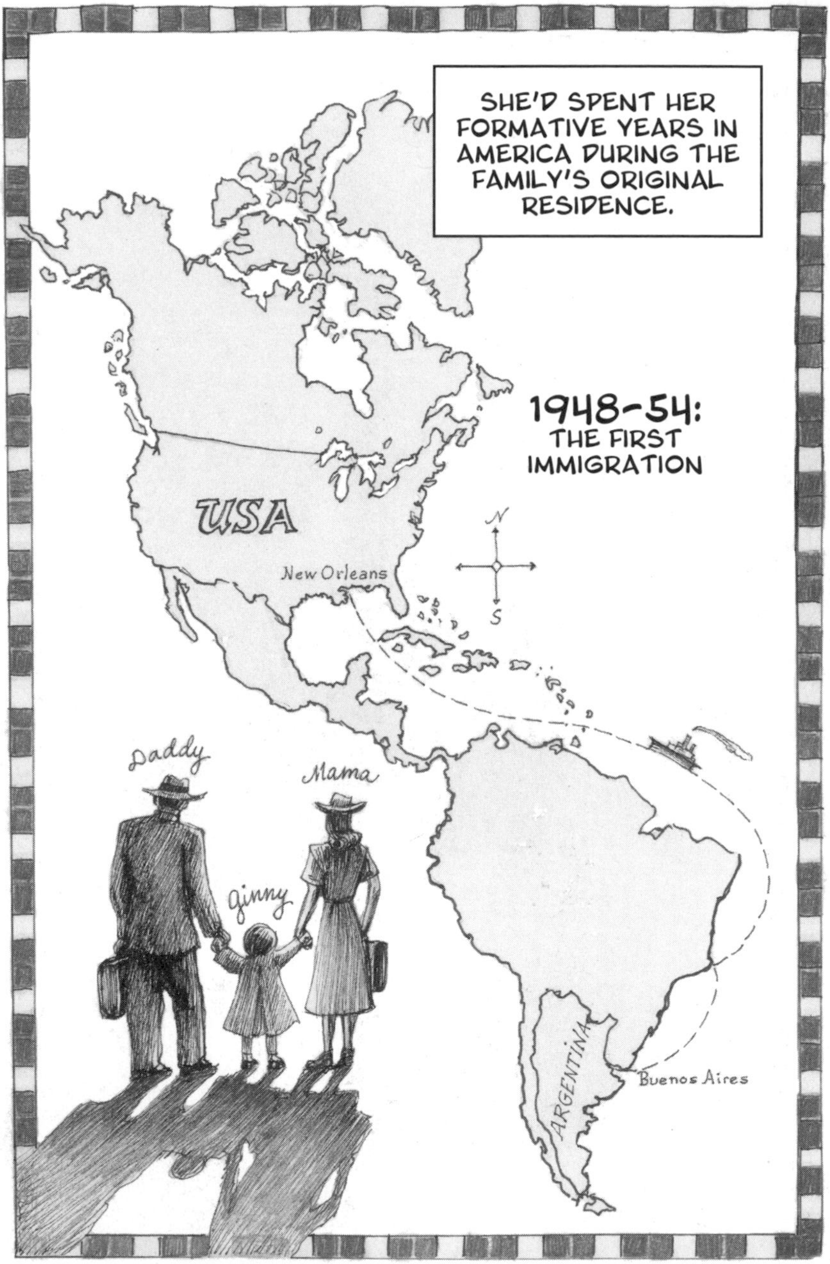
SHE'D SPENT HER FORMATIVE YEARS IN AMERICA DURING THE FAMILY'S ORIGINAL RESIDENCE.
1948–54: THE FIRST IMMIGRATION
USA
N
S
New Orleans
Daddy
Mama
Ginny
ARGENTINA
Buenos Aires

FOR LISSY, ALL THAT WAS REVERSED. SHE WAS BORN IN AMERICA IN 1951, RETURNED TO ARGENTINA AT THE AGE OF THREE, AND SPENT SEVEN CRITICAL YEARS THERE.

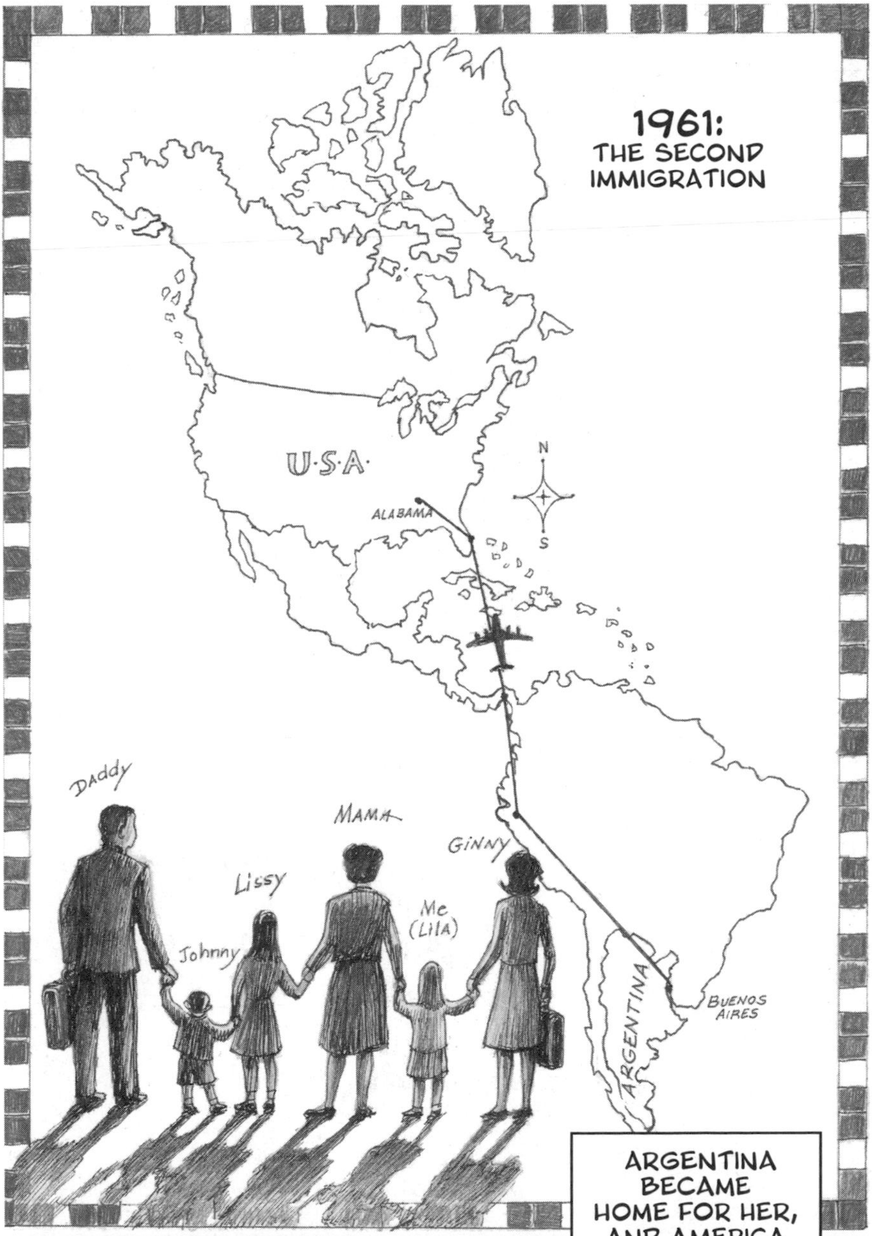

1961:
THE SECOND IMMIGRATION
U.S.A.
N
S
ALABAMA
ARGENTINA
BUENOS AIRES
DADDY
MAMA
GINNY
LISSY
JOHNNY
ME (LILA)
ARGENTINA BECAME HOME FOR HER, AND AMERICA WAS AN ALIEN LAND.

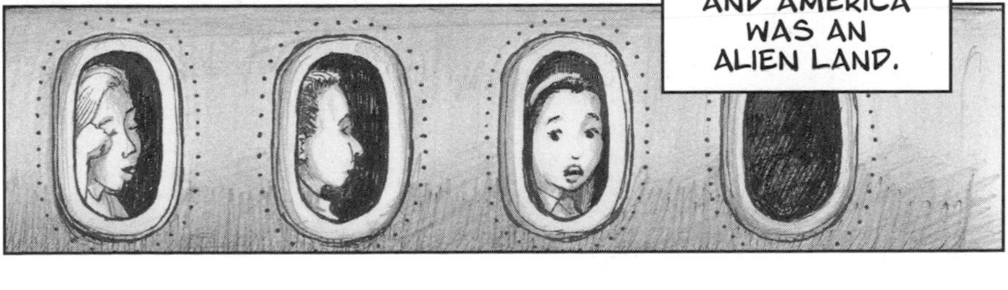

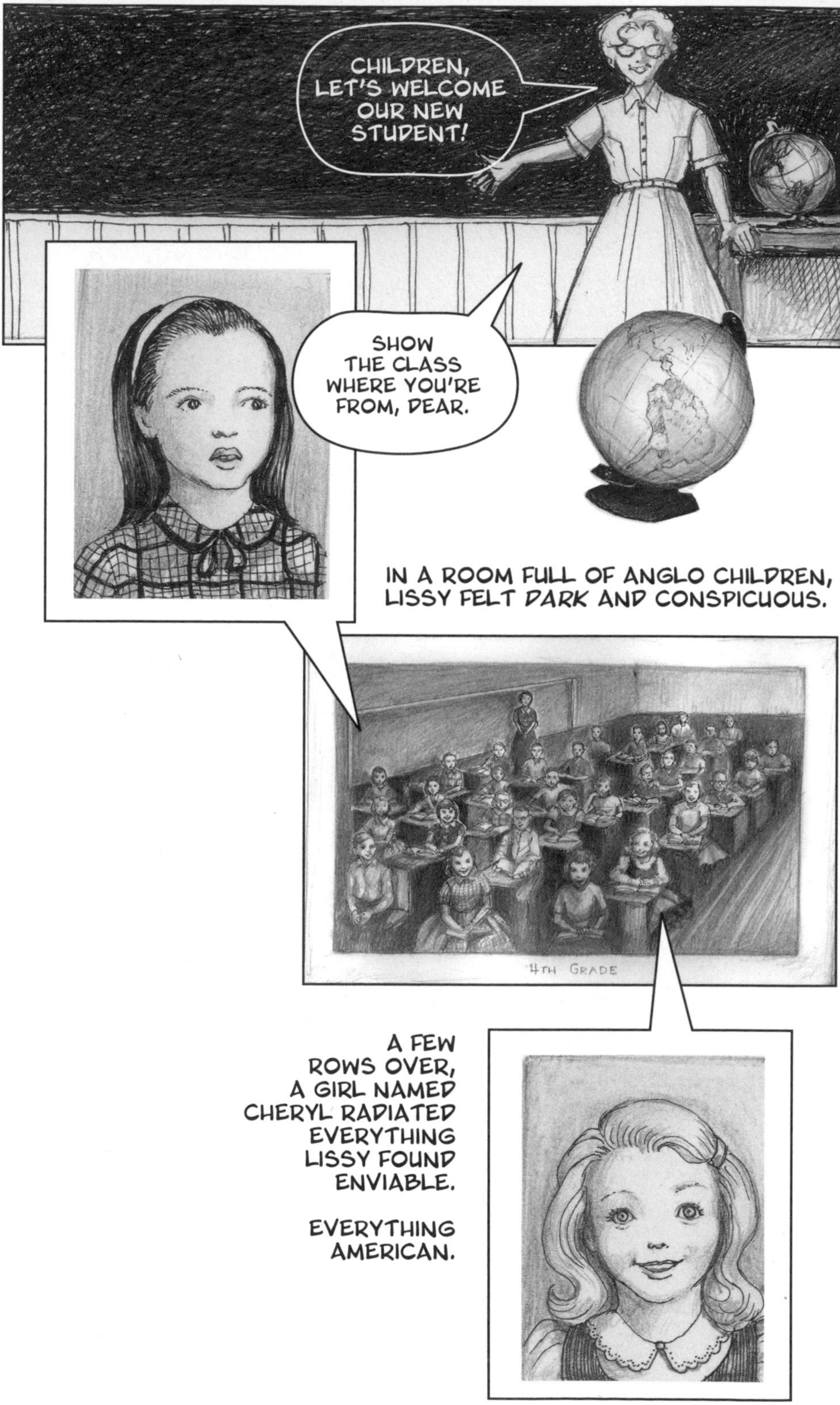
CHILDREN, LET'S WELCOME OUR NEW STUDENT!
SHOW THE CLASS WHERE YOU'RE FROM, DEAR.
IN A ROOM FULL OF ANGLO CHILDREN, LISSY FELT *DARK* AND CONSPICUOUS.
4TH GRADE
A FEW ROWS OVER, A GIRL NAMED CHERYL RADIATED EVERYTHING LISSY FOUND ENVIABLE.
EVERYTHING AMERICAN.

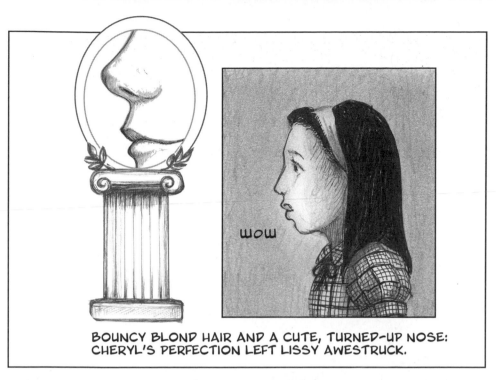

BOUNCY BLOND HAIR AND A CUTE, TURNED-UP NOSE: CHERYL'S PERFECTION LEFT LISSY AWESTRUCK.

SHE DEVISED A METHOD TO RETRAIN HER OWN NOSE, BUT TO NO AVAIL.

WHAT IF IT HAD WORKED?

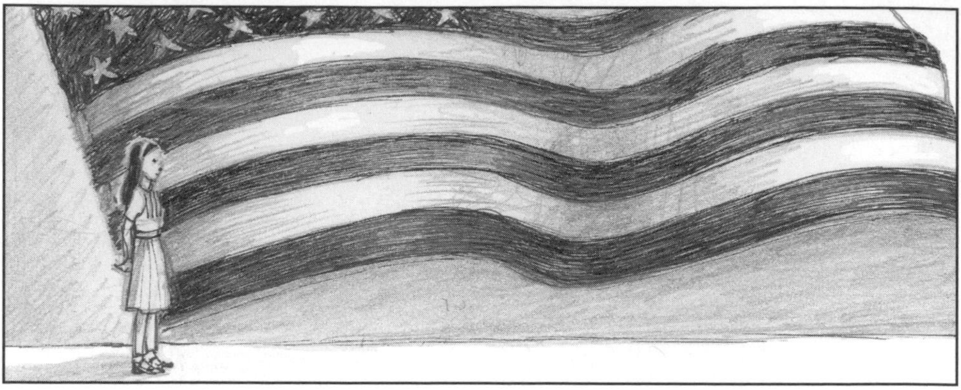

LISSY'S VISION OF AMERICA CAME FROM THE PAGES OF *MCCALL'S* AND OTHER WOMEN'S MAGAZINES SHE'D STUDIED BACK IN ARGENTINA.

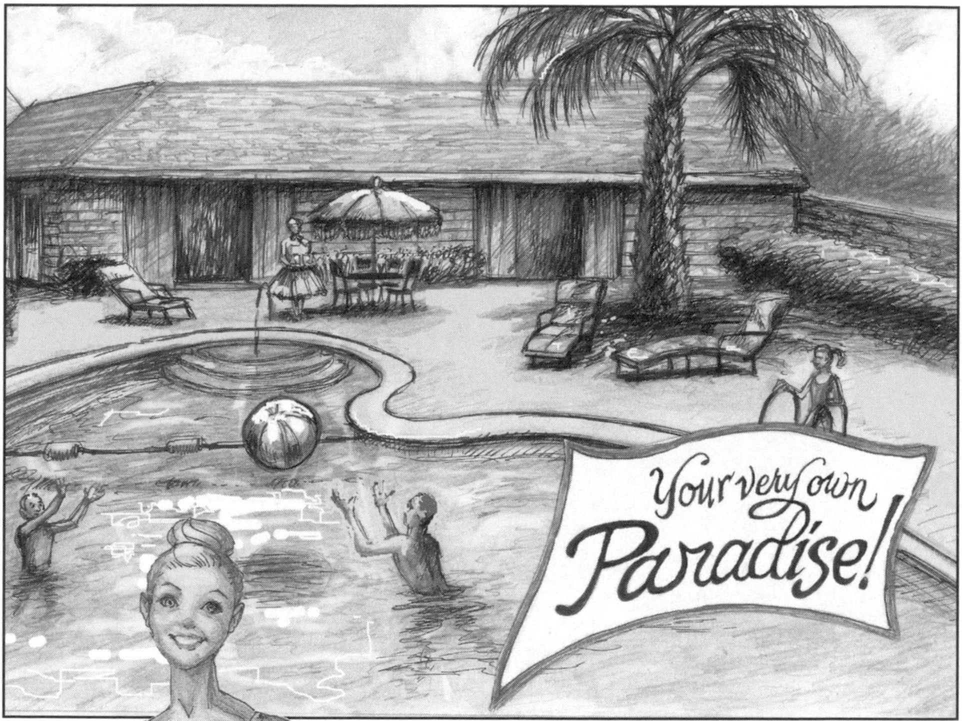
Your very own
Paradise!

CHERYL COULD'VE PASSED FOR A CUTOUT FROM THIS BLOND WONDERLAND OF SPARKLING PROMISE.

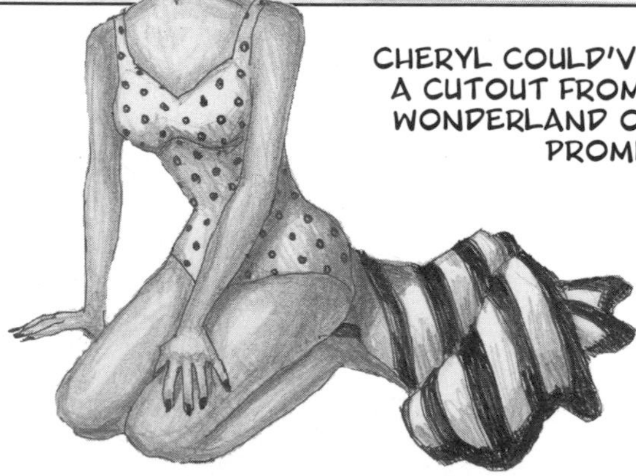

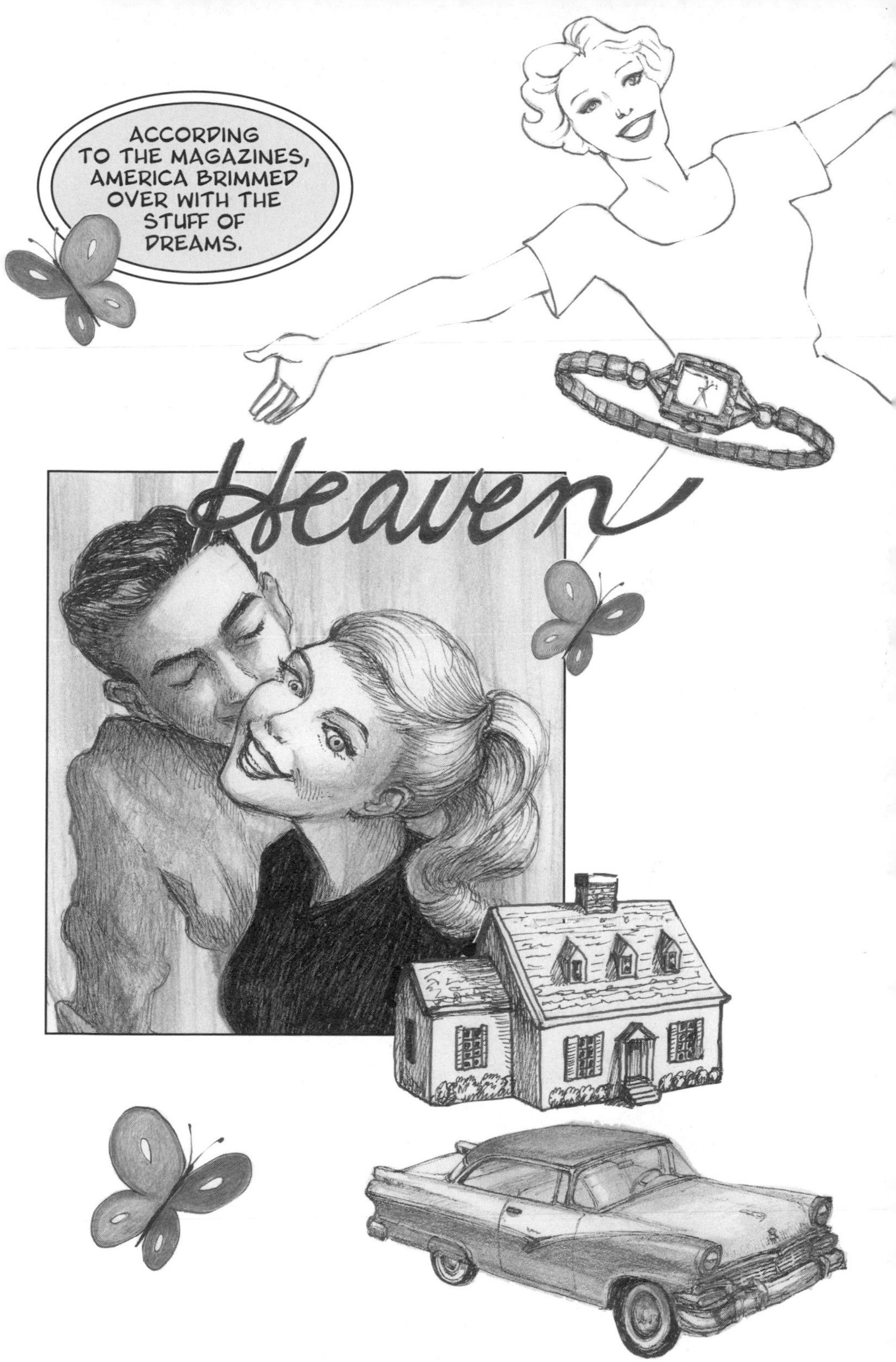
ACCORDING TO THE MAGAZINES, AMERICA BRIMMED OVER WITH THE STUFF OF DREAMS.
Heaven

BUT MARION FELL SHORT
OF LISSY'S GLAMOROUS
EXPECTATIONS.

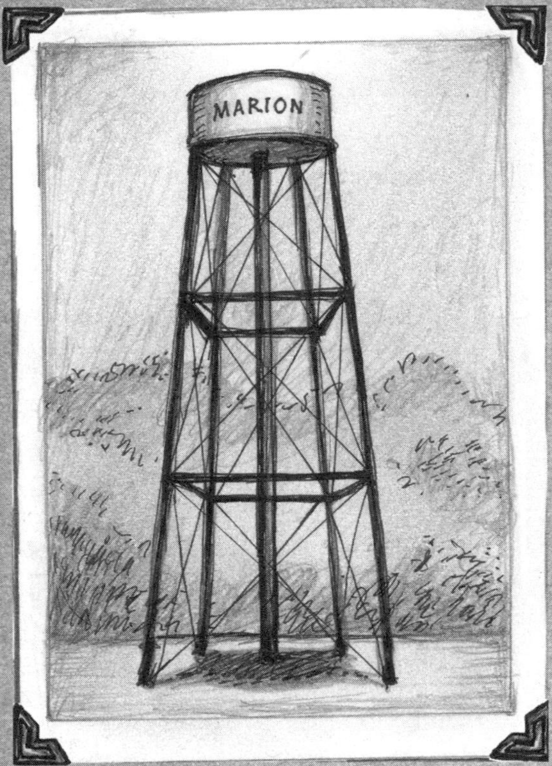
MARION

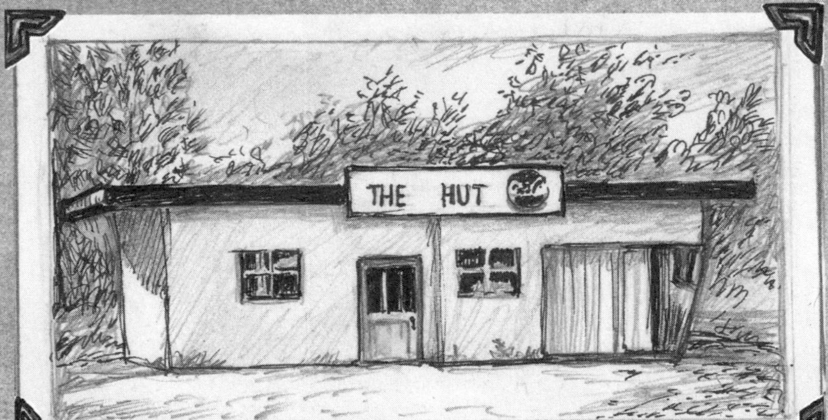
THE HUT

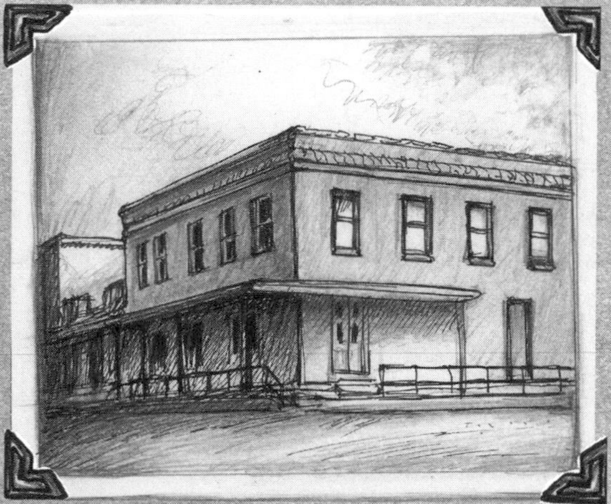

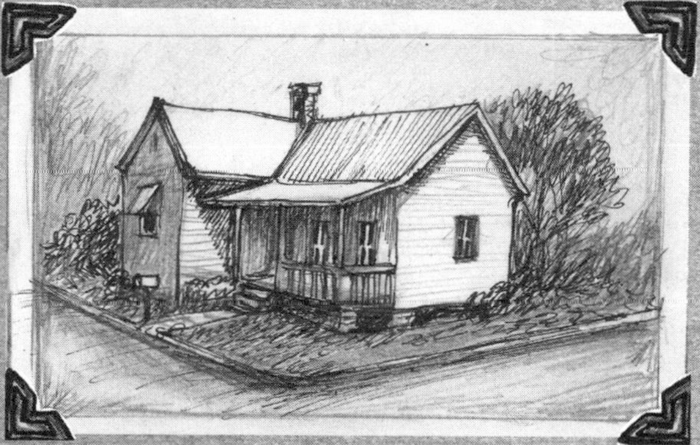

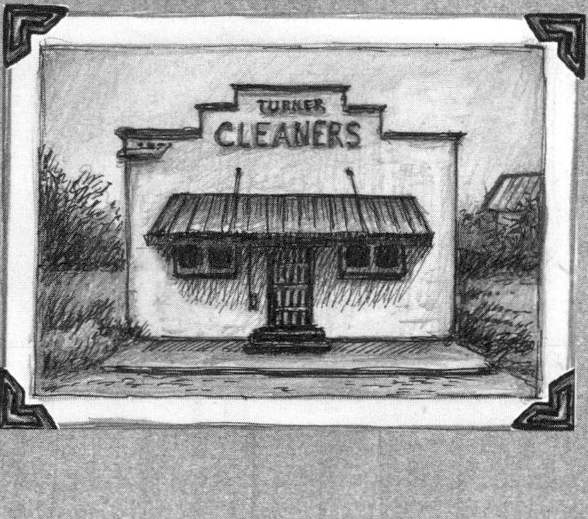
TURNER
CLEANERS

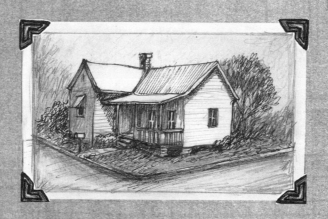

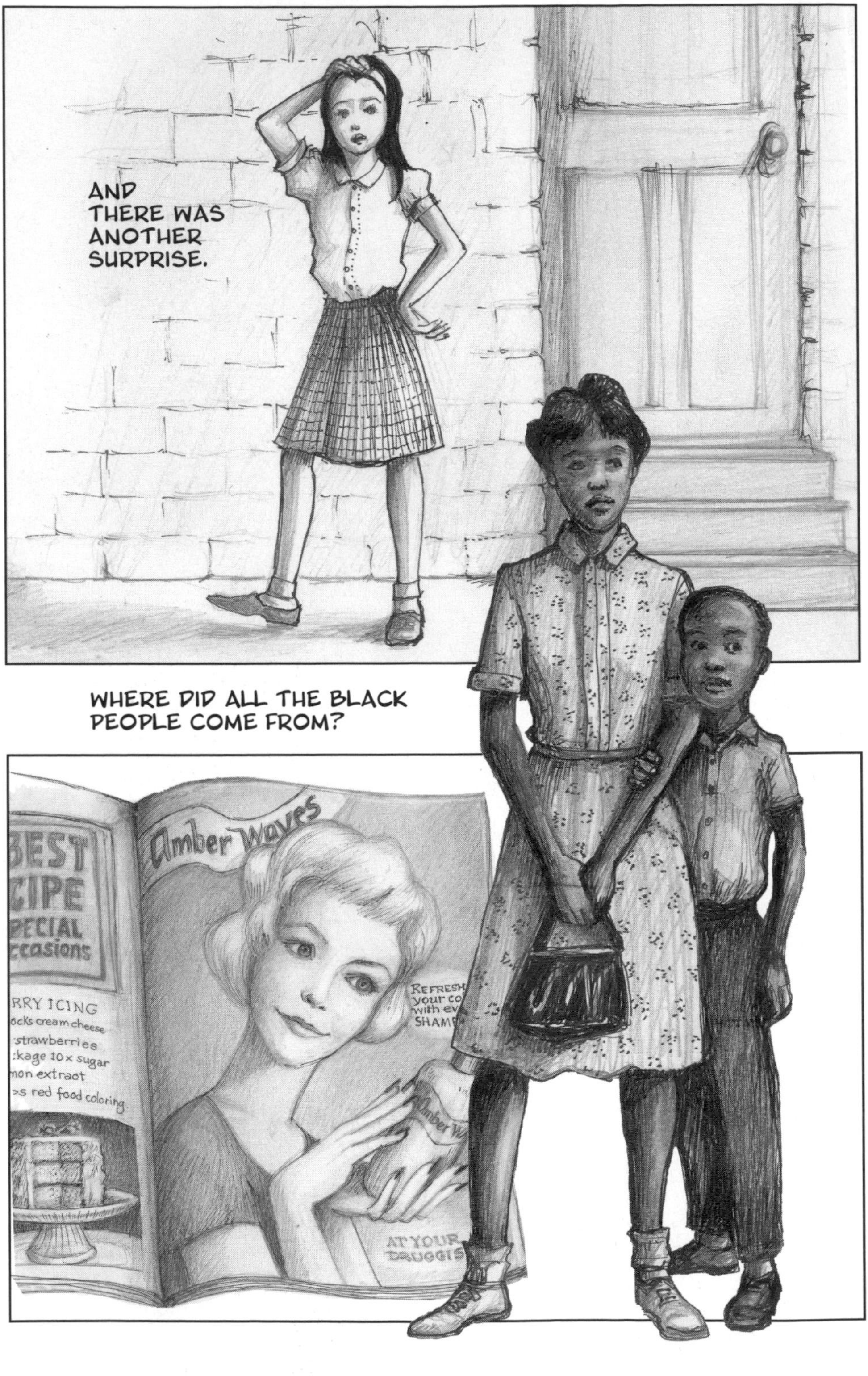
AND THERE WAS ANOTHER SURPRISE.
WHERE DID ALL THE BLACK PEOPLE COME FROM?
BEST
CIPE
PECIAL
ccasions
RRY ICING
ocks cream cheese
strawberries
kage 10x sugar
mon extract
s red food coloring
Amber Waves
REFRESH
your co
with ev
SHAMP
AT YOUR
DRUGGIS

THE MAGAZINES HAD NEVER SHOWN THEM.

IN ARGENTINA, PEOPLE OF AFRICAN ORIGIN WERE A RARE SIGHT.

WHEN WE ARRIVED IN ALABAMA, MY BROTHER GOT HIS FIRST GLIMPSE.

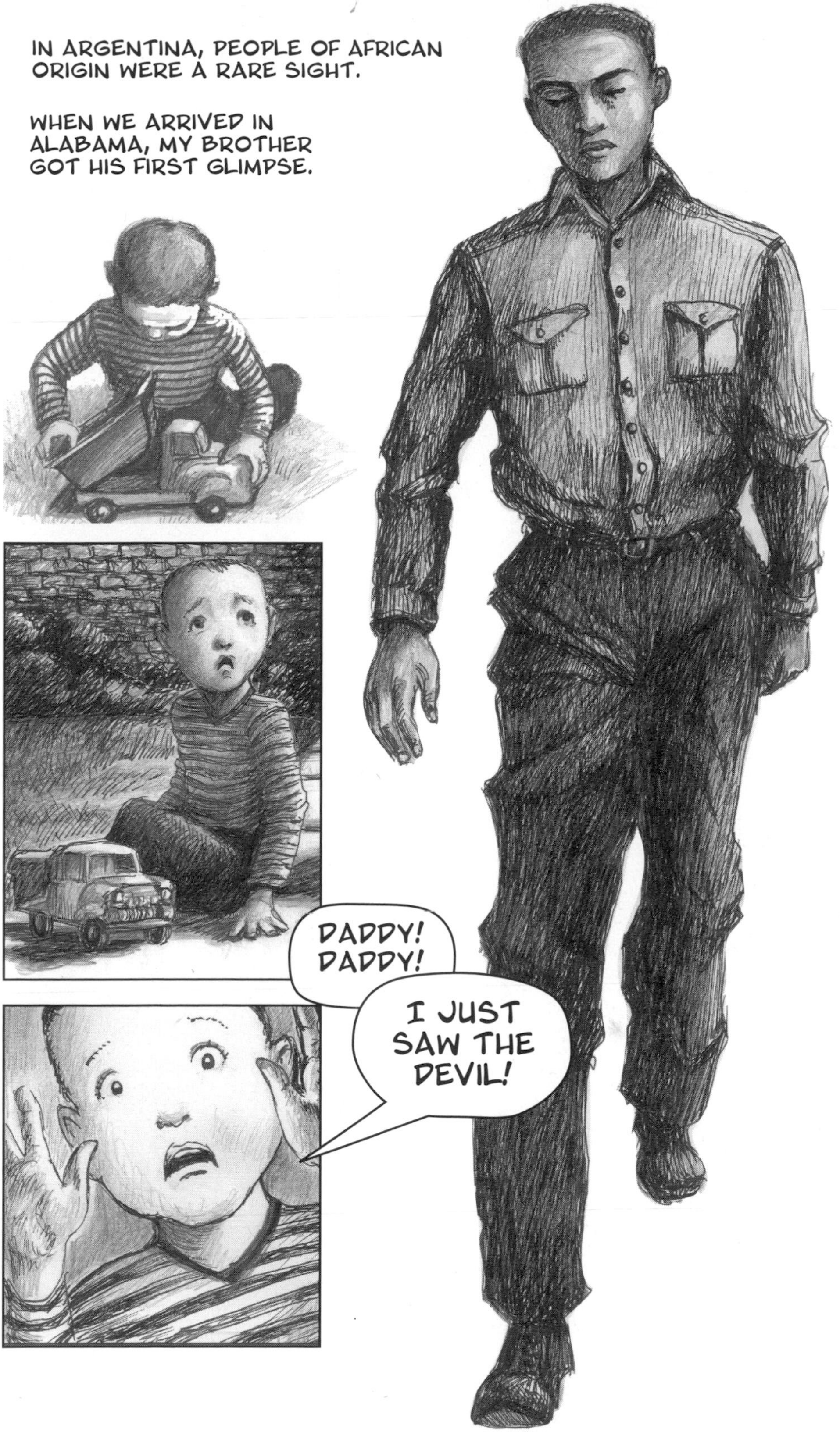
DADDY! DADDY!
I JUST SAW THE DEVIL!

chapter 3

BLENDING IN

VENUS
PINK
PEARL
30
100
WHITE
IVORY BLACK
Winsor&

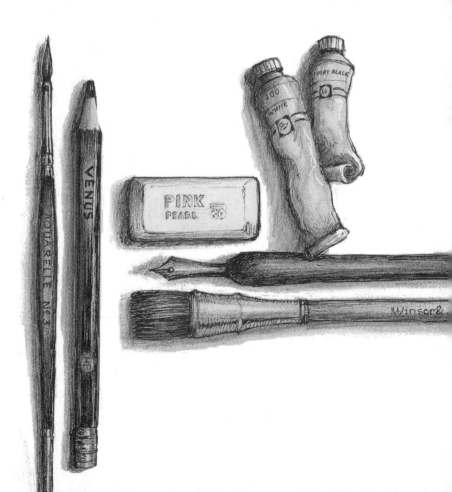

WE WEREN'T MEANT TO PUT DOWN ROOTS IN ALABAMA.

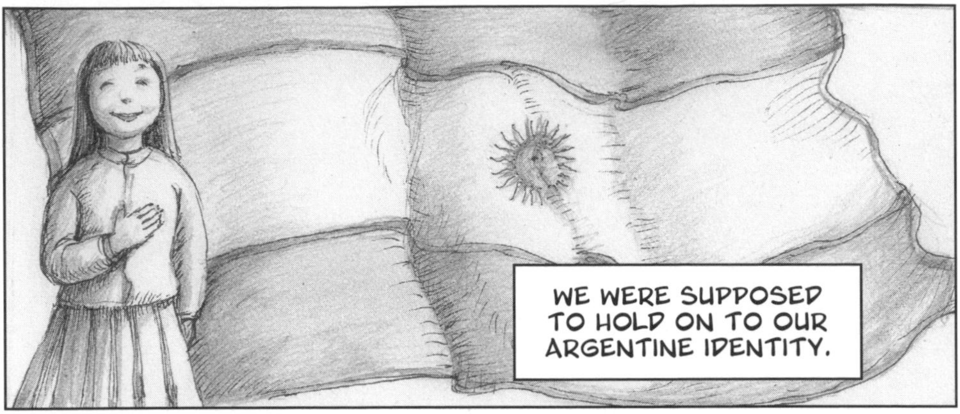
WE WERE SUPPOSED TO HOLD ON TO OUR ARGENTINE IDENTITY.

AND SOMEDAY, RESUME OUR LIVES IN BUENOS AIRES,

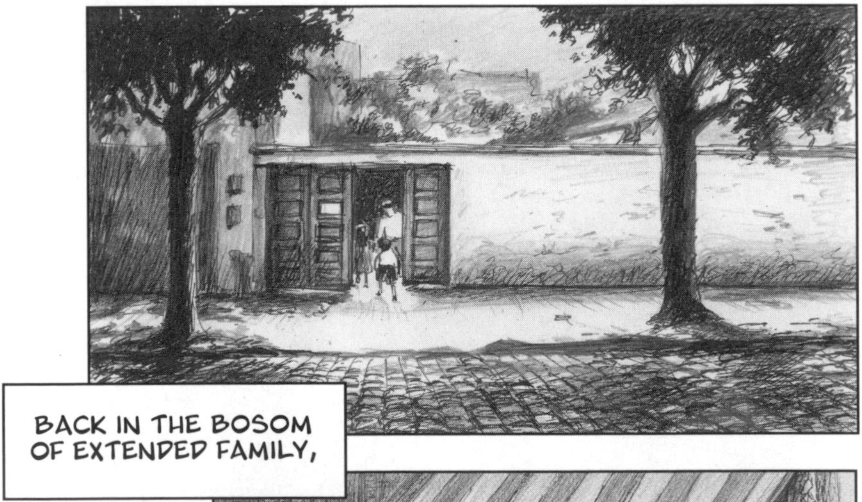
BACK IN THE BOSOM OF EXTENDED FAMILY,

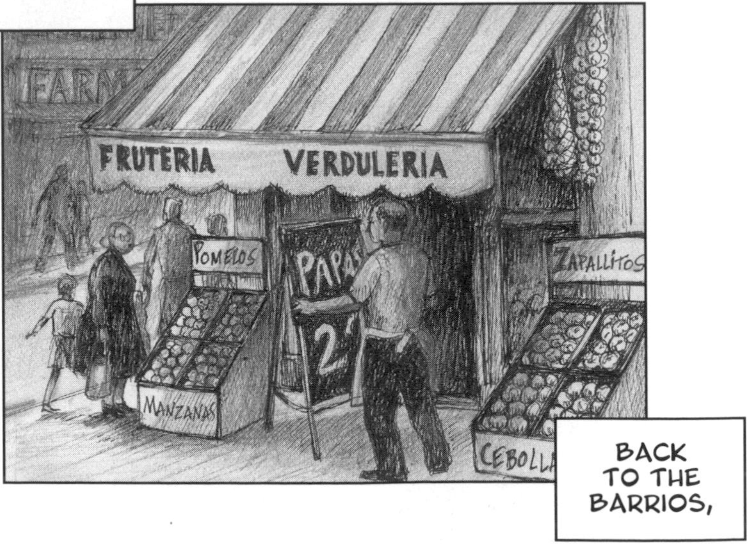
FRUTERIA
VERDULERIA
POMELOS
ZAPALLITOS
MANZANAS
BACK TO THE BARRIOS,

BACK TO THE LIFE A GIRL IN ARGENTINA WOULD'VE FOLLOWED,

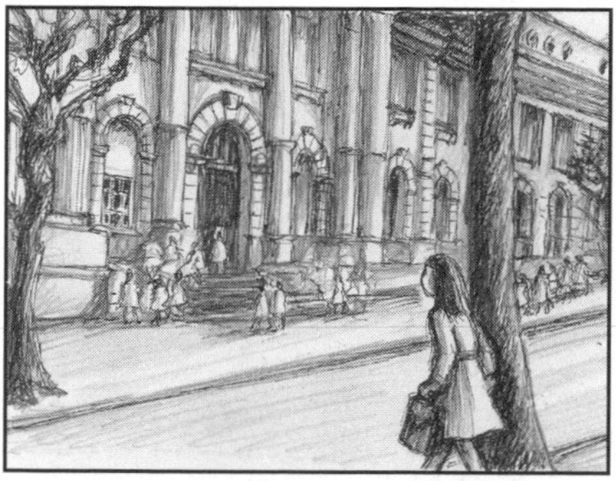

STARTING WITH *LA ESCUELA PRIMARIA*,

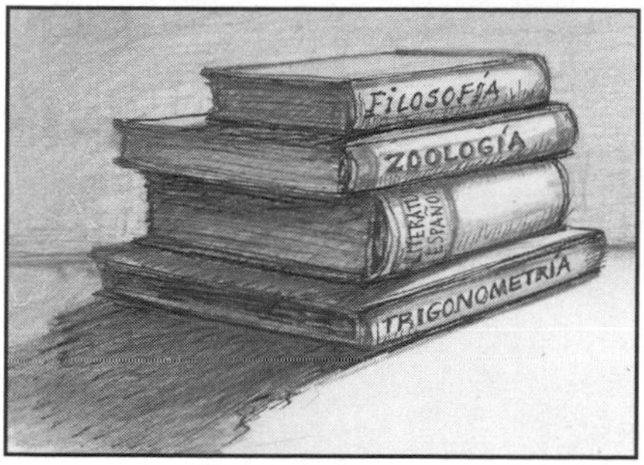

FILOSOFÍA
ZOOLOGÍA
TRIGONOMETRÍA

THEN THE *LICEO* FOR YOUNG LADIES,

NEXT UNIVERSITY, AND THEN...

?

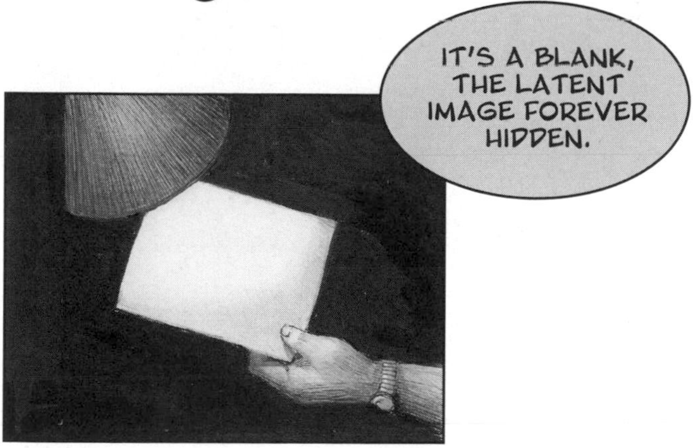

IT'S A BLANK, THE LATENT IMAGE FOREVER HIDDEN.

AND ALTHOUGH FOR SOME YEARS MAMA AND DADDY WOULD SAY, "WHEN WE GO BACK," IT NEVER HAPPENED. WE STAYED IN THE U.S. AND LIVED A DIFFERENT LIFE.

MY PARENTS TOOK A HARD LINE AGAINST THE UNDESIRABLE WAYS OF OUR NEW CULTURE.

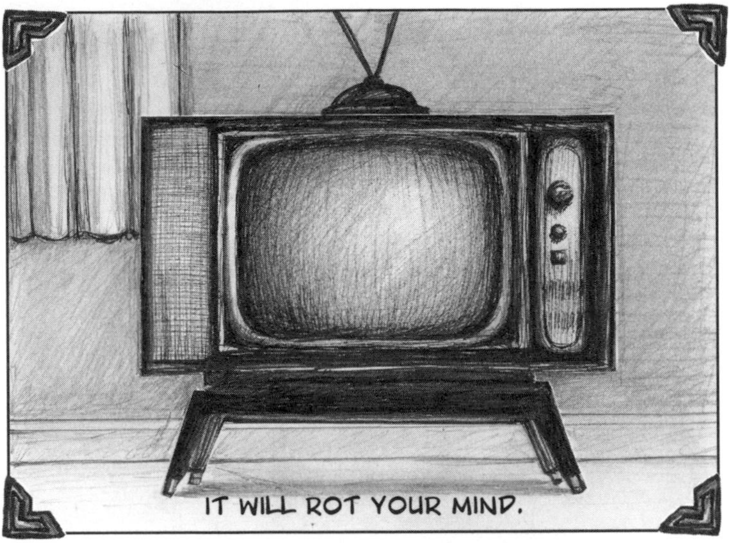
IT WILL ROT YOUR MIND.

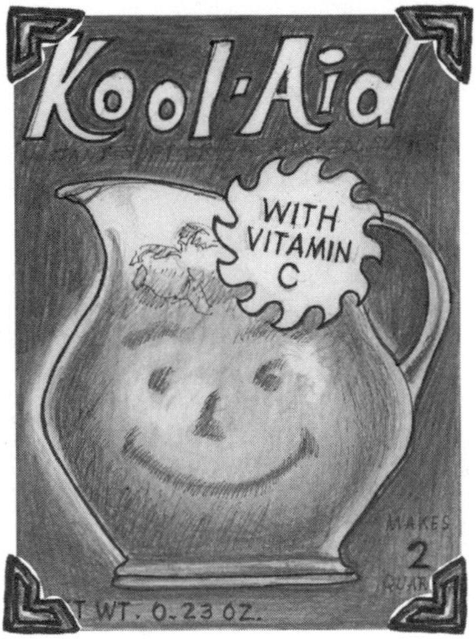
Kool-Aid
WITH VITAMIN C
MAKES 2
T WT. 0.23 OZ.

IT WILL ROT YOUR TEETH.

IT WILL ROT YOUR TONGUE.

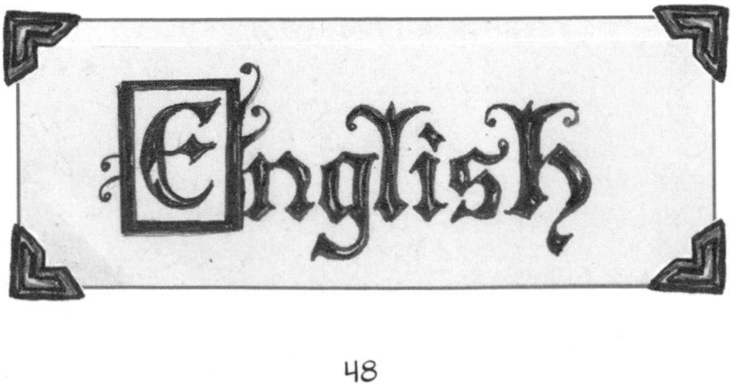
English

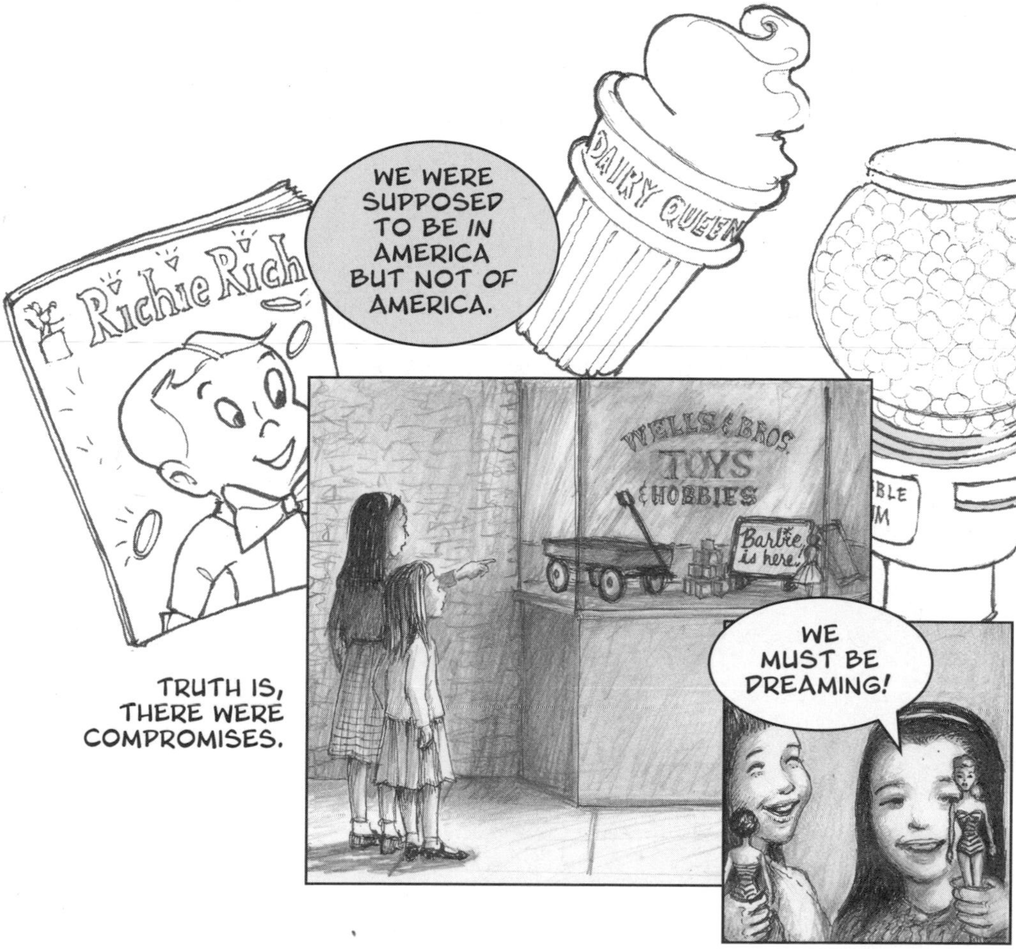
Richie Rich
WE WERE SUPPOSED TO BE IN AMERICA BUT NOT OF AMERICA.
DAIRY QUEEN
WELLS & BROS. TOYS & HOBBIES
Barbie is here!
TRUTH IS, THERE WERE COMPROMISES.
WE MUST BE DREAMING!

AND I LEARNED HOW TO SNEAK.

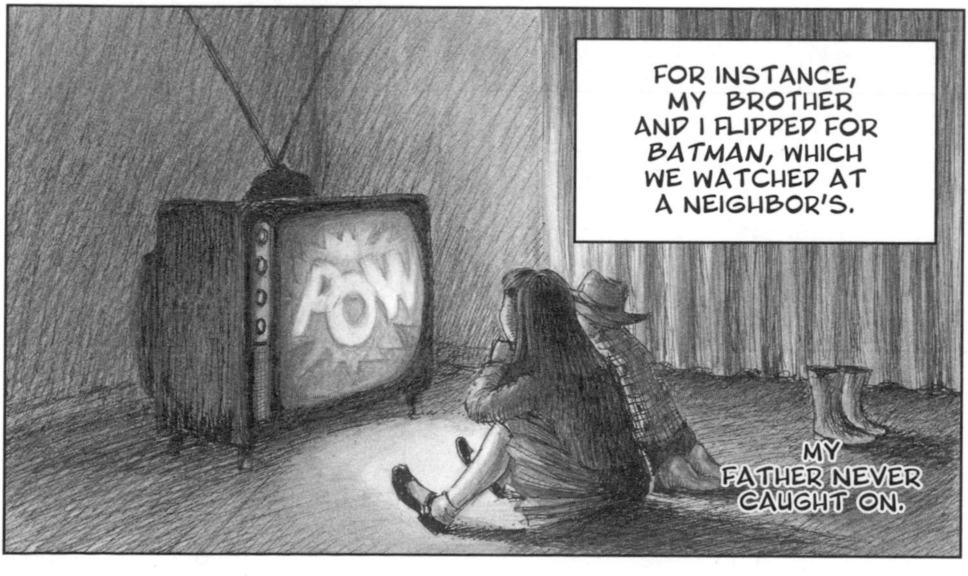
FOR INSTANCE, MY BROTHER AND I FLIPPED FOR BATMAN, WHICH WE WATCHED AT A NEIGHBOR'S.
POW
MY FATHER NEVER CAUGHT ON.

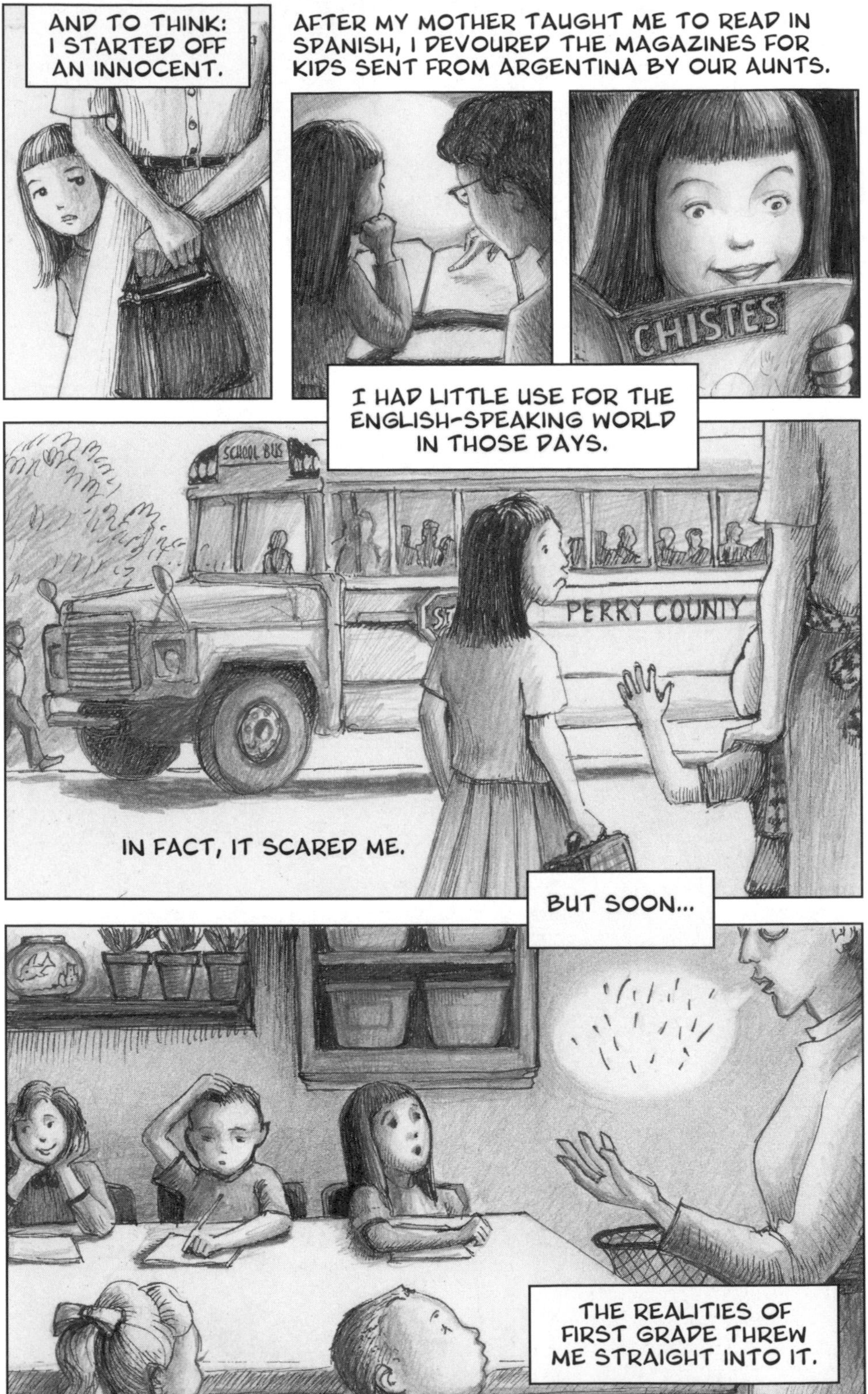
AND TO THINK: I STARTED OFF AN INNOCENT.
AFTER MY MOTHER TAUGHT ME TO READ IN SPANISH, I DEVOURED THE MAGAZINES FOR KIDS SENT FROM ARGENTINA BY OUR AUNTS.
CHISTES
I HAD LITTLE USE FOR THE ENGLISH-SPEAKING WORLD IN THOSE DAYS.
SCHOOL BUS
PERRY COUNTY
IN FACT, IT SCARED ME.
BUT SOON...
THE REALITIES OF FIRST GRADE THREW ME STRAIGHT INTO IT.

I CAN'T EXPLAIN HOW, BUT IT SEEMS AS IF COMPREHENSION CAME TO ME ALL AT ONCE.

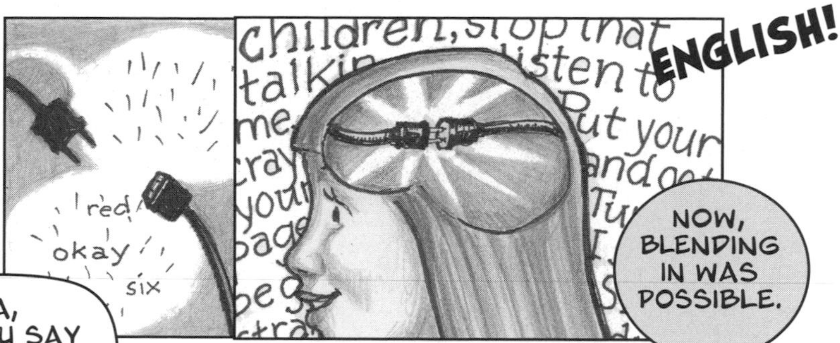

red
okay
six
ENGLISH!
NOW, BLENDING IN WAS POSSIBLE.

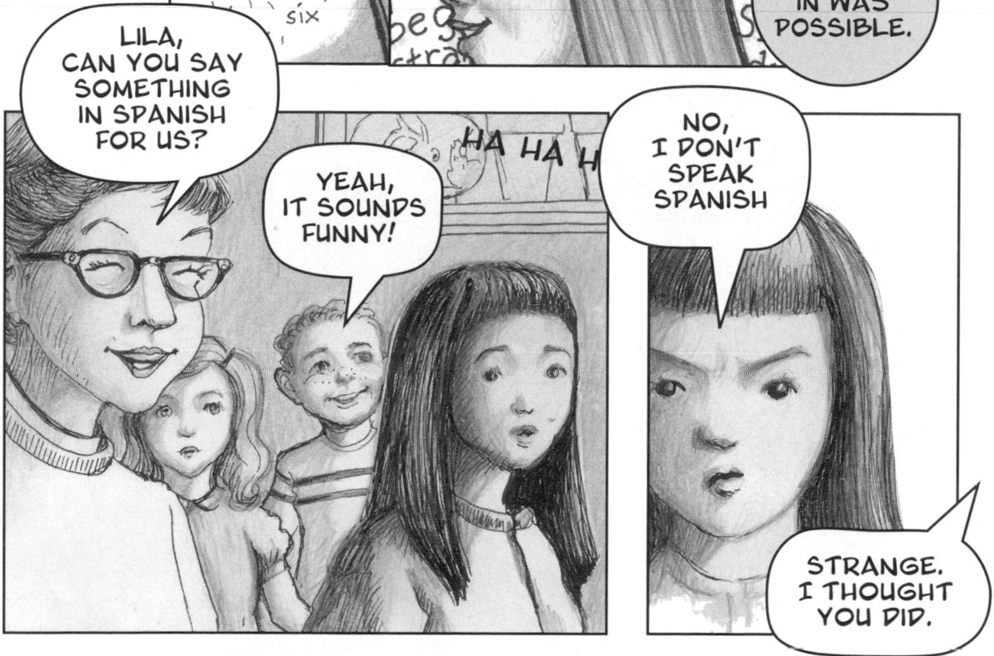

LILA, CAN YOU SAY SOMETHING IN SPANISH FOR US?
YEAH, IT SOUNDS FUNNY!
HA HA
NO, I DON'T SPEAK SPANISH
STRANGE. I THOUGHT YOU DID.

AS I RESISTED MY NATIVE TONGUE, IT BEGAN TO RECEDE INTO DUSTY CORNERS.

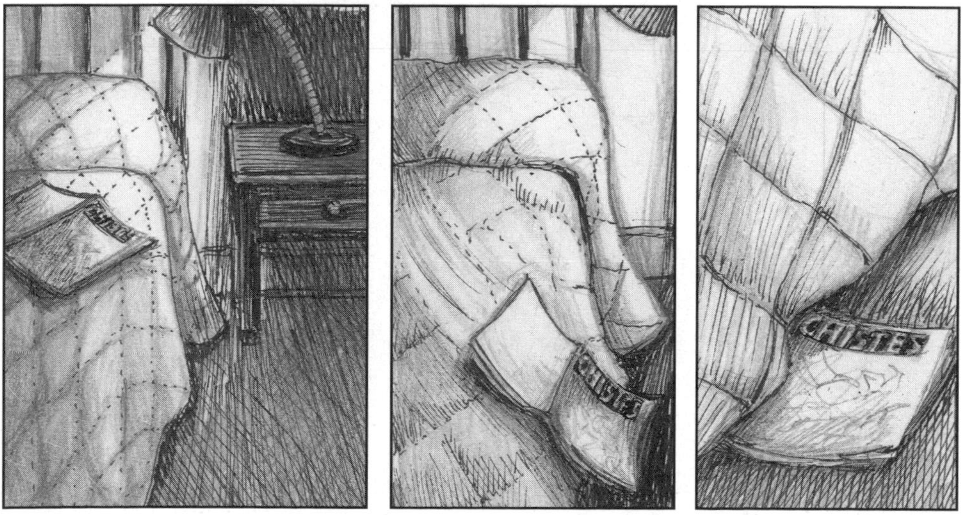

BUT MY PARENTS FELT NO SUCH HESITATION. THEY KEPT SPEAKING SPANISH AT HOME AND IN PUBLIC,

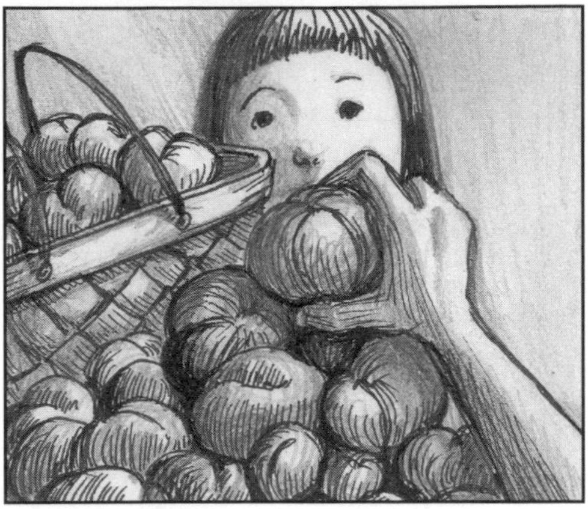
MUY LINDOS TOMATES.*

AS IF IT WERE THE MOST NORMAL THING—WHICH IN MARION, IT WAS *NOT.*

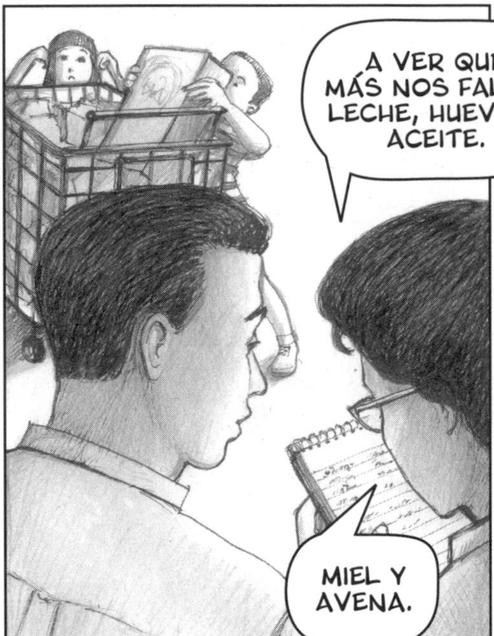
A VER QUE MÁS NOS FALTA: LECHE, HUEVOS, ACEITE.
MIEL Y AVENA.

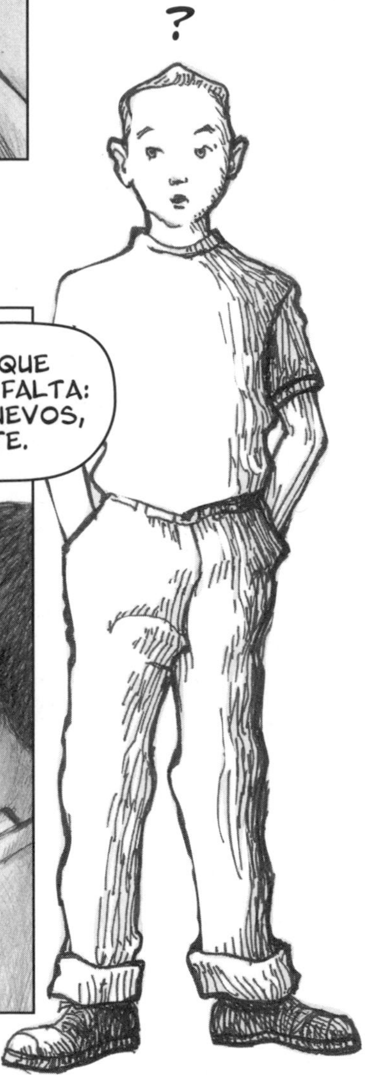
?

*TRANSLATION:
VERY NICE TOMATOES.
LET'S SEE WHAT ELSE WE NEED. MILK, EGGS, OIL.
HONEY AND OATMEAL.

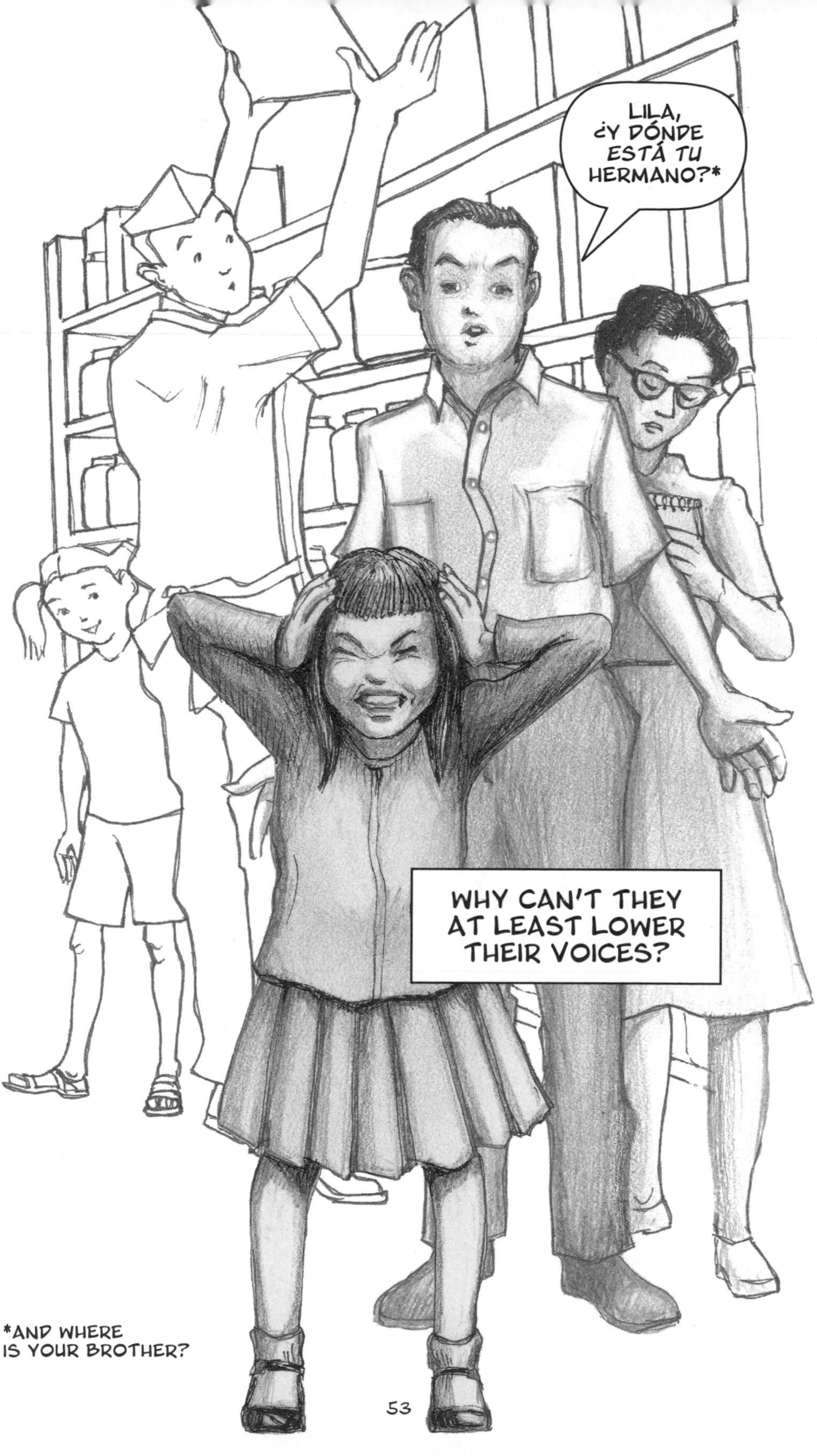
LILA, ¿Y DÓNDE ESTÁ TU HERMANO?*
WHY CAN'T THEY AT LEAST LOWER THEIR VOICES?
*AND WHERE IS YOUR BROTHER?

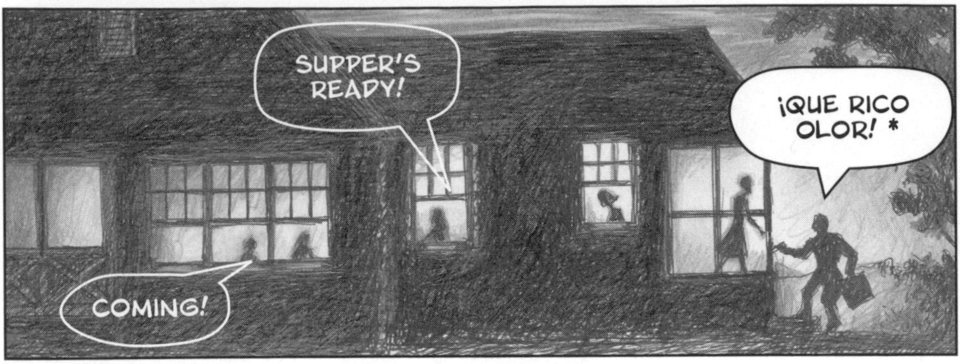
SUPPER'S READY!
¡QUE RICO OLOR! *
COMING!

AT HOME, WHERE I DIDN'T CARE WHAT LANGUAGE WAS SPOKEN, CREATIVITY FLOURISHED.

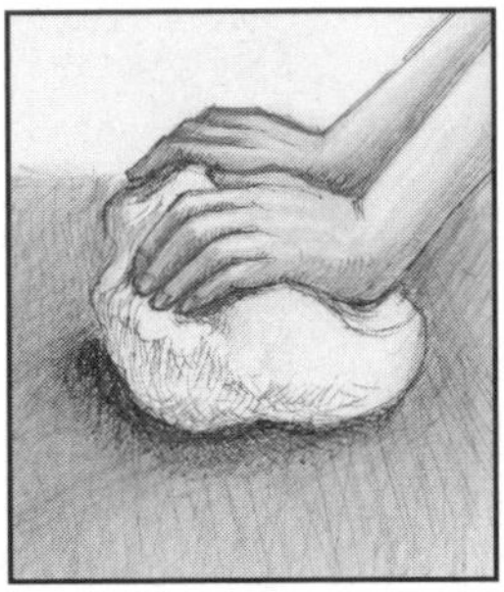

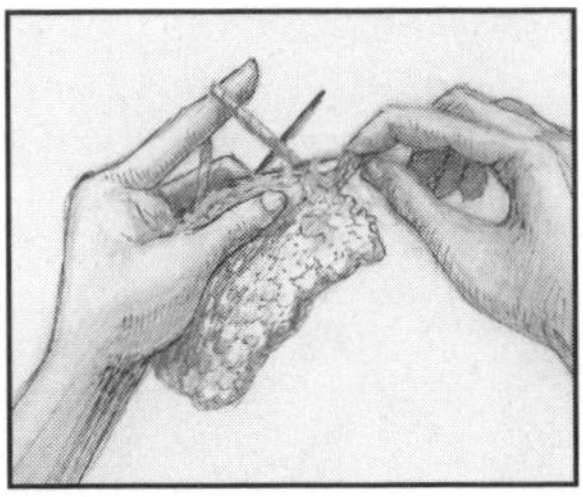

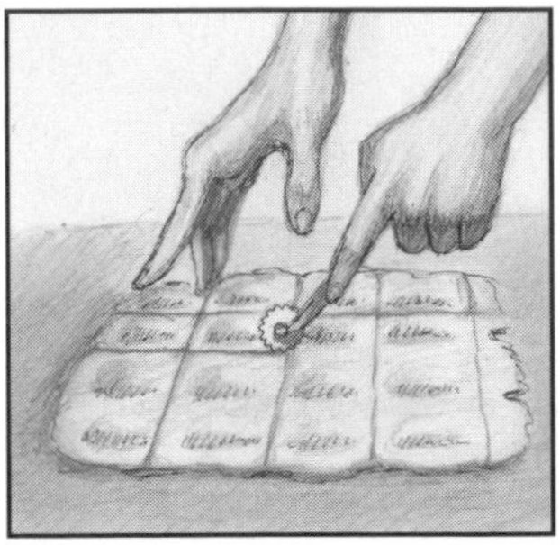

MAMA BAKED FRENCH BREAD, KNITTED SWEATERS, AND PREPARED GASTRONOMIC DELIGHTS LIKE RAVIOLI.

SHE ALSO PAINTED PORTRAITS FOR CLIENTS ALL OVER ALABAMA AND POINTS BEYOND.

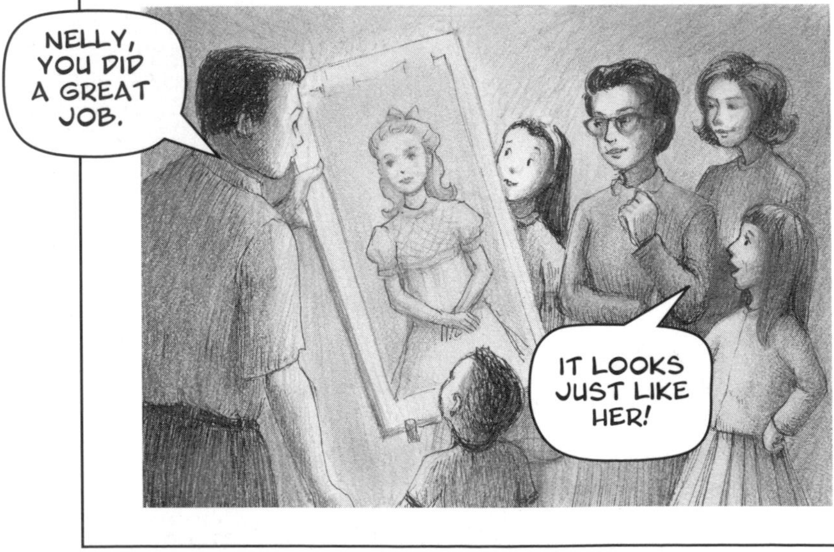
NELLY, YOU DID A GREAT JOB.
IT LOOKS JUST LIKE HER!

* WHAT A DELICIOUS SMELL!

I OFTEN LOST MYSELF IN MAKING ART.

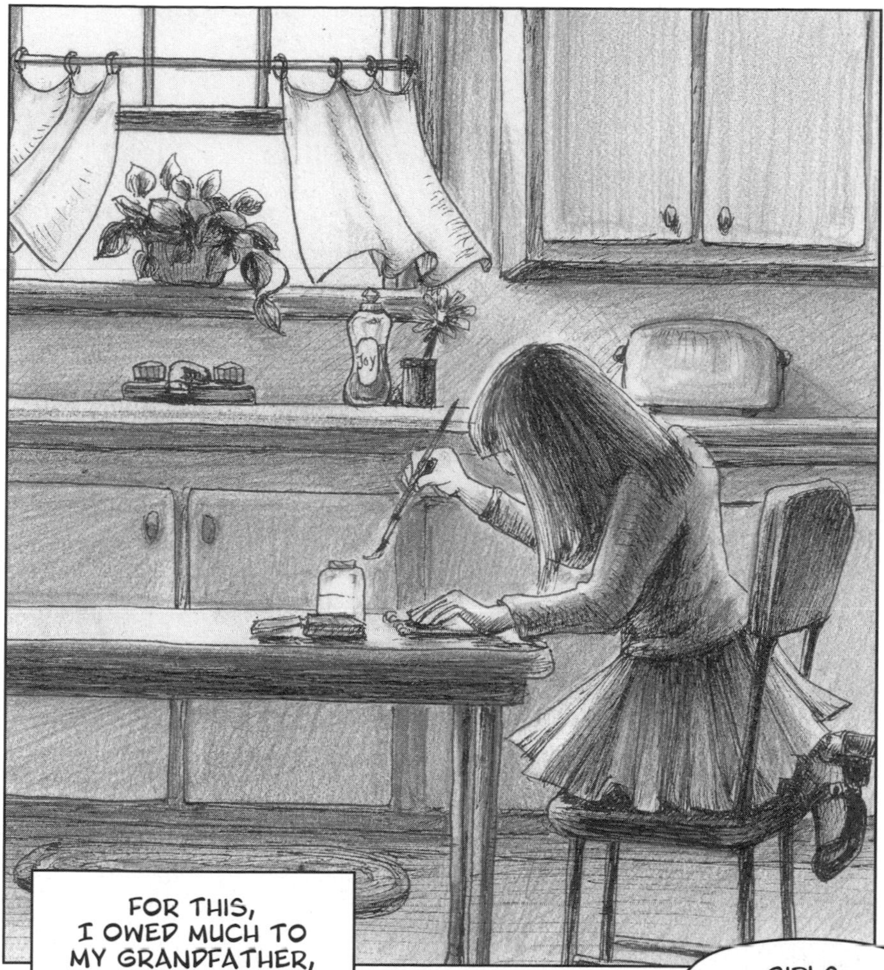

FOR THIS, I OWED MUCH TO MY GRANDFATHER, WHO TAUGHT HIS DAUGHTERS THE RIGORS OF DRAFTSMANSHIP.

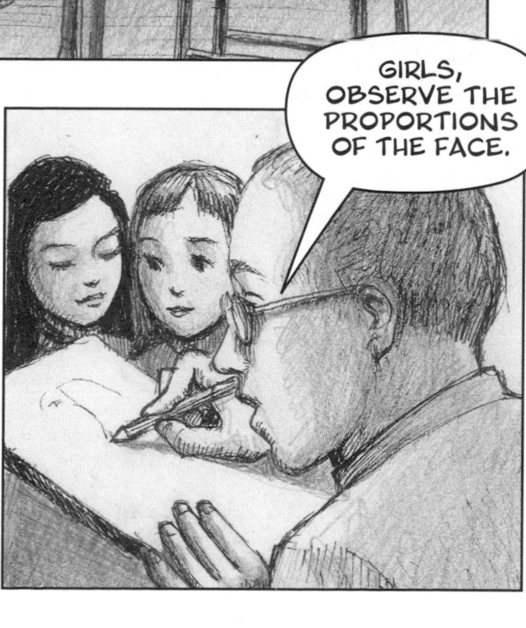
GIRLS, OBSERVE THE PROPORTIONS OF THE FACE.

MAMA PASSED THESE LESSONS ON TO US, HER CHILDREN.

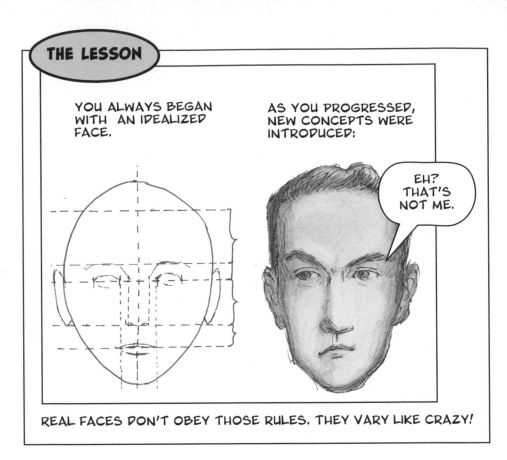

YOU ALWAYS BEGAN WITH AN IDEALIZED FACE.

AS YOU PROGRESSED, NEW CONCEPTS WERE INTRODUCED:

EH? THAT'S NOT ME.

REAL FACES DON'T OBEY THOSE RULES. THEY VARY LIKE CRAZY!

AND THE FACE ISN'T COMPOSED OF FLAT SHAPES.

INSTEAD, EVERY PLANE, EVERY FEATURE,

IS A FULLY DIMENSIONAL STRUCTURE WHOSE APPEARANCE VARIES DEPENDING ON THE ANGLE OF VIEW.

AND THE ONLY WAY TO DRAW IT CORRECTLY IS TO LOOK— *REALLY LOOK.*

THE LESSON CONTINUED WITH PROPORTIONS OF THE HUMAN BODY.

1
2
3
4
5
6
7
8

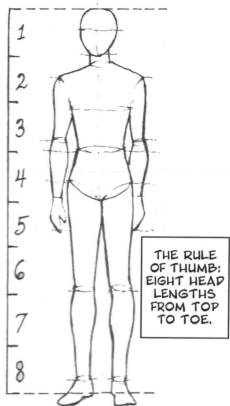

THE RULE OF THUMB: EIGHT HEAD LENGTHS FROM TOP TO TOE.

1
2
3
4
5
6
7

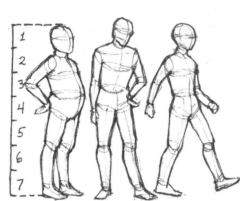

AS YOU LEARNED TO LOOK—*REALLY* LOOK—YOU BEGAN TO SEE THE WISHFUL THINKING BEHIND THAT FORMULA.

LISSY AND I WERE NOWHERE NEAR RELINQUISHING THOSE IDEALS WHEN WE LAID EYES ON THE RAVISHING ELKE SOMMER, A SCREEN STAR OF THE 1960S.

A SHOT IN THE DARK
PETER SELLERS ELKE SOMMER
WOW! SHE'S GORGEOUS!

WE PERSUADED MAMA TO DRAW A PAPER DOLL FOR US BASED ON ELKE. WE DREW AND COLORED HER GLAMOROUS WARDROBE.

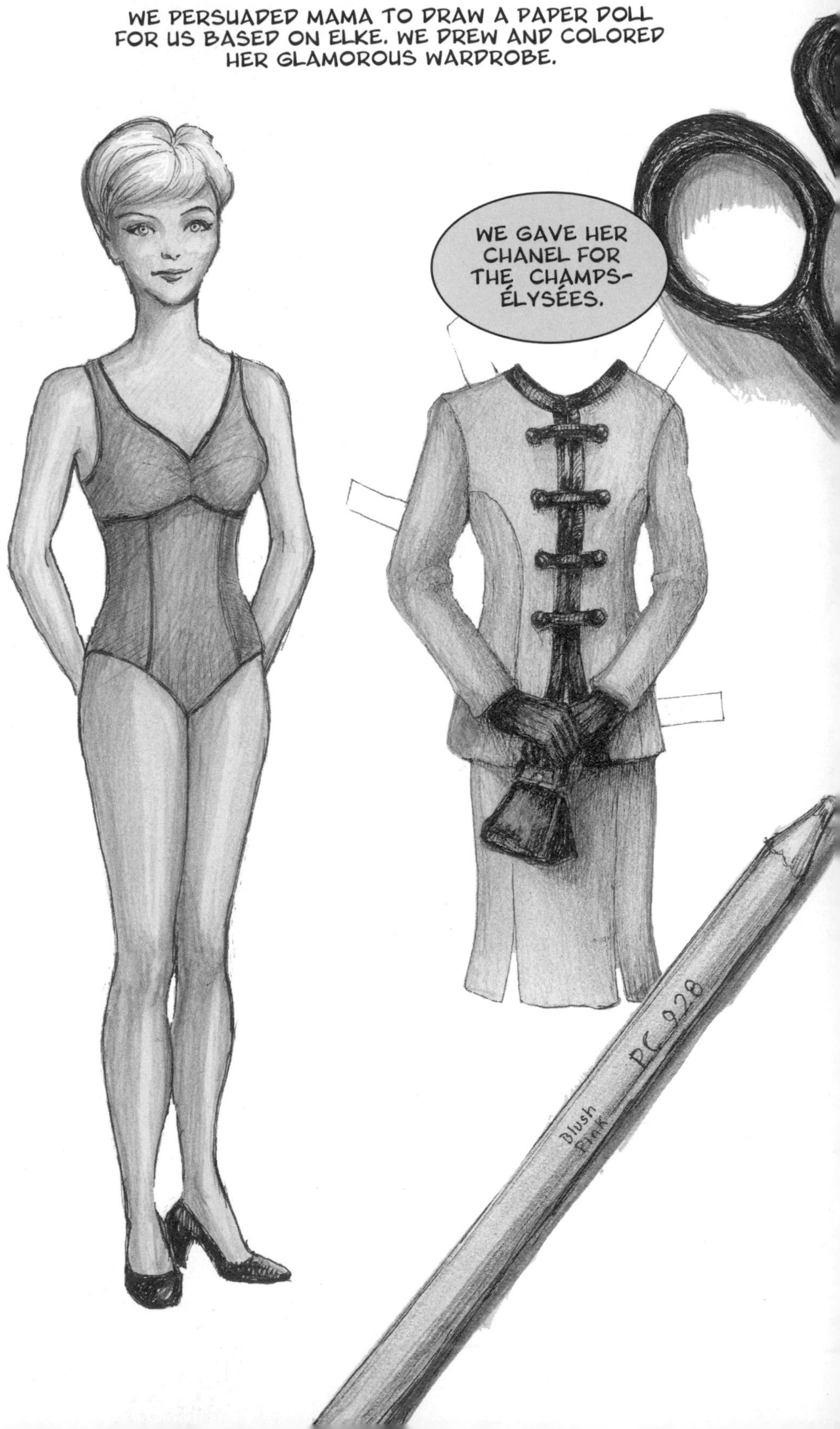
WE GAVE HER CHANEL FOR THE CHAMPS-ÉLYSÉES.
PC 928
Blush Pink

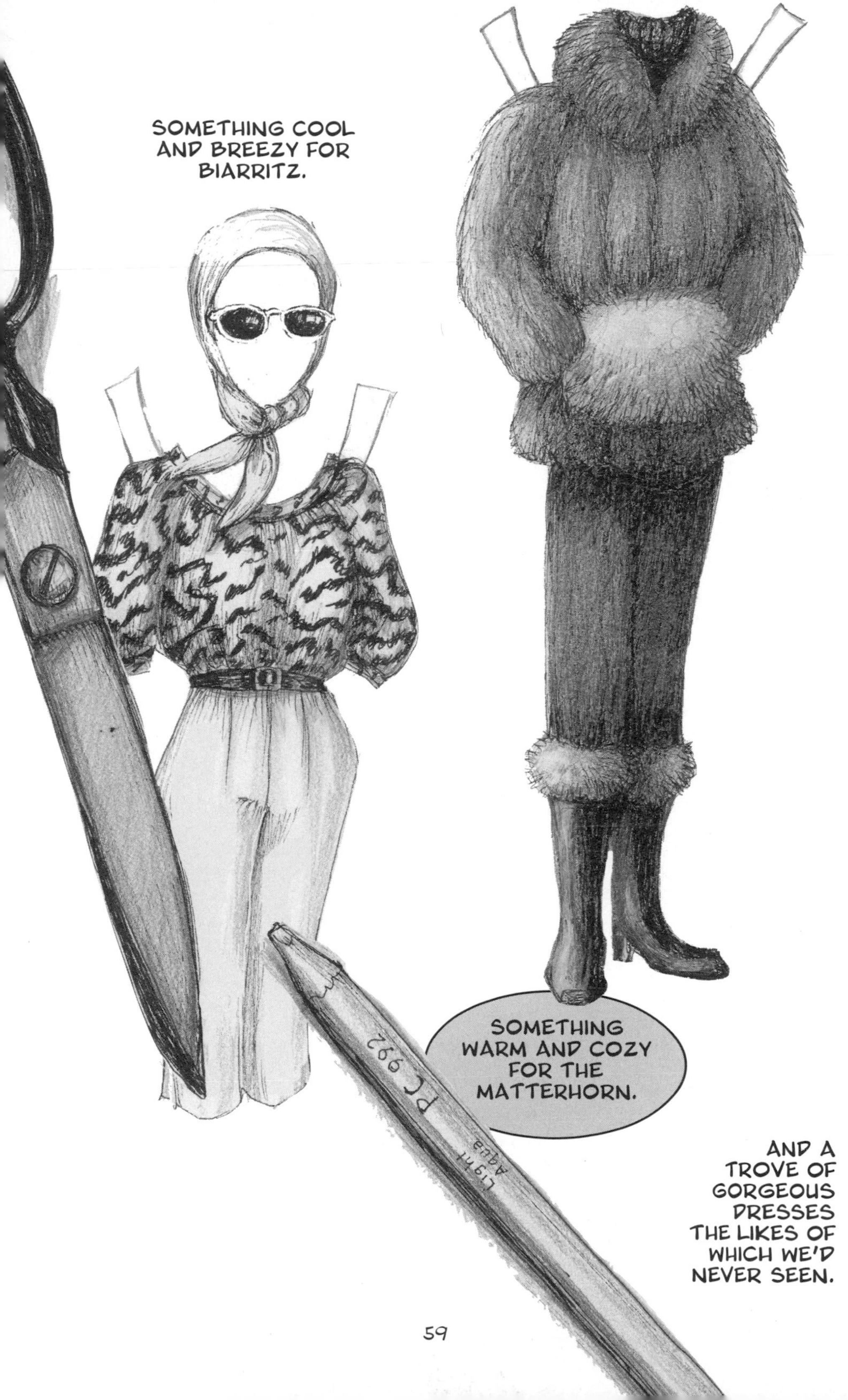
SOMETHING COOL AND BREEZY FOR BIARRITZ.
SOMETHING WARM AND COZY FOR THE MATTERHORN.
PC 992
Light Aqua
AND A TROVE OF GORGEOUS DRESSES THE LIKES OF WHICH WE'D NEVER SEEN.

chapter 4

GINNY'S BOOKS

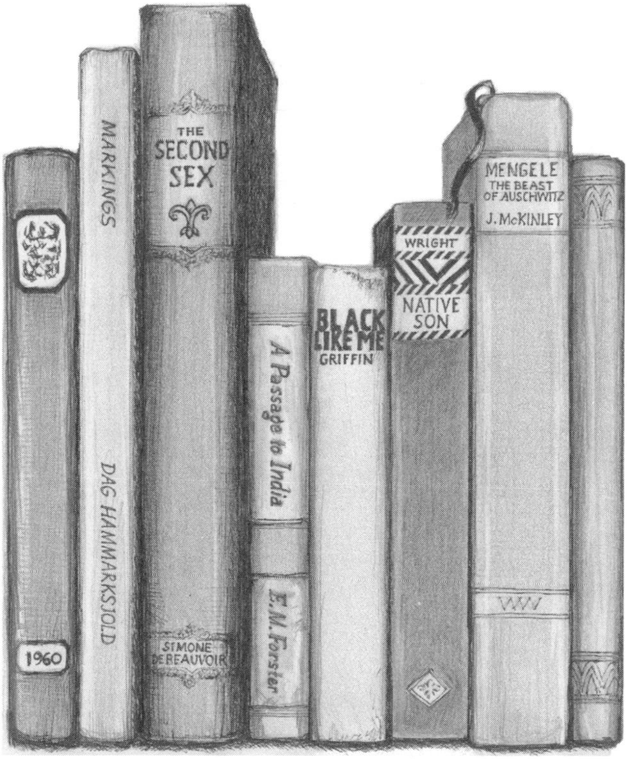

1960
MARKINGS
DAG HAMMARKSJOLD
THE SECOND SEX
SIMONE DE BEAUVOIR
A Passage to India
E.M. Forster
BLACK LIKE ME
GRIFFIN
WRIGHT
NATIVE SON
MENGELE
THE BEAST OF AUSCHWITZ
J. McKINLEY

We arrived in an Alabama simmering with racial strife.

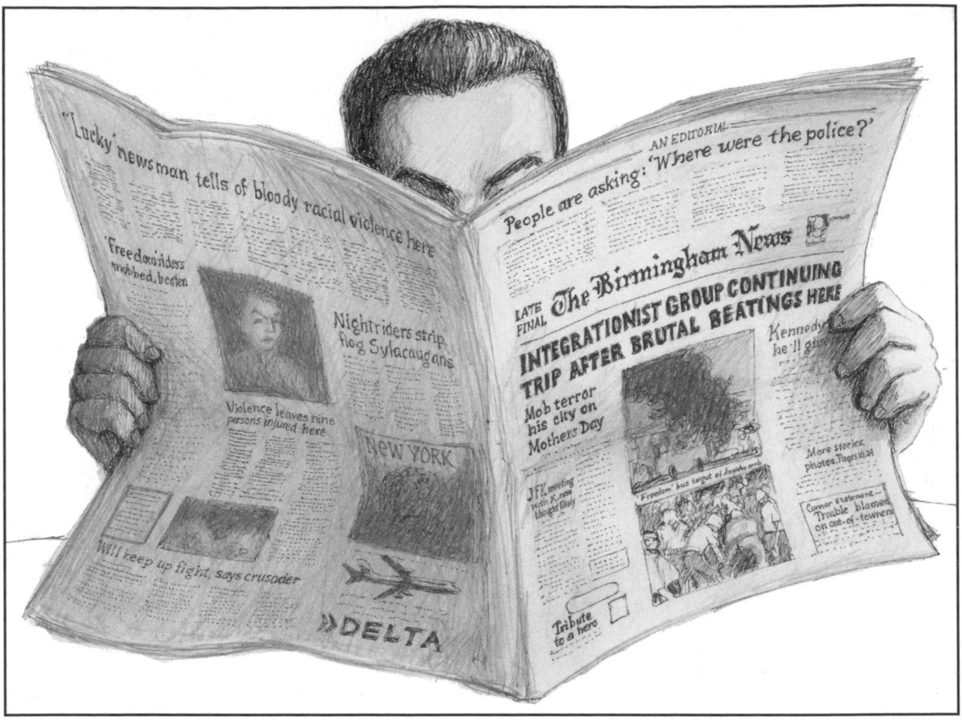
"Lucky" newsman tells of bloody racial violence here
'Freedom riders mobbed, beaten
Nightriders strip, flog Sylacaugans
Violence leaves nine persons injured here
NEW YORK
Will keep up fight, says crusader
»DELTA
AN EDITORIAL
People are asking: 'Where were the police?'
LATE FINAL
The Birmingham News
INTEGRATIONIST GROUP CONTINUING TRIP AFTER BRUTAL BEATINGS HERE
Mob terror his city on Mothers Day
Connor statement— Trouble blamed on out-of-towners
Tribute to a hero

Of which I remained completely oblivious.

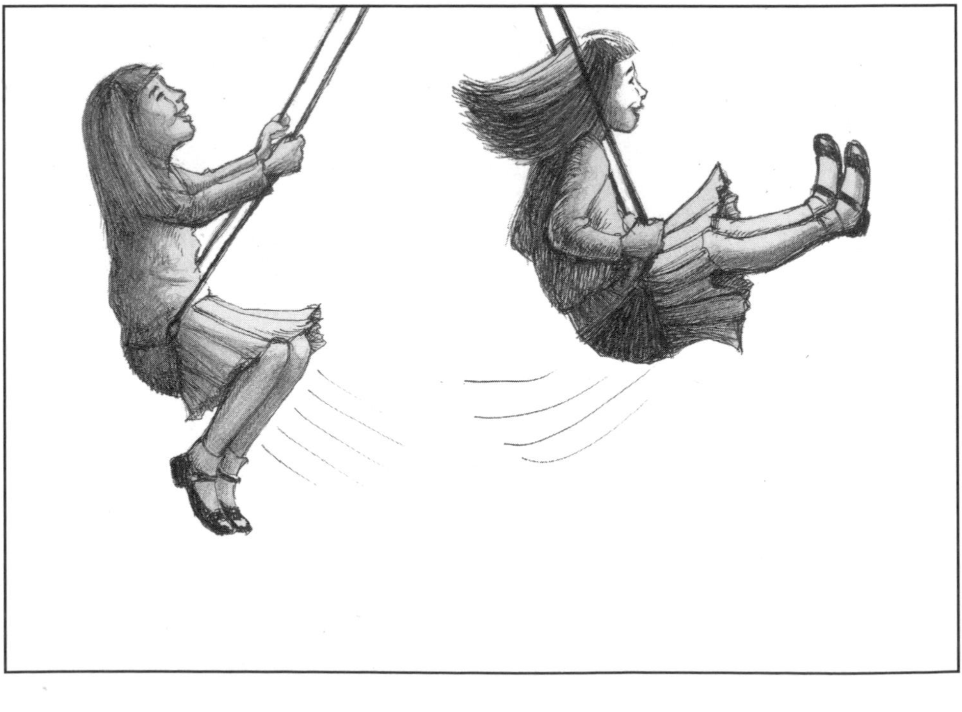

ALL OVER THE SOUTH, "OUR WAY OF LIFE" HAD COME UNDER SIEGE.

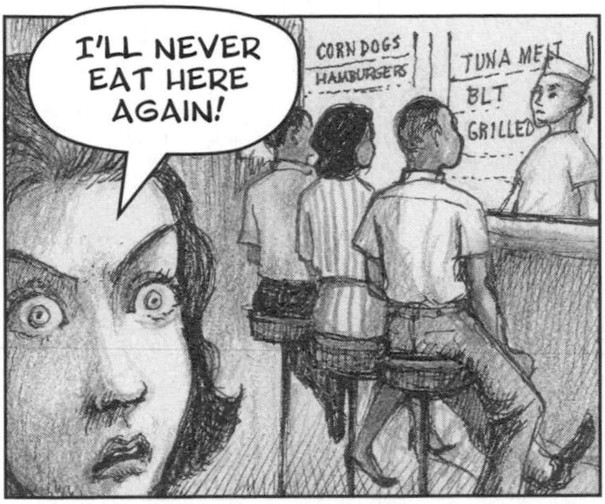
I'LL NEVER EAT HERE AGAIN!
CORN DOGS
HAMBURGERS
TUNA MELT
BLT
GRILLED

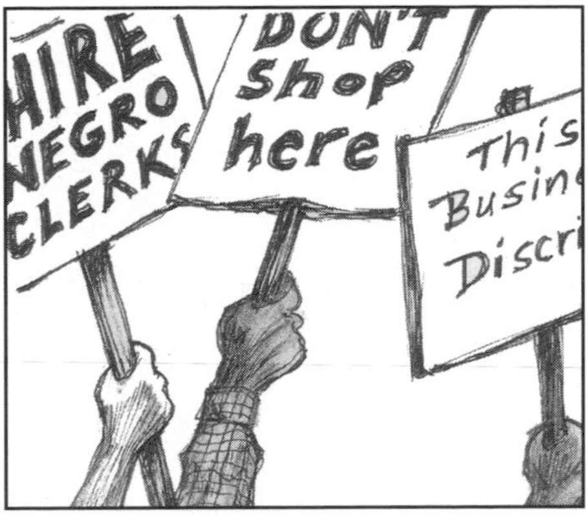
HIRE NEGRO CLERKS
DON'T Shop here
This Busin Discri

DEEP IN THE HEART OF DIXIE, JIM CROW HADN'T YET SURRENDERED TO THE INEVITABLE. BUT HIS DAYS WERE NUMBERED.

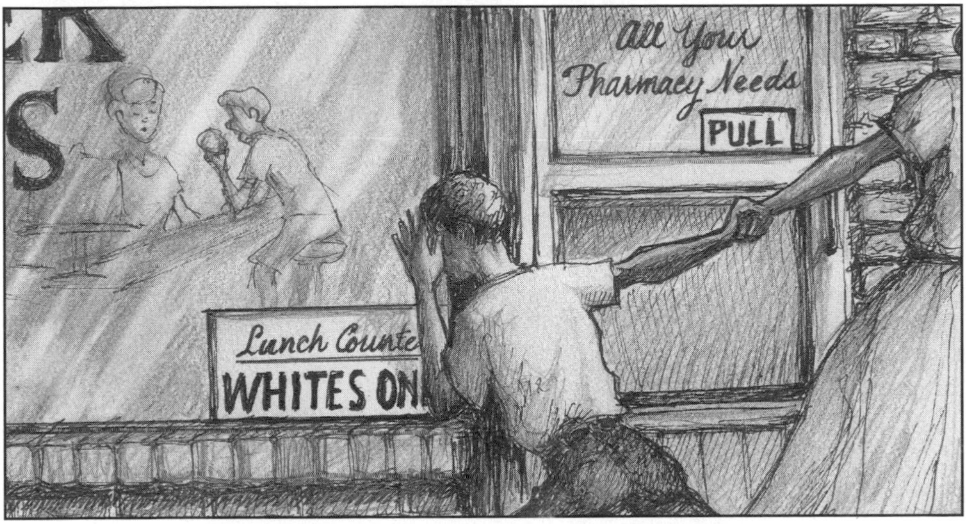
All Your Pharmacy Needs
PULL
Lunch Counte
WHITES ON

IT WAS THE SIGNS THAT HELPED ME SEE.

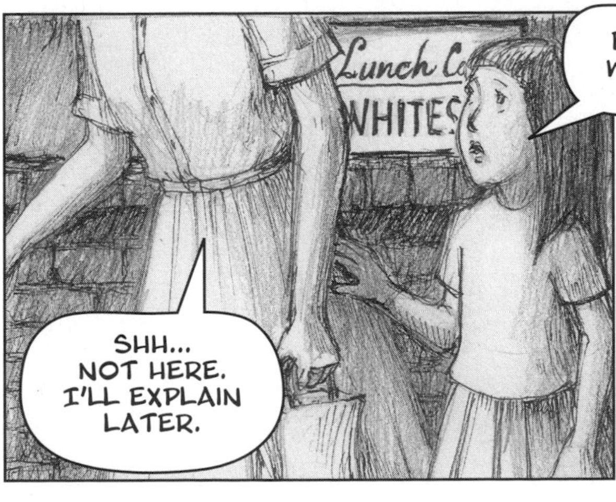
Lunch Co
WHITES
BUT, WHY?
SHH... NOT HERE. I'LL EXPLAIN LATER.

MY SISTER GINNY,
11 YEARS OLDER,
OPENED MY EYES
TO MANY THINGS.

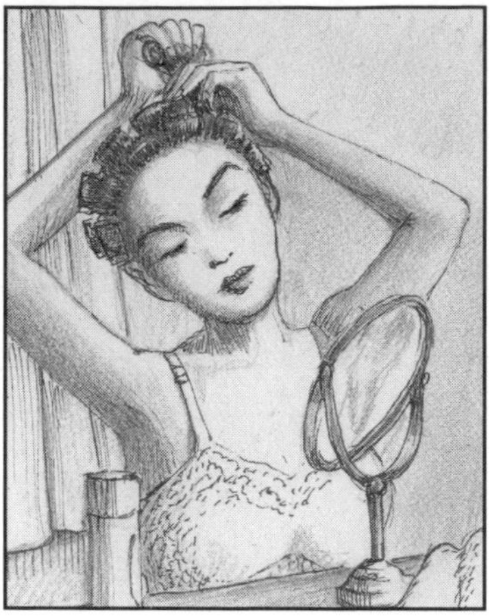

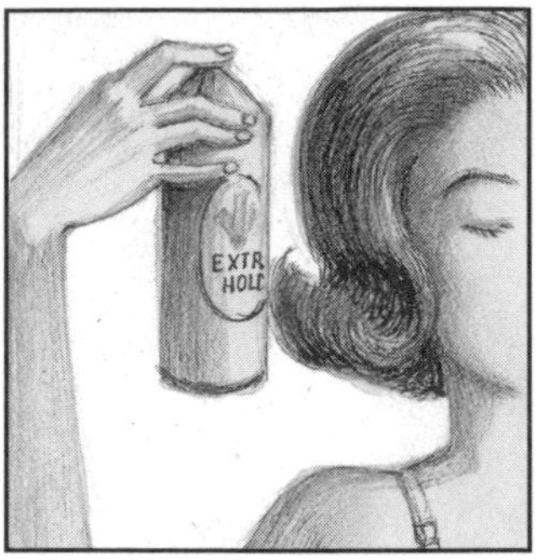

SHE WAS HIP AND GAVE
BRAINS GLAMOUR,
UNLIKE ANY OTHER
SMART GIRL I KNEW.

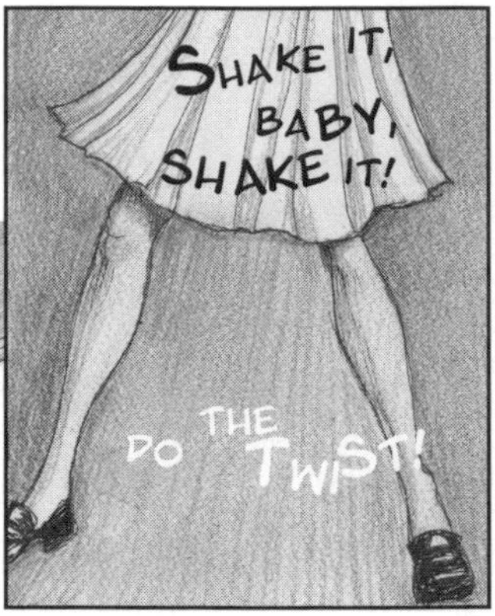
SHAKE IT, BABY, SHAKE IT!
DO THE TWIST!

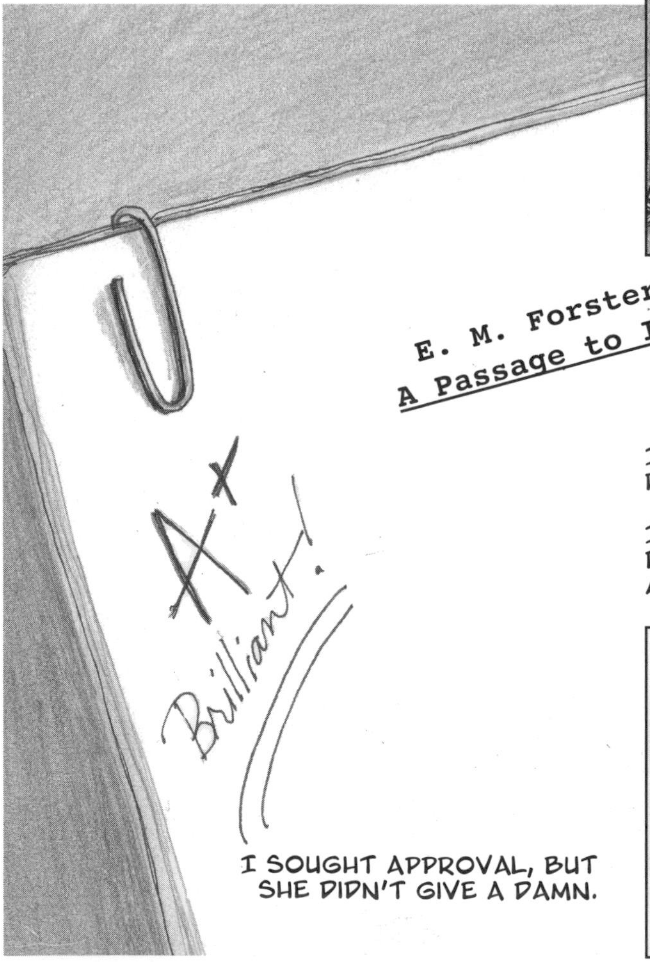
E. M. Forster's
A Passage to India
A+
Brilliant!

I MOLDED, BUT GINNY
REFUSED TO CONFORM.

I TREMBLED, BUT SHE
DARED TO QUESTION
AUTHORITY.

I SOUGHT APPROVAL, BUT
SHE DIDN'T GIVE A DAMN.

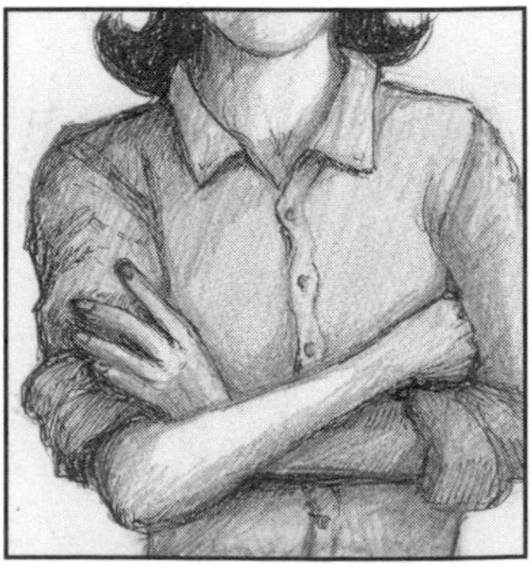

JUDSON COLLEGE, WHERE GINNY STUDIED, SHAPED YOUNG LADIES INTO SCHOLARS AND SOUTHERN BELLES.

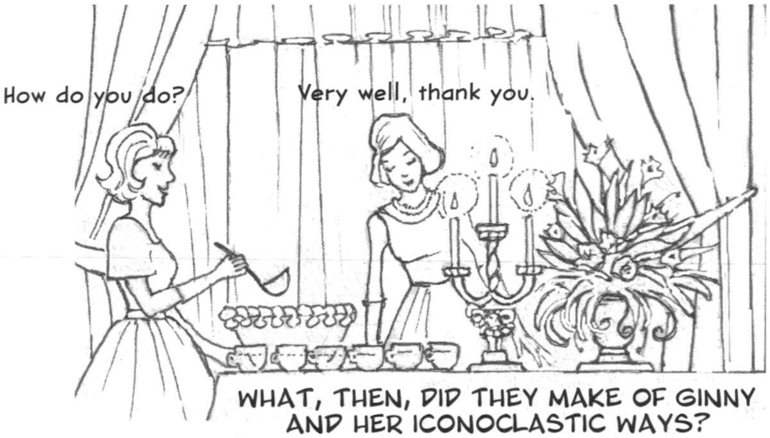
How do you do?
Very well, thank you.
WHAT, THEN, DID THEY MAKE OF GINNY AND HER ICONOCLASTIC WAYS?

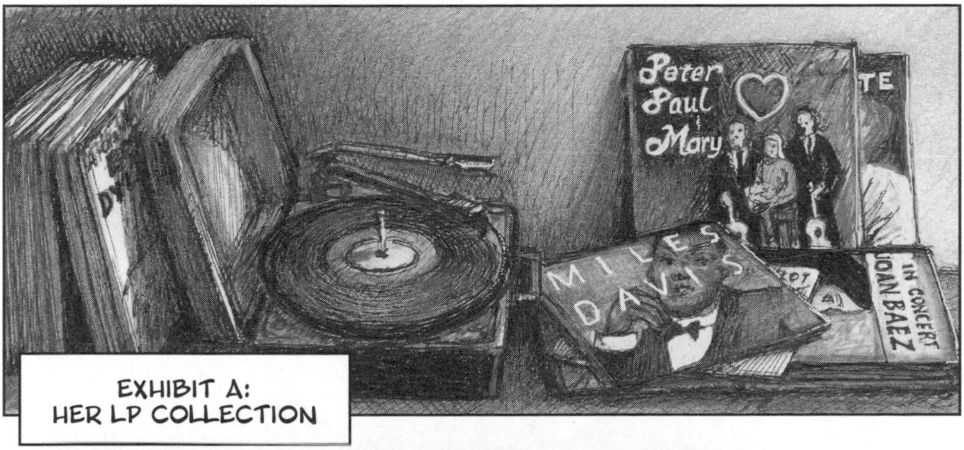
Peter Paul & Mary
MILES DAVIS
IN CONCERT JOAN BAEZ
EXHIBIT A: HER LP COLLECTION

EXHIBIT B: HER BOOKS

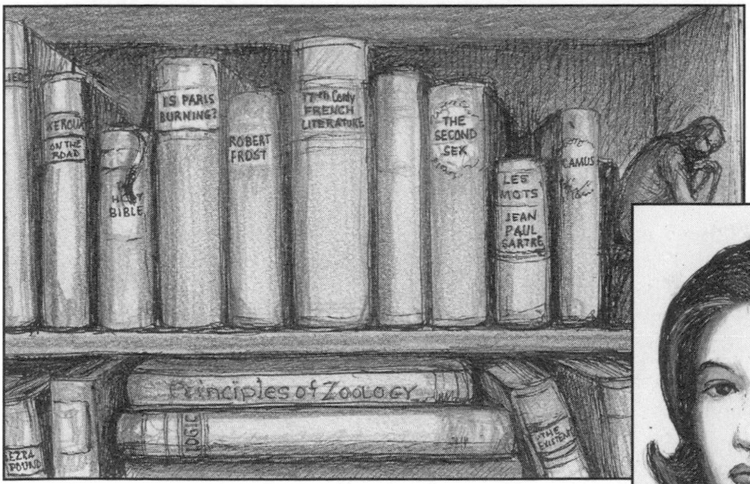
ON THE ROAD
HOLY BIBLE
IS PARIS BURNING?
ROBERT FROST
FRENCH LITERATURE
THE SECOND SEX
LES MOTS JEAN PAUL SARTRE
CAMUS
Principles of Zoology
LOGIC
EZRA POUND

EXHIBIT C: HER EYES.

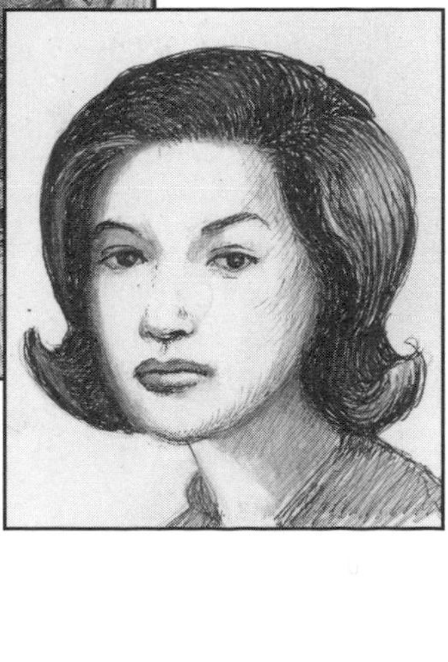

SHE'D RAISED THE DROP-DEAD STARE TO AN ART FORM.

I IDOLIZED HER.

READING GINNY'S BOOKS FILLED OUT MY EDUCATION.

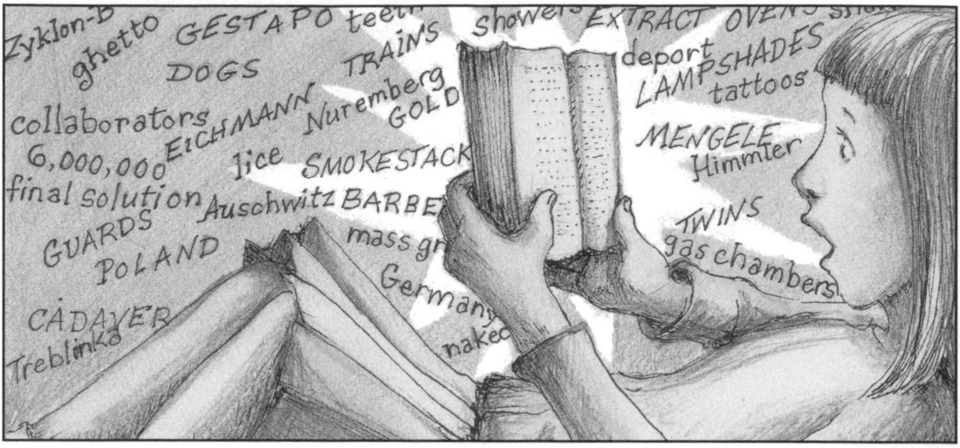
Zyklon-B
ghetto
GESTAPO
DOGS
TRAINS
EXTRACT
deport
LAMPSHADES
tattoos
collaborators
EICHMANN
Nuremberg
GOLD
6,000,000
lice
SMOKESTACK
MENGELE
Himmler
final solution
Auschwitz
GUARDS
POLAND
TWINS
gas chambers
CADAVER
Treblinka

I LEARNED ABOUT THINGS THAT TEACHERS NEVER MENTIONED.

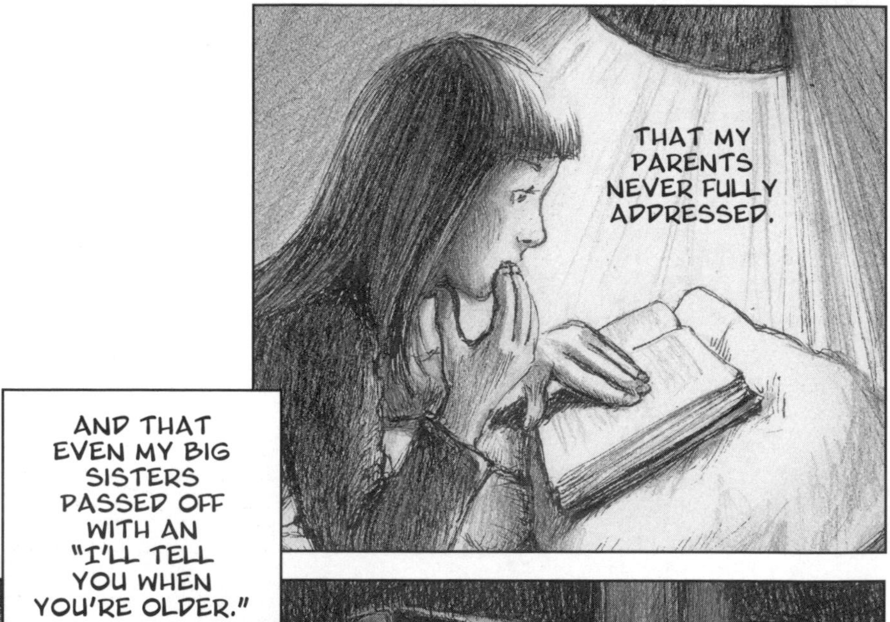
THAT MY PARENTS NEVER FULLY ADDRESSED.
AND THAT EVEN MY BIG SISTERS PASSED OFF WITH AN "I'LL TELL YOU WHEN YOU'RE OLDER."

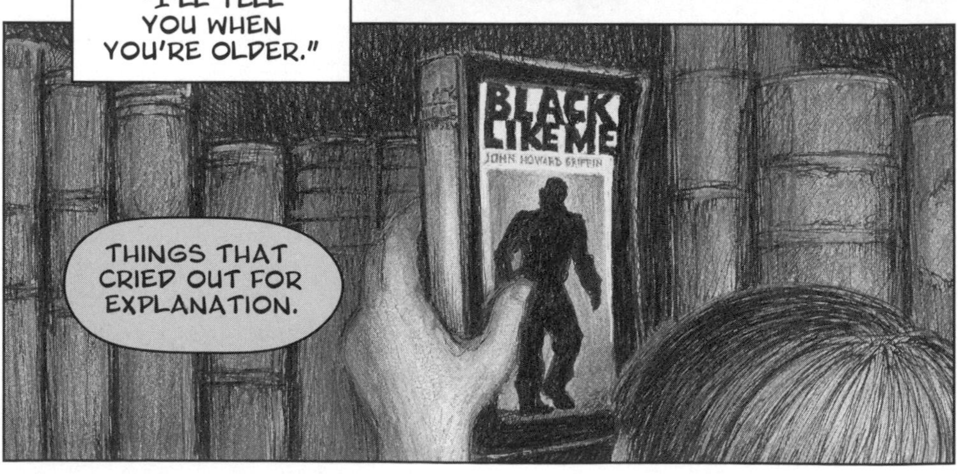
BLACK LIKE ME
JOHN HOWARD GRIFFIN
THINGS THAT CRIED OUT FOR EXPLANATION.

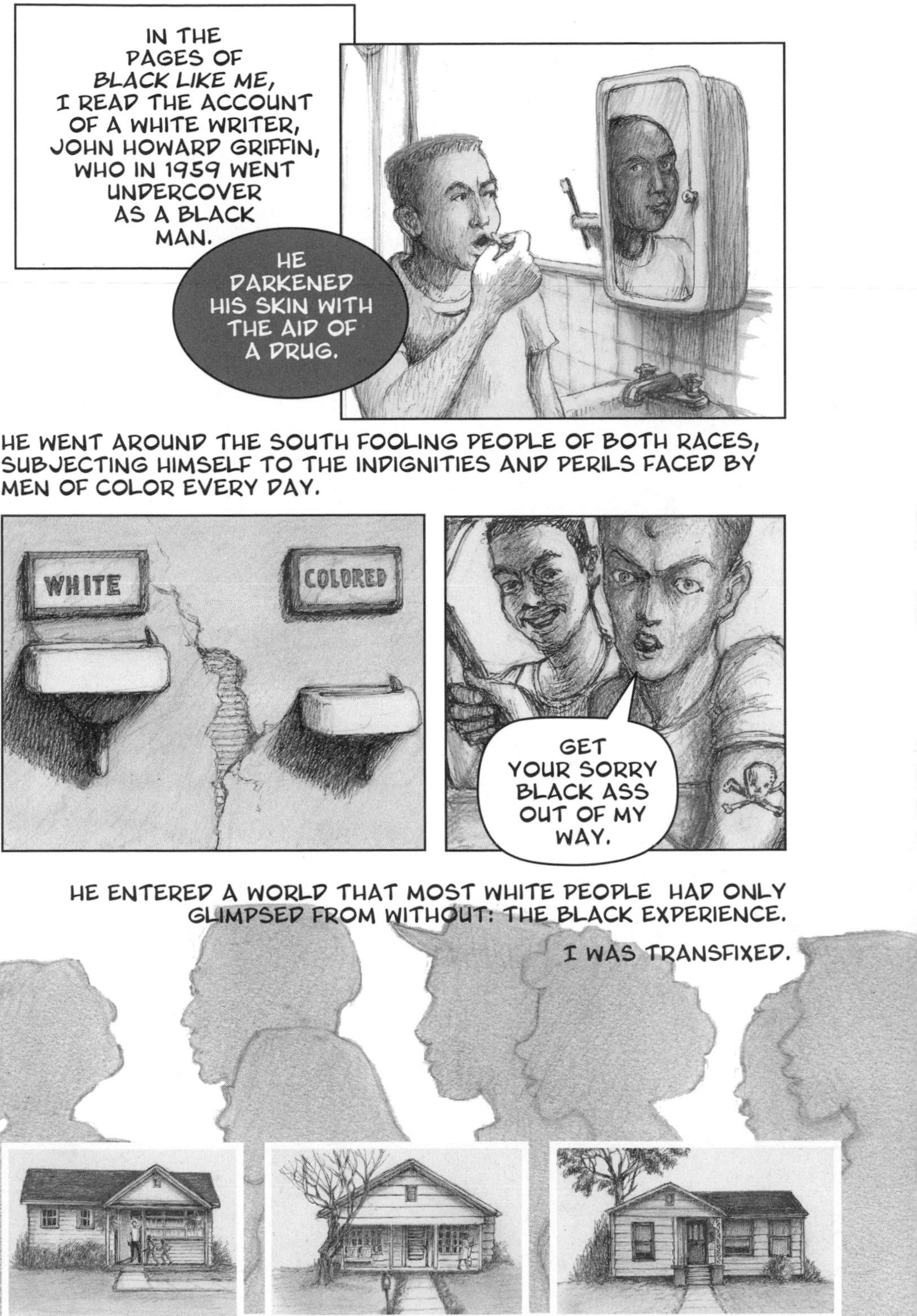

IN THE PAGES OF *BLACK LIKE ME*, I READ THE ACCOUNT OF A WHITE WRITER, JOHN HOWARD GRIFFIN, WHO IN 1959 WENT UNDERCOVER AS A BLACK MAN.

HE DARKENED HIS SKIN WITH THE AID OF A DRUG.

HE WENT AROUND THE SOUTH FOOLING PEOPLE OF BOTH RACES, SUBJECTING HIMSELF TO THE INDIGNITIES AND PERILS FACED BY MEN OF COLOR EVERY DAY.

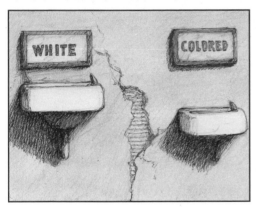

WHITE

COLORED

GET YOUR SORRY BLACK ASS OUT OF MY WAY.

HE ENTERED A WORLD THAT MOST WHITE PEOPLE HAD ONLY GLIMPSED FROM WITHOUT: THE BLACK EXPERIENCE.

I WAS TRANSFIXED.

JUST BENEATH THE VENEER OF MY HOMETOWN WAS SUCH A WORLD.

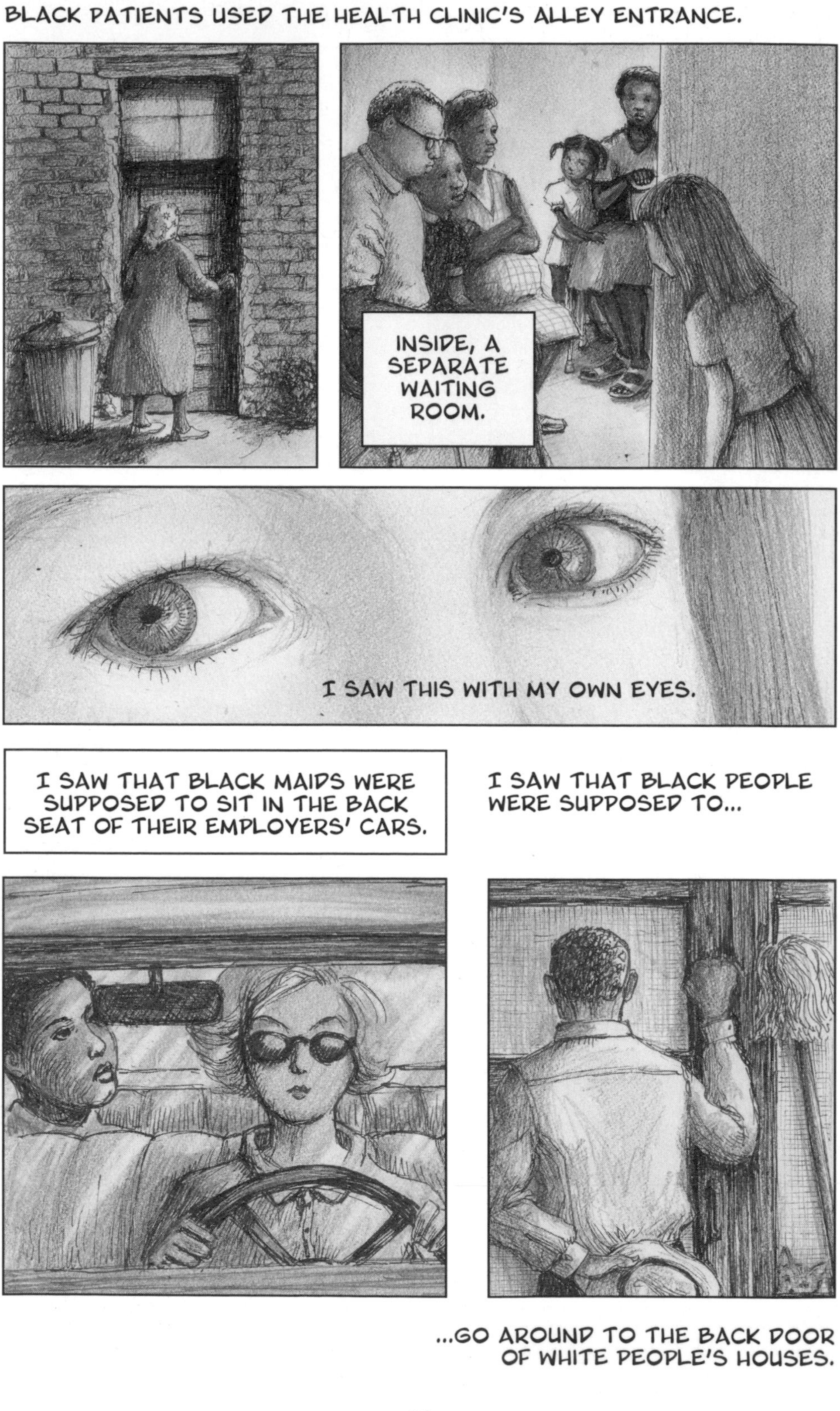
BLACK PATIENTS USED THE HEALTH CLINIC'S ALLEY ENTRANCE.
INSIDE, A SEPARATE WAITING ROOM.
I SAW THIS WITH MY OWN EYES.
I SAW THAT BLACK MAIDS WERE SUPPOSED TO SIT IN THE BACK SEAT OF THEIR EMPLOYERS' CARS.
I SAW THAT BLACK PEOPLE WERE SUPPOSED TO...
...GO AROUND TO THE BACK DOOR OF WHITE PEOPLE'S HOUSES.

I SAW THAT EACH SIDE AFFORDED THE OTHER A DISTINCT INTERPRETATION OF RESPECT.

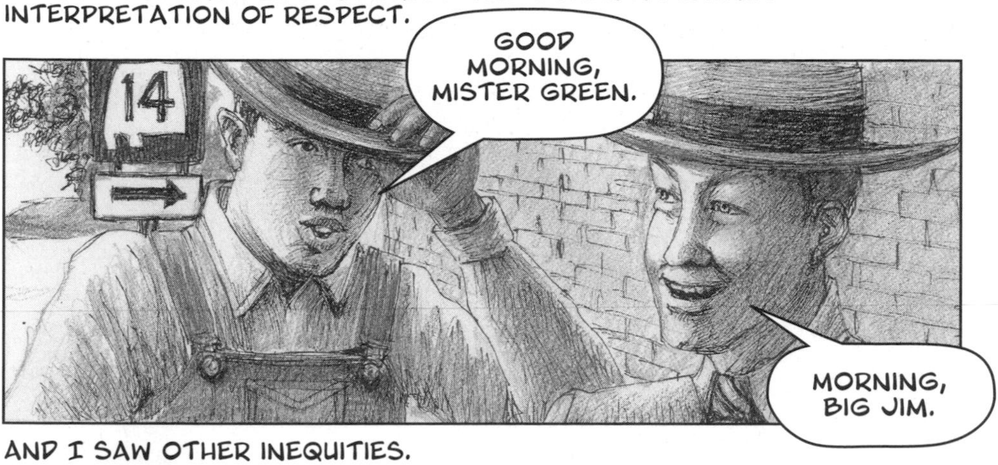
GOOD MORNING, MISTER GREEN.
MORNING, BIG JIM.

AND I SAW OTHER INEQUITIES.

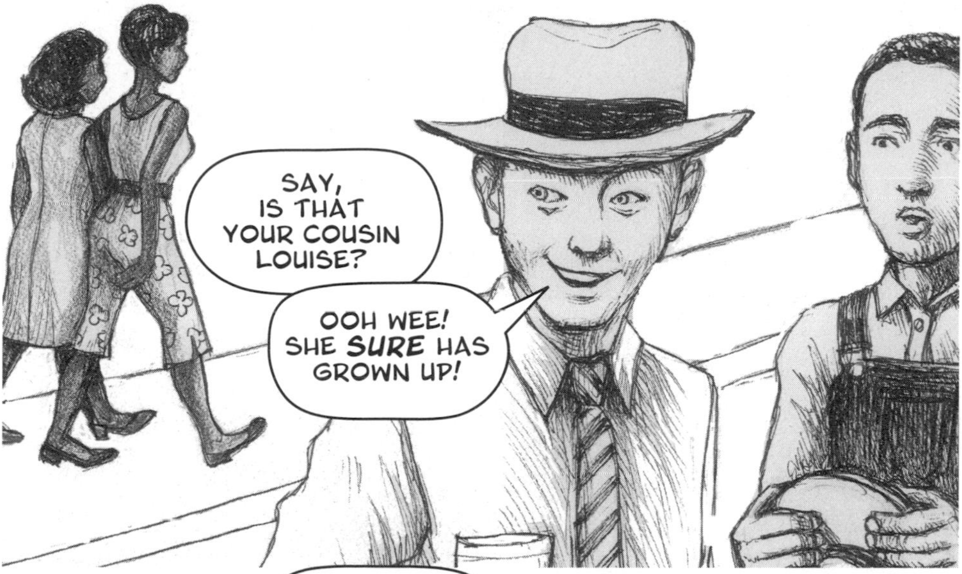
SAY, IS THAT YOUR COUSIN LOUISE?
OOH WEE! SHE *SURE* HAS GROWN UP!

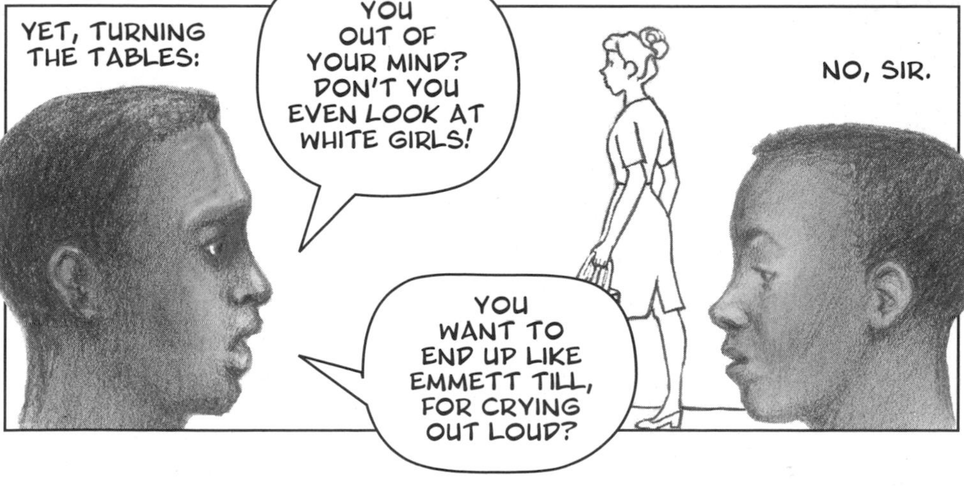
YET, TURNING THE TABLES:
YOU OUT OF YOUR MIND? DON'T YOU EVEN *LOOK* AT WHITE GIRLS!
NO, SIR.
YOU WANT TO END UP LIKE EMMETT TILL, FOR CRYING OUT LOUD?

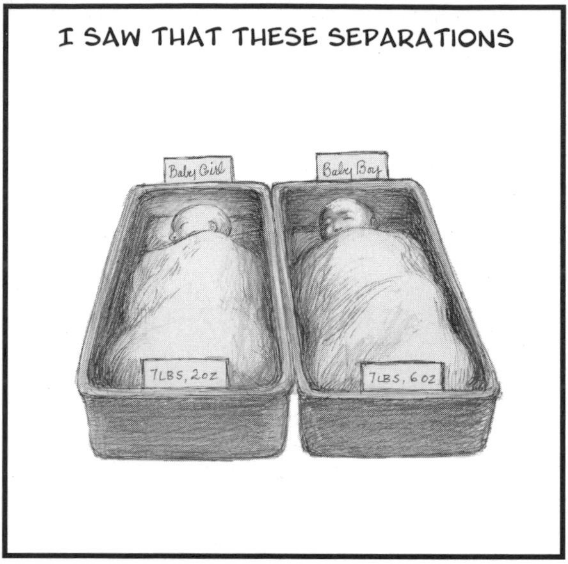
I SAW THAT THESE SEPARATIONS
Baby Girl
Baby Boy
7LBS, 2oz
7LBS, 6oz

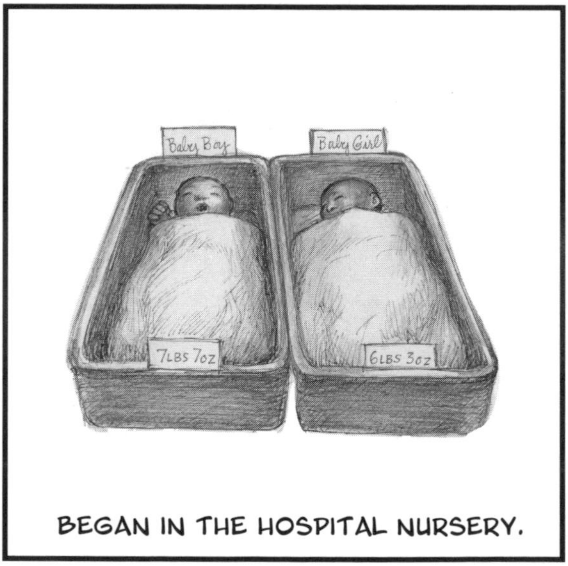
Baby Boy
Baby Girl
7LBS 7oz
6LBS 3oz
BEGAN IN THE HOSPITAL NURSERY.

AND RAN STRAIGHT TO THE GRAVEYARD.

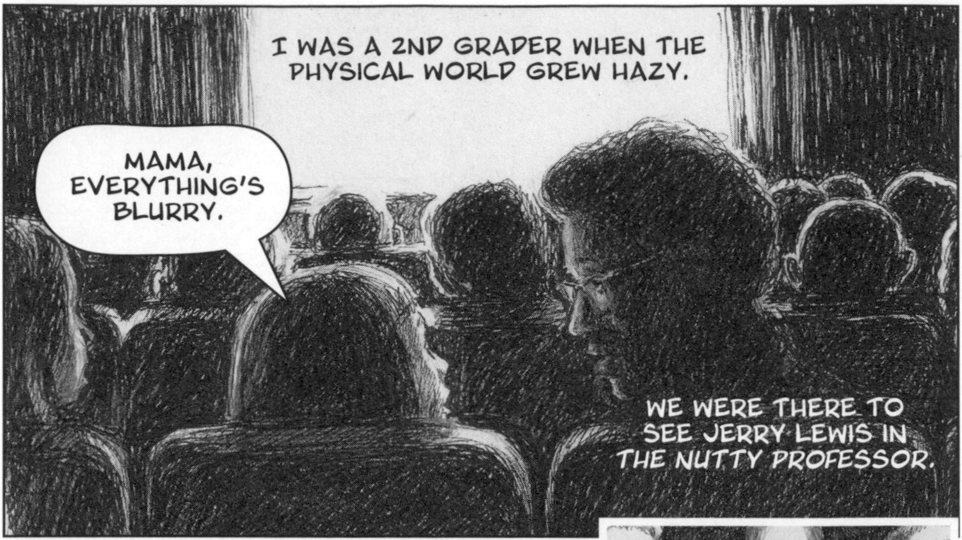
I WAS A 2ND GRADER WHEN THE PHYSICAL WORLD GREW HAZY.
MAMA, EVERYTHING'S BLURRY.
WE WERE THERE TO SEE JERRY LEWIS IN THE NUTTY PROFESSOR.

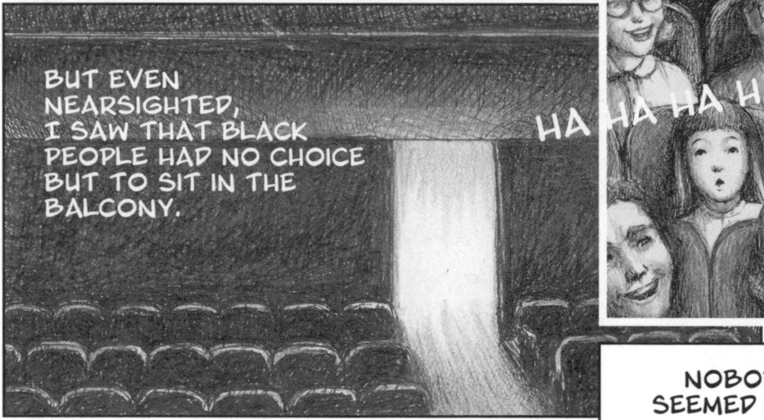
BUT EVEN NEARSIGHTED, I SAW THAT BLACK PEOPLE HAD NO CHOICE BUT TO SIT IN THE BALCONY.

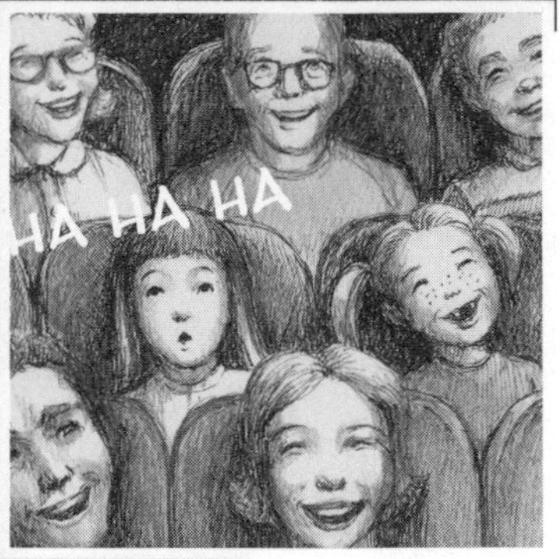
HA HA HA HA

NOBODY ELSE SEEMED HORRIFIED.

SOMETIMES PEOPLE IN THE BALCONY STOMPED AND WHISTLED AND JEERED.

SOMETIMES THEY RAINED POPCORN DOWN ON OUR HEADS.

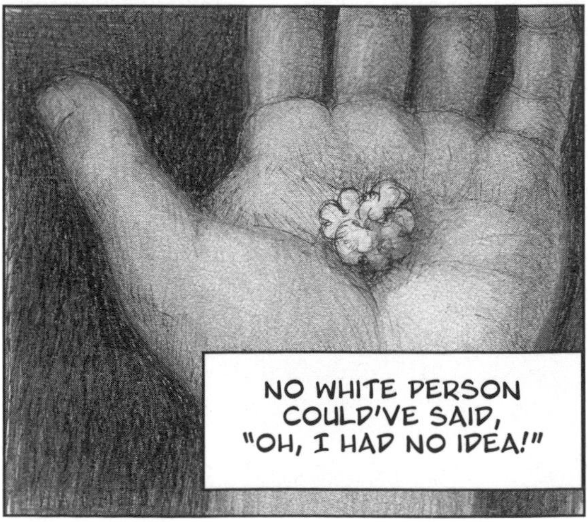
NO WHITE PERSON COULD'VE SAID, "OH, I HAD NO IDEA!"

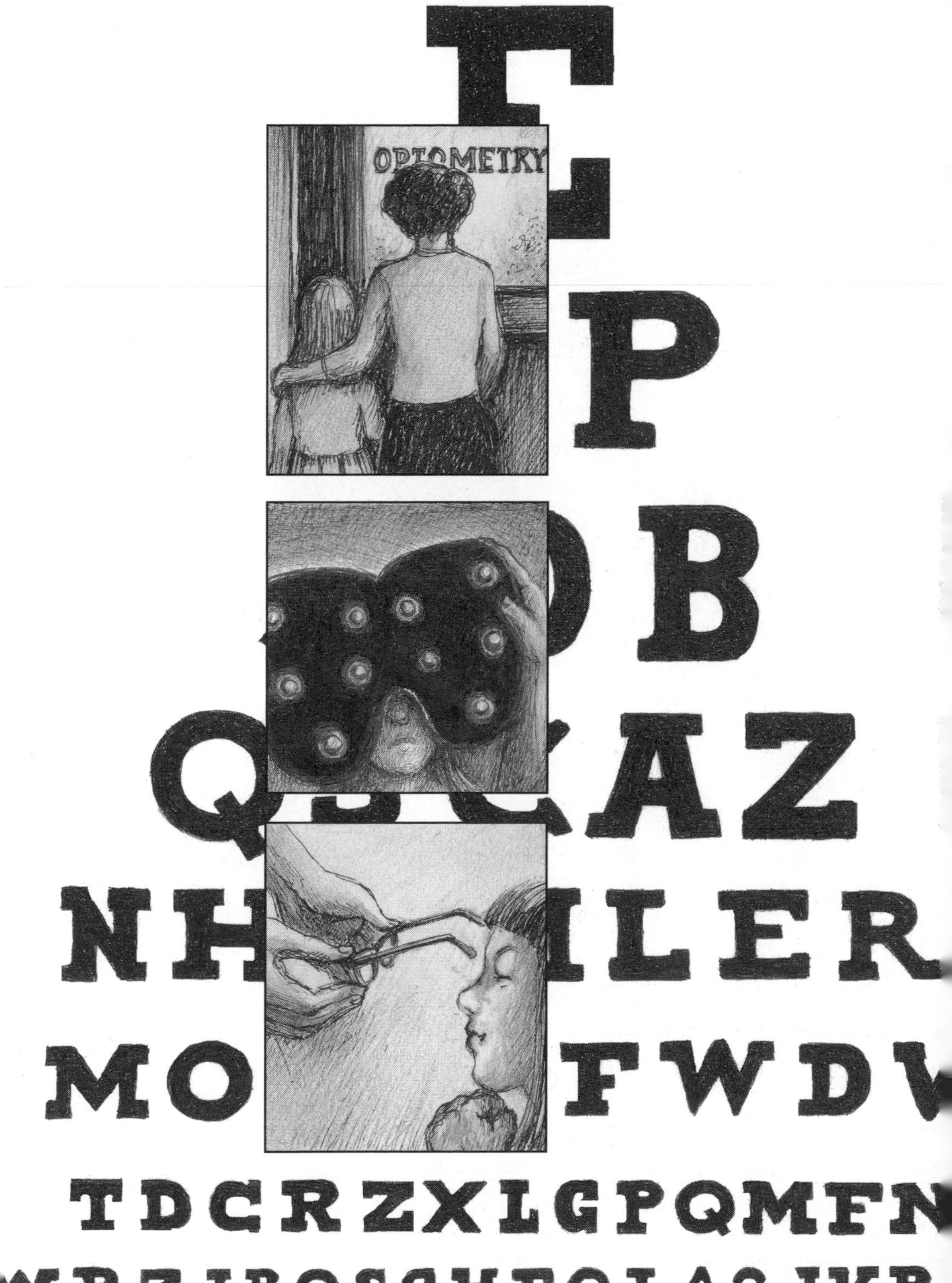
OPTOMETRY
TDCRZXLGPQMFN
WRZJBQSGHFOLACJKR

WHAT A DISCOVERY.

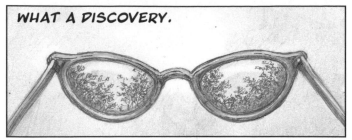

THE VISUAL WORLD WAS A THING OF WONDER. I HADN'T SUSPECTED ITS BREADTH AND RICHNESS. BUT NOW I SAW.

STILL, MY EYEGLASSES DIDN'T CORRECT A PARTICULAR BLINDSPOT:

THE FACES OF BLACK PEOPLE LOOKED INTERCHANGEABLE TO ME.

I KNEW ONLY ONE BLACK PERSON IN THOSE DAYS—MRS. JACKSON, THE LADY THAT HELPED OUT WITH IRONING NOW AND THEN.

SHE REFUSED INVITATIONS TO JOIN THE FAMILY AT LUNCH, WHICH LEFT ME ASKING,

WHY?

I COULDN'T BEAR TO SEE HER EATING ALONE, SO I SAT WITH HER.

BUT NEITHER OF US SPOKE.

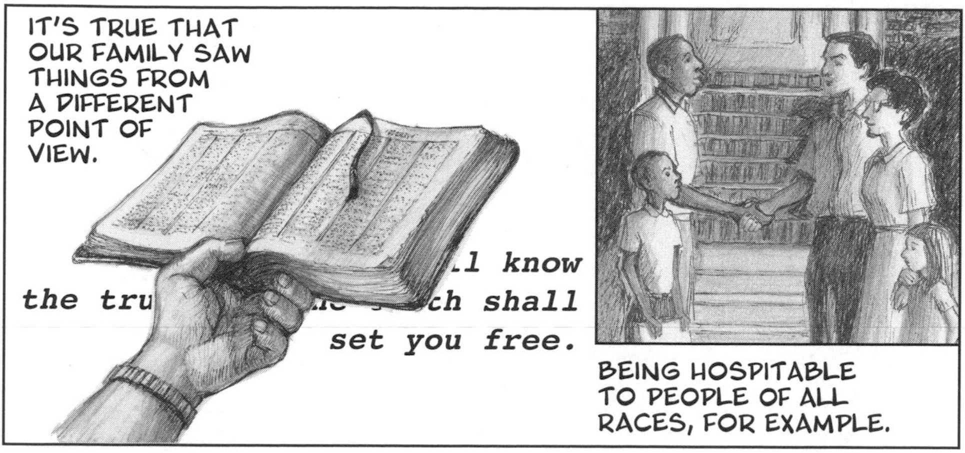
IT'S TRUE THAT OUR FAMILY SAW THINGS FROM A DIFFERENT POINT OF VIEW.
ll know
the tru
ch shall
set you free.
BEING HOSPITABLE TO PEOPLE OF ALL RACES, FOR EXAMPLE.

ONCE, A FATHER AND SON CAME TO OUR HOUSE TO SEEK MAMA'S ASSESSMENT OF THE BOY'S ARTISTIC TALENT.

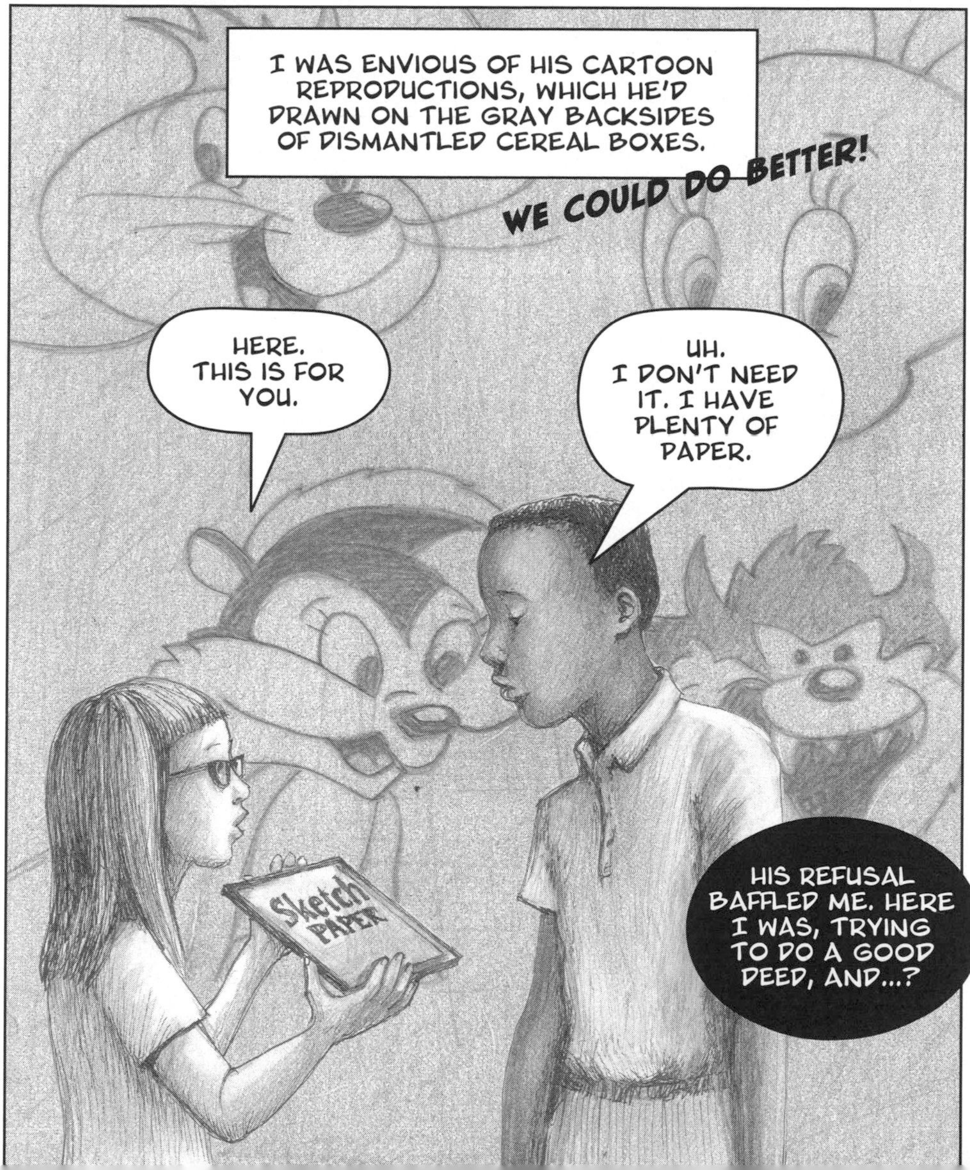
I WAS ENVIOUS OF HIS CARTOON REPRODUCTIONS, WHICH HE'D DRAWN ON THE GRAY BACKSIDES OF DISMANTLED CEREAL BOXES.
WE COULD DO BETTER!
HERE. THIS IS FOR YOU.
UH. I DON'T NEED IT. I HAVE PLENTY OF PAPER.
Sketch PAPER
HIS REFUSAL BAFFLED ME. HERE I WAS, TRYING TO DO A GOOD DEED, AND...?

THE RULES THAT GOVERNED RACE RELATIONS WERE WRITTEN DOWN NOWHERE, BUT YOU WERE SUPPOSED TO KNOW THEM ANYWAY.

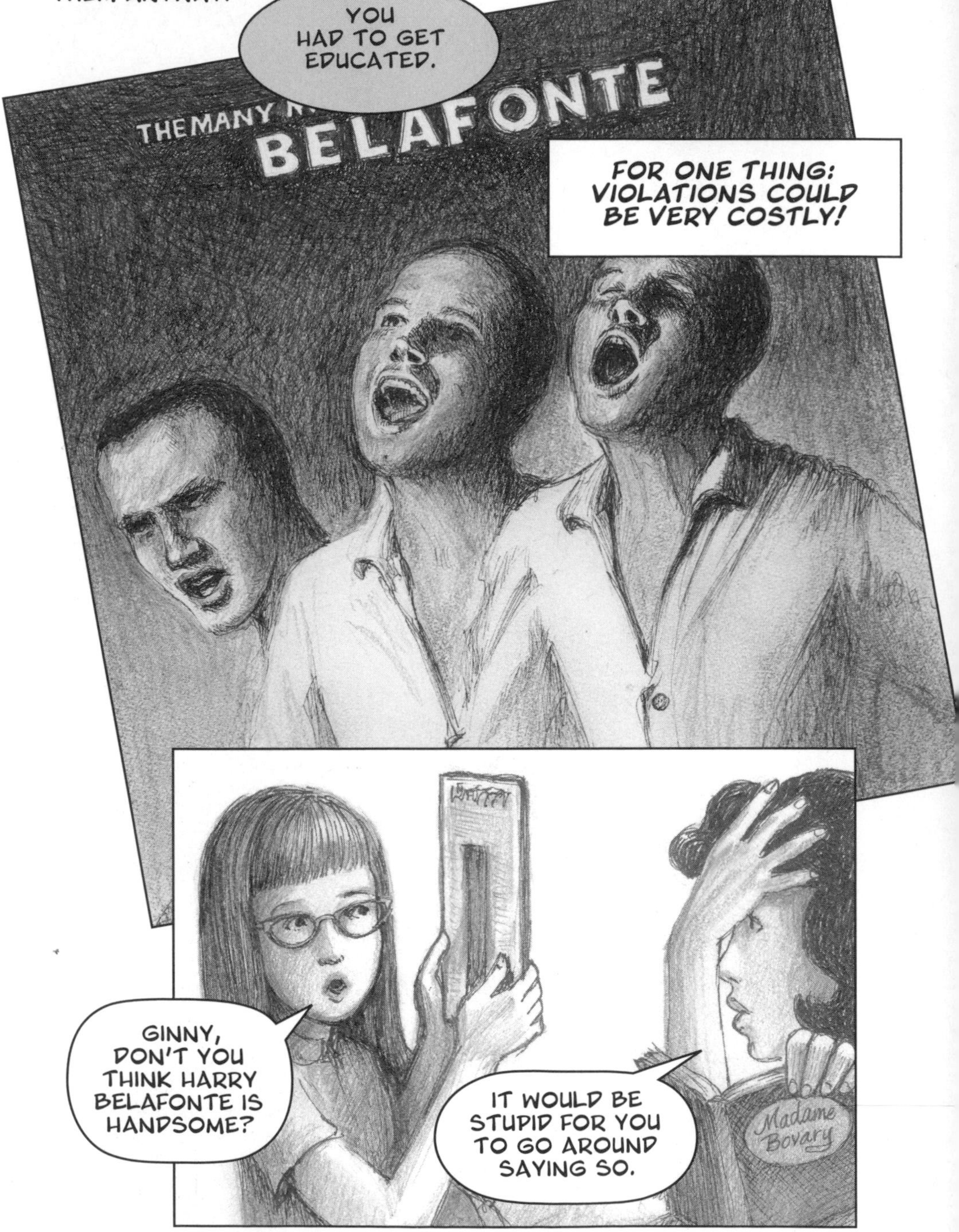

YOU HAD TO GET EDUCATED.
THEMANY
BELAFONTE
FOR ONE THING: VIOLATIONS COULD BE VERY COSTLY!
GINNY, DON'T YOU THINK HARRY BELAFONTE IS HANDSOME?
IT WOULD BE STUPID FOR YOU TO GO AROUND SAYING SO.
Madame Bovary

AS MUCH AS I ADMIRED GINNY'S DEFIANCE, I DARED NOT DISRESPECT ***THAT*** RULE.

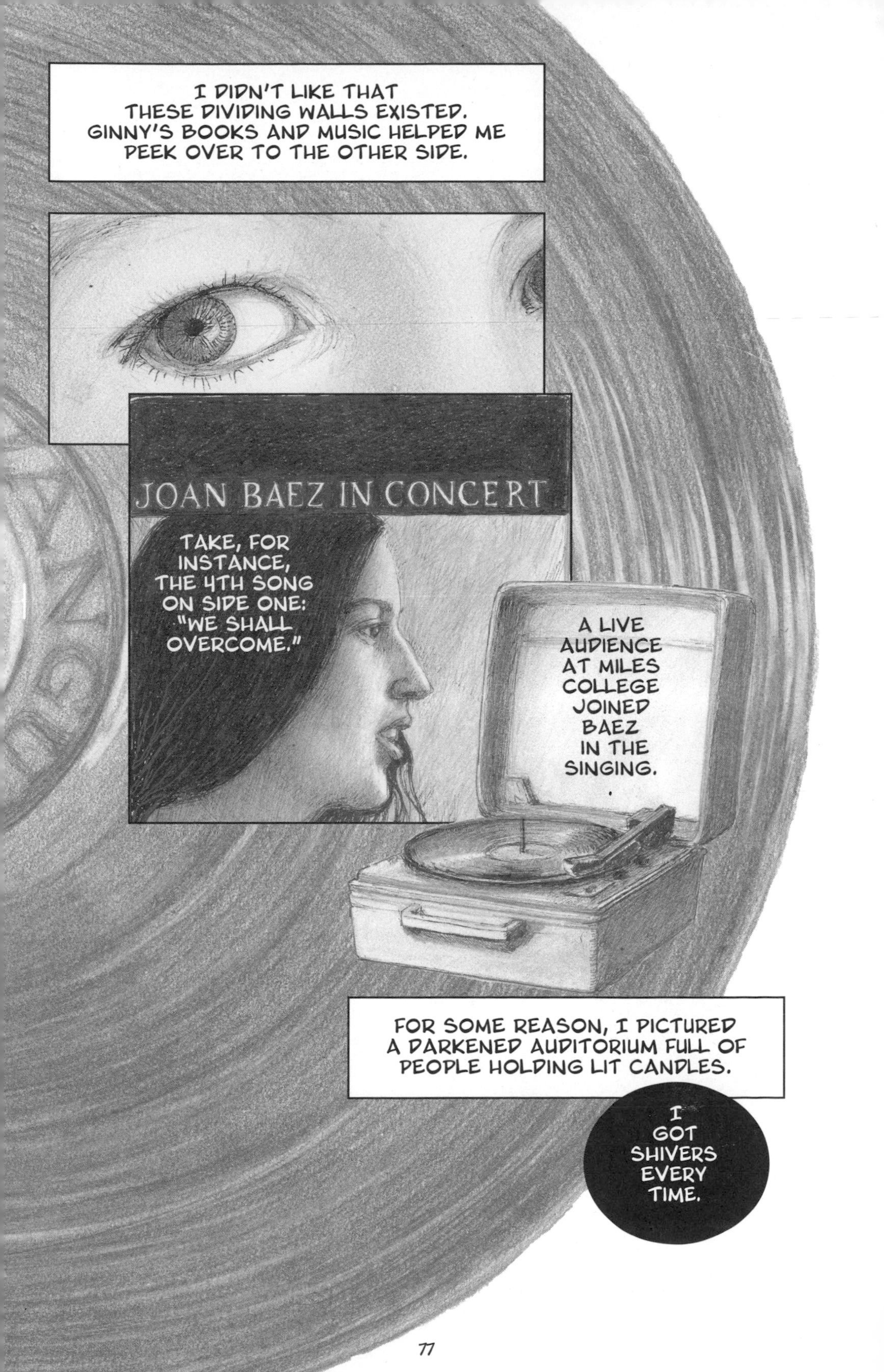

I DIDN'T LIKE THAT THESE DIVIDING WALLS EXISTED. GINNY'S BOOKS AND MUSIC HELPED ME PEEK OVER TO THE OTHER SIDE.
JOAN BAEZ IN CONCERT
TAKE, FOR INSTANCE, THE 4TH SONG ON SIDE ONE: "WE SHALL OVERCOME."
A LIVE AUDIENCE AT MILES COLLEGE JOINED BAEZ IN THE SINGING.
FOR SOME REASON, I PICTURED A DARKENED AUDITORIUM FULL OF PEOPLE HOLDING LIT CANDLES.
I GOT SHIVERS EVERY TIME.

chapter 5
ANCESTRAL LINES

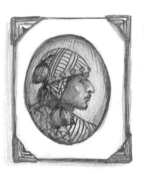

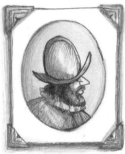

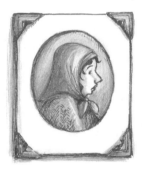

BEFORE COLLAGEN

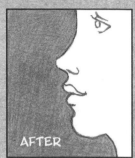

AFTER

LISSY WAS BORN WITH A MOUTH THAT WOMEN NOWADAYS PAY GOOD MONEY FOR.

BUT NOT IN 1962, HER 5TH-GRADE YEAR.

HEY, LOOK!

THE GIRL WITH NIGGER LIPS!

HA HA HA HA HA HA

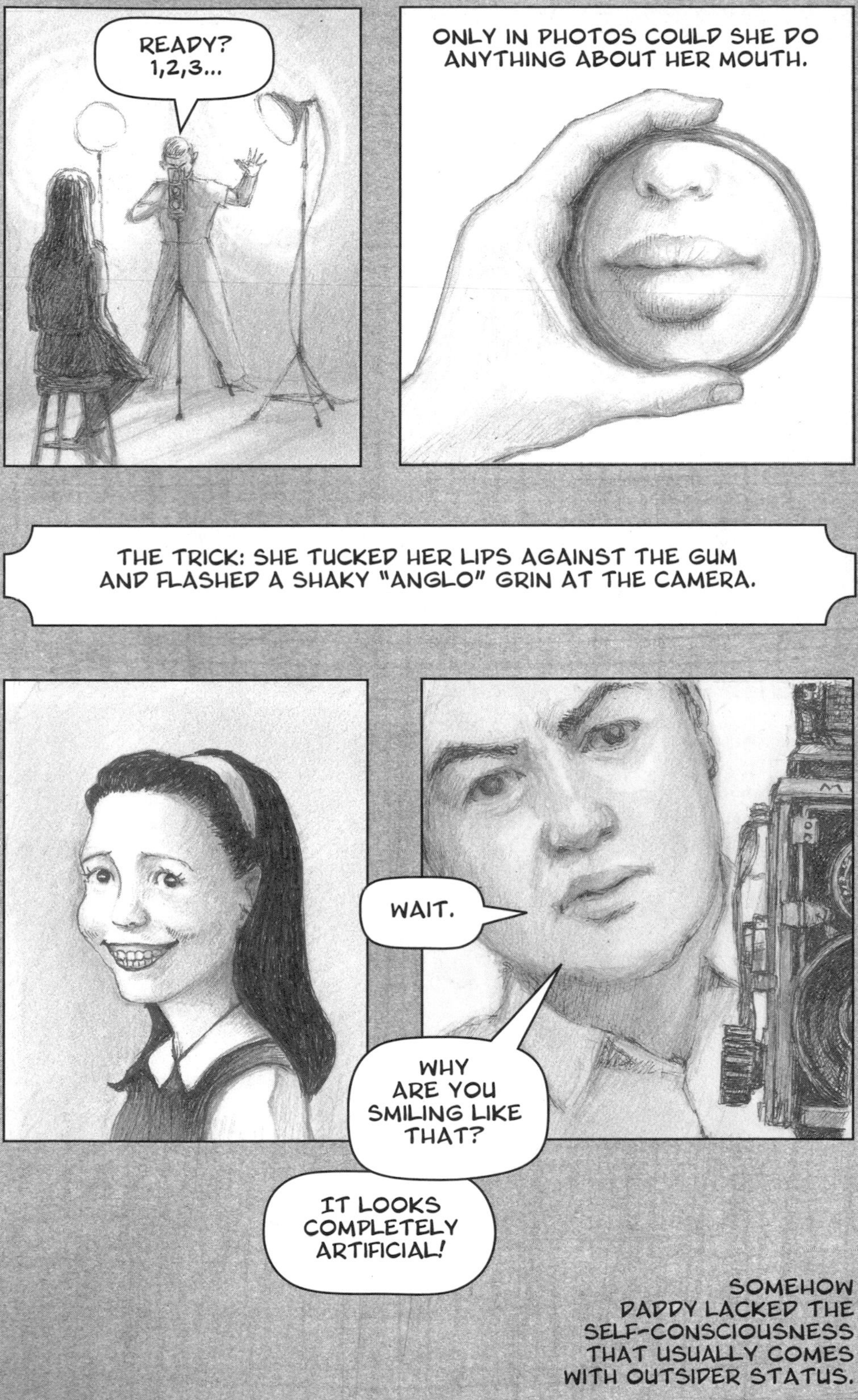
READY? 1,2,3...
ONLY IN PHOTOS COULD SHE DO ANYTHING ABOUT HER MOUTH.
THE TRICK: SHE TUCKED HER LIPS AGAINST THE GUM AND FLASHED A SHAKY "ANGLO" GRIN AT THE CAMERA.
WAIT.
WHY ARE YOU SMILING LIKE THAT?
IT LOOKS COMPLETELY ARTIFICIAL!
SOMEHOW DADDY LACKED THE SELF-CONSCIOUSNESS THAT USUALLY COMES WITH OUTSIDER STATUS.

HE'D ALWAYS BEEN ON THE OUTSIDE. AS A PENNILESS TEENAGER, HE MOVED FROM THE MOUNTAIN PROVINCE OF MENDOZA TO BUENOS AIRES IN SEARCH OF EDUCATION.

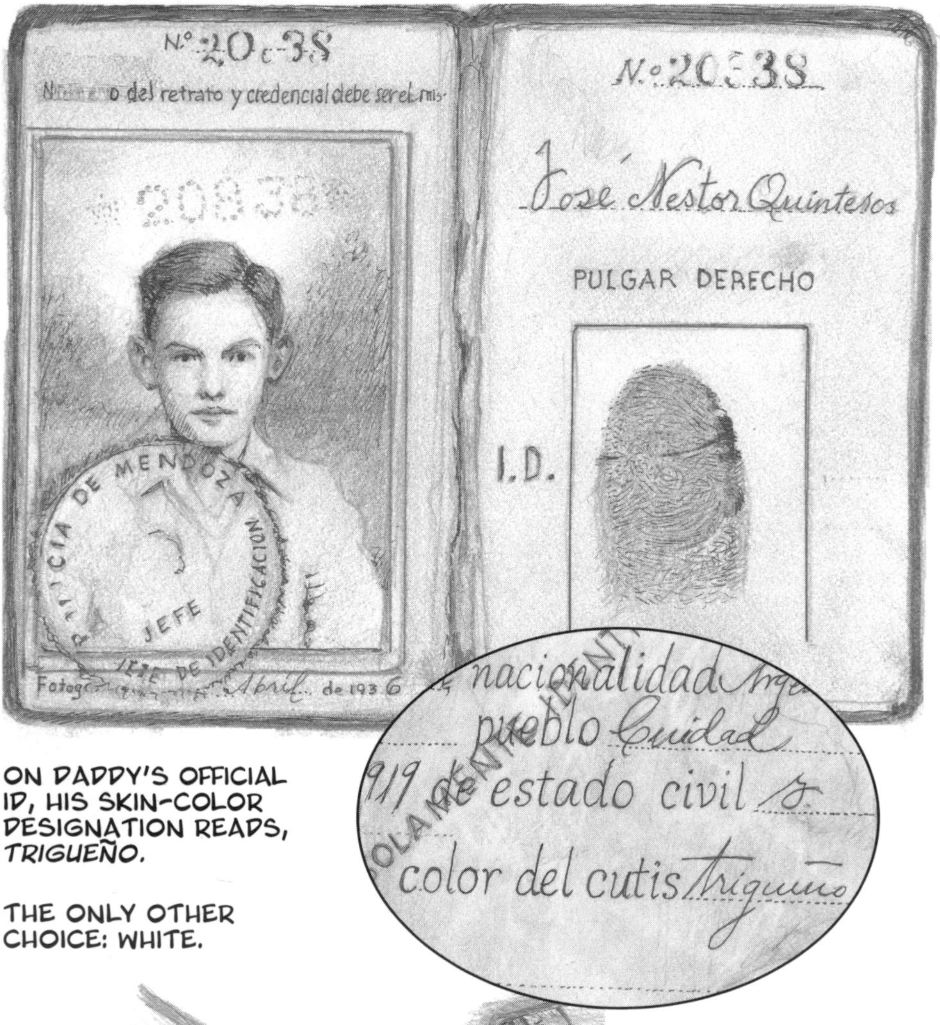

o del retrato y credencial debe ser el mis-
N.º 20838
José Nestor Quinteros
PULGAR DERECHO
I.D.
DE MENDOZA
JEFE
JEFE DE IDENTIFICACION
Abril de 1936
nacionalidad
pueblo Ciudad
estado civil
color del cutis Trigueño

ON DADDY'S OFFICIAL ID, HIS SKIN-COLOR DESIGNATION READS, *TRIGUEÑO.*

THE ONLY OTHER CHOICE: WHITE.

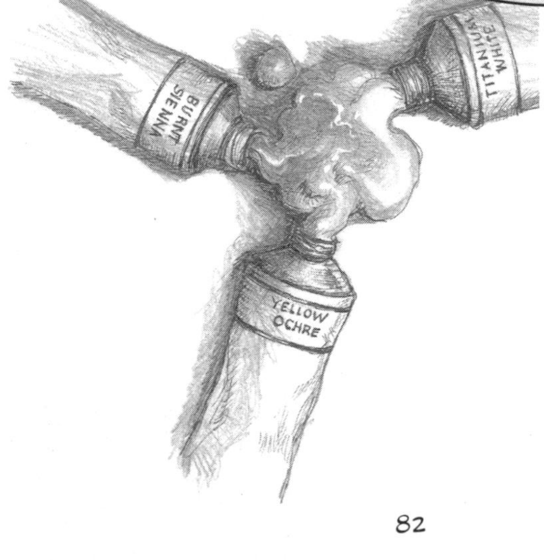

BURNT SIENNA
TITANIUM WHITE
YELLOW OCHRE

TRIGUEÑO IS A TERM DERIVED FROM *TRIGO*—SPANISH FOR WHEAT. IT APPLIES TO A PALETTE OF SKIN TONES BELONGING TO MIXED-RACE PEOPLE IN LATINO CULTURES.

MAMA, OFFICIALLY DEEMED WHITE, DEFIED SOCIAL CONVENTION BY MARRYING THIS *TRIGUEÑO*.

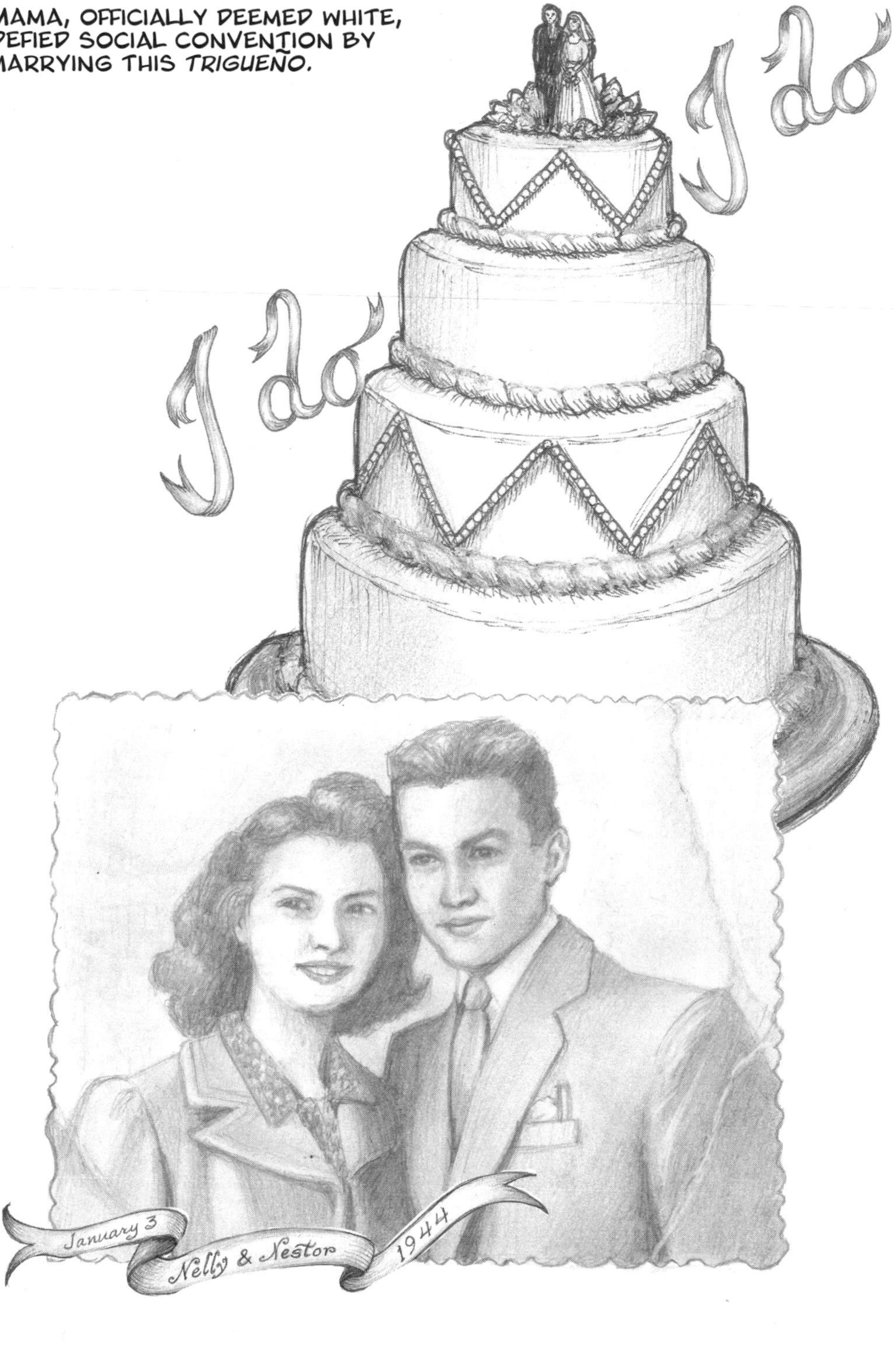
I do
I do
January 3
Nelly & Nestor
1944

LIKE MOST BUENOS AIRES NATIVES, SHE CAME FROM PURE EUROPEAN STOCK.

DADDY'S ANCESTRAL LINE CONSISTED OF WANDERERS,

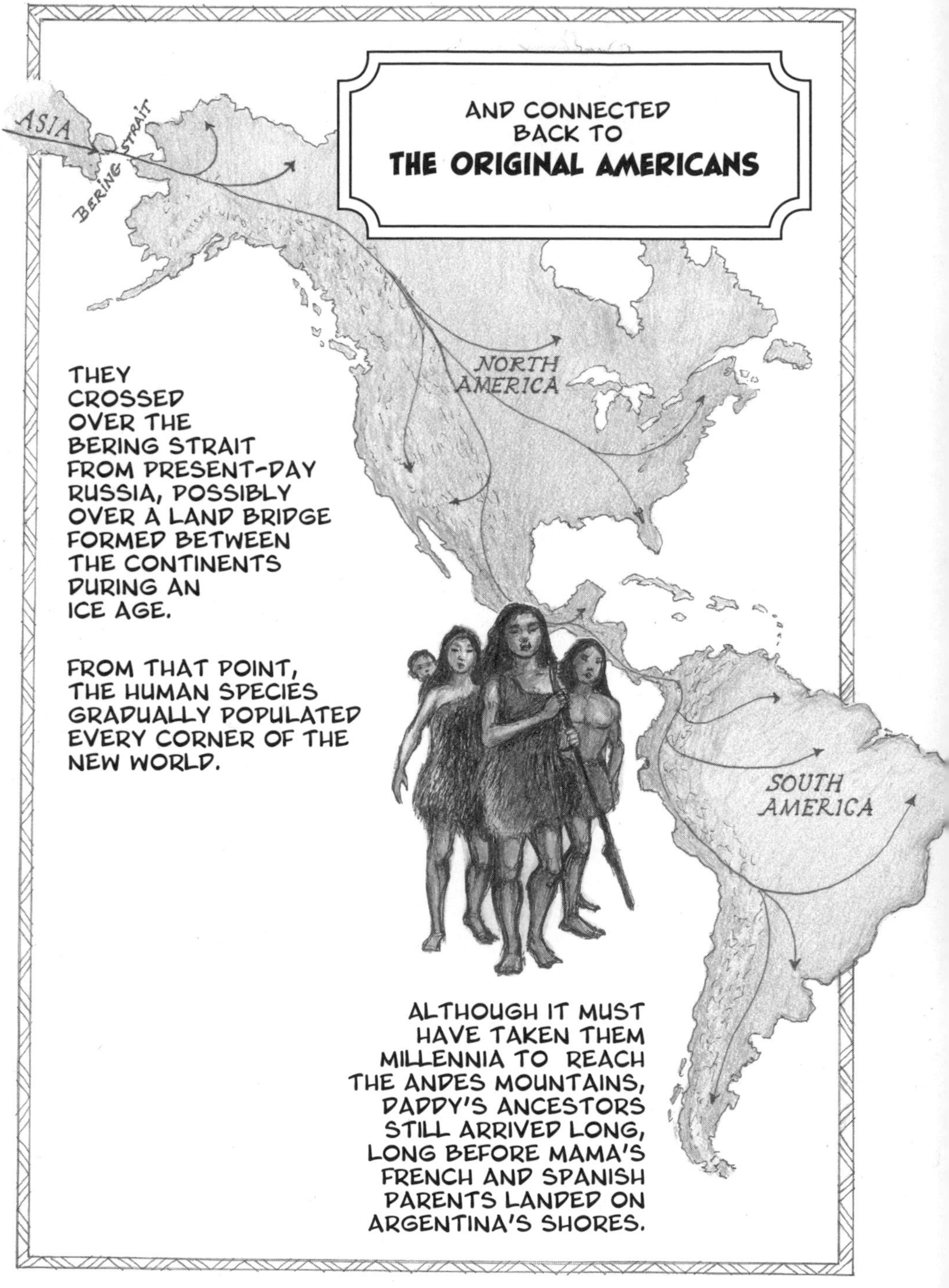
AND CONNECTED BACK TO THE ORIGINAL AMERICANS
ASIA
BERING STRAIT
NORTH AMERICA
THEY CROSSED OVER THE BERING STRAIT FROM PRESENT-DAY RUSSIA, POSSIBLY OVER A LAND BRIDGE FORMED BETWEEN THE CONTINENTS DURING AN ICE AGE.
FROM THAT POINT, THE HUMAN SPECIES GRADUALLY POPULATED EVERY CORNER OF THE NEW WORLD.
SOUTH AMERICA
ALTHOUGH IT MUST HAVE TAKEN THEM MILLENNIA TO REACH THE ANDES MOUNTAINS, DADDY'S ANCESTORS STILL ARRIVED LONG, LONG BEFORE MAMA'S FRENCH AND SPANISH PARENTS LANDED ON ARGENTINA'S SHORES.

MY FATHER PROUDLY IDENTIFIED WITH NATIVE AMERICANS ACROSS THE SPECTRUM.

TRACES OF THEIR COMMON ANCESTORS LIVED ON IN HIM AND HIS OFFSPRING.

YOU COULD SEE IT IN THEIR EYELID FOLDS, IN THE TEXTURE OF THEIR HAIR, IN THEIR LIPS, IN THEIR SKIN TONES THAT RANGED FROM MAHOGANY TO WHEAT.

MOST SOUTHERNERS HAD NO IDEA HOW TO LABEL US. THEY TOOK IN OUR DARK FEATURES, HISPANIC OLIVE SKIN, AND FULL LIPS, AND IF THEIR MOUTHS DIDN'T ASK THE QUESTION, THEIR EYES DID:

WHAT ARE YOU?

EVEN OUR GEOGRAPHICAL ORIGIN DREW BLANK STARES.

ARGENTINA. HMM...

OH!

IS THAT IN SOUTH ALABAMA?

LONG BEFORE THE TERM "HISPANIC" GAINED RECOGNTION IN THE SOUTH, NO SUITABLE CATEGORIES FOR OUR ETHNIC TYPE EXISTED.

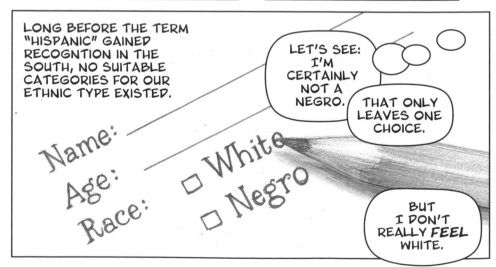

LET'S SEE: I'M CERTAINLY NOT A NEGRO.

THAT ONLY LEAVES ONE CHOICE.

Name:
Age:
Race: ☐ White
☐ Negro

BUT I DON'T REALLY *FEEL* WHITE.

I GOT THE IMPRESSION THAT WHITENESS WAS A PRIVILEGE, IF YOU WANTED TO SEE IT AS SUCH, RESERVED FOR DESCENDANTS OF NORTHERN EUROPEANS.

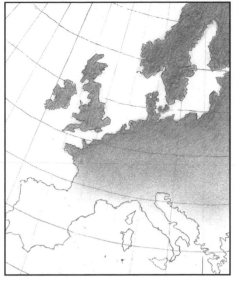

EVEN JESUS GOT DRAWN INTO THIS FOLD. BLUE-EYED PORTRAITS OF HIM WERE EVERYWHERE IN OUR BIBLE BELT STATE.

IS IT TRUE THAT GALILEANS HAD BLUE EYES AND BLOND HAIR?

WHERE DID YOU HEAR THAT, SUNDAY SCHOOL?

THAT'S COMPLETE NONSENSE.

ACCORDING TO DADDY, JESUS WOULD'VE BEEN AS DARK-SKINNED AS AN ARAB, NOT THE MILKY WHITE WISHED ON HIM BY SOUTHERNERS.

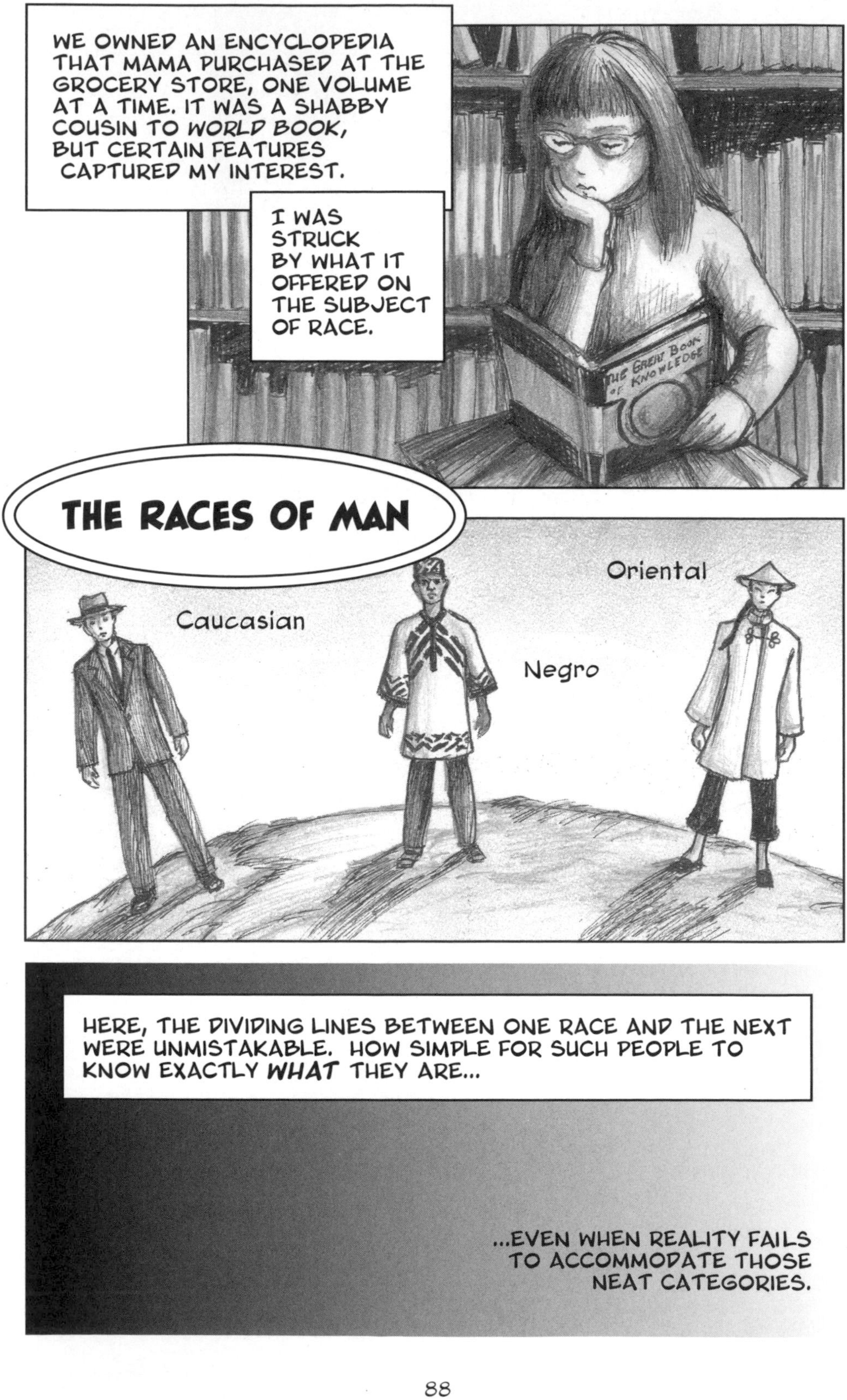
WE OWNED AN ENCYCLOPEDIA THAT MAMA PURCHASED AT THE GROCERY STORE, ONE VOLUME AT A TIME. IT WAS A SHABBY COUSIN TO *WORLD BOOK*, BUT CERTAIN FEATURES CAPTURED MY INTEREST.
I WAS STRUCK BY WHAT IT OFFERED ON THE SUBJECT OF RACE.
THE GREAT BOOK OF KNOWLEDGE
THE RACES OF MAN
Caucasian
Negro
Oriental
HERE, THE DIVIDING LINES BETWEEN ONE RACE AND THE NEXT WERE UNMISTAKABLE. HOW SIMPLE FOR SUCH PEOPLE TO KNOW EXACTLY *WHAT* THEY ARE...
...EVEN WHEN REALITY FAILS TO ACCOMMODATE THOSE NEAT CATEGORIES.

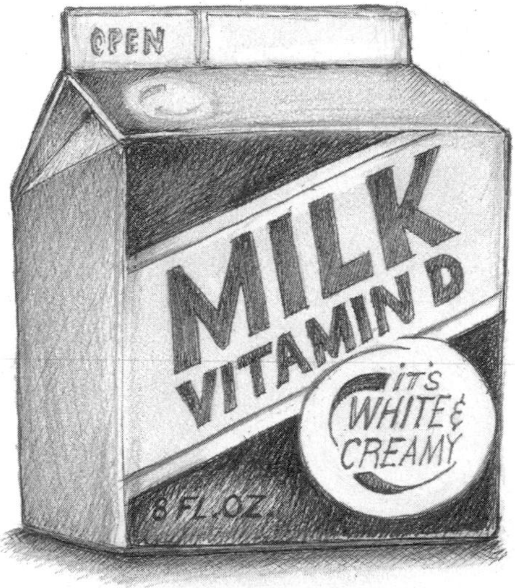
OPEN
MILK
VITAMIN D
IT'S WHITE & CREAMY
8 FL. OZ.

BUT FEW WHITE SOUTHERNERS TOLERATED RACIAL AMBIGUITY. THEY DISPENSED WITH SUCH FUZZY BOUNDARIES BY APPLYING ***THE ONE-DROP RULE.***

ACCORDING TO THE ONE-DROP RULE, NO ONE WHO HAS THE SLIGHTEST TRACE OF AFRICAN ANCESTRY CAN CLAIM TO BE WHITE.

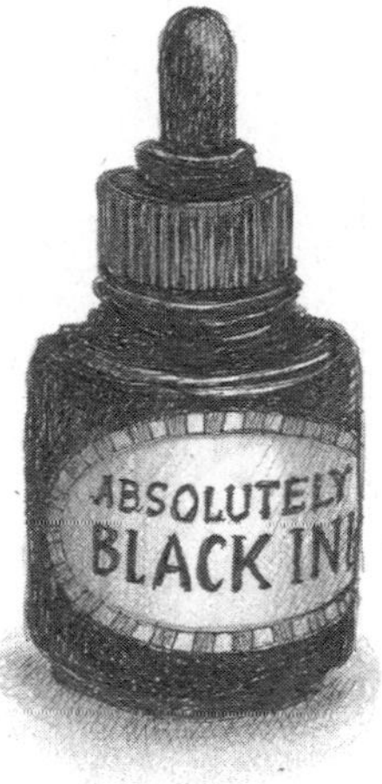
ABSOLUTELY
BLACK INK

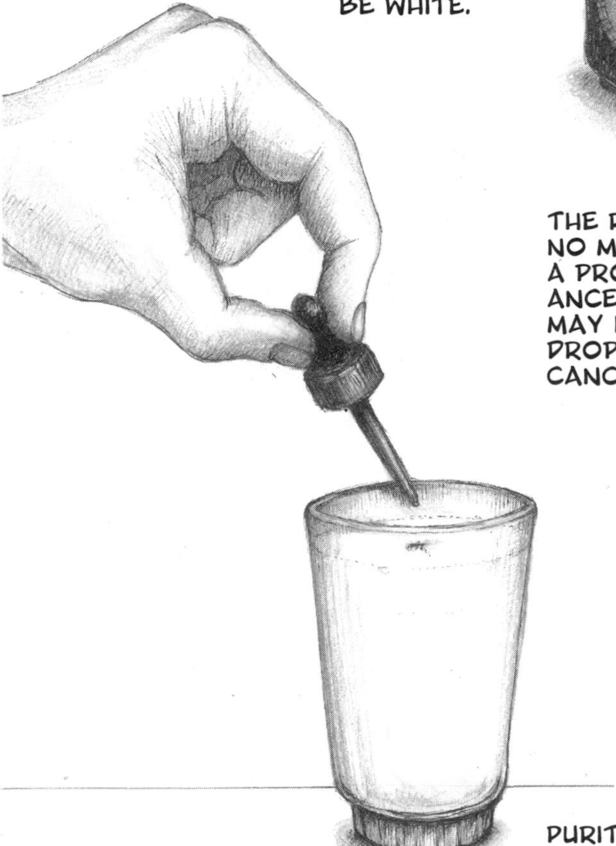

THE RULE IS UNYIELDING. NO MATTER HOW HIGH A PROPORTION OF WHITE ANCESTRY A PERSON MAY HAVE, JUST ONE DROP OF BLACKNESS CANCELS IT OUT.

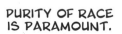

PURITY OF RACE IS PARAMOUNT.

WHITE ALABAMIANS' OBSESSION WITH KEEPING THE RACES APART PROPELLED A POLITICALLY ASTUTE JUDGE TO THE OFFICE OF GOVERNOR. IT HAPPENED SHORTLY AFTER OUR ARRIVAL.

FROM THIS CRADLE OF THE CONFEDERACY, FROM THIS VERY HEART OF THE GREAT ANGLO-SAXON SOUTHLAND...

...I draw the line in the dust and toss the gauntlet before the feet of tyranny, and I say segregation now, segregation tomorrow, and segregation forever.

—Gov. George C. Wallace
January 14, 1963

chapter 6
AN AMERICAN EDUCATION

DELTA LINE
NEW ORLEANS

NAME OF PASSENGER
J. Nestor Quintero

STEAMER Del Mundo
ROOM Nº.

SAILING
DESTINATION New Orleans

STATE ROOM
BAGGAGE

IT WAS 1948
WHEN DADDY LANDED
IN NEW ORLEANS
FOR THE PURPOSE
OF ENROLLING
IN SEMINARY.

I WONDER ABOUT HIS FIRST
IMPRESSIONS OF AMERICA.

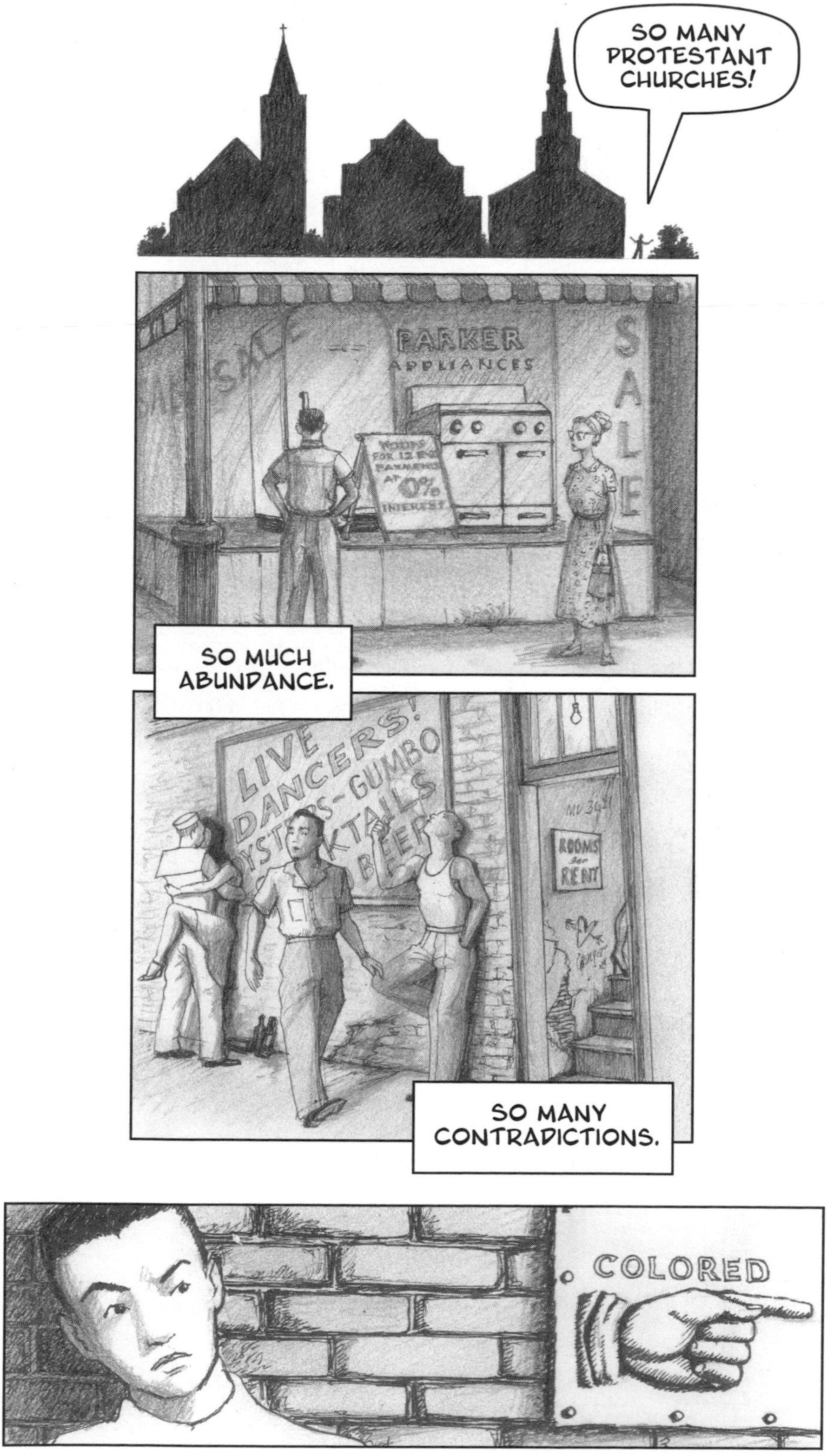
SO MANY PROTESTANT CHURCHES!
PARKER APPLIANCES
SALE
SO MUCH ABUNDANCE.
LIVE DANCERS!
ROOMS for RENT
SO MANY CONTRADICTIONS.
COLORED

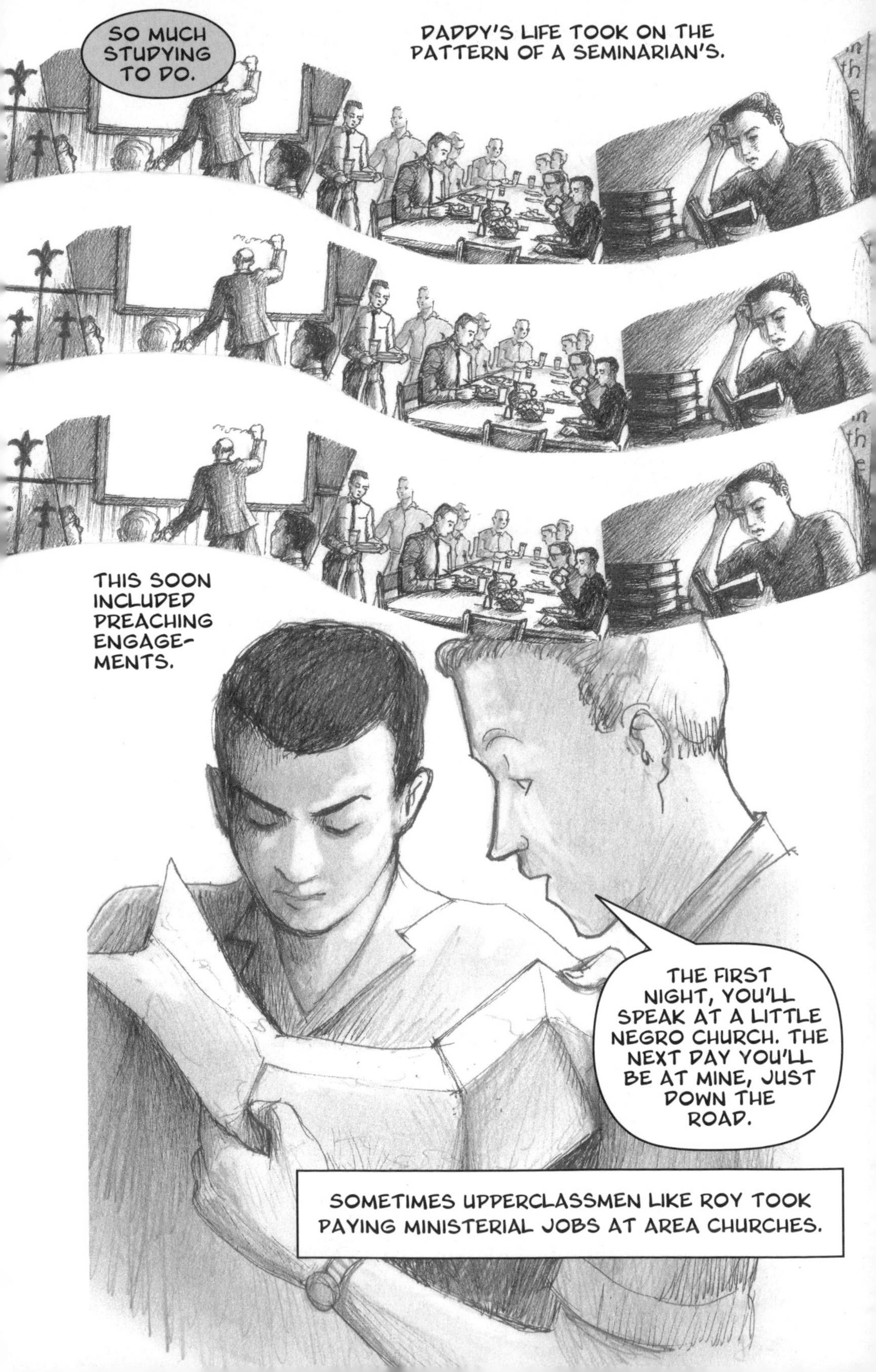
SO MUCH STUDYING TO DO.
DADDY'S LIFE TOOK ON THE PATTERN OF A SEMINARIAN'S.
THIS SOON INCLUDED PREACHING ENGAGE-MENTS.
THE FIRST NIGHT, YOU'LL SPEAK AT A LITTLE NEGRO CHURCH. THE NEXT DAY YOU'LL BE AT MINE, JUST DOWN THE ROAD.
SOMETIMES UPPERCLASSMEN LIKE ROY TOOK PAYING MINISTERIAL JOBS AT AREA CHURCHES.

ON A SATURDAY NIGHT, SOMEWHERE IN RURAL LOUISIANA:

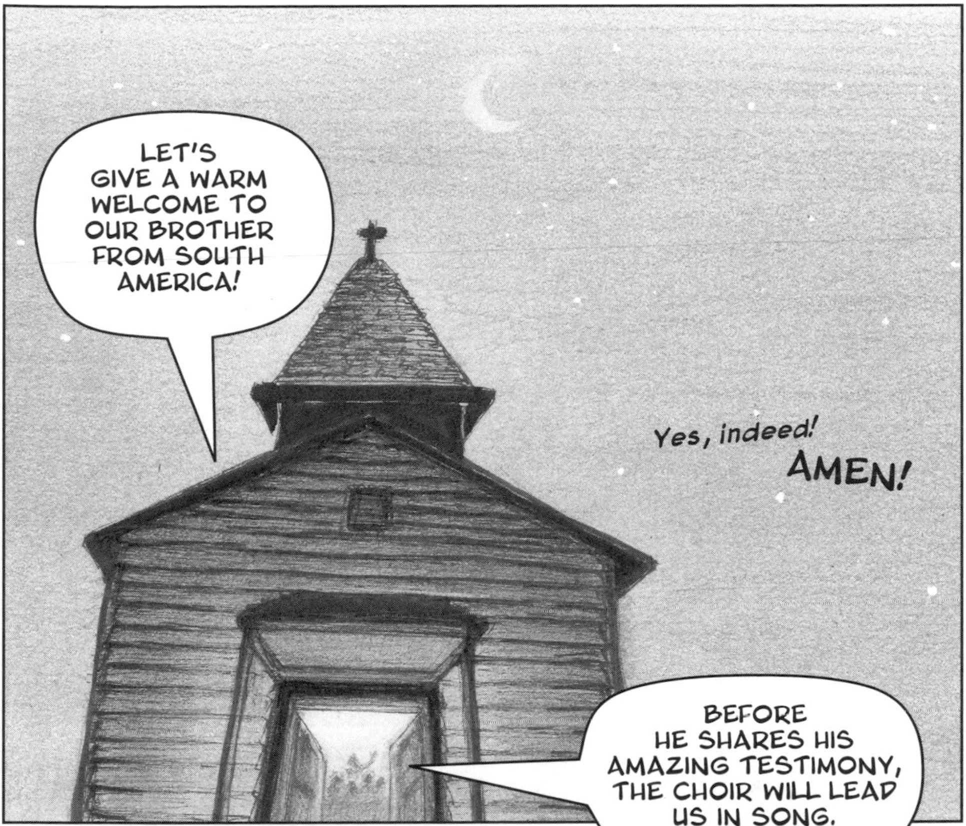
LET'S GIVE A WARM WELCOME TO OUR BROTHER FROM SOUTH AMERICA!
Yes, indeed!
AMEN!
BEFORE HE SHARES HIS AMAZING TESTIMONY, THE CHOIR WILL LEAD US IN SONG.

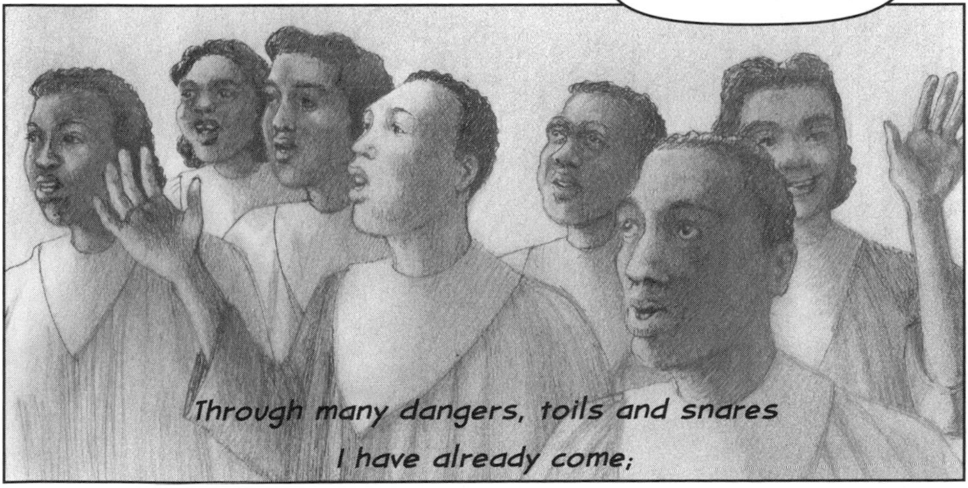
Through many dangers, toils and snares
I have already come;

'Tis Grace that brought me safe thus far

and Grace will lead me home.

THIS WAS UNLIKE ANYTHING MY FATHER HAD EVER HEARD.

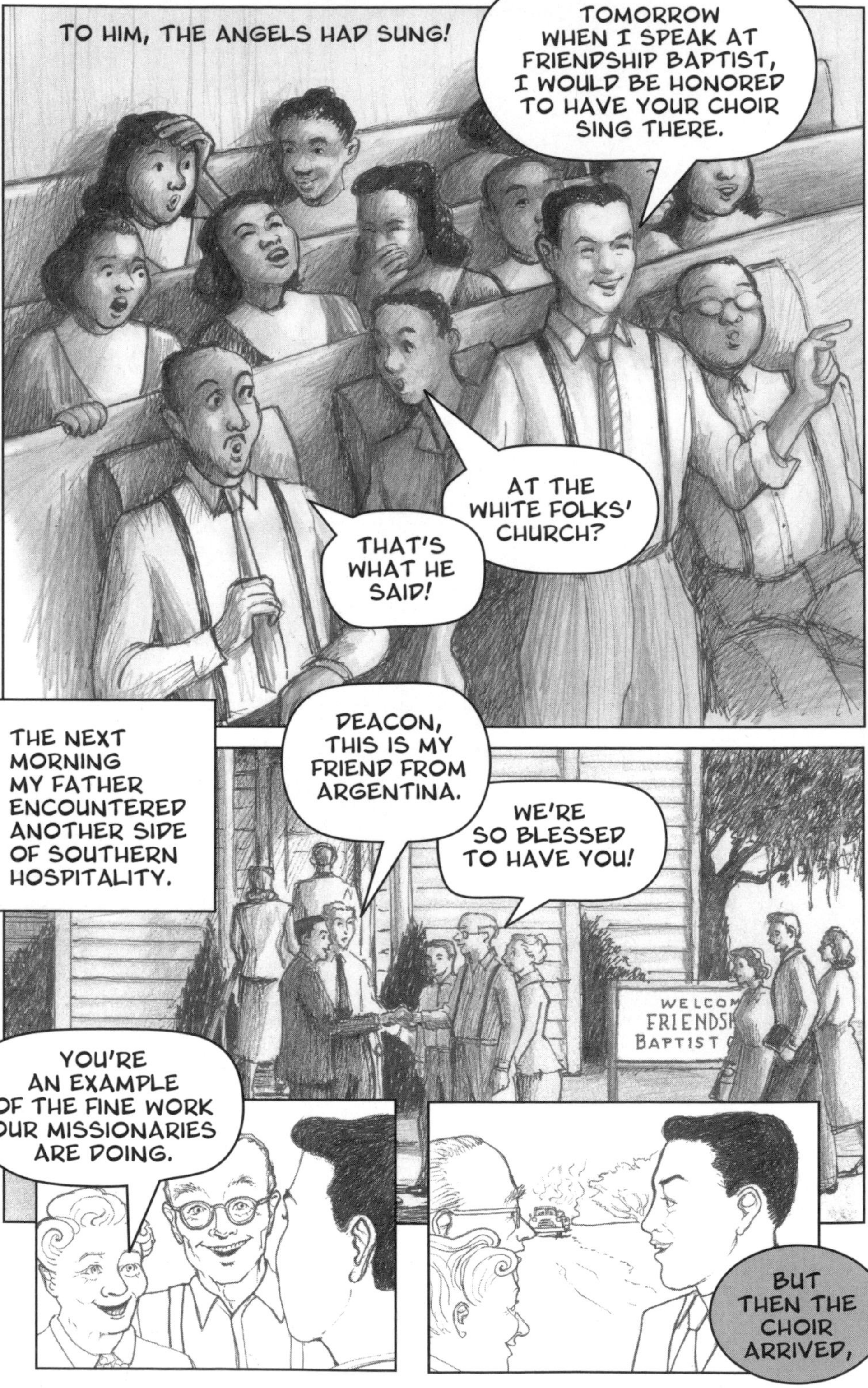
TO HIM, THE ANGELS HAD SUNG!
TOMORROW WHEN I SPEAK AT FRIENDSHIP BAPTIST, I WOULD BE HONORED TO HAVE YOUR CHOIR SING THERE.
AT THE WHITE FOLKS' CHURCH?
THAT'S WHAT HE SAID!
THE NEXT MORNING MY FATHER ENCOUNTERED ANOTHER SIDE OF SOUTHERN HOSPITALITY.
DEACON, THIS IS MY FRIEND FROM ARGENTINA.
WE'RE SO BLESSED TO HAVE YOU!
WELCOM
FRIENDSH
BAPTIST C
YOU'RE AN EXAMPLE OF THE FINE WORK OUR MISSIONARIES ARE DOING.
BUT THEN THE CHOIR ARRIVED,
AND THINGS TOOK AN UGLY TURN.

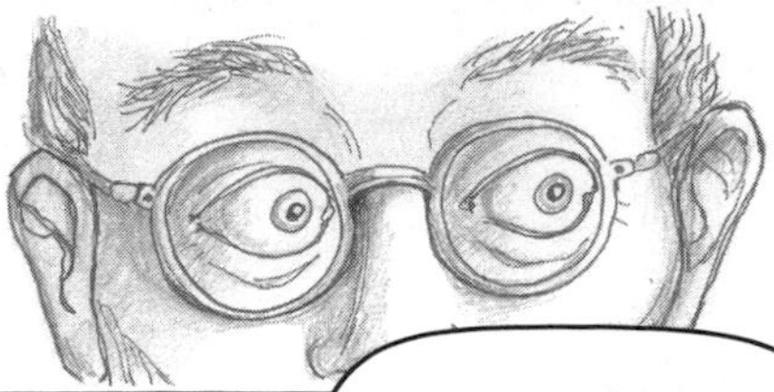
HUH?

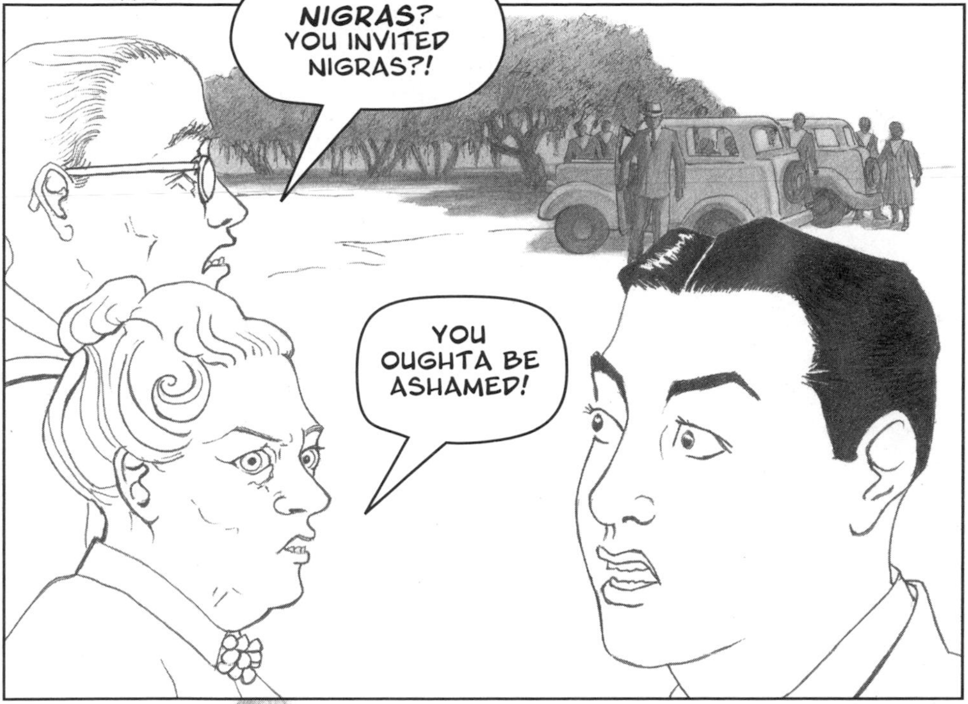
NIGRAS? YOU INVITED NIGRAS?!
YOU OUGHTA BE ASHAMED!

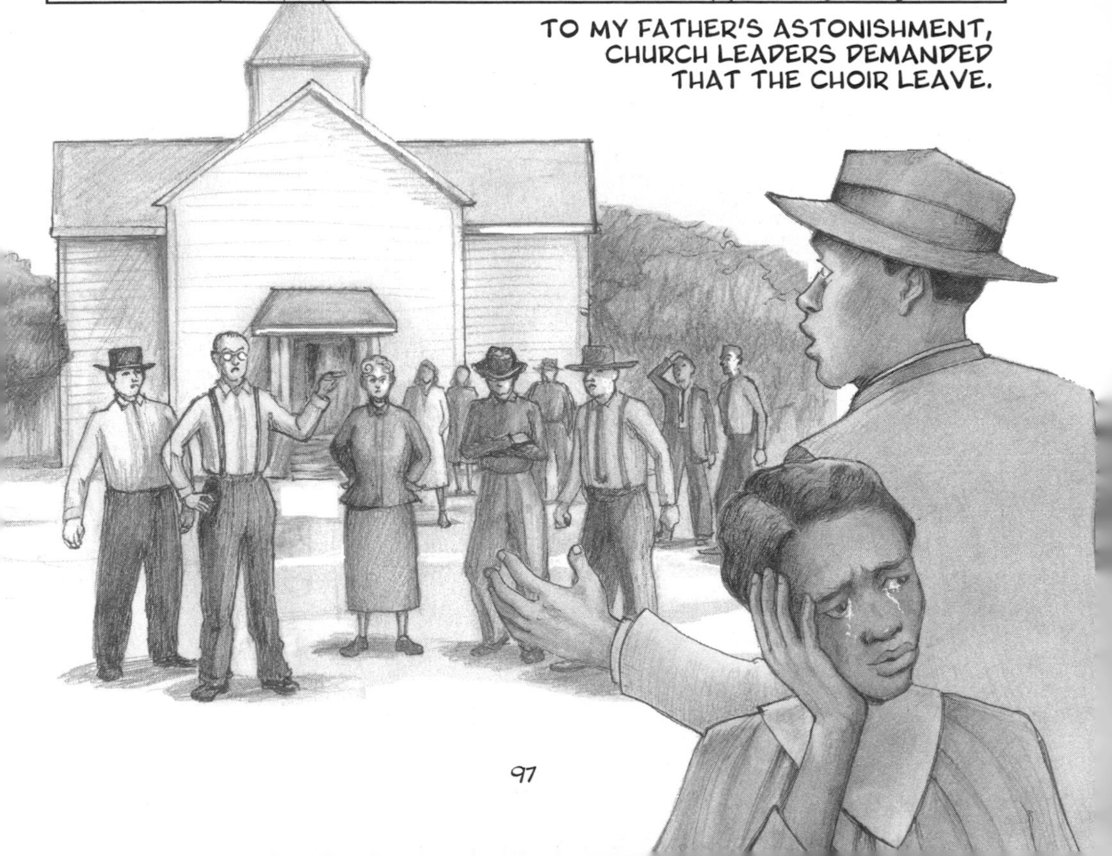
TO MY FATHER'S ASTONISHMENT, CHURCH LEADERS DEMANDED THAT THE CHOIR LEAVE.

I IMAGINE THAT HIS NEXT LETTER HOME MUST'VE CONTAINED SOMETHING ABOUT THIS INCIDENT.

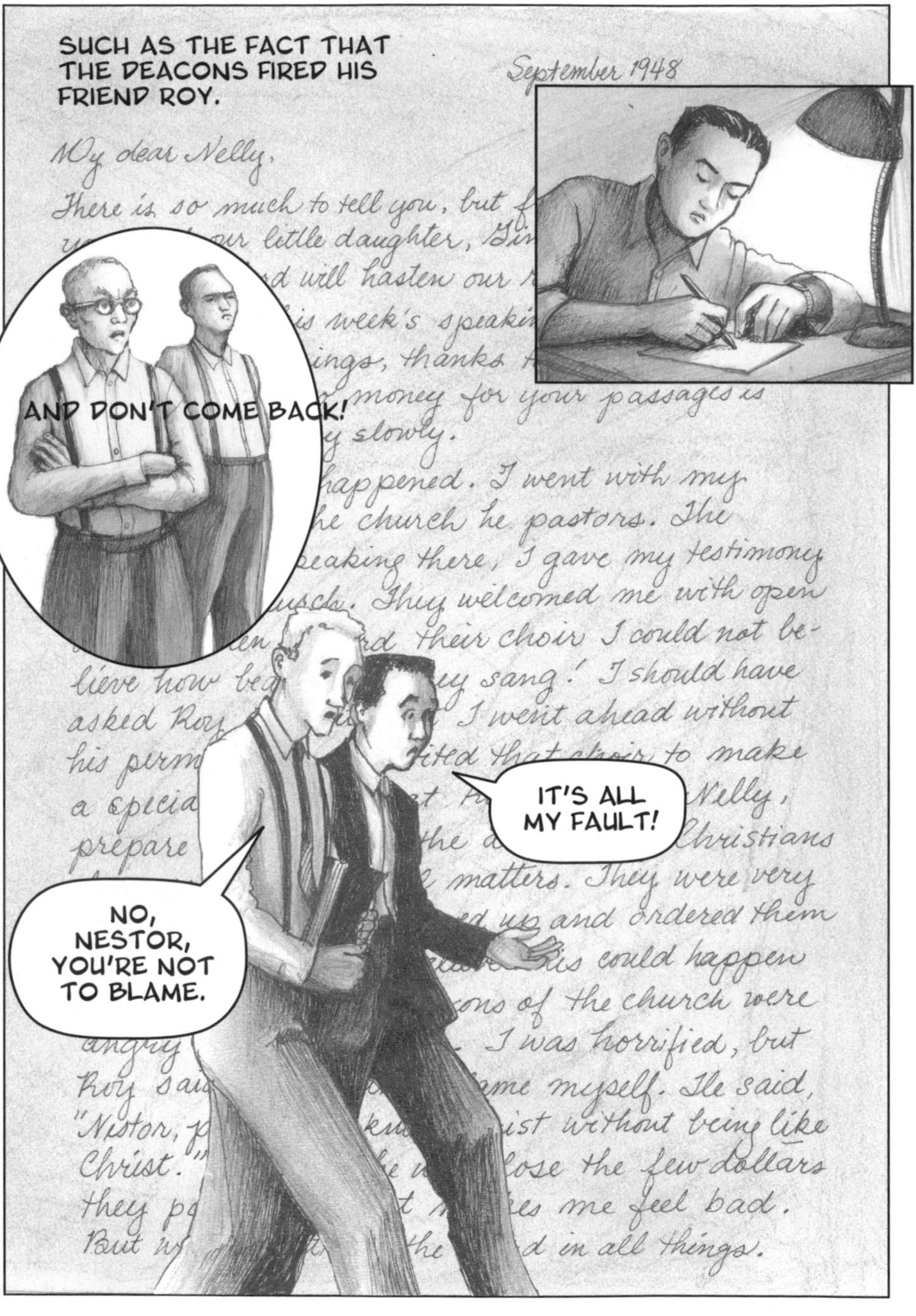
SUCH AS THE FACT THAT THE DEACONS FIRED HIS FRIEND ROY.
September 1948
My dear Nelly,
AND DON'T COME BACK!
IT'S ALL MY FAULT!
NO, NESTOR, YOU'RE NOT TO BLAME.

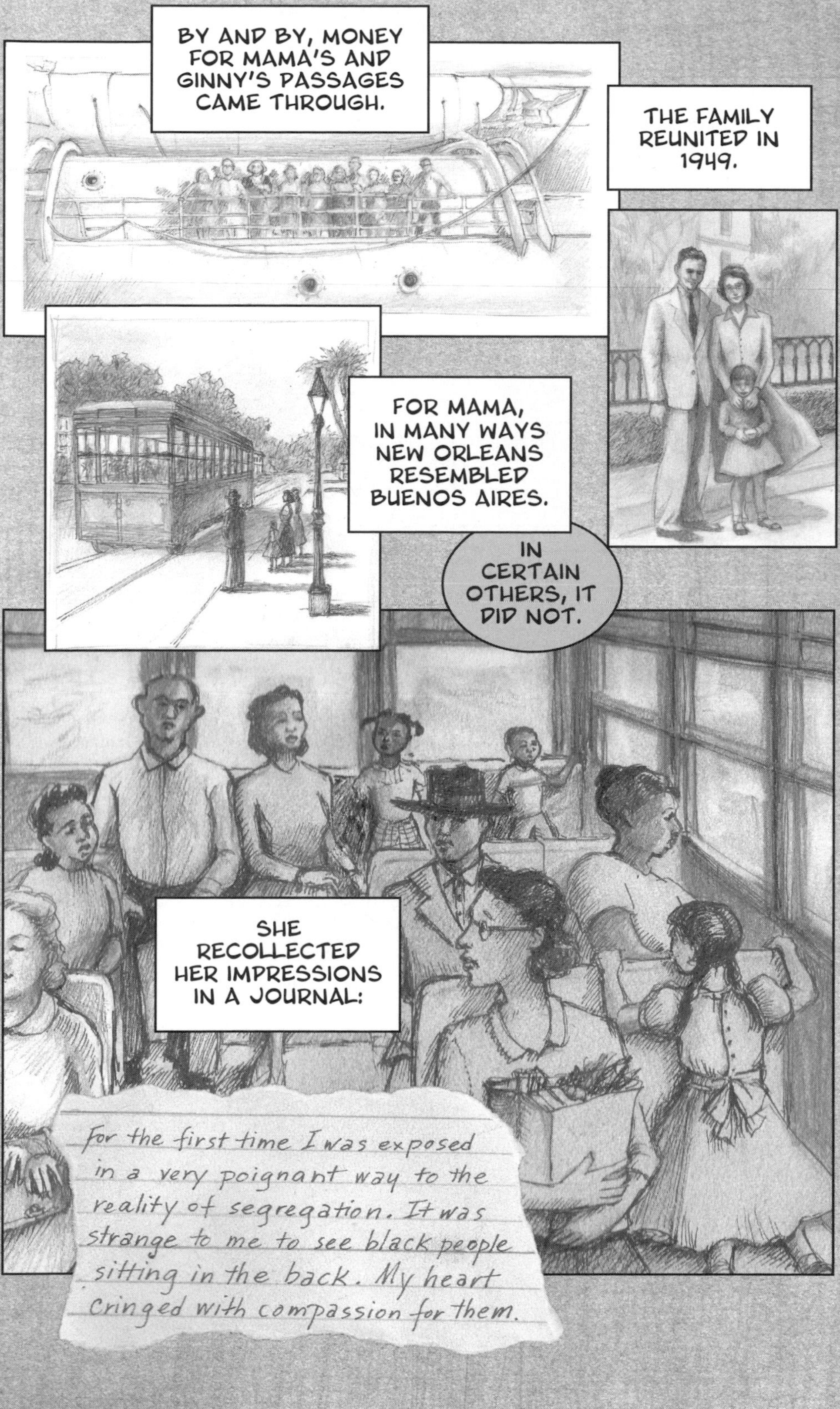

BY AND BY, MONEY FOR MAMA'S AND GINNY'S PASSAGES CAME THROUGH.
THE FAMILY REUNITED IN 1949.
FOR MAMA, IN MANY WAYS NEW ORLEANS RESEMBLED BUENOS AIRES.
IN CERTAIN OTHERS, IT DID NOT.
SHE RECOLLECTED HER IMPRESSIONS IN A JOURNAL:
For the first time I was exposed in a very poignant way to the reality of segregation. It was strange to me to see black people sitting in the back. My heart cringed with compassion for them.

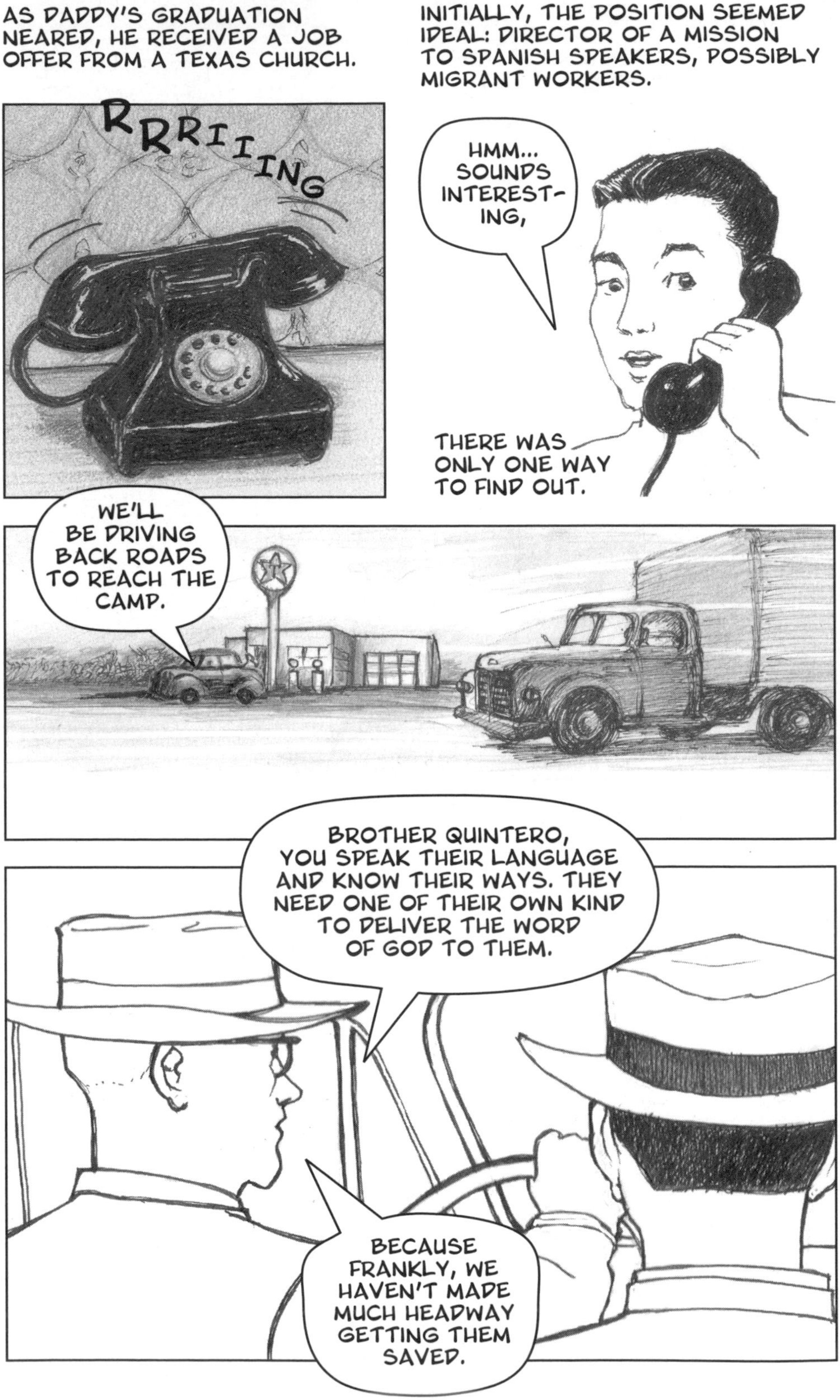
AS DADDY'S GRADUATION NEARED, HE RECEIVED A JOB OFFER FROM A TEXAS CHURCH.
INITIALLY, THE POSITION SEEMED IDEAL: DIRECTOR OF A MISSION TO SPANISH SPEAKERS, POSSIBLY MIGRANT WORKERS.
RRRIIIING
HMM... SOUNDS INTEREST-ING,
THERE WAS ONLY ONE WAY TO FIND OUT.
WE'LL BE DRIVING BACK ROADS TO REACH THE CAMP.
BROTHER QUINTERO, YOU SPEAK THEIR LANGUAGE AND KNOW THEIR WAYS. THEY NEED ONE OF THEIR OWN KIND TO DELIVER THE WORD OF GOD TO THEM.
BECAUSE FRANKLY, WE HAVEN'T MADE MUCH HEADWAY GETTING THEM SAVED.

THERE WAS A CERTAIN RING TO THE MAN'S WORDS.

DOWN THE WAY IS YOUR LIVING QUARTERS. YOUR WIFE WILL WANT TO FIX IT UP A BIT. ACTUALLY, THE WHOLE PLACE NEEDS WORK, BUT WE DON'T HAVE THE FUNDS RIGHT NOW.

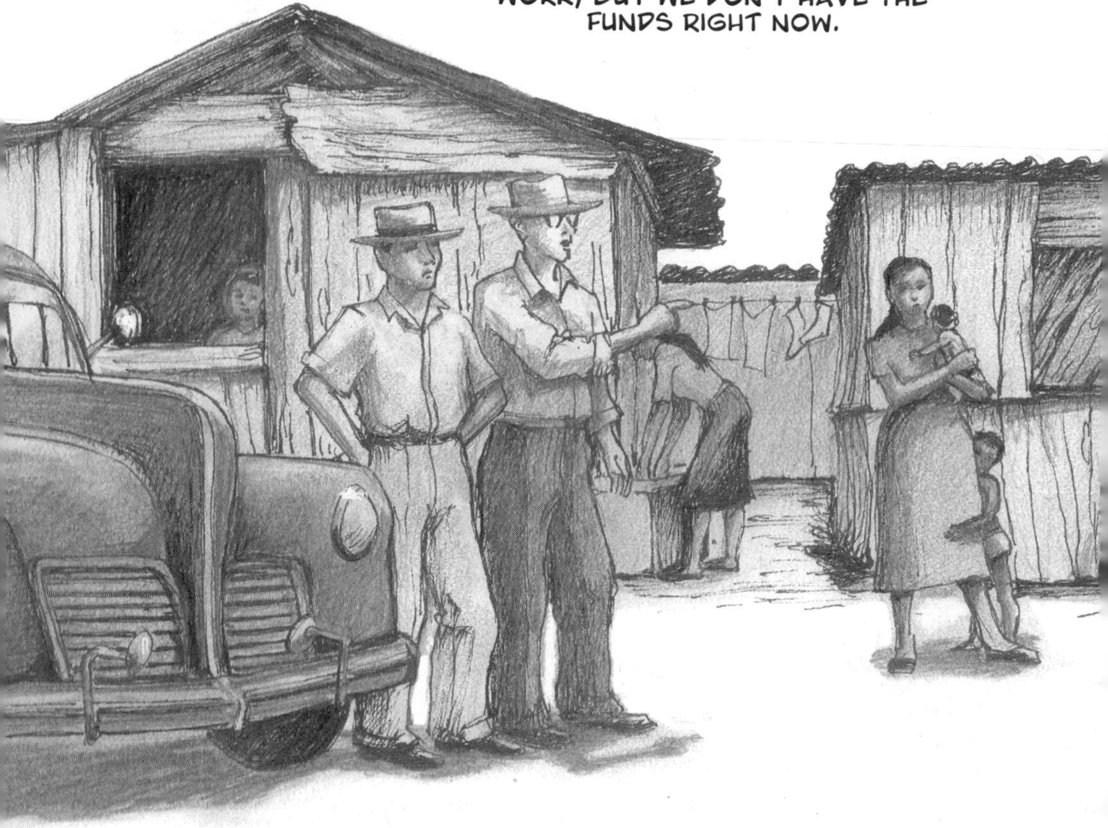

BUT SINCE YOU WERE A HOMELESS ORPHAN, YOU MUST BE USED TO THE LACK OF INDOOR PLUMBING AND ELECTRICITY.

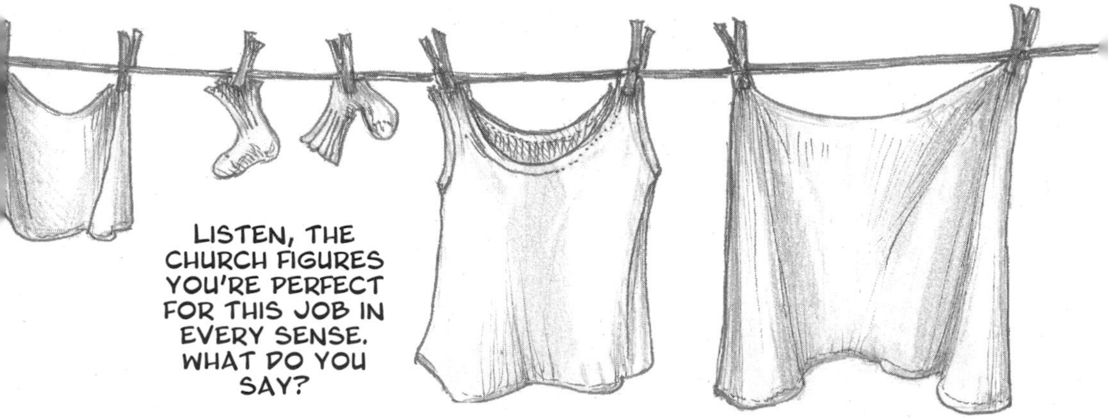
LISTEN, THE CHURCH FIGURES YOU'RE PERFECT FOR THIS JOB IN EVERY SENSE. WHAT DO YOU SAY?

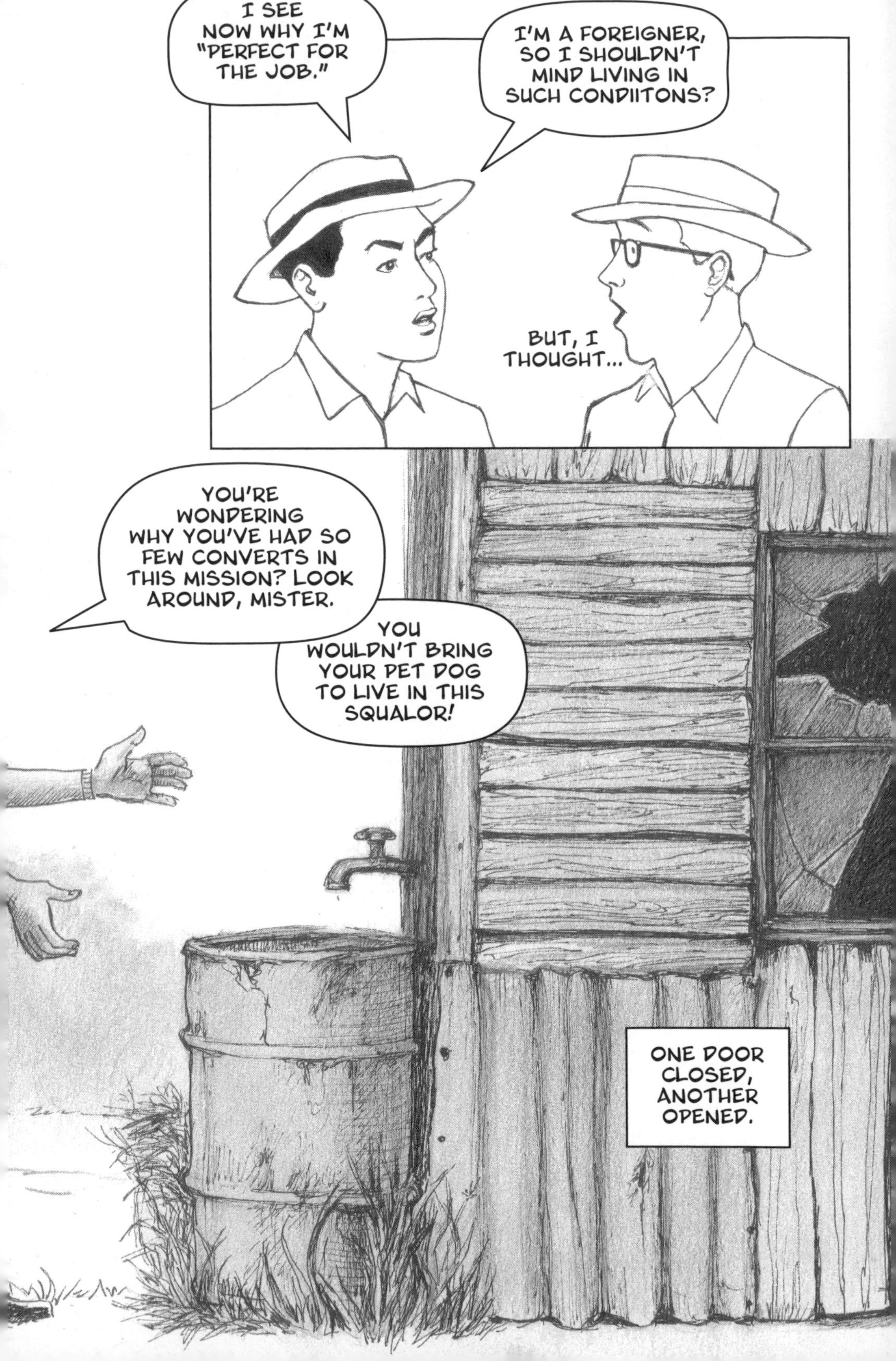

I SEE NOW WHY I'M "PERFECT FOR THE JOB."
I'M A FOREIGNER, SO I SHOULDN'T MIND LIVING IN SUCH CONDIITONS?
BUT, I THOUGHT...
YOU'RE WONDERING WHY YOU'VE HAD SO FEW CONVERTS IN THIS MISSION? LOOK AROUND, MISTER.
YOU WOULDN'T BRING YOUR PET DOG TO LIVE IN THIS SQUALOR!
ONE DOOR CLOSED, ANOTHER OPENED.

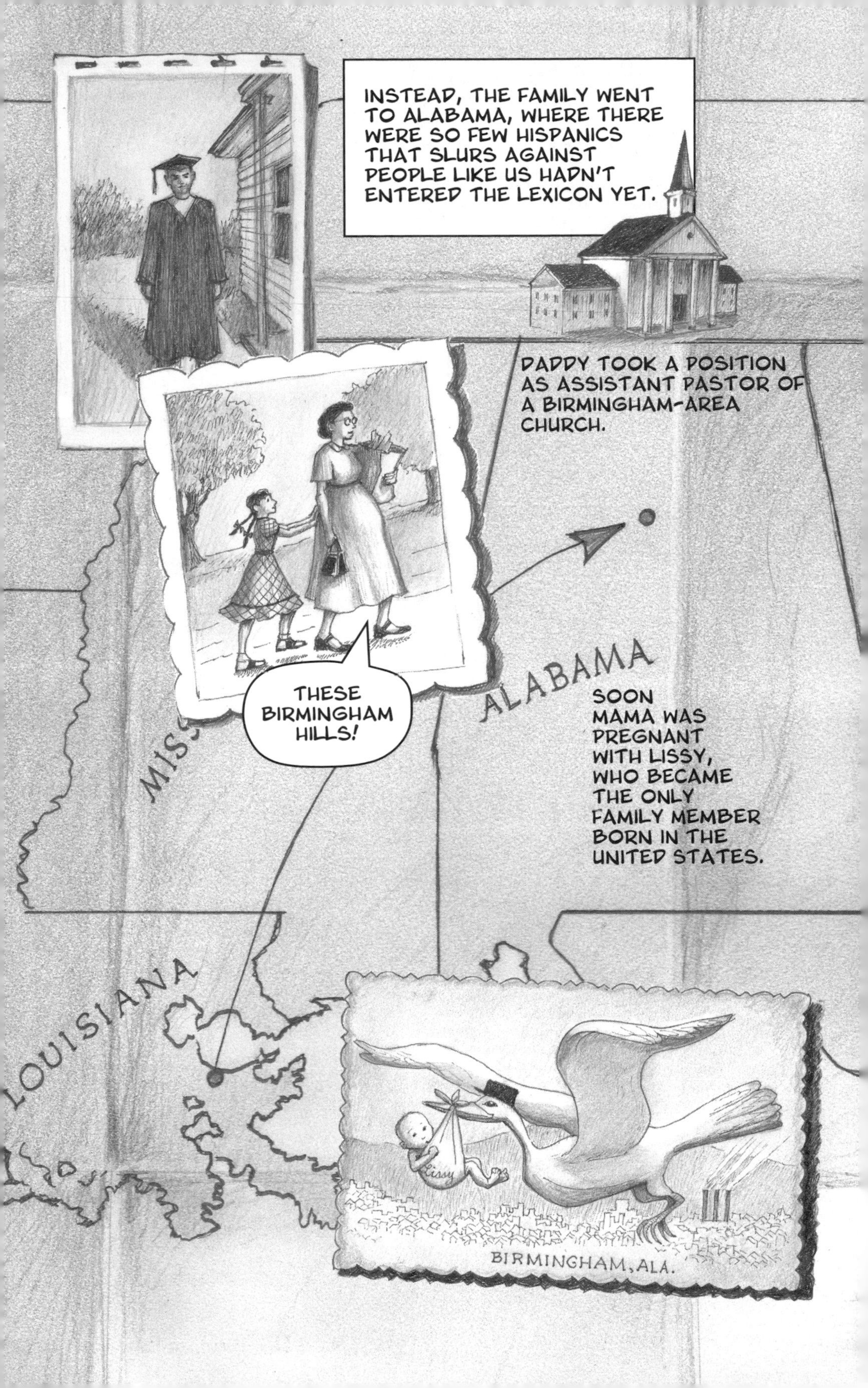
INSTEAD, THE FAMILY WENT TO ALABAMA, WHERE THERE WERE SO FEW HISPANICS THAT SLURS AGAINST PEOPLE LIKE US HADN'T ENTERED THE LEXICON YET.
DADDY TOOK A POSITION AS ASSISTANT PASTOR OF A BIRMINGHAM-AREA CHURCH.
THESE BIRMINGHAM HILLS!
ALABAMA
MISS
SOON MAMA WAS PREGNANT WITH LISSY, WHO BECAME THE ONLY FAMILY MEMBER BORN IN THE UNITED STATES.
LOUISIANA
Lissy
BIRMINGHAM, ALA.

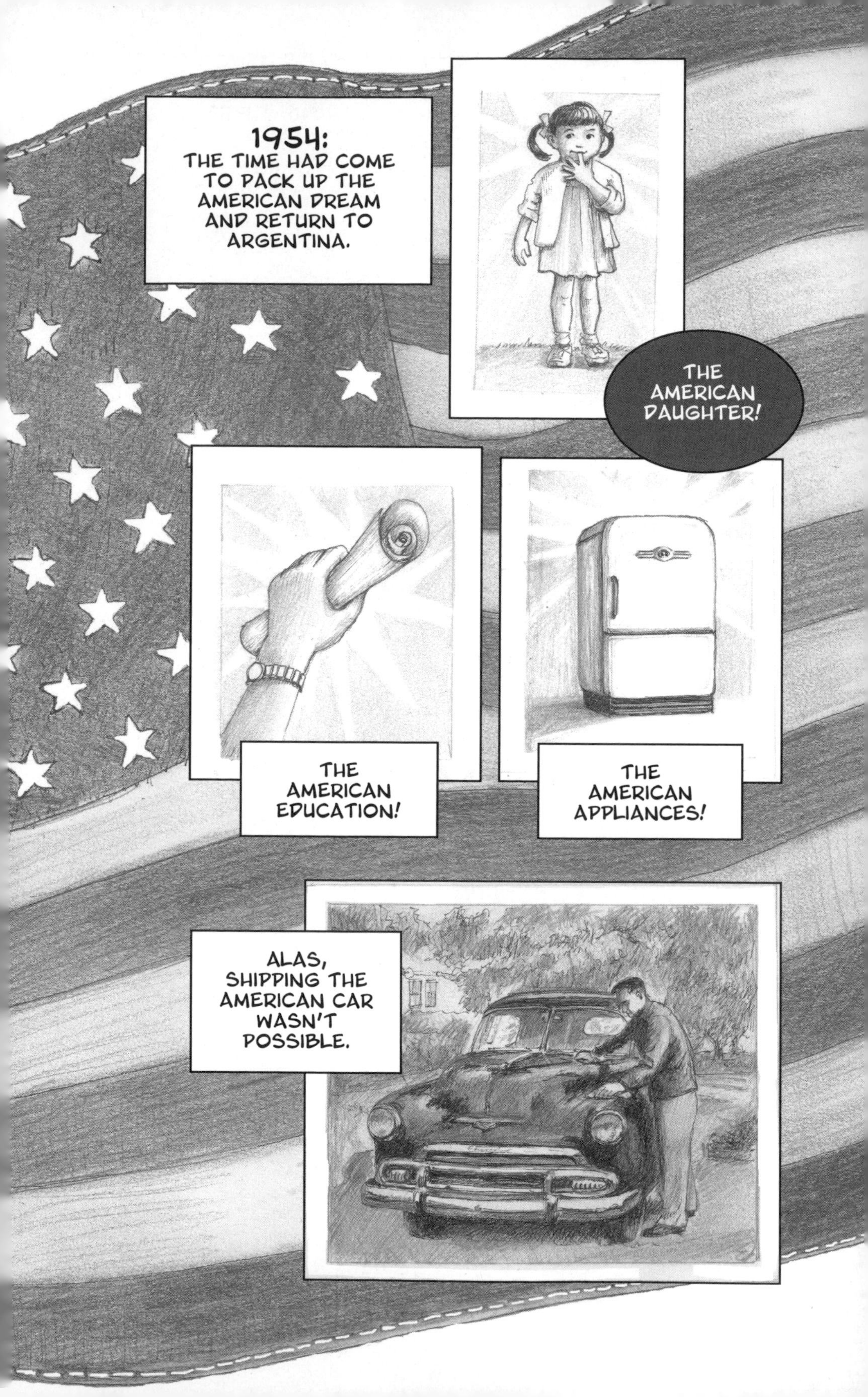
1954:
THE TIME HAD COME TO PACK UP THE AMERICAN DREAM AND RETURN TO ARGENTINA.
THE AMERICAN DAUGHTER!
THE AMERICAN EDUCATION!
THE AMERICAN APPLIANCES!
ALAS, SHIPPING THE AMERICAN CAR WASN'T POSSIBLE.

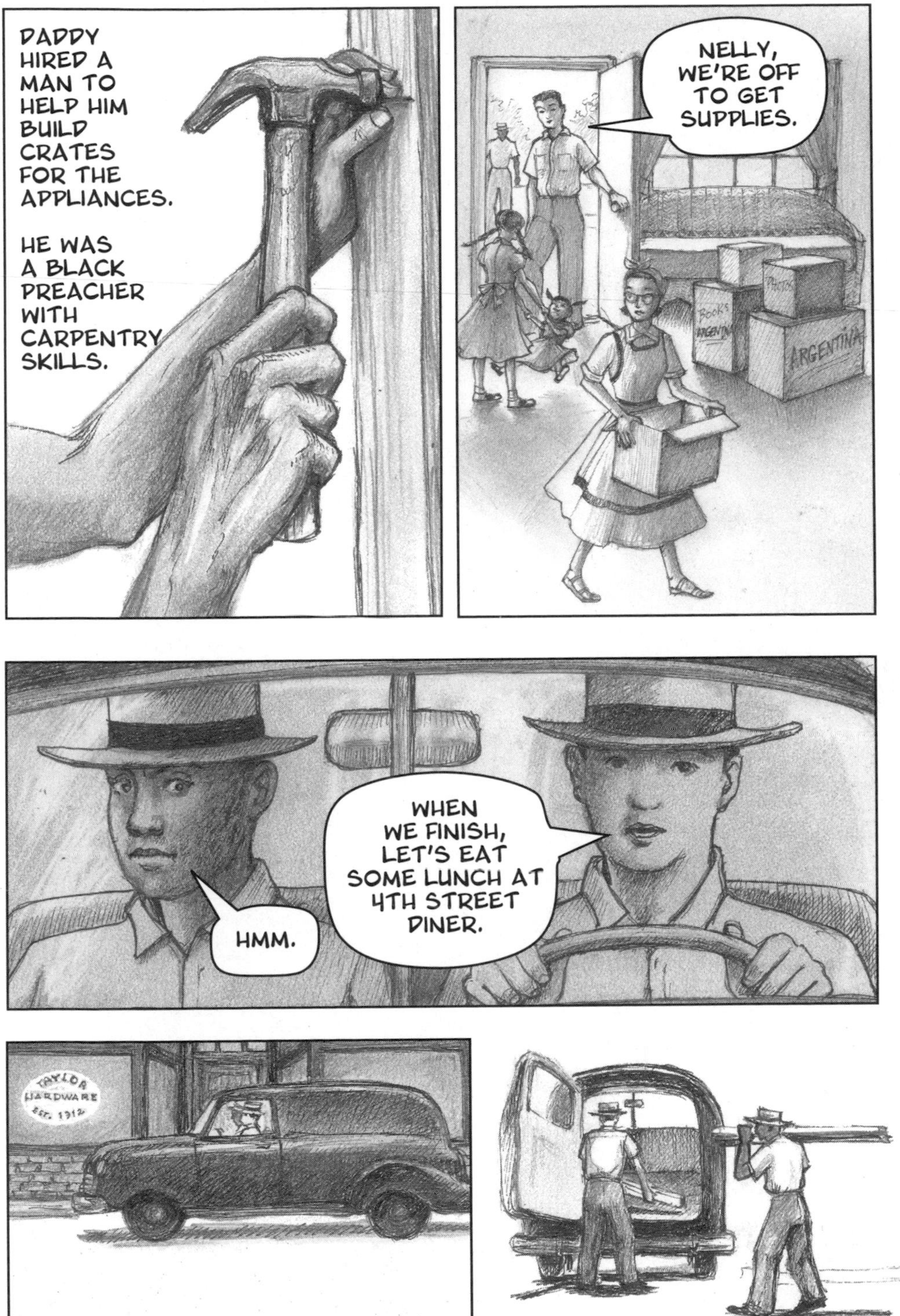
DADDY HIRED A MAN TO HELP HIM BUILD CRATES FOR THE APPLIANCES.
HE WAS A BLACK PREACHER WITH CARPENTRY SKILLS.
NELLY, WE'RE OFF TO GET SUPPLIES.
ARGENTINA
WHEN WE FINISH, LET'S EAT SOME LUNCH AT 4TH STREET DINER.
HMM.
HARDWARE
EST. 1912

BY NOW, SIX YEARS HAD PASSED SINCE DADDY'S UNHAPPY INITIATION TO THE SOUTH'S RACIAL CODE. HE WAS NO LONGER NAIVE.

WHEN HE DEFIED THE RULES, IT WOULD'VE BEEN INTENTIONAL.

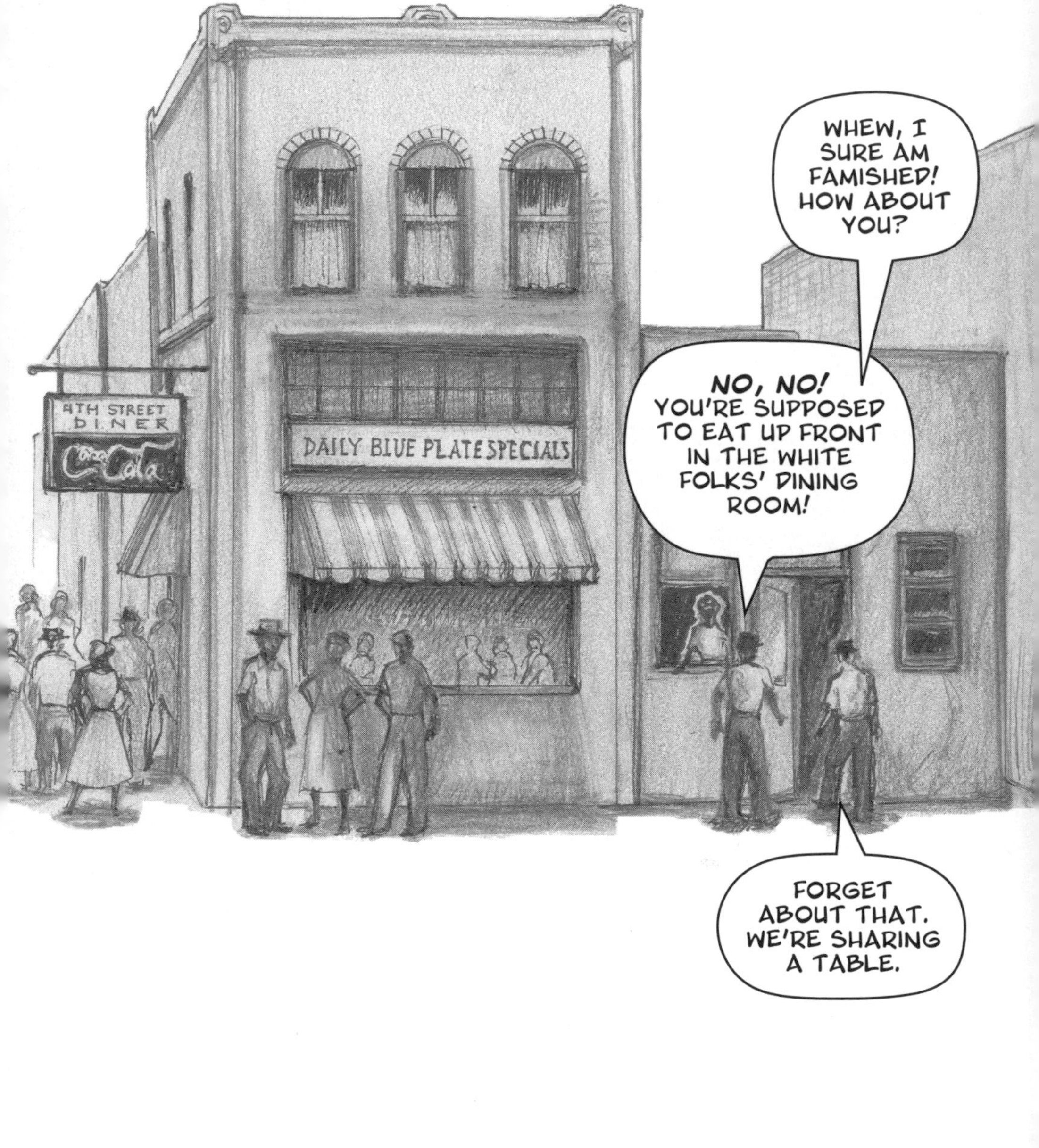
4TH STREET DINER
Coca-Cola
DAILY BLUE PLATE SPECIALS
WHEW, I SURE AM FAMISHED! HOW ABOUT YOU?
NO, NO! YOU'RE SUPPOSED TO EAT UP FRONT IN THE WHITE FOLKS' DINING ROOM!
FORGET ABOUT THAT. WE'RE SHARING A TABLE.

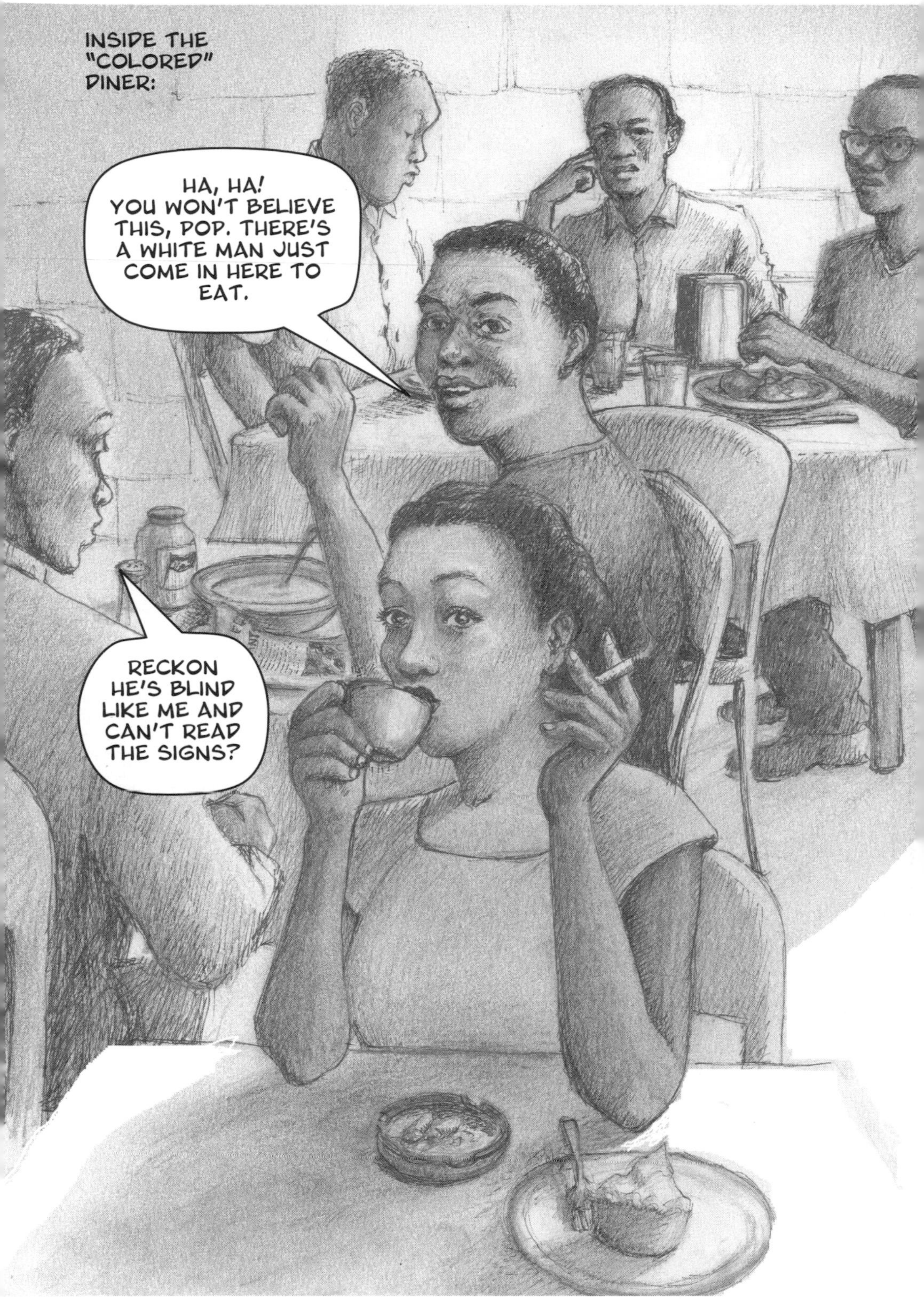
INSIDE THE "COLORED" DINER:
HA, HA! YOU WON'T BELIEVE THIS, POP. THERE'S A WHITE MAN JUST COME IN HERE TO EAT.
RECKON HE'S BLIND LIKE ME AND CAN'T READ THE SIGNS?

chapter 7

DEAR ARGENTINA

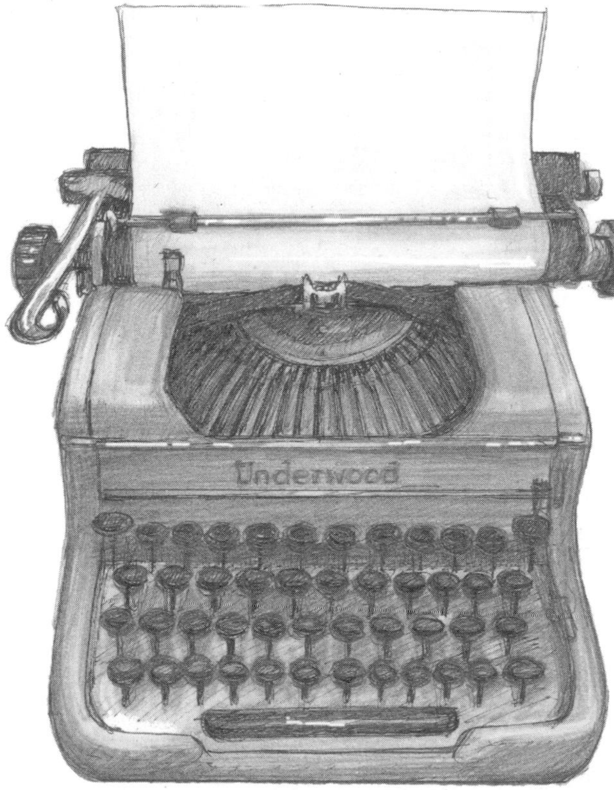
Underwood

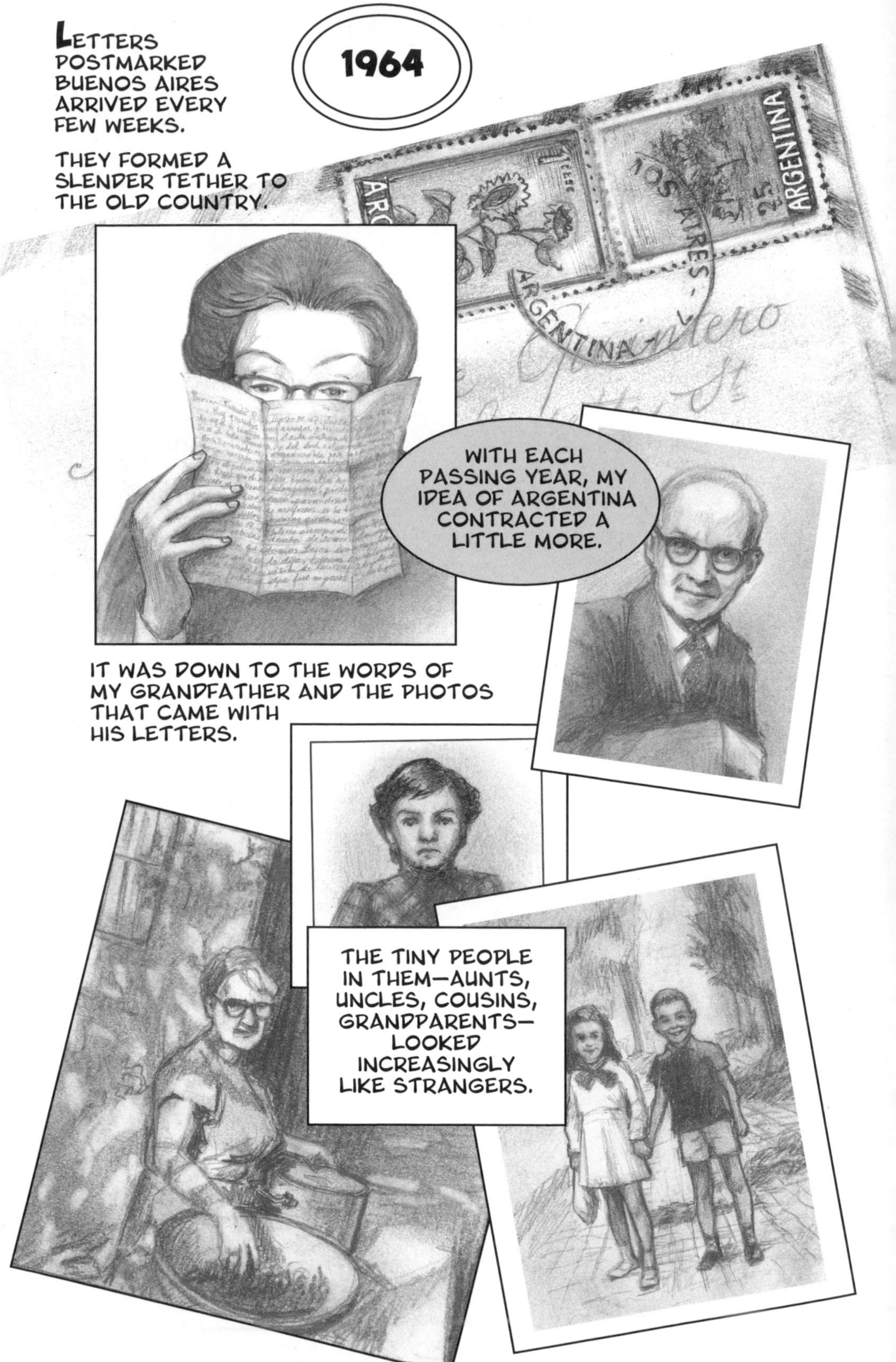
1964
LETTERS POSTMARKED BUENOS AIRES ARRIVED EVERY FEW WEEKS.
THEY FORMED A SLENDER TETHER TO THE OLD COUNTRY.
ARGENTINA
WITH EACH PASSING YEAR, MY IDEA OF ARGENTINA CONTRACTED A LITTLE MORE.
IT WAS DOWN TO THE WORDS OF MY GRANDFATHER AND THE PHOTOS THAT CAME WITH HIS LETTERS.
THE TINY PEOPLE IN THEM—AUNTS, UNCLES, COUSINS, GRANDPARENTS—LOOKED INCREASINGLY LIKE STRANGERS.

MAMA'S AND DADDY'S STORIES ABOUT THE OLD COUNTRY TOOK ON THE FEEL OF FAIRY TALES ON YELLOWED PAPER.

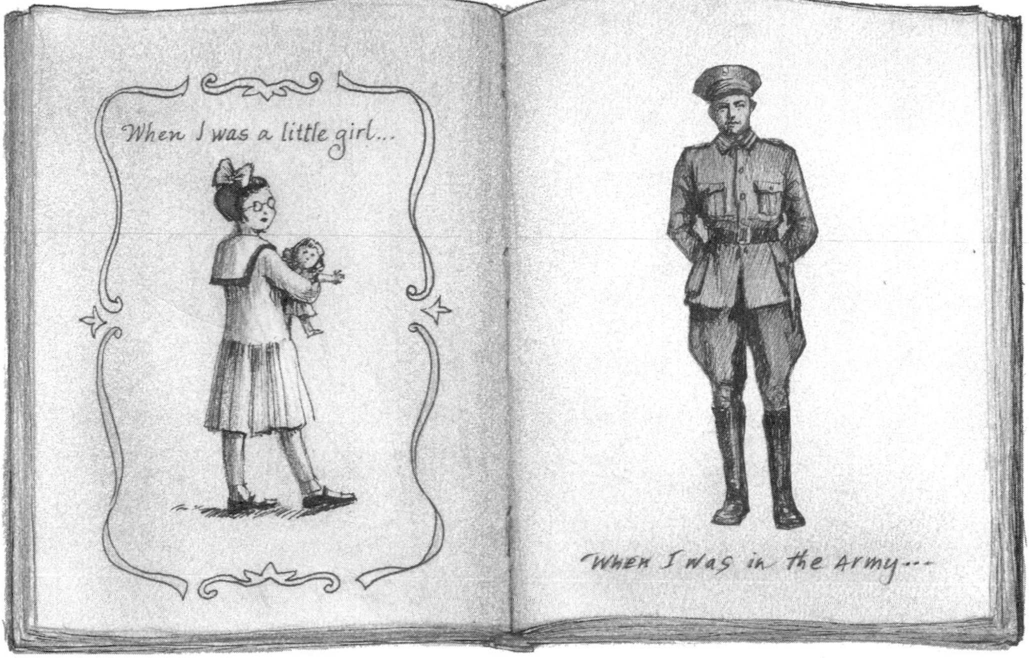
When I was a little girl...
When I was in the Army...

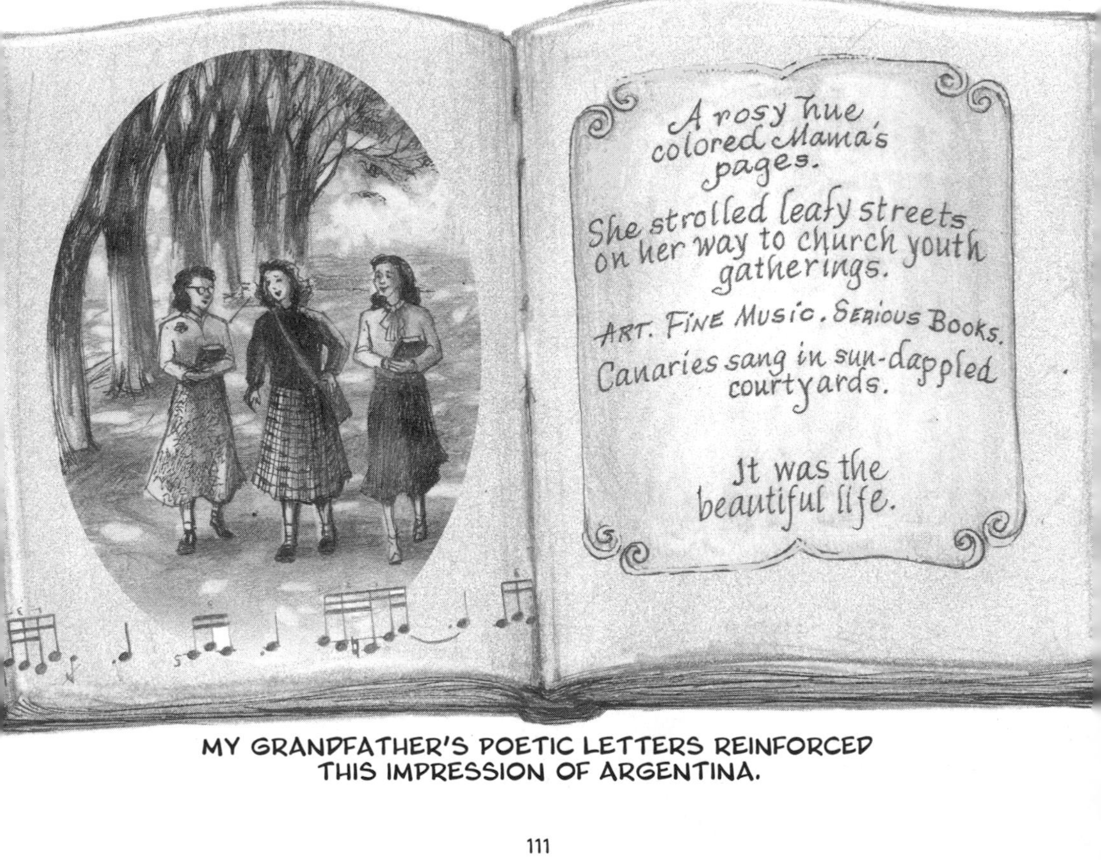
A rosy hue colored Mama's pages.
She strolled leafy streets on her way to church youth gatherings.
Art. Fine Music. Serious Books.
Canaries sang in sun-dappled courtyards.
It was the beautiful life.

MY GRANDFATHER'S POETIC LETTERS REINFORCED THIS IMPRESSION OF ARGENTINA.

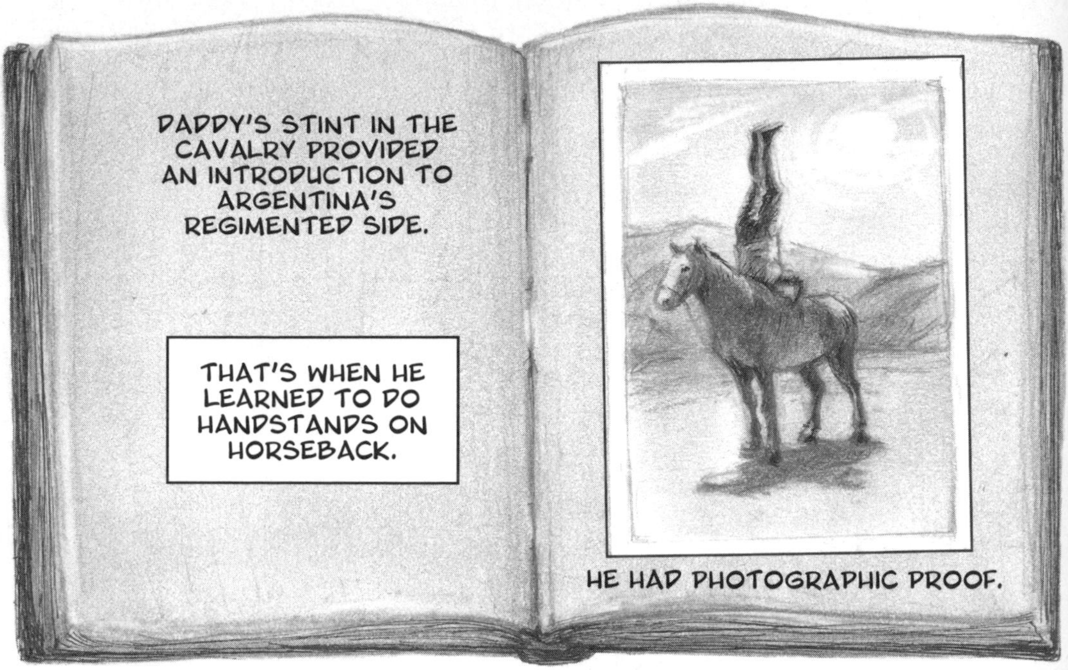
DADDY'S STINT IN THE CAVALRY PROVIDED AN INTRODUCTION TO ARGENTINA'S REGIMENTED SIDE.
THAT'S WHEN HE LEARNED TO DO HANDSTANDS ON HORSEBACK.
HE HAD PHOTOGRAPHIC PROOF.

THEN THERE WAS HIS HORRIFYING ACCOUNT OF AN OVERLOADED PACKHORSE WHOSE SPINE SNAPPED WHILE CROSSING A RAVINE.

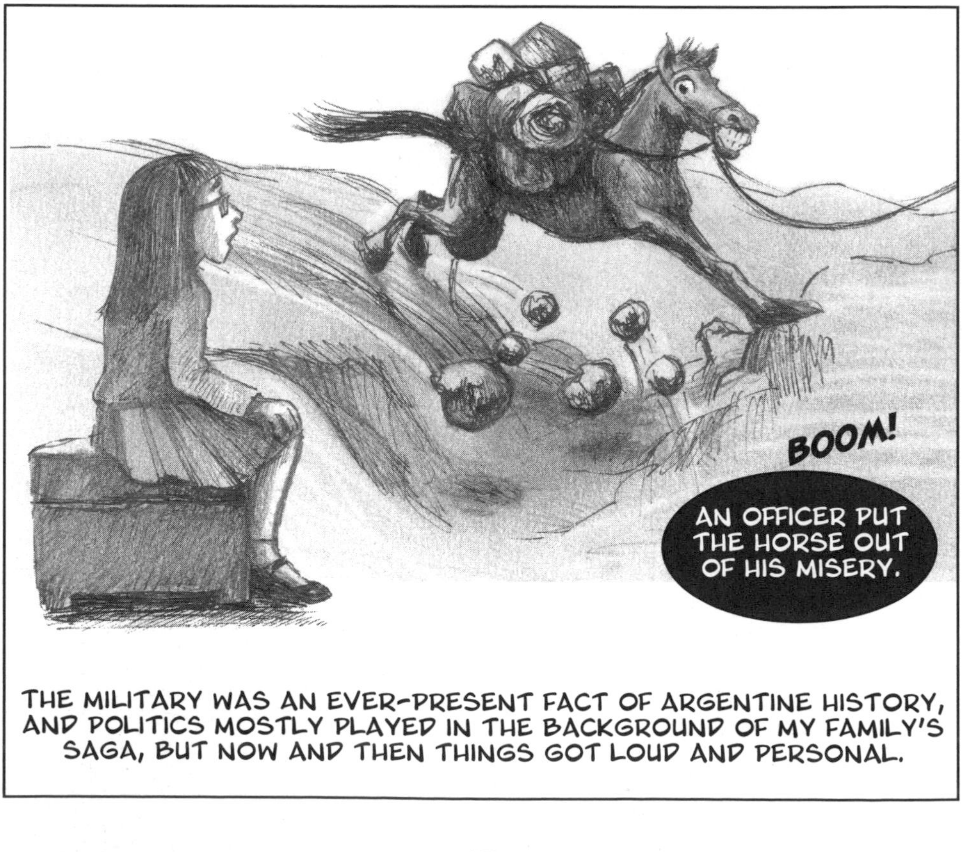
BOOM!
AN OFFICER PUT THE HORSE OUT OF HIS MISERY.
THE MILITARY WAS AN EVER-PRESENT FACT OF ARGENTINE HISTORY, AND POLITICS MOSTLY PLAYED IN THE BACKGROUND OF MY FAMILY'S SAGA, BUT NOW AND THEN THINGS GOT LOUD AND PERSONAL.

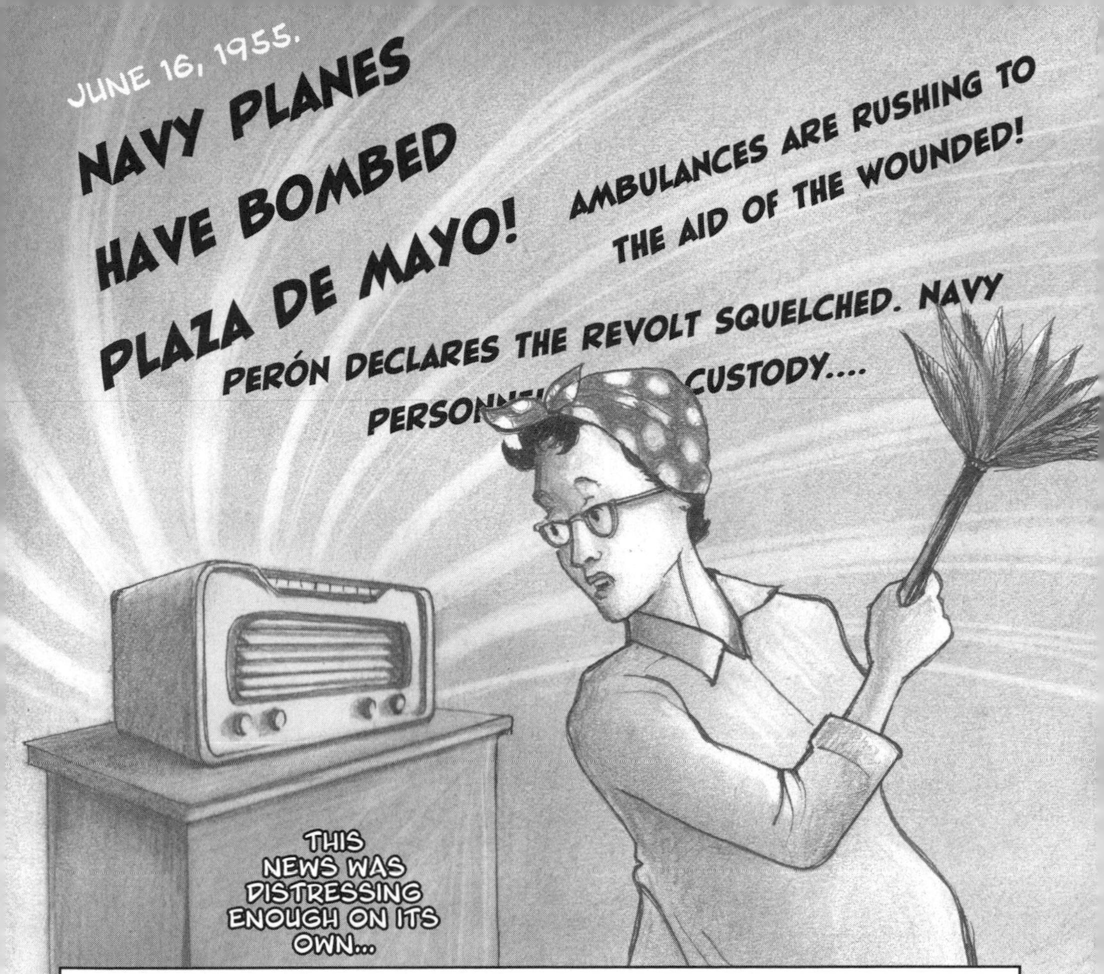
JUNE 16, 1955.
NAVY PLANES HAVE BOMBED PLAZA DE MAYO!
AMBULANCES ARE RUSHING TO THE AID OF THE WOUNDED!
PERÓN DECLARES THE REVOLT SQUELCHED. NAVY
PERSON
CUSTODY....
THIS NEWS WAS DISTRESSING ENOUGH ON ITS OWN...
...BUT BECAUSE GINNY WAS AT THAT MOMENT RECOVERING FROM MINOR SURGERY AT A HOSPITAL NOT FAR FROM THE BOMBING, IT BECAME A FAMILY EMERGENCY.

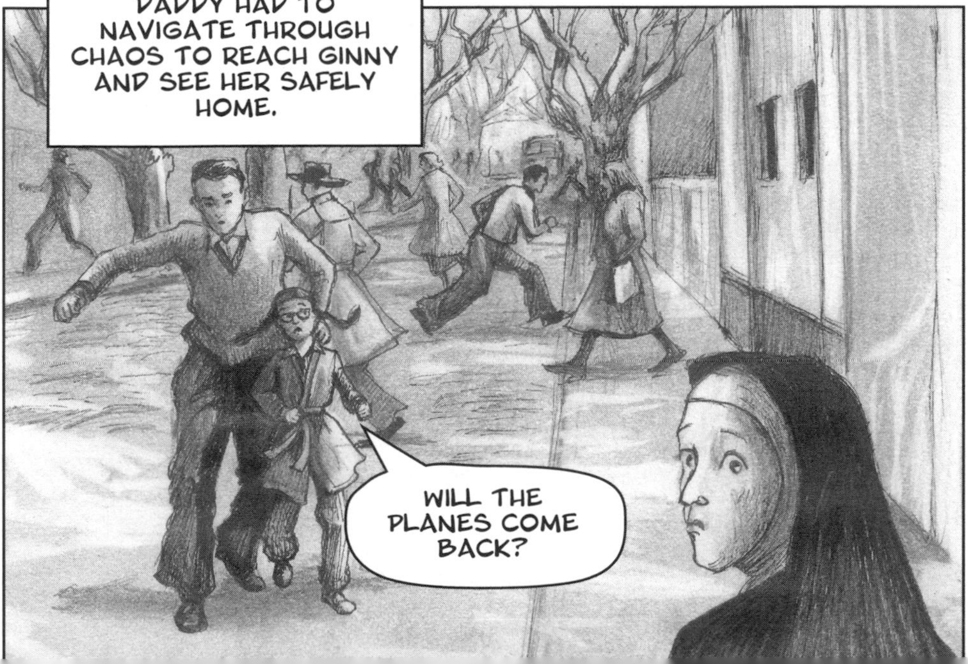
DADDY HAD TO NAVIGATE THROUGH CHAOS TO REACH GINNY AND SEE HER SAFELY HOME.
WILL THE PLANES COME BACK?

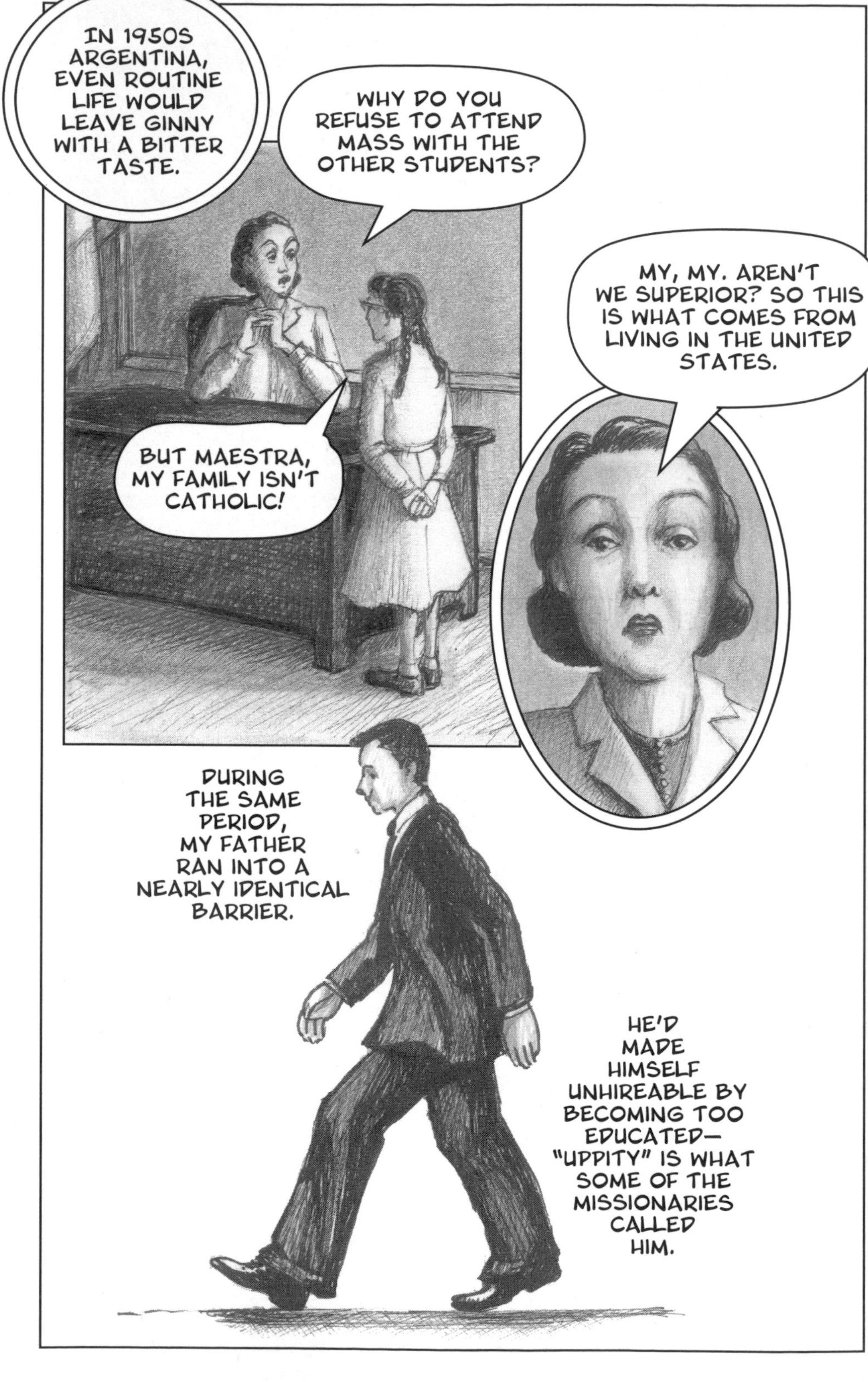
IN 1950S ARGENTINA, EVEN ROUTINE LIFE WOULD LEAVE GINNY WITH A BITTER TASTE.
WHY DO YOU REFUSE TO ATTEND MASS WITH THE OTHER STUDENTS?
BUT MAESTRA, MY FAMILY ISN'T CATHOLIC!
MY, MY. AREN'T WE SUPERIOR? SO THIS IS WHAT COMES FROM LIVING IN THE UNITED STATES.
DURING THE SAME PERIOD, MY FATHER RAN INTO A NEARLY IDENTICAL BARRIER.
HE'D MADE HIMSELF UNHIREABLE BY BECOMING TOO EDUCATED— "UPPITY" IS WHAT SOME OF THE MISSIONARIES CALLED HIM.

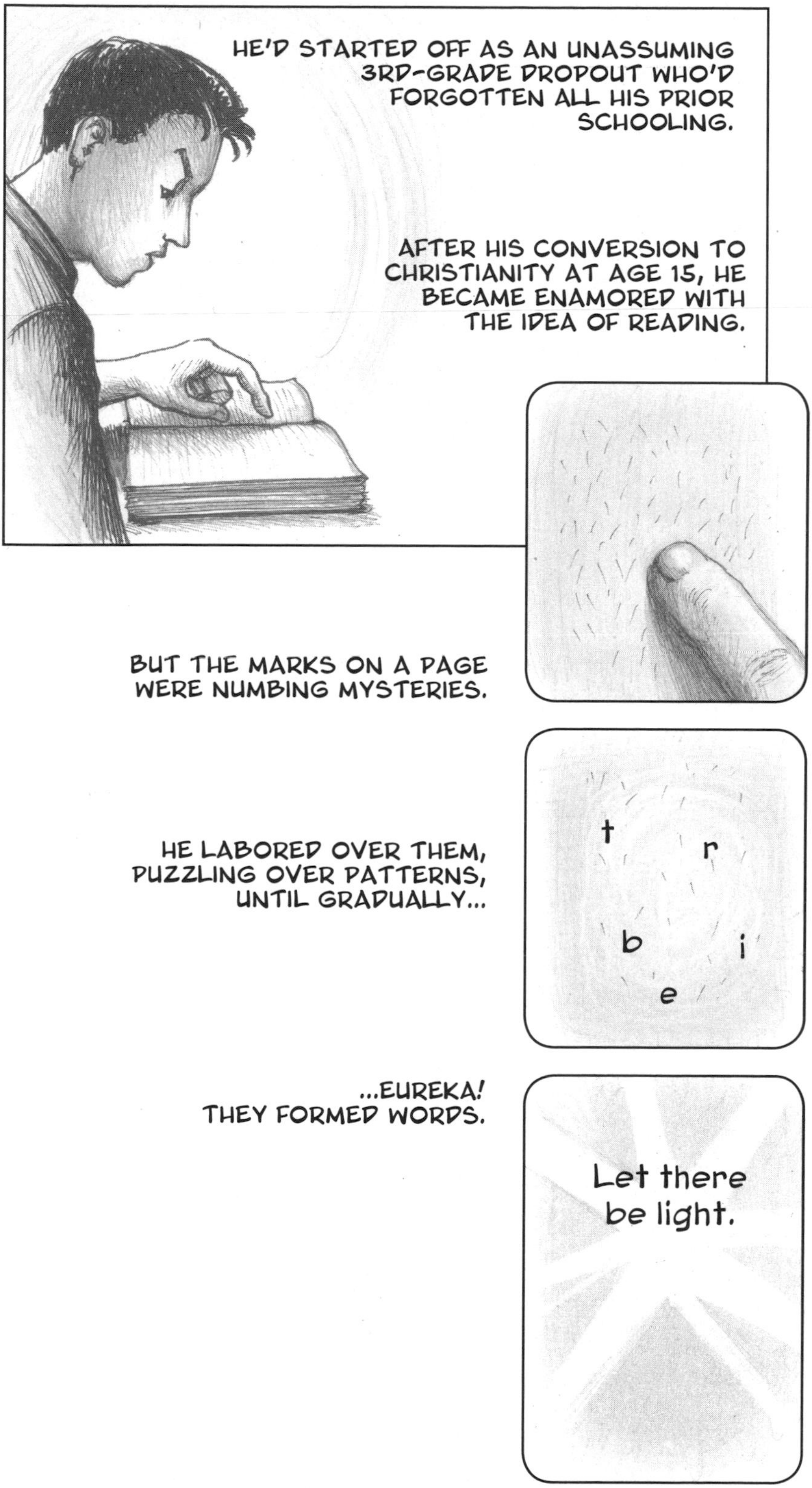

HE'D STARTED OFF AS AN UNASSUMING 3RD-GRADE DROPOUT WHO'D FORGOTTEN ALL HIS PRIOR SCHOOLING.
AFTER HIS CONVERSION TO CHRISTIANITY AT AGE 15, HE BECAME ENAMORED WITH THE IDEA OF READING.
BUT THE MARKS ON A PAGE WERE NUMBING MYSTERIES.
HE LABORED OVER THEM, PUZZLING OVER PATTERNS, UNTIL GRADUALLY...
t r b i e
...EUREKA! THEY FORMED WORDS.
Let there be light.

EVENTUALLY, HE FOUND A CHURCH THAT DIDN'T MIND A PASTOR WITH SCHOLARLY INTERESTS. THOSE WERE GOOD YEARS.

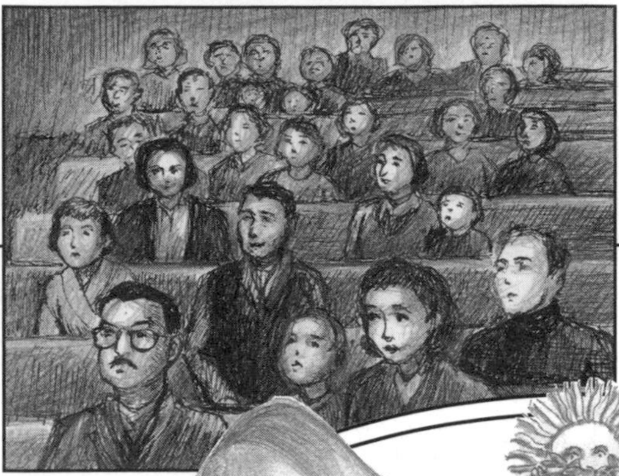

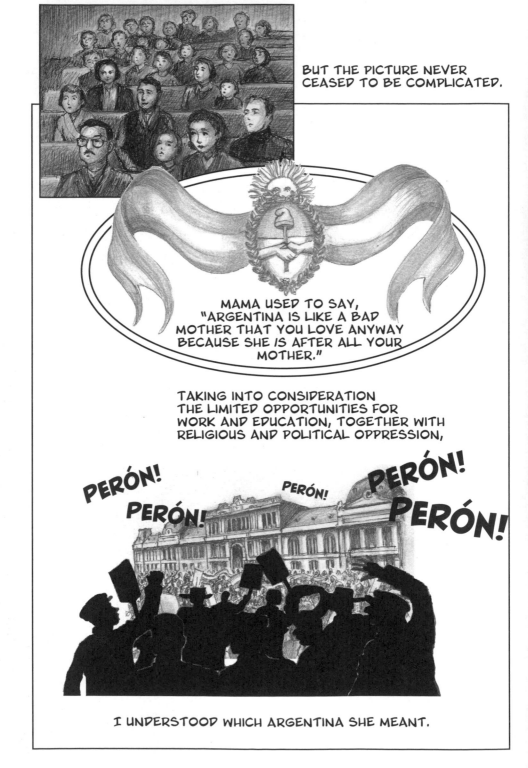

BUT THE PICTURE NEVER CEASED TO BE COMPLICATED.

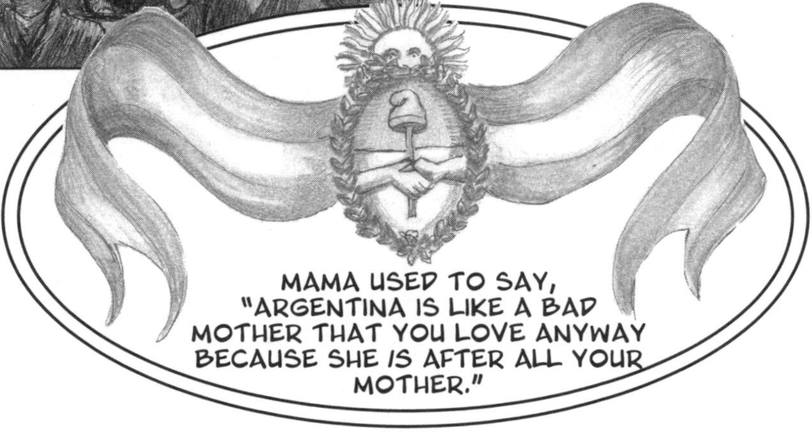
MAMA USED TO SAY, "ARGENTINA IS LIKE A BAD MOTHER THAT YOU LOVE ANYWAY BECAUSE SHE *IS* AFTER ALL YOUR MOTHER."

TAKING INTO CONSIDERATION THE LIMITED OPPORTUNITIES FOR WORK AND EDUCATION, TOGETHER WITH RELIGIOUS AND POLITICAL OPPRESSION,

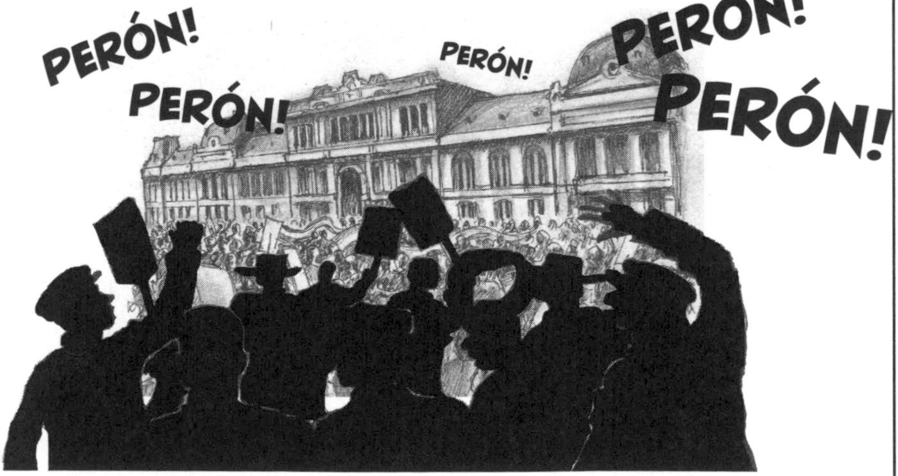
PERÓN!
PERÓN!
PERÓN!
PERÓN!
PERÓN!

I UNDERSTOOD WHICH ARGENTINA SHE MEANT.

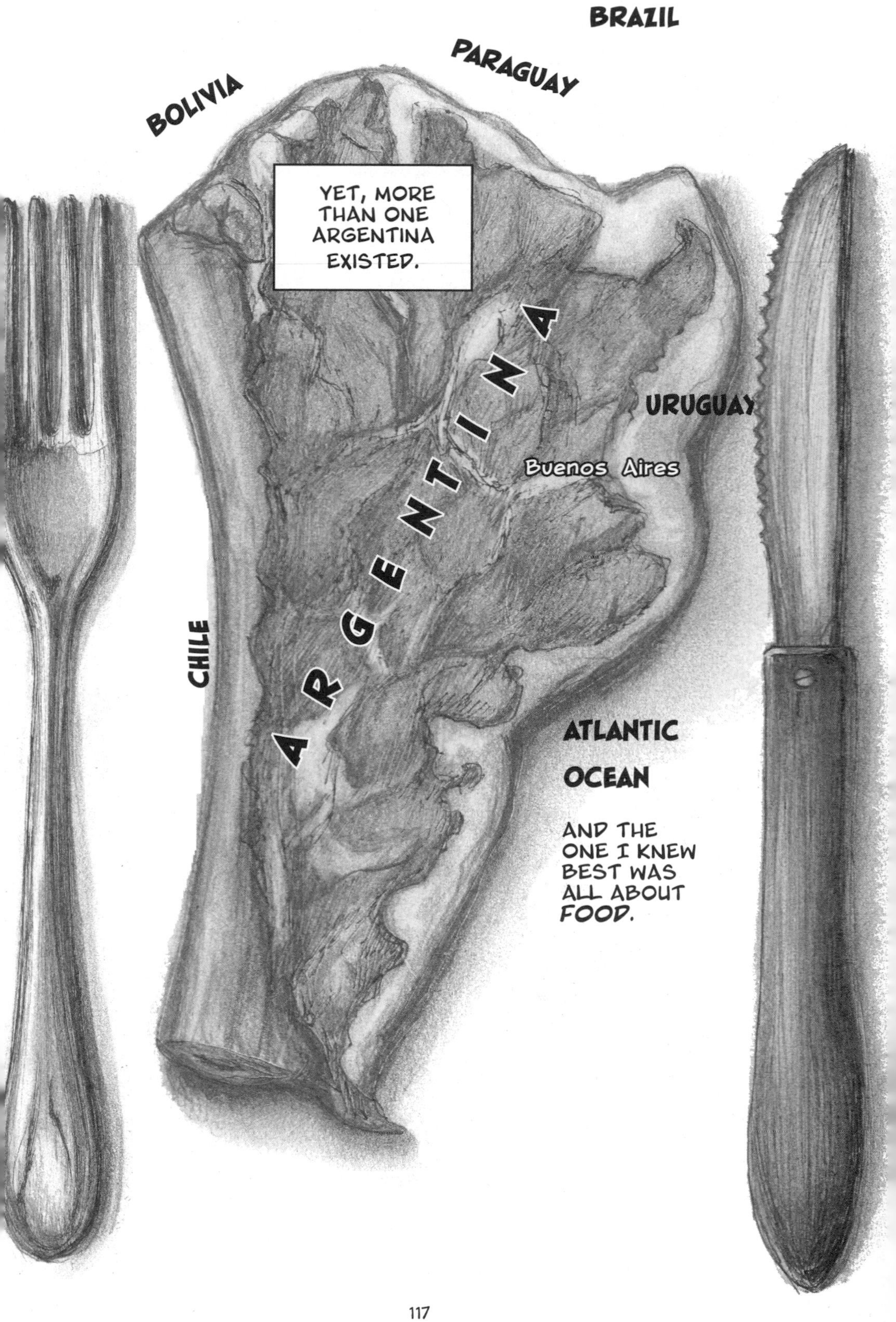
BRAZIL
PARAGUAY
BOLIVIA
YET, MORE THAN ONE ARGENTINA EXISTED.
ARGENTINA
URUGUAY
Buenos Aires
CHILE
ATLANTIC OCEAN
AND THE ONE I KNEW BEST WAS ALL ABOUT FOOD.

ARGENTINE SPECIALTIES

AS PERFECTED IN ALABAMA BY MY MOTHER.

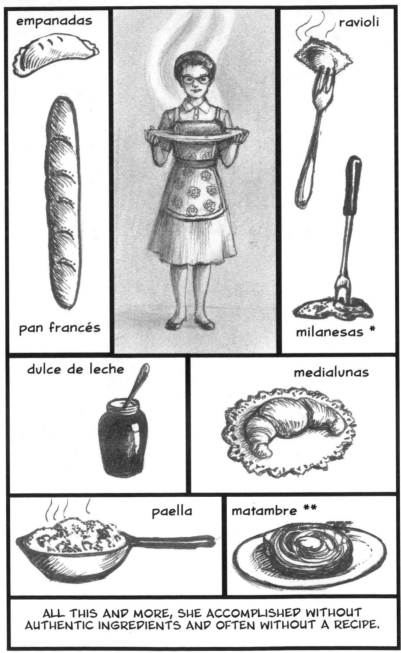

empanadas

pan francés

ravioli

milanesas *

dulce de leche

medialunas

paella

matambre **

ALL THIS AND MORE, SHE ACCOMPLISHED WITHOUT AUTHENTIC INGREDIENTS AND OFTEN WITHOUT A RECIPE.

* A BREADED & FRIED STEAK   ** A STUFFED ROLL OF BEEF

MY TASTE BUDS HAD BEEN TRAINED ON SOUTH AMERICAN FARE. BUT I HAD HANKERINGS THAT COULDN'T BE SATISFIED AT HOME.

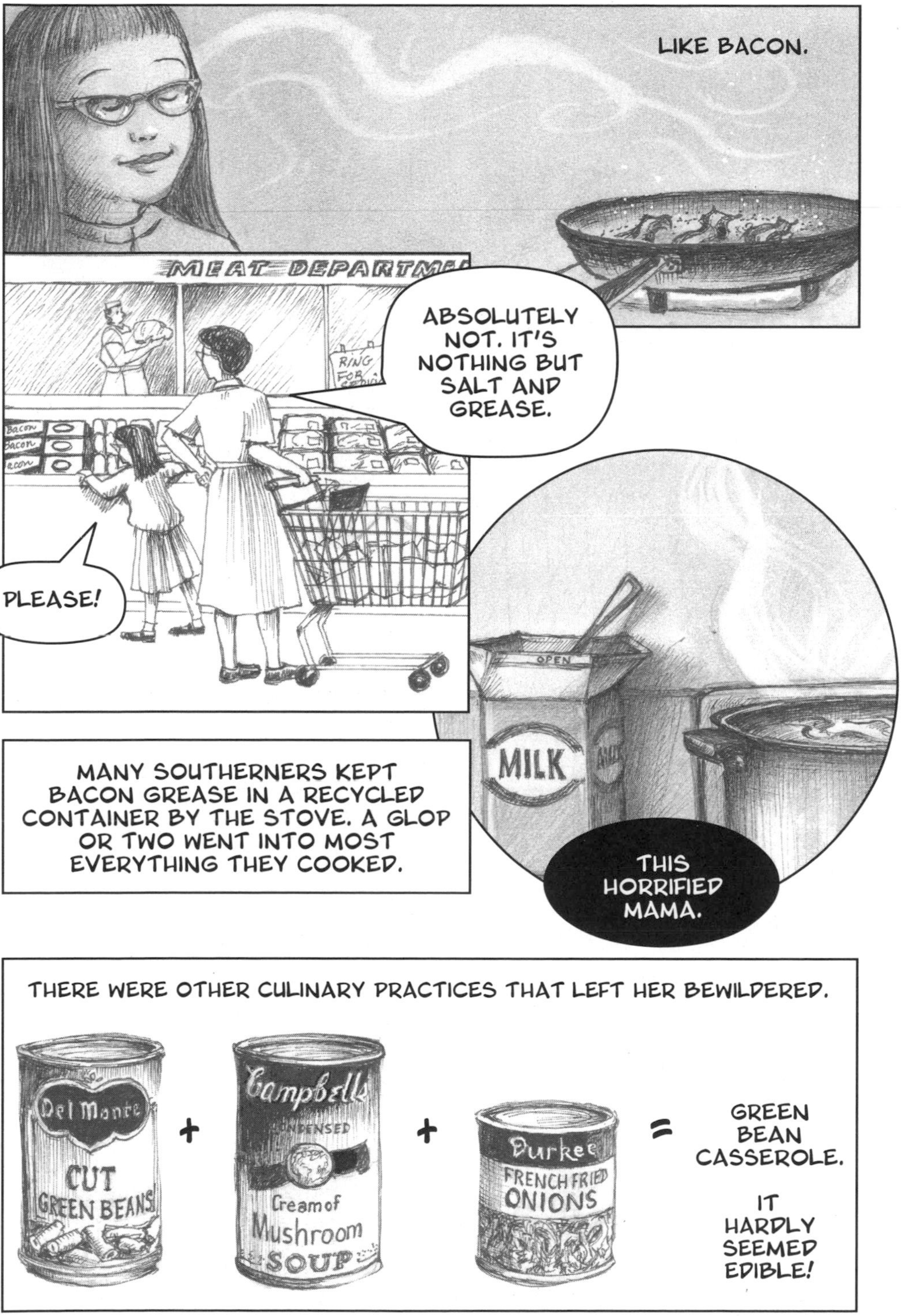

LIKE BACON.
ABSOLUTELY NOT. IT'S NOTHING BUT SALT AND GREASE.
PLEASE!
MILK
MANY SOUTHERNERS KEPT BACON GREASE IN A RECYCLED CONTAINER BY THE STOVE. A GLOP OR TWO WENT INTO MOST EVERYTHING THEY COOKED.
THIS HORRIFIED MAMA.
THERE WERE OTHER CULINARY PRACTICES THAT LEFT HER BEWILDERED.
Del Monte CUT GREEN BEANS
+
Campbell's CONDENSED Cream of Mushroom SOUP
+
Durkee FRENCH FRIED ONIONS
=
GREEN BEAN CASSEROLE.
IT HARDLY SEEMED EDIBLE!

WHEN MY 3RD-GRADE TEACHER ANNOUNCED A BREAKFAST COMPETITION, THAT'S WHEN THE CULTURAL FOOD WARS BEGAN TO ENCROACH ON MY PEACE.

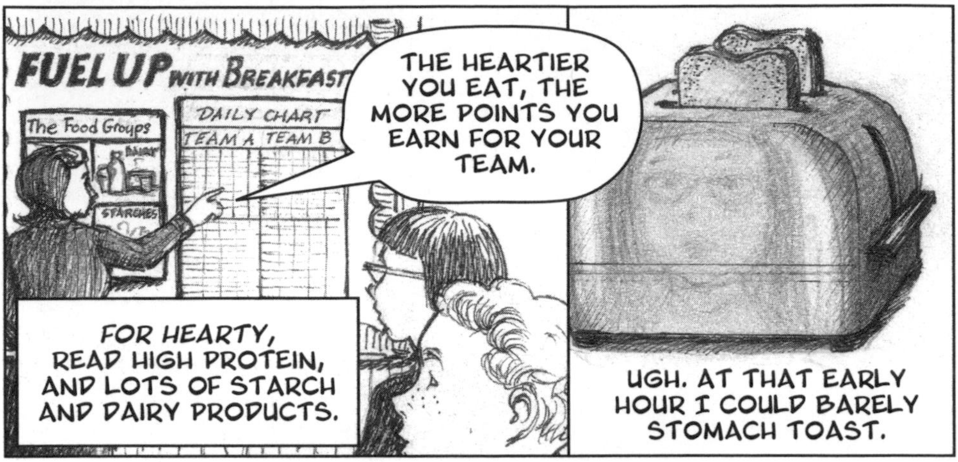
FUEL UP WITH BREAKFAST
The Food Groups
DAILY CHART
TEAM A TEAM B
STARCHES
THE HEARTIER YOU EAT, THE MORE POINTS YOU EARN FOR YOUR TEAM.
FOR HEARTY, READ HIGH PROTEIN, AND LOTS OF STARCH AND DAIRY PRODUCTS.
UGH. AT THAT EARLY HOUR I COULD BARELY STOMACH TOAST.

AND HOW WAS I, A KID, SUPPOSED TO GET MY HANDS ON HIGH-SCORING BREAKFAST FOODS?

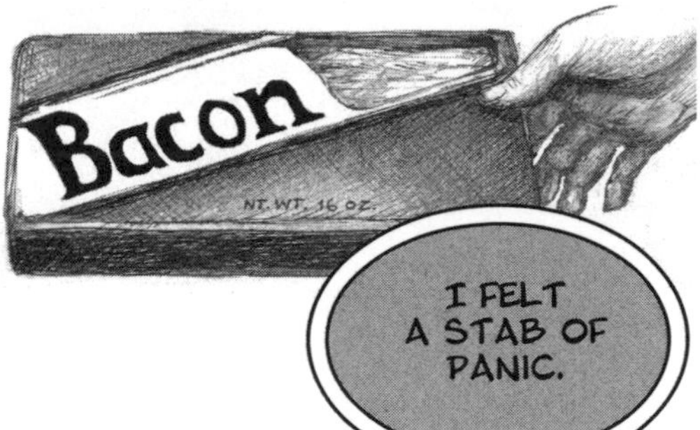
Bacon
NT. WT. 16 OZ.
I FELT A STAB OF PANIC.

I HAD YET ANOTHER PROBLEM THAT KEPT ME FROM APPEALING FOR HELP AT HOME: DADDY'S SCORN OF AMERICAN EDUCATIONAL METHODS.

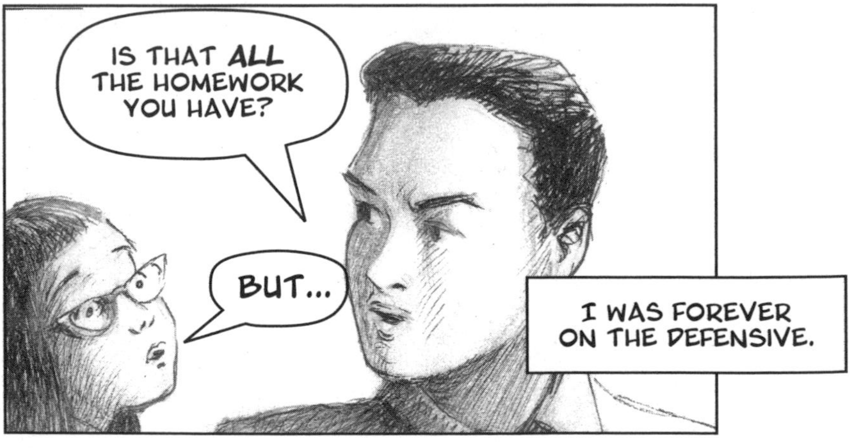
IS THAT **ALL** THE HOMEWORK YOU HAVE?
BUT...
I WAS FOREVER ON THE DEFENSIVE.

ACCORDING TO HIM, MY TEACHERS LET US PLAY TOO MUCH. THEY SOFTBALLED TOUGH SUBJECTS. THEY RELIED ON GIMMICKS RATHER THAN BOOKS.

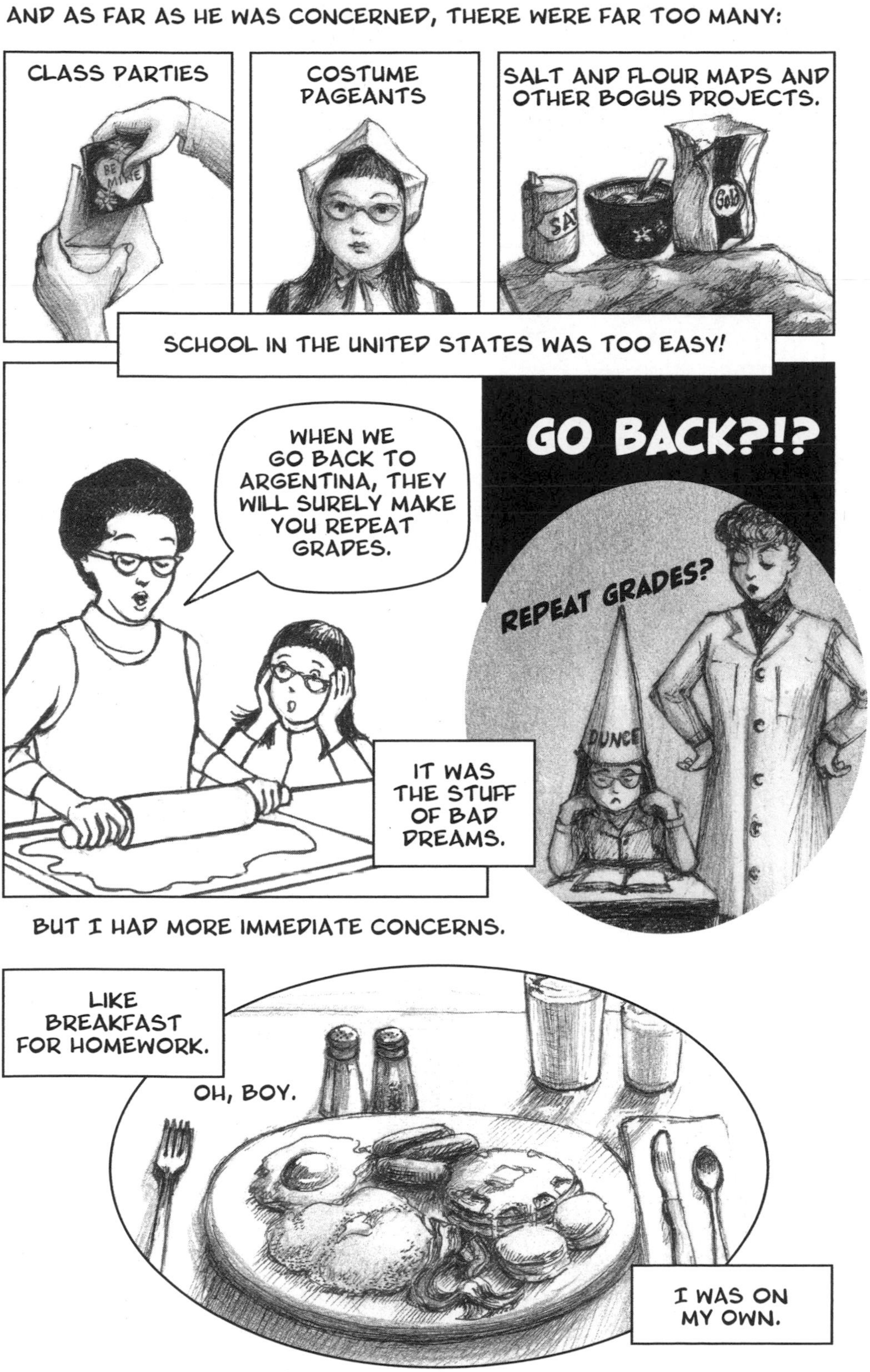
AND AS FAR AS HE WAS CONCERNED, THERE WERE FAR TOO MANY:
CLASS PARTIES
BE MINE
COSTUME PAGEANTS
SALT AND FLOUR MAPS AND OTHER BOGUS PROJECTS.
SCHOOL IN THE UNITED STATES WAS TOO EASY!
WHEN WE GO BACK TO ARGENTINA, THEY WILL SURELY MAKE YOU REPEAT GRADES.
IT WAS THE STUFF OF BAD DREAMS.
GO BACK?!?
REPEAT GRADES?
DUNCE
BUT I HAD MORE IMMEDIATE CONCERNS.
LIKE BREAKFAST FOR HOMEWORK.
OH, BOY.
I WAS ON MY OWN.

MORE AND MORE, I FOUND MYSELF ON MY OWN, SHUTTLING BACK AND FORTH BETWEEN MY TWO WORLDS.

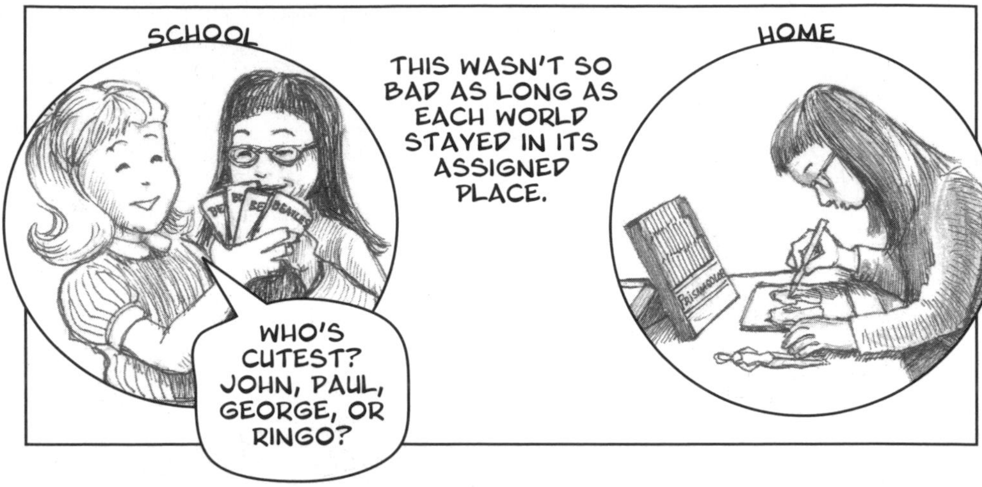
SCHOOL
HOME
THIS WASN'T SO BAD AS LONG AS EACH WORLD STAYED IN ITS ASSIGNED PLACE.
WHO'S CUTEST? JOHN, PAUL, GEORGE, OR RINGO?

BUT SOMETIMES, DESPITE MY BEST EFFORTS, THESE TWO WORLDS COLLIDED.

SUCH AS ANY TIME A SCHOOLMATE CAUGHT A GLIMPSE OF MY HOME LIFE.

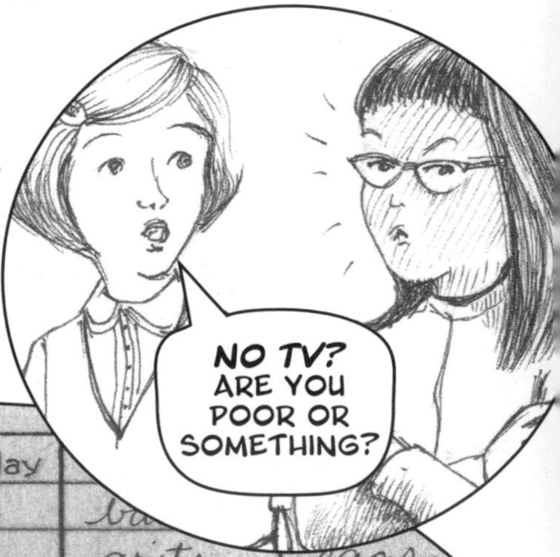
NO TV? ARE YOU POOR OR SOMETHING?

OR WHEN MY TEACHERS' EXPECTATIONS CLASHED WITH THOSE OF MY PARENTS.

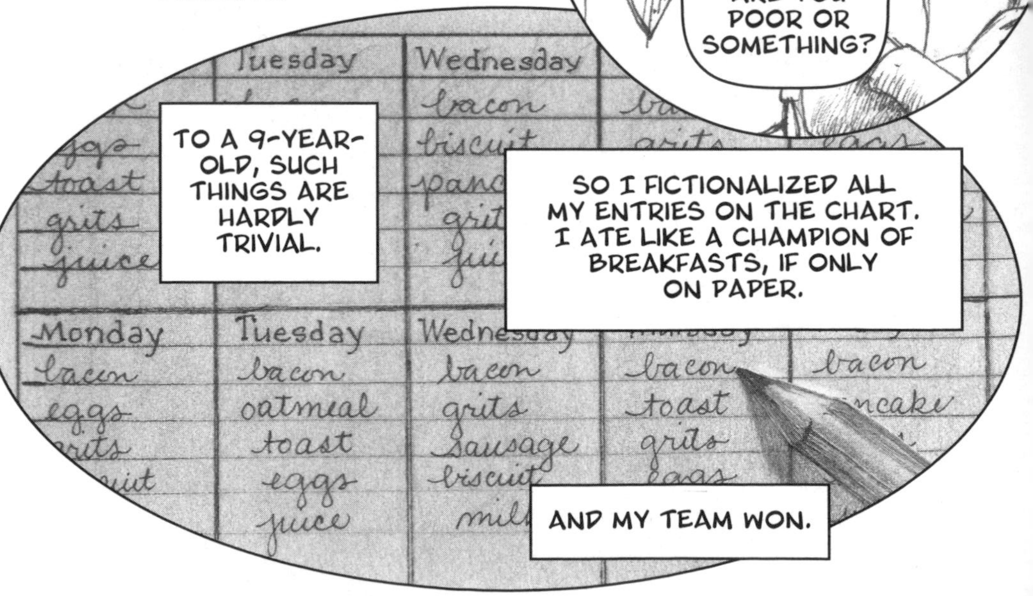
TO A 9-YEAR-OLD, SUCH THINGS ARE HARDLY TRIVIAL.
SO I FICTIONALIZED ALL MY ENTRIES ON THE CHART. I ATE LIKE A CHAMPION OF BREAKFASTS, IF ONLY ON PAPER.
AND MY TEAM WON.

I SUMMONED WILINESS, AND IT CAME TO MY RESCUE. IT KEPT MY PARENTS IGNORANT OF THE BREAKAST LESSON AND MY TEACHER IGNORANT OF THEIR DISREGARD.

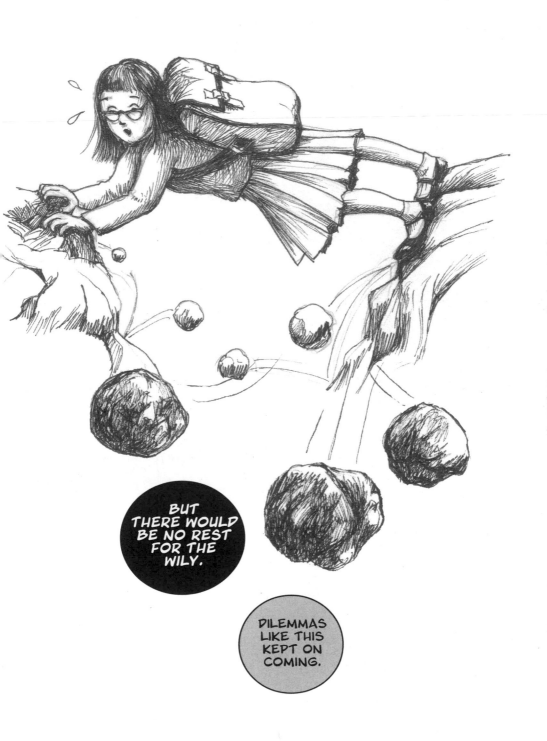

BUT THERE WOULD BE NO REST FOR THE WILY.

DILEMMAS LIKE THIS KEPT ON COMING.

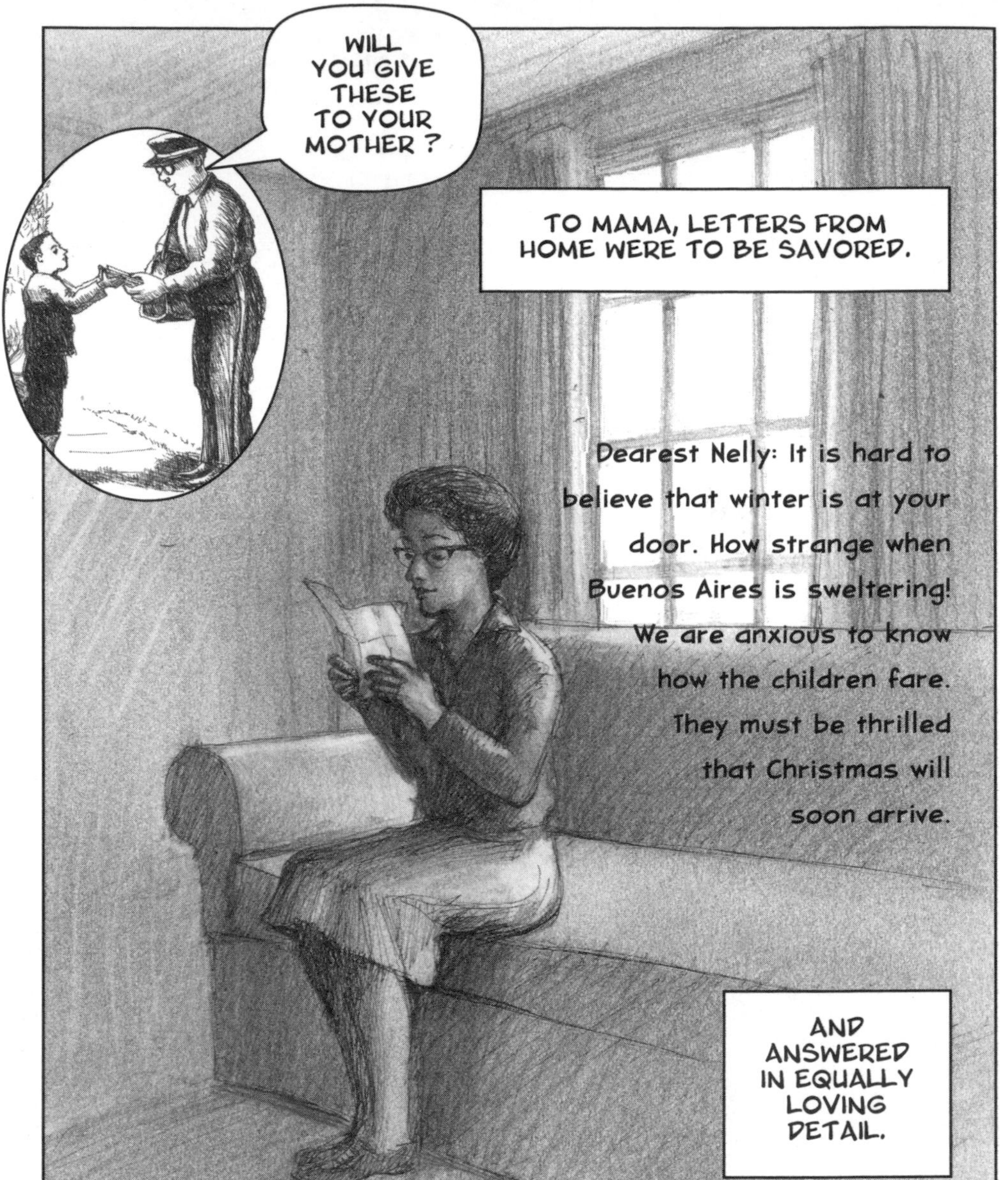
WILL YOU GIVE THESE TO YOUR MOTHER ?
TO MAMA, LETTERS FROM HOME WERE TO BE SAVORED.
Dearest Nelly: It is hard to believe that winter is at your door. How strange when Buenos Aires is sweltering! We are anxious to know how the children fare. They must be thrilled that Christmas will soon arrive.
AND ANSWERED IN EQUALLY LOVING DETAIL.

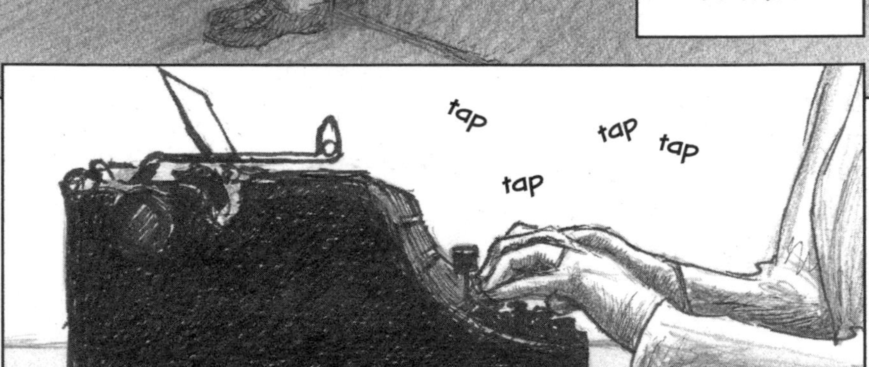
tap
tap
tap
tap

We are all busy in our own way. Nestor's day
consists of teaching or preparing to teach. He is
truly in his element in the classroom. Ginny and
Bill are settling in as newlyweds. Lissy is
doing very well in school. She started the
7th grade and is collecting butterflies for
a science project. I'm glad she's conscientious.
There's little time to supervise anyone's homework, as I have several portraits to complete
by Christmas. Johnny is the exception, of
course, since he's learning to read and needs
practice. Unless the weather's bad, he and Lila
walk to school. I don't know what to do about
Lila. She is our little neurotic! Her recurring
nightmare is that she arrives at school
without her books, although it has never
happened—that I know of; she's rather secretive.

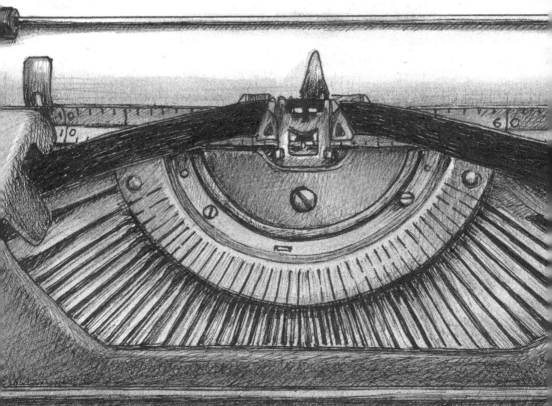

AT THAT MOMENT, I HAD FEW WORRIES. I WAS PUTTING THE FINISHING TOUCHES ON MY SET DESIGN FOR THE NATIVITY PLAY.

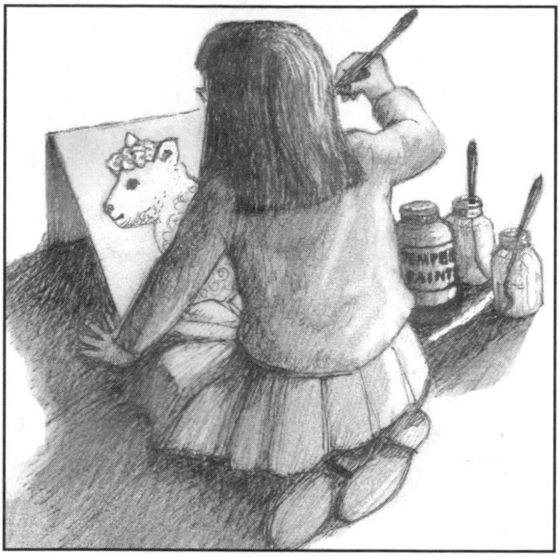

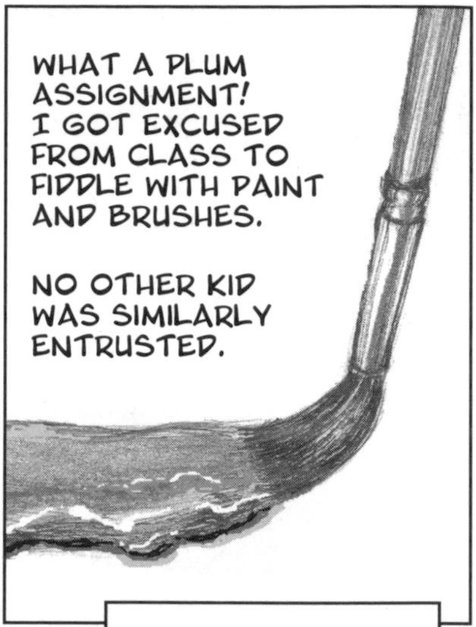
WHAT A PLUM ASSIGNMENT! I GOT EXCUSED FROM CLASS TO FIDDLE WITH PAINT AND BRUSHES.
NO OTHER KID WAS SIMILARLY ENTRUSTED.

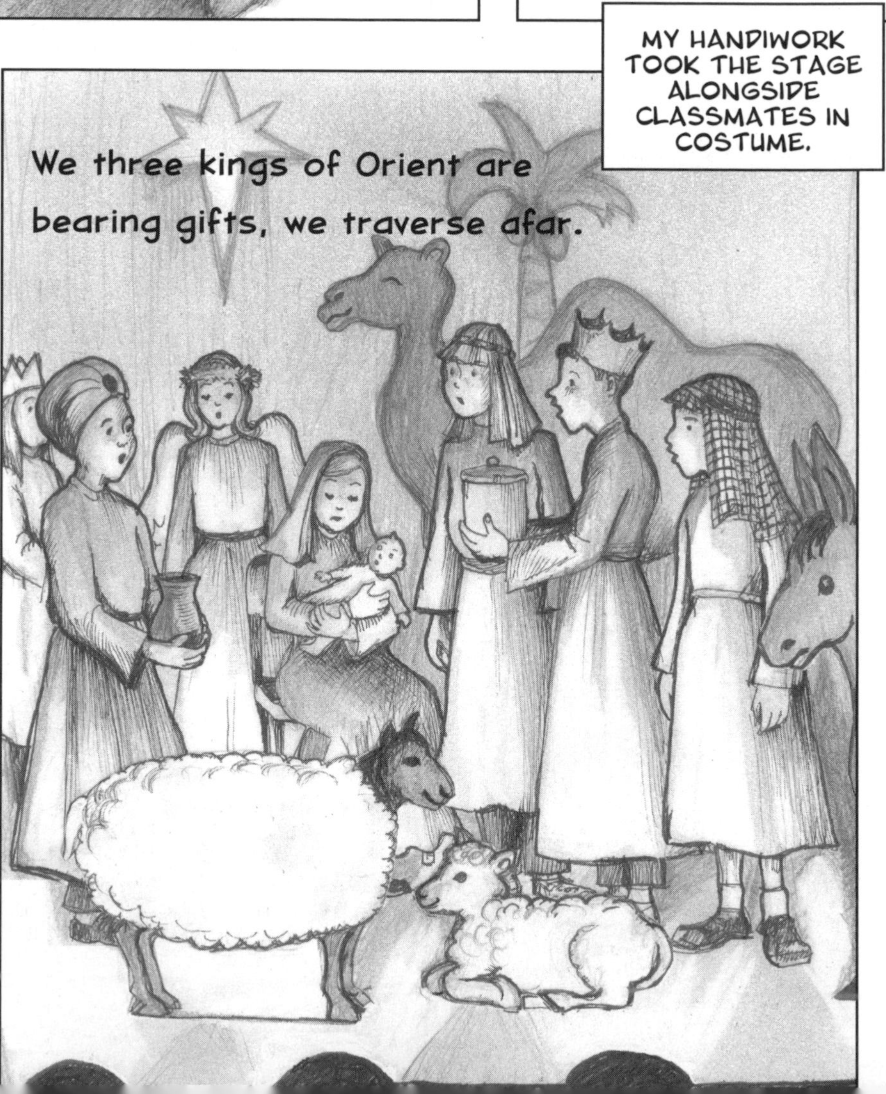
MY HANDIWORK TOOK THE STAGE ALONGSIDE CLASSMATES IN COSTUME.
We three kings of Orient are bearing gifts, we traverse afar.

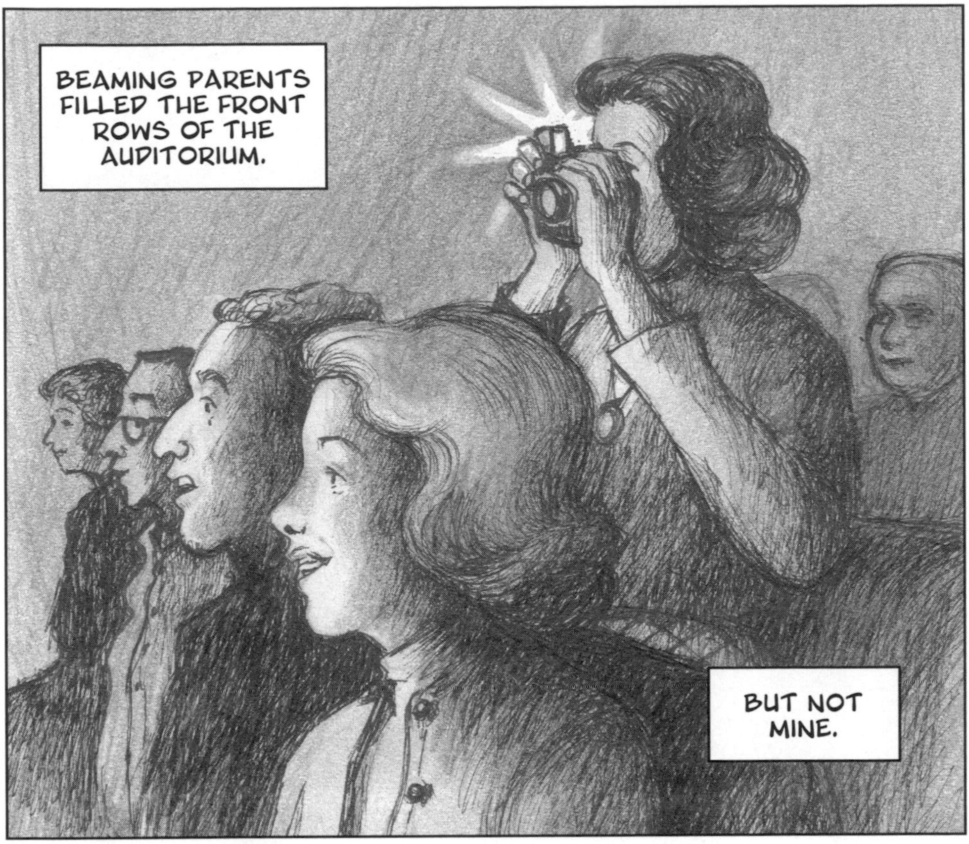
BEAMING PARENTS FILLED THE FRONT ROWS OF THE AUDITORIUM.
BUT NOT MINE.

MY MOM AND DAD WERE GOING ABOUT THEIR NORMAL ACTIVITIES, OBLIVIOUS OF THE PLAY AND MY ROLE IN ITS STAGING.

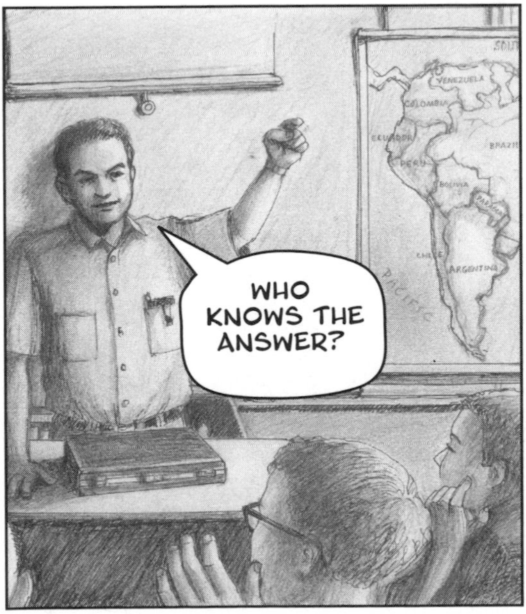
WHO KNOWS THE ANSWER?

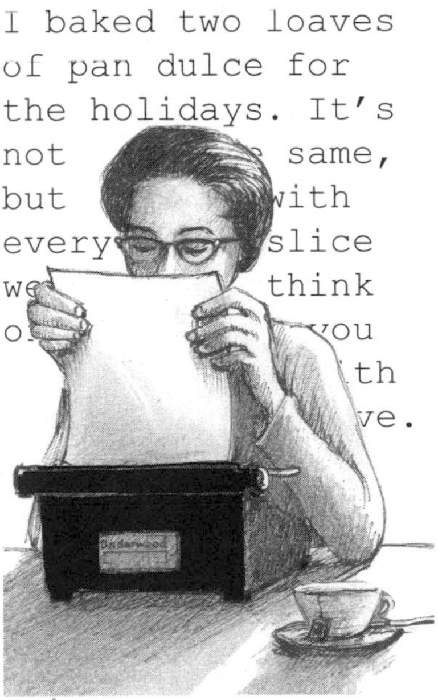
I baked two loaves
of pan dulce for
the holidays. It's
not
same,
but
with
every
slice
think
you
th
ve.

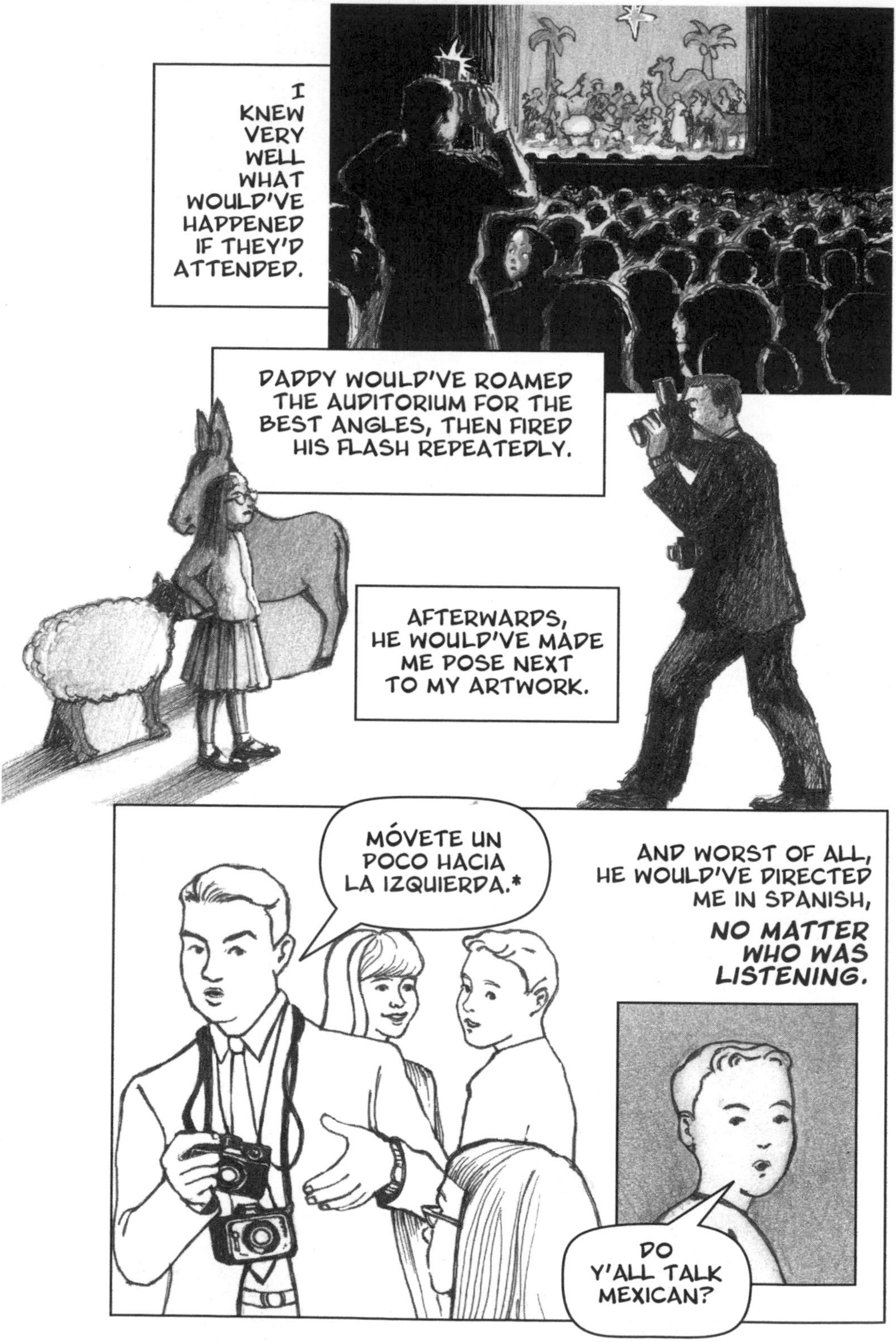
I KNEW VERY WELL WHAT WOULD'VE HAPPENED IF THEY'D ATTENDED.
DADDY WOULD'VE ROAMED THE AUDITORIUM FOR THE BEST ANGLES, THEN FIRED HIS FLASH REPEATEDLY.
AFTERWARDS, HE WOULD'VE MADE ME POSE NEXT TO MY ARTWORK.
MÓVETE UN POCO HACIA LA IZQUIERDA.*
AND WORST OF ALL, HE WOULD'VE DIRECTED ME IN SPANISH,
NO MATTER WHO WAS LISTENING.
DO Y'ALL TALK MEXICAN?

* MOVE A LITTLE TO THE LEFT.

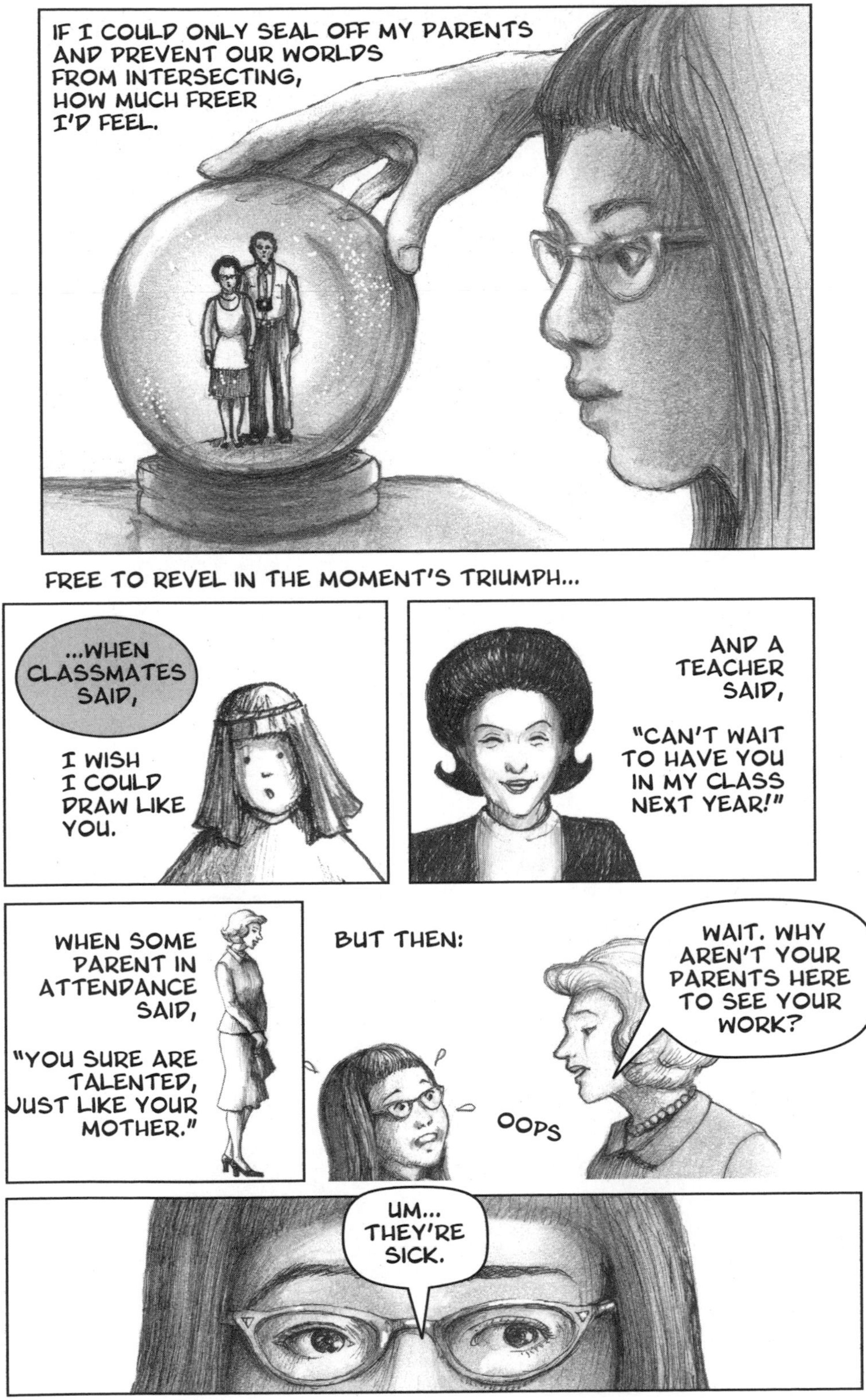
IF I COULD ONLY SEAL OFF MY PARENTS AND PREVENT OUR WORLDS FROM INTERSECTING, HOW MUCH FREER I'D FEEL.
FREE TO REVEL IN THE MOMENT'S TRIUMPH...
...WHEN CLASSMATES SAID,
I WISH I COULD DRAW LIKE YOU.
AND A TEACHER SAID,
"CAN'T WAIT TO HAVE YOU IN MY CLASS NEXT YEAR!"
WHEN SOME PARENT IN ATTENDANCE SAID,
"YOU SURE ARE TALENTED, JUST LIKE YOUR MOTHER."
BUT THEN:
WAIT. WHY AREN'T YOUR PARENTS HERE TO SEE YOUR WORK?
OOPS
UM... THEY'RE SICK.

I THOUGHT I HAD THE SITUATION UNDER CONTROL, BUT A FEW DAYS LATER:

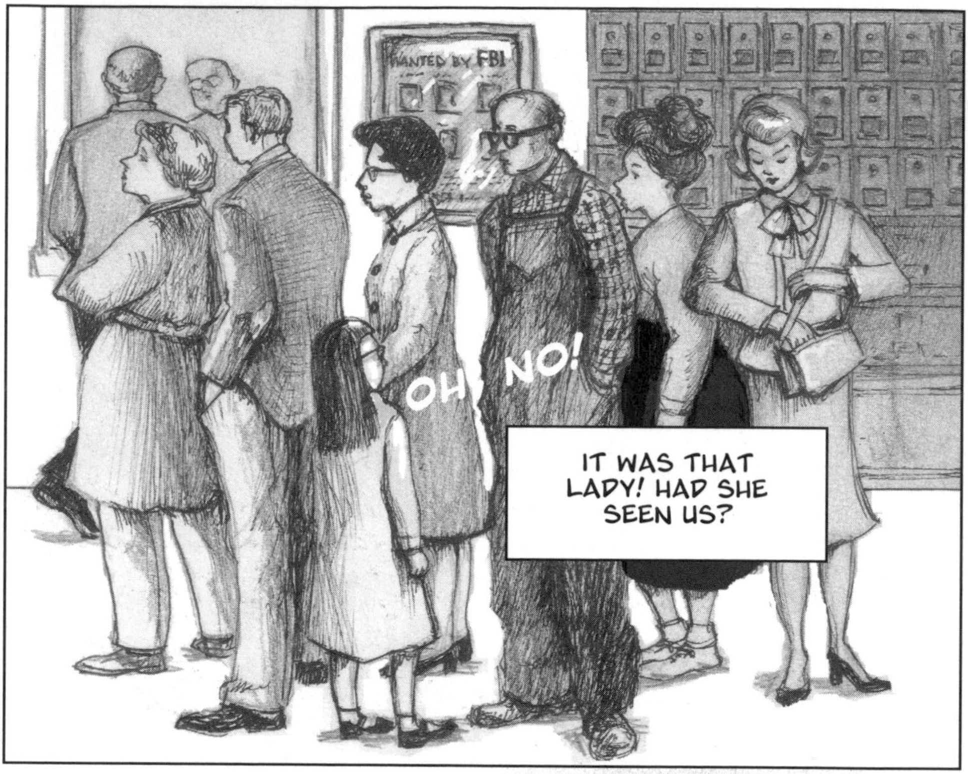
WANTED BY FBI
OH, NO!
IT WAS THAT LADY! HAD SHE SEEN US?

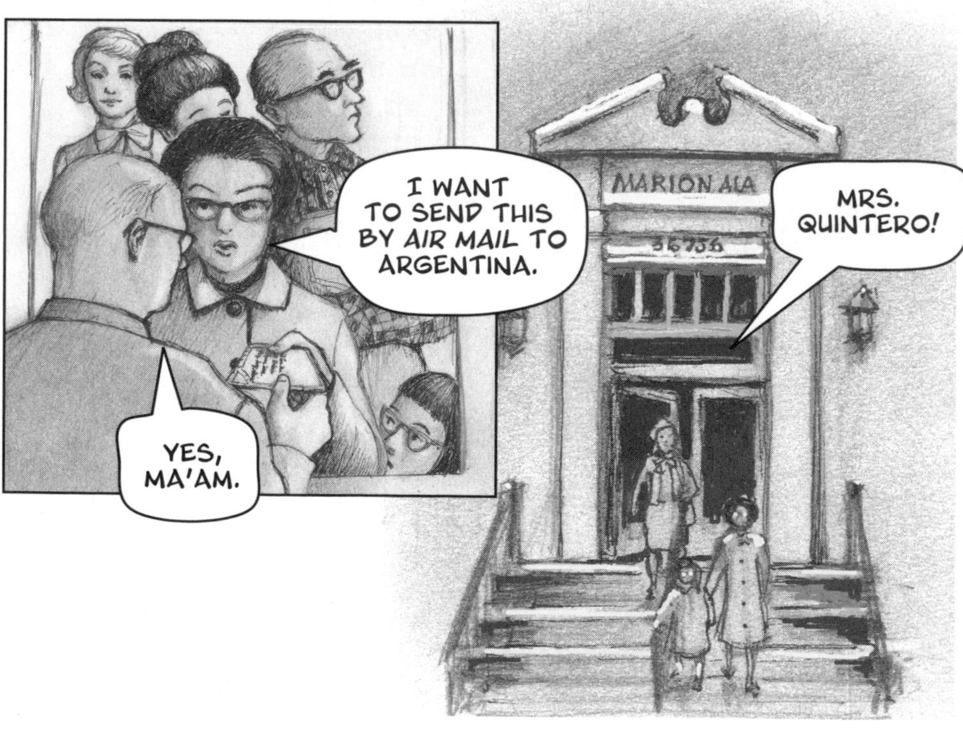
I WANT TO SEND THIS BY *AIR MAIL* TO ARGENTINA.
YES, MA'AM.
MARION ALA
MRS. QUINTERO!

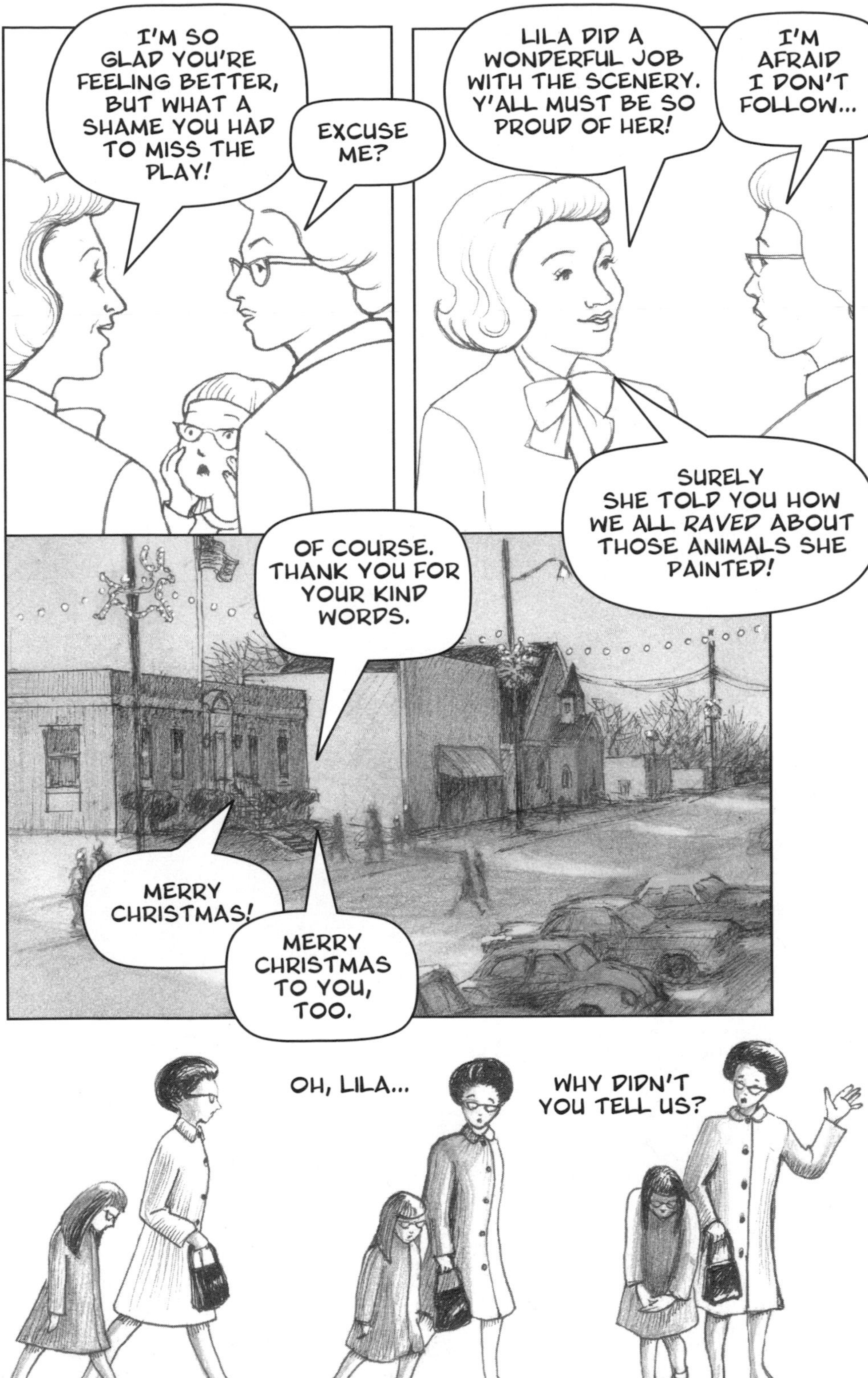
I'M SO GLAD YOU'RE FEELING BETTER, BUT WHAT A SHAME YOU HAD TO MISS THE PLAY!
EXCUSE ME?
LILA DID A WONDERFUL JOB WITH THE SCENERY. Y'ALL MUST BE SO PROUD OF HER!
I'M AFRAID I DON'T FOLLOW...
SURELY SHE TOLD YOU HOW WE ALL *RAVED* ABOUT THOSE ANIMALS SHE PAINTED!
OF COURSE. THANK YOU FOR YOUR KIND WORDS.
MERRY CHRISTMAS!
MERRY CHRISTMAS TO YOU, TOO.
OH, LILA...
WHY DIDN'T YOU TELL US?

chapter 8
GOOD NEWS, BAD NEWS

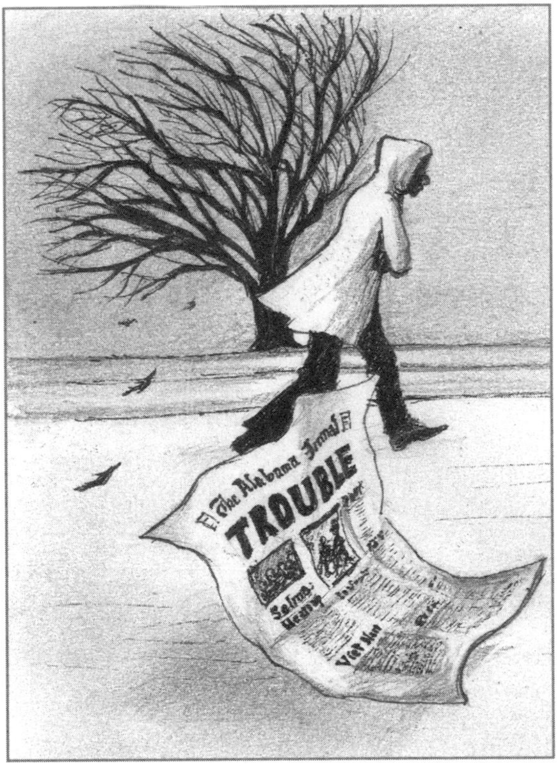
TROUBLE

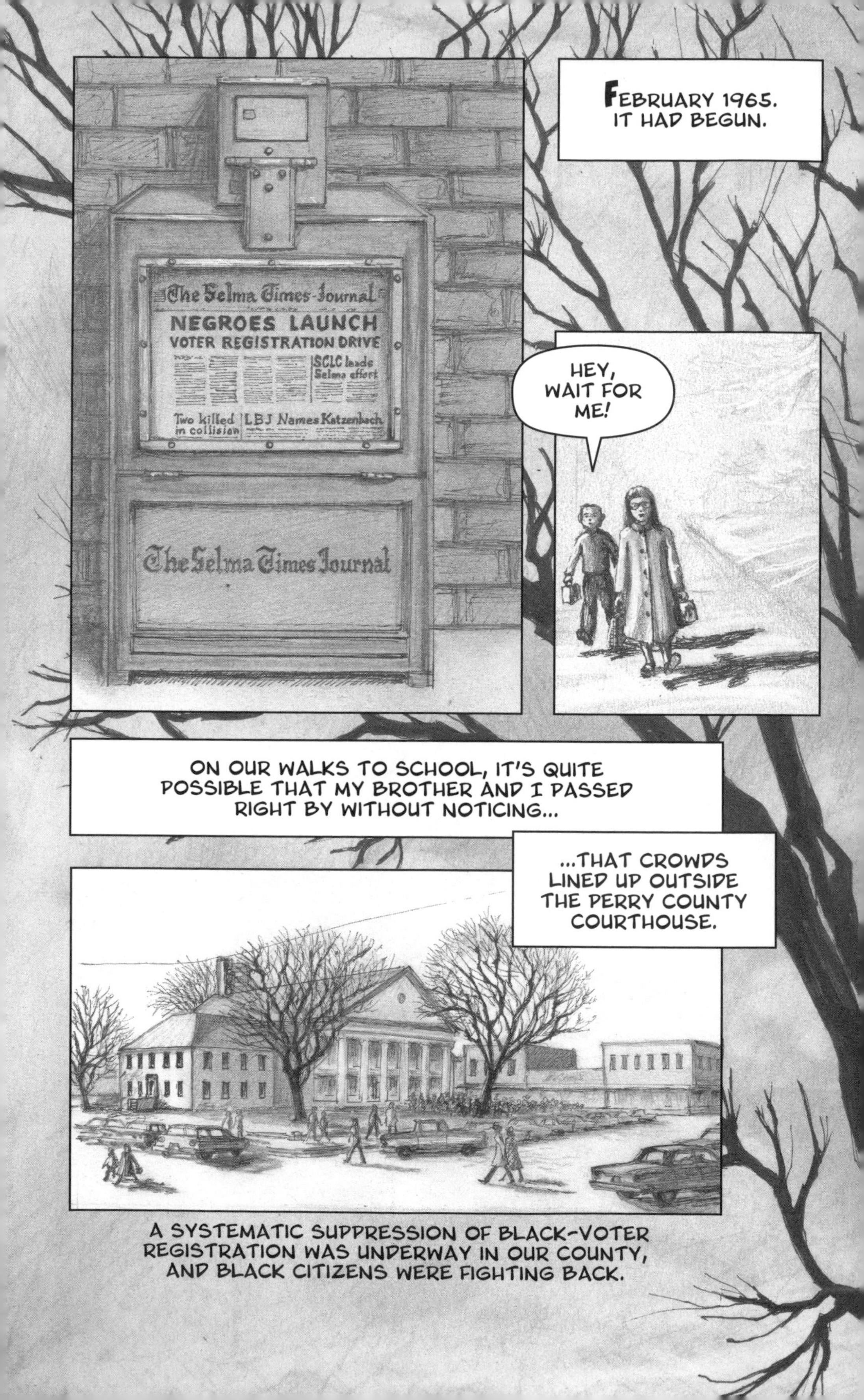

The Selma Times-Journal
NEGROES LAUNCH VOTER REGISTRATION DRIVE
SCLC leads Selma effort
Two killed in collision
LBJ Names Katzenbach
The Selma Times Journal
FEBRUARY 1965. IT HAD BEGUN.
HEY, WAIT FOR ME!
ON OUR WALKS TO SCHOOL, IT'S QUITE POSSIBLE THAT MY BROTHER AND I PASSED RIGHT BY WITHOUT NOTICING...
...THAT CROWDS LINED UP OUTSIDE THE PERRY COUNTY COURTHOUSE.
A SYSTEMATIC SUPPRESSION OF BLACK-VOTER REGISTRATION WAS UNDERWAY IN OUR COUNTY, AND BLACK CITIZENS WERE FIGHTING BACK.

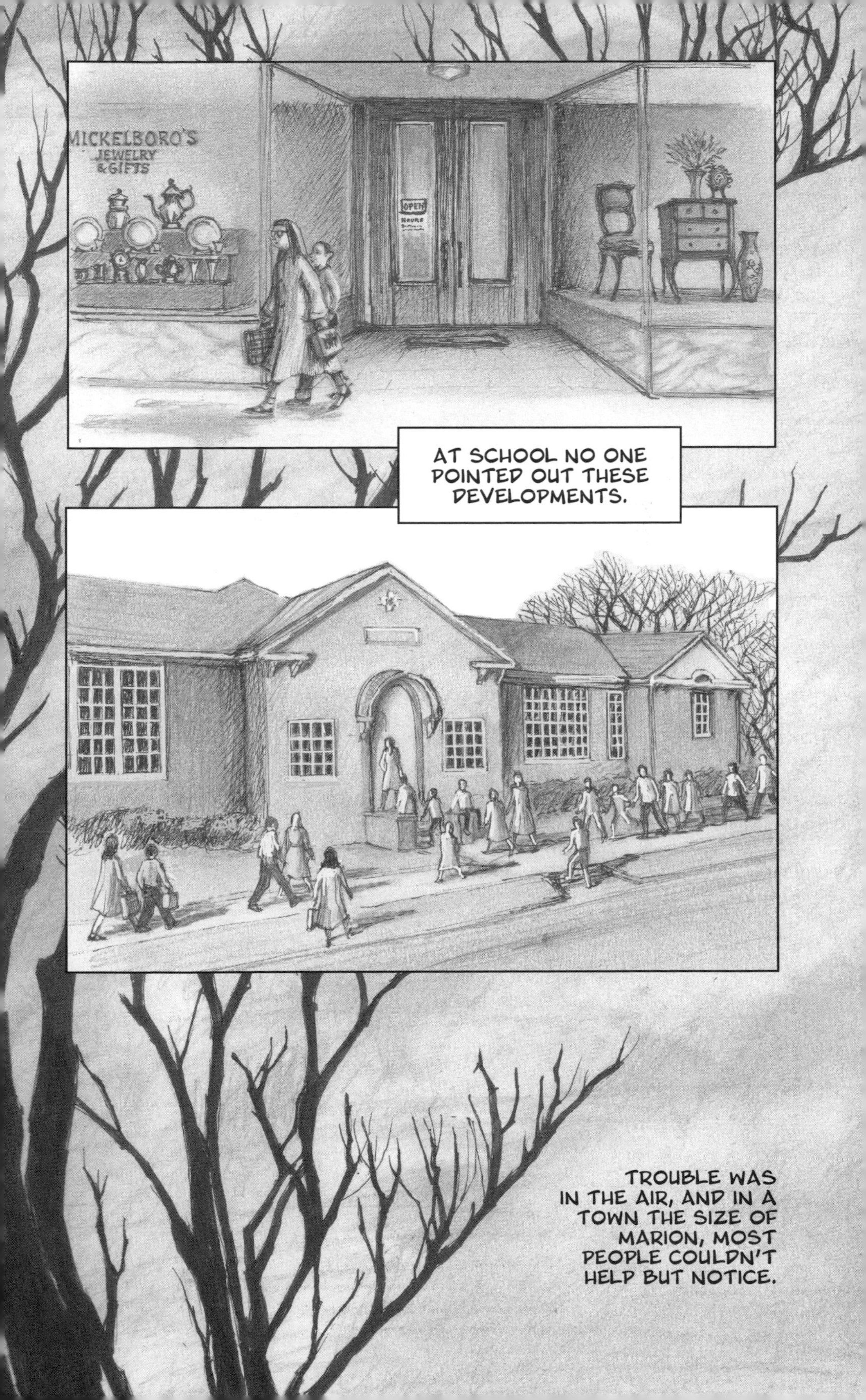
MICKELBORO'S
JEWELRY
& GIFTS
OPEN
AT SCHOOL NO ONE POINTED OUT THESE DEVELOPMENTS.
TROUBLE WAS IN THE AIR, AND IN A TOWN THE SIZE OF MARION, MOST PEOPLE COULDN'T HELP BUT NOTICE.

WE LIVED JUST ONE BLOCK FROM WHERE EVERYTHING HAPPENED.

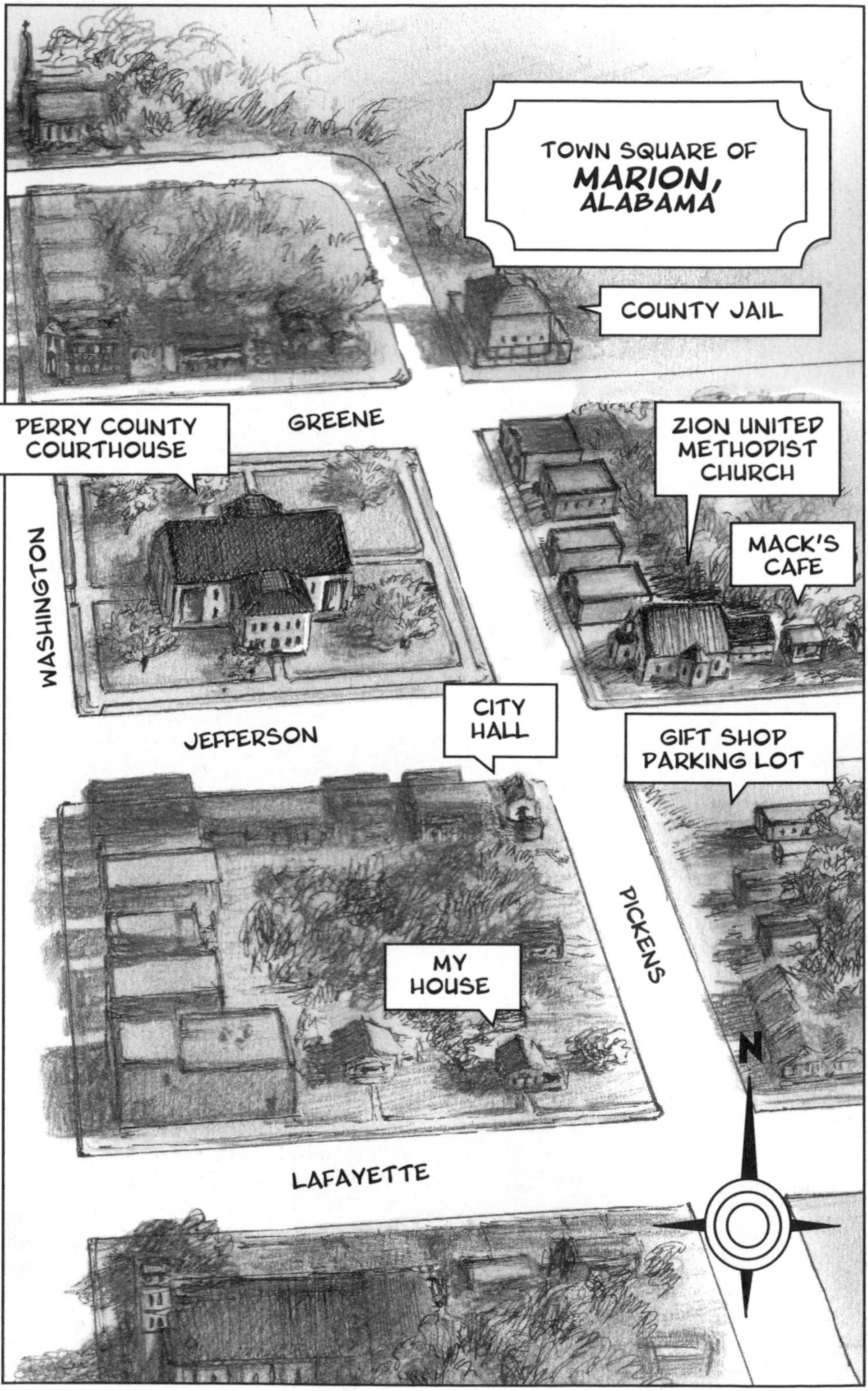

TOWN SQUARE OF MARION, ALABAMA
COUNTY JAIL
PERRY COUNTY COURTHOUSE
GREENE
ZION UNITED METHODIST CHURCH
MACK'S CAFE
WASHINGTON
CITY HALL
JEFFERSON
GIFT SHOP PARKING LOT
PICKENS
MY HOUSE
N
LAFAYETTE

INSIDE
THE COURTHOUSE,
A DAILY DRAMA
UNFOLDED.

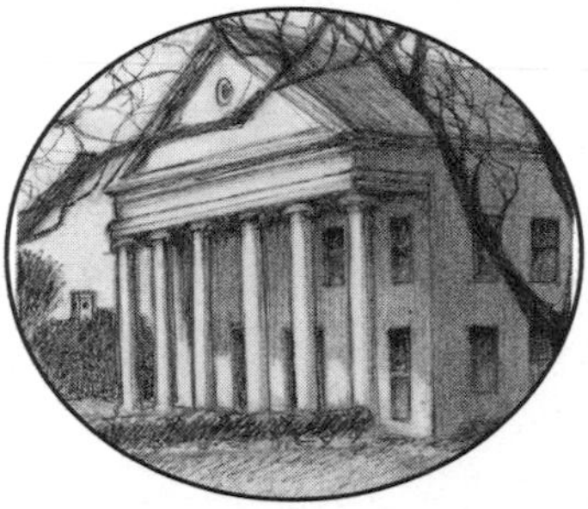

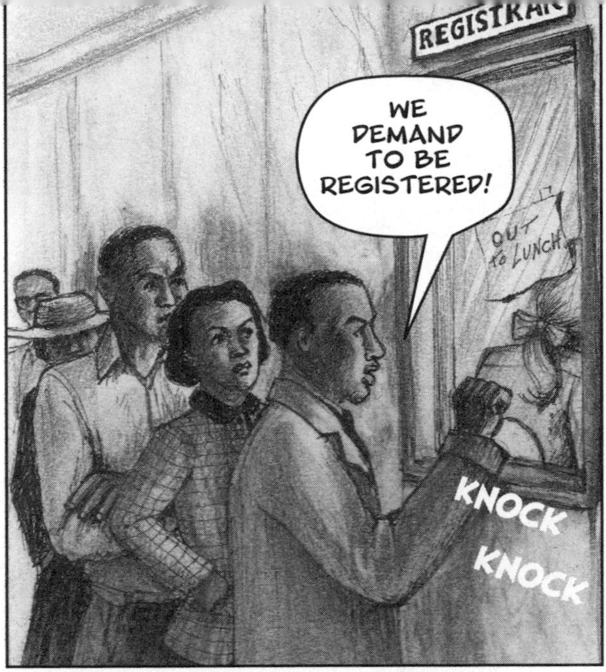
WE DEMAND TO BE REGISTERED!
OUT TO LUNCH
KNOCK
KNOCK

BUT THE BOARD OF REGISTRARS WASN'T IN SESSION. NOT TODAY, NOT TOMORROW, NOT ANY TIME THAT BLACK CITIZENS LINED UP TO APPLY.

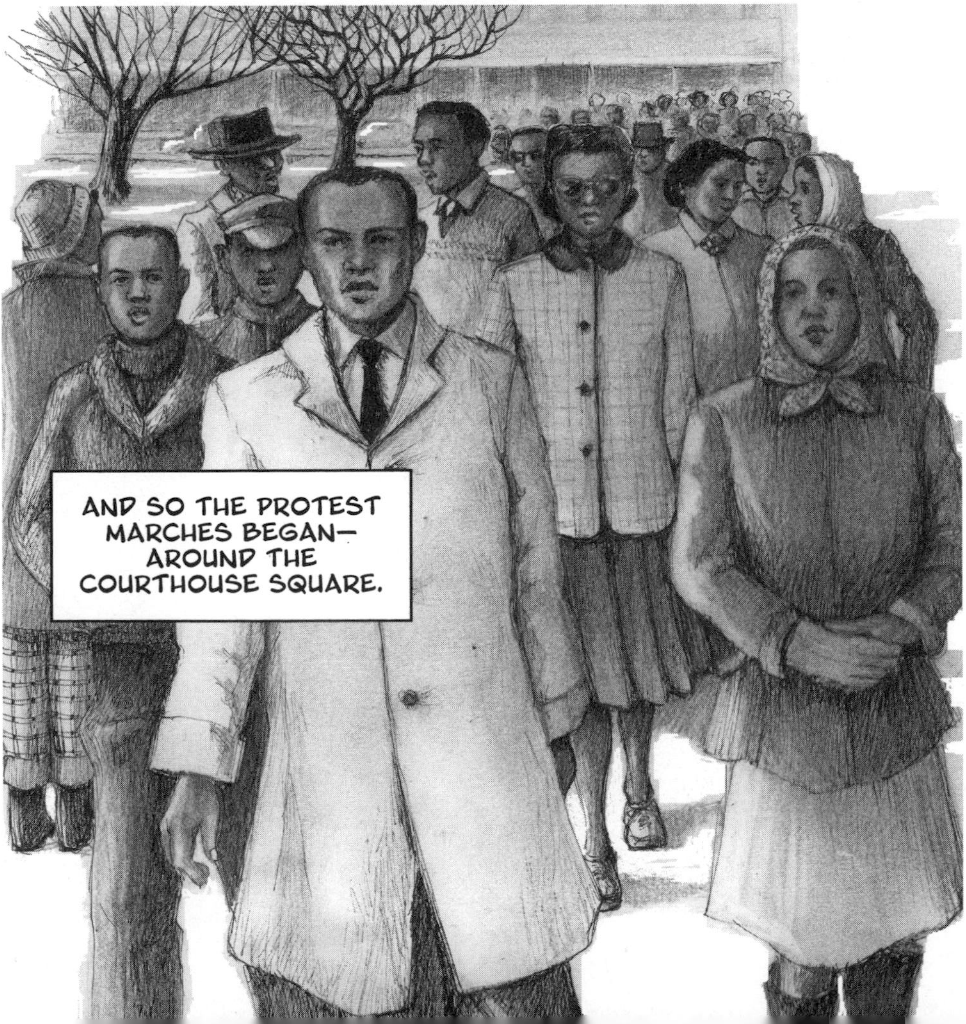
AND SO THE PROTEST MARCHES BEGAN— AROUND THE COURTHOUSE SQUARE.

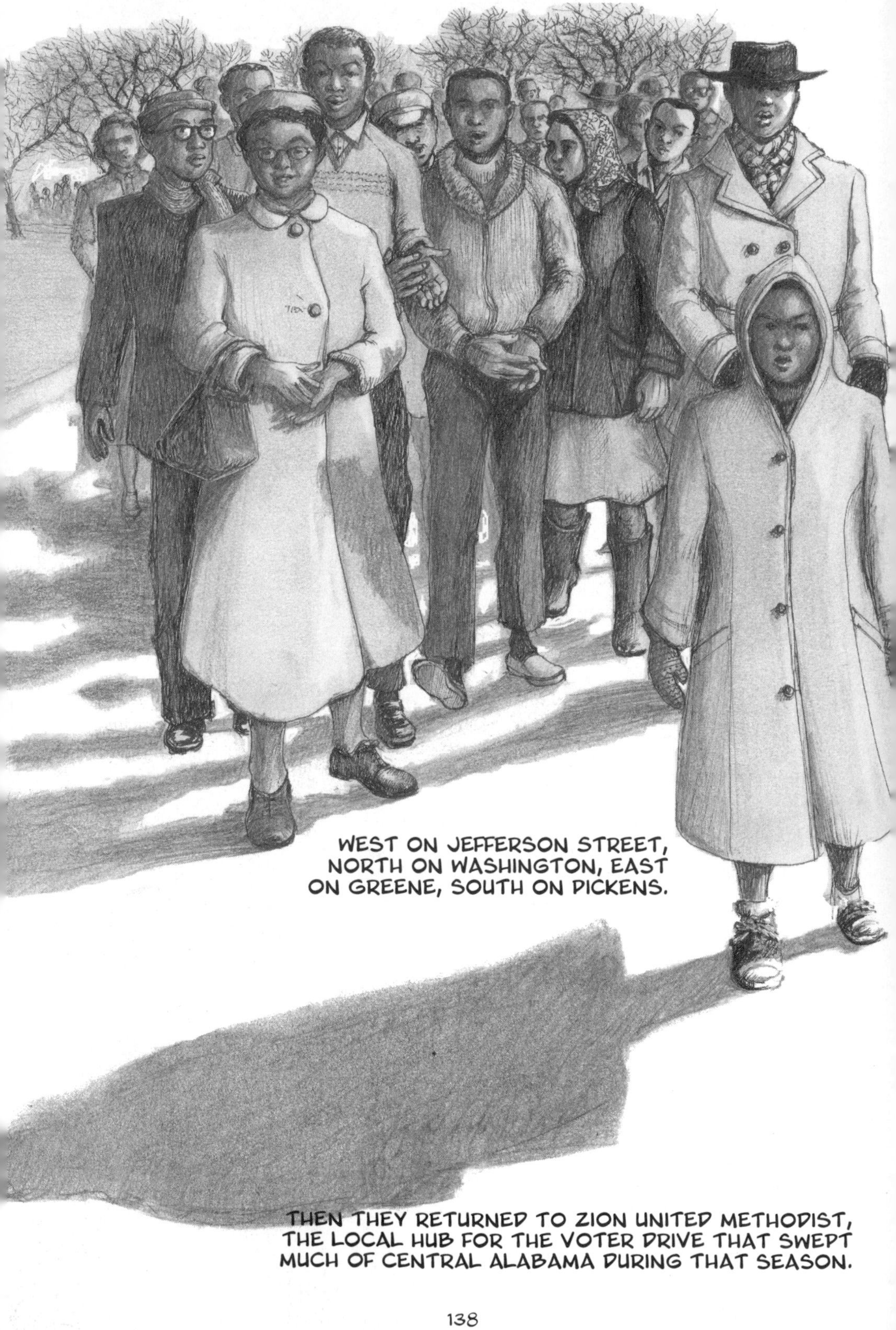
WEST ON JEFFERSON STREET, NORTH ON WASHINGTON, EAST ON GREENE, SOUTH ON PICKENS.
THEN THEY RETURNED TO ZION UNITED METHODIST, THE LOCAL HUB FOR THE VOTER DRIVE THAT SWEPT MUCH OF CENTRAL ALABAMA DURING THAT SEASON.

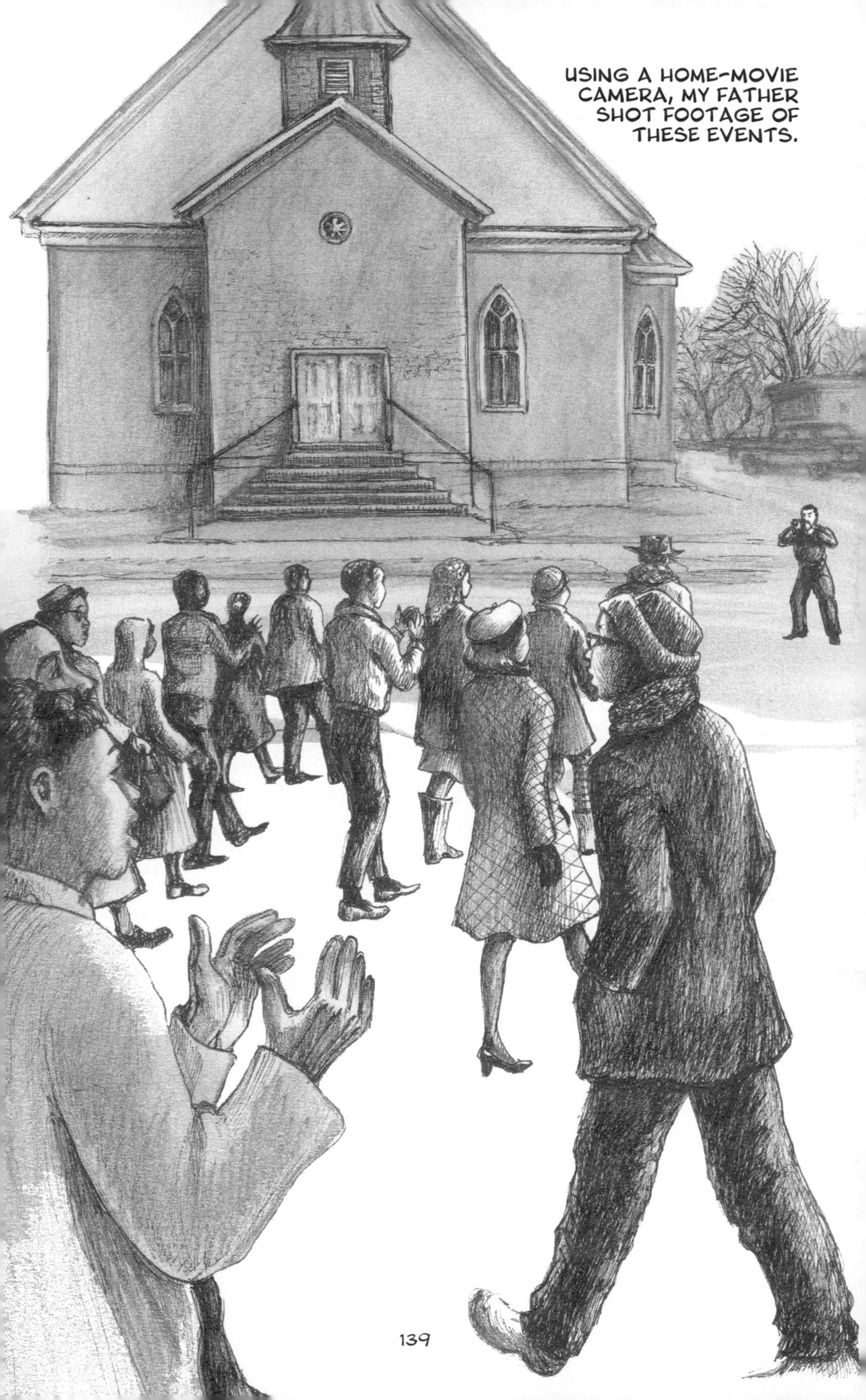
USING A HOME-MOVIE CAMERA, MY FATHER SHOT FOOTAGE OF THESE EVENTS.

WEEKS PASSED. THE REGISTRARS ALLOWED NO MORE THAN A TRICKLE OF BLACK APPLICANTS TO PROCEED. THE MARCHING WENT ON, WITH PARTICIPATION SWELLING TO 400 PEOPLE AT TIMES.

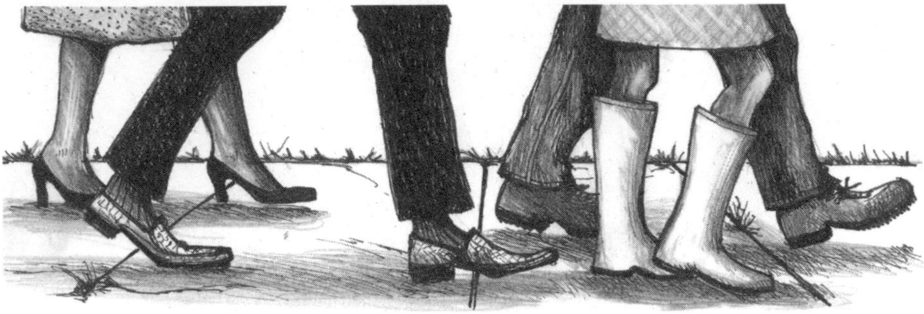

IN THE WHITE COMMUNITY, CONCERN GREW.

AMONG THE SPECTRUM OF REACTIONS, THERE WERE THOSE THAT REFUSED TO BELIEVE LOCAL AFRICAN AMERICANS WERE UNHAPPY WITH THEIR LOT.

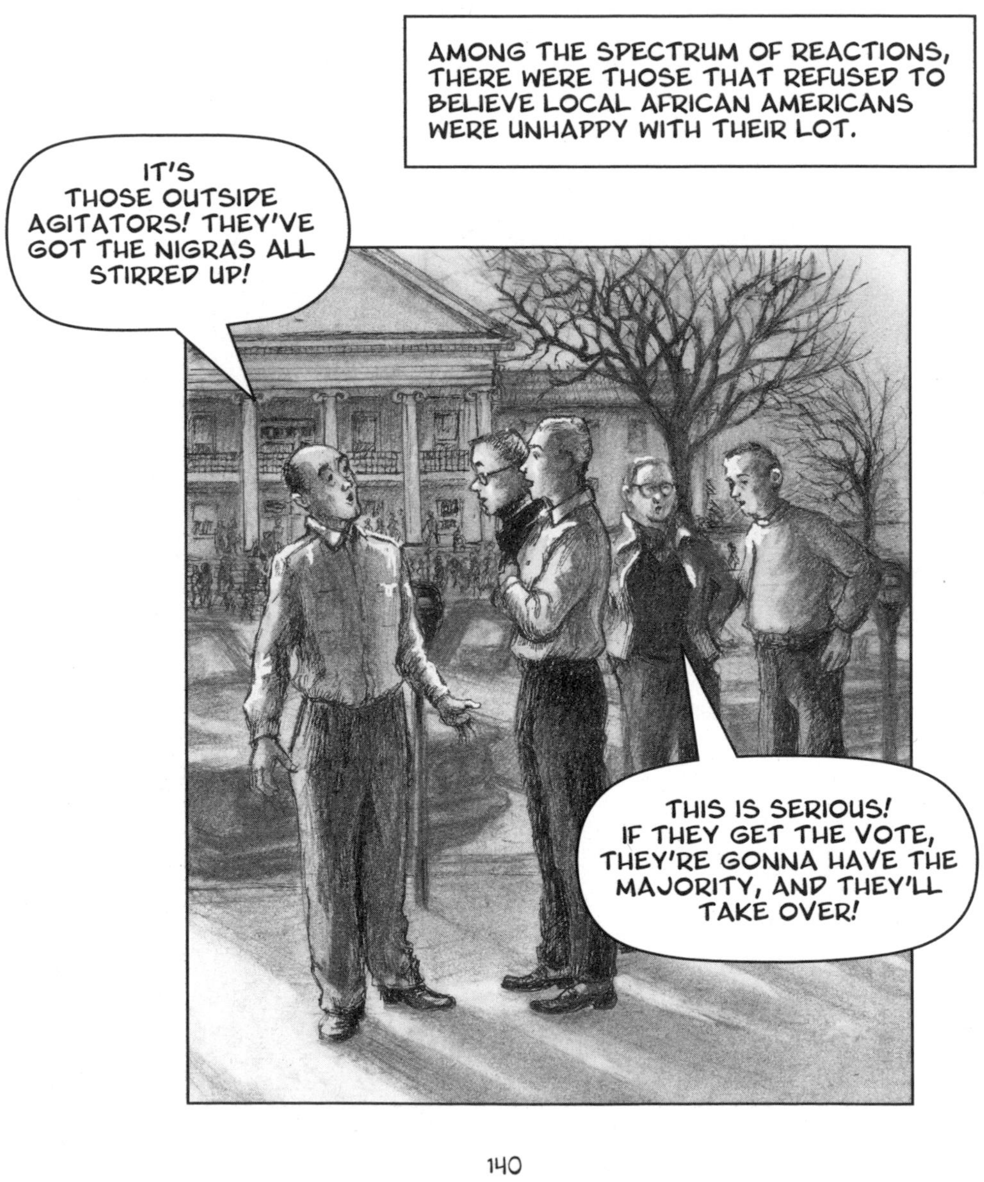
IT'S THOSE OUTSIDE AGITATORS! THEY'VE GOT THE NIGRAS ALL STIRRED UP!
THIS IS SERIOUS! IF THEY GET THE VOTE, THEY'RE GONNA HAVE THE MAJORITY, AND THEY'LL TAKE OVER!

LIKE THE SOUTH IN GENERAL, WHITE MARION HAD SOME RACIAL MODERATES AND GRADUALISTS, BUT ITS MOST OUTSPOKEN CITIZENS HELD A HARD LINE ON SEGREGATION.

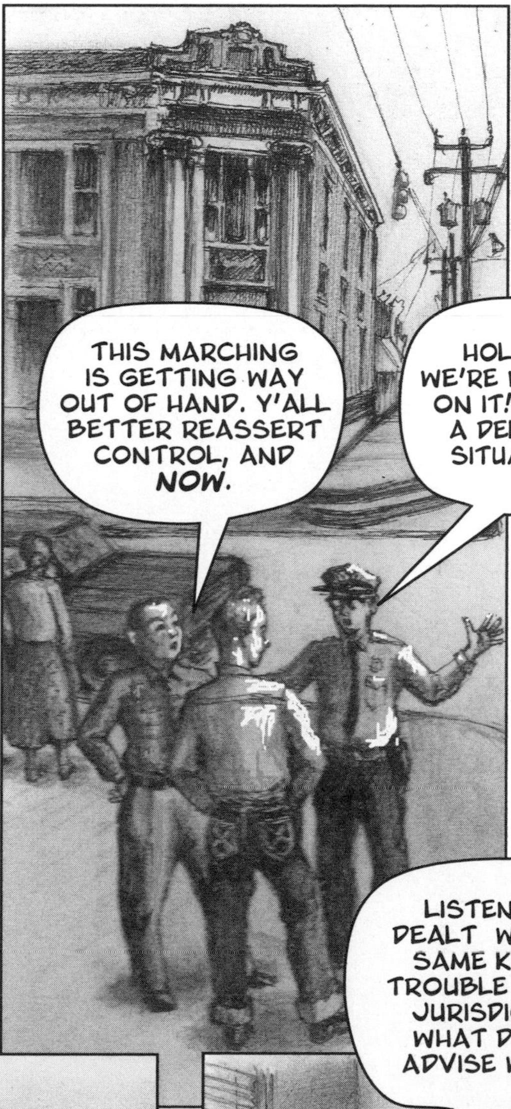
THIS MARCHING IS GETTING WAY OUT OF HAND. Y'ALL BETTER REASSERT CONTROL, AND **NOW**.
HOLD ON, WE'RE WORKING ON IT! THIS IS A DELICATE SITUATION!

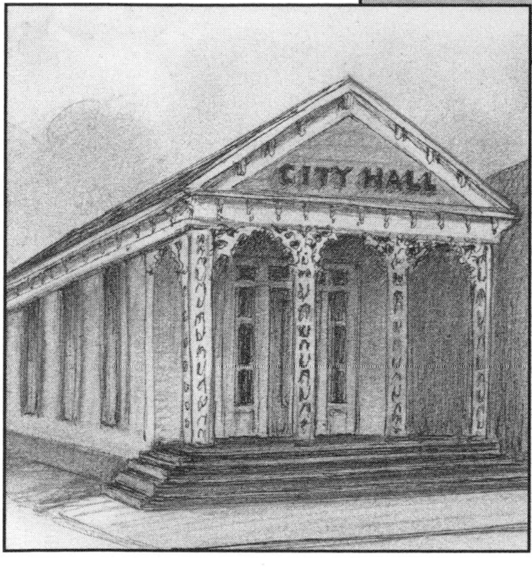
CITY HALL

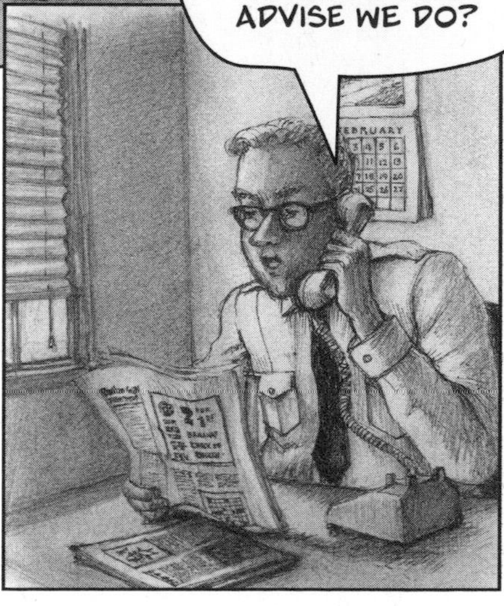
LISTEN, YOU DEALT WITH THE SAME KIND OF TROUBLE IN YOUR JURISDICTION. WHAT DO YOU ADVISE WE DO?
FEBRUARY

AT THE COURTHOUSE:

TEST 8

1. When thE Constitution was approved by the original colonies, how many states had to ra fect?

***--

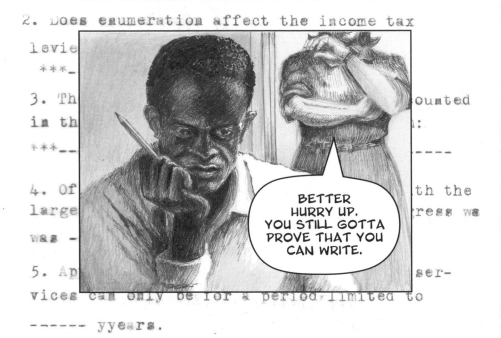

ANY APPLICANT THAT GOT PAST THE STALLING TACTICS FACED THE LITERACY TEST.

2. Does enumeration affect the income tax

levie

***_

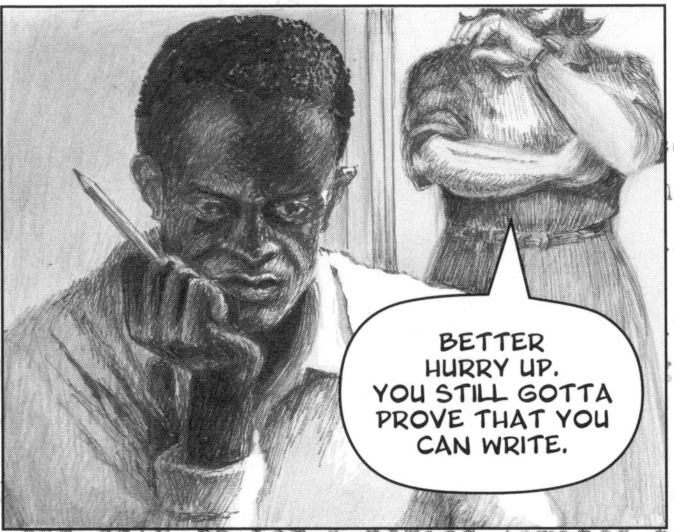
BETTER HURRY UP. YOU STILL GOTTA PROVE THAT YOU CAN WRITE.

3. Th ounted

in th :

***__ ----

4. Of th the

large gress was

was -

5. Ap ser-

vices can only be for a period limited to

------ yyears.

6. Cases tried before a court of law are two types, civil and--------------.

7. Check the offenses whic com-

victed of them, disqualif :

Murder----

Issuing worthless checks---

Petty larceny-----

Manufacturing whisky-----

WHITE VOTERS RECEIVED FAR EASIER VERSIONS OF THE TEST—OR NO TEST AT ALL.

8. Impeachmentsof U.S. officials are tried by

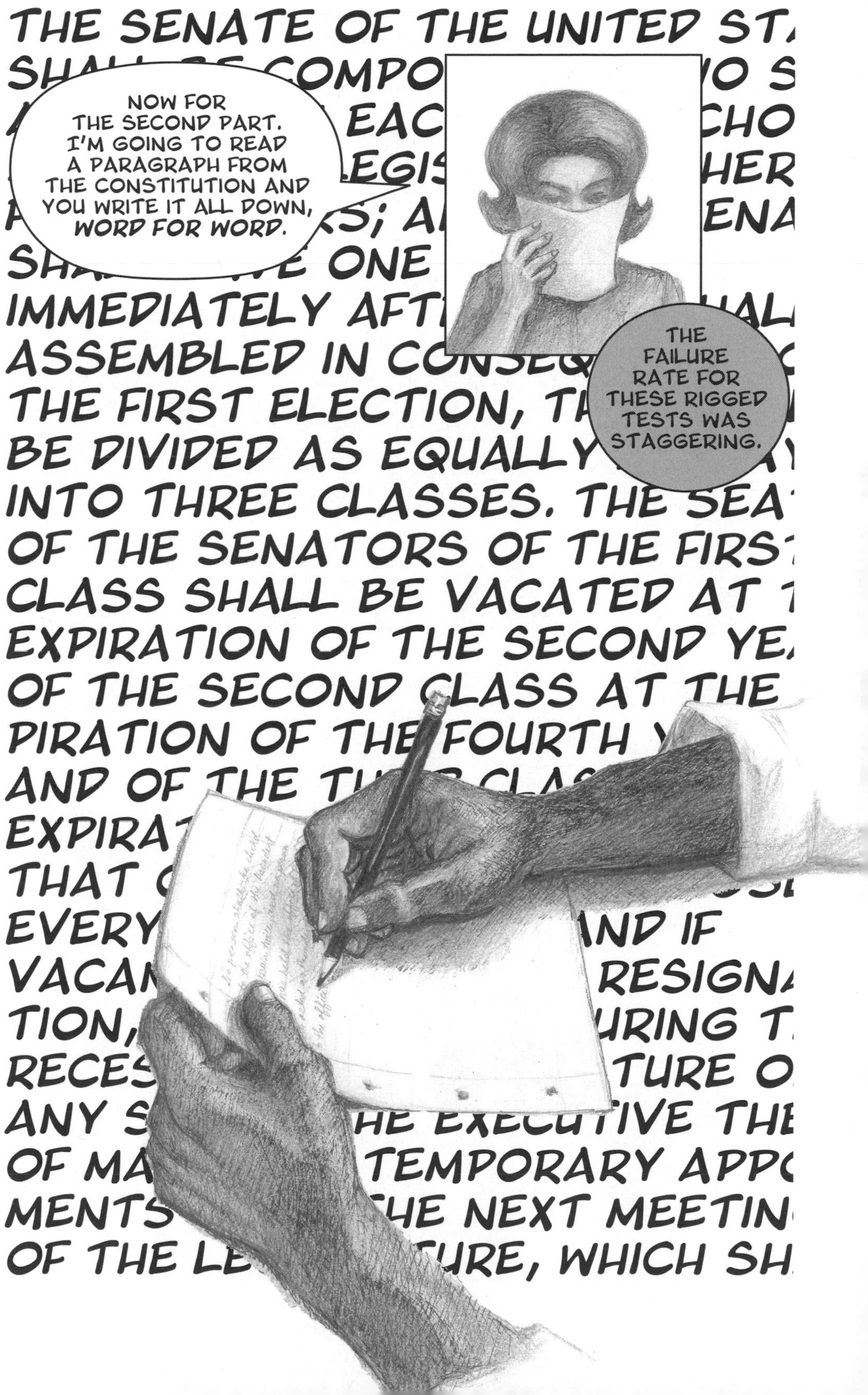
THE SENATE OF THE UNITED
IMMEDIATELY
ASSEMBLED IN
THE FIRST ELECTION,
BE DIVIDED AS EQUALLY
INTO THREE CLASSES. THE
OF THE SENATORS OF THE
CLASS SHALL BE VACATED AT
EXPIRATION OF THE SECOND
OF THE SECOND CLASS AT THE
PIRATION OF THE FOURTH
AND OF THE
TEMPORARY
NOW FOR THE SECOND PART. I'M GOING TO READ A PARAGRAPH FROM THE CONSTITUTION AND YOU WRITE IT ALL DOWN, WORD FOR WORD.
THE FAILURE RATE FOR THESE RIGGED TESTS WAS STAGGERING.

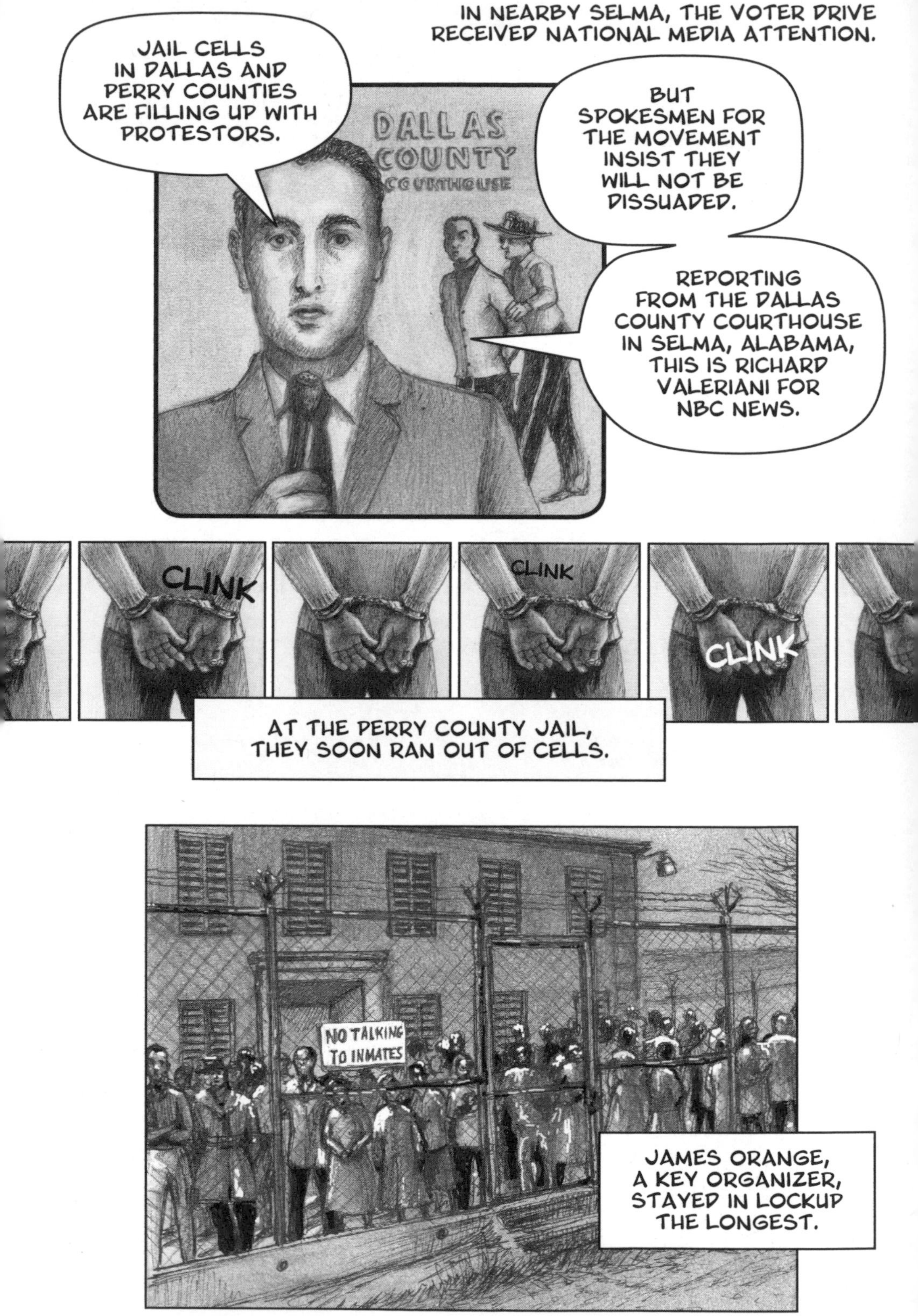
IN NEARBY SELMA, THE VOTER DRIVE RECEIVED NATIONAL MEDIA ATTENTION.
JAIL CELLS IN DALLAS AND PERRY COUNTIES ARE FILLING UP WITH PROTESTORS.
DALLAS COUNTY COURTHOUSE
BUT SPOKESMEN FOR THE MOVEMENT INSIST THEY WILL NOT BE DISSUADED.
REPORTING FROM THE DALLAS COUNTY COURTHOUSE IN SELMA, ALABAMA, THIS IS RICHARD VALERIANI FOR NBC NEWS.
CLINK
CLINK
CLINK
AT THE PERRY COUNTY JAIL, THEY SOON RAN OUT OF CELLS.
NO TALKING TO INMATES
JAMES ORANGE, A KEY ORGANIZER, STAYED IN LOCKUP THE LONGEST.

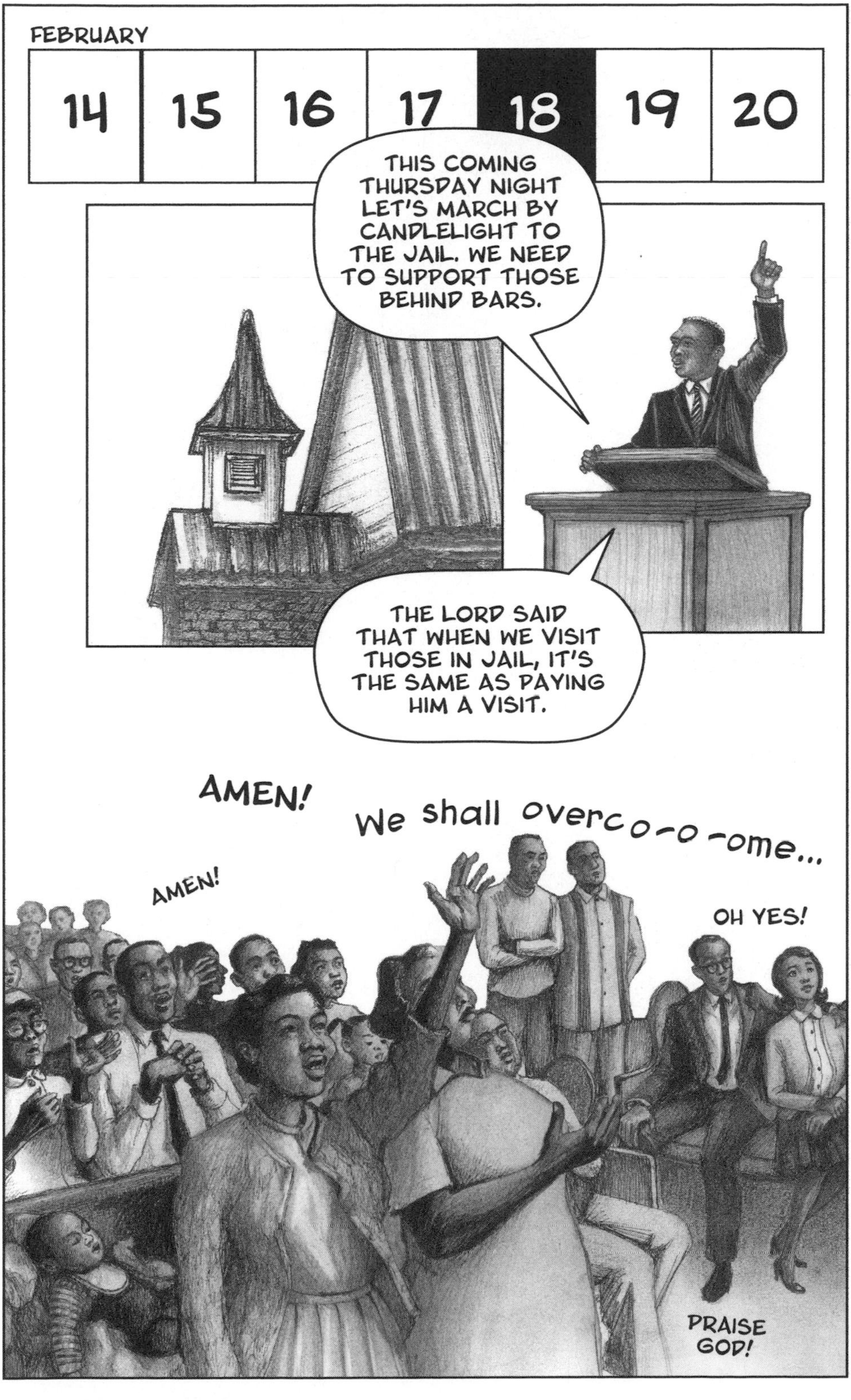
FEBRUARY
14 15 16 17 18 19 20
THIS COMING THURSDAY NIGHT LET'S MARCH BY CANDLELIGHT TO THE JAIL. WE NEED TO SUPPORT THOSE BEHIND BARS.
THE LORD SAID THAT WHEN WE VISIT THOSE IN JAIL, IT'S THE SAME AS PAYING HIM A VISIT.
AMEN!
We shall overco-o-ome...
AMEN!
OH YES!
PRAISE GOD!

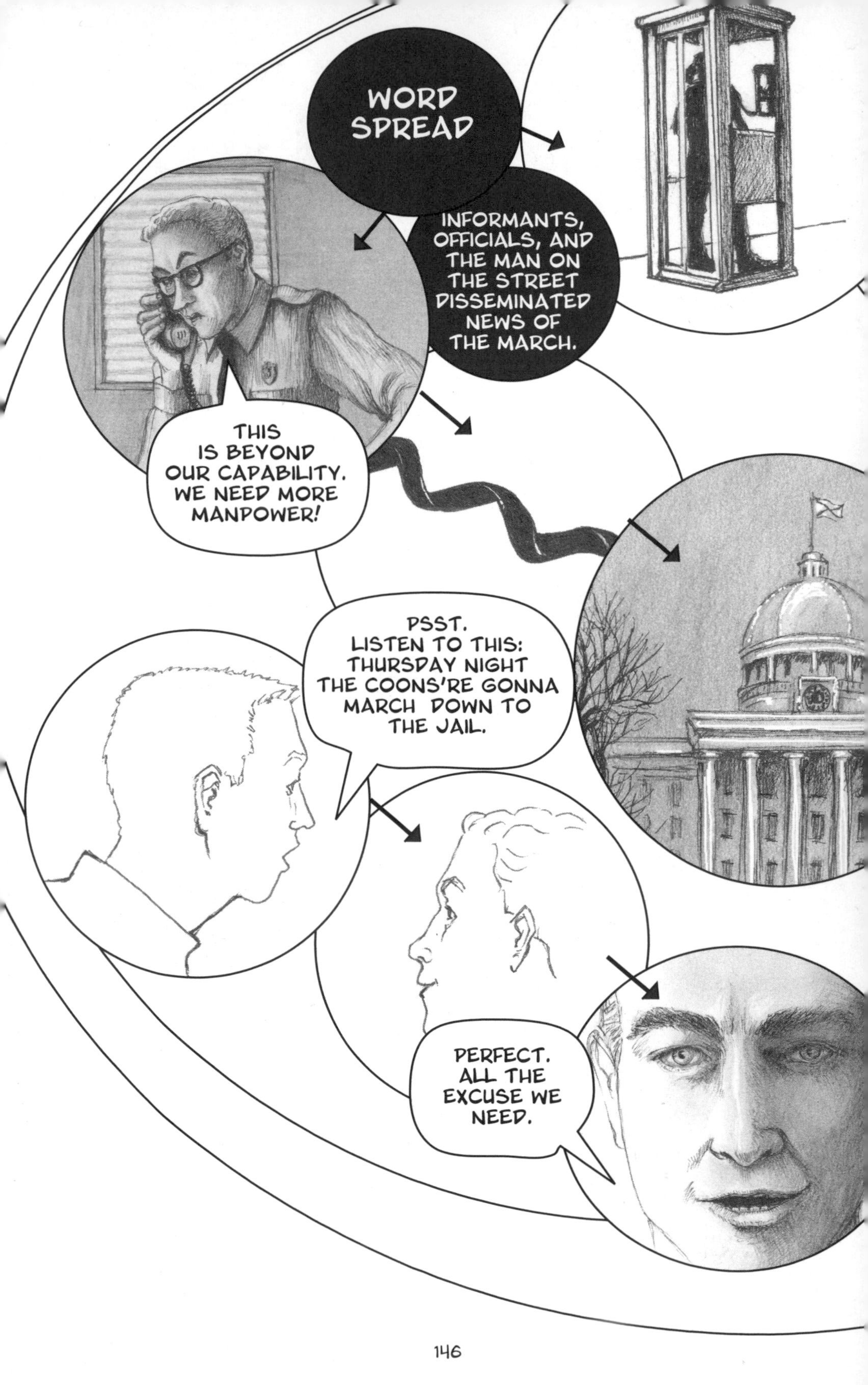
WORD SPREAD
INFORMANTS, OFFICIALS, AND THE MAN ON THE STREET DISSEMINATED NEWS OF THE MARCH.
THIS IS BEYOND OUR CAPABILITY. WE NEED MORE MANPOWER!
PSST. LISTEN TO THIS: THURSDAY NIGHT THE COONS'RE GONNA MARCH DOWN TO THE JAIL.
PERFECT. ALL THE EXCUSE WE NEED.

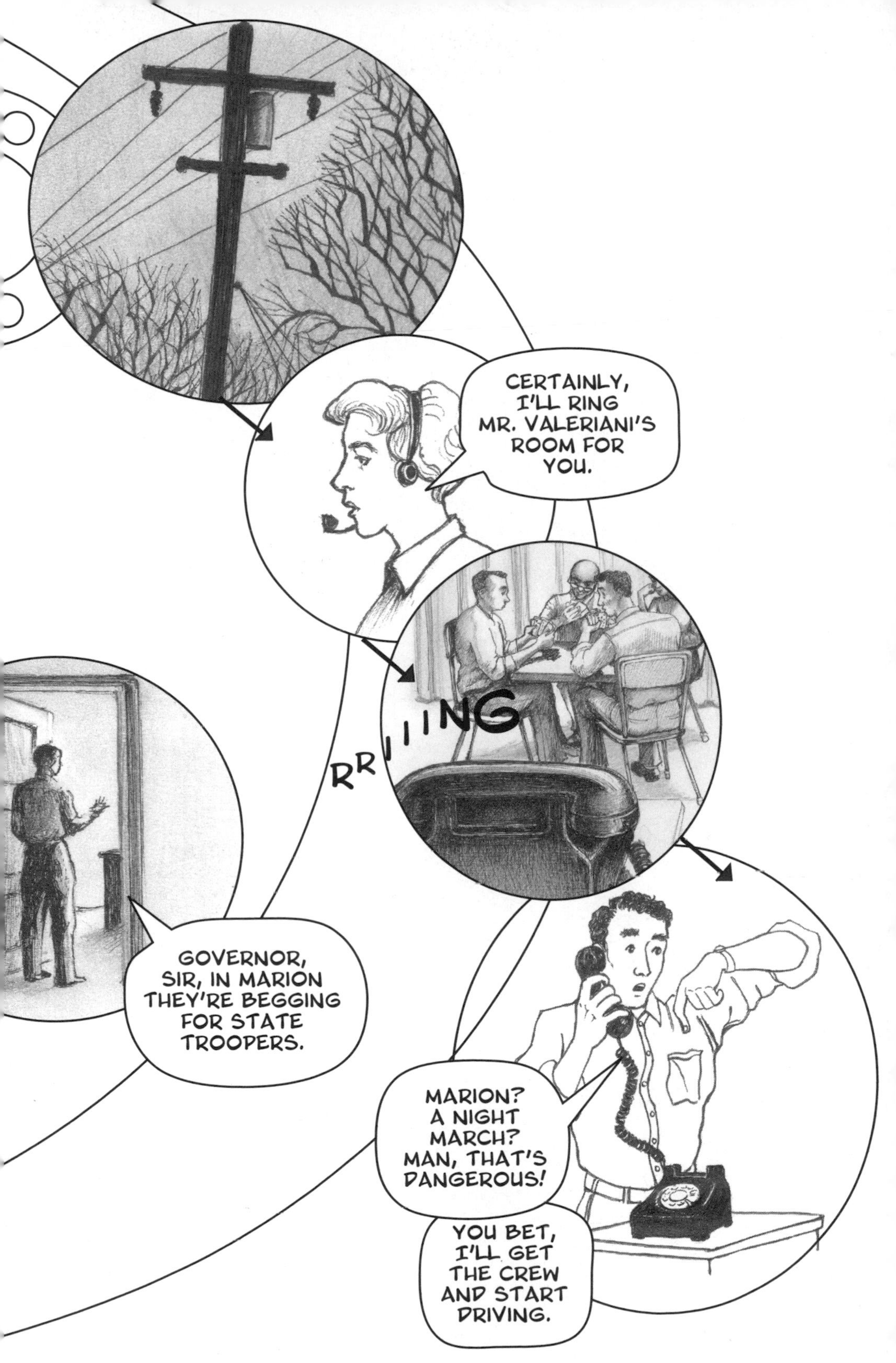
CERTAINLY, I'LL RING MR. VALERIANI'S ROOM FOR YOU.
RRIIING
MARION? A NIGHT MARCH? MAN, THAT'S DANGEROUS!
YOU BET, I'LL GET THE CREW AND START DRIVING.
GOVERNOR, SIR, IN MARION THEY'RE BEGGING FOR STATE TROOPERS.

DADDY HAD ALSO GOTTEN NEWS OF THAT NIGHT'S MARCH.

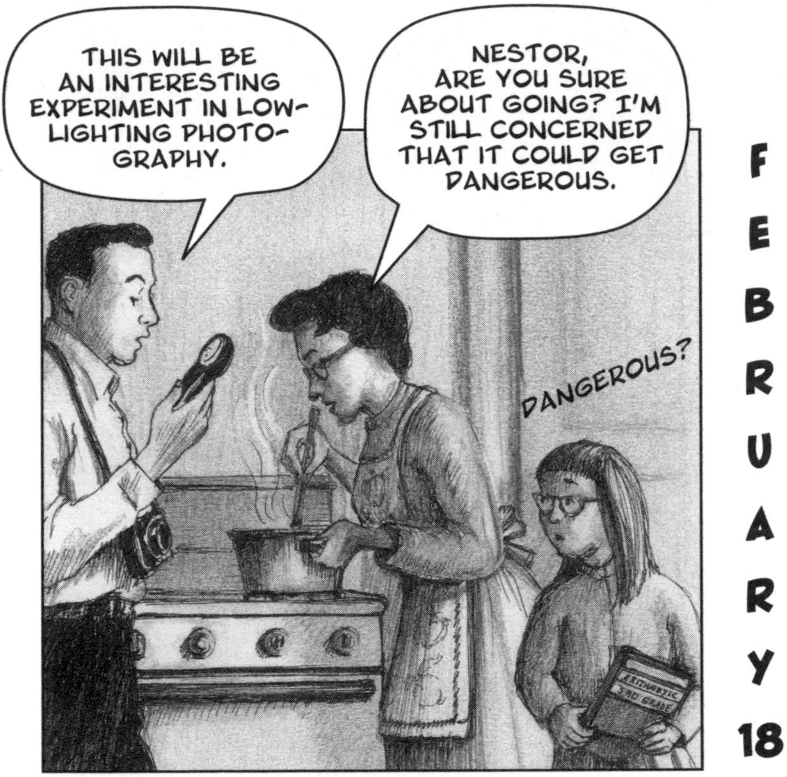
THIS WILL BE AN INTERESTING EXPERIMENT IN LOW-LIGHTING PHOTOGRAPHY.
NESTOR, ARE YOU SURE ABOUT GOING? I'M STILL CONCERNED THAT IT COULD GET DANGEROUS.
DANGEROUS?
FEBRUARY 18

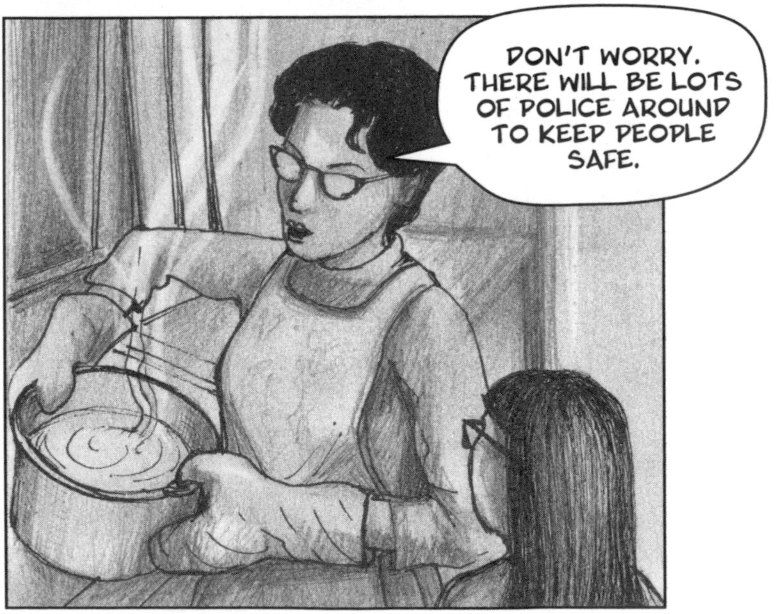
DON'T WORRY. THERE WILL BE LOTS OF POLICE AROUND TO KEEP PEOPLE SAFE.

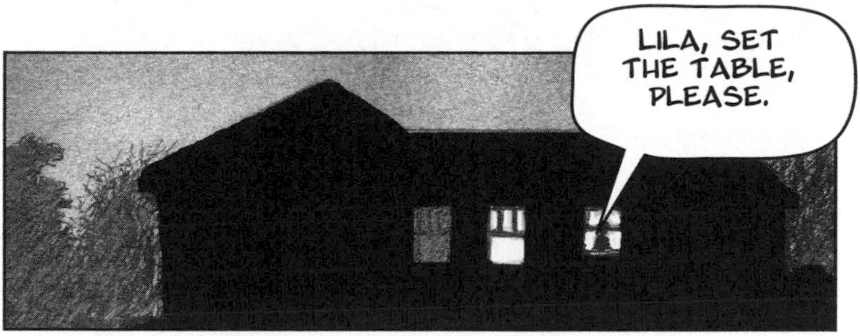
LILA, SET THE TABLE, PLEASE.

FOR EVERYONE BESIDES DADDY, IT WAS A REGULAR NIGHT AT HOME.

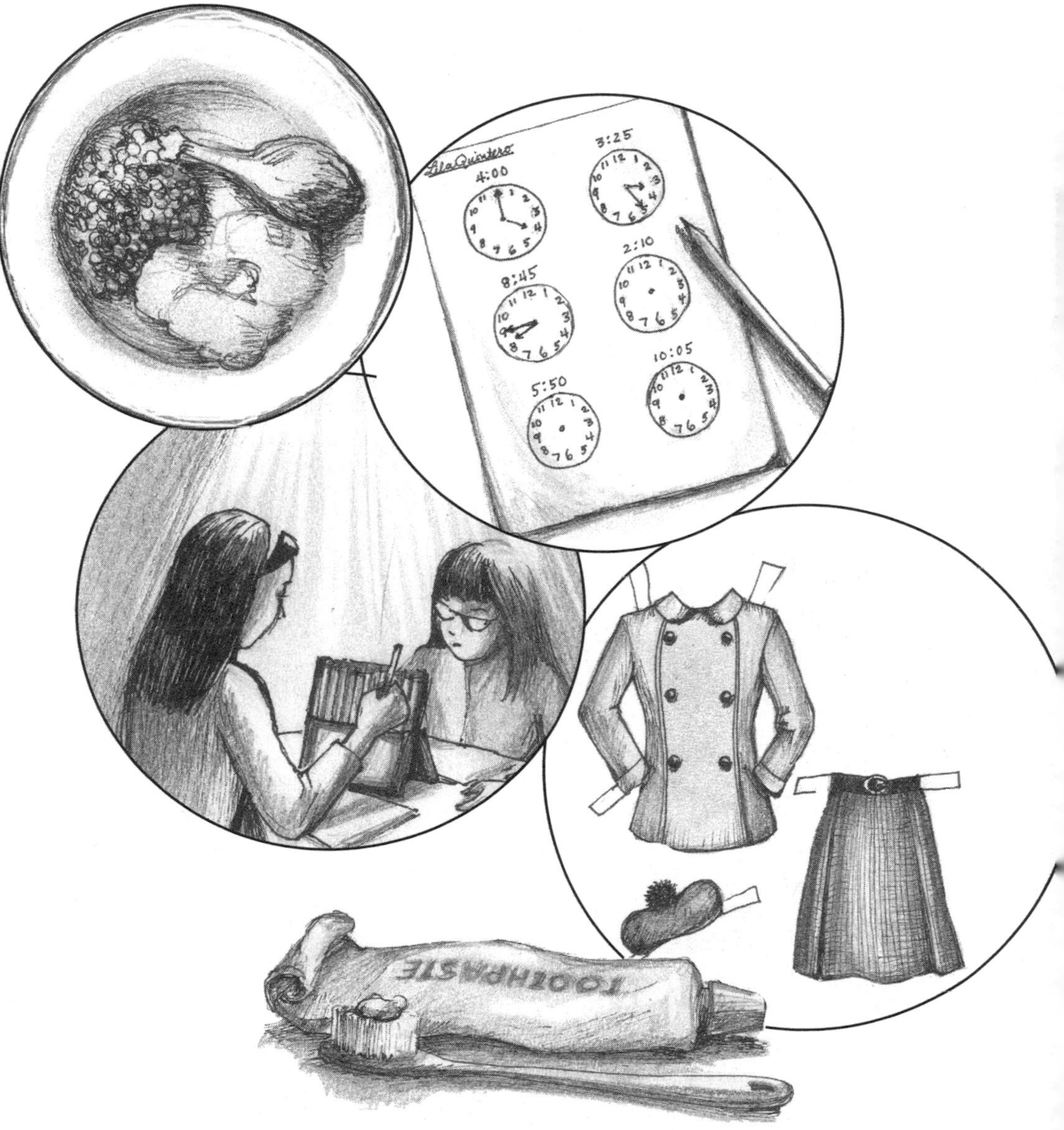
Lila Quintero
4:00
3:25
8:45
2:10
10:05
5:50

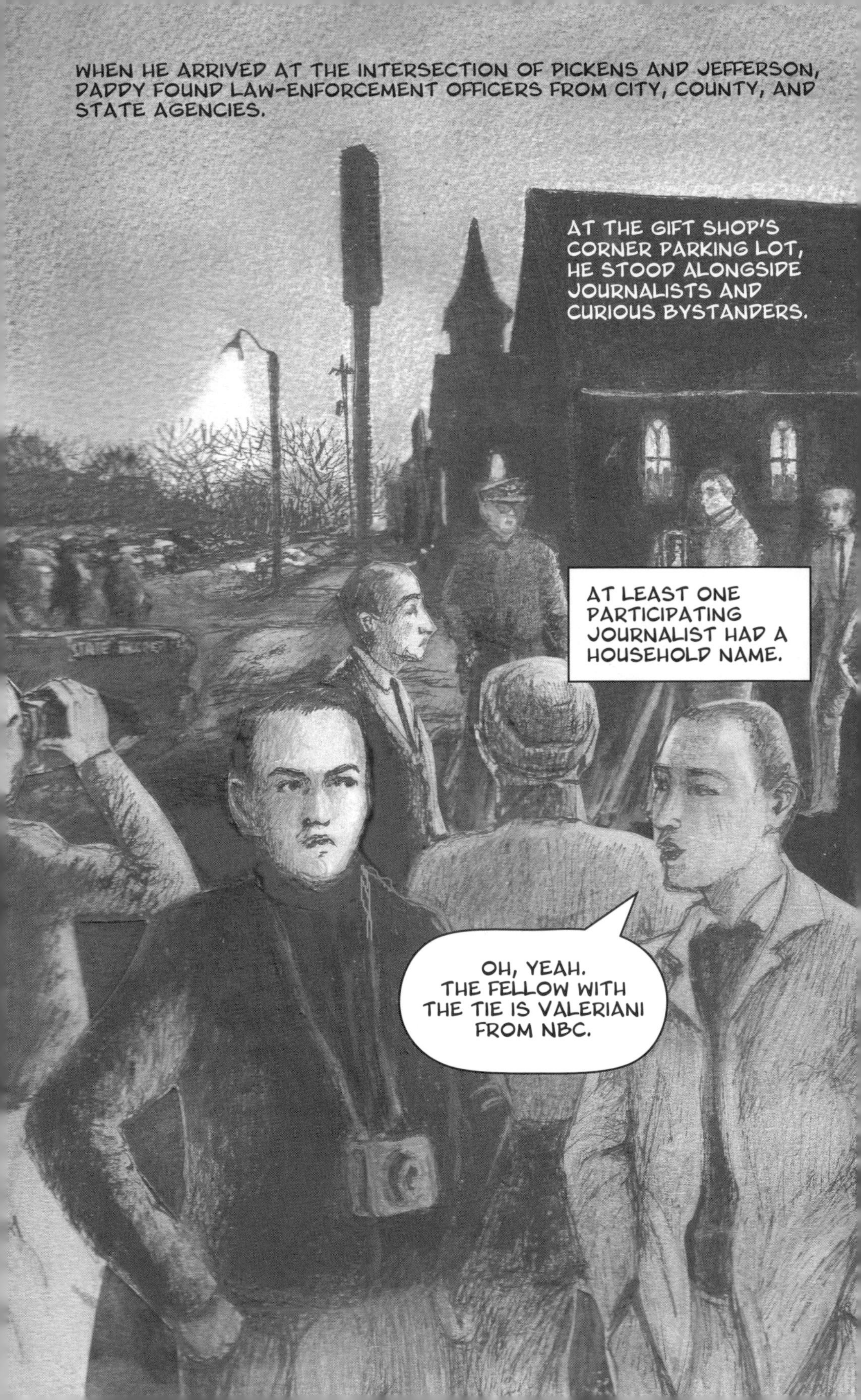
WHEN HE ARRIVED AT THE INTERSECTION OF PICKENS AND JEFFERSON, DADDY FOUND LAW-ENFORCEMENT OFFICERS FROM CITY, COUNTY, AND STATE AGENCIES.
AT THE GIFT SHOP'S CORNER PARKING LOT, HE STOOD ALONGSIDE JOURNALISTS AND CURIOUS BYSTANDERS.
AT LEAST ONE PARTICIPATING JOURNALIST HAD A HOUSEHOLD NAME.
OH, YEAH. THE FELLOW WITH THE TIE IS VALERIANI FROM NBC.

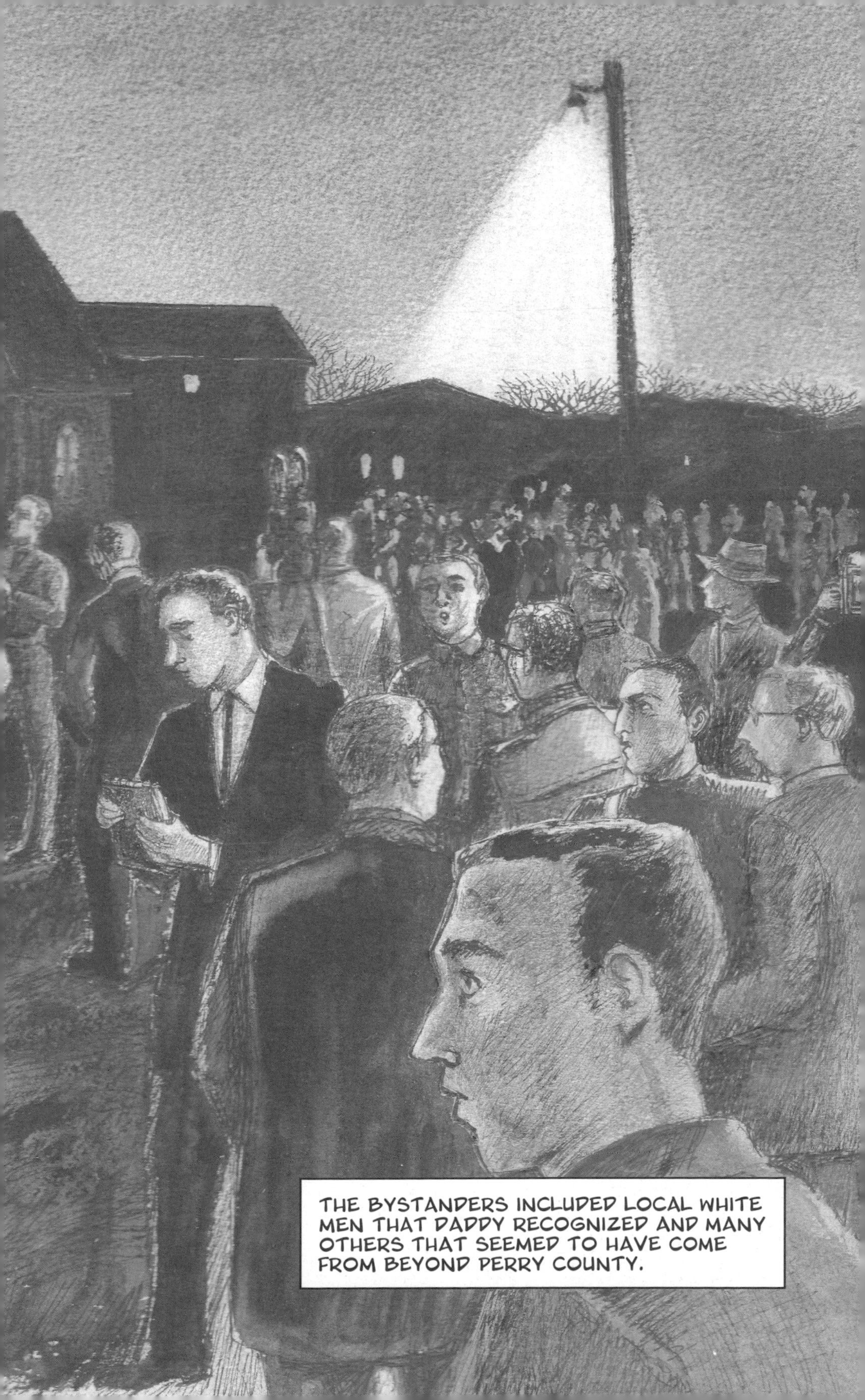
THE BYSTANDERS INCLUDED LOCAL WHITE MEN THAT DADDY RECOGNIZED AND MANY OTHERS THAT SEEMED TO HAVE COME FROM BEYOND PERRY COUNTY.

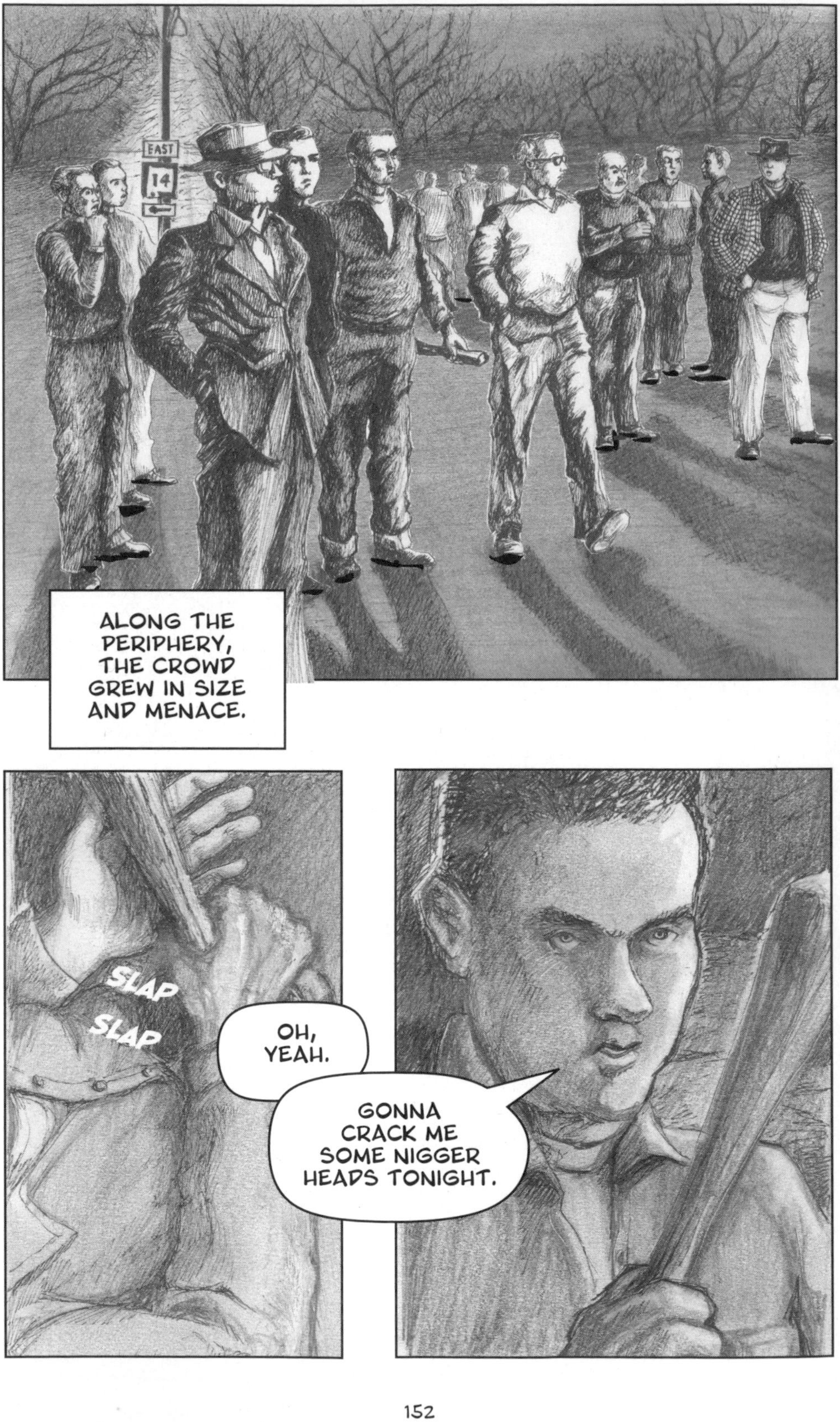
EAST
14
ALONG THE PERIPHERY, THE CROWD GREW IN SIZE AND MENACE.
SLAP
SLAP
OH, YEAH.
GONNA CRACK ME SOME NIGGER HEADS TONIGHT.

INSIDE THE CHURCH, PROTESTORS PREPARED TO FACE A HOSTILE CROWD. I CAN ONLY IMAGINE THE WORDS THAT STEELED THEM.

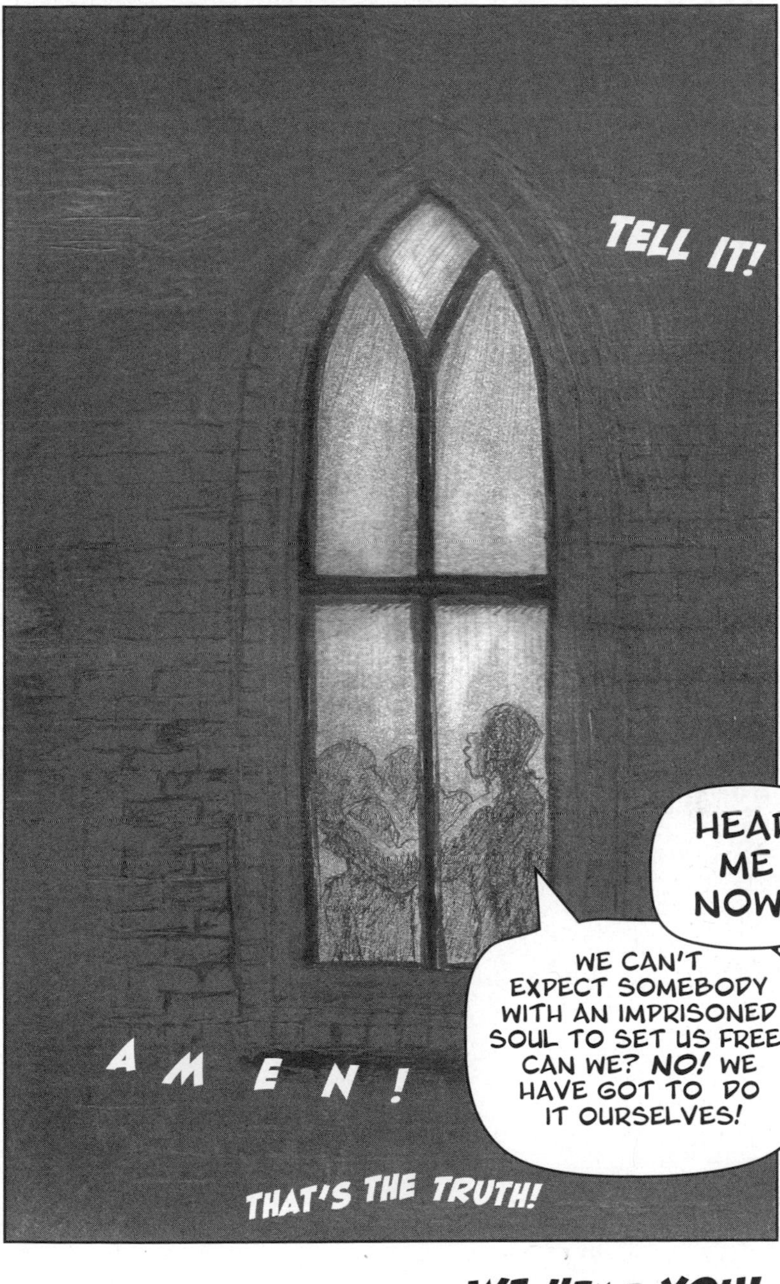
TELL IT!
HEAR ME NOW!
WE CAN'T EXPECT SOMEBODY WITH AN IMPRISONED SOUL TO SET US FREE, CAN WE? NO! WE HAVE GOT TO DO IT OURSELVES!
A M E N !
THAT'S THE TRUTH!

WE HEAR YOU!

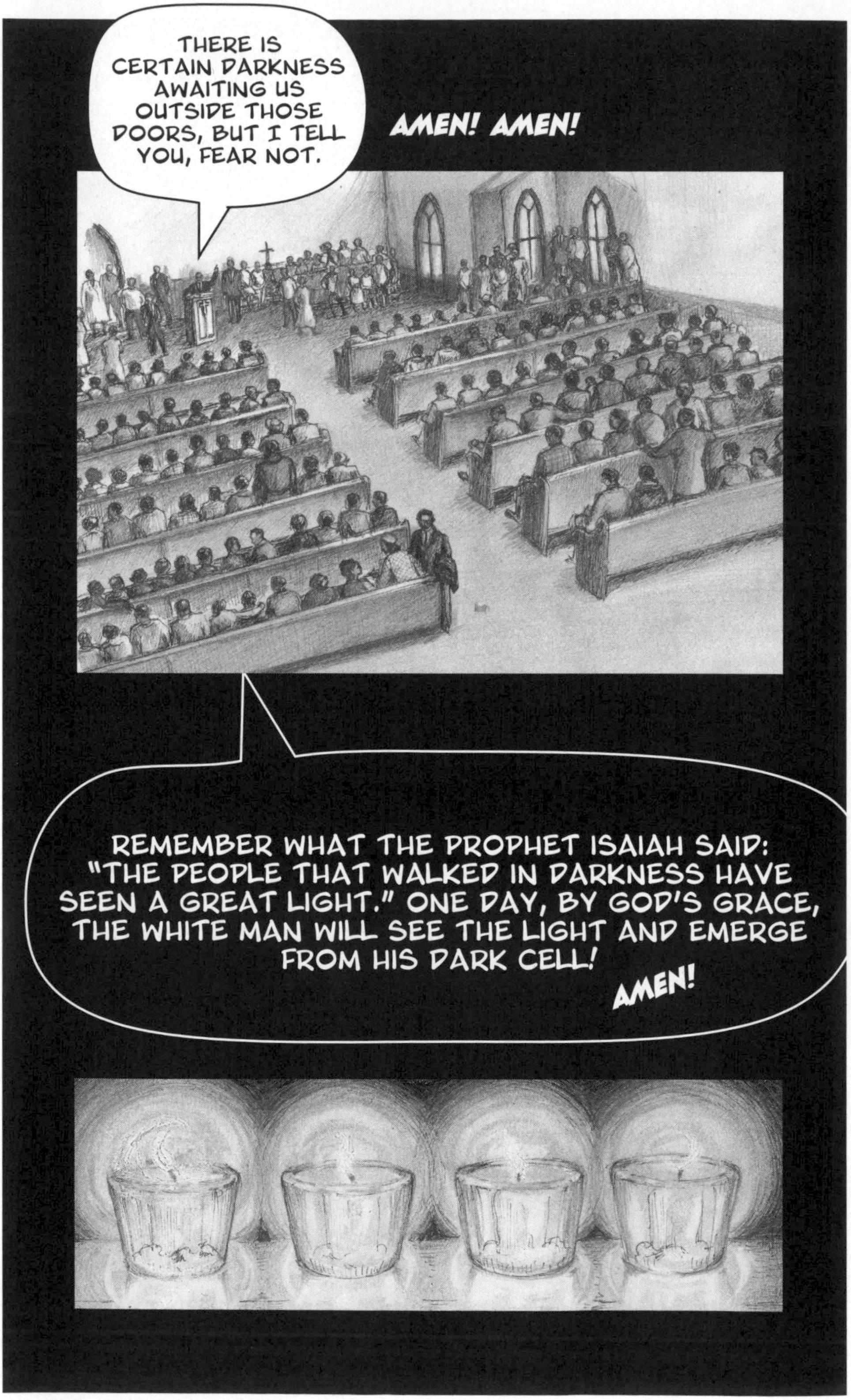
THERE IS CERTAIN DARKNESS AWAITING US OUTSIDE THOSE DOORS, BUT I TELL YOU, FEAR NOT.
AMEN! AMEN!
REMEMBER WHAT THE PROPHET ISAIAH SAID: "THE PEOPLE THAT WALKED IN DARKNESS HAVE SEEN A GREAT LIGHT." ONE DAY, BY GOD'S GRACE, THE WHITE MAN WILL SEE THE LIGHT AND EMERGE FROM HIS DARK CELL!
AMEN!

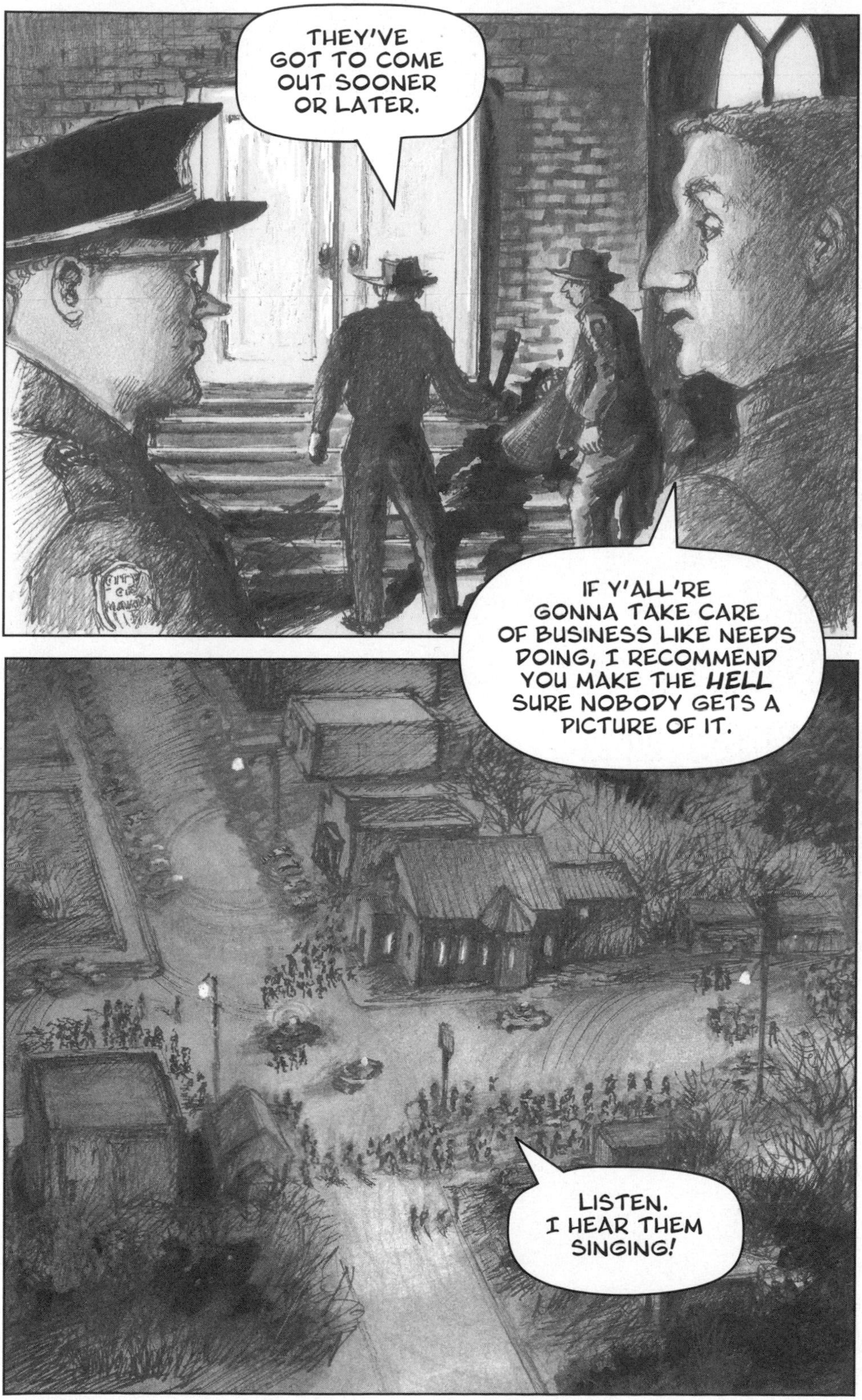
THEY'VE GOT TO COME OUT SOONER OR LATER.
IF Y'ALL'RE GONNA TAKE CARE OF BUSINESS LIKE NEEDS DOING, I RECOMMEND YOU MAKE THE ***HELL*** SURE NOBODY GETS A PICTURE OF IT.
LISTEN. I HEAR THEM SINGING!

We shall overcome...

we shall overcome,
we shall overcome
someday.
Oh, deep in my heart,
I do believe that,
we shall overcome
someday.
We are not afraid...

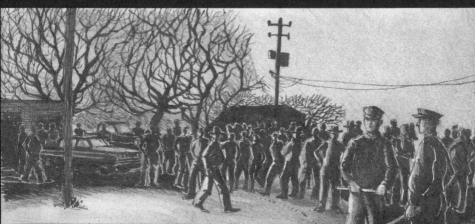

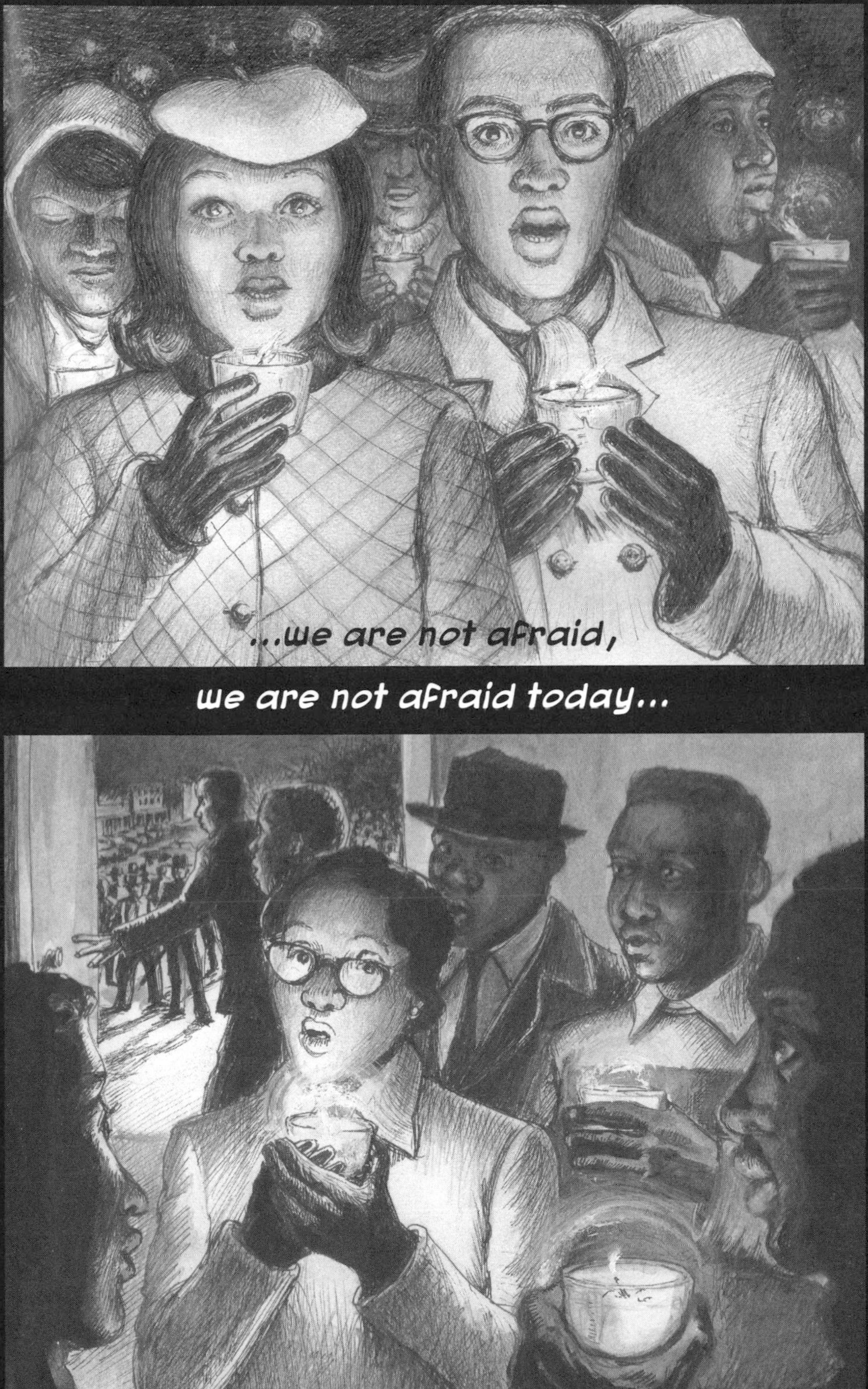
...we are not afraid,
we are not afraid today...

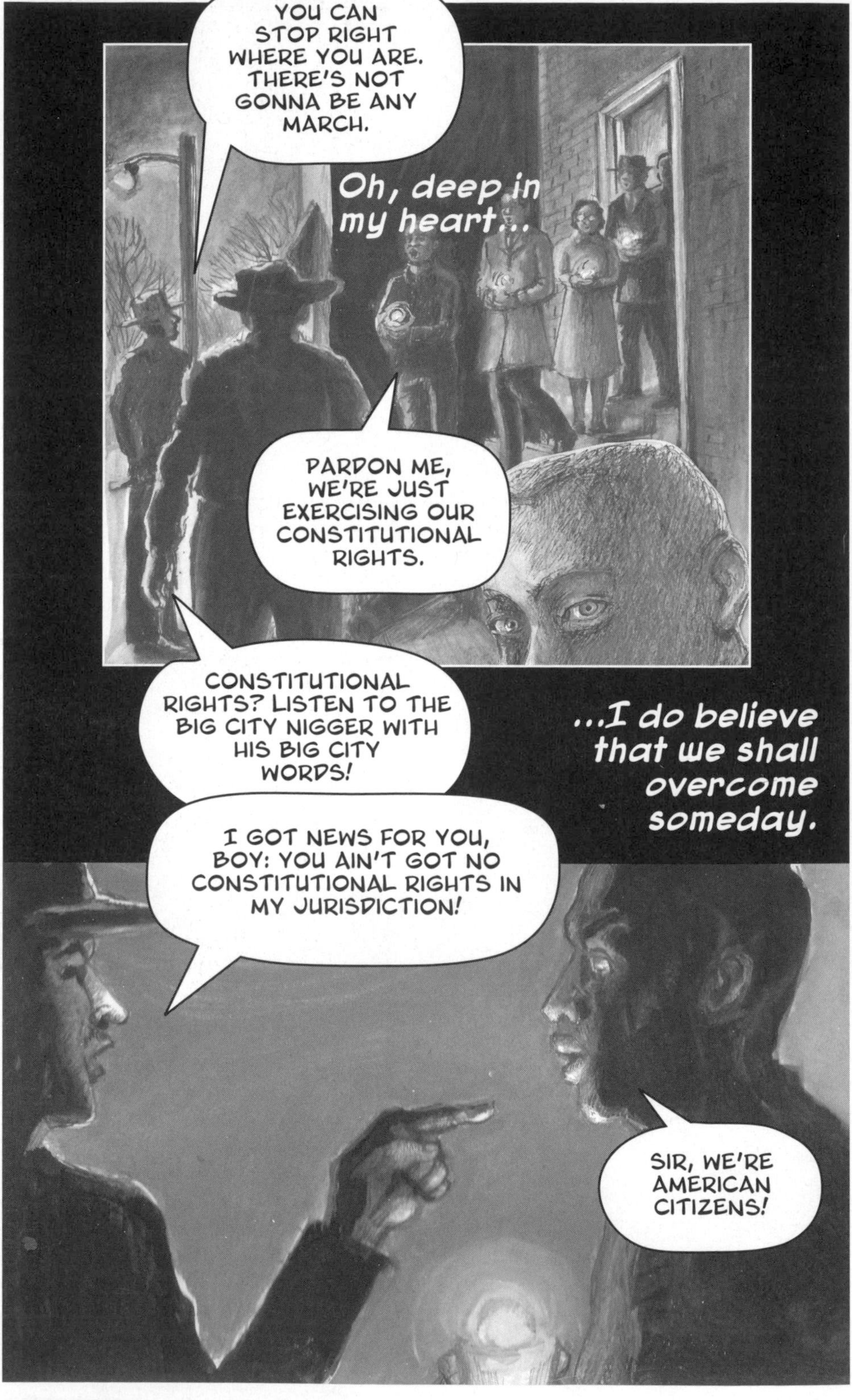
YOU CAN STOP RIGHT WHERE YOU ARE. THERE'S NOT GONNA BE ANY MARCH.
Oh, deep in my heart...
PARDON ME, WE'RE JUST EXERCISING OUR CONSTITUTIONAL RIGHTS.
CONSTITUTIONAL RIGHTS? LISTEN TO THE BIG CITY NIGGER WITH HIS BIG CITY WORDS!
...I do believe that we shall overcome someday.
I GOT NEWS FOR YOU, BOY: YOU AIN'T GOT NO CONSTITUTIONAL RIGHTS IN MY JURISDICTION!
SIR, WE'RE AMERICAN CITIZENS!

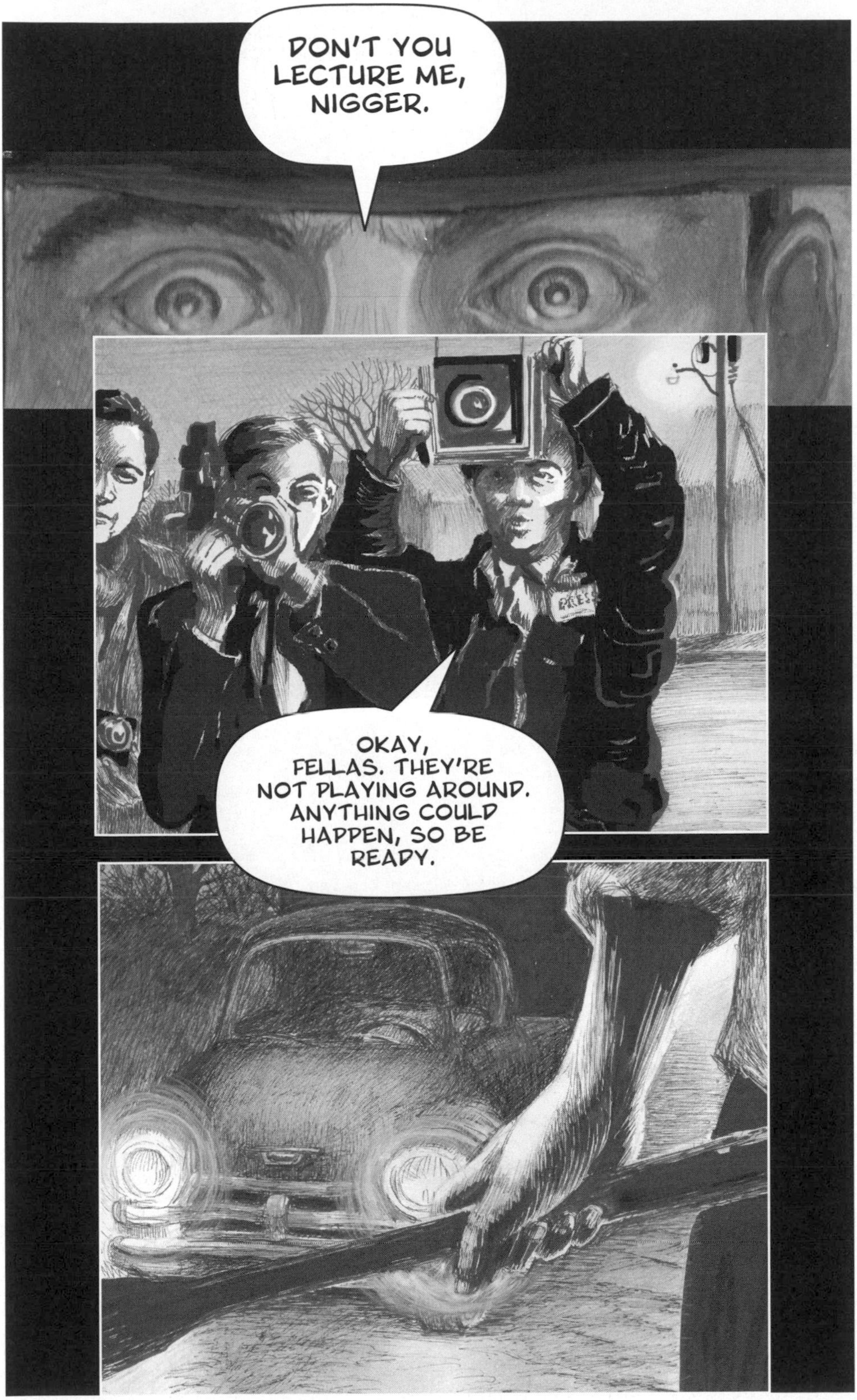
DON'T YOU LECTURE ME, NIGGER.
PRESS
OKAY, FELLAS. THEY'RE NOT PLAYING AROUND. ANYTHING COULD HAPPEN, SO BE READY.

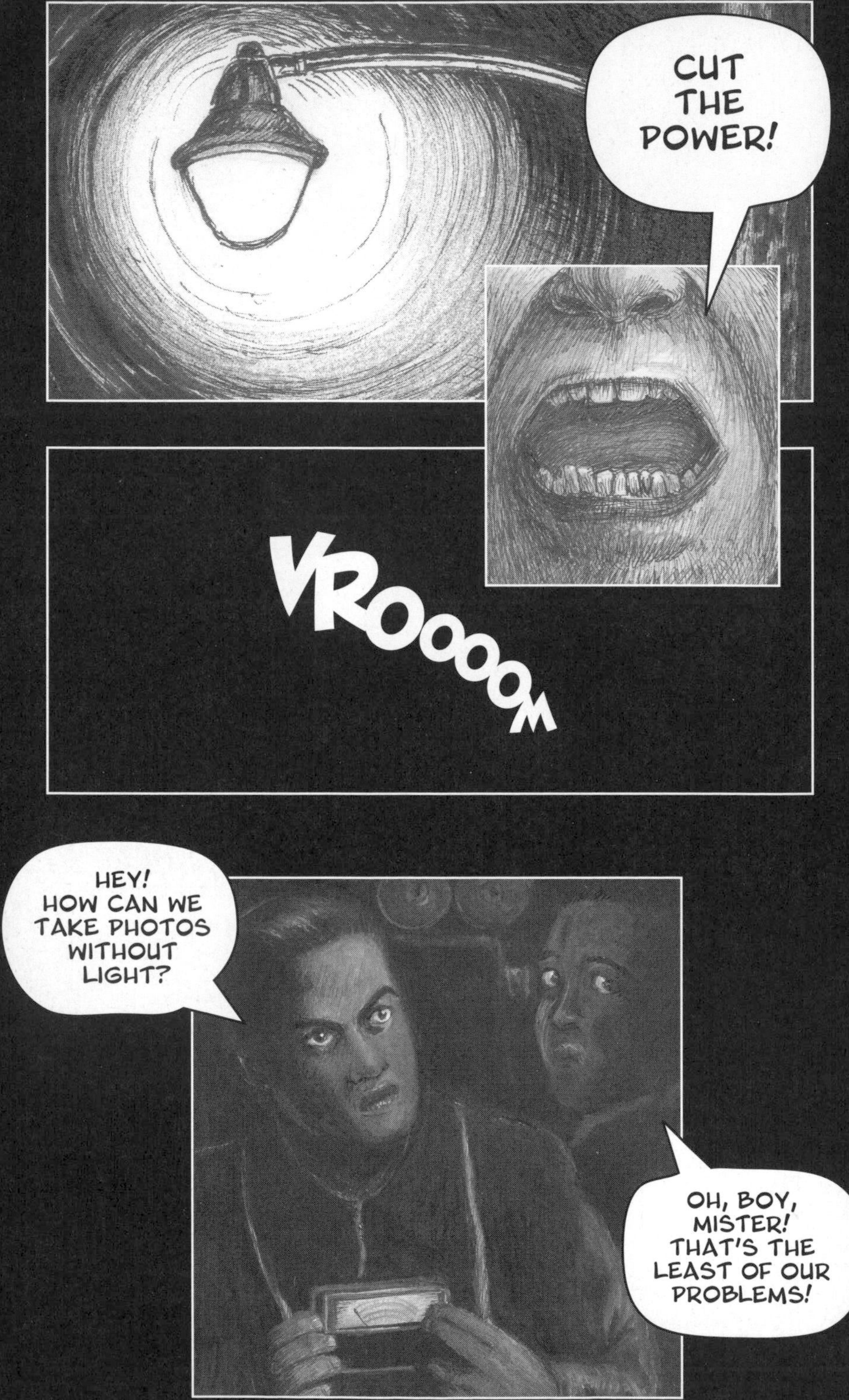
CUT THE POWER!
VROOOOOM
HEY! HOW CAN WE TAKE PHOTOS WITHOUT LIGHT?
OH, BOY, MISTER! THAT'S THE LEAST OF OUR PROBLEMS!

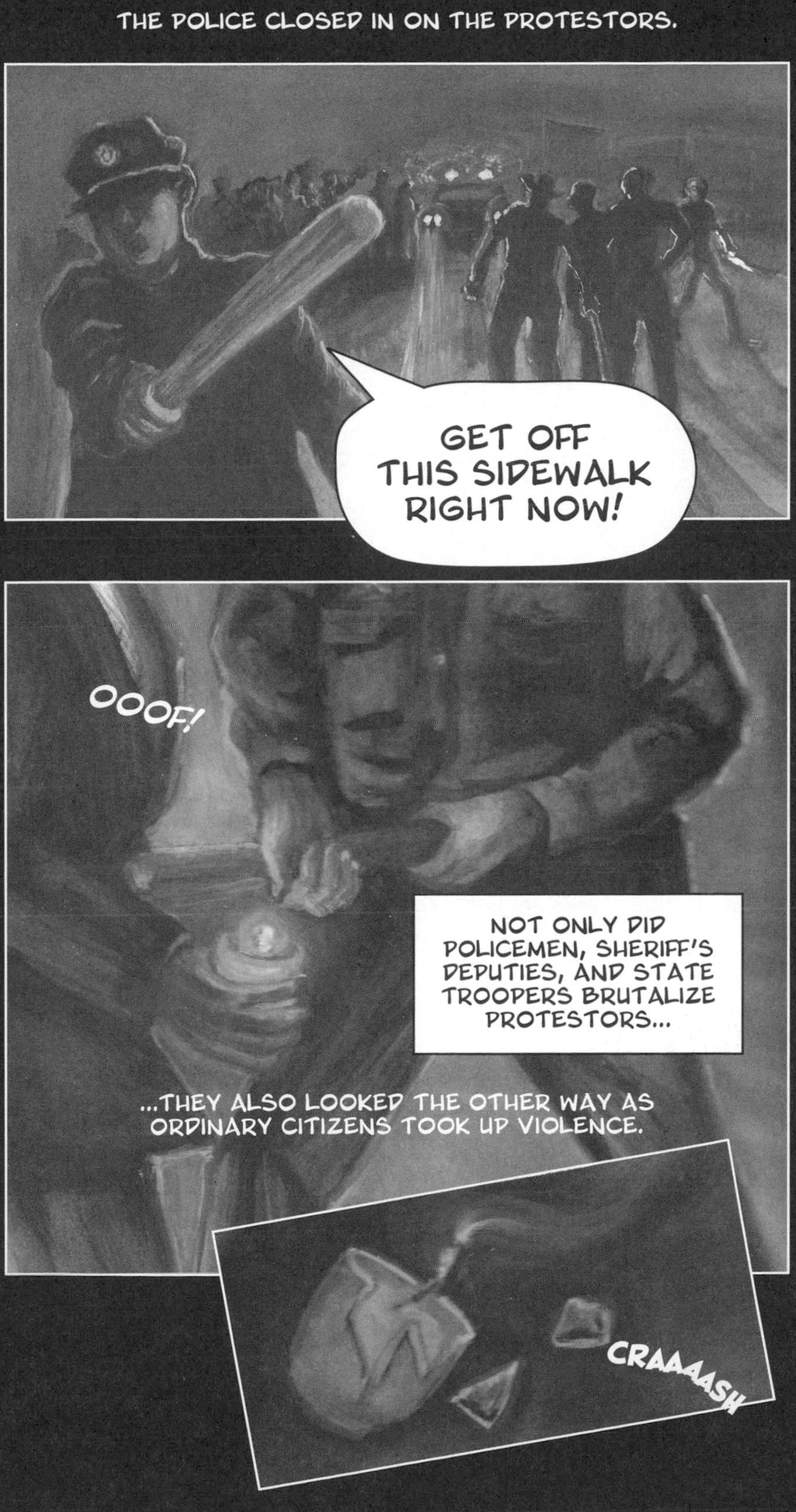
THE POLICE CLOSED IN ON THE PROTESTORS.
GET OFF THIS SIDEWALK RIGHT NOW!
OOOF!
NOT ONLY DID POLICEMEN, SHERIFF'S DEPUTIES, AND STATE TROOPERS BRUTALIZE PROTESTORS...
...THEY ALSO LOOKED THE OTHER WAY AS ORDINARY CITIZENS TOOK UP VIOLENCE.
CRAAAASH

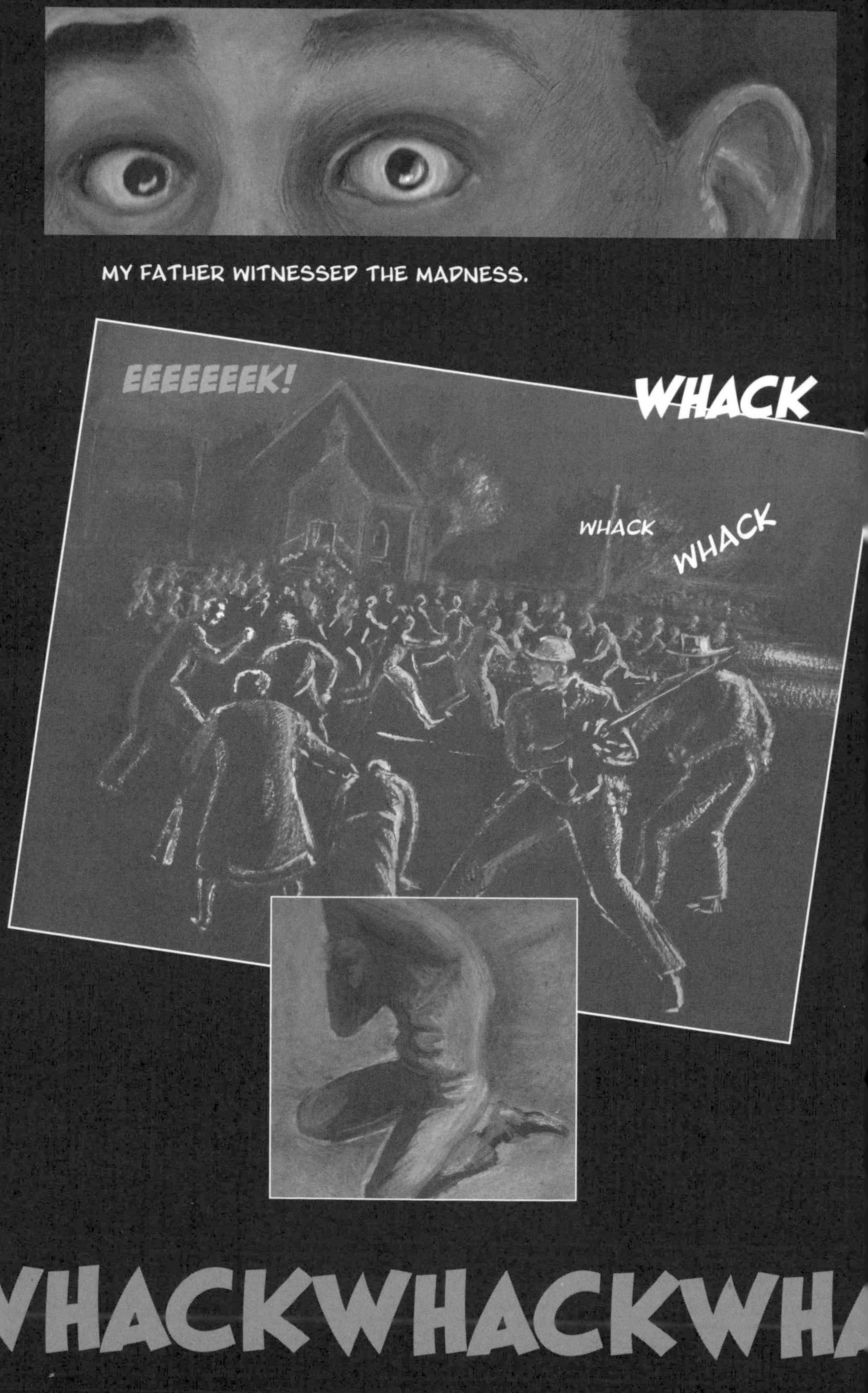
MY FATHER WITNESSED THE MADNESS.
EEEEEEEK!
WHACK
WHACK
WHACK
WHACKWHACKWHA

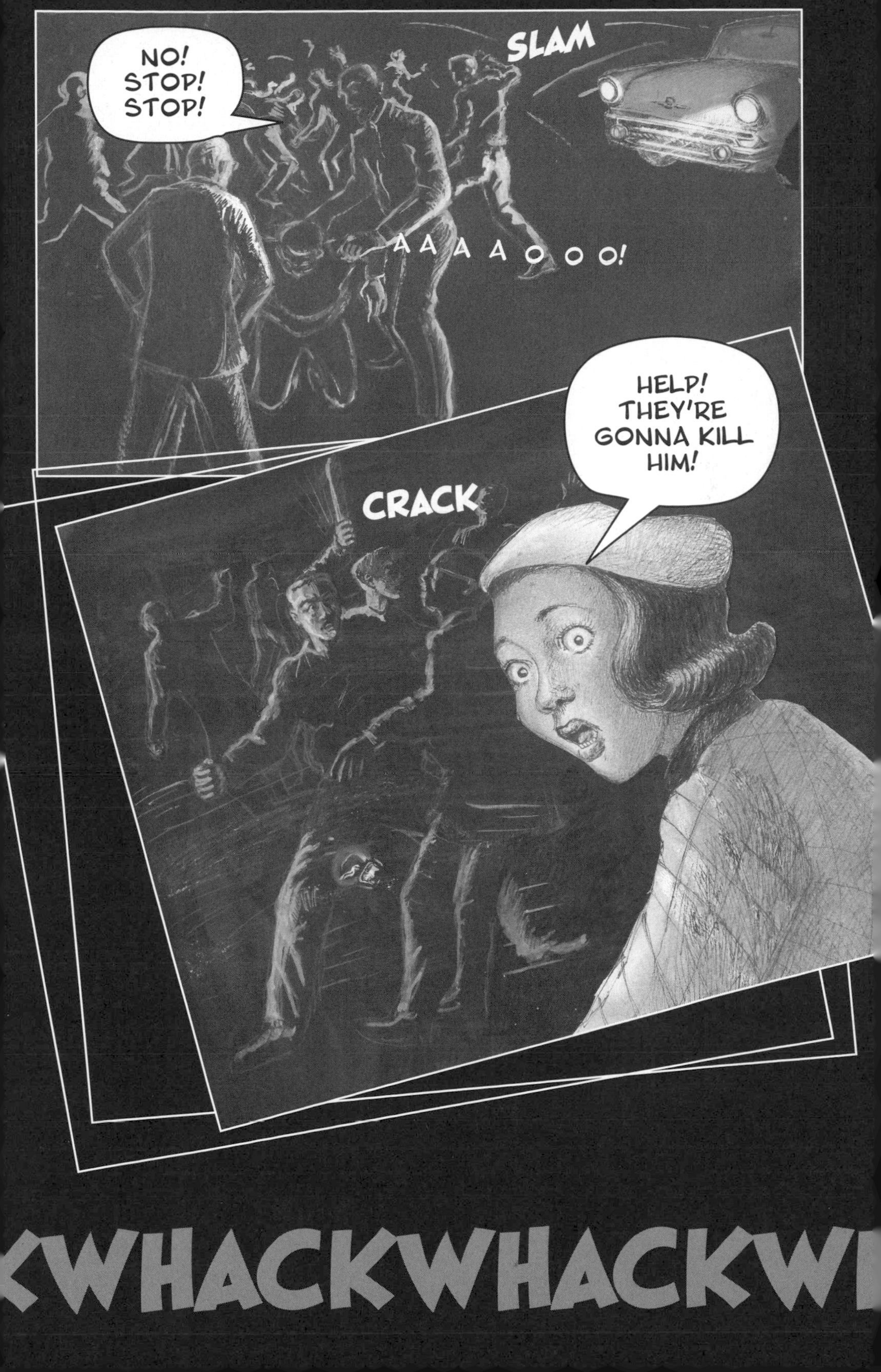
NO! STOP! STOP!
SLAM
AAAAOOO!
HELP! THEY'RE GONNA KILL HIM!
CRACK
WHACKWHACKWH

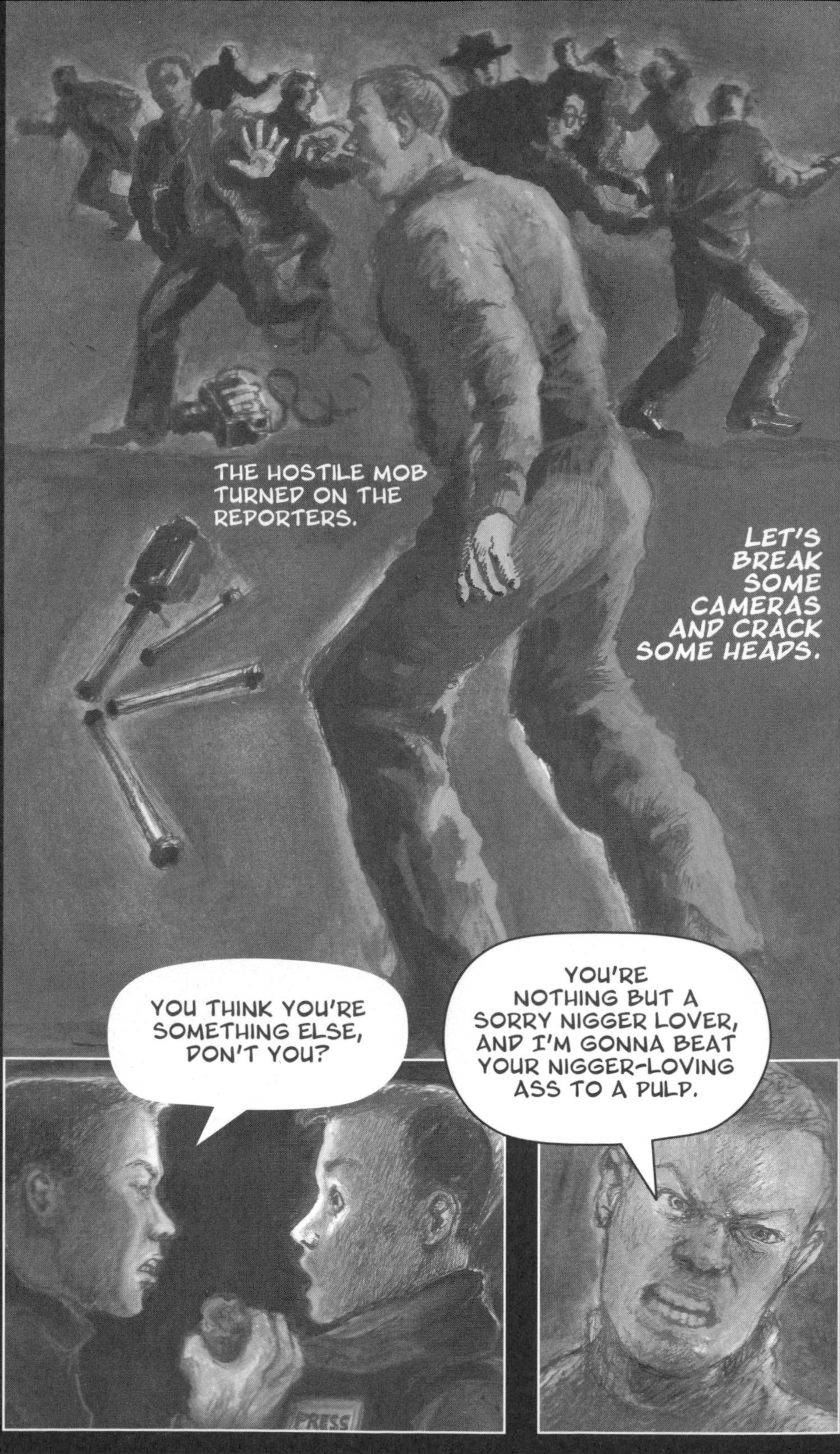
THE HOSTILE MOB TURNED ON THE REPORTERS.
LET'S BREAK SOME CAMERAS AND CRACK SOME HEADS.
YOU THINK YOU'RE SOMETHING ELSE, DON'T YOU?
YOU'RE NOTHING BUT A SORRY NIGGER LOVER, AND I'M GONNA BEAT YOUR NIGGER-LOVING ASS TO A PULP.
PRESS

THEY VANDALIZED PHOTOGRAPHIC EQUIPMENT.

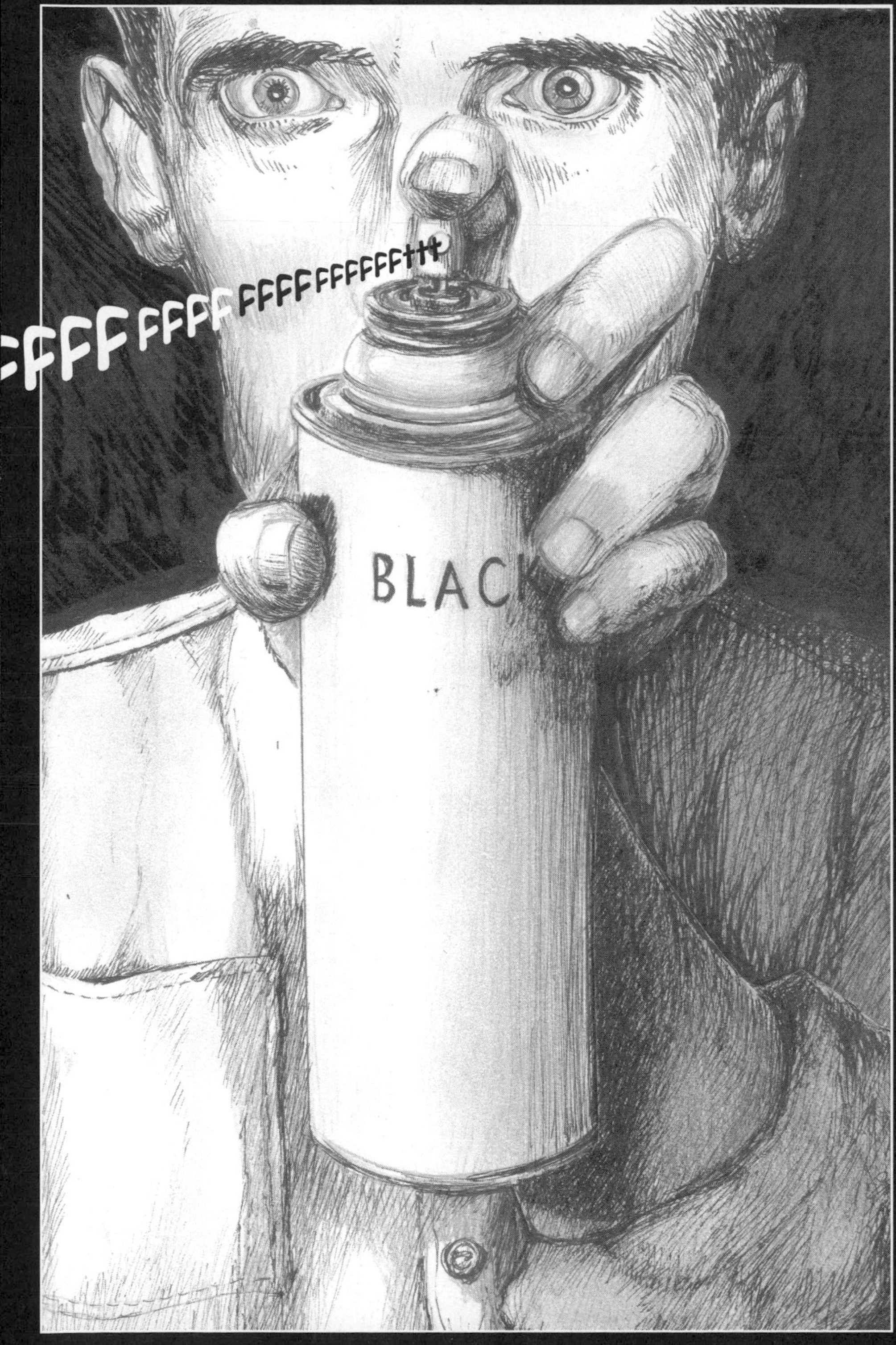
FFFFFFFFFFFFFFFFFFFFFFFtttt
BLAC

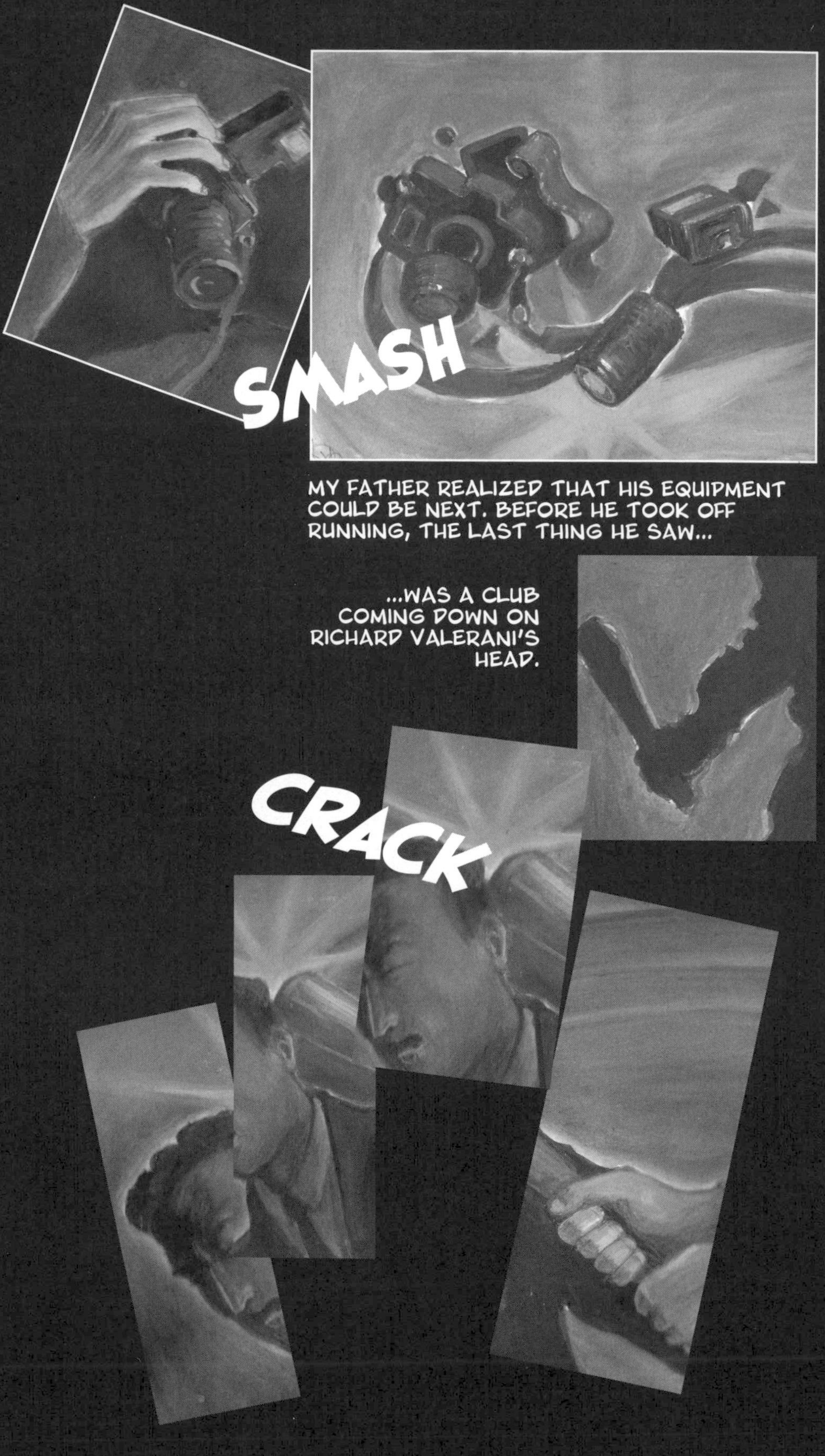
SMASH
MY FATHER REALIZED THAT HIS EQUIPMENT COULD BE NEXT. BEFORE HE TOOK OFF RUNNING, THE LAST THING HE SAW...
...WAS A CLUB COMING DOWN ON RICHARD VALERANI'S HEAD.
CRACK

THE MOB HARDLY PAUSED IN ITS RAMPAGE.

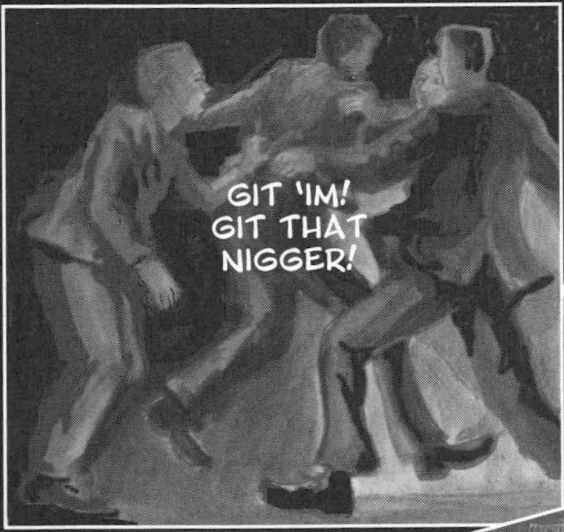
GIT 'IM! GIT THAT NIGGER!

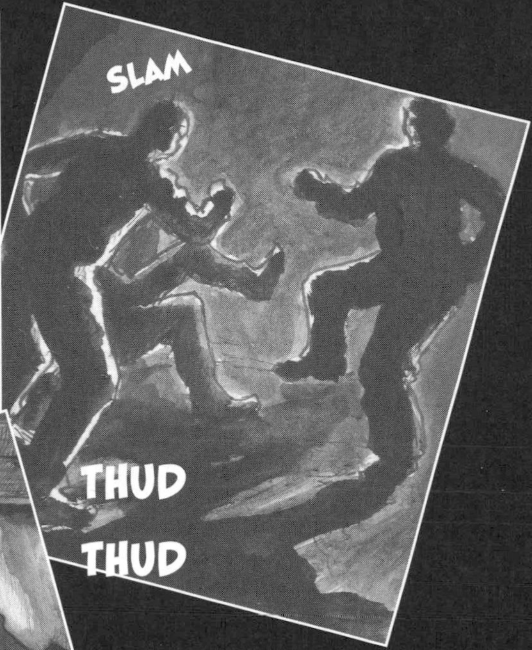
SLAM
THUD
THUD

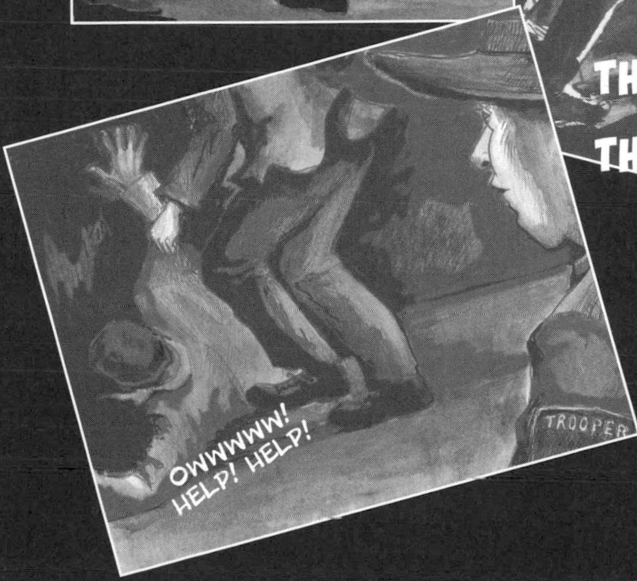
TROOPER
OWWWWW! HELP! HELP!

EYEWITNESS ACCOUNTS ARE CLEAR: POLICE OFTEN STOOD BY, GIVING TACIT APPROVAL.

IN THE MIDDLE OF THIS CHAOS, A YOUNG MAN NAMED JIMMIE LEE JACKSON HUSTLED HIS MOTHER AND GRANDFATHER TOWARD SAFETY.

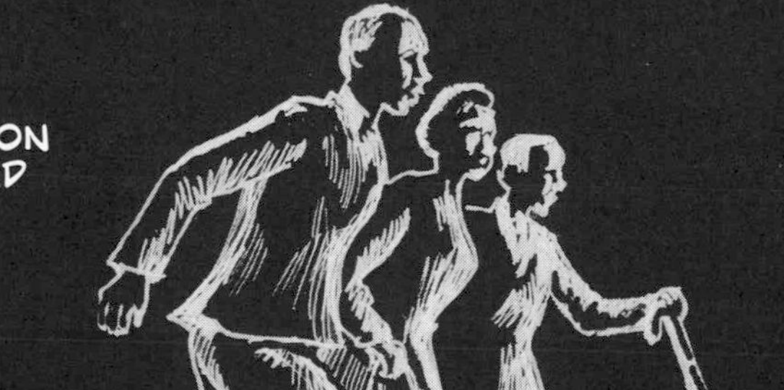

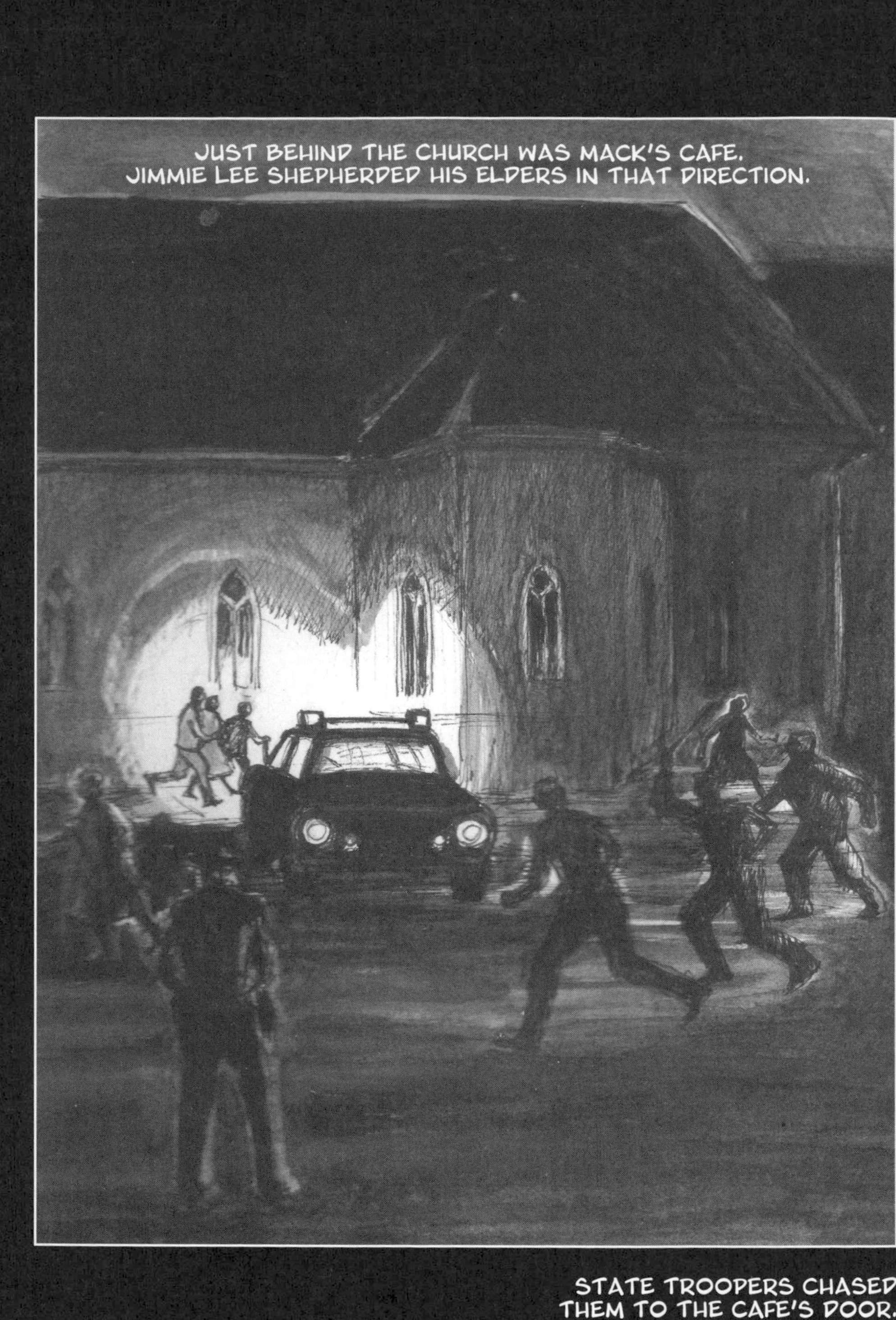
JUST BEHIND THE CHURCH WAS MACK'S CAFE.
JIMMIE LEE SHEPHERDED HIS ELDERS IN THAT DIRECTION.
STATE TROOPERS CHASED
THEM TO THE CAFE'S DOOR.

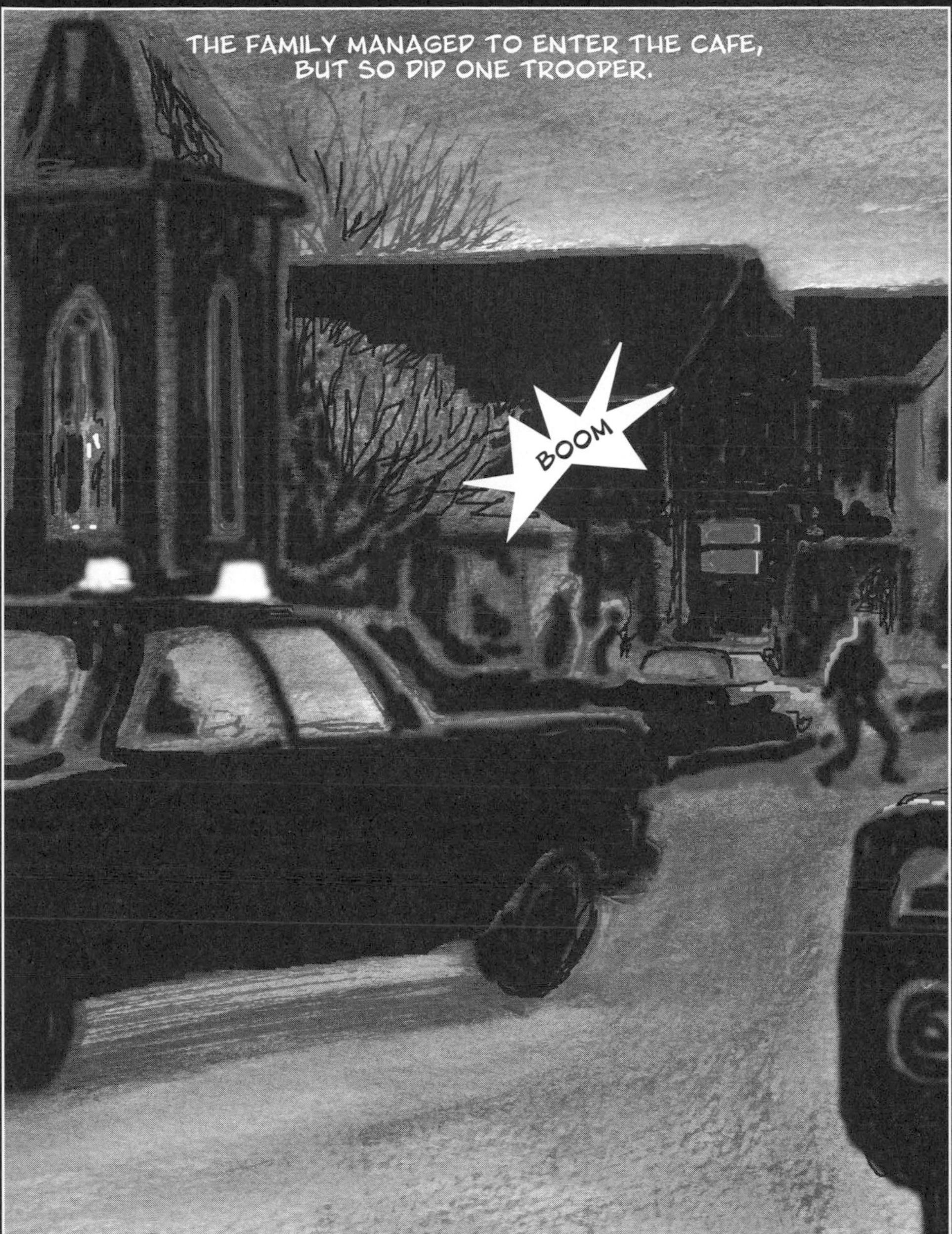
THE FAMILY MANAGED TO ENTER THE CAFE, BUT SO DID ONE TROOPER.
BOOM

A SHOT IN THE DARK.

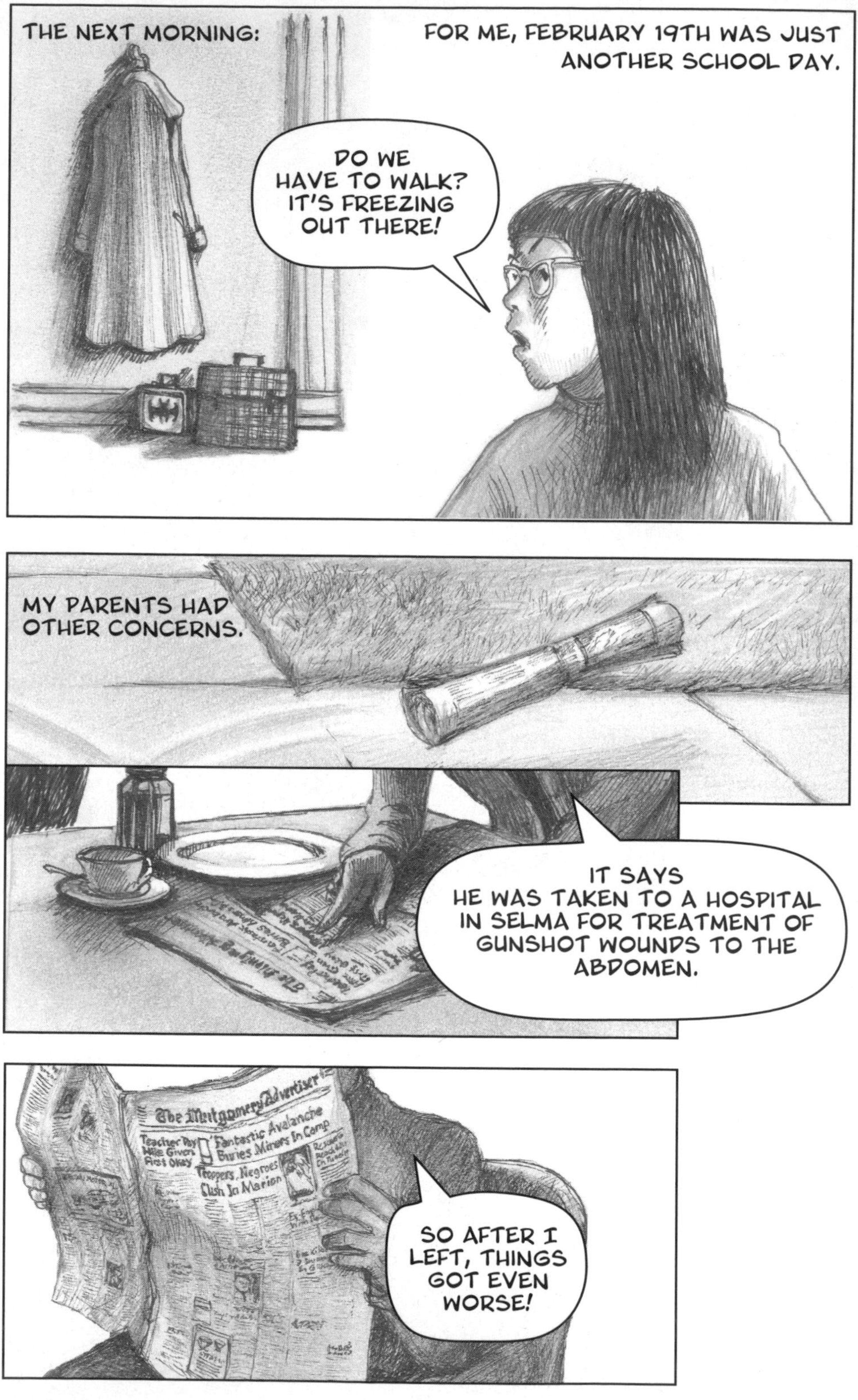
THE NEXT MORNING:
FOR ME, FEBRUARY 19TH WAS JUST ANOTHER SCHOOL DAY.
DO WE HAVE TO WALK? IT'S FREEZING OUT THERE!
MY PARENTS HAD OTHER CONCERNS.
IT SAYS HE WAS TAKEN TO A HOSPITAL IN SELMA FOR TREATMENT OF GUNSHOT WOUNDS TO THE ABDOMEN.
The Montgomery Advertiser
Fantastic Avalanche Buries Miners In Camp
Teacher Pay Hike Given First Okay
Troopers, Negroes Clash In Marion
SO AFTER I LEFT, THINGS GOT EVEN WORSE!

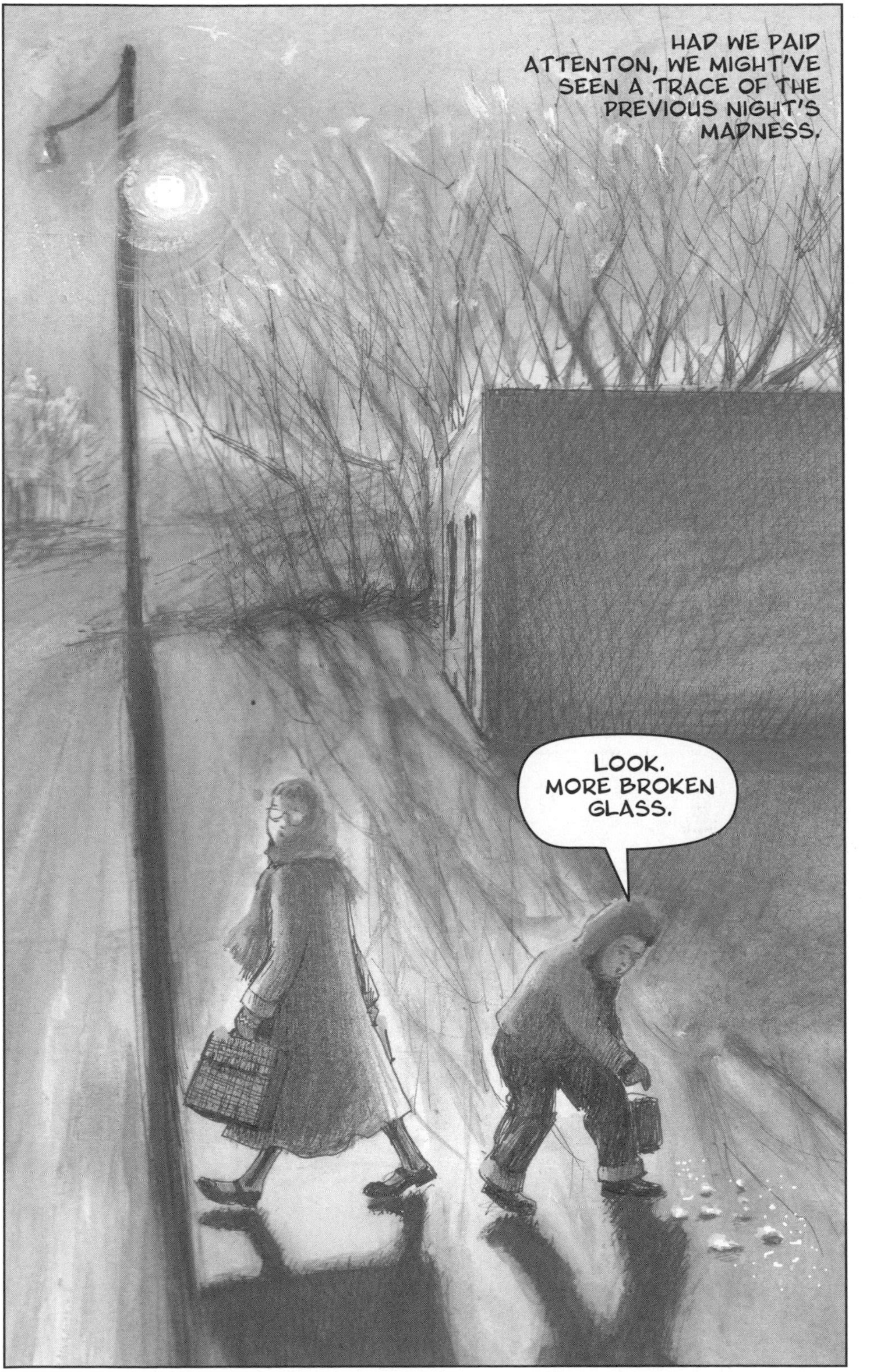
HAD WE PAID ATTENTON, WE MIGHT'VE SEEN A TRACE OF THE PREVIOUS NIGHT'S MADNESS.
LOOK. MORE BROKEN GLASS.

AT SCHOOL, THE INCIDENT RECEIVED LITTLE NOTICE.
BUT BY NOW, I KNEW WHAT SORT OF REACTION TO EXPECT.

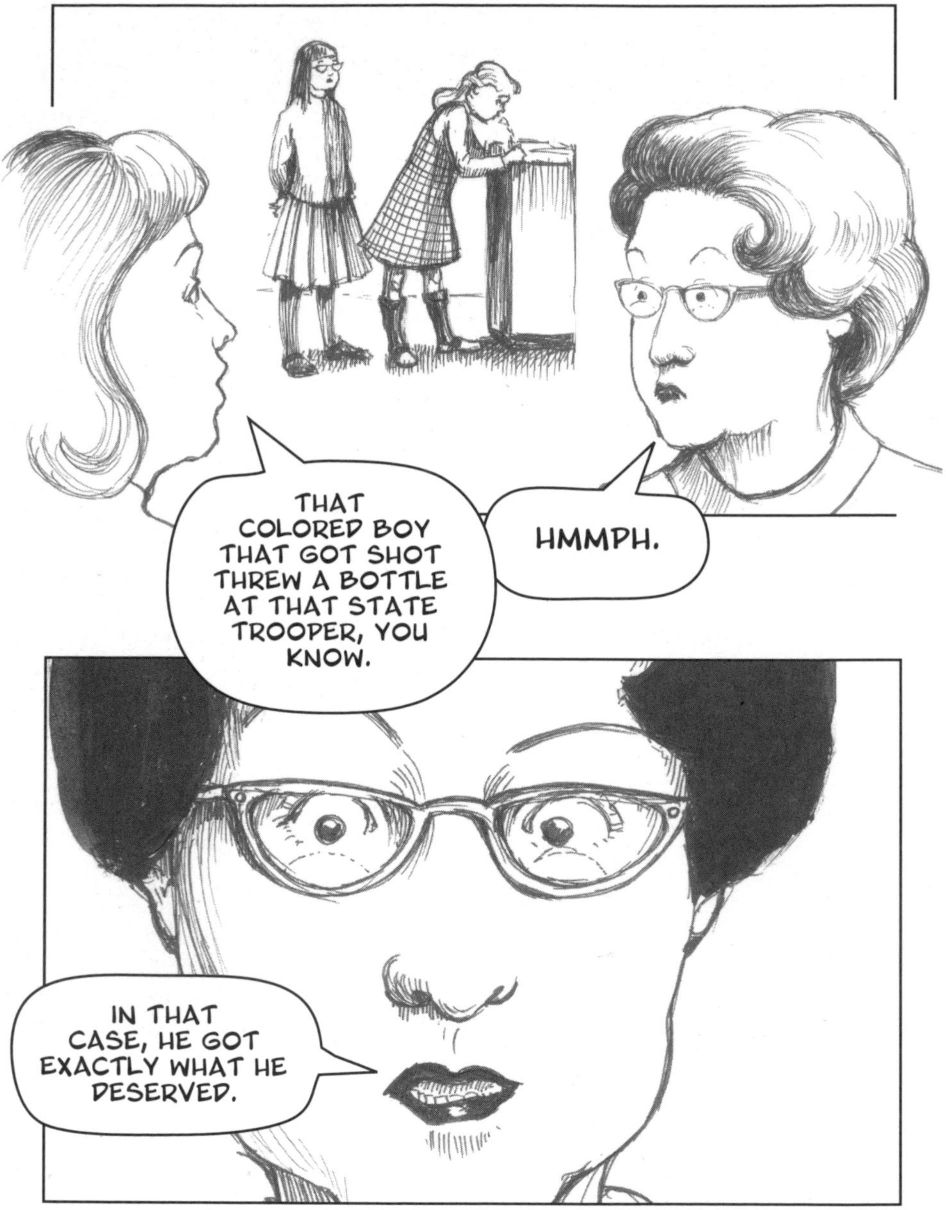
THAT COLORED BOY THAT GOT SHOT THREW A BOTTLE AT THAT STATE TROOPER, YOU KNOW.
HMMPH.
IN THAT CASE, HE GOT EXACTLY WHAT HE DESERVED.

FOR DECADES TO COME, THE STATE TROOPER WOULD INSIST THAT HE FIRED HIS GUN IN SELF-DEFENSE. THAT STORY PREVAILED AS THE OFFICIAL NARRATIVE FOR OVER FORTY YEARS UNTIL 2007, WHEN HE RECEIVED A GRAND-JURY INDICTMENT. HE EVENTUALLY PLED GUILTY TO A CHARGE OF 2ND-DEGREE MANSLAUGHTER.

EVEN BEFORE JACKSON DIED,
THE BLACK COMMUNITY SEETHED WITH
INDIGNATION AT THE CLAIM OF
SELF-DEFENSE.

Negro Shot Eight Days Ag
Succumbs In Selma Hospital

By REX THOMAS
SELMA, Ala. (AP) — A Ne-
gro who said he was shot by a
state trooper during a bloody
night of racial violence became
the first fatality Friday in Alabama's new civil rights strug-

when about 400 Negroes left
a church and started marching
to a county courthouse.
    Jackson, who also had a two-
inch gash on his head and
bruises on his back, told ho
tal attendants that he w
beaten by a troop

THEN NEWS CAME THAT
HE'D LOST THE FIGHT.

JIMMIE LEE
JACKSON,
DEAD AT 26.

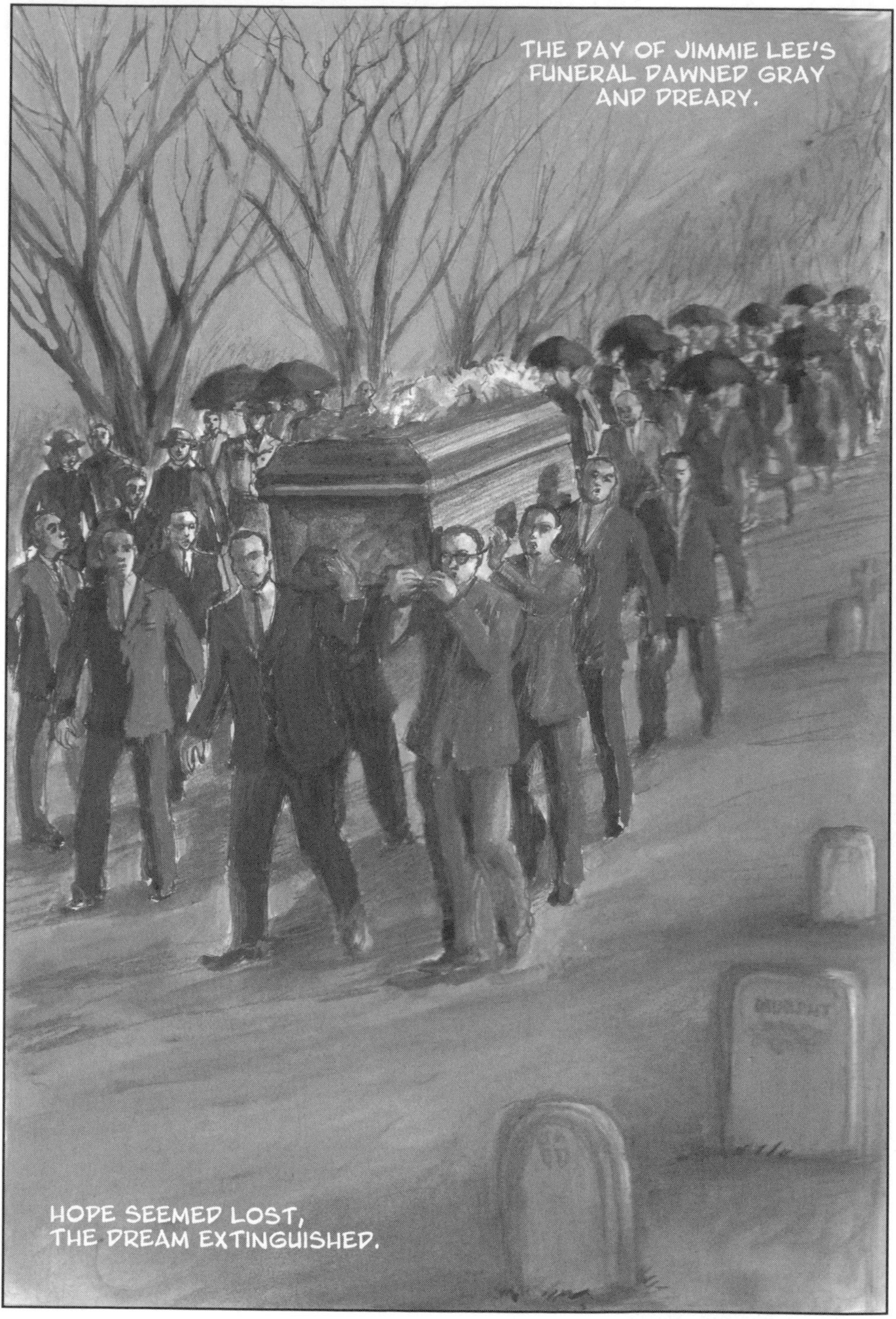
THE DAY OF JIMMIE LEE'S FUNERAL DAWNED GRAY AND DREARY.
HOPE SEEMED LOST, THE DREAM EXTINGUISHED.

AS THINGS STOOD, THE VOTER-REGISTRATION DRIVE HAD YIELDED SO LITTLE PROGRESS.

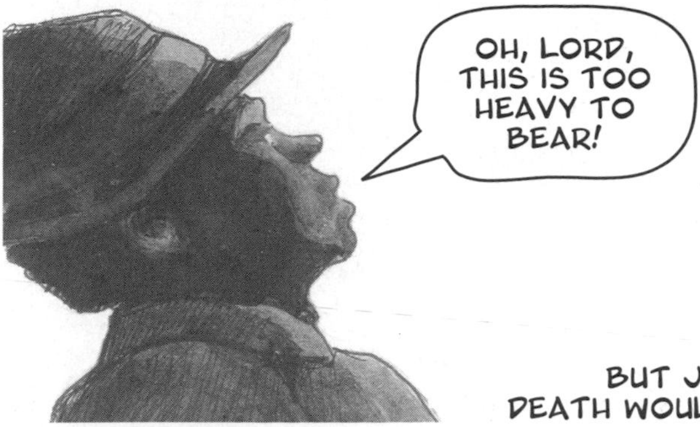
OH, LORD, THIS IS TOO HEAVY TO BEAR!

BUT JIMMIE LEE JACKSON'S DEATH WOULDN'T BE FORGOTTEN.

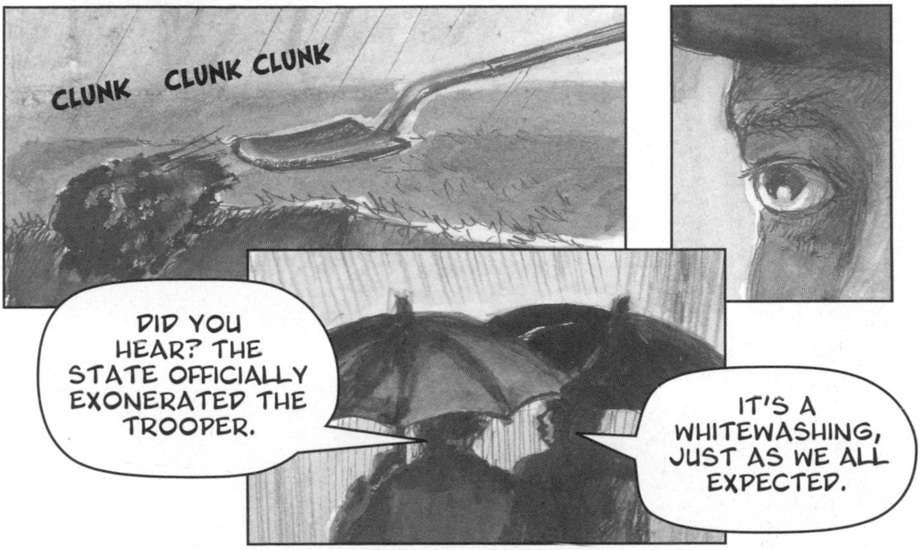
CLUNK CLUNK CLUNK
DID YOU HEAR? THE STATE OFFICIALLY EXONERATED THE TROOPER.
IT'S A WHITEWASHING, JUST AS WE ALL EXPECTED.

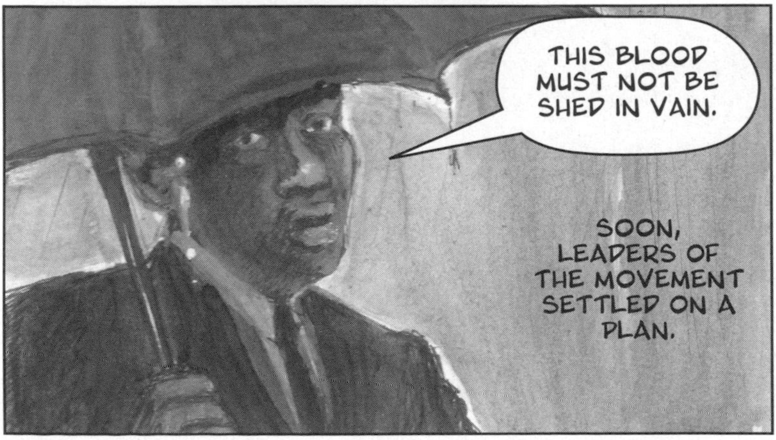
THIS BLOOD MUST NOT BE SHED IN VAIN.
SOON, LEADERS OF THE MOVEMENT SETTLED ON A PLAN.

THEY WOULD MARCH FROM SELMA TO MONTGOMERY BY THE HUNDREDS. WASHINGTON COULDN'T IGNORE THAT.

SELMA CHANGED EVERYTHING.

LEFT TURN LANE
80 THRU THIS LANE
EDMUND PETTUS BRIDGE 15'-1"

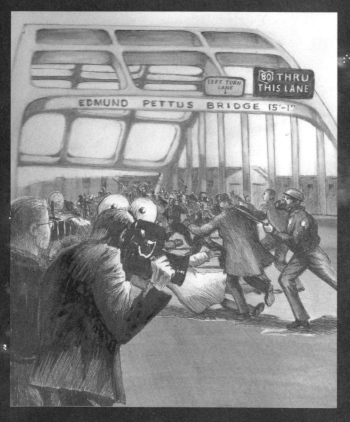

ON MARCH 7, 1965, THE FIRST ATTEMPT TO MARCH TO MONTGOMERY EXPOSED SOUTHERN POLICE BRUTALITY AS NEVER BEFORE.

THE SUN SHONE. CAMERAS ROLLED. ALABAMA STATE TROOPERS BEAT MARCHERS IN PLAIN VIEW.

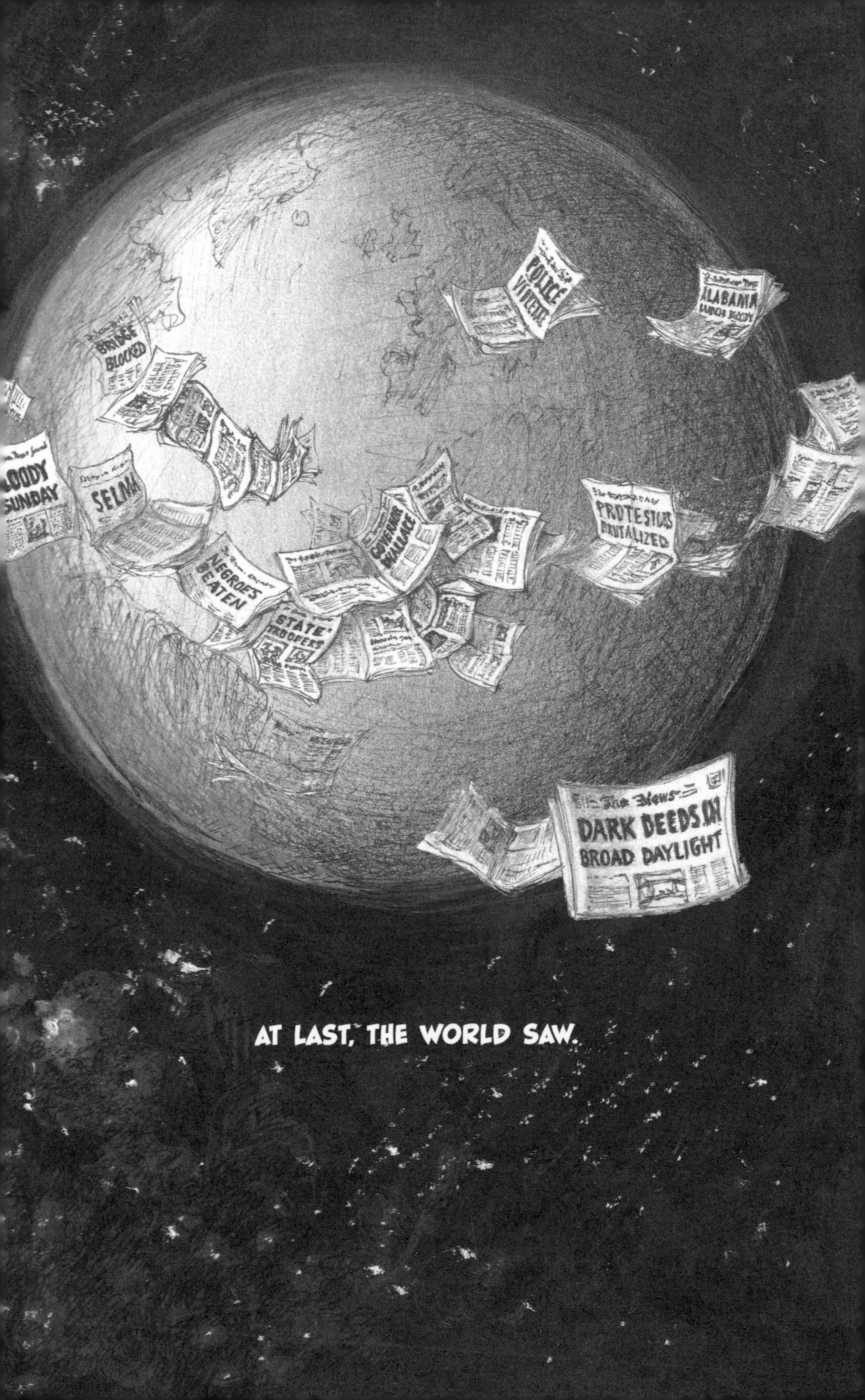
BRIDGE BLOCKED
POLICE VIOLENCE
ALABAMA
PROTESTORS BRUTALIZED
NEGROES BEATEN
STATE TROOPERS
The News
DARK DEEDS IN BROAD DAYLIGHT
AT LAST, THE WORLD SAW.

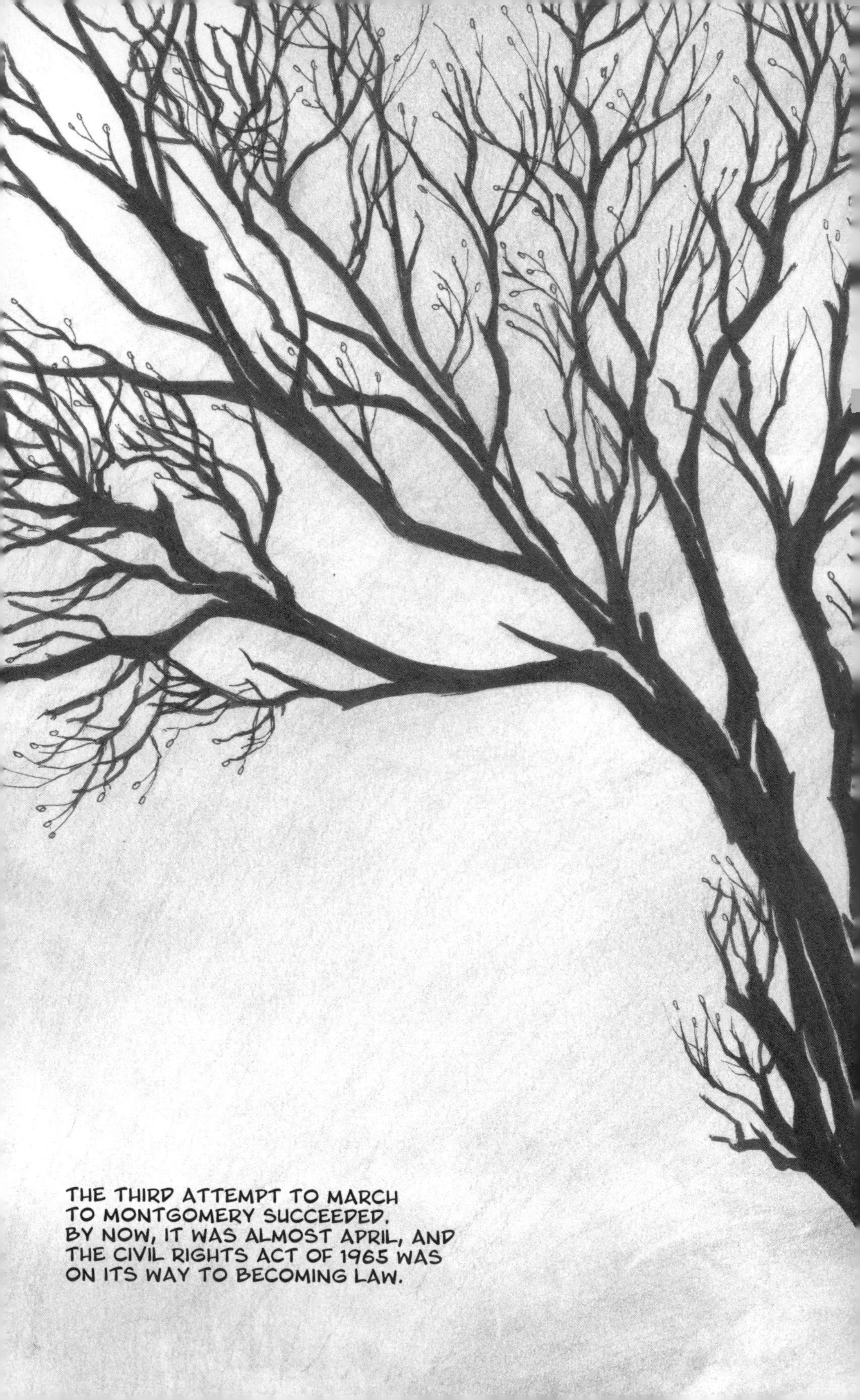
THE THIRD ATTEMPT TO MARCH TO MONTGOMERY SUCCEEDED. BY NOW, IT WAS ALMOST APRIL, AND THE CIVIL RIGHTS ACT OF 1965 WAS ON ITS WAY TO BECOMING LAW.

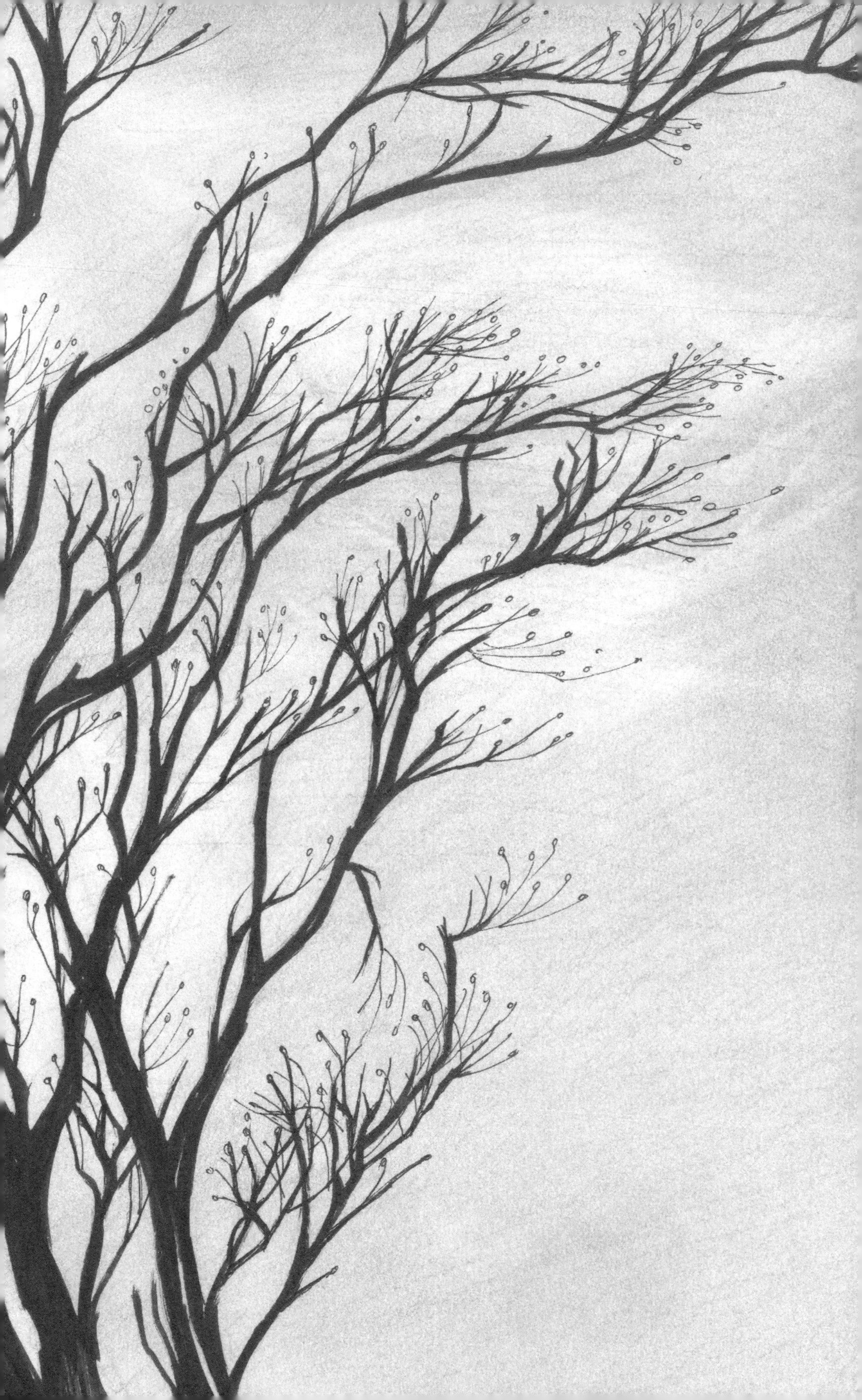

chapter 9
KNOW ALABAMA

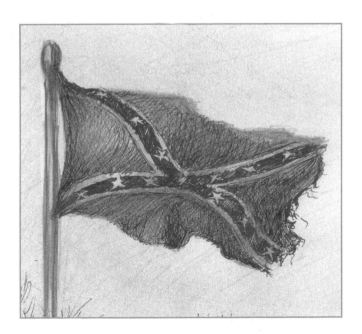

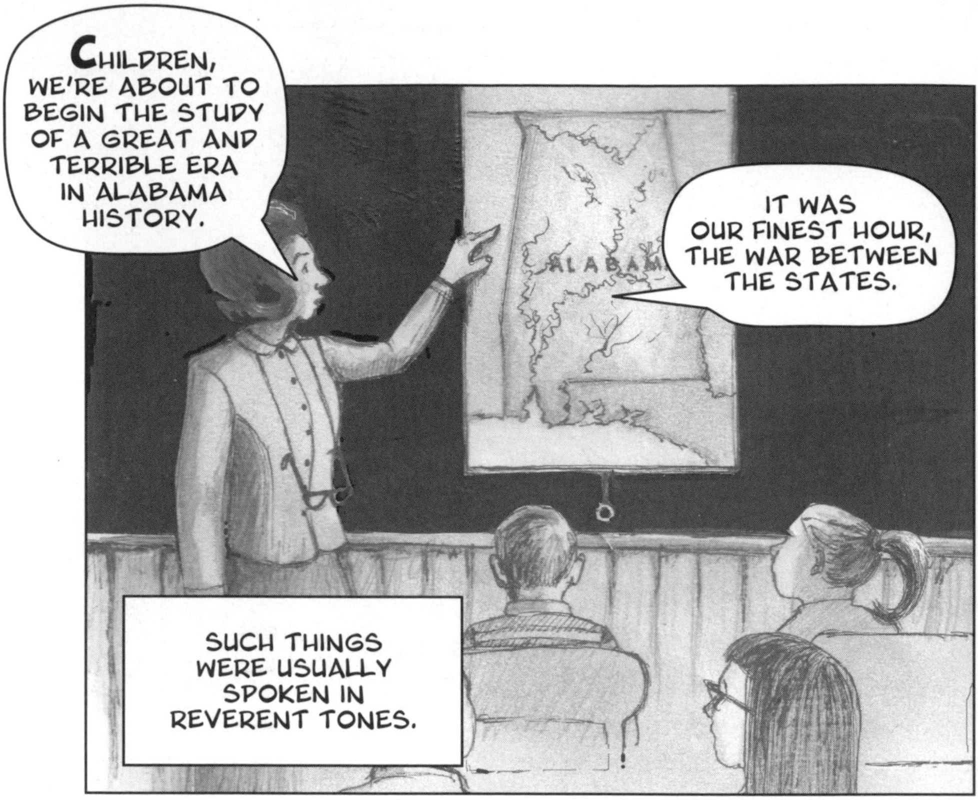
CHILDREN, WE'RE ABOUT TO BEGIN THE STUDY OF A GREAT AND TERRIBLE ERA IN ALABAMA HISTORY.
ALABAMA
IT WAS OUR FINEST HOUR, THE WAR BETWEEN THE STATES.
SUCH THINGS WERE USUALLY SPOKEN IN REVERENT TONES.

BY THE TIME MY 4TH-GRADE TEACHER PASSED OUT OUR KNOW ALABAMA TEXTBOOKS, TOO MUCH HAD HAPPENED FOR ME TO SWALLOW EVERYTHING THE AUTHORS CLAIMED.

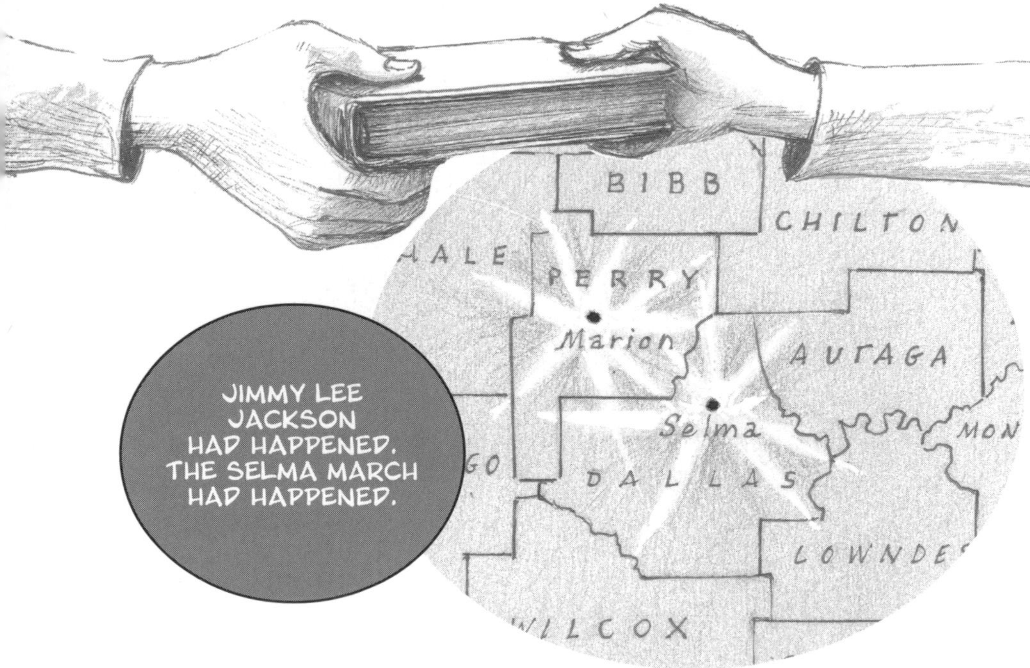
BIBB
CHILTON
PERRY
Marion
AUTAGA
Selma
DALLAS
JIMMY LEE JACKSON HAD HAPPENED. THE SELMA MARCH HAD HAPPENED.

I'D WITNESSED SEGREGATION; I'D SEEN RACISM.

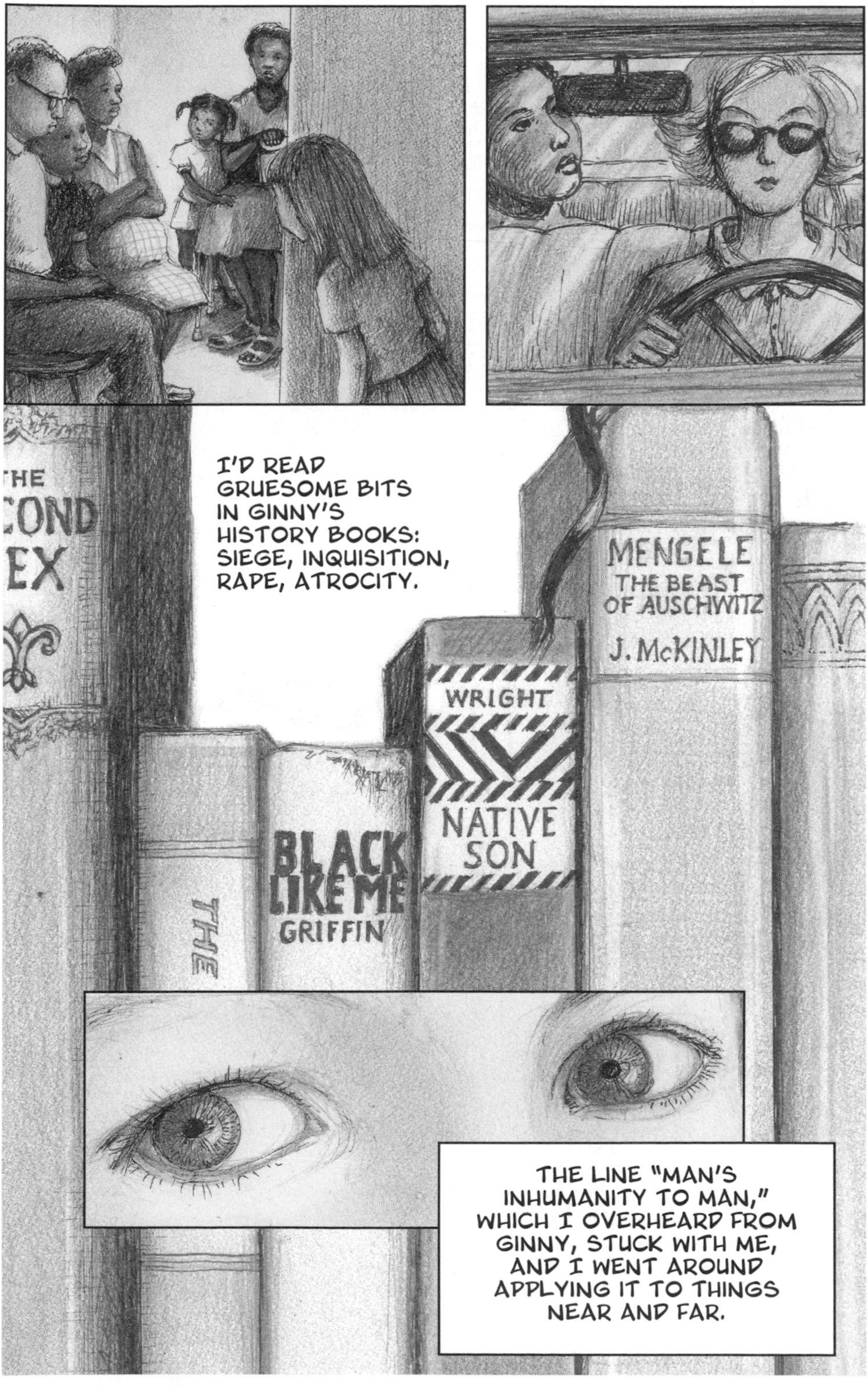

I'D READ GRUESOME BITS IN GINNY'S HISTORY BOOKS: SIEGE, INQUISITION, RAPE, ATROCITY.
MENGELE
THE BEAST OF AUSCHWITZ
J. McKINLEY
WRIGHT
NATIVE SON
BLACK LIKE ME
GRIFFIN
THE
THE LINE "MAN'S INHUMANITY TO MAN," WHICH I OVERHEARD FROM GINNY, STUCK WITH ME, AND I WENT AROUND APPLYING IT TO THINGS NEAR AND FAR.

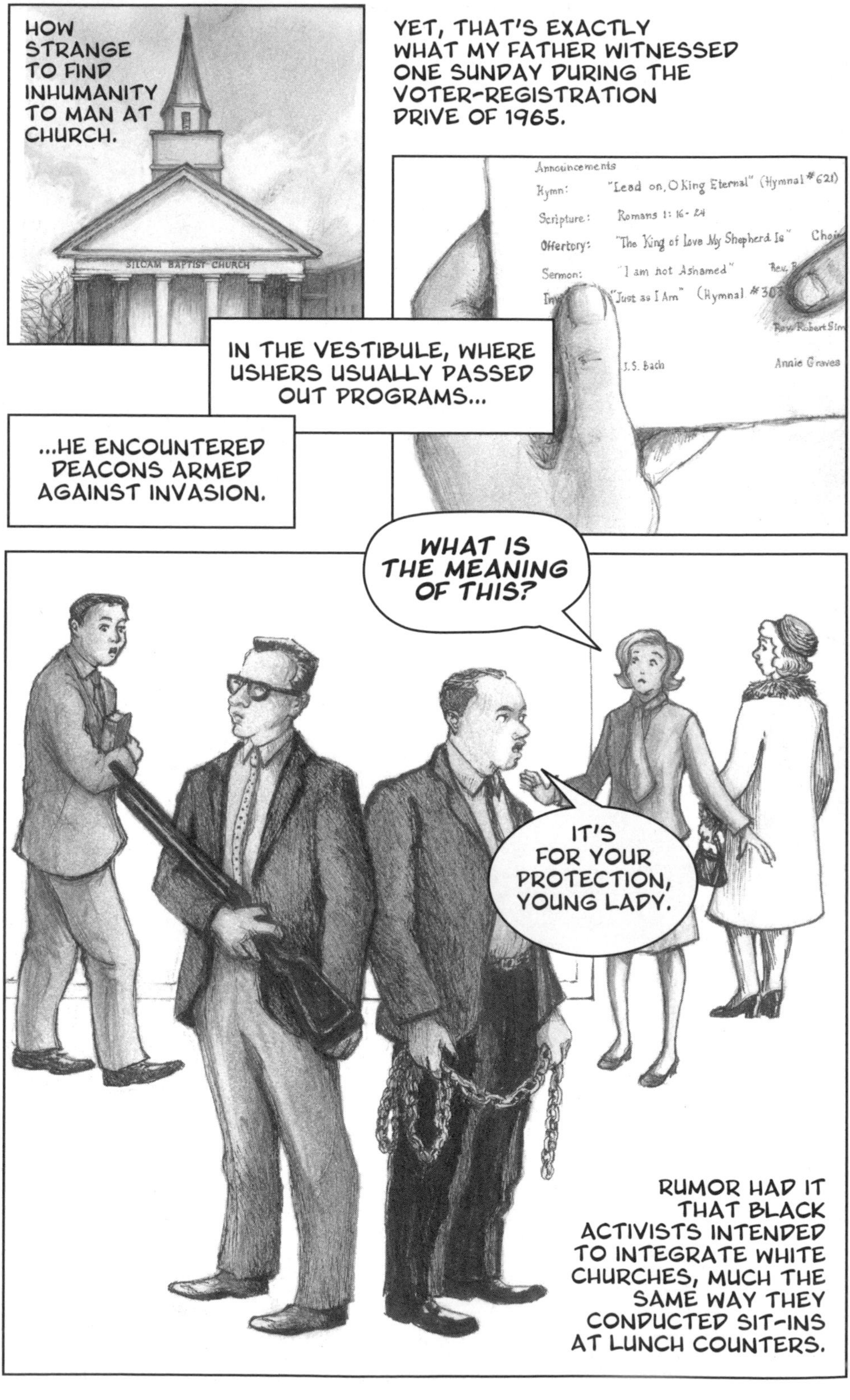
HOW STRANGE TO FIND INHUMANITY TO MAN AT CHURCH.
SILOAM BAPTIST CHURCH
YET, THAT'S EXACTLY WHAT MY FATHER WITNESSED ONE SUNDAY DURING THE VOTER-REGISTRATION DRIVE OF 1965.
Announcements
Hymn: "Lead on, O King Eternal" (Hymnal #621)
Scripture: Romans 1: 16-24
Offertory: "The King of Love My Shepherd Is"
Sermon: "I am not Ashamed"
"Just as I Am" (Hymnal
J.S. Bach
Annie Graves
IN THE VESTIBULE, WHERE USHERS USUALLY PASSED OUT PROGRAMS...
...HE ENCOUNTERED DEACONS ARMED AGAINST INVASION.
WHAT IS THE MEANING OF THIS?
IT'S FOR YOUR PROTECTION, YOUNG LADY.
RUMOR HAD IT THAT BLACK ACTIVISTS INTENDED TO INTEGRATE WHITE CHURCHES, MUCH THE SAME WAY THEY CONDUCTED SIT-INS AT LUNCH COUNTERS.

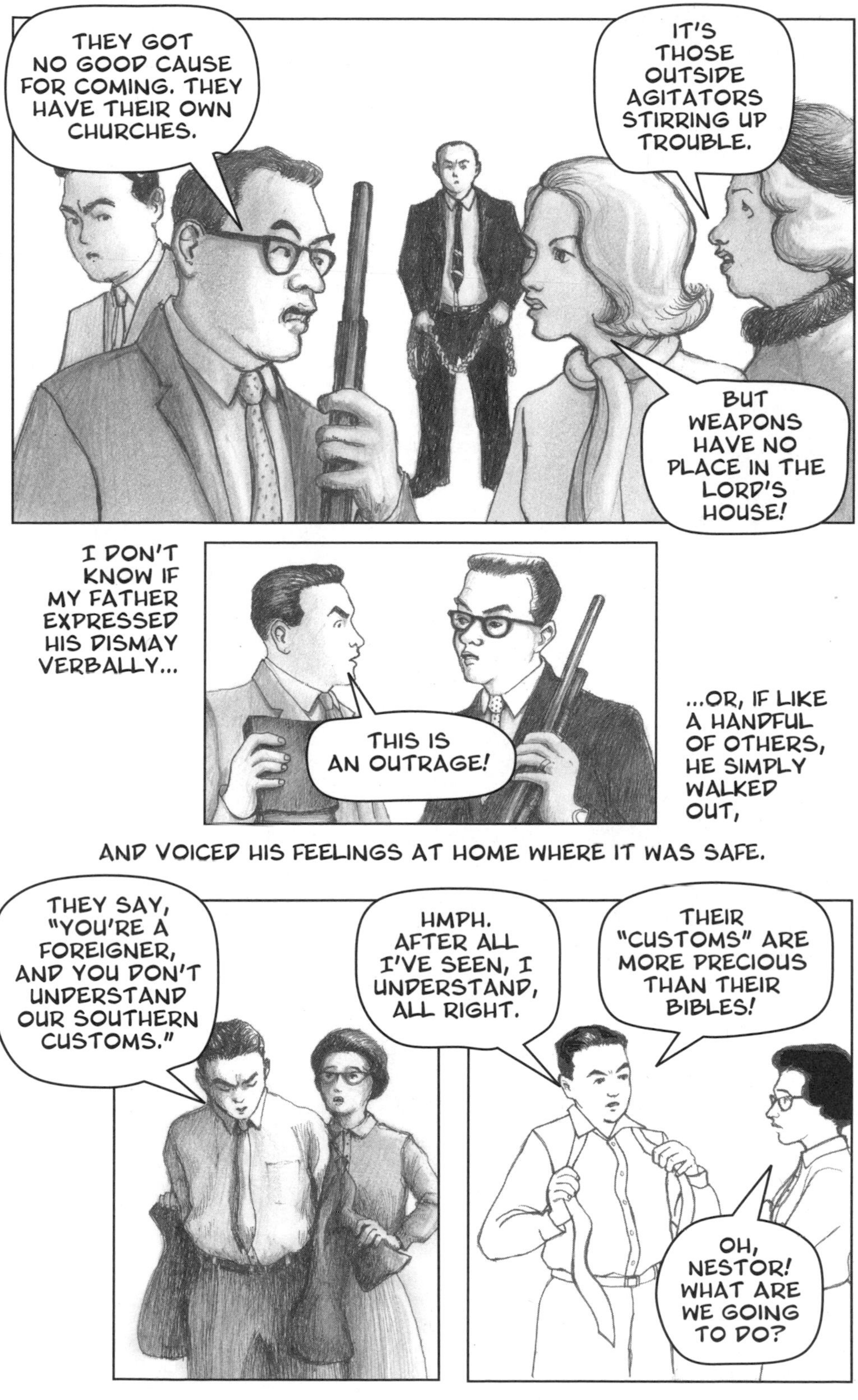
THEY GOT NO GOOD CAUSE FOR COMING. THEY HAVE THEIR OWN CHURCHES.
IT'S THOSE OUTSIDE AGITATORS STIRRING UP TROUBLE.
BUT WEAPONS HAVE NO PLACE IN THE LORD'S HOUSE!
I DON'T KNOW IF MY FATHER EXPRESSED HIS DISMAY VERBALLY...
THIS IS AN OUTRAGE!
...OR, IF LIKE A HANDFUL OF OTHERS, HE SIMPLY WALKED OUT,
AND VOICED HIS FEELINGS AT HOME WHERE IT WAS SAFE.
THEY SAY, "YOU'RE A FOREIGNER, AND YOU DON'T UNDERSTAND OUR SOUTHERN CUSTOMS."
HMPH. AFTER ALL I'VE SEEN, I UNDERSTAND, ALL RIGHT.
THEIR "CUSTOMS" ARE MORE PRECIOUS THAN THEIR BIBLES!
OH, NESTOR! WHAT ARE WE GOING TO DO?

AT THE FAR END OF WASHINGTON STREET, WHERE MY FATHER WOULD HEAD NEXT, THE METHODISTS HAD THEIR HANDS FULL WITH AN OUTSPOKEN MINISTER.

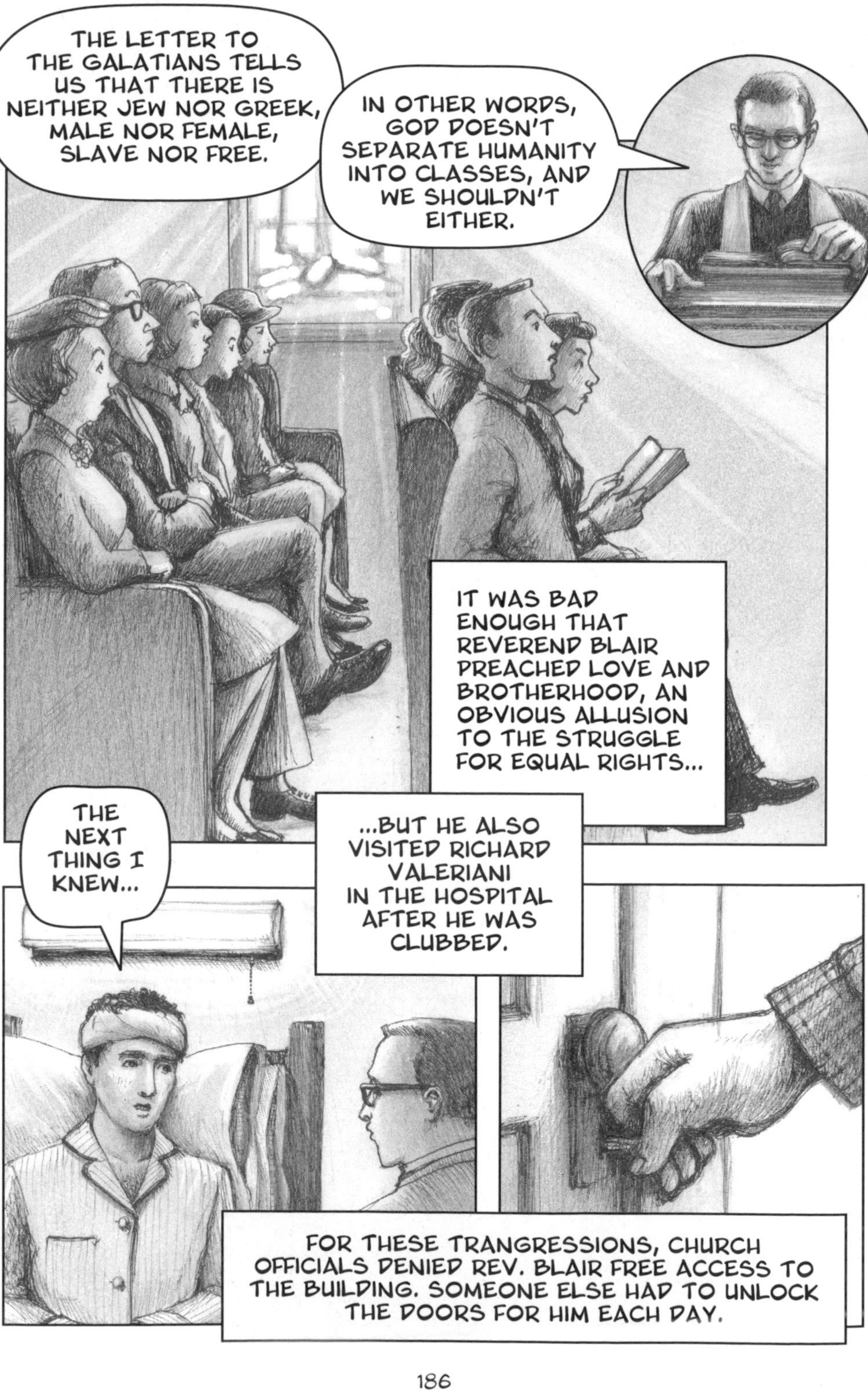

THE LETTER TO THE GALATIANS TELLS US THAT THERE IS NEITHER JEW NOR GREEK, MALE NOR FEMALE, SLAVE NOR FREE.
IN OTHER WORDS, GOD DOESN'T SEPARATE HUMANITY INTO CLASSES, AND WE SHOULDN'T EITHER.
IT WAS BAD ENOUGH THAT REVEREND BLAIR PREACHED LOVE AND BROTHERHOOD, AN OBVIOUS ALLUSION TO THE STRUGGLE FOR EQUAL RIGHTS...
...BUT HE ALSO VISITED RICHARD VALERIANI IN THE HOSPITAL AFTER HE WAS CLUBBED.
THE NEXT THING I KNEW...
FOR THESE TRANGRESSIONS, CHURCH OFFICIALS DENIED REV. BLAIR FREE ACCESS TO THE BUILDING. SOMEONE ELSE HAD TO UNLOCK THE DOORS FOR HIM EACH DAY.

SO THE METHODISTS DIDN'T PAN OUT EITHER, AND MY FATHER ABANDONED CHURCH ATTENDANCE FOR YEARS TO COME.

HE DEVOTED HIMSELF TO OTHER PASSIONS, SUCH AS THE POSTGRADUATE STUDY OF ROMANCE LANGUAGES.

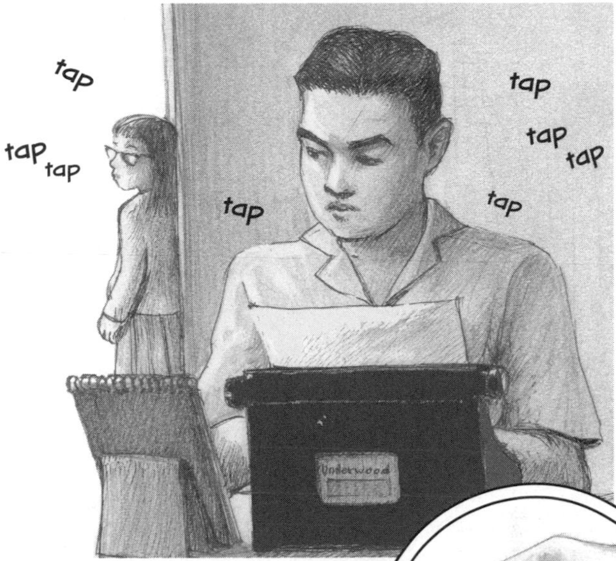
tap
tap
tap
tap
tap
tap
tap
tap
Underwood

HE TOOK PHOTOS.

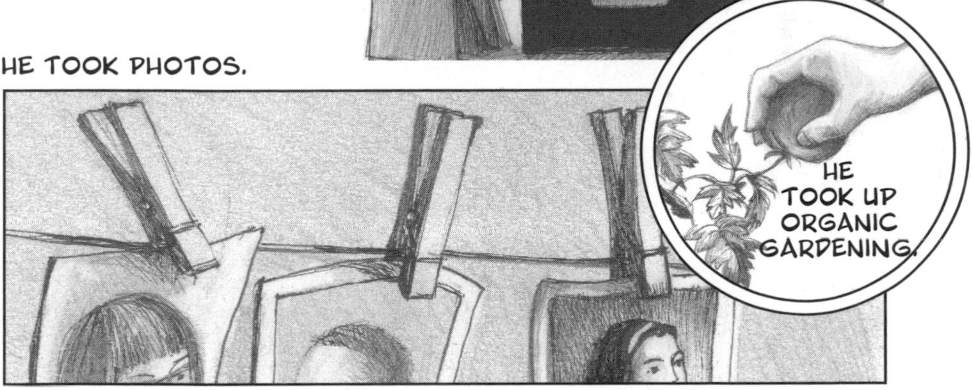
HE TOOK UP ORGANIC GARDENING.

HE ENFORCED A HOUSEHOLD STANDARD OF ACADEMIC DEVOTION.

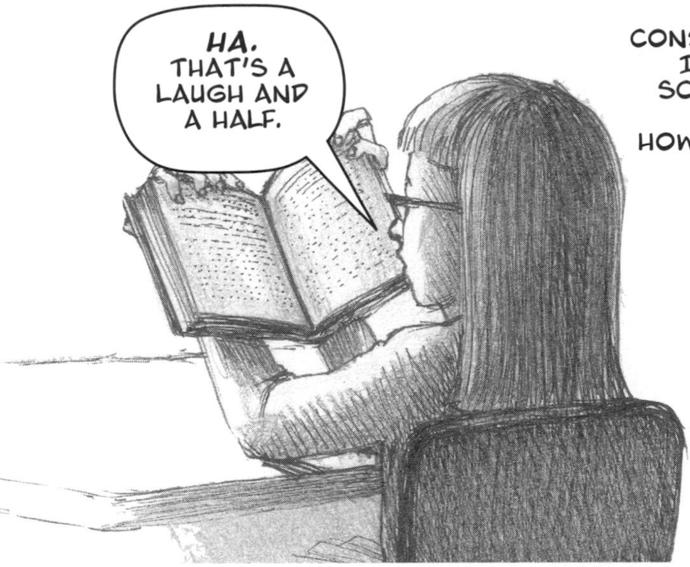
HA. THAT'S A LAUGH AND A HALF.

CONSEQUENTLY, I DID ALL MY SCHOOLWORK, NO MATTER HOW AWFUL THE TEXTBOOK, WHICH WAS ESPECIALLY TRUE OF *KNOW ALABAMA*.

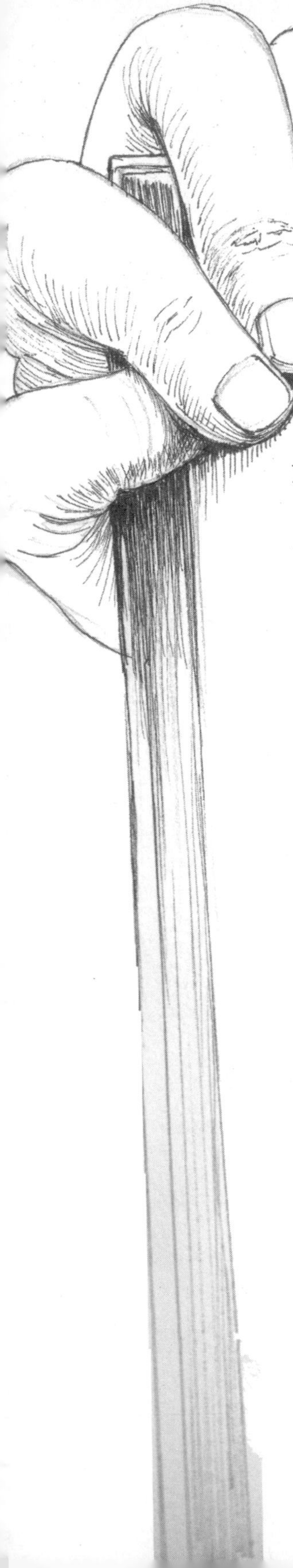

[THE FOLLOWING EXCERPTS COME FROM THE TEXT OF *KNOW ALABAMA*, EXCLUDING ILLUSTRATIONS.]

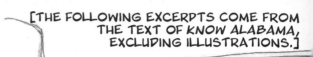

CHAPTER VIII
PLANTATION LIFE

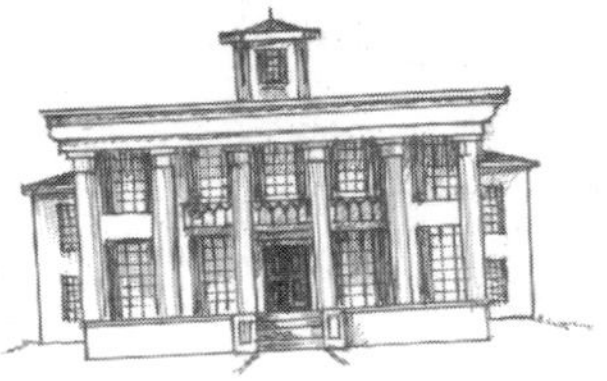

Now we have come to the happiest way of life in Alabama before the War Between the States.

Now suppose you were a little boy or girl and lived in one of the plantation homes many years ago. You wake up early in the morning, bathe, dress, and run down the long stairs to have breakfast with your family.

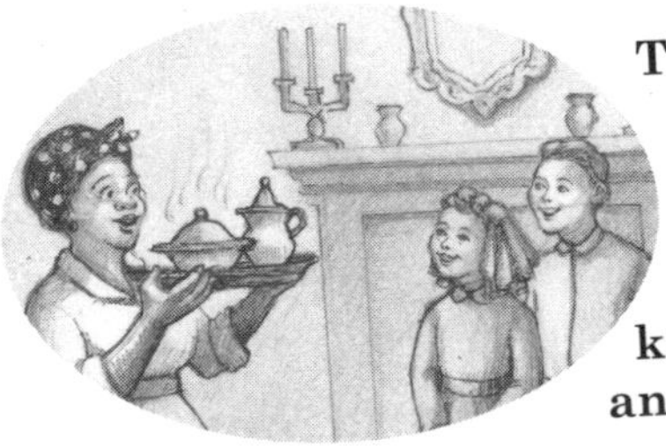

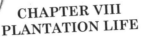

The Negro cook whom you call "Mammy" comes in bringing a great tray of food. You have known her all your life and love her very much.

"Good morning, Miss Mary; good morning, Mr. John," she says.

"Good morning, Mammy," you reply.

And Mammy smiles and sets the dishes of hot food on the table.

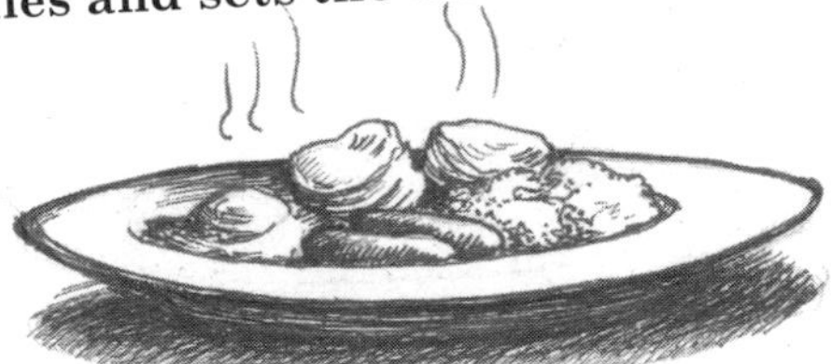

You eat a big breakfast because you are hungry and looking forward to a long day of fun on the plantation.

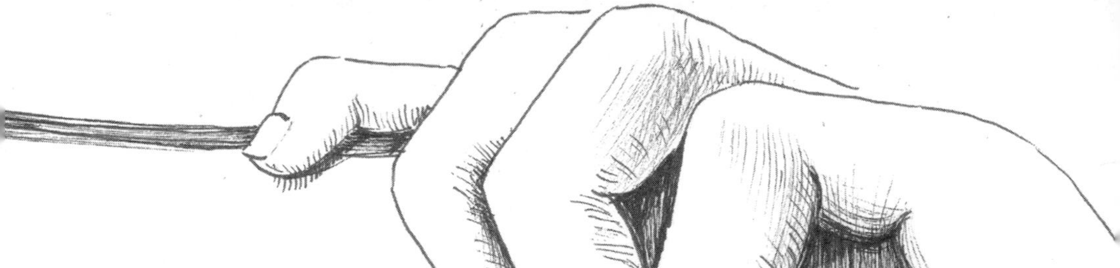

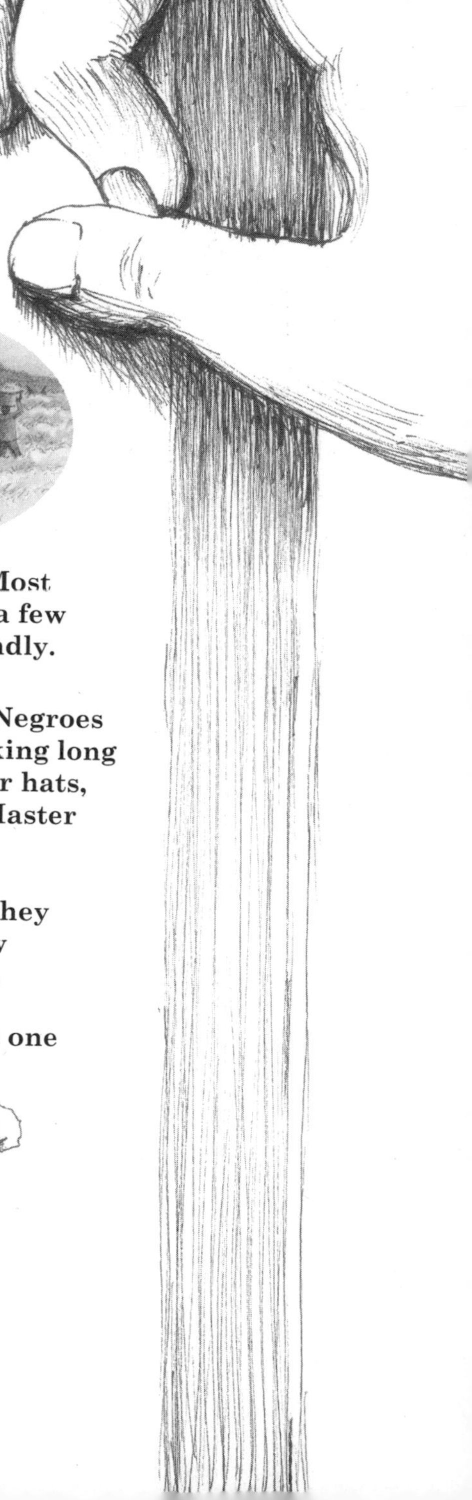

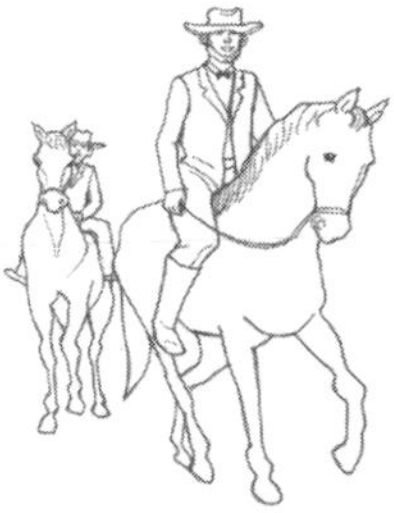

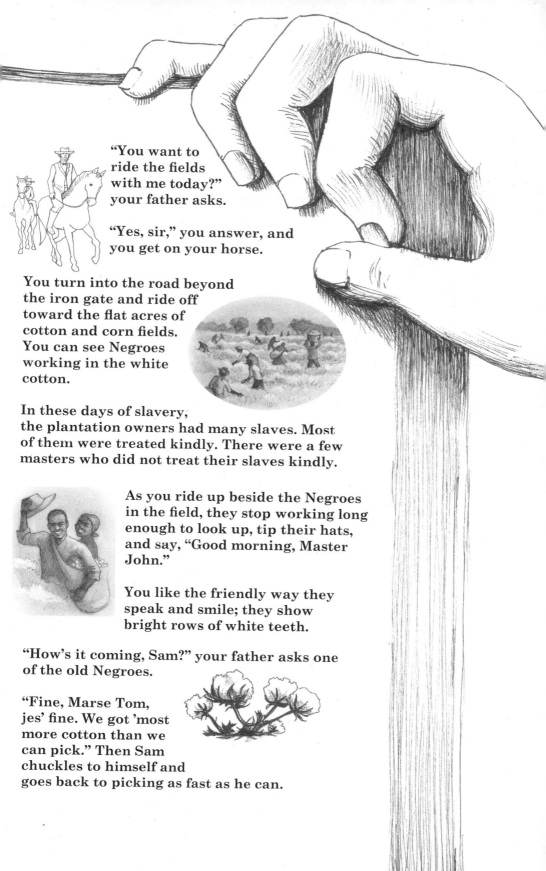

"You want to ride the fields with me today?" your father asks.

"Yes, sir," you answer, and you get on your horse.

You turn into the road beyond the iron gate and ride off toward the flat acres of cotton and corn fields. You can see Negroes working in the white cotton.

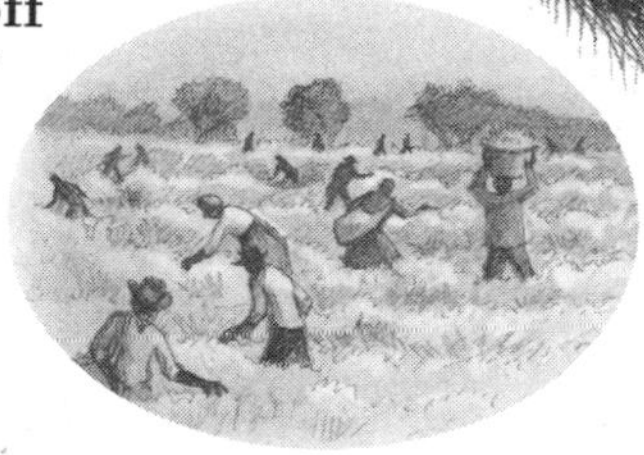

In these days of slavery, the plantation owners had many slaves. Most of them were treated kindly. There were a few masters who did not treat their slaves kindly.

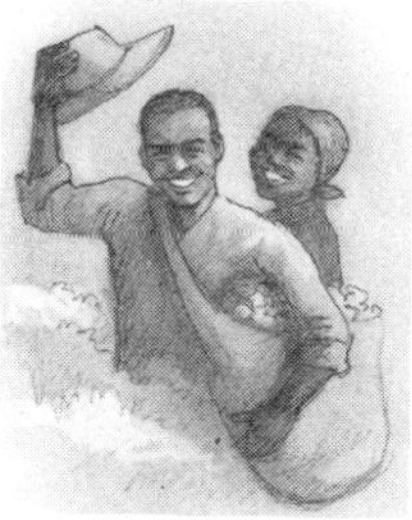

As you ride up beside the Negroes in the field, they stop working long enough to look up, tip their hats, and say, "Good morning, Master John."

You like the friendly way they speak and smile; they show bright rows of white teeth.

"How's it coming, Sam?" your father asks one of the old Negroes.

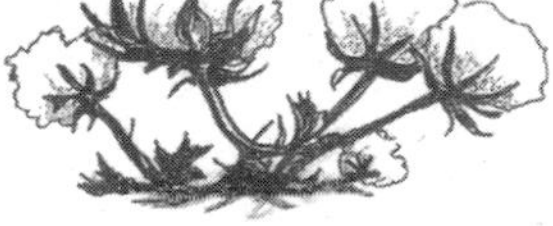

"Fine, Marse Tom, jes' fine. We got 'most more cotton than we can pick." Then Sam chuckles to himself and goes back to picking as fast as he can.

IN SCHOOL ASSEMBLY, WE SANG SONGS RANGING FROM PATRIOTIC TO FOLK. MY FAVORITE WAS "OLD BLACK JOE," BY STEPHEN FOSTER. I WAS A FAN OF PATHOS IN THOSE DAYS.

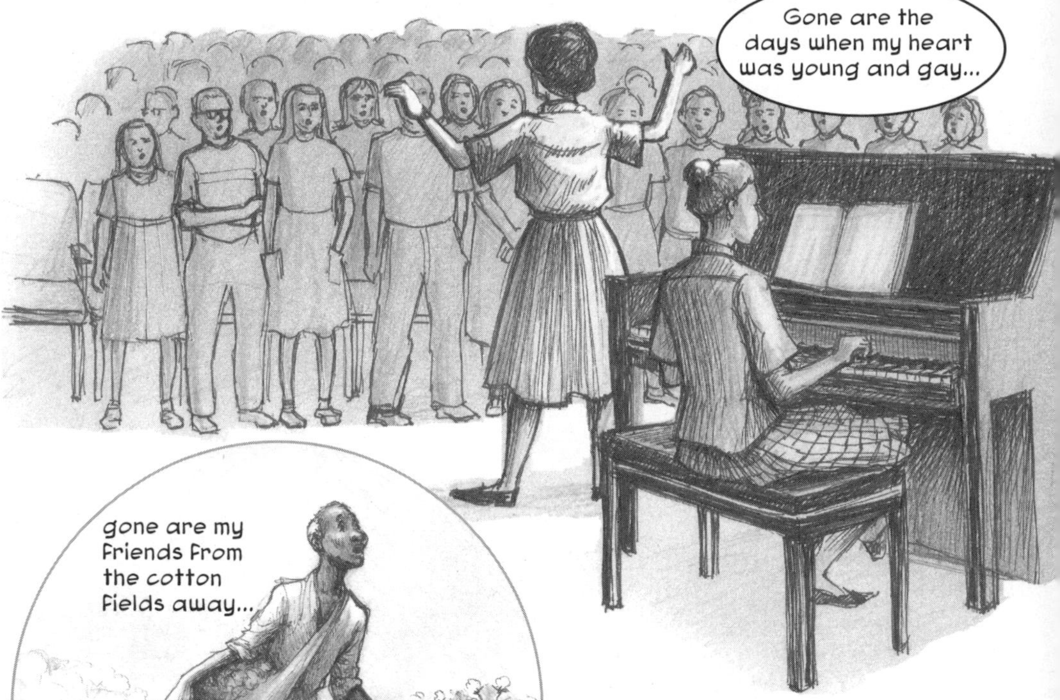
Gone are the days when my heart was young and gay...

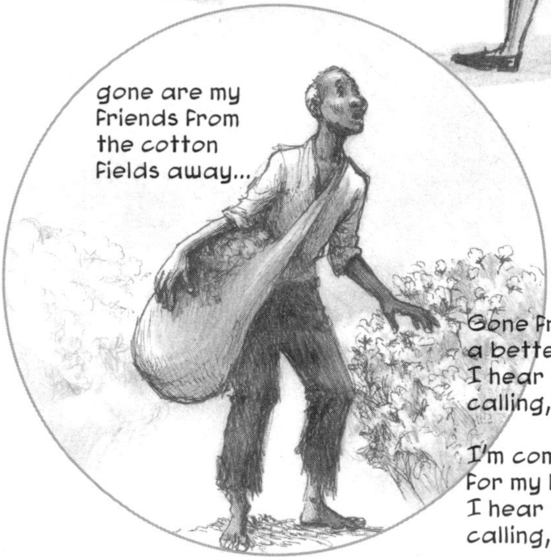
gone are my friends from the cotton fields away...
Gone from the Earth to
a better land I know,
I hear their gentle voices
calling, "Old Black Joe."
I'm coming, I'm coming,
For my head is bending low.
I hear those gentle voices
calling, "Old Black Joe."

SOMETIMES I FELT A LUMP IN MY THROAT FOR POOR OLD JOE.

THE OLDER BOYS LOVED THIS SONG FOR THE COMIC OPPORTUNITY IT GAVE THEM. THEY ROUTINELY TURNED THE LAST LINE INTO A MOCK HOWL.

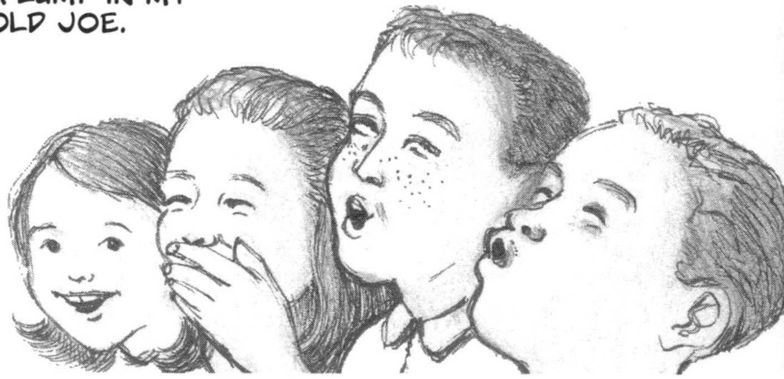
Ooooold Blaaaaaack Joooooooe!

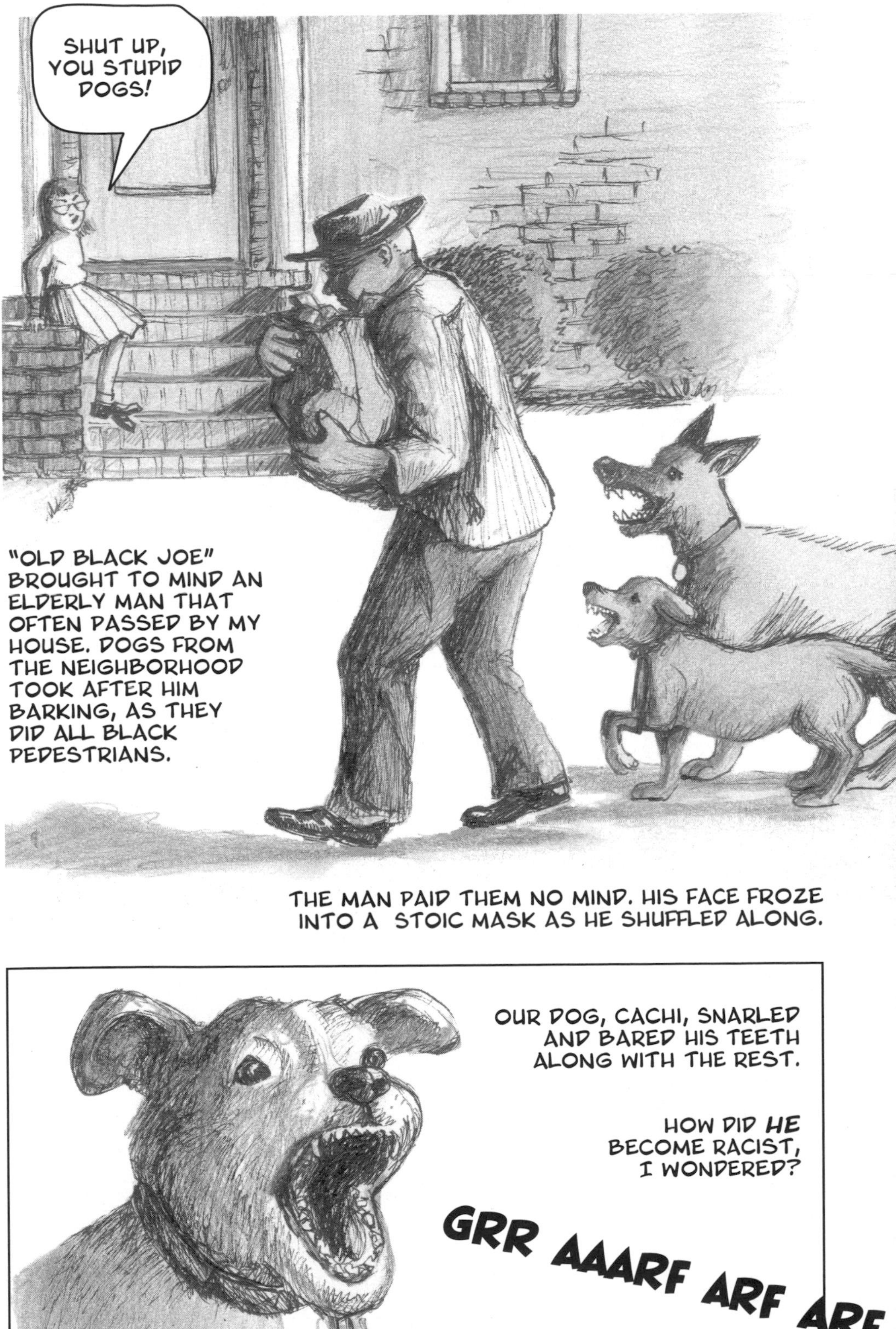
SHUT UP, YOU STUPID DOGS!
"OLD BLACK JOE" BROUGHT TO MIND AN ELDERLY MAN THAT OFTEN PASSED BY MY HOUSE. DOGS FROM THE NEIGHBORHOOD TOOK AFTER HIM BARKING, AS THEY DID ALL BLACK PEDESTRIANS.
THE MAN PAID THEM NO MIND. HIS FACE FROZE INTO A STOIC MASK AS HE SHUFFLED ALONG.
OUR DOG, CACHI, SNARLED AND BARED HIS TEETH ALONG WITH THE REST.
HOW DID **HE** BECOME RACIST, I WONDERED?
GRR AAARF ARF ARF

AS WE PROGRESSED IN OUR STUDY OF THE CIVIL WAR, THE TEXTBOOK BECAME EVEN MORE SURREAL.

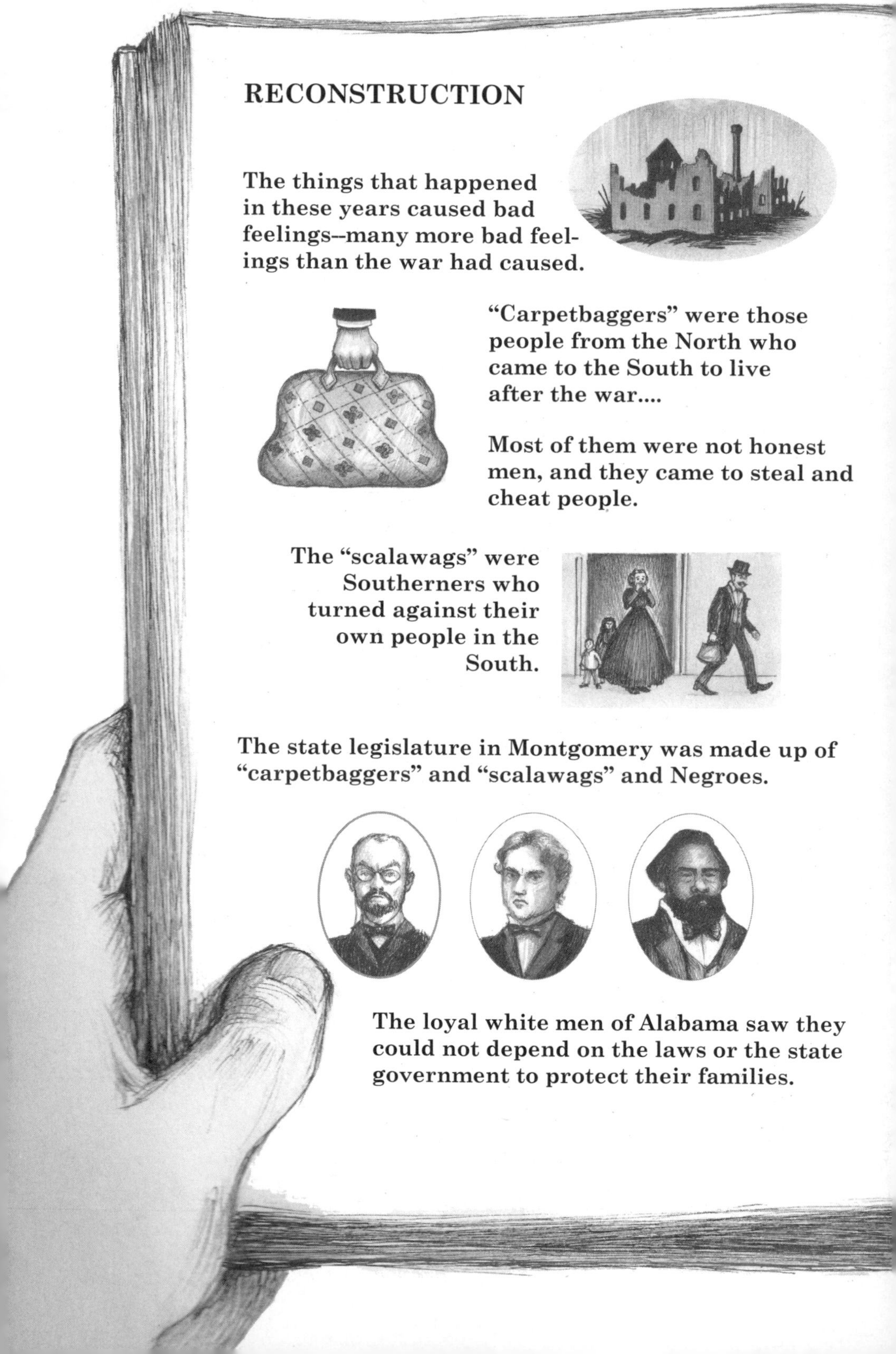

RECONSTRUCTION

The things that happened in these years caused bad feelings--many more bad feelings than the war had caused.

"Carpetbaggers" were those people from the North who came to the South to live after the war....

Most of them were not honest men, and they came to steal and cheat people.

The "scalawags" were Southerners who turned against their own people in the South.

The state legislature in Montgomery was made up of "carpetbaggers" and "scalawags" and Negroes.

The loyal white men of Alabama saw they could not depend on the laws or the state government to protect their families.

[ALL EXCERPTS COME FROM THE TEXT OF KNOW ALABAMA, EXCLUDING ILLUSTRATIONS.]

A band of white-robed figures appeared on the streets of Pulaski, Tennessee. No one knew who they were.

The Klan did not ride often, only when it had to.

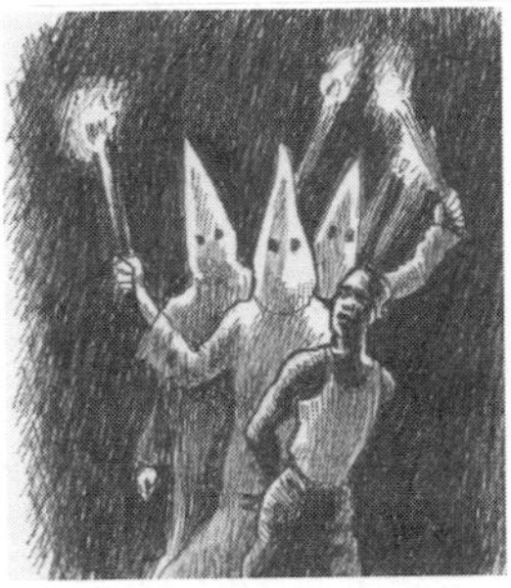

They held their courts in the dark forest at night; they passed sentence on the criminals and carried out the sentence.

The sign of the Klan was a large fiery cross. Whenever the cross was seen burning on a hillside at night, people knew that the Klan had struck again.

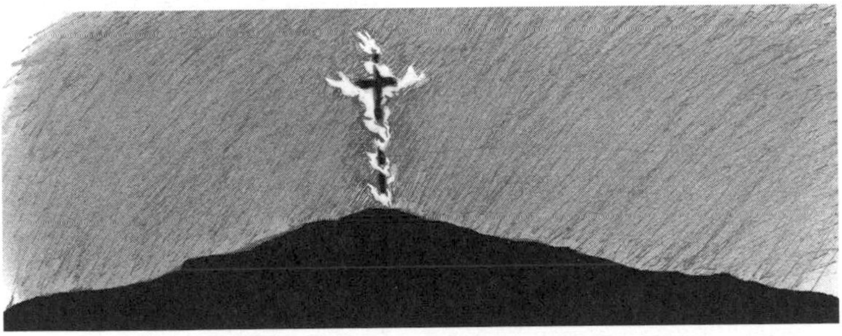

Sometimes in the quiet night the sound of galloping horses would be heard in the streets; the Klansmen would pass like ghosts and disappear.

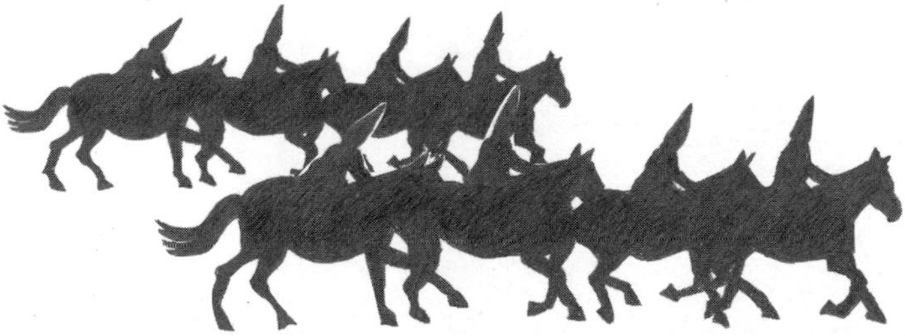

EVER SINCE OUR ARRIVAL IN ALABAMA, WE'D HEARD PLENTY OF KLAN STORIES.

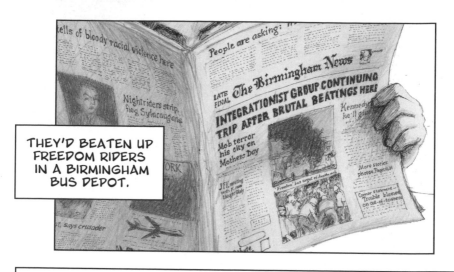

tells of bloody racial violence here
Nightriders strip, flog Sylacaugans
says crusader
People are asking:
The Birmingham News
LATE FINAL
INTEGRATIONIST GROUP CONTINUING TRIP AFTER BRUTAL BEATINGS HERE
Mob terror his city on Mothers Day
JFK meeting with K. now thought likely
Kennedy he'll give
More stories, photos, Pages 14,34
Connor statement—Trouble blamed on out-of-towners
THEY'D BEATEN UP FREEDOM RIDERS IN A BIRMINGHAM BUS DEPOT.

THEY'D BOMBED THE SIXTEENTH STREET BAPTIST CHURCH IN BIRMINGHAM, KILLING FOUR CHILDREN IN THE PROCESS.

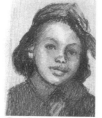

Denise McNair, 11 | Carole Robertson, 14 | Addie Mae Collins, 14 | Cynthia Wesley, 14

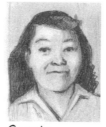

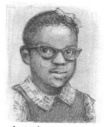

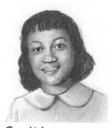

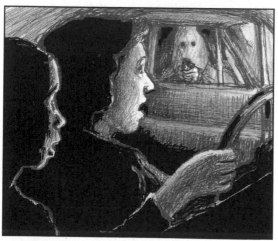

MOST RECENTLY, THEY'D GUNNED DOWN CIVIL RIGHTS VOLUNTEER VIOLA LIUZZO AS SHE AND HER PASSENGER DROVE ALONG A DARK HIGHWAY.

THESE THINGS HAPPENED LESS THAN A TWO-HOUR DRIVE FROM OUR HOUSE.

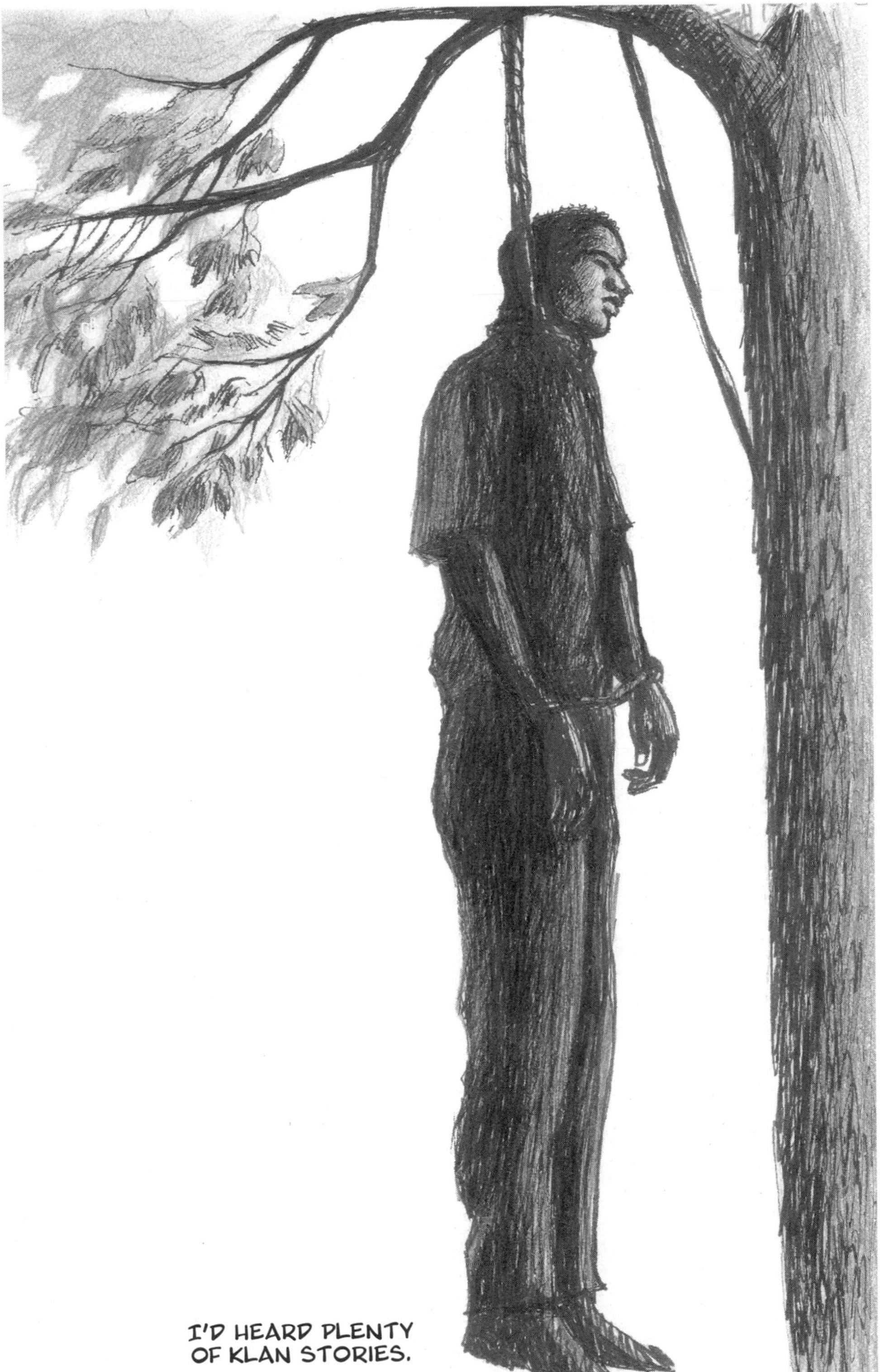
I'D HEARD PLENTY
OF KLAN STORIES.

A NATIONAL MAGAZINE WE SUBSCRIBED TO PUBLISHED A FEATURE ON THE KLAN THAT INCLUDED A SHOCKING PHOTO.

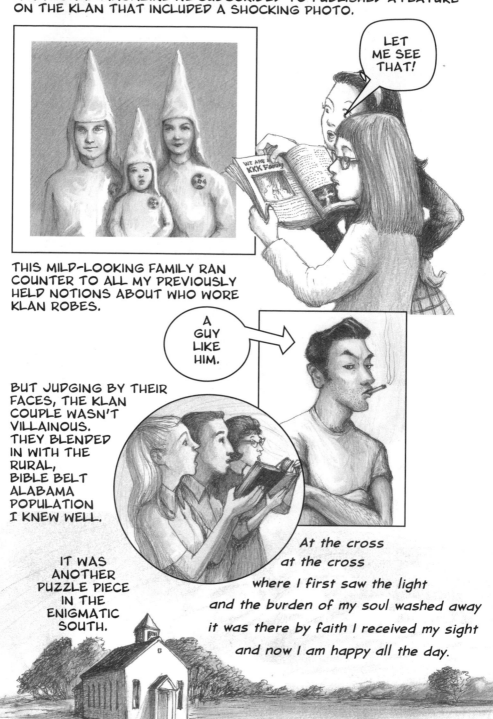

THIS MILD-LOOKING FAMILY RAN COUNTER TO ALL MY PREVIOUSLY HELD NOTIONS ABOUT WHO WORE KLAN ROBES.

LET ME SEE THAT!

A GUY LIKE HIM.

BUT JUDGING BY THEIR FACES, THE KLAN COUPLE WASN'T VILLAINOUS. THEY BLENDED IN WITH THE RURAL, BIBLE BELT ALABAMA POPULATION I KNEW WELL.

IT WAS ANOTHER PUZZLE PIECE IN THE ENIGMATIC SOUTH.

At the cross
at the cross
where I first saw the light
and the burden of my soul washed away
it was there by faith I received my sight
and now I am happy all the day.

TWELVE YEARS AFTER THE SUPREME COURT RULED THAT *SEPARATE* WAS IN NO WAY *EQUAL*, PUBLIC SCHOOLS IN PERRY COUNTY FINALLY TOOK A STEP TOWARD DESEGREGATION.

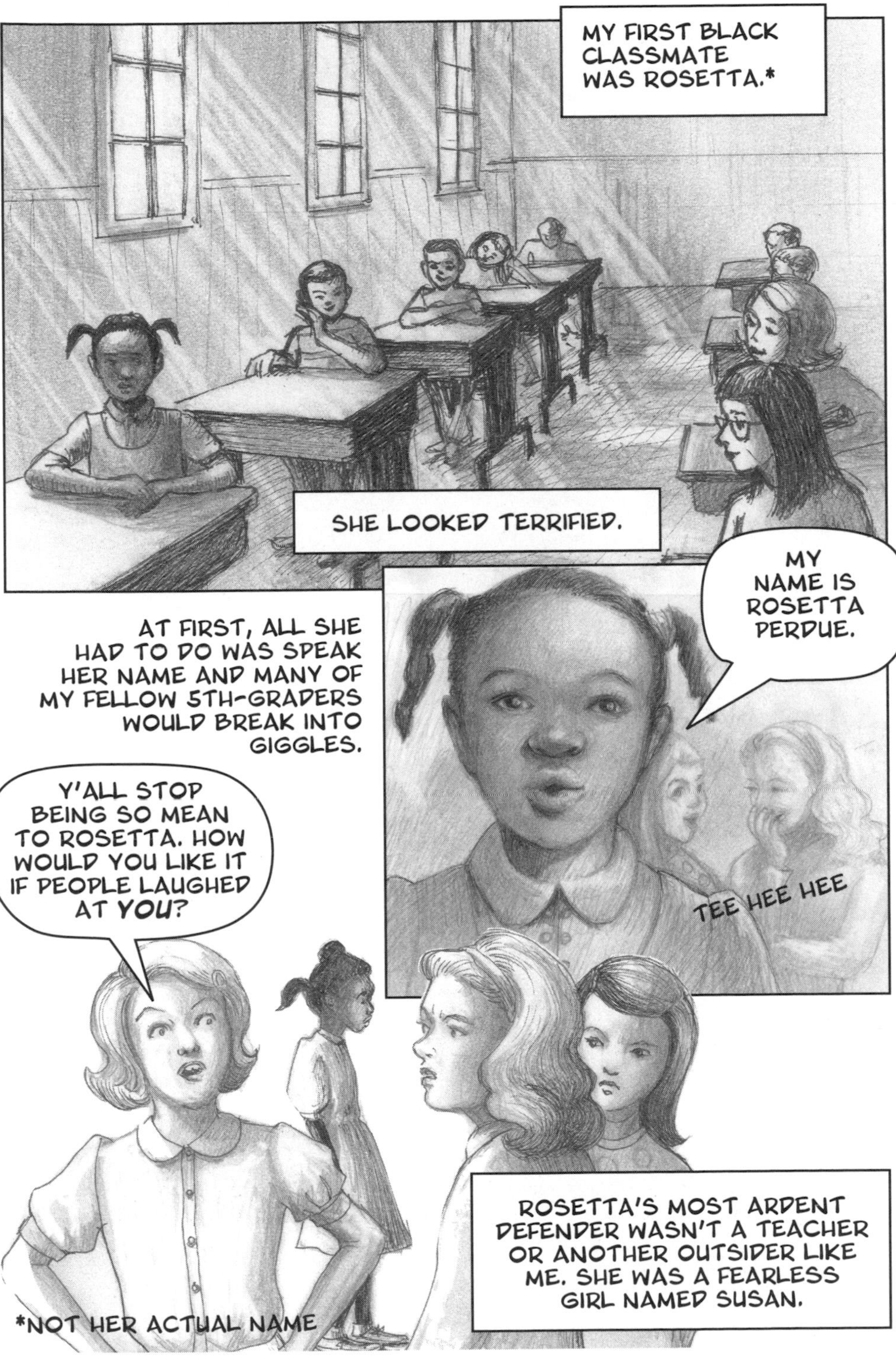
MY FIRST BLACK CLASSMATE WAS ROSETTA.*
SHE LOOKED TERRIFIED.
AT FIRST, ALL SHE HAD TO DO WAS SPEAK HER NAME AND MANY OF MY FELLOW 5TH-GRADERS WOULD BREAK INTO GIGGLES.
MY NAME IS ROSETTA PERDUE.
TEE HEE HEE
Y'ALL STOP BEING SO MEAN TO ROSETTA. HOW WOULD YOU LIKE IT IF PEOPLE LAUGHED AT **YOU**?
ROSETTA'S MOST ARDENT DEFENDER WASN'T A TEACHER OR ANOTHER OUTSIDER LIKE ME. SHE WAS A FEARLESS GIRL NAMED SUSAN.

*NOT HER ACTUAL NAME

I WAS NO SUSAN. MY OVERTURES TOWARD ROSETTA WERE CLUMSY AND INEFFECTIVE.

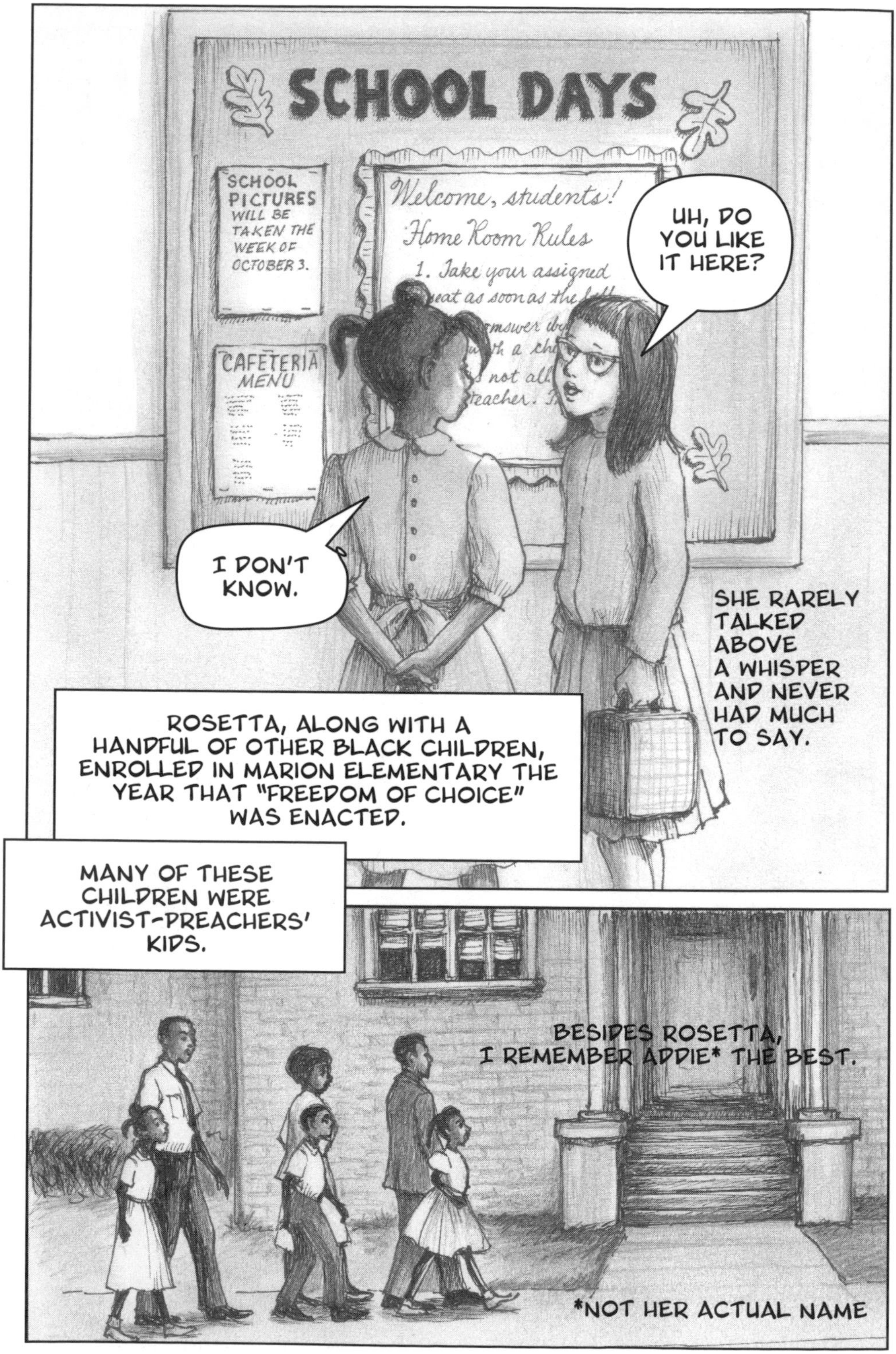
SCHOOL DAYS
SCHOOL PICTURES WILL BE TAKEN THE WEEK OF OCTOBER 3.
CAFETERIA MENU
Welcome, students!
Home Room Rules
1. Take your assigned
UH, DO YOU LIKE IT HERE?
I DON'T KNOW.
SHE RARELY TALKED ABOVE A WHISPER AND NEVER HAD MUCH TO SAY.
ROSETTA, ALONG WITH A HANDFUL OF OTHER BLACK CHILDREN, ENROLLED IN MARION ELEMENTARY THE YEAR THAT "FREEDOM OF CHOICE" WAS ENACTED.
MANY OF THESE CHILDREN WERE ACTIVIST-PREACHERS' KIDS.
BESIDES ROSETTA, I REMEMBER ADDIE* THE BEST.
*NOT HER ACTUAL NAME

FOR ONE THING, SHE WAS AN ALL-A STUDENT, AND ALTHOUGH SHE WAS A YEAR OR TWO YOUNGER, SHE HAD ENOUGH FIRE FOR HERSELF ***AND*** ROSETTA.

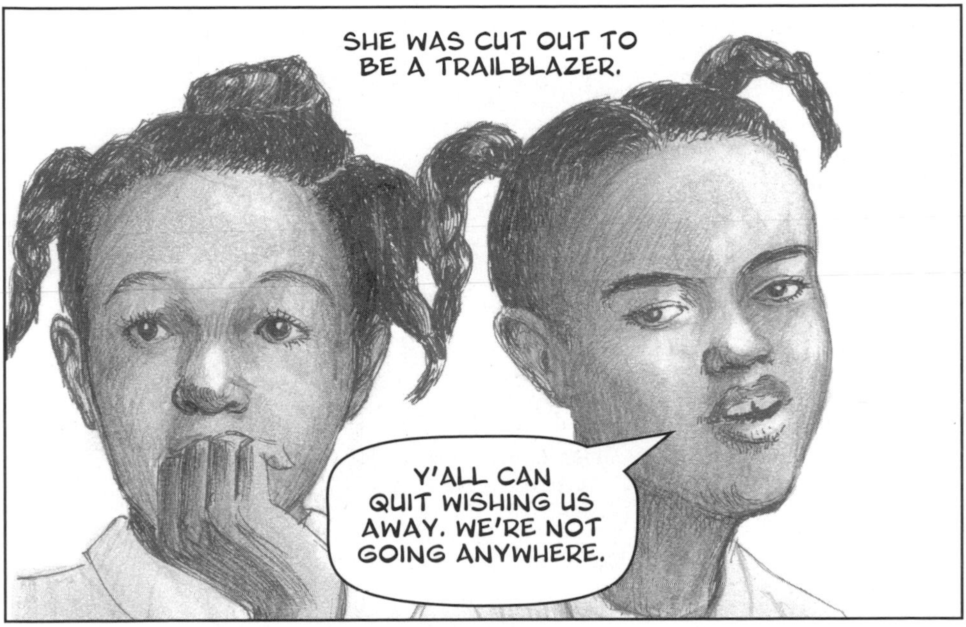
SHE WAS CUT OUT TO BE A TRAILBLAZER.
Y'ALL CAN QUIT WISHING US AWAY. WE'RE NOT GOING ANYWHERE.

ONE DAY BEFORE THE BELL FOR HOMEROOM SOUNDED, ADDIE AND I CAME FACE-TO-FACE.

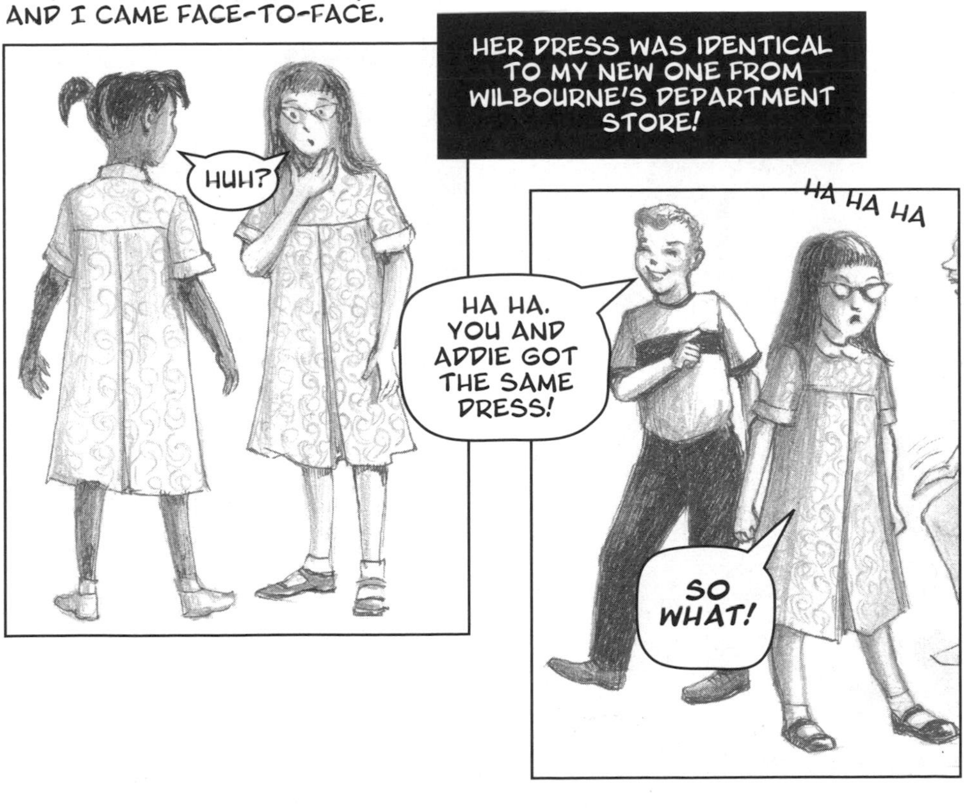
HER DRESS WAS IDENTICAL TO MY NEW ONE FROM WILBOURNE'S DEPARTMENT STORE!
HUH?
HA HA HA
HA HA. YOU AND ADDIE GOT THE SAME DRESS!
SO WHAT!

ONE DAY, THAT "FREEDOM OF CHOICE" YEAR, THE PRINCIPAL MYSTERIOUSLY CALLED A GROUP OF HONOR ROLL STUDENTS TO HIS OFFICE.

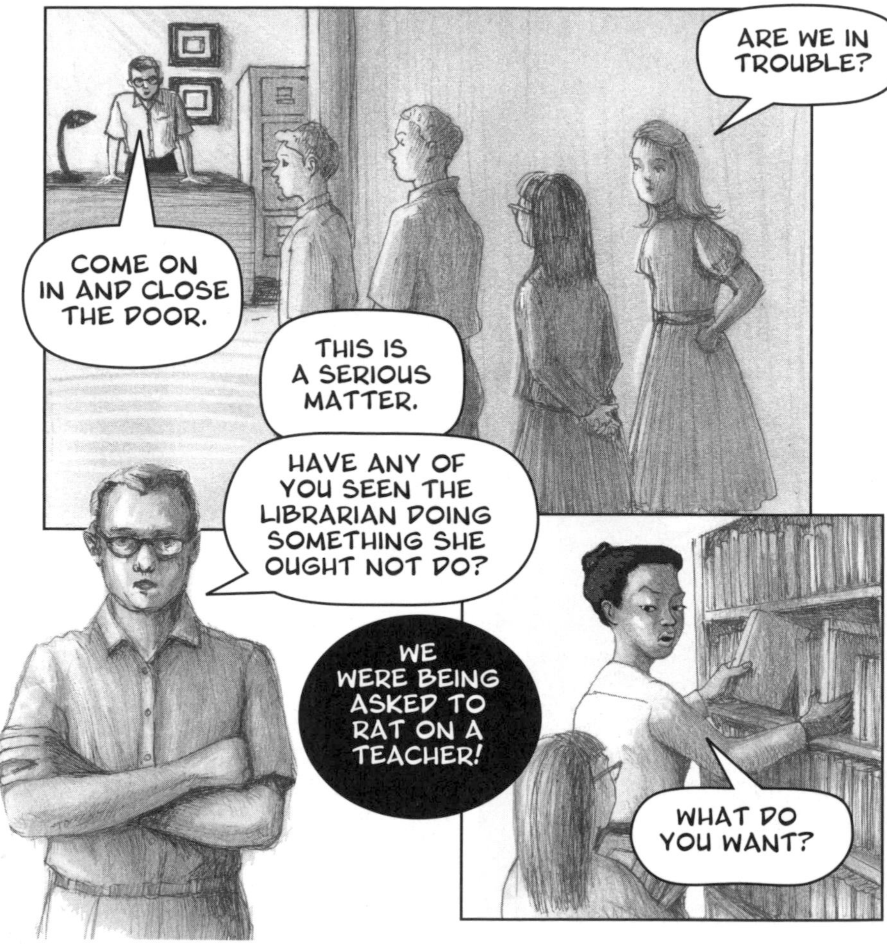
COME ON IN AND CLOSE THE DOOR.
ARE WE IN TROUBLE?
THIS IS A SERIOUS MATTER.
HAVE ANY OF YOU SEEN THE LIBRARIAN DOING SOMETHING SHE OUGHT NOT DO?
WE WERE BEING ASKED TO RAT ON A TEACHER!
WHAT DO YOU WANT?

THE NEW LIBRARIAN, WHO WAS ALSO THE FIRST BLACK AUTHORITY FIGURE IN MY LIFE, HAD COMMITTED A SERIES OF ERRORS.

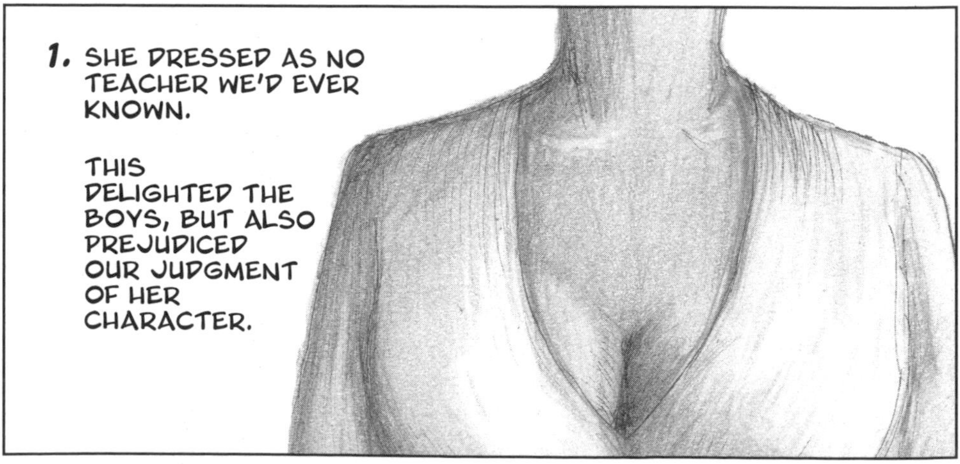
1. SHE DRESSED AS NO TEACHER WE'D EVER KNOWN.
THIS DELIGHTED THE BOYS, BUT ALSO PREJUDICED OUR JUDGMENT OF HER CHARACTER.

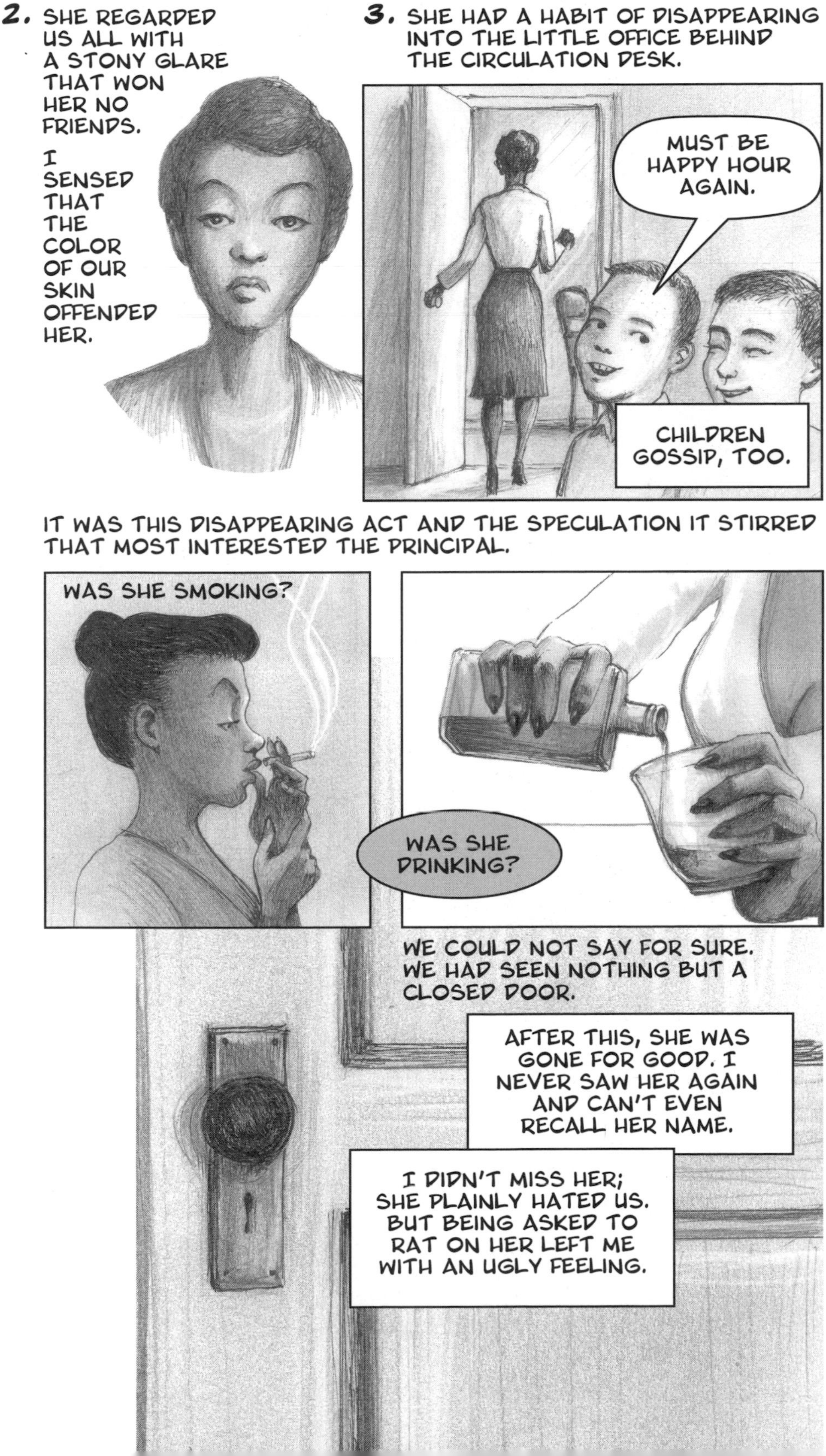
2. SHE REGARDED US ALL WITH A STONY GLARE THAT WON HER NO FRIENDS.
I SENSED THAT THE COLOR OF OUR SKIN OFFENDED HER.
3. SHE HAD A HABIT OF DISAPPEARING INTO THE LITTLE OFFICE BEHIND THE CIRCULATION DESK.
MUST BE HAPPY HOUR AGAIN.
CHILDREN GOSSIP, TOO.
IT WAS THIS DISAPPEARING ACT AND THE SPECULATION IT STIRRED THAT MOST INTERESTED THE PRINCIPAL.
WAS SHE SMOKING?
WAS SHE DRINKING?
WE COULD NOT SAY FOR SURE. WE HAD SEEN NOTHING BUT A CLOSED DOOR.
AFTER THIS, SHE WAS GONE FOR GOOD. I NEVER SAW HER AGAIN AND CAN'T EVEN RECALL HER NAME.
I DIDN'T MISS HER; SHE PLAINLY HATED US. BUT BEING ASKED TO RAT ON HER LEFT ME WITH AN UGLY FEELING.

chapter 10
SCHOOL LESSONS

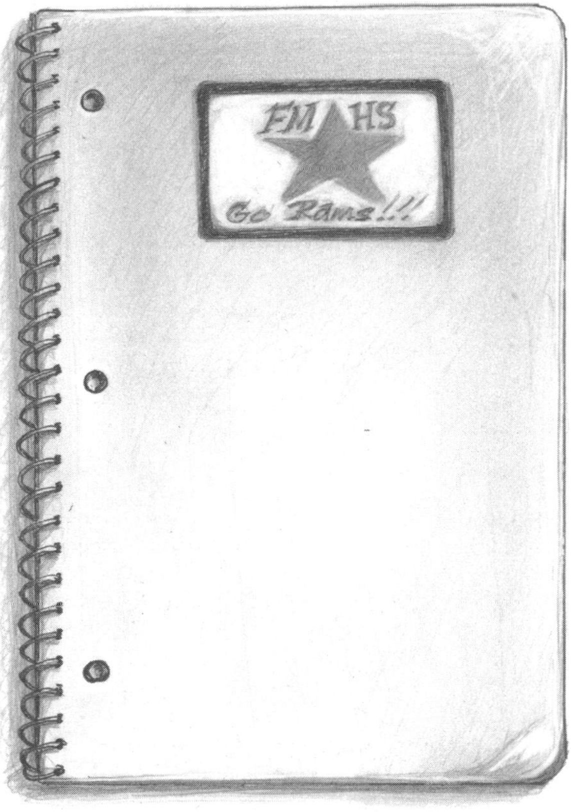
FM HS
Go Rams!!!

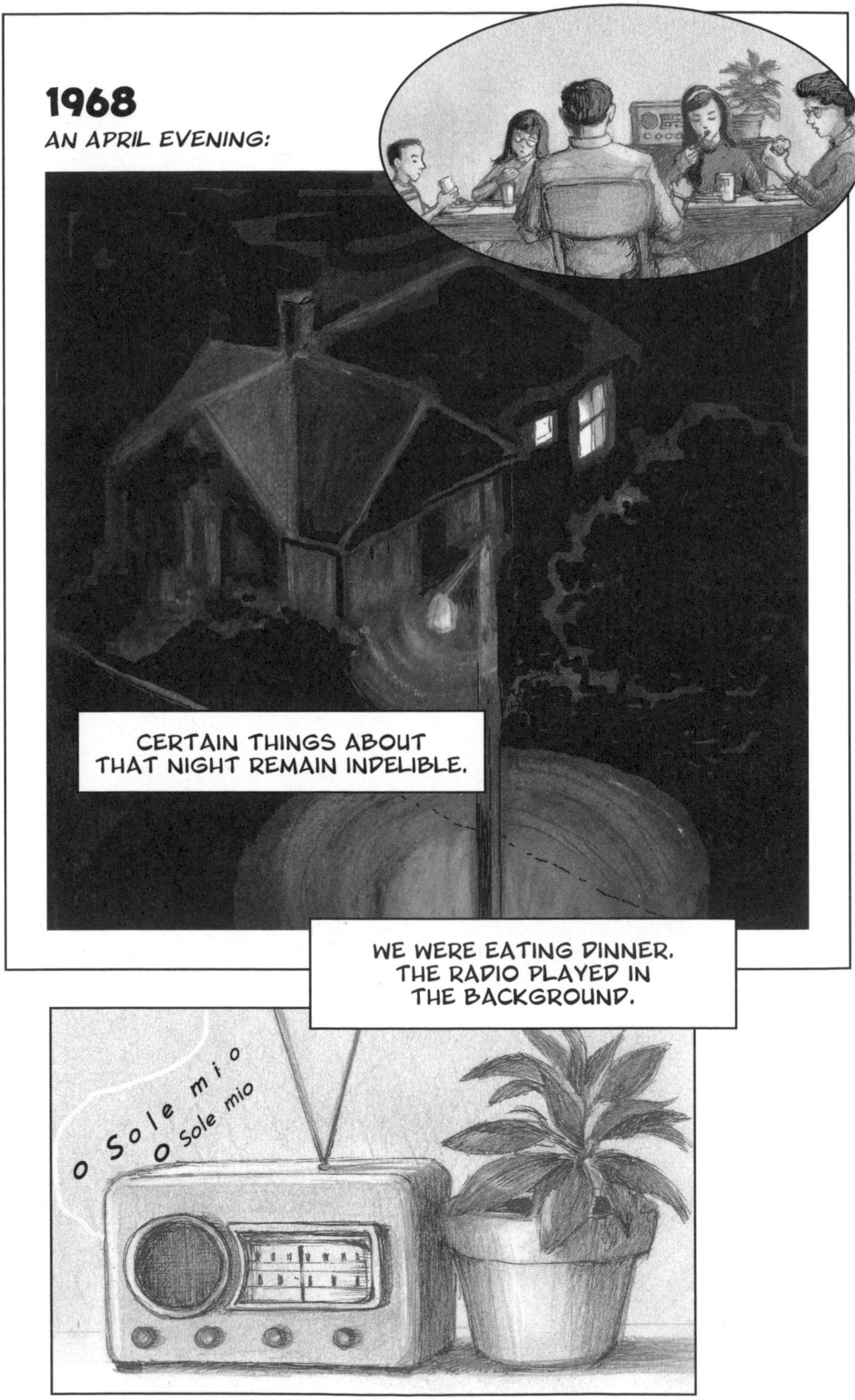
1968
AN APRIL EVENING:
CERTAIN THINGS ABOUT THAT NIGHT REMAIN INDELIBLE.
WE WERE EATING DINNER. THE RADIO PLAYED IN THE BACKGROUND.
O Sole mio
O Sole mio

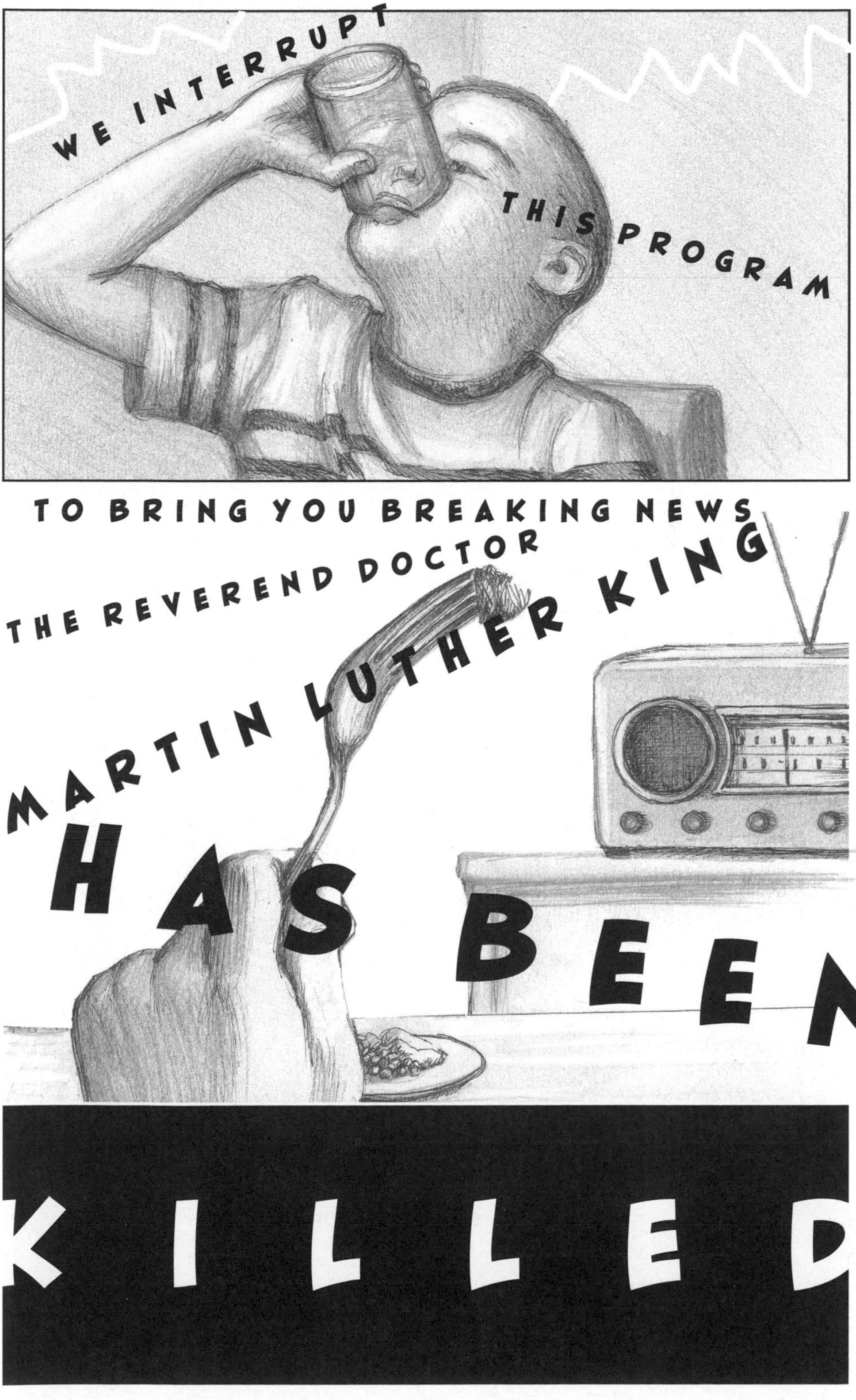
WE INTERRUPT
THIS PROGRAM
TO BRING YOU BREAKING NEWS
THE REVEREND DOCTOR
MARTIN LUTHER KING
HAS BEEN
KILLED

MY MIND'S EYE RECORDED DADDY'S EXPRESSION.
HIS WORDS ECHO IN MY HEAD.

OH, NO! NOW THERE'S REALLY GOING TO BE TROUBLE!

TROUBLE
TROUBLE
TROUBLE

BUT HIS PREMONITION DIDN'T COME TRUE.
THOUGH OTHER CITIES BLAZED WITH OUTRAGE,
MARION STAYED QUIET. IT LOOKED AS IF OUR
DAYS OF TROUBLE WERE BEHIND US.

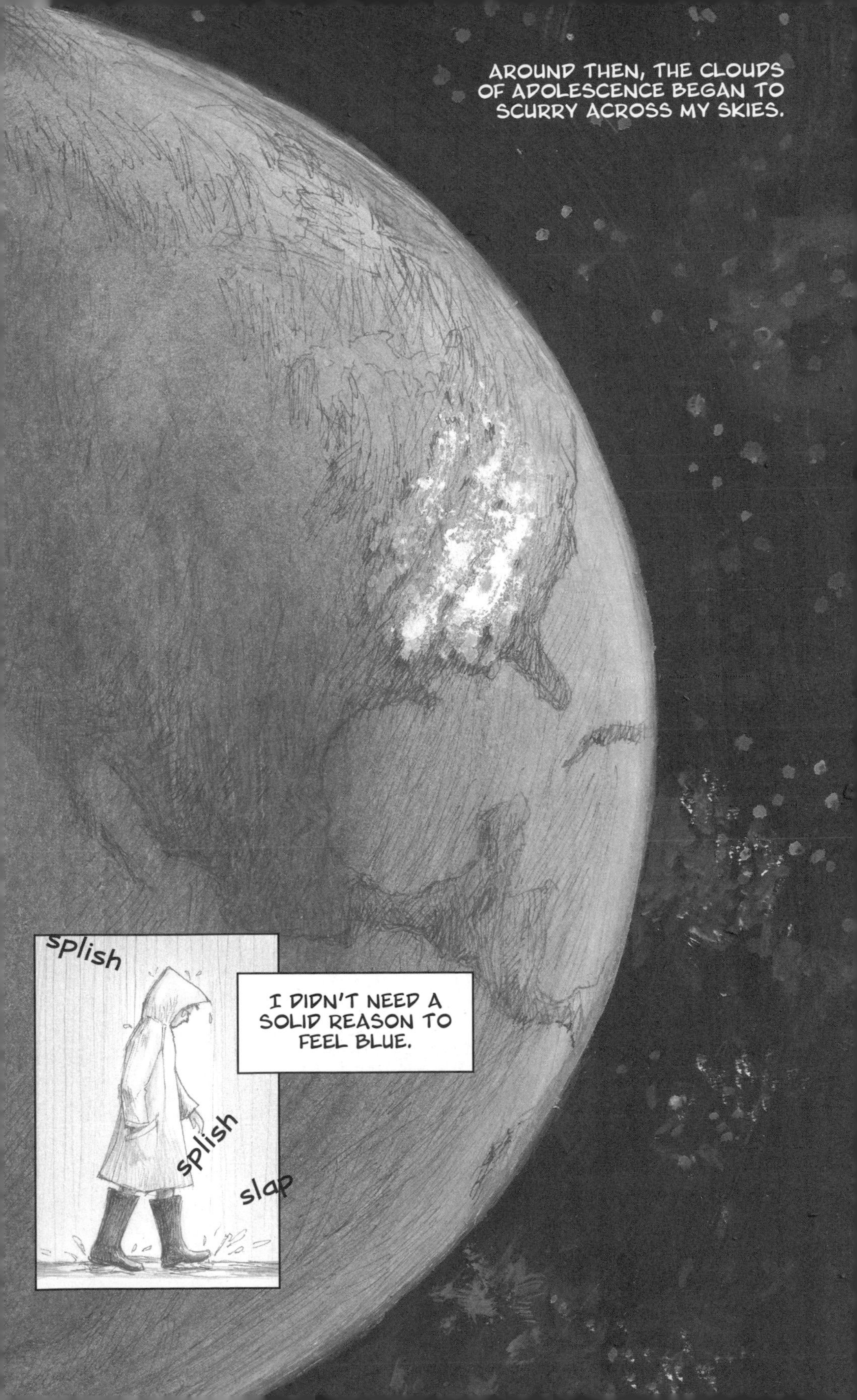
AROUND THEN, THE CLOUDS OF ADOLESCENCE BEGAN TO SCURRY ACROSS MY SKIES.
splish
I DIDN'T NEED A SOLID REASON TO FEEL BLUE.
splish
slap

BUT I FELT I HAD GOOD CAUSE FOR SELF-LOATHING WHEN I AWOKE TO THE SPECTER OF CROOKED TEETH AND SHRUNKEN EYES.

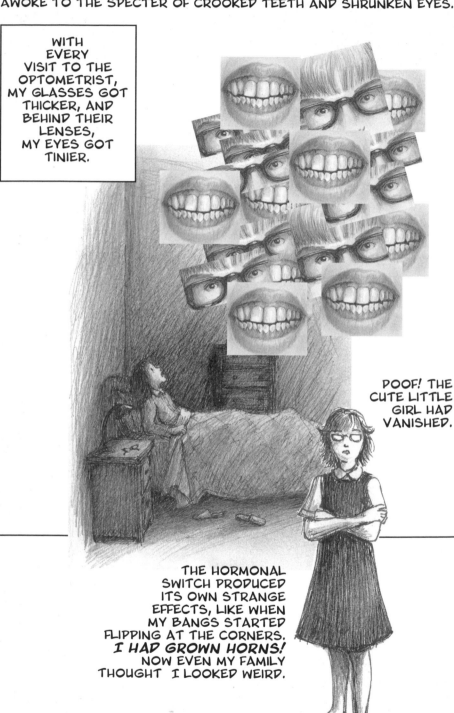

WITH EVERY VISIT TO THE OPTOMETRIST, MY GLASSES GOT THICKER, AND BEHIND THEIR LENSES, MY EYES GOT TINIER.

POOF! THE CUTE LITTLE GIRL HAD VANISHED.

THE HORMONAL SWITCH PRODUCED ITS OWN STRANGE EFFECTS, LIKE WHEN MY BANGS STARTED FLIPPING AT THE CORNERS. *I HAD GROWN HORNS!* NOW EVEN MY FAMILY THOUGHT I LOOKED WEIRD.

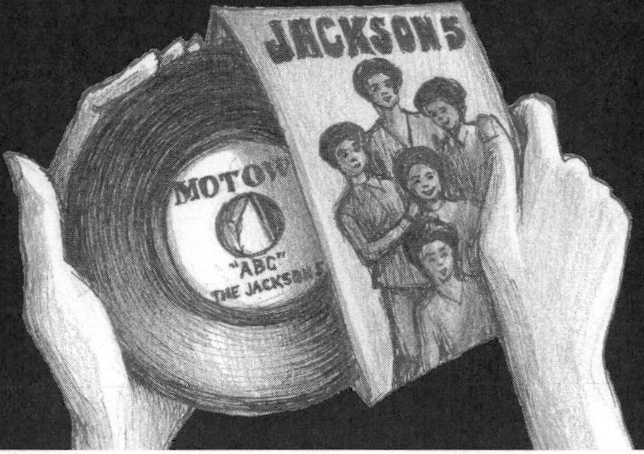
JACKSON5
"ABC"

THIS HAPPENED AT THE WORST TIME, JUST WHEN LOOKS BEGAN TO MATTER LIKE NEVER BEFORE.

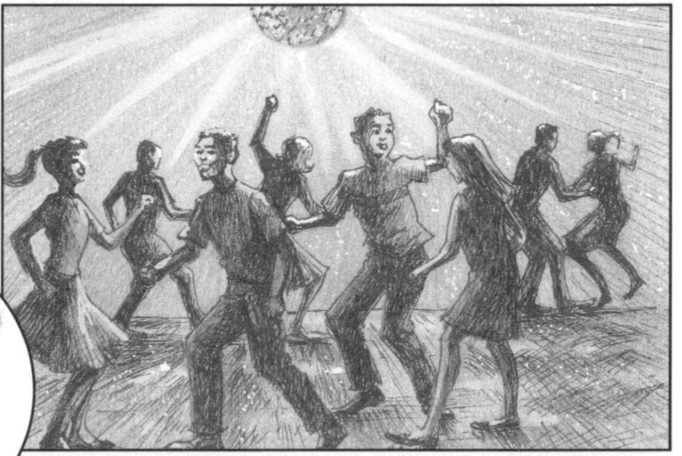

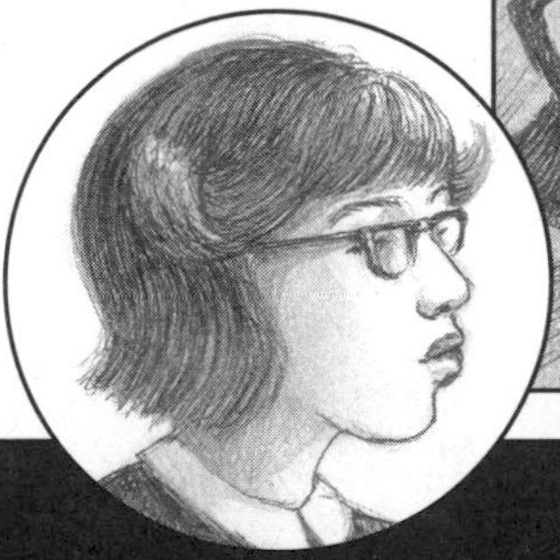

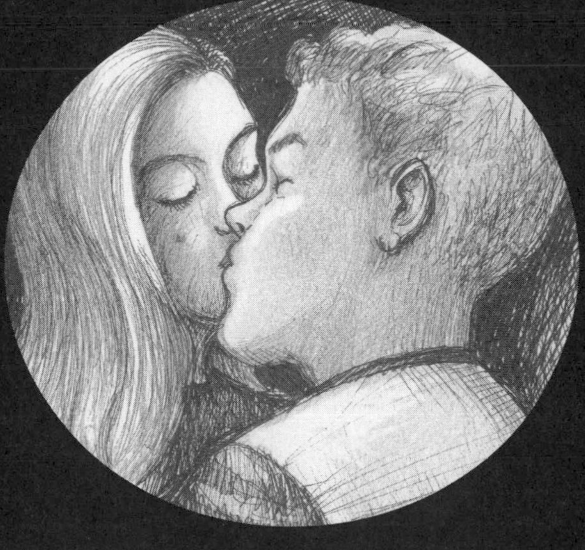

YOU HAD TO BE COOL AND BEAUTIFUL TO SECURE YOUR SPOT. I WAS NEITHER, AND BOY-GIRL PARTIES BECAME HELLISH REMINDERS OF THOSE DEFICITS.

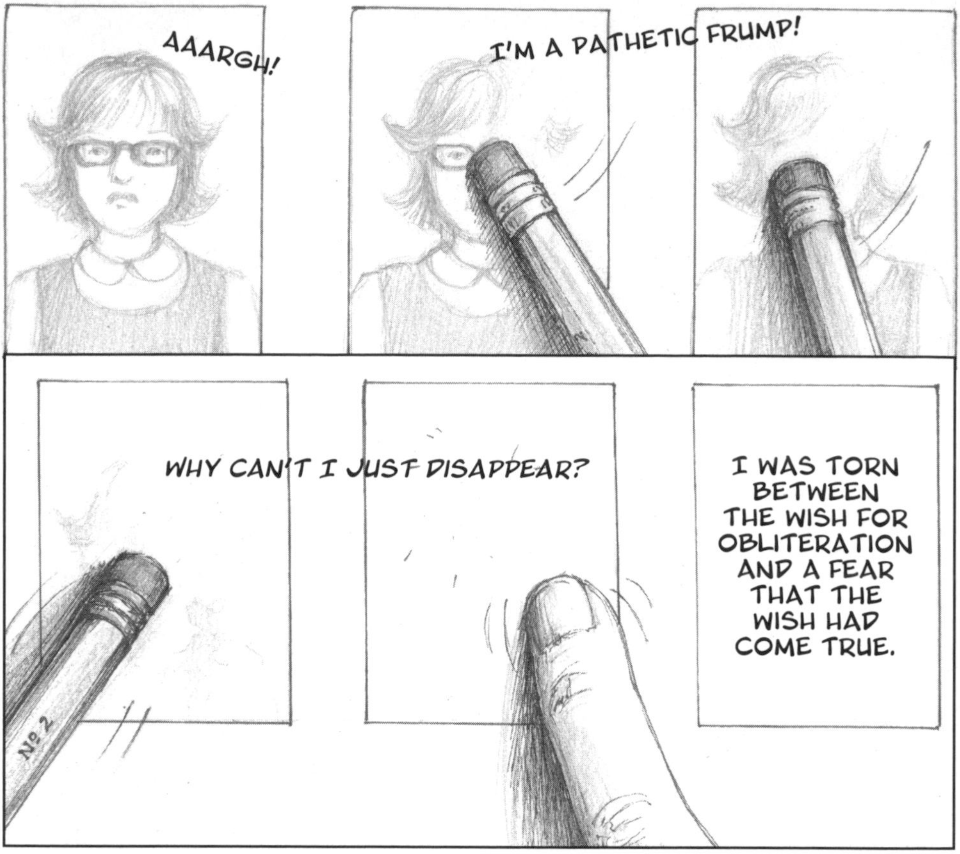
AAARGH!
I'M A PATHETIC FRUMP!
WHY CAN'T I JUST DISAPPEAR?
I WAS TORN BETWEEN THE WISH FOR OBLITERATION AND A FEAR THAT THE WISH HAD COME TRUE.
Nº 2

I HEARD ABOUT A RABBI FROM A NEARBY TOWN WHO'D CONVINCED HIMSELF THAT PASSERSBY MUTTERED, "THERE GOES A JEW," EACH TIME THEY SAW HIM. MY INSTINCT TOLD ME HE HAD IT WRONG.

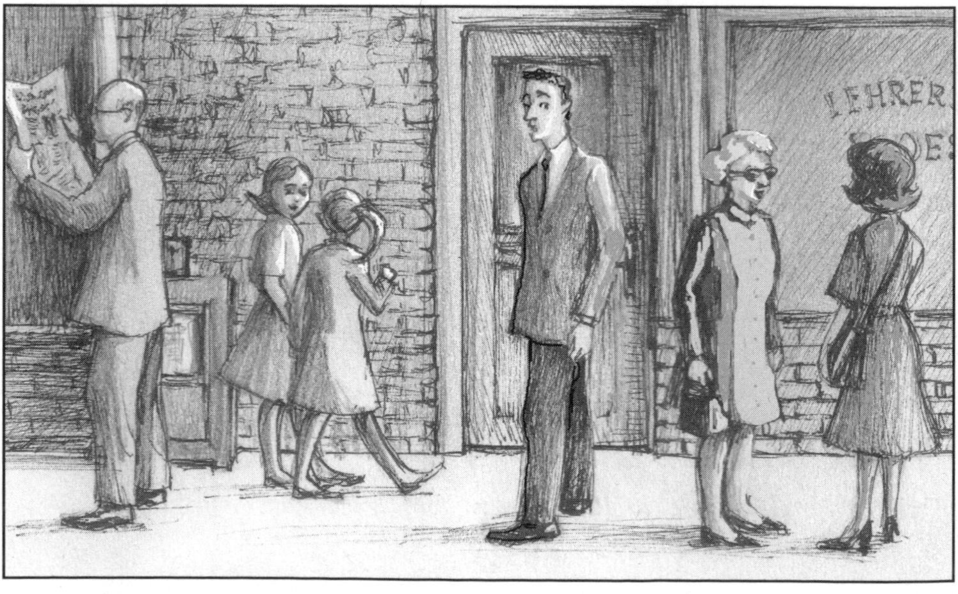

IT'S POSSIBLE THAT SOMETHING SIMILAR HAPPENED TO ME AS I WALKED AROUND MARION.

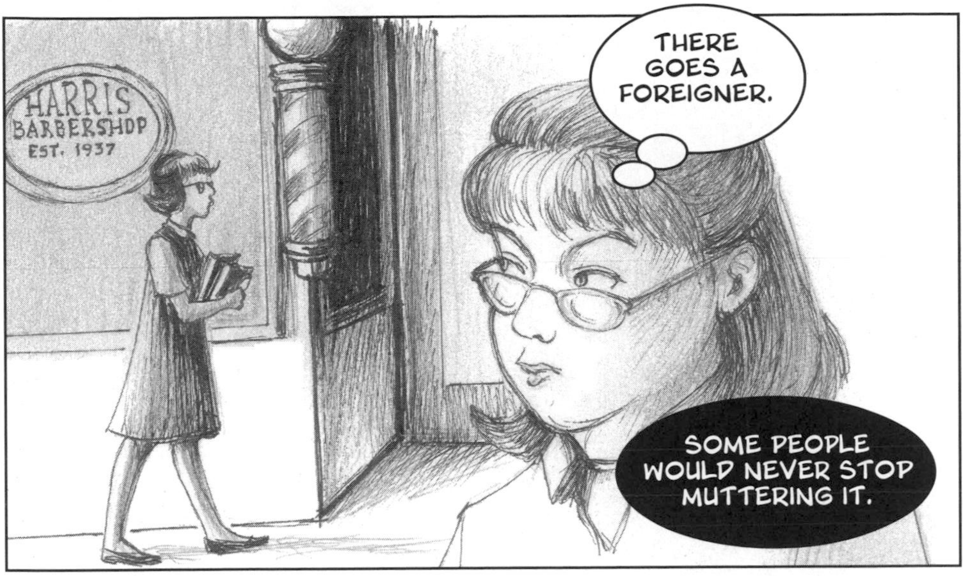
HARRIS
BARBERSHOP
EST. 1937
THERE GOES A FOREIGNER.
SOME PEOPLE WOULD NEVER STOP MUTTERING IT.

BUT THAT WASN'T NECESSARILY TOPMOST IN PEOPLE'S MINDS. IT'S MORE LIKELY THAT THEY DIDN'T SEE ME AT ALL.

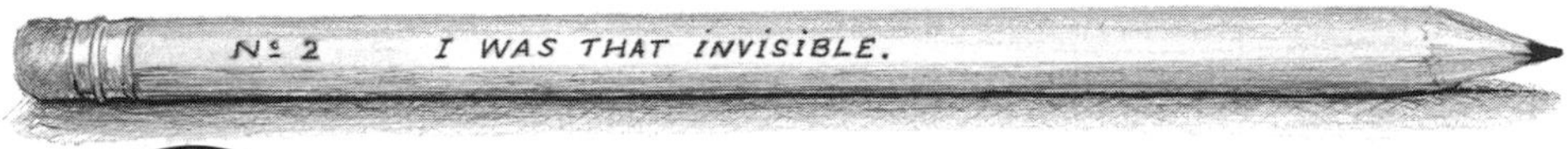
No 2
I WAS THAT INVISIBLE.

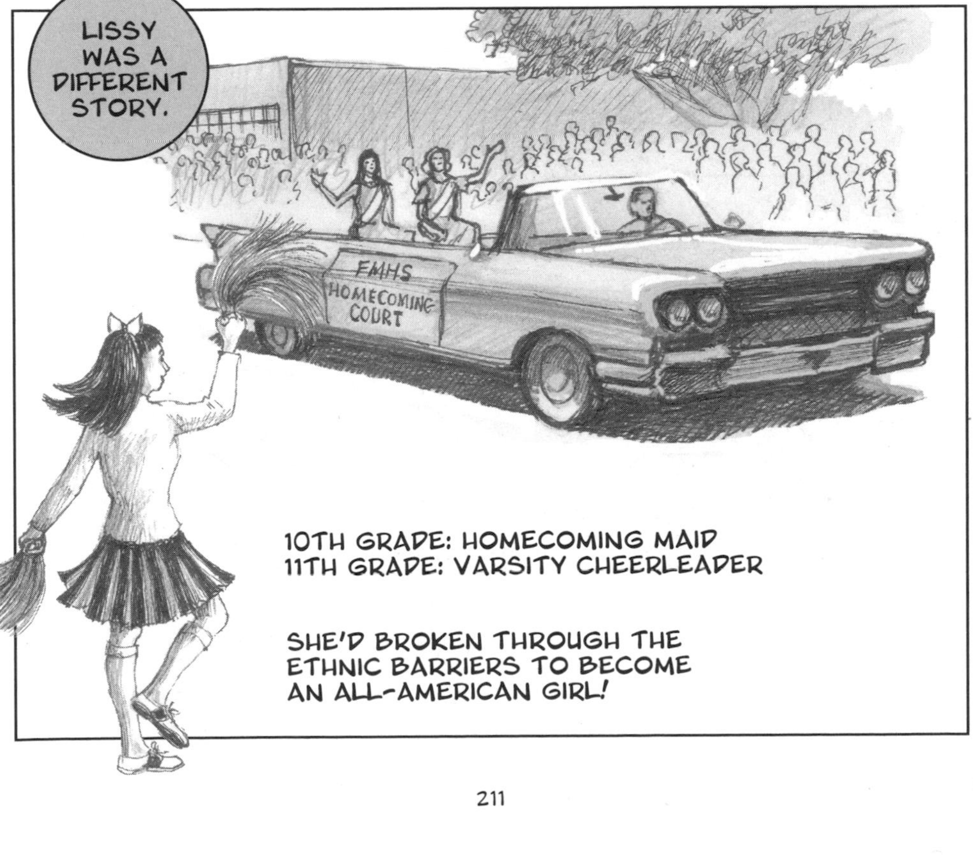
LISSY WAS A DIFFERENT STORY.
FMHS
HOMECOMING COURT
10TH GRADE: HOMECOMING MAID
11TH GRADE: VARSITY CHEERLEADER
SHE'D BROKEN THROUGH THE ETHNIC BARRIERS TO BECOME AN ALL-AMERICAN GIRL!

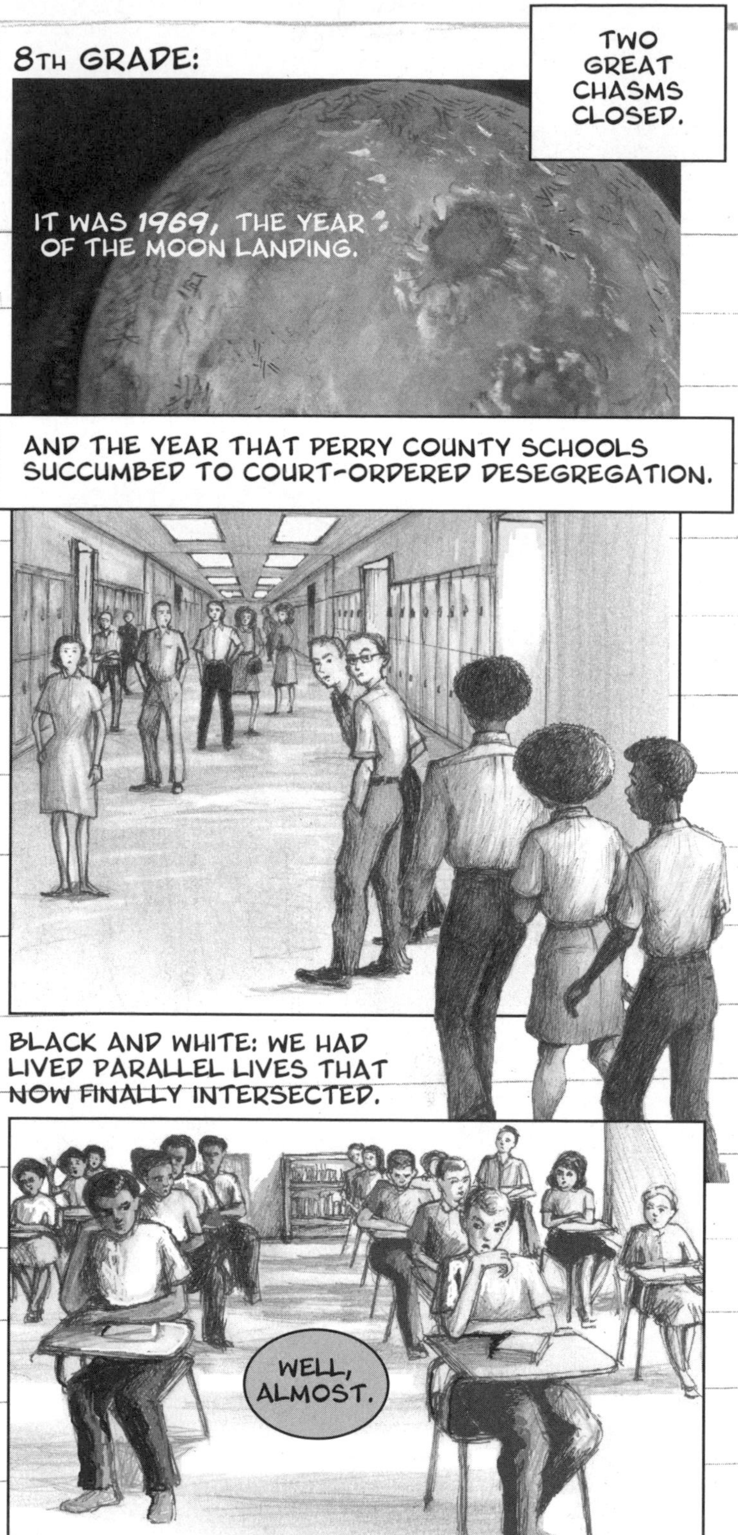
8TH GRADE:
TWO GREAT CHASMS CLOSED.
IT WAS 1969, THE YEAR OF THE MOON LANDING.
AND THE YEAR THAT PERRY COUNTY SCHOOLS SUCCUMBED TO COURT-ORDERED DESEGREGATION.
BLACK AND WHITE: WE HAD LIVED PARALLEL LIVES THAT NOW FINALLY INTERSECTED.
WELL, ALMOST.

EACH DAY PRESENTED A NEW FIRST AT FRANCIS MARION HIGH SCHOOL.

MANY WHITE KIDS HAD NEVER ADDRESSED BLACK ADULTS WITH TITLES OF RESPECT.

THE THREE BRANCHES OF GOVERNMENT

1. LEGISLATIVE
   CONGRESS → SENATE
   HOUSE OF REPRESENTATIVES

EXECUTIVE
   PRESIDENT VICE-PRESIDENT

COURT
CHIEF JUSTICE - JUSTICES

THEY DID NOW.

MOST WHITE KIDS HAD NEVER SEEN AFRO PICKS OR DAISHIKIS UP CLOSE—UNTIL NOW.

WHITE ATHLETES HAD NEVER SHARED A FIELD OR A COURT WITH BLACK ATHLETES.

WHITE CHEERLEADERS HAD NEVER CHEERED FOR BLACK PLAYERS. THEY DID NOW.

IT DIDN'T TAKE LONG FOR INGRAINED BIASES TO EMERGE.

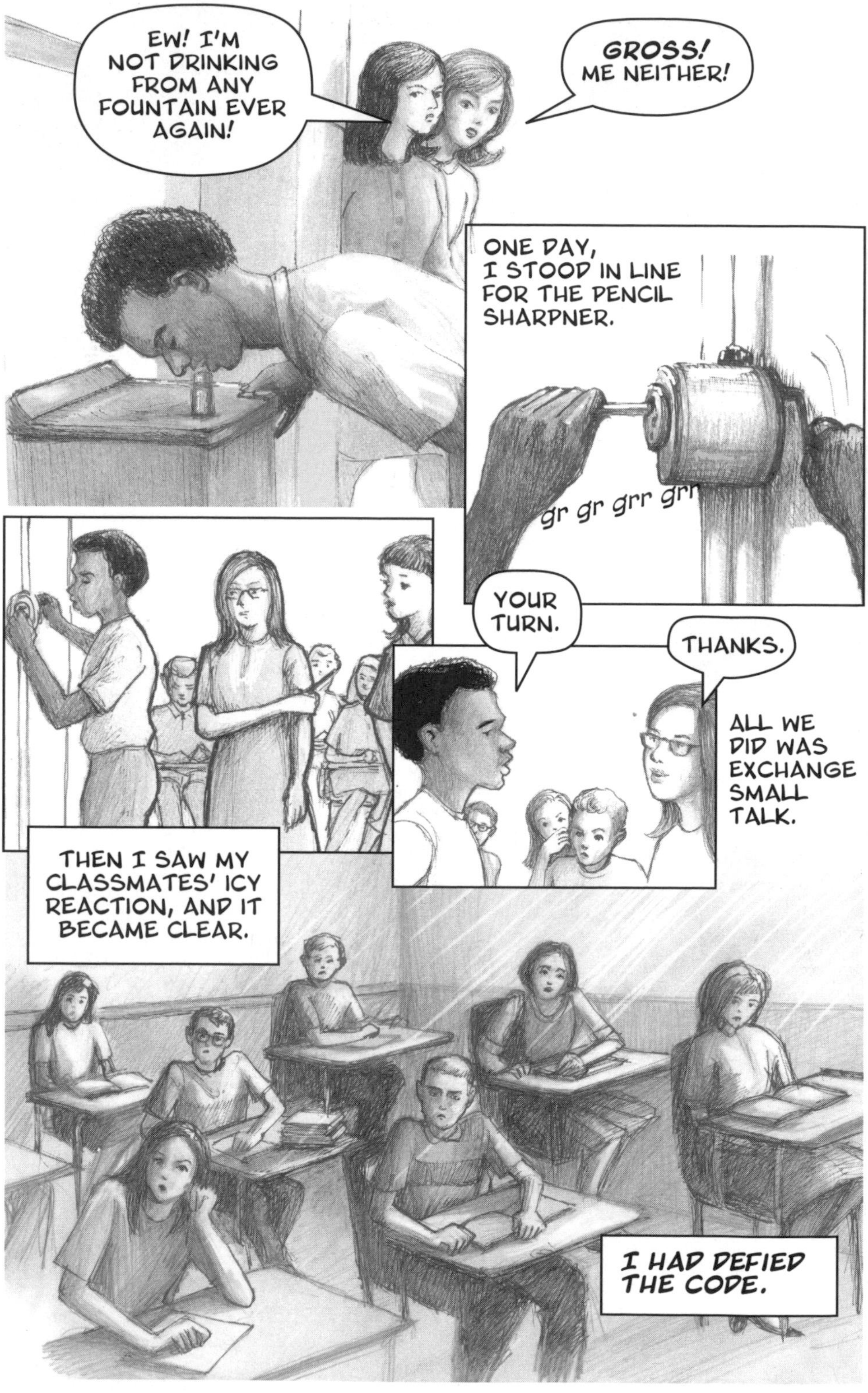

OUR NEW SCHOOLMATES FLAUNTED THE RULES LEFT AND RIGHT.

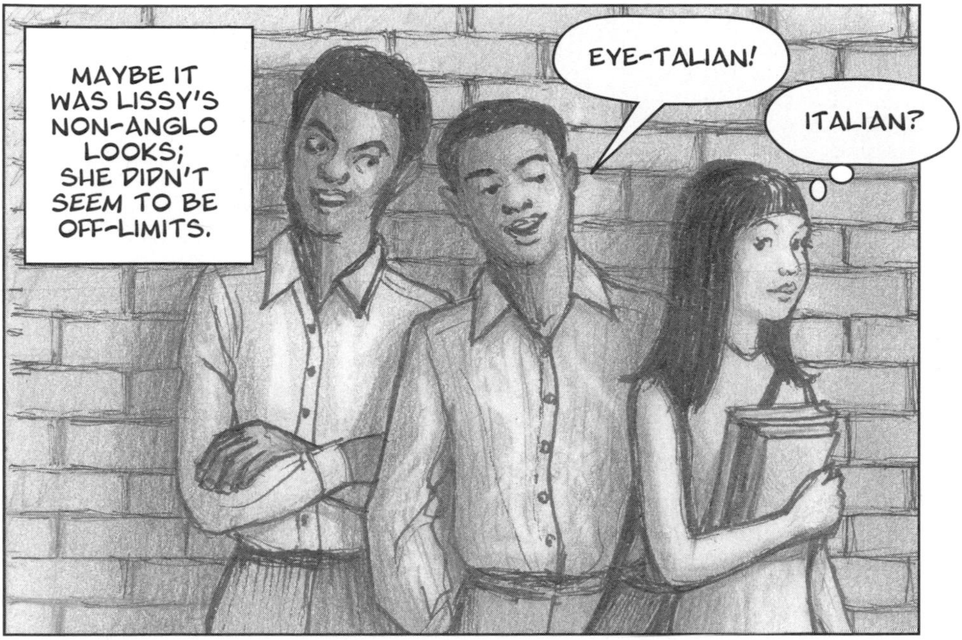
MAYBE IT WAS LISSY'S NON-ANGLO LOOKS; SHE DIDN'T SEEM TO BE OFF-LIMITS.
EYE-TALIAN!
ITALIAN?

MY REGARD FOR THE RULES WAS GIVING WAY TO THE CURRENT SITUATION, NAMELY, A RAPPORT WITH MY BLACK CLASSMATES.

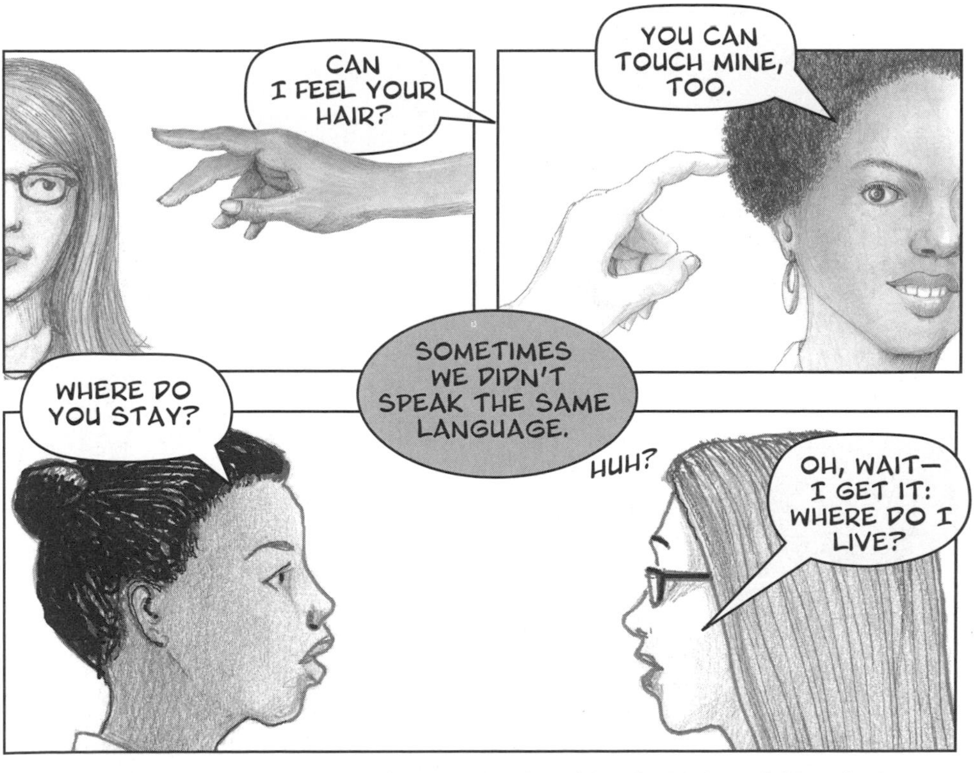
CAN I FEEL YOUR HAIR?
YOU CAN TOUCH MINE, TOO.
SOMETIMES WE DIDN'T SPEAK THE SAME LANGUAGE.
WHERE DO YOU STAY?
HUH?
OH, WAIT— I GET IT: WHERE DO I LIVE?

BUT THE SPARK OF CONNECTION LEAPT OVER THESE INITIAL GAPS.

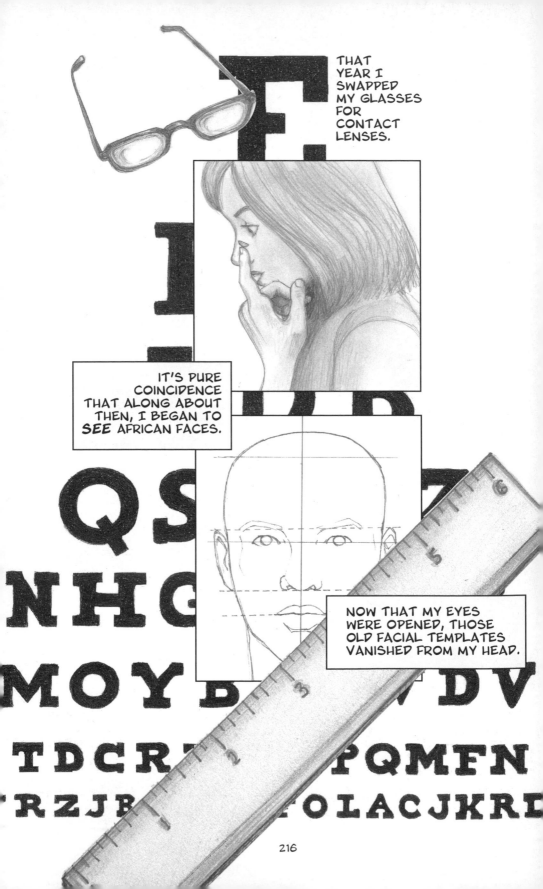

THAT YEAR I SWAPPED MY GLASSES FOR CONTACT LENSES.

IT'S PURE COINCIDENCE THAT ALONG ABOUT THEN, I BEGAN TO *SEE* AFRICAN FACES.

NOW THAT MY EYES WERE OPENED, THOSE OLD FACIAL TEMPLATES VANISHED FROM MY HEAD.

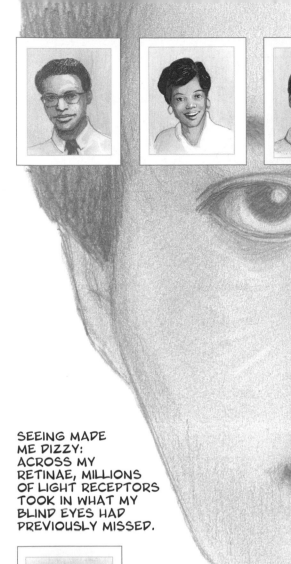

SEEING MADE ME DIZZY: ACROSS MY RETINAE, MILLIONS OF LIGHT RECEPTORS TOOK IN WHAT MY BLIND EYES HAD PREVIOUSLY MISSED.

GONE WERE THE DAYS WHEN I WAS DESPERATE TO BLEND IN. NOW I FORMED ALLIANCES WITH KIDS WHO EMBRACED RACIAL HARMONY.

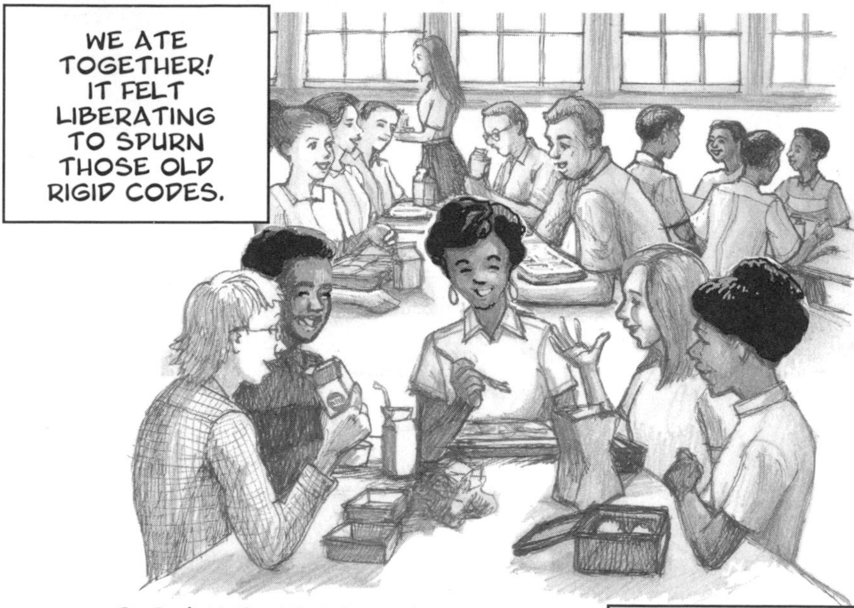
WE ATE TOGETHER! IT FELT LIBERATING TO SPURN THOSE OLD RIGID CODES.

THE VIOLENCE OF 1965 SEEMED LIKE SOMETHING FROM EONS PAST.

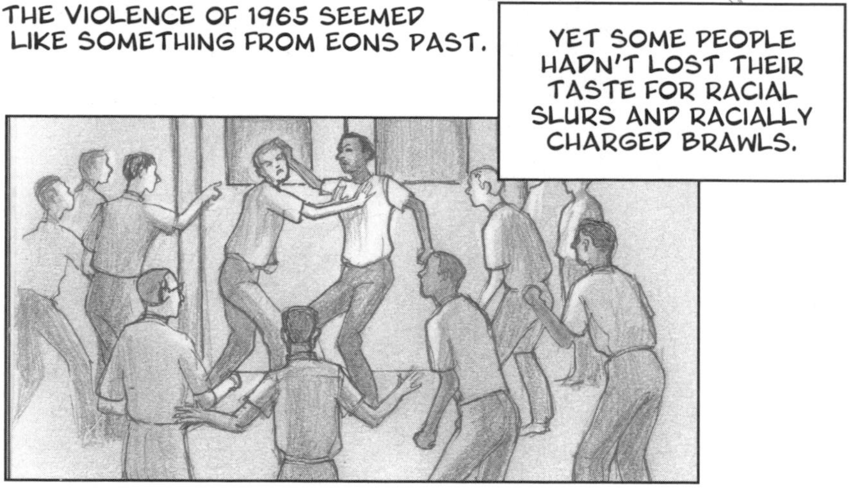
YET SOME PEOPLE HADN'T LOST THEIR TASTE FOR RACIAL SLURS AND RACIALLY CHARGED BRAWLS.

BEYOND THE VIOLENCE LAY MANY MORE EXPRESSIONS OF RACISM.

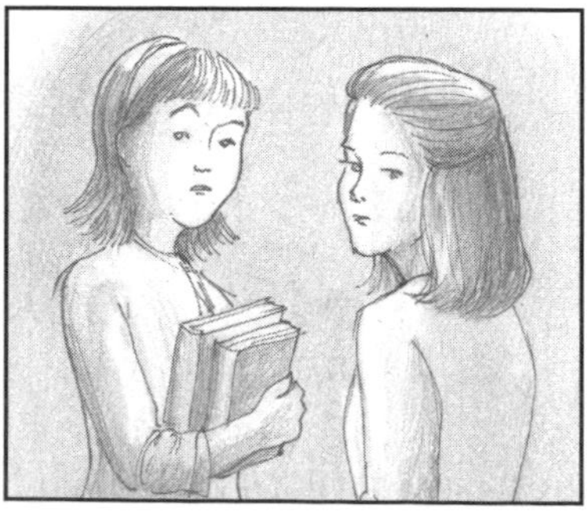

FRATERNIZING WITH BLACK KIDS GOT ME LOOKS OF CONTEMPT ON A DAILY BASIS. SOMETIMES THEY CAME FROM OLD FRIENDS, AND THAT HURT.

STILL, I FIGURED MY DEFIANCE WOULDN'T COST ME MUCH BESIDES REJECTION.

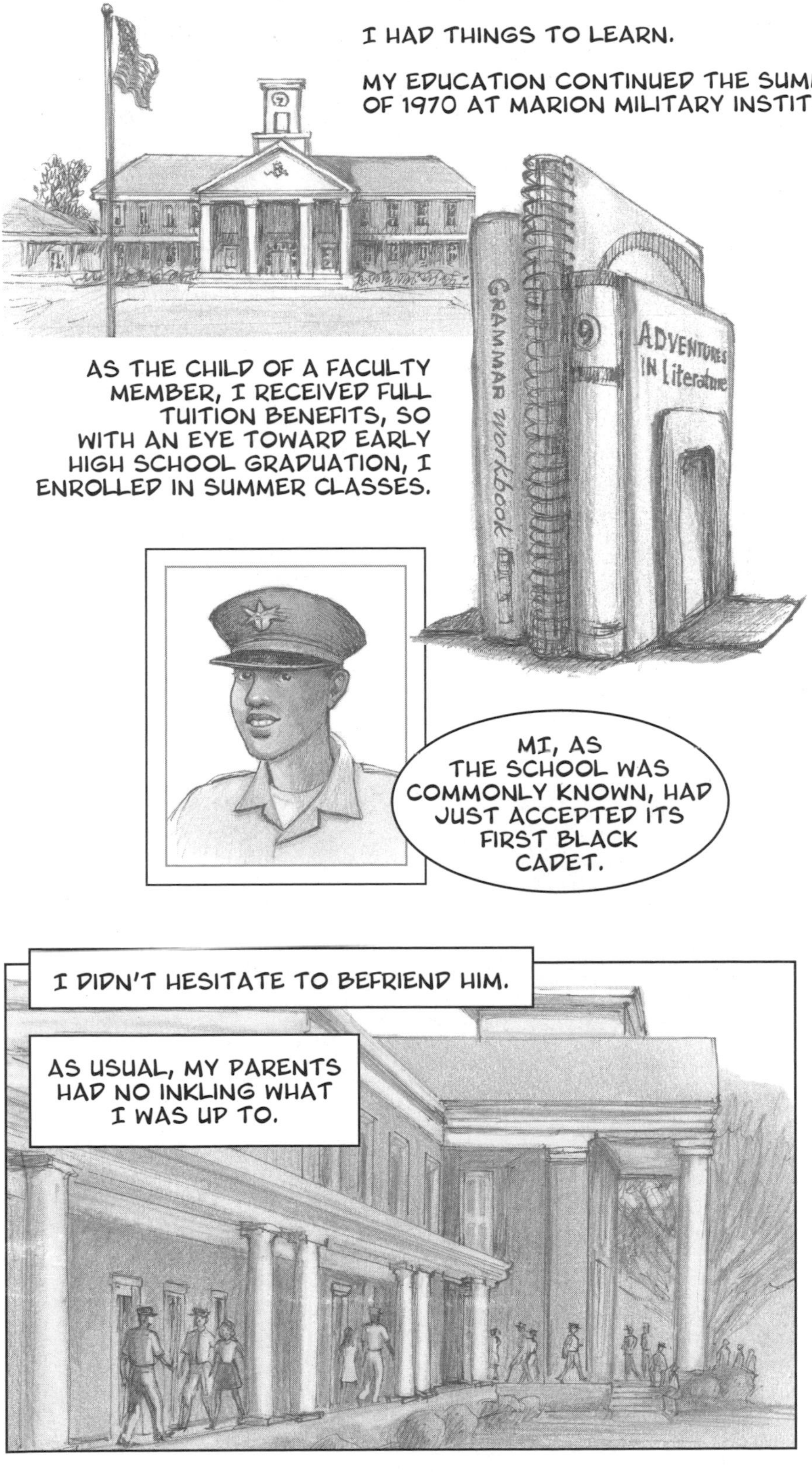
I HAD THINGS TO LEARN.
MY EDUCATION CONTINUED THE SUMMER OF 1970 AT MARION MILITARY INSTITUTE.
GRAMMAR WORKBOOK
ADVENTURES IN LITERATURE
AS THE CHILD OF A FACULTY MEMBER, I RECEIVED FULL TUITION BENEFITS, SO WITH AN EYE TOWARD EARLY HIGH SCHOOL GRADUATION, I ENROLLED IN SUMMER CLASSES.
MI, AS THE SCHOOL WAS COMMONLY KNOWN, HAD JUST ACCEPTED ITS FIRST BLACK CADET.
I DIDN'T HESITATE TO BEFRIEND HIM.
AS USUAL, MY PARENTS HAD NO INKLING WHAT I WAS UP TO.

ALL WE EVER DID WAS WALK AROUND CAMPUS BETWEEN CLASSES.

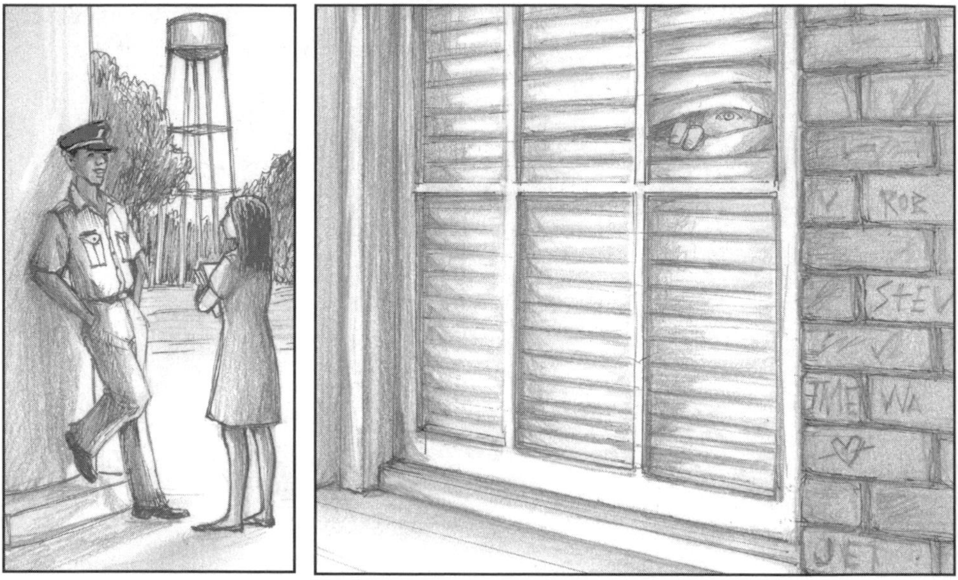

ON OUR STROLLS, WE NEVER NOTICED RAISED EYEBROWS OR SIDE-LONG GLANCES. I GUESS WE NEVER LOOKED AROUND THAT MUCH.

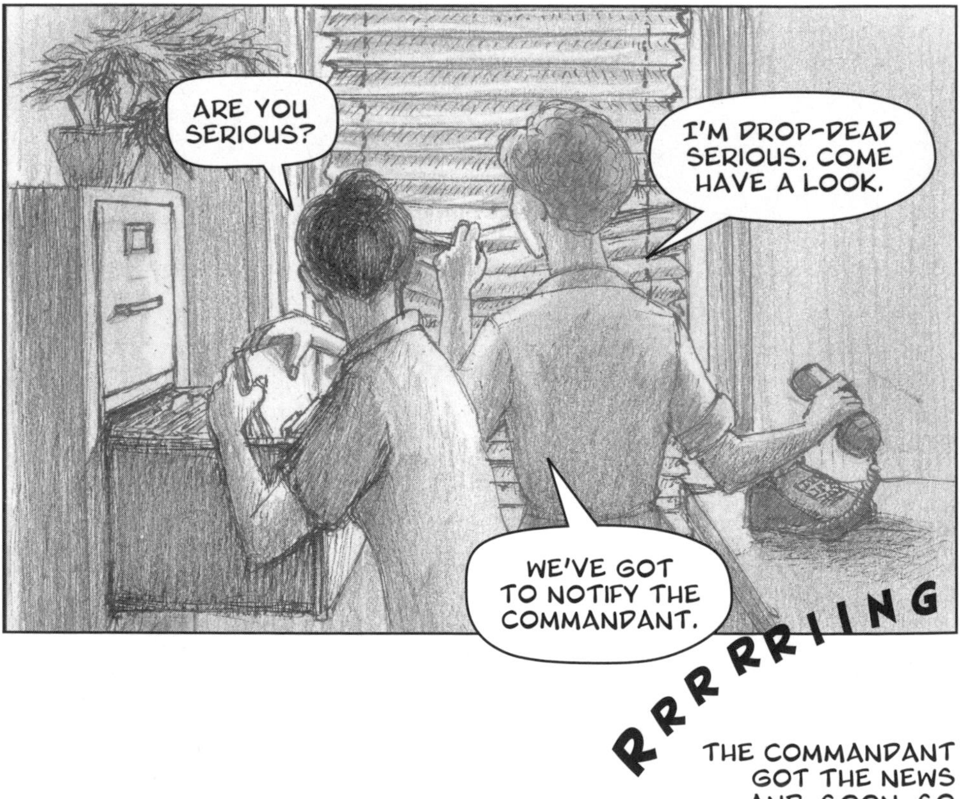
ARE YOU SERIOUS?
I'M DROP-DEAD SERIOUS. COME HAVE A LOOK.
WE'VE GOT TO NOTIFY THE COMMANDANT.
RRRRRIING

THE COMMANDANT GOT THE NEWS AND, SOON, SO DID THE TOWN.

THIS IS HOW I IMAGINE THE GRAPEVINE IN OPERATION:

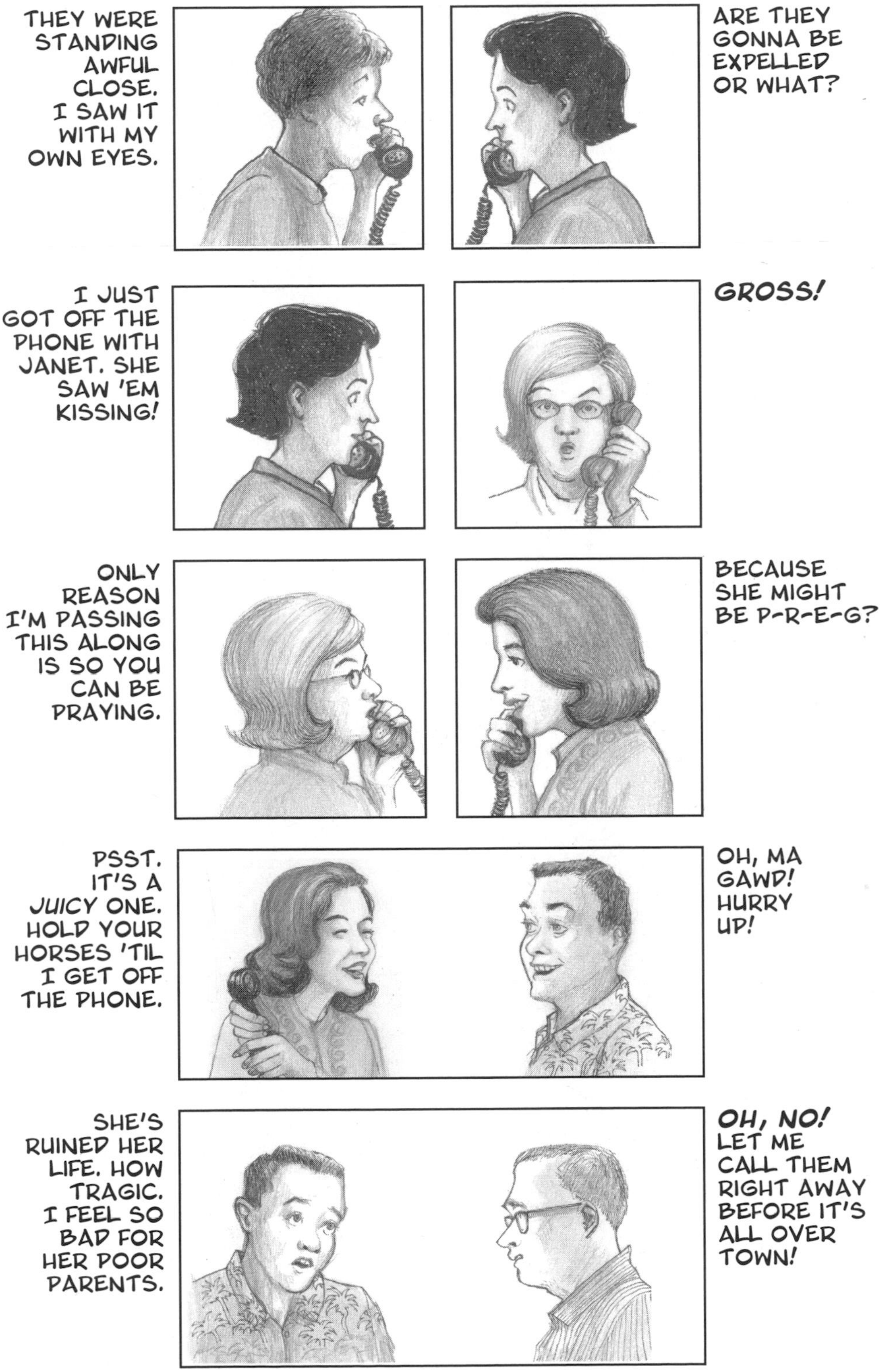
THEY WERE STANDING AWFUL CLOSE. I SAW IT WITH MY OWN EYES.
ARE THEY GONNA BE EXPELLED OR WHAT?
I JUST GOT OFF THE PHONE WITH JANET. SHE SAW 'EM KISSING!
GROSS!
ONLY REASON I'M PASSING THIS ALONG IS SO YOU CAN BE PRAYING.
BECAUSE SHE MIGHT BE P-R-E-G?
PSST. IT'S A JUICY ONE. HOLD YOUR HORSES 'TIL I GET OFF THE PHONE.
OH, MA GAWD! HURRY UP!
SHE'S RUINED HER LIFE. HOW TRAGIC. I FEEL SO BAD FOR HER POOR PARENTS.
OH, NO! LET ME CALL THEM RIGHT AWAY BEFORE IT'S ALL OVER TOWN!

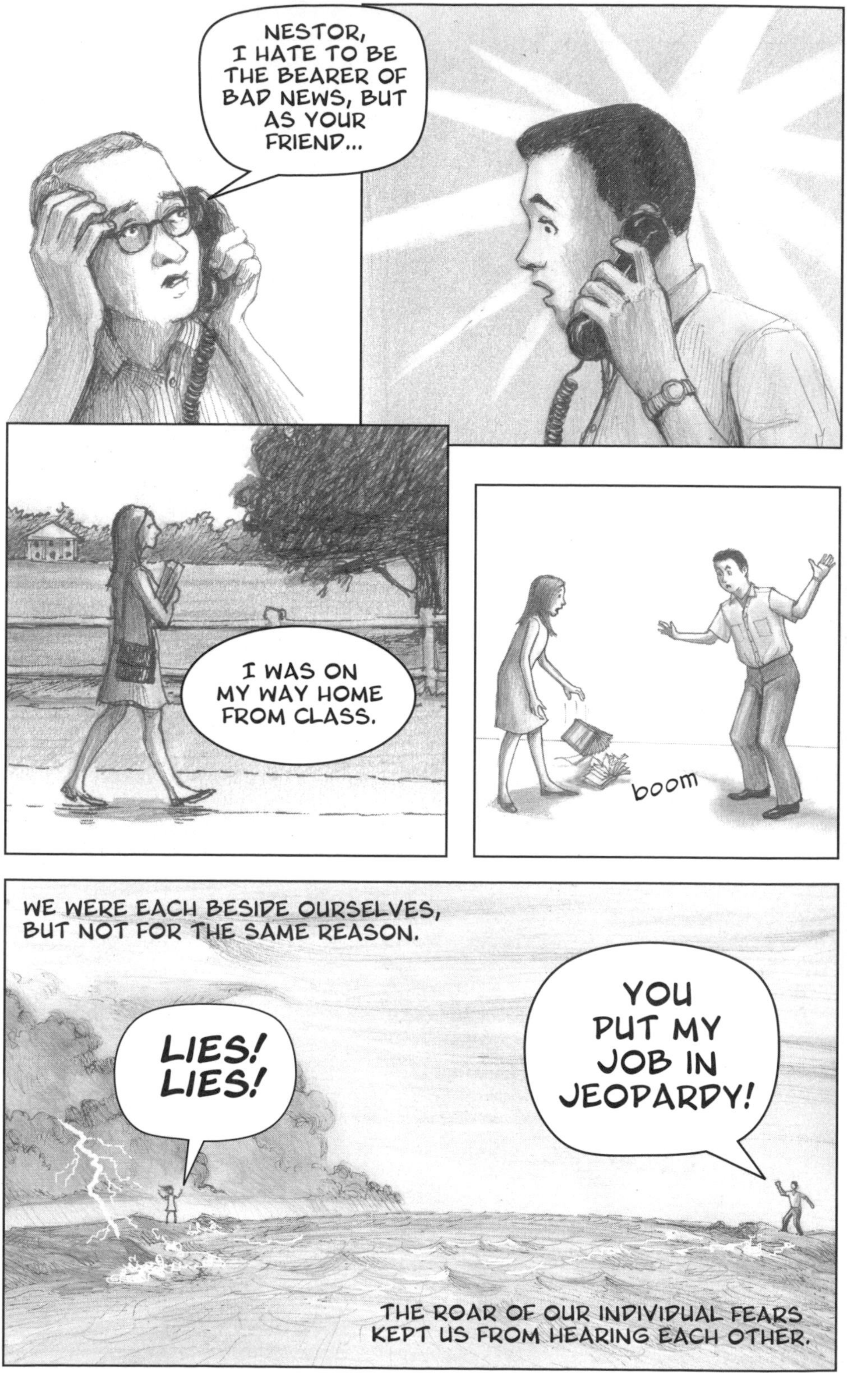
NESTOR, I HATE TO BE THE BEARER OF BAD NEWS, BUT AS YOUR FRIEND...
I WAS ON MY WAY HOME FROM CLASS.
boom
WE WERE EACH BESIDE OURSELVES, BUT NOT FOR THE SAME REASON.
LIES! LIES!
YOU PUT MY JOB IN JEOPARDY!
THE ROAR OF OUR INDIVIDUAL FEARS KEPT US FROM HEARING EACH OTHER.

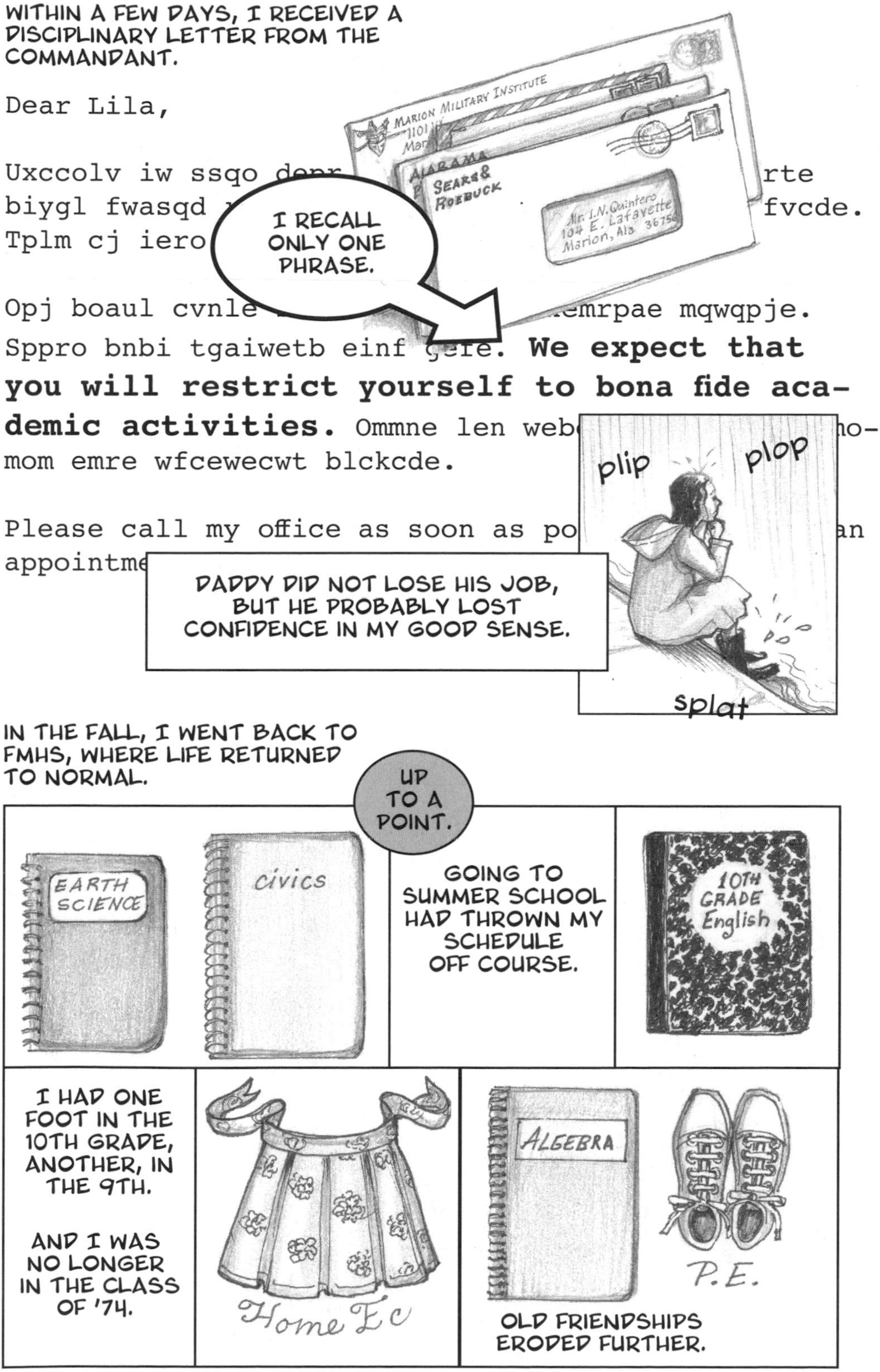

WITHIN A FEW DAYS, I RECEIVED A DISCIPLINARY LETTER FROM THE COMMANDANT.
Dear Lila,
Uxccolv iw ssqo depr rte biygl fwasqd fvcde. Tplm cj iero
I RECALL ONLY ONE PHRASE.
MARION MILITARY INSTITUTE
SEARS & ROEBUCK
Mr. J.N. Quintero 104 E. Lafayette Marion, Ala 36756
Opj boaul cvnle emrpae mqwqpje. Sppro bnbi tgaiwetb einf gere. **We expect that you will restrict yourself to bona fide academic activities.** Ommne len web mom emre wfcewecwt blckcde.
Please call my office as soon as po an appointme
DADDY DID NOT LOSE HIS JOB, BUT HE PROBABLY LOST CONFIDENCE IN MY GOOD SENSE.
plip
plop
splat
IN THE FALL, I WENT BACK TO FMHS, WHERE LIFE RETURNED TO NORMAL.
UP TO A POINT.
EARTH SCIENCE
civics
GOING TO SUMMER SCHOOL HAD THROWN MY SCHEDULE OFF COURSE.
10TH GRADE English
I HAD ONE FOOT IN THE 10TH GRADE, ANOTHER, IN THE 9TH.
AND I WAS NO LONGER IN THE CLASS OF '74.
Home Ec
ALGEBRA
P.E.
OLD FRIENDSHIPS ERODED FURTHER.

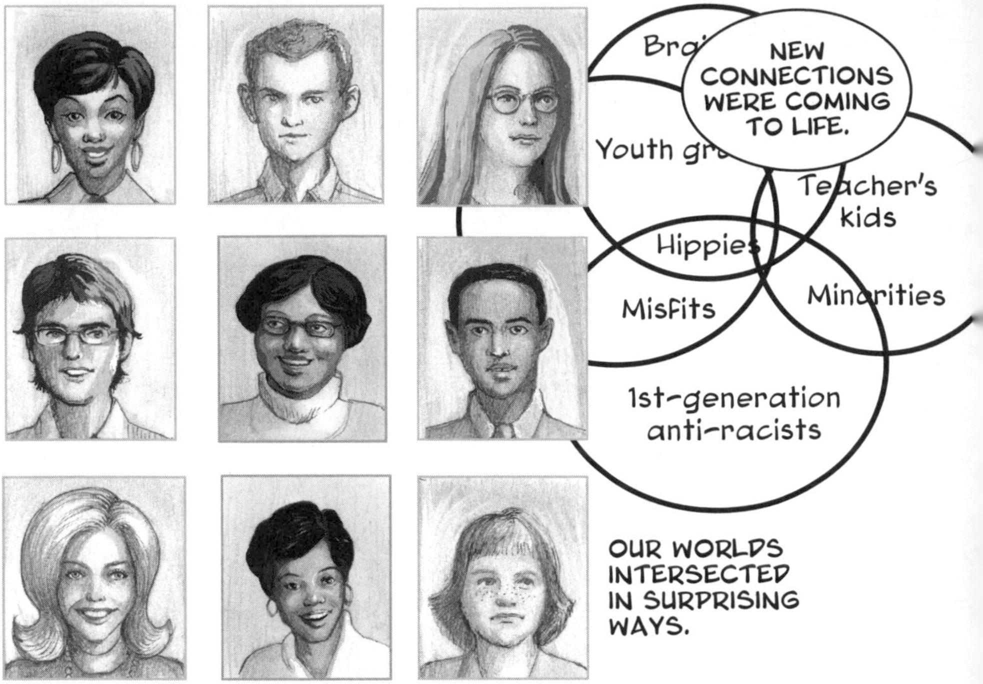
NEW CONNECTIONS WERE COMING TO LIFE.
Teacher's kids
Hippies
Misfits
Minorities
1st-generation anti-racists
OUR WORLDS INTERSECTED IN SURPRISING WAYS.

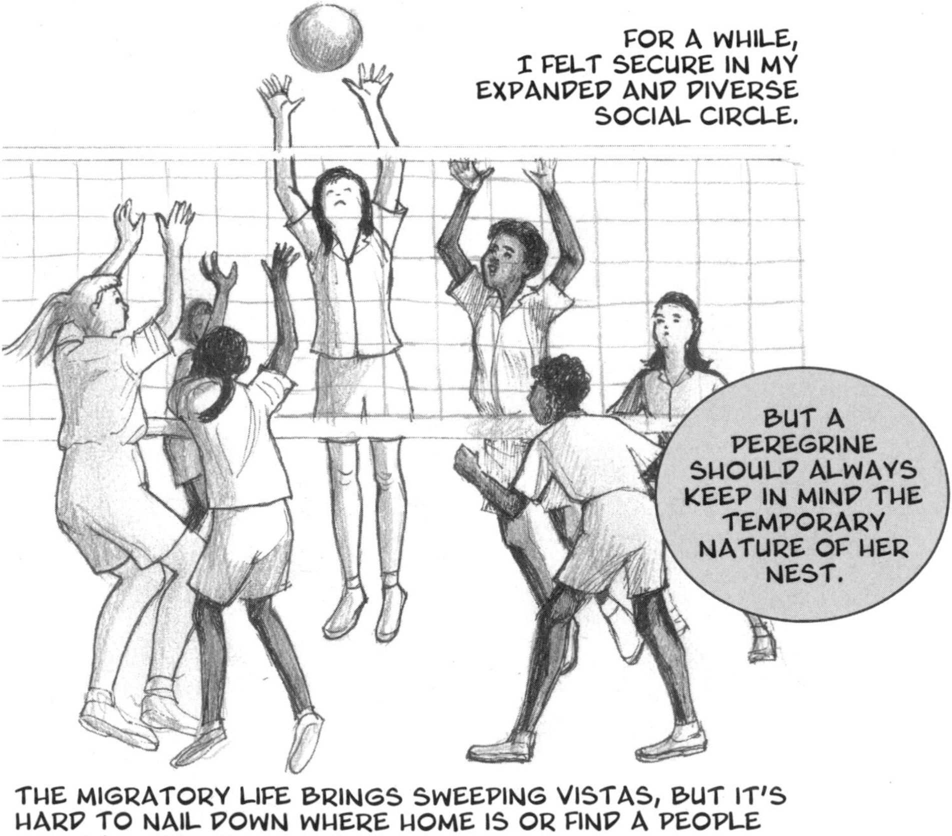
FOR A WHILE, I FELT SECURE IN MY EXPANDED AND DIVERSE SOCIAL CIRCLE.
BUT A PEREGRINE SHOULD ALWAYS KEEP IN MIND THE TEMPORARY NATURE OF HER NEST.

THE MIGRATORY LIFE BRINGS SWEEPING VISTAS, BUT IT'S HARD TO NAIL DOWN WHERE HOME IS OR FIND A PEOPLE YOU CAN CALL YOUR OWN.

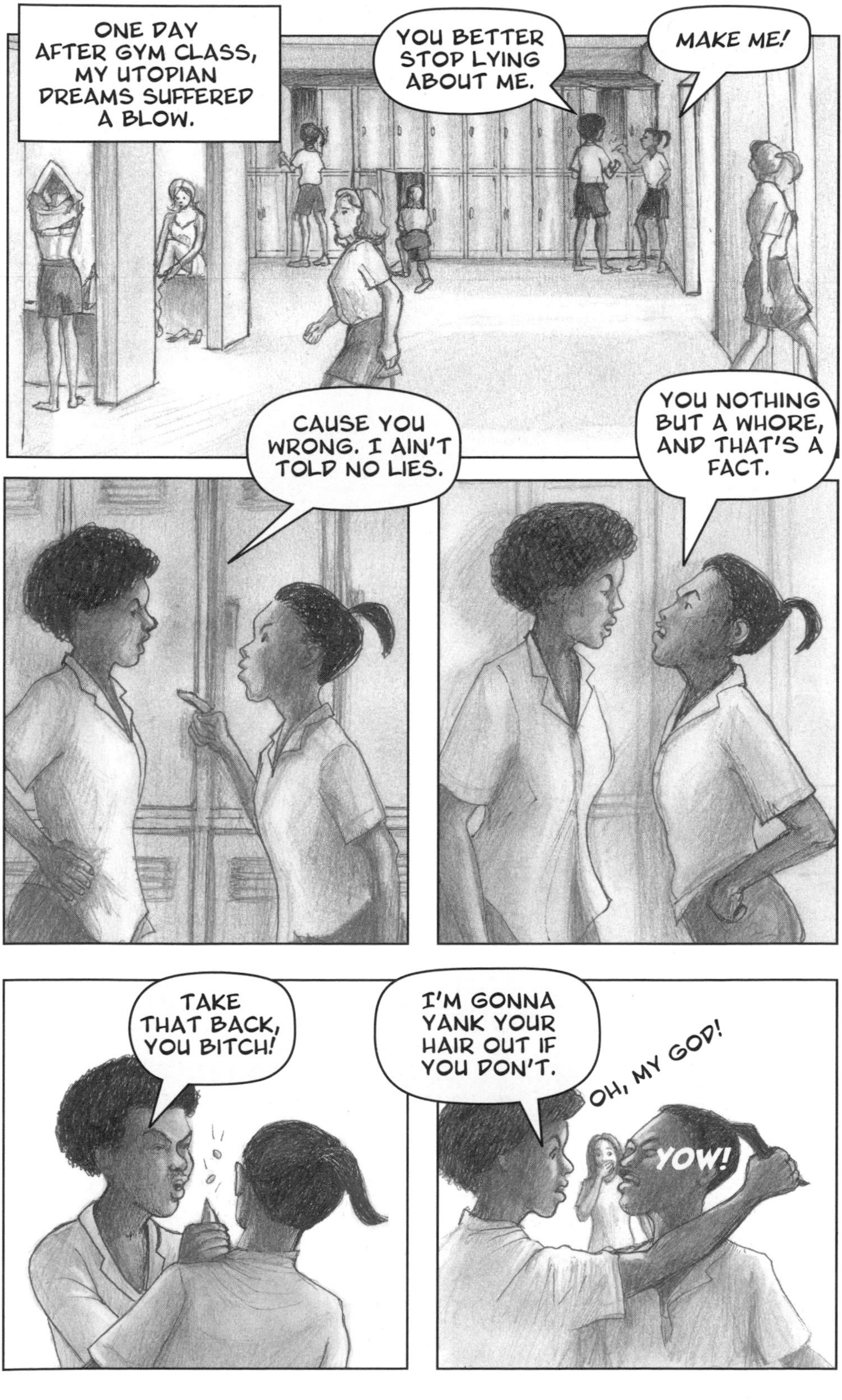
ONE DAY AFTER GYM CLASS, MY UTOPIAN DREAMS SUFFERED A BLOW.
YOU BETTER STOP LYING ABOUT ME.
MAKE ME!
CAUSE YOU WRONG. I AIN'T TOLD NO LIES.
YOU NOTHING BUT A WHORE, AND THAT'S A FACT.
TAKE THAT BACK, YOU BITCH!
I'M GONNA YANK YOUR HAIR OUT IF YOU DON'T.
OH, MY GOD!
YOW!

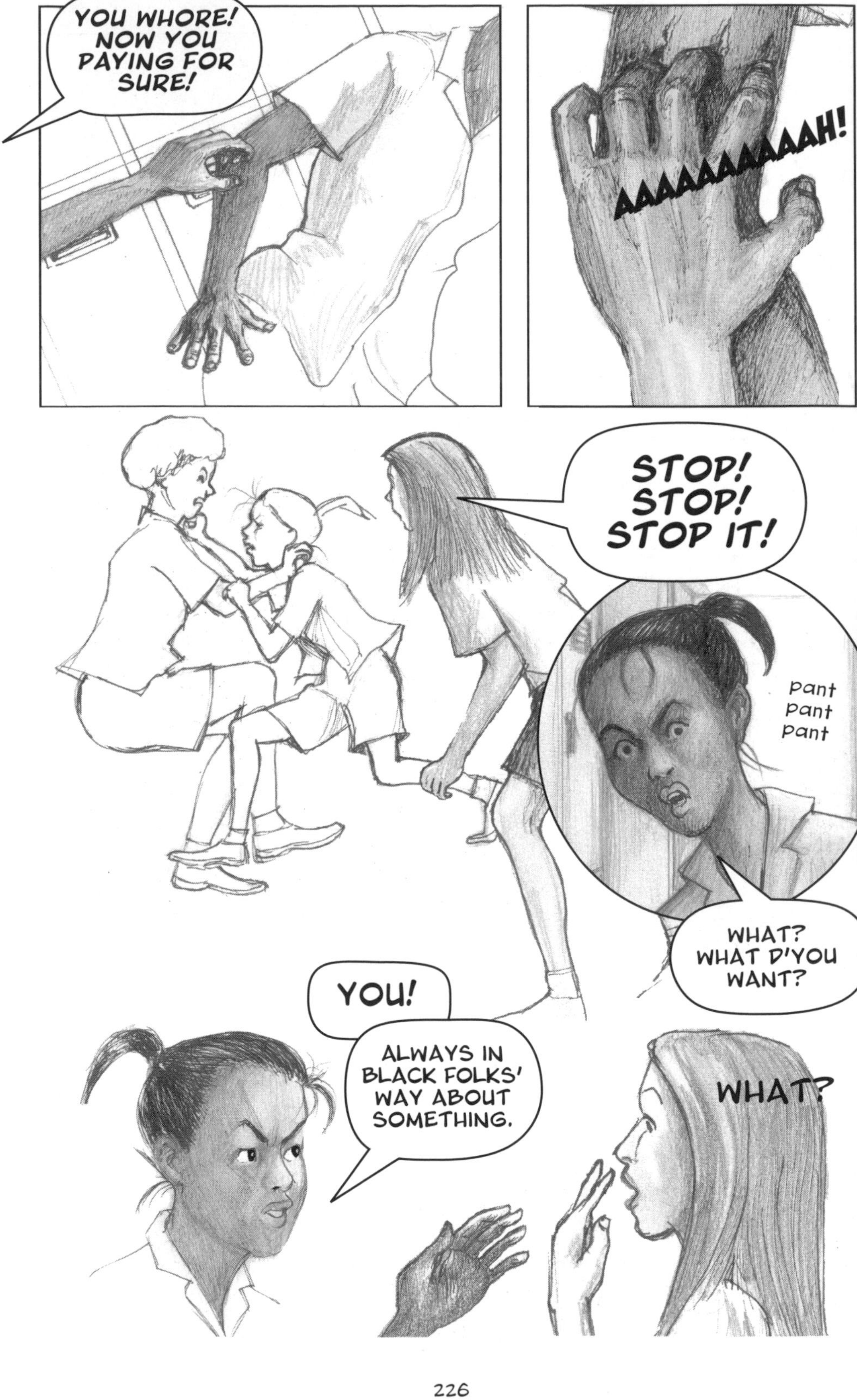
YOU WHORE! NOW YOU PAYING FOR SURE!
AAAAAAAAAAH!
STOP! STOP! STOP IT!
pant pant pant
WHAT? WHAT D'YOU WANT?
YOU!
ALWAYS IN BLACK FOLKS' WAY ABOUT SOMETHING.
WHAT?

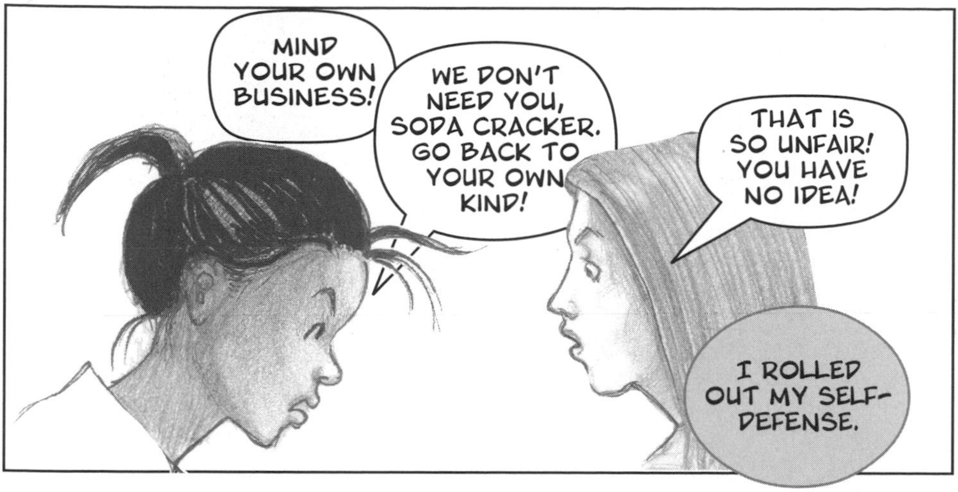
MIND YOUR OWN BUSINESS!
WE DON'T NEED YOU, SODA CRACKER. GO BACK TO YOUR OWN KIND!
THAT IS SO UNFAIR! YOU HAVE NO IDEA!
I ROLLED OUT MY SELF-DEFENSE.

IT GOT RATHER IMPASSIONED.

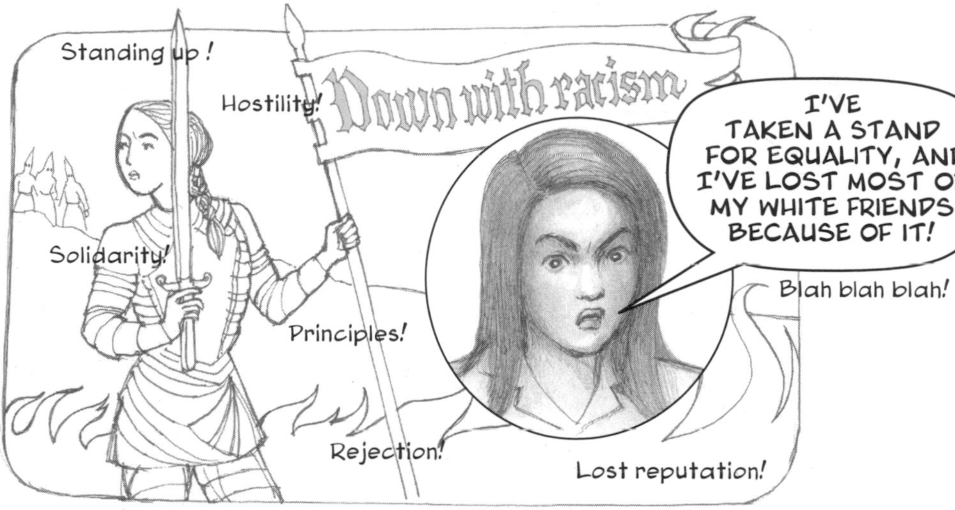
Standing up!
Hostility!
Down with racism
I'VE TAKEN A STAND FOR EQUALITY, AND I'VE LOST MOST OF MY WHITE FRIENDS BECAUSE OF IT!
Solidarity!
Blah blah blah!
Principles!
Rejection!
Lost reputation!

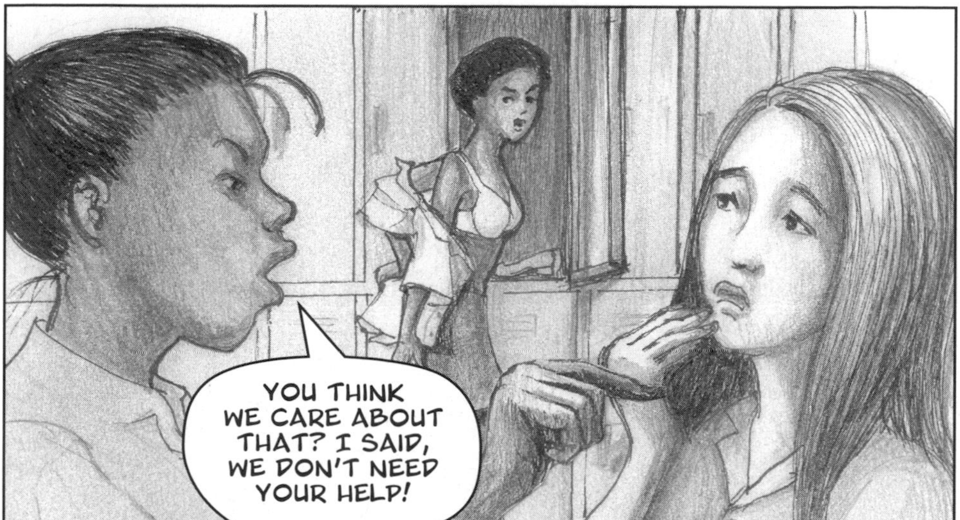
YOU THINK WE CARE ABOUT THAT? I SAID, WE DON'T NEED YOUR HELP!

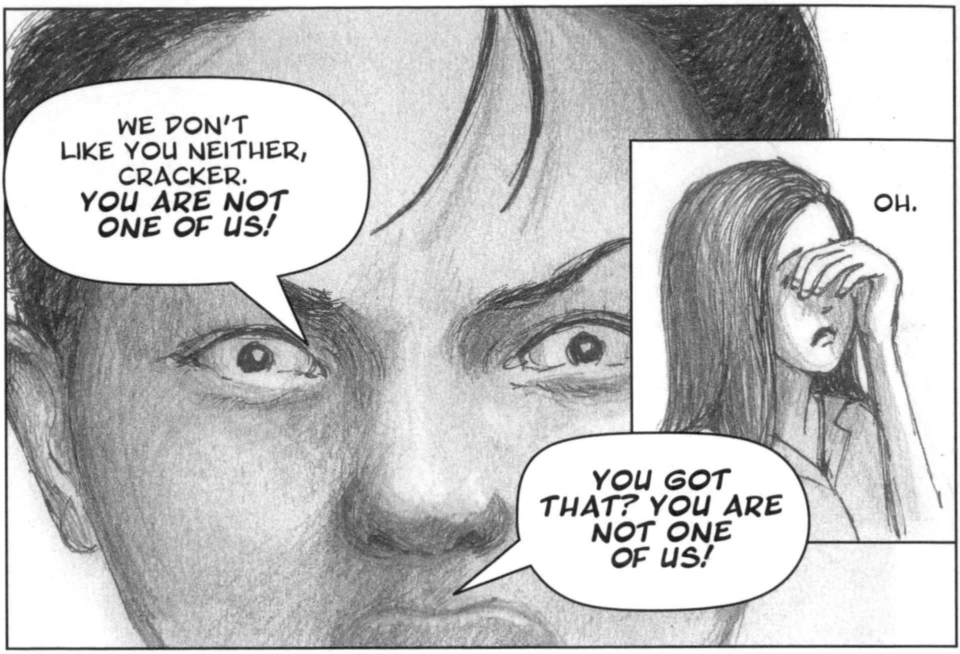
WE DON'T LIKE YOU NEITHER, CRACKER. **YOU ARE NOT ONE OF US!**
OH.
YOU GOT THAT? YOU ARE NOT ONE OF US!

I DON'T KNOW WHEN IT HAPPENED, BUT THE LOCKER ROOM HAD EMPTIED OUT. ONLY TWO OF US REMAINED.

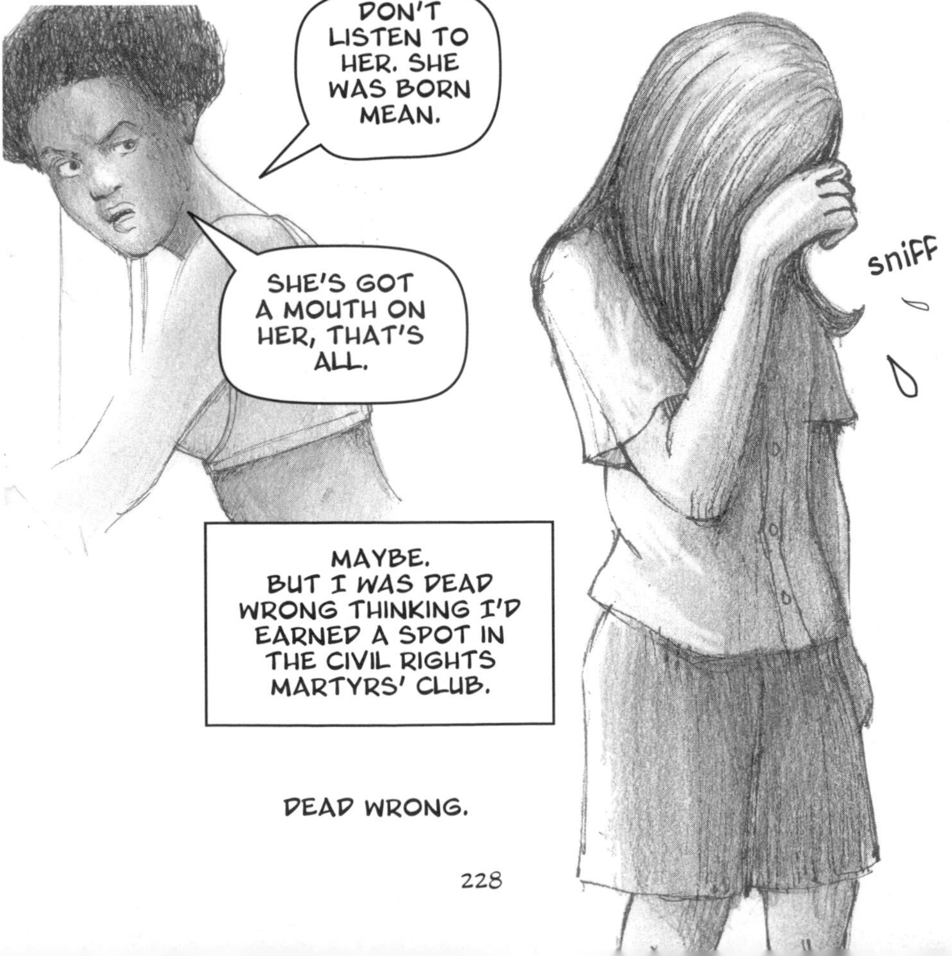
DON'T LISTEN TO HER. SHE WAS BORN MEAN.
SHE'S GOT A MOUTH ON HER, THAT'S ALL.
sniff
MAYBE. BUT I WAS DEAD WRONG THINKING I'D EARNED A SPOT IN THE CIVIL RIGHTS MARTYRS' CLUB.
DEAD WRONG.

1971

A NEW SCHOOL YEAR MEANT NEW SCHOOL SUPPLIES: SHARP PENCIL POINTS, CLEAN PAPER, FRESH PAGES. I LOVED ALL THAT.

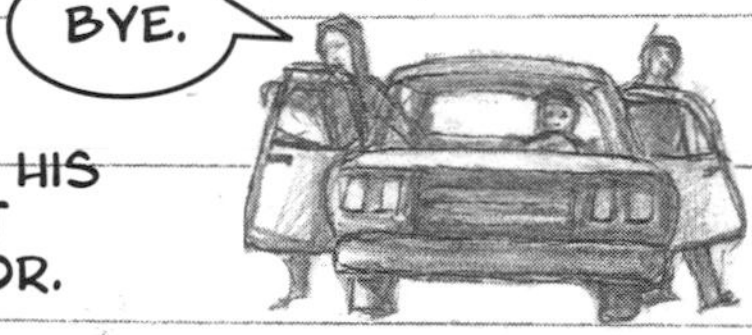
BYE.

MY BROTHER BEGAN HIS STINT AT FMHS THAT YEAR. I WAS A JUNIOR.

OUR WALK NOW WAS ONLY AS LONG AS THE PATH FROM THE CAR TO THE SCHOOL'S FRONT DOOR.

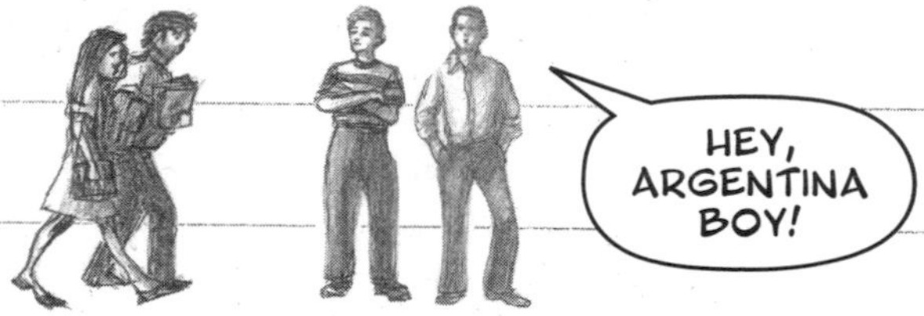
HEY, ARGENTINA BOY!

I WOULD LIKE TO REPORT FMHS AS A WONDERFUL FRESH START FOR JOHNNY, BUT RIGHT AWAY HE HAD DETRACTORS.

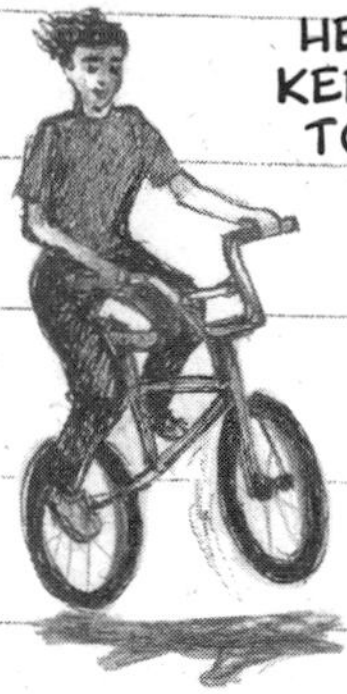

HE WASN'T TOO KEEN ON SCHOOL TO BEGIN WITH.

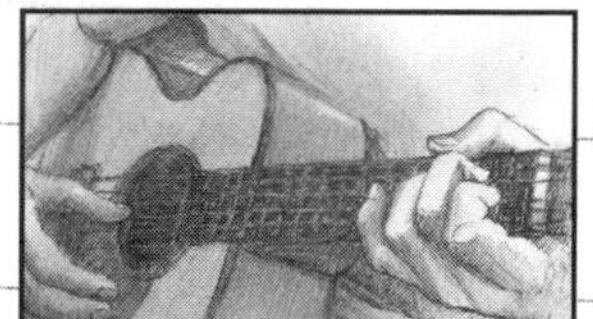

Am

G

C

D

HE WOULD RATHER HAVE BEEN POPPING WHEELIES SOMEWHERE OR LEARNING NEW CHORDS ON HIS GUITAR.

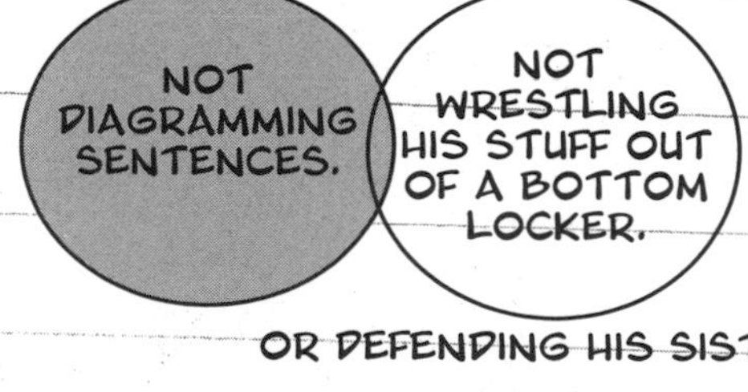
NOT DIAGRAMMING SENTENCES.
NOT WRESTLING HIS STUFF OUT OF A BOTTOM LOCKER.

OR DEFENDING HIS SISTER'S HONOR.

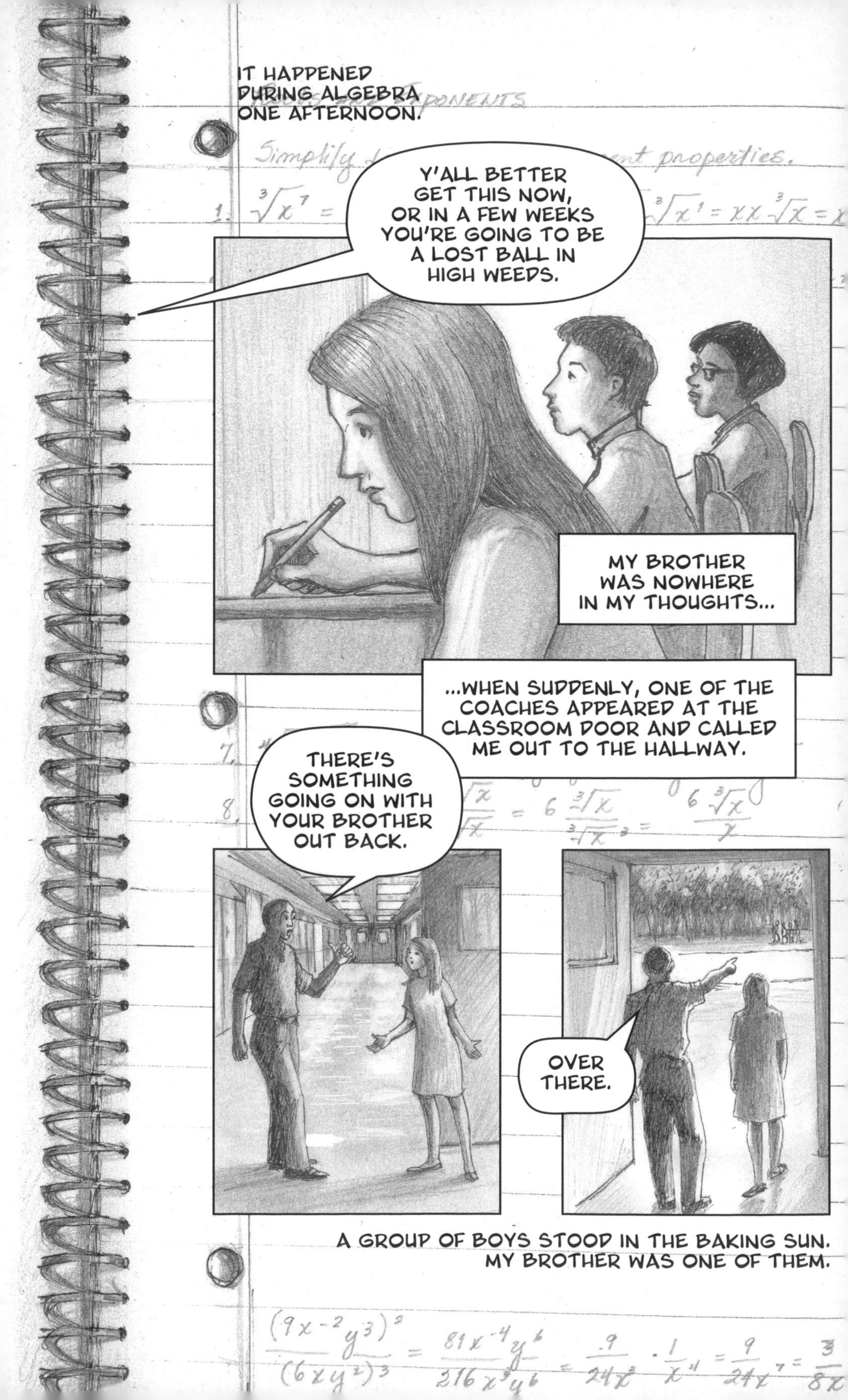
IT HAPPENED DURING ALGEBRA ONE AFTERNOON.
Y'ALL BETTER GET THIS NOW, OR IN A FEW WEEKS YOU'RE GOING TO BE A LOST BALL IN HIGH WEEDS.
MY BROTHER WAS NOWHERE IN MY THOUGHTS...
...WHEN SUDDENLY, ONE OF THE COACHES APPEARED AT THE CLASSROOM DOOR AND CALLED ME OUT TO THE HALLWAY.
THERE'S SOMETHING GOING ON WITH YOUR BROTHER OUT BACK.
OVER THERE.
A GROUP OF BOYS STOOD IN THE BAKING SUN. MY BROTHER WAS ONE OF THEM.

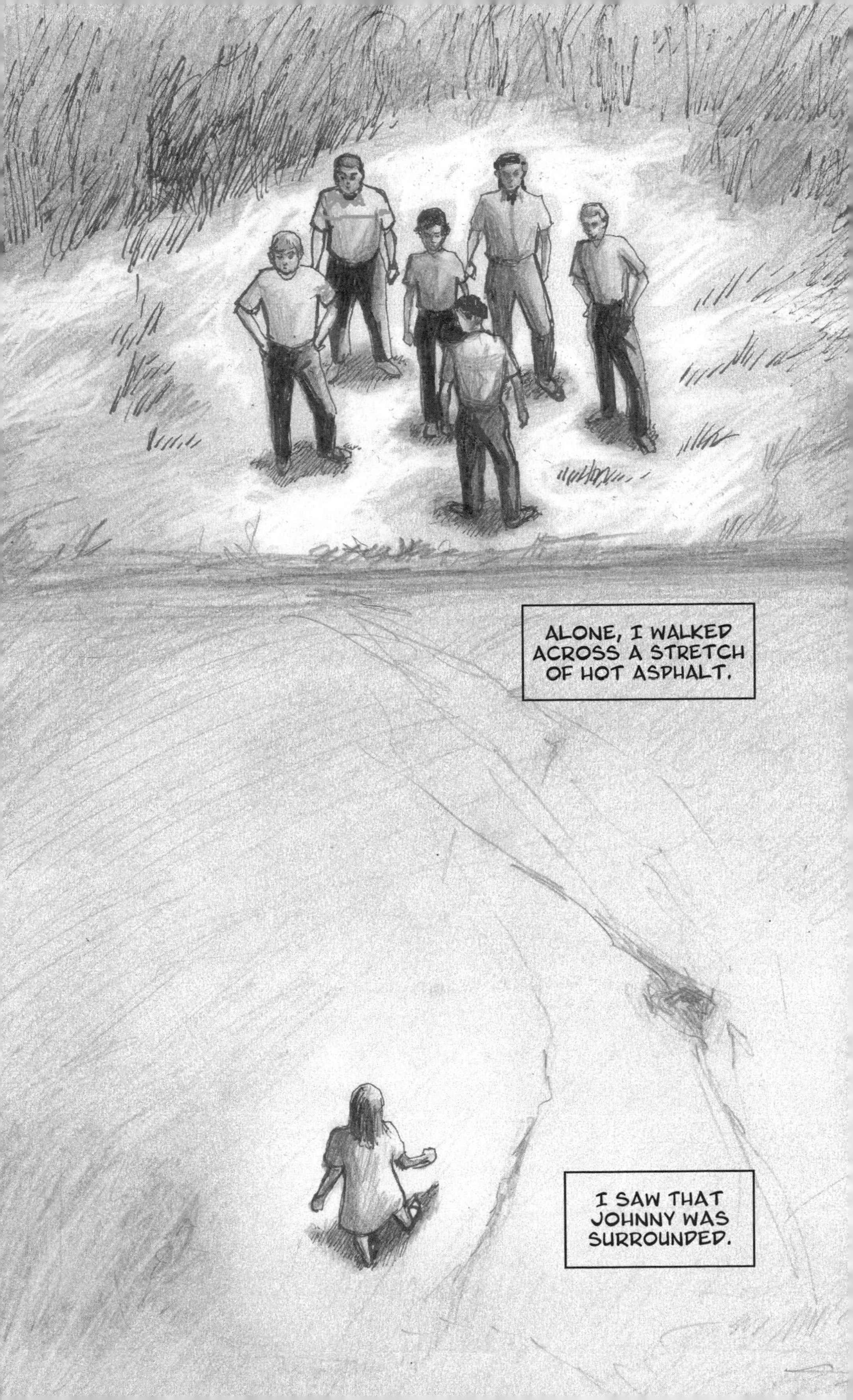
ALONE, I WALKED ACROSS A STRETCH OF HOT ASPHALT.
I SAW THAT JOHNNY WAS SURROUNDED.

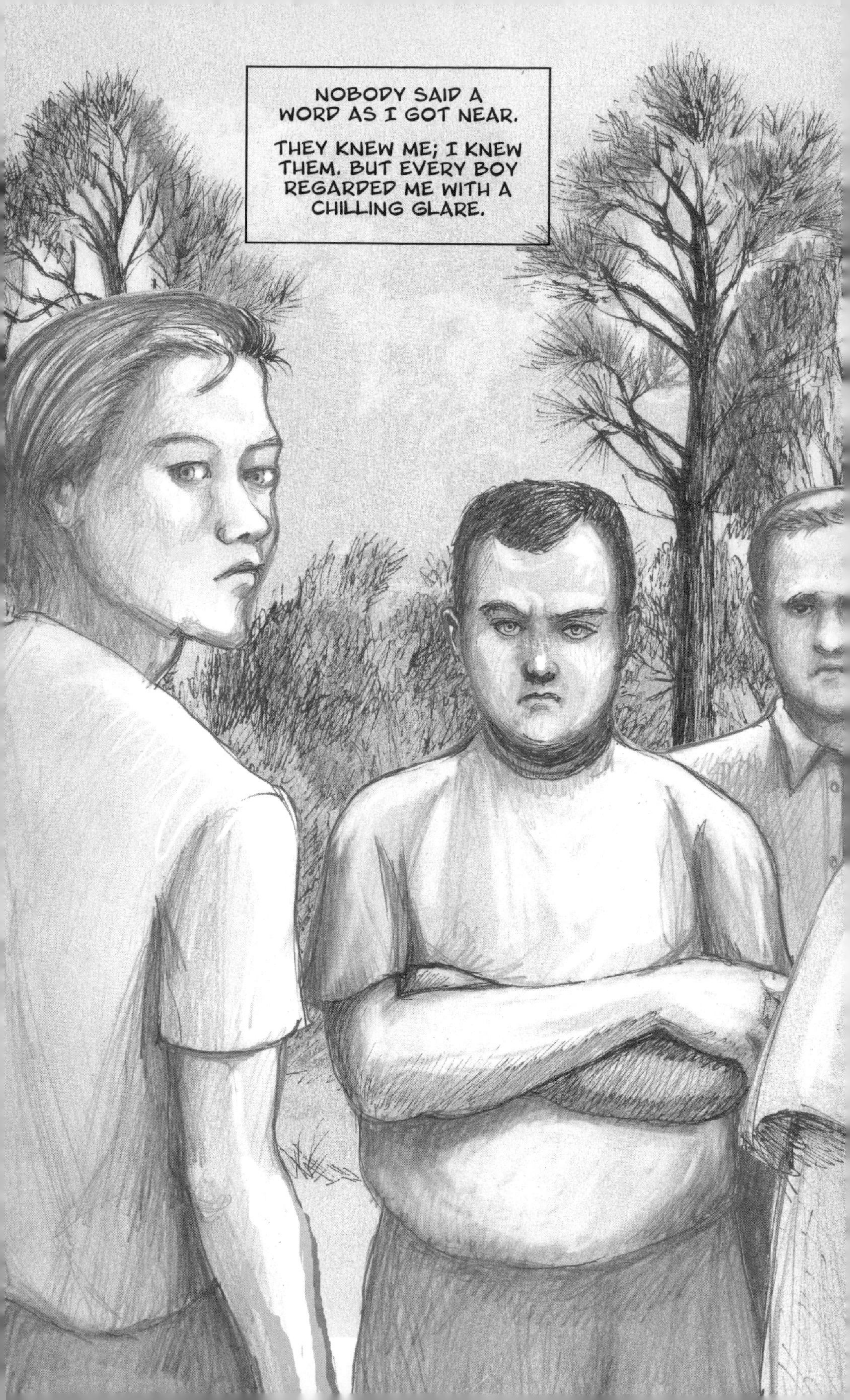
NOBODY SAID A WORD AS I GOT NEAR.
THEY KNEW ME; I KNEW THEM. BUT EVERY BOY REGARDED ME WITH A CHILLING GLARE.

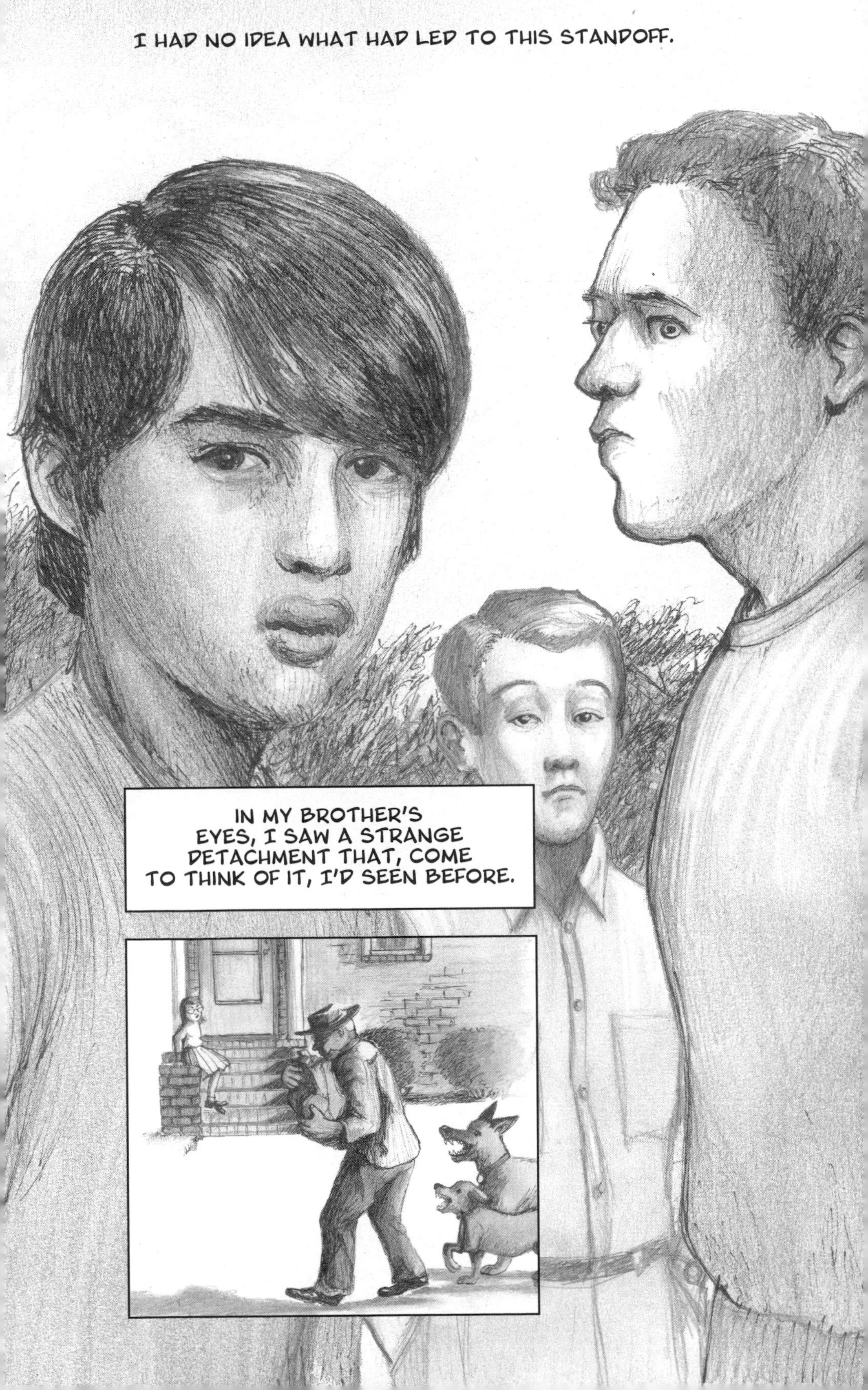
I HAD NO IDEA WHAT HAD LED TO THIS STANDOFF.
IN MY BROTHER'S EYES, I SAW A STRANGE DETACHMENT THAT, COME TO THINK OF IT, I'D SEEN BEFORE.

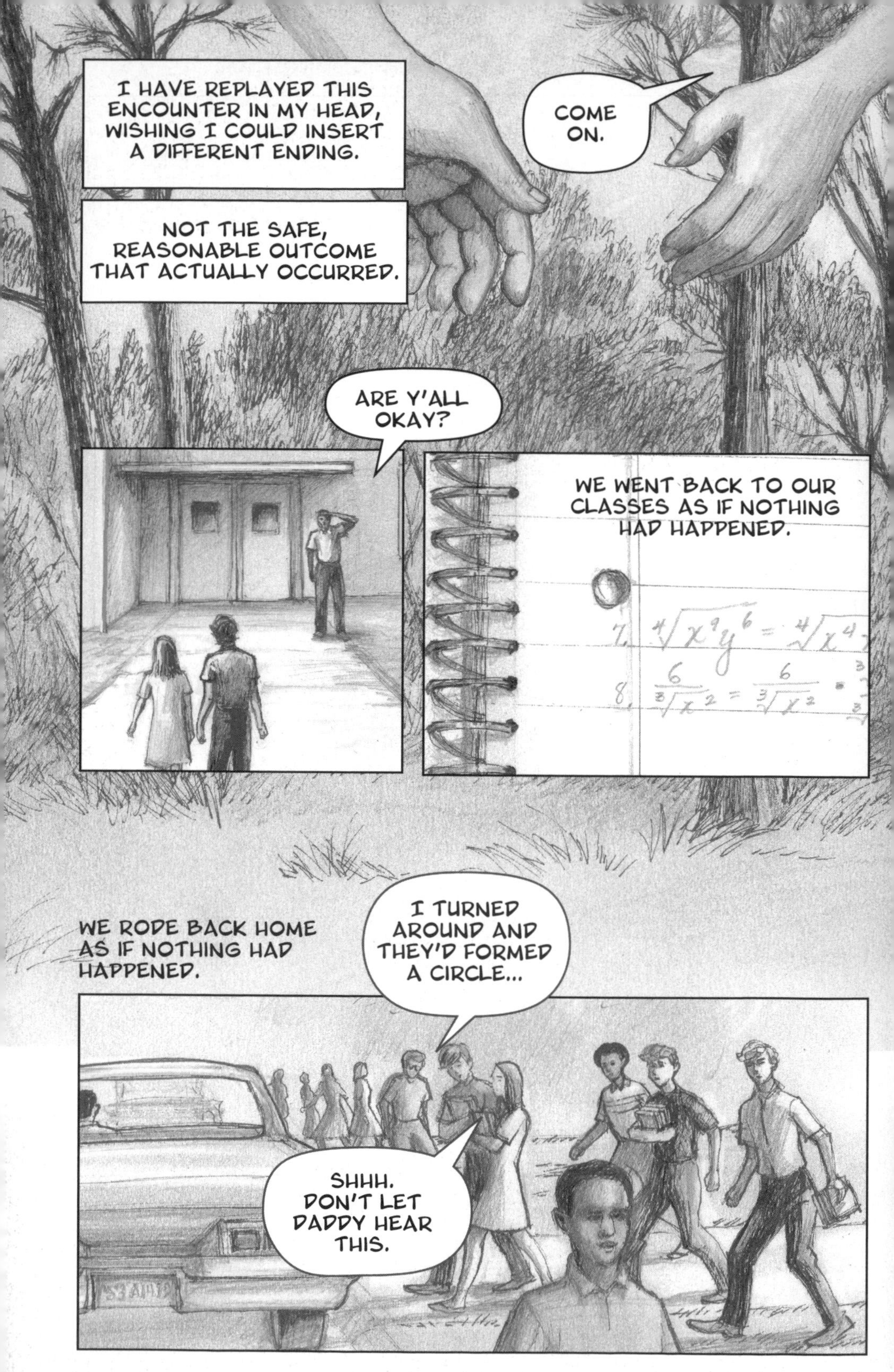
I HAVE REPLAYED THIS ENCOUNTER IN MY HEAD, WISHING I COULD INSERT A DIFFERENT ENDING.
NOT THE SAFE, REASONABLE OUTCOME THAT ACTUALLY OCCURRED.
COME ON.
ARE Y'ALL OKAY?
WE WENT BACK TO OUR CLASSES AS IF NOTHING HAD HAPPENED.
WE RODE BACK HOME AS IF NOTHING HAD HAPPENED.
I TURNED AROUND AND THEY'D FORMED A CIRCLE...
SHHH. DON'T LET DADDY HEAR THIS.

EVENTUALLY, JOHNNY TOLD ME THE REST OF THE STORY, BUT I CAN'T SEEM TO PLACE THAT CONVERSATION.

WAS IT SOMEWHERE AROUND THE HOUSE, OUT OF EARSHOT, SWALLOWED UP BY THE SOUNDS OF NORMALCY?

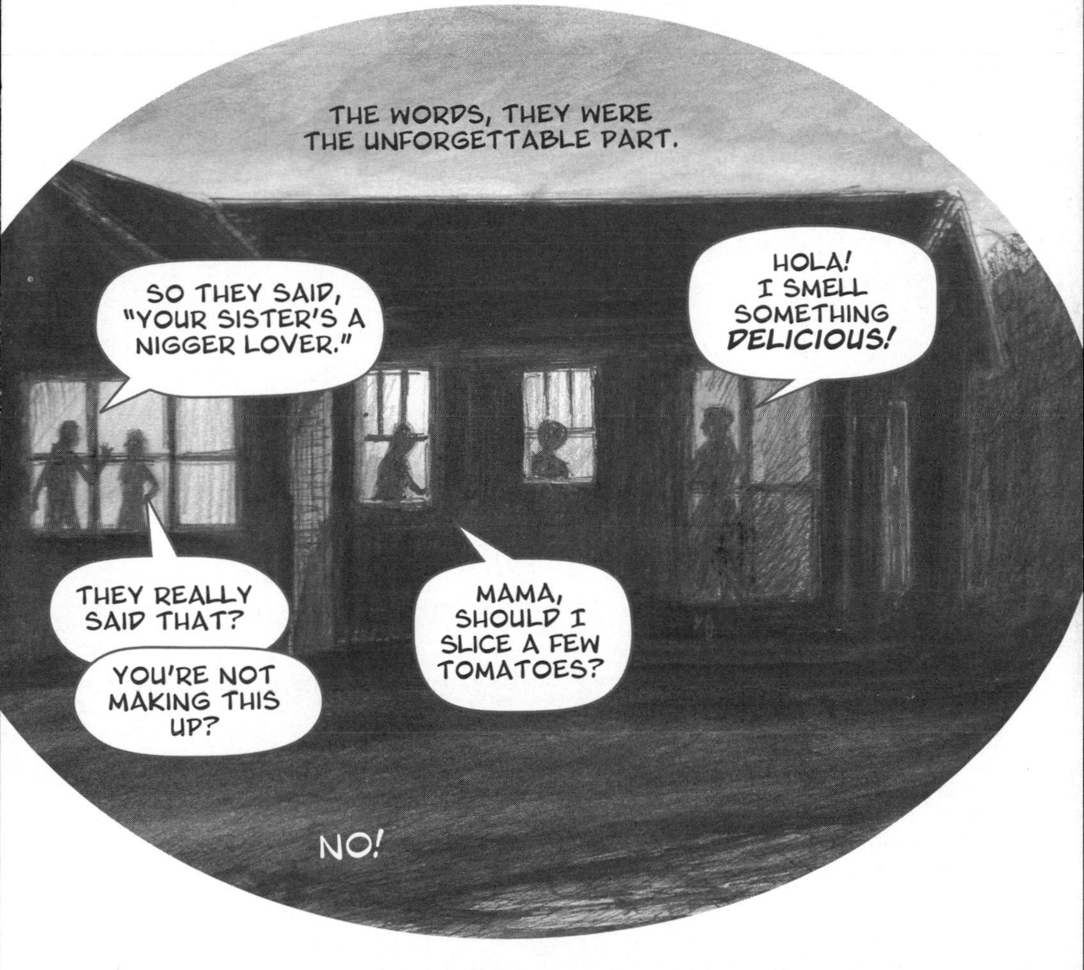

NOW HE TELLS ME.

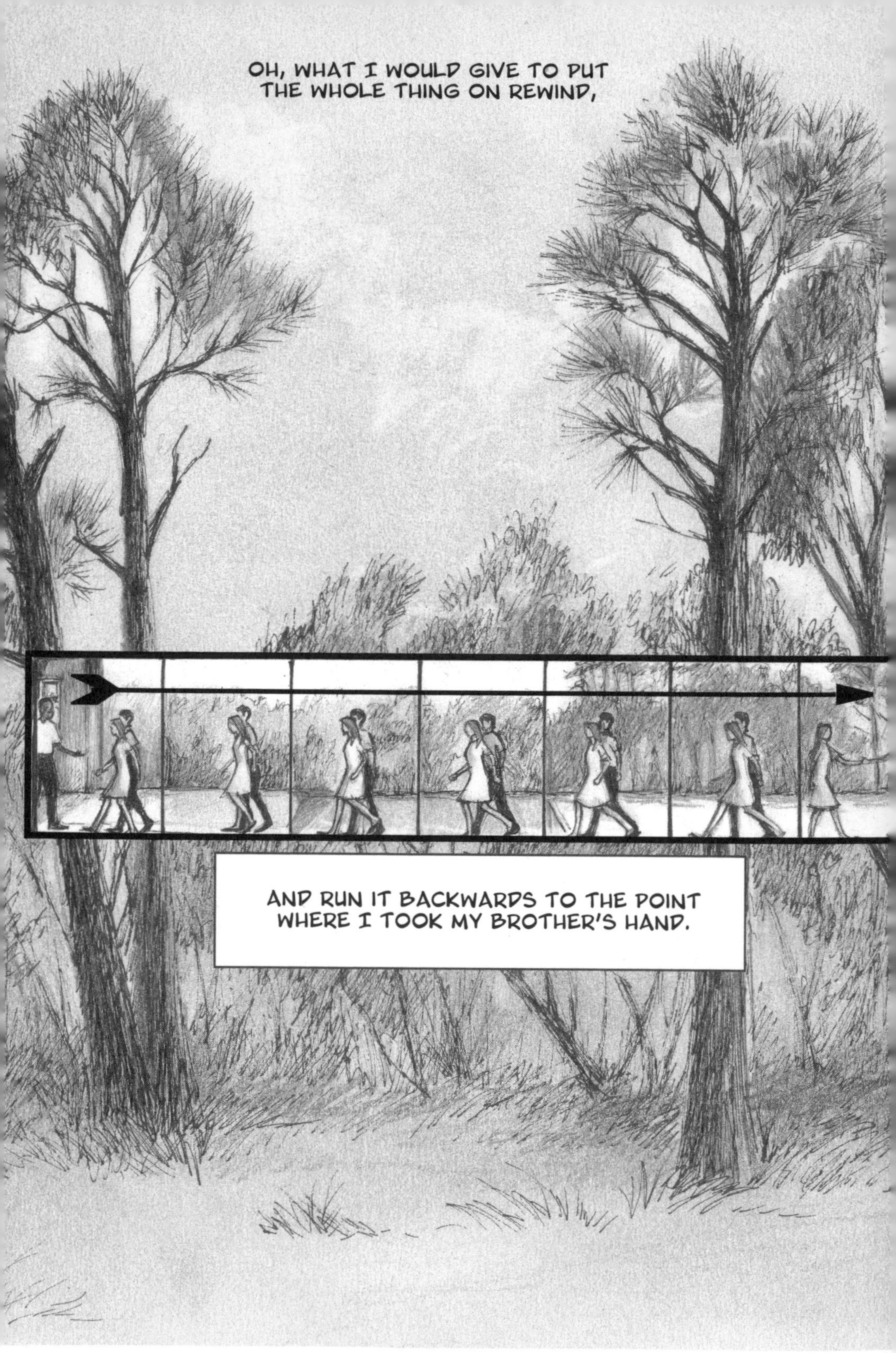
OH, WHAT I WOULD GIVE TO PUT THE WHOLE THING ON REWIND,
AND RUN IT BACKWARDS TO THE POINT WHERE I TOOK MY BROTHER'S HAND.

EXCEPT THIS TIME,
I'D LOOK THE RINGLEADER IN HIS HATE-FILLED EYES AND DEMAND HE
SAY *IT* TO MY *FACE*.

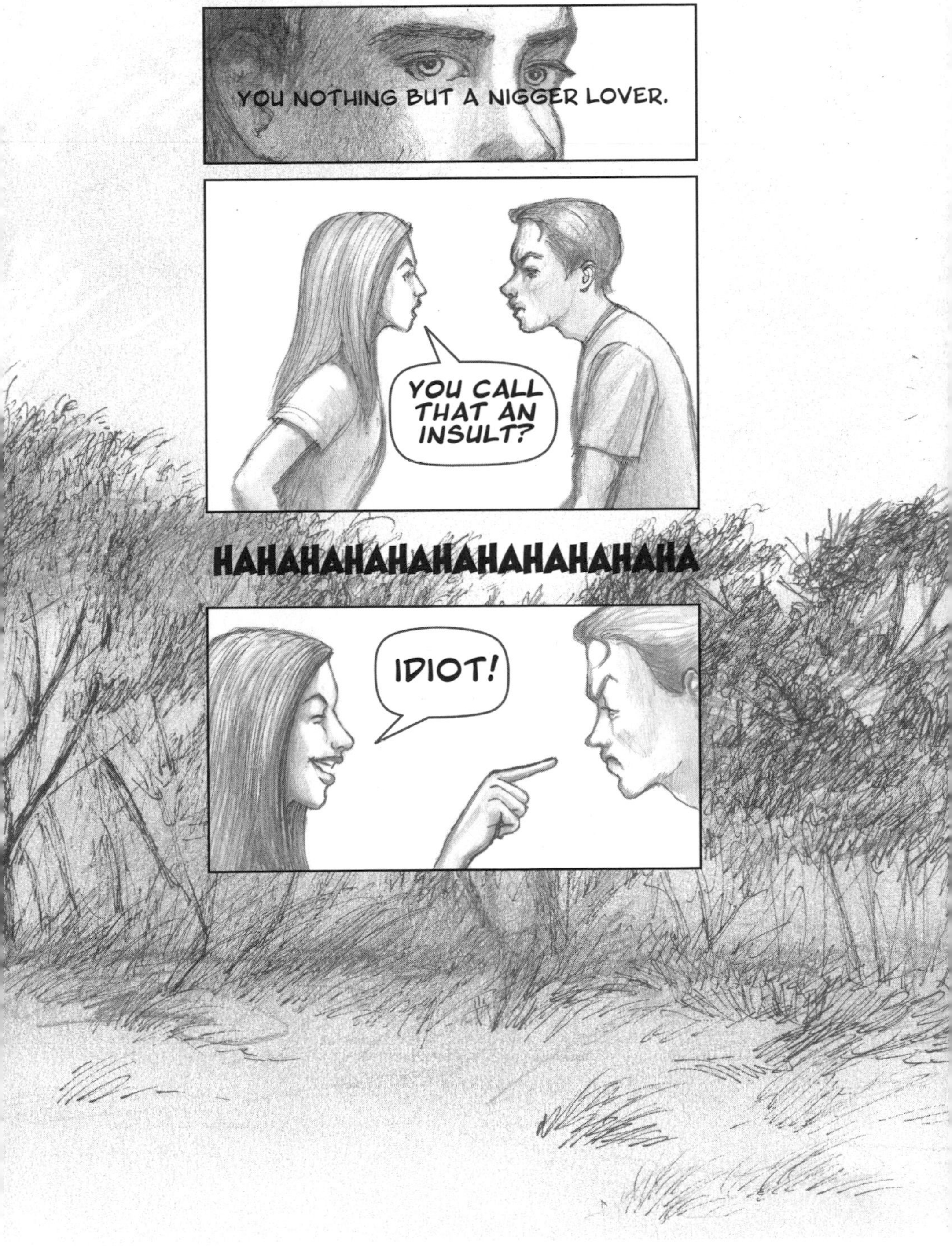

YOU NOTHING BUT A NIGGER LOVER.
YOU CALL THAT AN INSULT?
HAHAHAHAHAHAHAHAHAHAHA
IDIOT!

Epilogue

LONG NIGHT'S JOURNEY INTO DAY

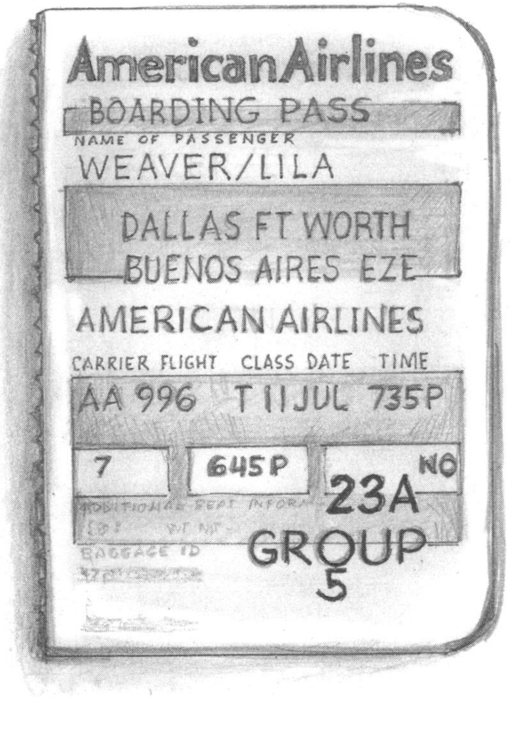

AmericanAirlines
BOARDING PASS
NAME OF PASSENGER
WEAVER/LILA
DALLAS FT WORTH
BUENOS AIRES EZE
AMERICAN AIRLINES
CARRIER FLIGHT CLASS DATE TIME
AA 996 T 11JUL 735P
7
645P
23A
NO
GROUP
5

ONLY 3 A.M.!

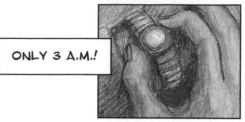

THE SOUTH AMERICAN CONTINENT LIES DARK AND SOMBER BELOW US.

CLOUDS PREVENT THE SLIGHTEST WINK OF CITY LIGHTS FROM PEEKING THROUGH.

THERE'S NO MOON.

JULY 2005

MOST OF THE PASSENGERS SLEEP.

NOT I.

IT'S MY FIRST TRIP BACK TO ARGENTINA SINCE WE IMMIGRATED. BEN, MY 21-YEAR-OLD SON, IS MY TRAVELING COMPANION.

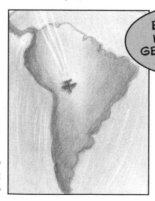

BUT WILL WE EVER GET THERE?

DALLAS, TX, TO BUENOS AIRES: 11 HOURS

REPEATED GLANCES AT THE ROUTE MONITOR CONVINCE ME THAT WE'RE ONLY CRAWLING.

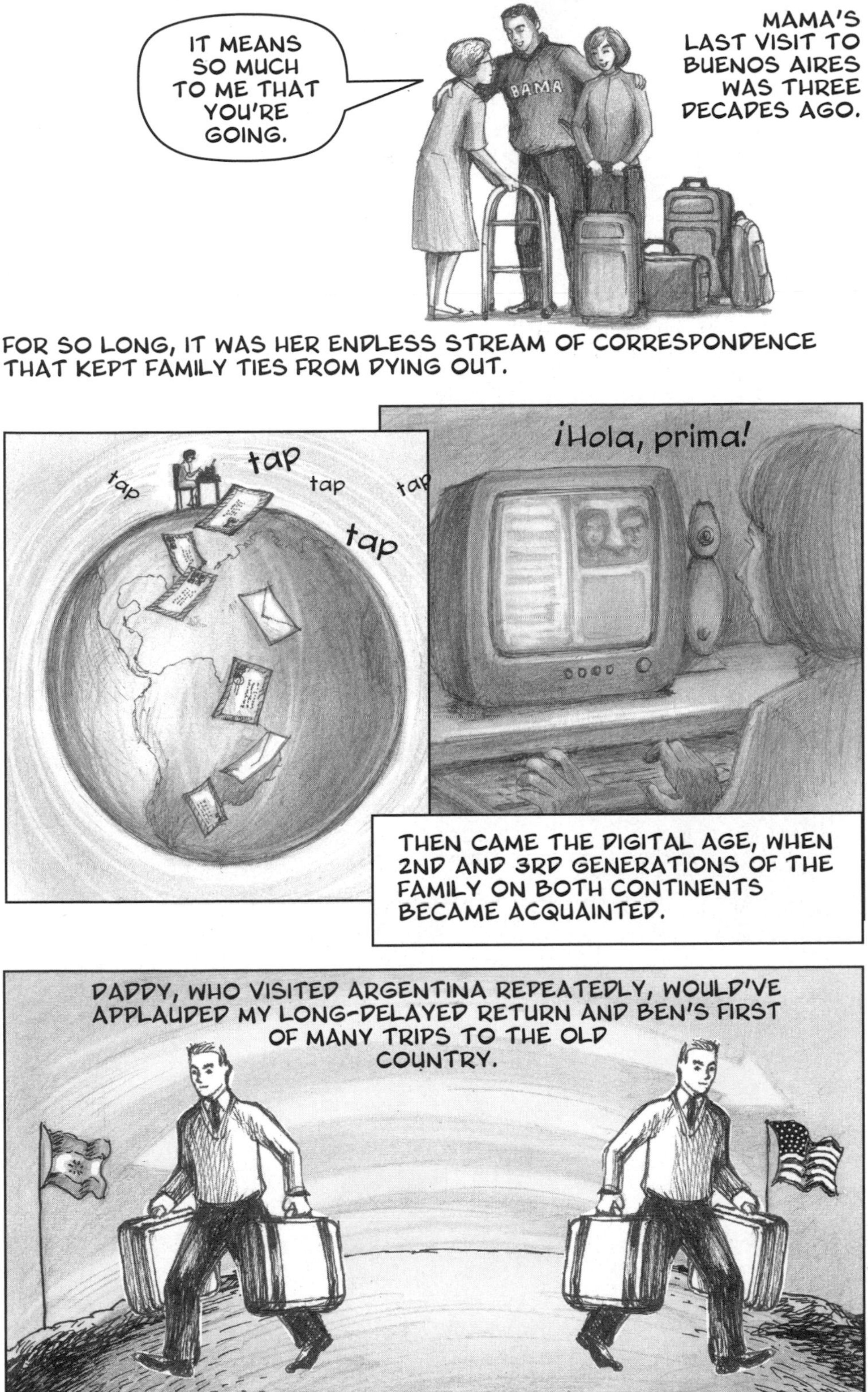
IT MEANS SO MUCH TO ME THAT YOU'RE GOING.
BAMA
MAMA'S LAST VISIT TO BUENOS AIRES WAS THREE DECADES AGO.
FOR SO LONG, IT WAS HER ENDLESS STREAM OF CORRESPONDENCE THAT KEPT FAMILY TIES FROM DYING OUT.
tap
tap
tap
tap
tap
¡Hola, prima!
THEN CAME THE DIGITAL AGE, WHEN 2ND AND 3RD GENERATIONS OF THE FAMILY ON BOTH CONTINENTS BECAME ACQUAINTED.
DADDY, WHO VISITED ARGENTINA REPEATEDLY, WOULD'VE APPLAUDED MY LONG-DELAYED RETURN AND BEN'S FIRST OF MANY TRIPS TO THE OLD COUNTRY.

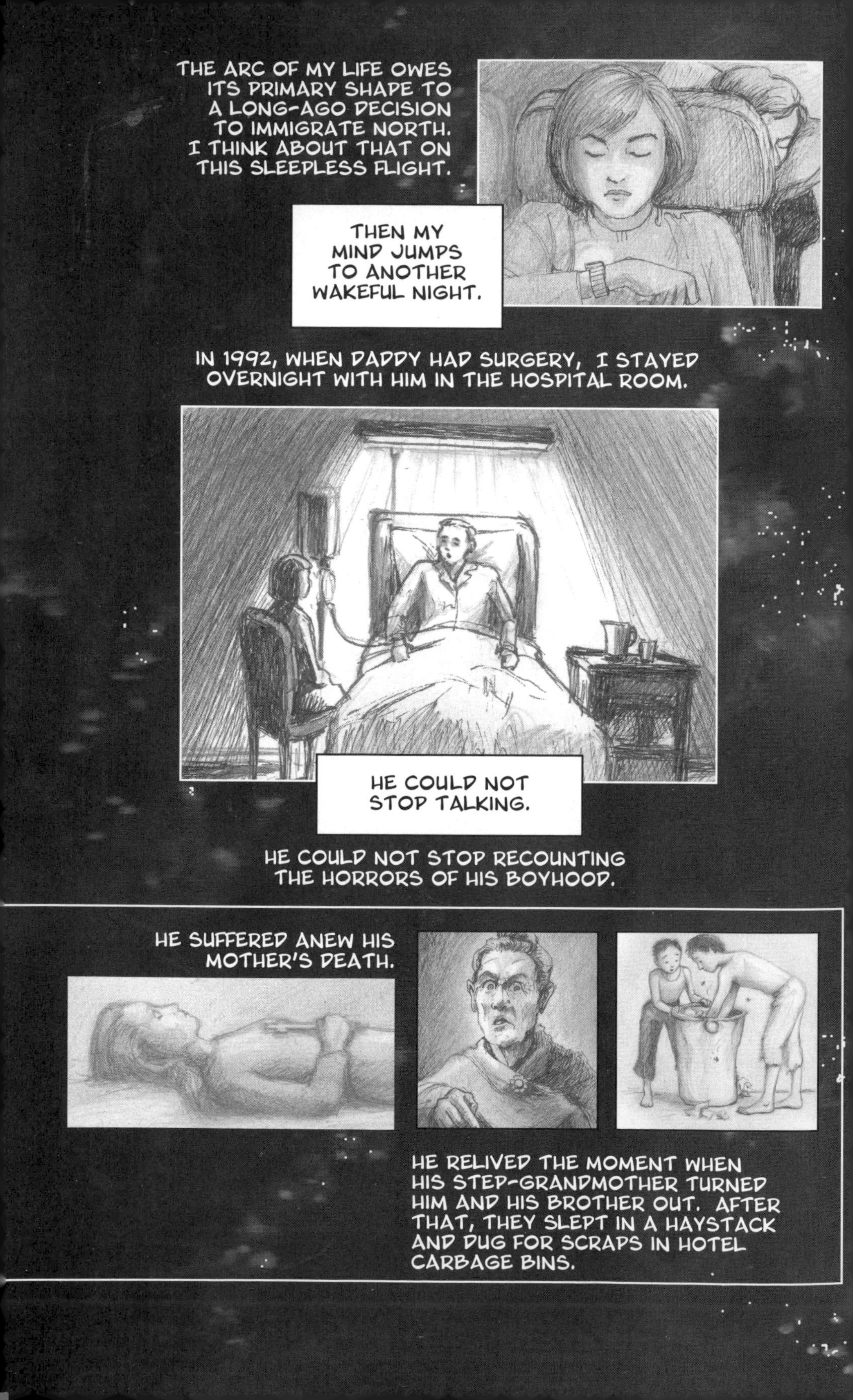

THE ARC OF MY LIFE OWES ITS PRIMARY SHAPE TO A LONG-AGO DECISION TO IMMIGRATE NORTH. I THINK ABOUT THAT ON THIS SLEEPLESS FLIGHT.

THEN MY MIND JUMPS TO ANOTHER WAKEFUL NIGHT.

IN 1992, WHEN DADDY HAD SURGERY, I STAYED OVERNIGHT WITH HIM IN THE HOSPITAL ROOM.

HE COULD NOT STOP TALKING.

HE COULD NOT STOP RECOUNTING THE HORRORS OF HIS BOYHOOD.

HE SUFFERED ANEW HIS MOTHER'S DEATH.

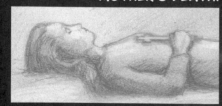

HE RELIVED THE MOMENT WHEN HIS STEP-GRANDMOTHER TURNED HIM AND HIS BROTHER OUT. AFTER THAT, THEY SLEPT IN A HAYSTACK AND DUG FOR SCRAPS IN HOTEL CARBAGE BINS.

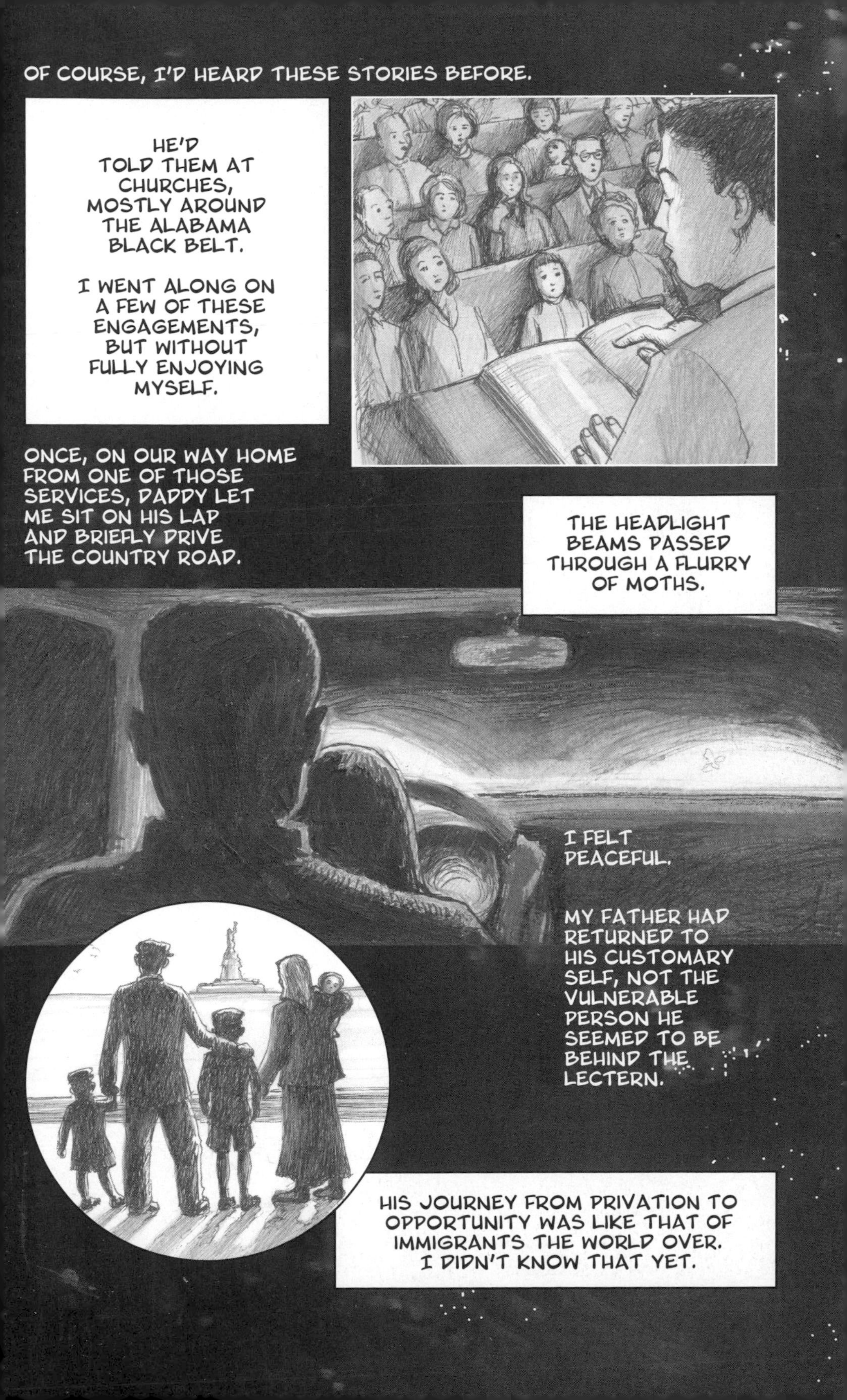
OF COURSE, I'D HEARD THESE STORIES BEFORE.
HE'D TOLD THEM AT CHURCHES, MOSTLY AROUND THE ALABAMA BLACK BELT.
I WENT ALONG ON A FEW OF THESE ENGAGEMENTS, BUT WITHOUT FULLY ENJOYING MYSELF.
ONCE, ON OUR WAY HOME FROM ONE OF THOSE SERVICES, DADDY LET ME SIT ON HIS LAP AND BRIEFLY DRIVE THE COUNTRY ROAD.
THE HEADLIGHT BEAMS PASSED THROUGH A FLURRY OF MOTHS.
I FELT PEACEFUL.
MY FATHER HAD RETURNED TO HIS CUSTOMARY SELF, NOT THE VULNERABLE PERSON HE SEEMED TO BE BEHIND THE LECTERN.
HIS JOURNEY FROM PRIVATION TO OPPORTUNITY WAS LIKE THAT OF IMMIGRANTS THE WORLD OVER. I DIDN'T KNOW THAT YET.

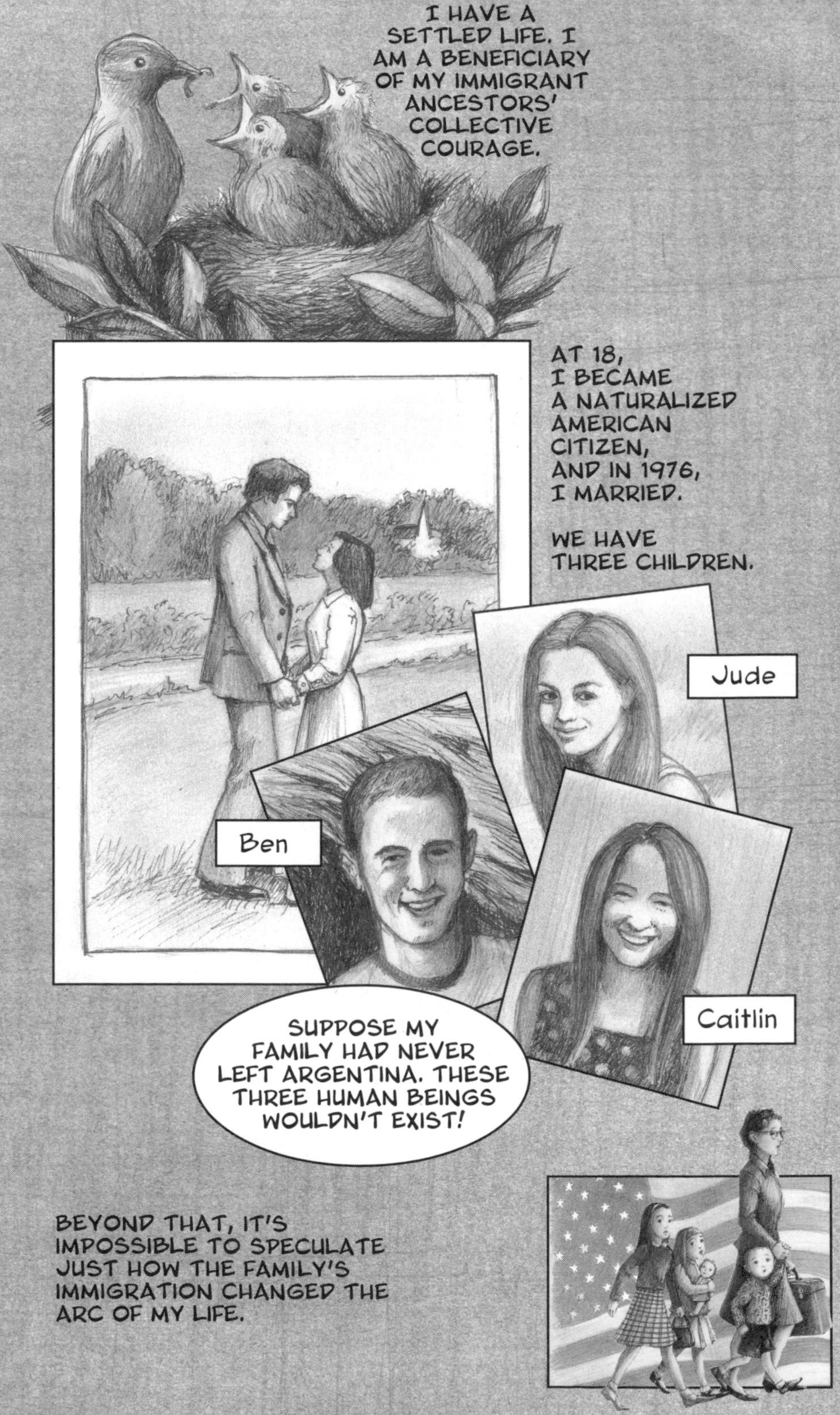
I HAVE A SETTLED LIFE. I AM A BENEFICIARY OF MY IMMIGRANT ANCESTORS' COLLECTIVE COURAGE.
AT 18, I BECAME A NATURALIZED AMERICAN CITIZEN, AND IN 1976, I MARRIED.
WE HAVE THREE CHILDREN.
Jude
Ben
Caitlin
SUPPOSE MY FAMILY HAD NEVER LEFT ARGENTINA. THESE THREE HUMAN BEINGS WOULDN'T EXIST!
BEYOND THAT, IT'S IMPOSSIBLE TO SPECULATE JUST HOW THE FAMILY'S IMMIGRATION CHANGED THE ARC OF MY LIFE.

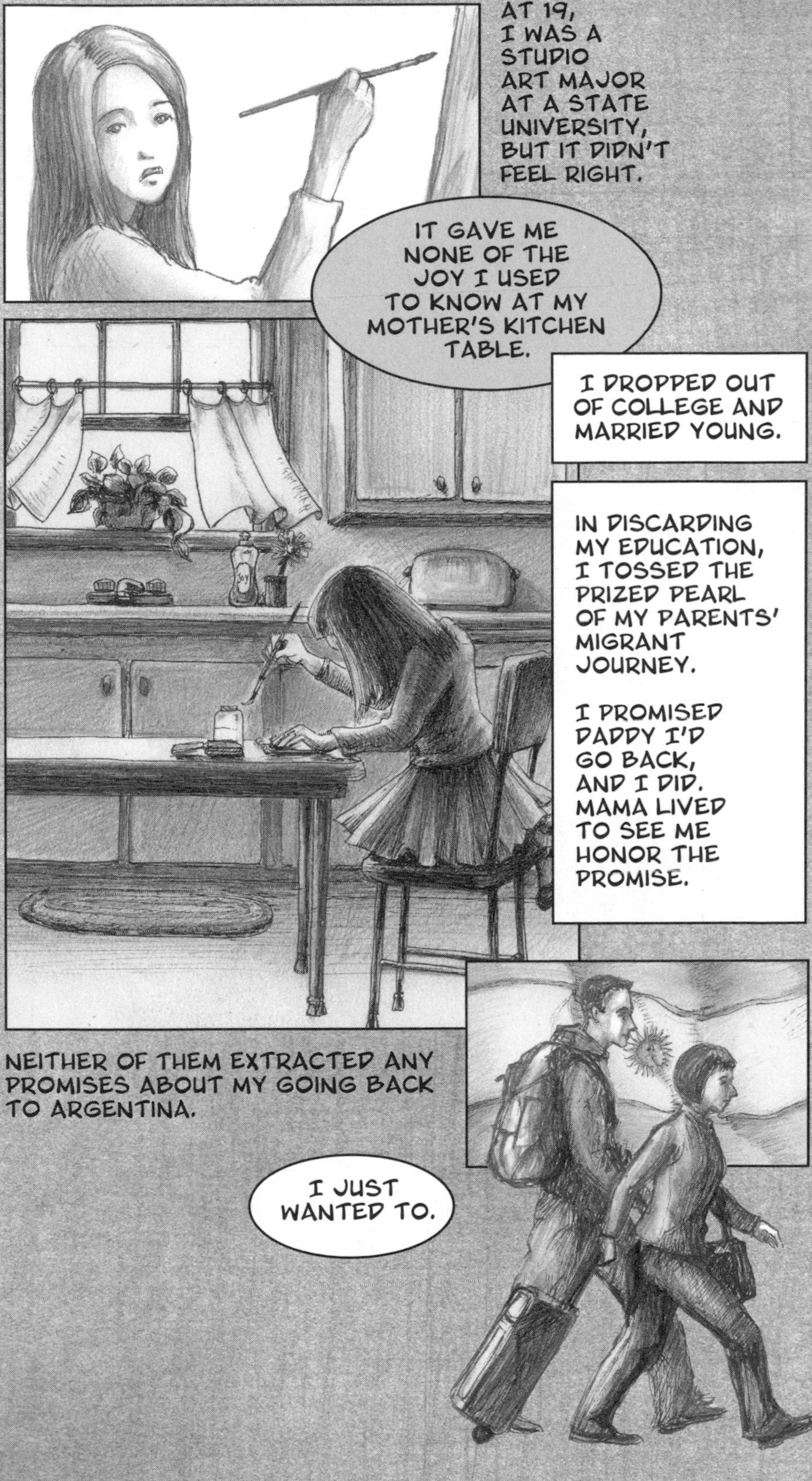
AT 19, I WAS A STUDIO ART MAJOR AT A STATE UNIVERSITY, BUT IT DIDN'T FEEL RIGHT.
IT GAVE ME NONE OF THE JOY I USED TO KNOW AT MY MOTHER'S KITCHEN TABLE.
I DROPPED OUT OF COLLEGE AND MARRIED YOUNG.
IN DISCARDING MY EDUCATION, I TOSSED THE PRIZED PEARL OF MY PARENTS' MIGRANT JOURNEY.
I PROMISED DADDY I'D GO BACK, AND I DID. MAMA LIVED TO SEE ME HONOR THE PROMISE.
NEITHER OF THEM EXTRACTED ANY PROMISES ABOUT MY GOING BACK TO ARGENTINA.
I JUST WANTED TO.

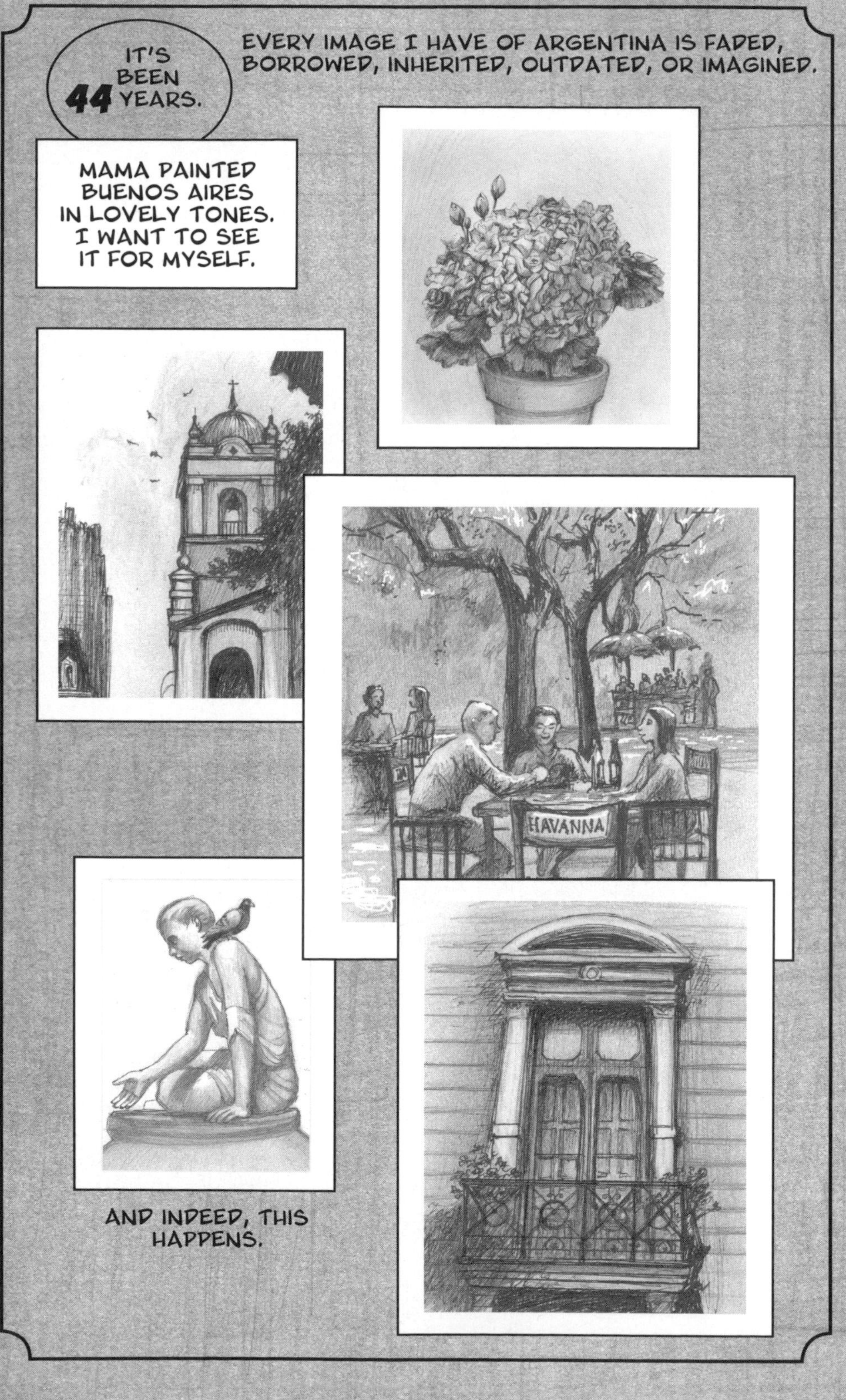
IT'S BEEN 44 YEARS.
EVERY IMAGE I HAVE OF ARGENTINA IS FADED, BORROWED, INHERITED, OUTDATED, OR IMAGINED.
MAMA PAINTED BUENOS AIRES IN LOVELY TONES. I WANT TO SEE IT FOR MYSELF.
HAVANNA
AND INDEED, THIS HAPPENS.

I WILL ALSO SEE THE ARGENTINA THAT DADDY EXPERIENCED.

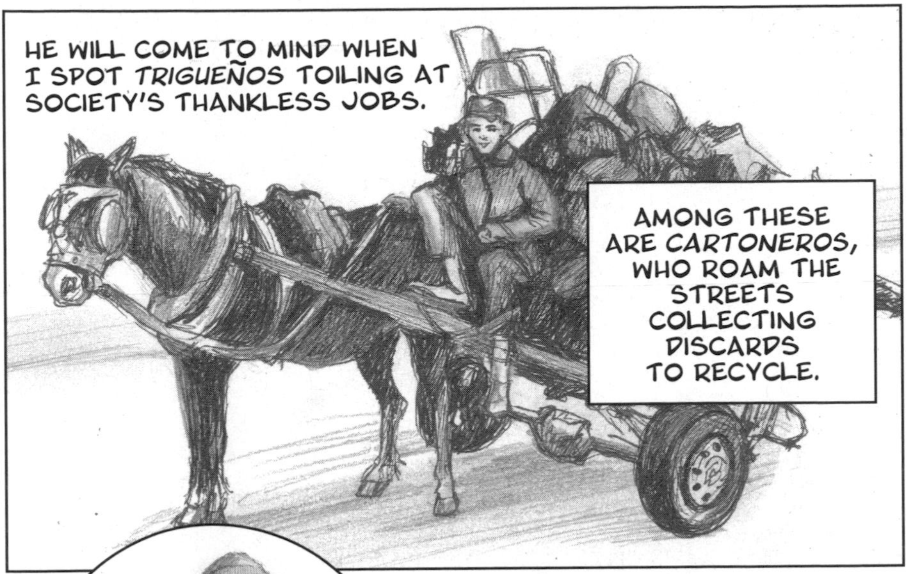
HE WILL COME TO MIND WHEN I SPOT *TRIGUEÑOS* TOILING AT SOCIETY'S THANKLESS JOBS.
AMONG THESE ARE *CARTONEROS*, WHO ROAM THE STREETS COLLECTING DISCARDS TO RECYCLE.

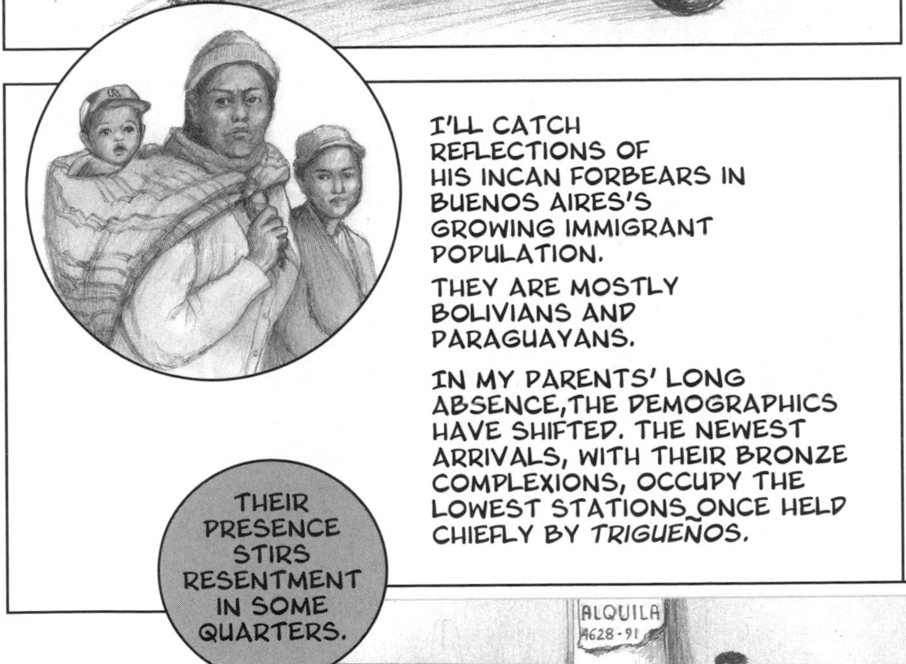
I'LL CATCH REFLECTIONS OF HIS INCAN FORBEARS IN BUENOS AIRES'S GROWING IMMIGRANT POPULATION.
THEY ARE MOSTLY BOLIVIANS AND PARAGUAYANS.
IN MY PARENTS' LONG ABSENCE, THE DEMOGRAPHICS HAVE SHIFTED. THE NEWEST ARRIVALS, WITH THEIR BRONZE COMPLEXIONS, OCCUPY THE LOWEST STATIONS ONCE HELD CHIEFLY BY *TRIGUEÑOS*.
THEIR PRESENCE STIRS RESENTMENT IN SOME QUARTERS.

AT LEAST, THAT'S WHAT I OBSERVE. I USED TO THINK OF RACISM AS A SPECIALTY OF THE AMERICAN SOUTH. HOW WRONG I WAS.

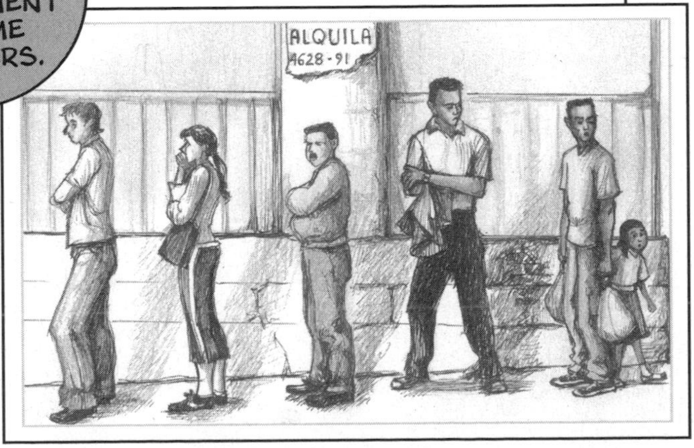
ALQUILA
4628-91

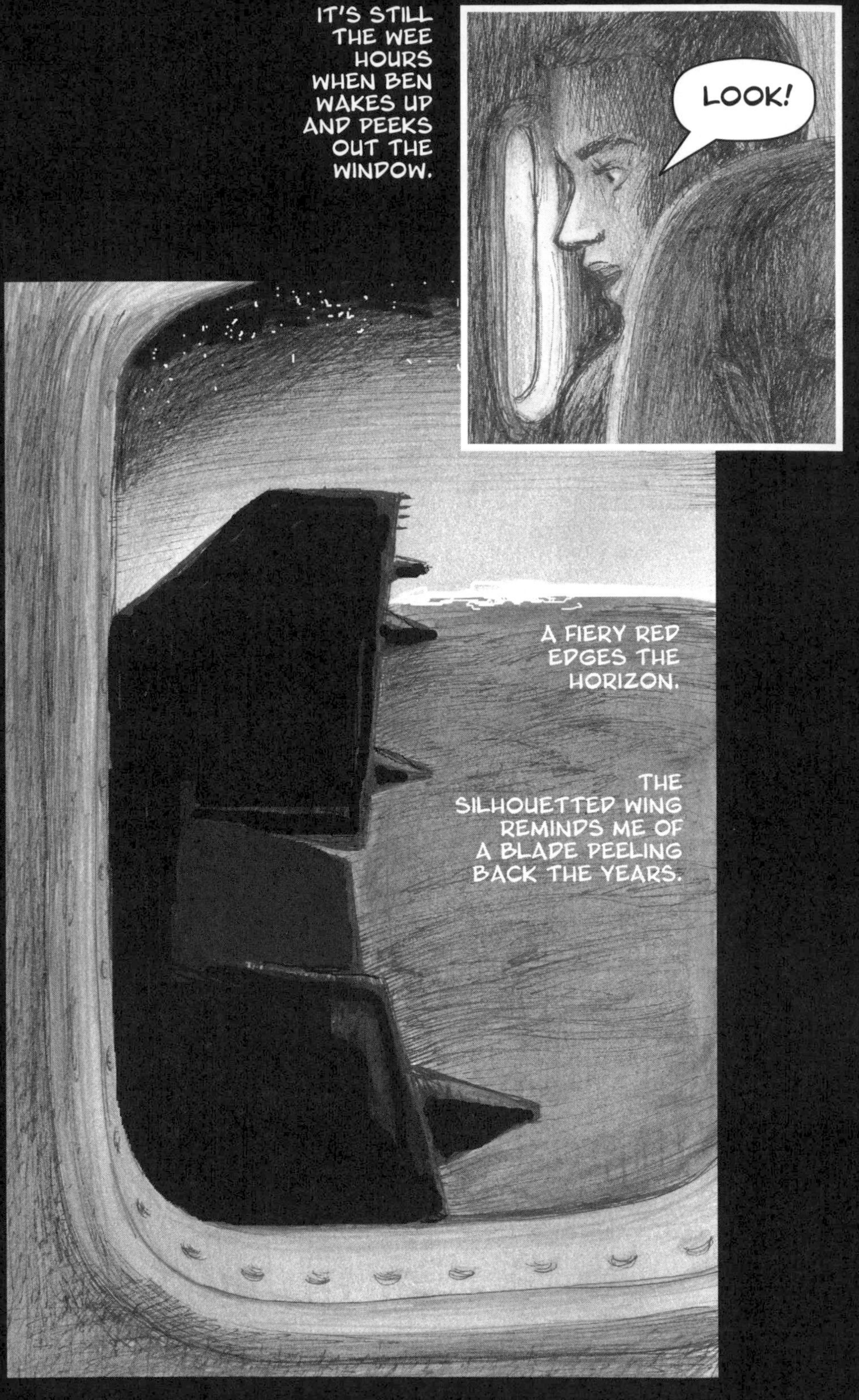
IT'S STILL THE WEE HOURS WHEN BEN WAKES UP AND PEEKS OUT THE WINDOW.
LOOK!
A FIERY RED EDGES THE HORIZON.
THE SILHOUETTED WING REMINDS ME OF A BLADE PEELING BACK THE YEARS.

MY LAST GLIMPSE OF ARGENTINA RUSHES BACK TO MEMORY.

SOON, THOSE TINY PEOPLE,
GRAINY AND OUT OF FOCUS,
WILL BE MADE REAL AGAIN.

AS THE
SOFT LIGHT OF
DAWN ENTERS
THE CABIN,
THE BREAKFAST
CARTS ROLL OUT.

WE ARE DESCENDING, AND WILL SOON
PASS THROUGH THE CLOUD COVER. ONLY
THEN WILL ARGENTINA COME INTO VIEW.

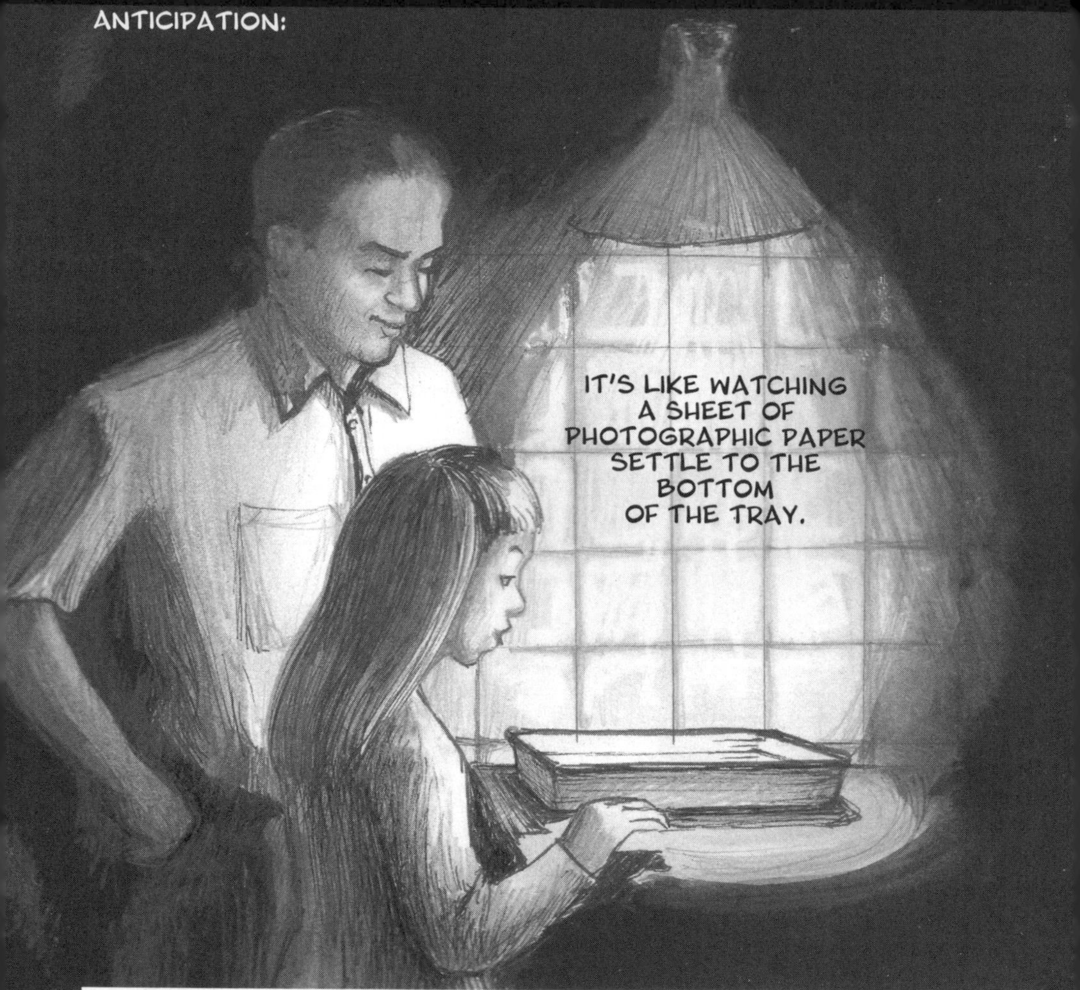
ANTICIPATION:
IT'S LIKE WATCHING A SHEET OF PHOTOGRAPHIC PAPER SETTLE TO THE BOTTOM OF THE TRAY.

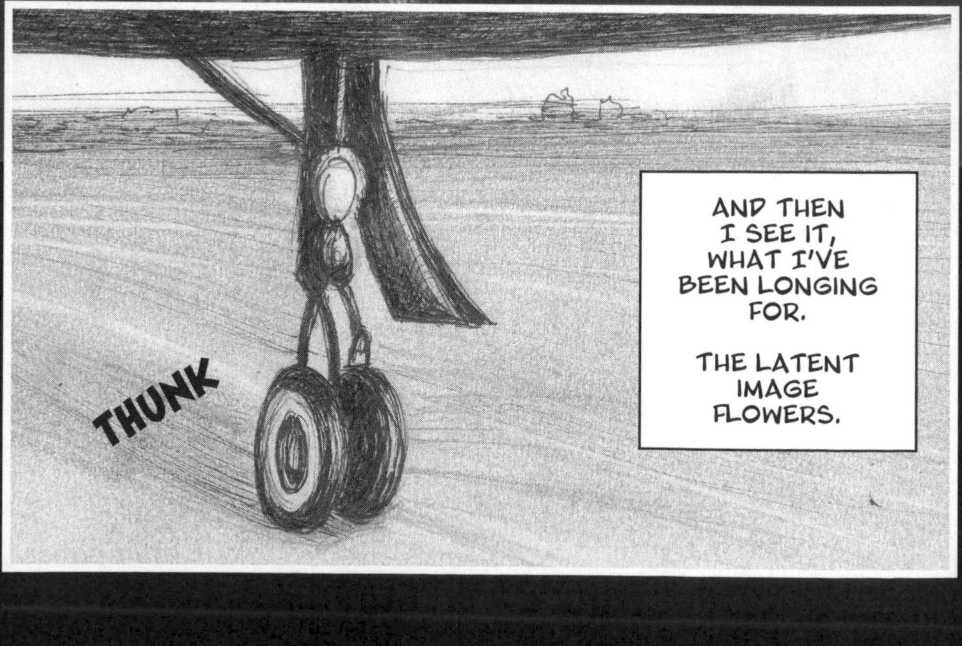
AND THEN I SEE IT, WHAT I'VE BEEN LONGING FOR.
THE LATENT IMAGE FLOWERS.
THUNK

ACKNOWLEDGEMENTS

This book began in 2007 as the senior project I submitted for the completion of my undergraduate work at The University of Alabama External Degree Program. That program has since been renamed New College LifeTrack. It exists to help late bloomers like me complete our college educations. My advisor at External Degree, Sandra Perkins, never steered me wrong, and if she hadn't urged me to show my project to Dr. James C. Hall, there would be no book. I want to also thank faculty member Ric Dice for overseeing my project in its academic phase and for supporting my writing interests ever since.

Dr. Hall, the director of New College, is the key that opened the publishing door. I owe him immense gratitude. He is the first person that looked at my work and recognized its book potential. He arranged for New College to host an exhibit based on the project and made sure that acquisition editors at The University of Alabama Press knew about it.

At The University of Alabama, two professors stirred my passion for the study of American culture, which underlies this book. They are Dr. James Salem of American studies and Dr. Dabney Gray at the External Degree Program. Their courses on the American fifties and the film and literature of the Vietnam War, respectively, inspired me to take a closer look at the current events of my childhood. I began to ask myself: What about the violence that took place in my hometown? What role did it play in the larger unfolding of civil rights?

I'm also grateful to Jim Hilgartner, who opened my eyes to intriguing possibilities through the creative-writing class he taught in Tuscaloosa. The writing group that grew from his class has become a second family. I thank Roger and Sherry Myers for years of hospitality and enthusiastic reception of my creative efforts. The group that met in their home for so long includes lifelong friends Mary Ann Shirley, Dot Franklin, Marcia Lehman, Carolyn Watson, and Joanna Hutt. I am profoundly richer for the love and support of these women. I especially thank Joanna for mentoring and cheering me through the anxious territory of preparing drafts and meeting professional expectations, and for coaching me through times of self-doubt. Those seven rules to work by remain tacked to my office wall.

The stories in this book are based primarily on personal and family memory. But to flesh out the events related in chapters 8 and 9, I needed more. I turned to the voluminous history of the civil rights movement. Many books, articles, and films lent dimension to my words and images. Of these, I want to specifically acknowledge three works. A document known as the "Alabama Literacy Test" is widely published on the Internet and difficult to attribute to its original source; nevertheless, I relied on it for an authentic representation of what black voter applicants experienced. My depiction of Marion's night march owes much to the eyewitness accounts recorded in Howell Raines's *My Soul is Rested: The Story of the Civil Rights Movement in the Deep South.* And until I discovered *When the Church Bell Rang Racist: The Methodist Church and the Civil Rights Movement in Alabama,* by Donald E. Collins, I had but a flimsy recollection of Rev. Joe Neal Blair's tenure in Marion.

Surely The University of Alabama Press never before dealt with so accidental an author. I am grateful for the support of its entire editorial and production staff, many of whom labored in the interest of this book without my specific knowledge. From receptionist to interns, the friendliness and assurance that I encountered at every visit to the press followed me back to my home desk.

At the press, I thank Crissie E. Johnson for her bilingual abilities as editor; Rebecca Todd Minder for her vigorous efforts in promotion; Rick Cook for his expertise; Beth Motherwell for her encouragement; and Michele Myatt Quinn who prepared the manuscript for the printer and also guided me through the daunting world of Adobe Creative Suite. I thank her for this and for never saying, "what a dumb question."

I owe special gratitude to my editor, Dan Waterman. When I arrived at his office, I had only the germ of a book and scant knowledge about how to grow one. Over three-and-a-half years, he directed me through tedious manuscript development and did so with extraordinary patience, honesty, humor, respect, and vision. I can never thank him enough.

Several volunteer readers contributed their insights toward late-draft improvements. One of these is Amanda Gayle Moore, whose literary discernment is topnotch and who has become like an extra daughter to Paul and me. Carol Lynn Robertson and Victoria Robertson tested the clarity of the narrative and made astute observations, all while on family vacation. Thank you!

I thank the Reverend Dr. Catherine Collier for her interest in my work and for helping me confront the spiritual questions that memoir writing often raises.

For their friendship and enthusiastic support of my writing, I warmly thank Christopher D. L. Johnson, Gary and Patricia Falls, Stephen Royce Mills, Jeff Beans, and the Reverend Hoyt Winslett.

Many people that played no specific role in the development of this book have also contributed to my creative life. Space prohibits me from naming them all. I want to make special mention of Dorothy Davis Hollingsworth, my childhood friend from Marion with whom I share a deep bond and who remembers many of the incidents told in these pages, and Candace Weaver, who happens to be my sister-in-law but is also the best friend a person could ever ask for.

I thank my dear cousin Susana Bazzini, her late husband Roberto Gavarini, and their children for reintroducing me to Argentina in exquisite fashion. It's also been my joy to rediscover other lost family members in Buenos Aires: my cousins Annie and Irene Salnicov, Adriana and Edgardo Bazzini, their respective families, and my aunt Esther Maisonnave. Additional extended family members are scattered across the Americas. We've also established new levels of connection. They are my cousin Sergio Salnicov in Uruguay and my aunt Emilia Maisonnave and her children and grandchildren in Costa Rica and the United States. The once broken circle is now redrawn.

Paul is the most supportive husband imaginable. He is equal parts coach and arts patron. The more hours I put into my work, the crazier life got, yet he never complained. I owe everything to his encouragement and unflappable nature.

For our children, Jude, Benjamin and Caitlin, this book is a glimpse into family history. But these stories are hardly static. The Quintero DNA of artistic skill, foreign-language acquisition, and passion for Argentine culture lives on through them in unique incarnations that would've delighted their grandparents as surely as they delight me.

My siblings, Virginia Nettles, Lisa Quintero Prewitt, and John Quintero, have been remarkably gracious throughout this venture. I thank them for their gift of trust. They each supplied stories and details I barely knew or had forgotten. They allowed me to tell our shared history without interference. Such generosity is hardly automatic in sibling contracts and only makes me love them more. My brother-in-law Bill Nettles deserves special mention in this context. When he married Ginny in 1964, he became a big brother to the rest of us and, ultimately, the patriarch of our tribe.

My siblings and I had extraordinary parents and a remarkable upbringing. We can never know what our lives would've been like had our parents not immigrated to the United States or made similarly consequential choices of faith, education, and personal growth. Furthermore, my parents' belief in me is a priceless gift beyond the scope of words. This book is an ode that only hints at the deeper levels of their contribution. I only wish they were alive to see it, hold it, and experience the ever-fuller esteem that I hold them in.

I have one more set of people to thank. They are the heroes of the civil rights struggle that changed my hometown. I especially honor the memory of Jimmie Lee Jackson, who gave his utmost. I pay tribute to the countless local heroes who marched for the vote, endured jail time, and received physical blows, all without assurance that their efforts would ever pay off. I don't know how they withstood the hardships, but I thank them for their exemplary courage. And in those days, few white people dared to voice support of the cause. Of these, the late Reverend Joe Neal Blair shines like a beacon in the dark. I aspire to be more like him.